To Glenn All the best

WITC… S
WELL
CHRONICLES

A Trilogy of Adventures in Time and History

THE WITCHFINDER'S WELL
THE ALCHEMIST'S ARMS
THE SOVEREIGN'S SECRET

JONATHAN POSNER

ISBN: 9781739702793

Published by Winter & Drew Publishing.

The Witchfinder's Well, The Alchemist's Arms, The Sovereign's Secret
The Witchfinder's Well Chronicles

jonathanposnerauthor.com

All cover designs by Jonathan Posner, with images purchased royalty-free from Dreamstime.com

INTRODUCTION

The Witchfinder's Well was originally written back in the early 1990s as a musical called Spirit of History, with music by John Gauntley and Chris Smellie. It then got upcycled into the 'book that the musical would have come from' and published in 2015 – although necessary plot changes were made to reflect the move from stage to page.

But when I had finished this book, I found it hard to let the characters go; there was definitely another story to be told, or maybe even two! So The Alchemist's Arms was published in 2019, picking the main characters up ten years later.

This story then set up so many interesting plot opportunities, that I decided to make part 3 of the trilogy follow on only a few weeks later from its dramatic events. The result was The Sovereign's Secret, published in 2022. And although it does draw the story started in The Witchfinder's Well to a close – who knows, maybe there are still more tales to be told!

Historical note

These books are set in Elizabethan England. While I have tried to make the period setting feel authentic, I have avoided making it *too* accurate – mainly because I didn't want the accuracy of things like the language and social norms to get in the way of great action and adventure. Instead I have tried to capture the sights, smells and *feel* of Elizabethan England, so you can enjoy the fast-paced action without getting too bogged down in period detail.

There are also a few 'liberties' taken in the story – such as how I have depicted the trial of witches by ducking, or having the death penalty for witchcraft being burning, when at that time it was by hanging. I also have Francis Walsingham living at Barn Elms in 1575, when he didn't actually move there until a couple of years later. Liberties such as these (and there are more) are there to serve the story, and if you are offended by them, then I do apologise! I hope the pace and tension are adequate compensation.

I do hope you enjoy reading these stories as much as I have enjoyed writing them!

This book is dedicated to the memory of
John Gauntley, a talented composer, wine expert and great friend,
without whom this book would never have happened.

CONTENTS

PART 1

THE WITCHFINDER'S WELL

CHAPTER ONE

As she surveyed the royal banquet from her high vantage point in the Minstrel's Gallery, Justine Parker twisted slightly to get more comfortable in the tight bodice of her gown.

All things considered, the banquet was going pretty well.

An army of servants had brought exotic dishes up from the kitchens into the Great Hall and presented them to the assembled ladies, gentlemen, knights and courtiers for their appreciation and amazement.

There were dishes such as the noble roast peacock with its plumage dancing in the light, guinea fowl in a deep crusty pie and legs of mutton surrounded by mountains of peas and carrots. Fine red claret was drunk copiously from silver goblets, with the servants replenishing them from silver pitchers as they weaved around the tables.

Justine leaned on the railing of the gallery and let the warm sound of conversation and laughter wash over her; the rich hubbub of noise that rose up to the furthest corners of the magnificent ornate plaster roof. Down below her, the face of every guest was bright with enjoyment, bathed in the golden glow of a thousand flickering candles.

In the middle of the high table, Her Majesty Queen Elizabeth sat bolt upright, her bright eyes dancing round the room as the courtier to her right engaged her in conversation.

Justine admired her pale beauty, set off by her striking bodice of red velvet edged with gold lace and sparkling with a thousand shimmering pearls, together with the single flashing emerald at her neck that brought out the green fire in her eyes. Then there was her red-bronze hair adorned with its simple, elegant gold crown, framed by the high pearl-edged lace ruff that flared up from her shoulders.

With a small raise of her hand, the Queen paused the conversation with the courtier beside her and looked up at the gallery. Maybe Justine's small twisting movement had caught her eye. She held Justine's gaze a moment, then gave the smallest nod of her head – so small that it could easily have been missed – as if to congratulate Justine on the success of the banquet she had organised.

With a smile Justine bowed her own head and gave a gentle curtsey. The Queen nodded again, then turned back to the courtier and resumed their conversation.

In the gallery Justine smiled again, this time to herself.

Yes, all things considered, the banquet was going pretty well.

She looked down across the room, taking in the full scene. The long high table ran along the back wall under the big windows with the Queen in the centre. On either side Justine had seated her most important courtiers, looking resplendent in their richly-coloured silk doublets with slashed sleeves and fine white ruffs. Beyond the courtiers she had seated the women, elegant in their low-cut gowns, their hair carefully parted in the centre and tucked under their French hoods – a style introduced originally by Elizabeth's mother, Anne Boleyn.

Justine's gaze moved to the table down the left side of the room. The people here were less important and their clothes reflected this – the men wore plain doublets and the women wore their hair in simple cotton coifs rather than the more elaborate French hoods of the high table. Their behaviour was no less exuberant, if anything slightly more so, and Justine smiled as they all laughed at a joke from the jester who had been moving round the tables. His brightly-coloured motley costume consisted of a tunic split into a red half and a yellow half, while his hose had one red leg and one yellow leg on the opposite sides. In his hand was a small jester head on a stick, which he was using to entertain the guests.

From behind her came the sound of the minstrels; four elderly men with lutes playing light-hearted music that was all but lost against the loud noise of the room. Their piece came to an end, and she turned to them.

"You play well, good sirs," she said with a twinkling smile. "What is next?"

"We have not yet played Greensleeves," said the eldest minstrel. "But first we need a drink." All four reached down for the tankards by their stools and drained them with great satisfaction. The oldest man then examined the bottom of his empty tankard and looked up at Justine expectantly. She laughed and reached for the large pewter jug ready by her feet, then went to each in turn, pouring more beer into their proffered tankards.

"Ahh, thank you my girl," said the oldest man, "it is always a pleasure to play at one of your banquets."

Justine curtseyed in reply. The men drank some more, then put down their tankards and launched into Greensleeves.

She turned and resumed her gaze across the Great Hall.

To her right was a smaller table seating more people, with a carving table beside it. On the wall above was a large portrait of a handsome knight in a shining breastplate standing with a white stag in the background. Her gaze stopped on this portrait, as it so often did, and she gave a small sigh as she studied the man's long blond hair and trim beard.

The jester turned from the table he'd been entertaining and looked up, catching sight of Justine as she stared across at the portrait.

His gaze took in her shoulder-length cascade of russet-coloured ringlets trying to escape from under her French hood; her small, slightly snub nose, her pale blue eyes under thick, dark eyebrows staring with a faraway look at the portrait…

He gave a little dance and waved his stick to catch her eye.

She spotted him and gave a small wave back. He raised an enquiring eyebrow, then flicked the stick up behind his back so the little jester head on the end popped up on his shoulder.

He turned to it and appeared to have a brief conversation, then pointed up at her. The little head on his shoulder nodded. He made a 'doe-eyed' face – a gross over-exaggeration of hers, with a sickly grin and fluttering eyelashes – then pointed back at her. The head nodded again, then both the jester and the head turned to look up at her, with the jester smiling broadly.

She couldn't help but laugh and he laughed back. Then he gave a low courtly bow, while she applauded.

The jester turned back to the room and started dancing sideways up towards the high table.

Still chuckling, Justine's gaze moved upwards to the large tapestries depicting heroic scenes of hunts that were hanging round the hall between the sconces. In one scene knights attacked a stag with spears and arrows in a green forest; in another a different stag was running from a pack of baying hounds, followed by nobles on horses.

Justine looked back down at the hall. The servants had cleared the main courses away and were now circulating with bowls of fruit and more wine.

'Only an hour more and we'll be cleared and finished,' she thought, as she twisted once more in the tight bodice of her gown.

Just then she became aware of an insistent beeping sound over the noise of the room. Fishing her mobile from the pocket of her gown, she swiped the screen.

"Hello, Justine Parker here."

"The taxis have started arriving," said a voice. "They're early."

"Oh, bother. I put half-eleven on the schedule." She nudged up the end of her lace sleeve with her elbow, to reveal her watch. "It's only eleven fifteen. We've just served the fruit. Would you be a sweetie and tell them they'll have to wait?"

"OK."

"And please can you tell them to turn their meters off. I don't want one of their silly waiting charges when it's all their fault." Justine thought a moment. "It is their fault, isn't it? Oh bother and blast it, it had better be. I'll check the email I sent them. Can you be an absolute poppet and bluff it out or something?"

"Sure, no problem."

Justine tapped the email app on her phone and scrolled through to find the relevant message. There it was – 'please make sure the taxis arrive at 11:30pm'.

Tucking her mobile back into her pocket with a satisfied smile, Justine looked back down at the hall.

The Queen was dispensing her wisdom to the courtiers on either side, who were hanging on her every word and laughing sycophantically, even though Justine didn't think the Queen was actually trying to be funny.

Justine sighed deeply. For all that she liked to pretend to herself that events such as this were real, in truth this was just a modern-day re-enactment of a Tudor banquet. The setting was real enough – the magnificent Grangedean Manor genuinely dated back to the late 1400s – but now it was a National Trust property, purposefully restored to its Tudor period as a 'living museum'.

The costumes were all hired from the special fancy dress store in the old stables, and were held together with Velcro and poppers, not laced and tied as they should have been. They were a modern-day approximation of the Tudor costume; made for ease of putting on, not authenticity.

The dishes that had been served for the meal were cooked in a modern-day kitchen set up to standards demanded by the environmental health officer, and while the dishes were close enough to the Tudor recipes, the reality was that they were only interpretations for 21st century tastes. Even the peacock had really been a pheasant in disguise.

The 'courtiers' were the CEO and Board of an American corporate with offices in the UK, while the other guests were members of their teams. They had signed up for the Genuine Tudor Banquet Experience at Grangedean Manor – Complete with Her Majesty Queen Elizabeth I and as the events manager, Justine had been determined to give them their money's worth.

Looking down at the glow of the candles on the bright, happy faces, she thought she'd done OK.

She had wanted to welcome them on arrival with a full tour of the magnificent 15th century manor house and grounds, so a week before she had sought out Mrs Warburton, National Trust volunteer tour guide and retired schoolteacher, whose knowledge of Grangedean Manor was encyclopaedic and whose no-nonsense disciplined approach meant she could be relied upon to keep control of such a large party.

Justine had found Mrs. Warburton in the Master Bedroom; she was a tall, ramrod-straight woman with iron-grey hair wearing a tweed twinset that looked like it was straight out of the 1950s. She was in the middle of explaining to a family how Tudor people managed their clothing.

"Clothes were kept in wooden chests like these," she was saying, "rather than hanging in wardrobes like we do now."

"They couldn't have got much in there," said the mother, looking dubiously at the metal-bound oak chest at the end of the bed. It was about five feet long by three feet high and three feet wide.

"There may have been more than one chest in a bedroom, particularly for the nobility like Sir William de Beauvais, who owned the manor in the 1560s," explained Mrs. Warburton. "But the truth is they didn't have anywhere near as many clothes as we do now, and only really changed their underclothes to keep clean. Sometimes all they did was unlace the sleeves on their outfit and lace on new ones."

"Ugh!" exclaimed the daughter, who looked about fourteen. "Didn't they smell rank?"

"Very possibly," said Mrs. Warburton matter-of-factly, "but that would have been the same for most. Certainly the poorer people."

"So didn't they, like, have baths and stuff?" asked the girl incredulously.

"Occasionally, but only the nobility. A copper or wooden tub would be brought into the bedroom and filled with water heated on the fire. Herbs would be sprinkled on the water to make it smell good, and soap for the rich would be made with olive oil. The poor – they would wash in a stream or with a bucket of water and soap made of animal fat."

"Eww, gross," said the girl.

Justine couldn't let this go unchallenged. "No, no, no!" she interjected, her eyes shining brightly. "The Tudors were absolutely wonderful people!"

The family and Mrs. Warburton all turned to look at her in surprise.

"Sorry to butt in, Mrs. Warburton," she went on, "but I wouldn't want this young lady to think the Tudors were ghastly at all. Imagine you were in Tudor times," she said brightly. "There would be lots of dancing, great banquets that lasted for hours, riding in the park and handsome young men just itching to go out with you! It would be such fun!"

"Suppose," said the girl, not looking convinced.

"And beautiful gowns to wear and jewellery and dainty shoes…"

Just then the girl's father intervened. Casting concerned glances at Justine, he said, "Come, Shaz, time to go, I think."

The girl Shaz said, "But didn't they, like…?" then caught the expression on her father's face, and shut her mouth. The family shuffled quickly out, leaving Justine alone with Mrs. Warburton.

"You are very enthusiastic, my dear," observed the older lady drily. "Maybe just a little too much, perhaps? Although I am not sure that the girl, Shaz, wasn't starting to become just a tiny bit more interested in the Tudors."

Justine laughed. "Maybe. Maybe not. But Grangedean Manor can have that effect, can't it?"

Mrs. Warburton thought about this a moment, her hands clasped together and her lips pursed. "Yes, it can. It can certainly make you feel like the Tudors are alive, and may come through a door at any moment. But only if you're that kind of person. I am not sure that Shaz was really that kind of person." She smiled. "Anyway. Did you want me, Miss Parker?"

"Oh yes," said Justine, "Yes, yes, I did. In fact, you're absolutely the very person I wanted. I have a large party of Americans coming next Thursday for a banquet, and I would really love it if you could very kindly show them round before we get them changed into their Tudor outfits?" Justine smiled warmly. "I am sure you'll be absolutely brilliant at keeping them together and giving them a really wonderful tour. There's no one who knows more about Grangedean Manor than you."

"I suspect you actually know at least as much as I do, Miss Parker," observed Mrs. Warburton with just a hint of amusement in her voice. "But no matter. Of course I'll show them round."

"That's great! Great! Thanks!" said Justine happily. "I'm putting the schedule together and I'll email it to you later."

"I don't really look at emails," said Mrs. Warburton. "Can you not print it out for me?"

"Yes, of course," said Justine. Then she added, "But you really should use emails – they're so easy." She held up her phone. "I get them on my PC and on this phone, so I have them wherever I go."

"I am sure that works well for you, but I prefer the old fashioned methods of communication," observed Mrs. Warburton, "such as writing," she shook her head, "and talking."

"Ahh, but this talks as well," said Justine opening up the battered cover protecting her phone.

"It is a phone, so I suppose it does. Although it is actually the other person that does the talking, is it not?"

"No, no, it's the phone," Justine insisted. She tapped to open an app and held up the screen for Mrs. Warburton to peer at vaguely. "It actually talks if you want it to! It's brilliant! You can type text into this special app, then tap on a button here and it says what you've written. You can choose what voice you want it to talk in, as well. Look..." She quickly typed and tapped the screen. The phone said, "Hello, Missus Warburton." It was slightly robotic, but reasonably clear. Justine looked at the older lady in triumph, challenging her not to be impressed.

"What will they think of next?" said Mrs. Warburton politely.

Justine closed her phone cover and dropped it back in her pocket. "Anyway, I must be getting on. Thanks, Mrs. Warburton. I'll send you the schedule for next week." She turned to leave.

"Miss Parker," Mrs Warburton stopped her. "These Americans. Is there anything particular" – she emphasised the 'tic' in the middle – "that they want to see?"

Justine considered. "No – the standard tour should be fine. The CEO told me in one of his emails, that he wants to 'absorb all your English history'."

"He sounds fascinating. I very much look forward to meeting him."

"Me too," said Justine, brightly. "Me too!"

CHAPTER TWO

It was the following Thursday afternoon; Justine and Mrs Warburton were in the Great Hall, having greeted the corporate guests on their arrival.

The CEO stood in the middle of the hall, his hands thrust deep into the pockets of his jeans as he looked around him. He looked in his mid-forties, tall with short grey hair and small round glasses. His gaze stopped on the picture of the blond knight with the white stag.

"Who's that guy?" he asked

"That's Sir William de Beauvais, the owner of Grangedean Manor in the 1560s," said Justine. "A very interesting man indeed."

"Why so?"

"He never married for starters," she answered, "which was very unusual in those days."

"The guy was gay?"

"That's very unlikely," she said defensively. "In fact it is rumoured that he was very much the ladies' man and had many lovers."

The CEO studied Sir William's portrait. "Certainly looks gay," he observed. "Long blond hair and little beard..."

"No, no!" said Justine indignantly. "Of course, he was very handsome and apparently quite charming, but he was also rumoured to be a strong, rugged fighting man. In fact," she continued, as the CEO glanced at her with a raised eyebrow, "he actually died in a fight on the 31st July 1565, when he was only in his late 20s."

"Hence he never married."

"Exactly."

"Hmm." The CEO studied Sir William again. "How'd he die?"

Mrs. Warburton answered, "It is said he was stabbed in a brawl in a tavern."

"Over a woman?"

"We don't know," said Justine, "but maybe it was. Wouldn't that be just so romantic?"

"Waste of a young guy," said the CEO. "Think what he could have achieved if he'd lived a longer life."

"Oh yes," breathed Justine. "Such a waste."

The CEO chuckled and leaned in conspiratorially to Mrs. Warburton. "The kid's sweet on the dead guy," he said, then turned and moved on.

It was deliberately loud enough for Justine to hear and she felt her face flushing red as she stood rooted to the spot. What a strange idea – how could he possibly think she had anything other than purely historical interest in Sir William de Beauvais? She shook her head to clear the thought, then trotted after the CEO and Mrs. Warburton.

He was walking briskly; his Converse sneakers squeaking on the flagstones as he stared intently at each of the tapestries and the leaded windows in turn.

"Place like this has gotta be haunted?" he demanded.

"Certainly not," said Mrs. Warburton sharply. "Why does everyone assume old houses like this are always haunted? There are no spirits here apart from the spirit of history," she paused, "and the whisky in the private wing, of course." The CEO was sharp enough to recognise that this was meant as a joke and gave a polite laugh. "Sure. Whisky in the private wing. Cool. Yeah."

He turned to Justine. "Right," he said briskly, "let's get this Tudor show on the road. What's first on the agenda?"

Justine took out her phone and opened the notes app. "Mrs. Warburton will take you all around the manor for the full tour. She will finish in the tea rooms so you can grab a cup of tea and some scones, before I take you over to the stable block where we'll fit you into your Tudor costumes."

"Tea and scones?" asked the CEO. "How quaintly English. Do they do coffee and cookies there for us Yanks?"

"Of course," said Justine, trying to ignore Mrs. Warburton's derisive snort behind her. "And they do lovely cakes and tarts as well." She consulted her phone again. "After tea, we have archery, jousting, falconry and sword-fighting, then into the Great Hall for the Royal Banquet at 7pm. Taxis are at 11:30pm." She put her phone back in her pocket. "A full afternoon and evening living the life of the Tudors. Won't that be such great fun?"

---0---

And now it was nearly 11:30pm; the banquet was all but over and the taxis were ready to take the guests away.

Justine stood up from leaning on the gallery balcony and decided to pop down and see if all was well in the kitchens.

She turned and ducked through a low doorway and went down the short stairway into the hall. Then she went through another door and took the final flight of stone stairs down to the kitchens.

As she ran lightly down the stairs she marvelled as always at the sophistication of the Tudor builders who had constructed the magnificent Grangedean Manor over 500 years ago. Every stone fitted together perfectly and such was its quality that even after all this time and use there was only an inch or two of wear on each step. The wood panelling in the private rooms was still in excellent shape, and only in the Great Hall had there been any real renovation – mainly to correct some disastrous redecoration done by the Victorians.

Months of painstaking work had been undertaken under the watchful eye of the National Trust. They were keen to ensure that every detail was correct, even down to the position of the sconces on the wall – although these now had electric bulbs and silk 'flames' rather than actual candles due to health and safety concerns.

Arriving in the kitchens, Justine soon located Rick, the manager from the contract catering company that provided food for the banquets, as well as the lunches and teas for the day trippers in the canteen and tea rooms. He was an unshaven man in his late thirties, with dark spiky hair and large tattoos on both arms; a Colt 45 on the left arm and a pair of crossed hunting rifles on the right. Justine had never made a secret of her dislike of these tattoos, which she thought were unnecessarily aggressive.

"How's it going?" Justine asked neutrally.

"OK," he replied. "The fruit is out but they're hardly touching it. We're going to start clearing the tables now." He shrugged. "Serve them up effing burger and fries and they'd find room, believe me." Behind him a line of serving staff was forming to go out into the hall, all dressed as Tudor servants in smocks bearing the Grangedean Manor coat of arms. "OK, you lot," he barked as they moved past him and started up the stairs to the hall, "get out there and clear the effing tables."

Justine watched them go past. "This lot are quite good. Where d'you get them?"

"Acting school in West London graduated a couple of weeks ago," he answered. "I put a notice up on the board and got the pick of the effing bunch." His gaze lingered on the bottom of the last girl going past. "They were pathetically grateful for any job – especially one where they get to wear a costume."

Justine bit her lip to stop herself being provoked by his typically crass comment. She would be professional, she told herself. She would not let him get to her.

"Talking of actresses, the one playing the Queen has been a perfect darling," she said to change the subject. "Much better than the last one we tried. I'll have a word with her agent tomorrow and see if we can get her again. She's had the CEO eating out of the palm of her hand."

"Too bad they don't eat the effing food as well," muttered Rick.

"Rick, my sweet," said Justine with a forced smile, "they're here to make believe that this is a real Tudor banquet. We put them in Tudor clothes, we pretend the Queen is here and we serve them up the closest thing we can to Tudor food. We try and make it as lovely as we can for them, so they think it is real."

"Yeah. But if this was a real Tudor banquet, Justine, my hopeless little romantic, there'd be more meat than they could possibly stomach; whole deer, hares, pigs, rabbits, stuffed partridges – and that's just for starters. There'd be sugared fruits and marzipan, plums stewed in rose-water – all washed down with a thin ale for the riff-raff because the water was undrinkable, and wine for the nobles. Believe me, if we served them that lot we'd be seriously out of pocket and they'd be as sick as pigs."

"Oh for goodness sake, Rick, don't be such a party pooper," she snapped. She took a breath to steady herself, unsure as to whether she was annoyed with him for being a jerk, or for trying to out-do her on knowledge of the Tudors. "They have a lovely time and that's all that matters," she finished lamely.

"Yeah, well enough," he muttered with a small triumphant grin, then turned away as the first of the Tudor servants started coming back down into the kitchens with the plates.

Still annoyed with herself, Justine went to go back up the narrow stairs to the hall, but first she had to wait for one of the servants to come down carrying a big stack of pewter plates. The serving girl smiled as she went past and said "thanks", but then completely missed her footing on the bottom step; falling headlong and throwing all her plates into the air like an acrobat tossing a fellow performer up to a trapeze.

The plates and cutlery came tumbling down to the flagstone floor in a series of ear-splitting crashes, closely followed by the girl herself. Leftover food was splattered across the stainless steel units; while plates and cutlery spun off in all directions across the kitchens.

Everyone stopped what they were doing and turned to stare. One last plate rolled unsteadily across the flagstones with an unnaturally loud trundling noise, then slowed and toppled over like a drunk, flopping noisily around on its rim a couple of times before coming to rest.

There was a moment's shocked silence.

Then Rick barked out, "Oh effing, effing hell! What the frigging heck was that?"

The girl got up painfully. Justine caught a glimpse of blood on her leg before she smoothed her skirts down. "Sorry, Rick," the girl muttered.

"Sorry?" he said grimly. "Sorry? You'll be effing sorry if you don't clear up that effing mess. You'll be out on your effing ear!"

"Sorry," the girl repeated, and limped forward to pick up the first plate.

"Oh for goodness sake, Rick, that was totally and utterly uncalled for," Justine snapped, "now you've gone too far!" She rushed forward and started picking up plates as well. "It was only an accident!"

"Yeah, right…" Rick snapped back, "and it has to be effing cleared up!"

"You don't need to be such a pig about it." Justine grabbed a cloth and started wiping splattered food off the units. "Why do you always have to be so bolshie?" she hissed at him when she went to the sink to rinse it out.

Rick looked the anger flashing in her eyes. Some of the fight went out of him.

"Yeah. Well, sorry."

"Don't apologise to me," growled Justine. "Apologise to her."

"Yeah, whatever."

"I mean it, Rick. Now!"

Rick went over to the girl, who was standing alone in the centre of the kitchen, clutching some plates and quivering like a hunted stag.

"Sorry," he muttered.

"S'all right," she whispered.

Normal activity and noise levels were resumed in the kitchens. Justine went over to the girl.

"Thanks," the girl said quietly as she put the plates on the worktop.

"It wasn't your fault," said Justine, her voice equally low.

"I'm just a bit clumsy, that's all," the girl said, wincing as she shifted the weight on her leg.

"What's your name?"

"Rachael."

"Well, Rachael," said Justine, putting her hand on the girl's shoulder "I should get that leg bandaged up if I were you. Why don't you pop upstairs to the first aid cupboard? I'll meet you there in five minutes and see what I can do."

---0---

It was after one in the morning when Justine finally got out into the cold night air and made her way across the gravel at the rear of the manor, past the ancient well to where her battered little Ford was standing alone and forlorn in the staff car park. Its windows were misted white in the light of the modern overhead lamps.

She got in and started the car, put the demist on full blast to clear the windows then settled down for the usual long wait until they were clear enough to drive.

Often she would find herself falling asleep, but on this night, she took out her phone and flicked open its case. Scrolling through the screens of apps, she got to the book-reader app and tapped it. It opened where she'd last left off in one of her favourite books – a series of adventures featuring a courageous Tudor heroine called Mary Fox. This book was Mary Fox and the Broken Sword; the first in the series.

"Where was I…?" she muttered to herself. She scanned the first few lines of the chapter. The story quickly came back; Mary Fox has just escaped from the wicked Sir Reginald de Courtney and his henchmen once again…

She settled back in her seat to read, and was quickly absorbed in the story.

She had first come across the series of Mary Fox adventures in the Grangedean library, when she had been exploring the house by herself one summer's evening after work. The library was a lovely peaceful room with a central stone fireplace, which had oak panelling above and barley-twist columns supporting the great mantelpiece. Either side of the fireplace were two large alcoves, each with a gothic arch reaching right up to the white plaster ceiling, and each featuring a richly-decorated oak bookcase with shelves above a cabinet base.

Justine was fascinated by the rows and rows of beautiful leather-bound books, with their musty but evocative smell. There were complete sets of Shakespeare's plays, as well as the works of Jane Austen, Charles Dickens and George Eliot. She selected Middlemarch by George Eliot and opened it to read a random page. She quickly decided that Dorothea Brooke seemed a bit too worthy to hold her interest, so she put the book back. Idly she bent down and opened one of the cabinets. Inside were more books, but these were modern paperbacks. Justine crouched down level with the books for a closer look. Immediately she spotted a series of matching paperbacks with gold leaf titles in a mediaeval typeface. She twisted her head to one side to read them. Mary Fox and the River of Fire. Mary Fox and the Broken Sword. Mary Fox and the Tudor Prince. Fascinated, Justine pulled out the first book – The Broken Sword. She read the blurb on the back. It promised adventure, romance and intrigue, all in a Tudor period setting, with an all-action heroine called Mary Fox who had perilous challenges to face, a curse to defeat and a man's heart to win.

Walking over to a high-backed armchair by the window, Justine sat down, opened the book and started to read.

Two hours later, she finished the last page, closed the book slowly and sat back with a deep sigh. Never before had she read a book that had so completely absorbed her; so completely immersed her in its world, its plot and its characters. Mary Fox was the perfect heroine – idealistic, honest, clever, resourceful and never afraid to fight for what she thought was right. She also had a wide romantic streak – and her honesty, courage and integrity meant she had won the heart of the young man by the end of the book.

Justine then borrowed and read each of the books several times, before deciding that she wanted her own personal copies. She downloaded them all onto her phone so she could dip into any of them whenever she had a few minutes to spare.

Justine glanced up from her phone and saw that the windscreen had now fully cleared. With a small sigh she bade farewell to Mary, switched off her phone and dropped it back in her bag. Then she let out the clutch and the little car juddered forward out of the Grangedean Manor car park.

It was the darkest part of the night with not a star in the sky, or another car on the road, and soon Justine's headlights swept around the corner of her block of flats in Hammersmith, West London, before she parked in her designated space.

She got out and locked the car, then let herself into the flat, kicked off her shoes and changed into an old t-shirt. She padded into the kitchen and opened the fridge door, then peered in for half a minute without being really aware of what she was looking for.

With a grunt of annoyance at herself, she closed the fridge, went to her room and climbed into bed.

Lying on her back, she chuckled drowsily as she remembered the words of the CEO before getting into his taxi to go home.

"Good job, Justine," he had said. "The team bonded well, and having the Queen was a great piece of theatre. Only thing…" he had looked her squarely in the eye "…not sure about the food. A bit rich, even for us Yanks. I don't suppose next time you could bend history a bit and lay on some burger and fries?"

CHAPTER THREE

Justine's drive from her flat in Hammersmith back to Grangedean Manor the next morning was considerably slower in the busy traffic, until she got to the leafy lanes of the countryside. The sun shone weakly overhead, but out to the west she could see an ominous dark grey storm cloud approaching.

She turned into the car park and slowed to drive round the large ancient well before parking.

Seeing it brought back memories of the day she had first driven into the Grangedean Manor car park for her job interview a year before. She'd been working as an events manager for a corporate hospitality firm, organising events like lunches at Ascot and Henley – but she'd been feeling more and more disillusioned with these. Where was the satisfaction in delivering yet more smoked salmon to hordes of racegoers? How could she possibly get excited about catering to people who were really there just to 'see and be seen'? There must be more interesting events to organise, she had thought – a chance to create something with passion, something that people would remember for years to come. So when she saw the advert for the job of events manager at Grangedean Manor, she'd applied straight away.

On the morning of the interview, the ancient well had fascinated her as she had driven in, optimistically choosing the car park marked 'Staff'.

Once she'd parked, she walked up onto the raised dais to get a closer look. The well was built of thin red bricks that were worn down through years of weathering. Above it was a pitched roof finished with orange clay tiles, supported by two thick wooden struts. It stood on a raised dais that ran all the way round, lifting it up above the main cobbled car park.

She ran her hand over the worn bricks, wondering how many different people had done just that over the centuries. What had happened here – was it like a Tudor 'water cooler' where people would meet and gossip? What stories could this humble brick, wood and clay structure tell? What dramas had taken place beside it; what events had it witnessed?

She peered over the edge. There was a wooden board set a couple of feet below the lip, capping off the void below. She leaned over and tapped it curiously. There was a hollow, echoing sound that suggested great depth underneath.

Suddenly a wave of dizziness swept over her and she felt as if she was tipping forward into the well. Then it seemed like the wooden board had disappeared and all she could see below her was a dreadful blackness, rising up to swallow her. In terror she scrabbled at the sides and after a moment, managed to get a grip. With an effort she pushed herself back upright.

As she stood up, breathing hard, she looked back down at the well.

The wooden board was firmly in place – very solid and very real. There was no black void and she could never have been in any actual danger.

"Are you all right?"

She turned to see a tall, iron-haired lady in a tweed skirt and sensible brogues striding towards her across the courtyard.

"Yes, yes I'm fine," she said, glancing back into the well. The board was still there. Still solid. She took a deep breath and smiled. "Just a dizzy turn." She stepped down from the dais.

"This is the staff car park," said the lady, sounding as if she was trying to be helpful but betraying annoyance with her sharp tone. "The public car park is round the corner and on the other side of the cedars." She pointed across towards the exit.

"I'm actually here for an interview – for events manager."

"Oh, right. I see." The lady paused, looking Justine up and down, and seemed to soften. "Are you really all right? You look green."

"Really, I'm fine."

The lady shook her head. "Well, you don't look it. Quite green. Come into the house and we'll find you some water."

Justine suddenly felt very thirsty. "OK, thanks," she said.

"And I'll show you where to go. Is it Susan Holmes you're seeing? The general manager?"

"Yes."

"Right. Come on then." The lady turned and strode across the car park towards the house. "Mrs. Warburton," she said suddenly over her shoulder.

"I beg your pardon?"

"My name. Mrs. Warburton."

"Oh. Right. Justine. Justine Parker."

Mrs. Warburton stopped and turned, then shook Justine by the hand. Her handshake was very firm.

"Pleased to meet you, Miss Parker."

"And you, Mrs. Warburton," answered Justine, trying to restore feeling in her hand by flexing her fingers rapidly.

A few moments later Mrs. Warburton led Justine up a few steps through the front door and into the main entrance of the house.

Justine caught her breath as she took in the scene. They were in an imposing hallway with a single wooden staircase leading up to a gallery corridor. The wood of the banister finials and gallery vault posts was a fine dark oak, turned in a barley-twist style. The stair treads were also oak, with only the slightest wear in the centre of each tread. At the back of the hallway under the gallery was a hanging tapestry showing a hunting scene and next to it was a burnished suit of amour by a pair of imposing double doors.

"What a magnificent, lovely place," Justine whispered, letting her gaze move slowly up the stairs and onto the gallery. "So romantic."

As she looked around, she felt the house work its magic on her – she felt that this house belonged in the past, not the present. Its true reality was the golden age of the Tudors; an age of chivalrous men and romantic women, of intrigue and love, of beautiful clothes and fine foods. An age when the concerns of modern life – of mobile phones, traffic, televisions and social media – didn't matter anymore; when all that mattered was romance and a love of life. In this reality there were no electric bulbs lighting the hallway, the suit of armour was for battle not display, the tread on the stairs was new and there were no information leaflets on display for tourists...

What this reality needed was a romantic love scene.

Justine gazed up at the gallery. In this scene a beautiful girl in a narrow-waisted gown would open the door and step serenely onto the gallery. Justine half-closed her eyes and let several hundred years roll away. In the bright sunlight of a fresh Tudor morning, she imagined such a girl appearing.

Justine admired the elegant simplicity of the girl's green velvet gown with its lace trimmings at the sleeves, the wide neckline with a single pearl on a chain, the fine jeweled velvet French hood that framed her face, as she swept effortlessly to the top of the stairs and seemed to glide down. As she did so a tall, handsome man with curly blond hair and a trim beard stepped out to receive her. He gave a low bow. Justine admired his fine doublet, the deep slashes over red velvet in his breeches and sleeves, the grey hose and soft leather boots. He had a sword hanging from his left hip and a red silk cape on his shoulder.

Justine held her breath as the girl gazed into the man's eyes, then looked down demurely and curtseyed low. The girl held out her hand and he took it, brought it to his lips and kissed it gently as he raised her up. She lifted her eyes and smiled at him, a look of deep love that Justine knew was forever. The girl took the man's arm and swept her away through the double doors.

Justine sighed deeply.

"It's beautiful," she said. "I love it."

"Indeed," said Mrs. Warburton matter-of-factly. "Fascinating people, the Tudors." She pointed at the double doors. "You go through to the Great Hall while I'll get you some water." She marched off across the hall and disappeared through a side door.

Justine picked up a leaflet from a rack. 'Grangedean Manor was built in 1498 by a wealthy landowner called Sir Thomas de Beauvais and extended in 1560 when his grandson Sir William inherited it,' she read. 'The house has twelve bedrooms, a great hall, extensive kitchens and has its own chapel. Much of the original Tudor décor is still intact, and, while not on the scale of Tudor houses such as Burghley or Hatfield, Grangedean represents a significant historical insight into the lives of Tudor nobility. It is understood that Shakespeare stayed here in 1594 and that Charles I stopped here during the Civil War.'

Justine walked through into the Great Hall.

If the entrance had been beautiful, then this place was doubly magnificent. Light burst in through the leaded panes of square, clear glass in three main windows. The central window was a gothic arch that ran right up to the ornate plaster-decorated ceiling, and the two side windows each reached to about three quarters of its height.

Justine looked up and saw that she was standing under a minstrels' gallery. A large portrait of a Tudor knight caught her eye. He was wearing a burnished silver breastplate and was holding his sword up in his right hand. There was a noble-looking white stag standing behind him.

Justine moved closer to look at this man.

Suddenly she caught her breath. There was no mistaking the blond hair and beard – he was absolutely the romantic hero she'd imagined in the hallway…

"Sir William de Beauvais," said Mrs. Warburton from behind her. "Born 1539, died on the night of the 31st of July 1565; stabbed while in a tavern. He was reputed to be something of a wild man." Mrs. Warburton held out a glass. "Your water."

Suddenly the peace was broken by the sound of loud voices, the squeak of trainers on the flagstones and the clicking of smartphone cameras. Justine took the water, then turned and saw a party of tourists being led in by a woman in her mid-thirties with blond highlights. The woman was talking to the group.

"This is the Great Hall. Come on, everyone in? Good. The great hall was the heart of a Tudor manor and would have been used for banquets, dancing and entertaining. The painting on the wall is of Sir William de Beauvais, the squire who owned the house in the 1560s. The hall is undergoing restoration work to bring it to exactly how we believe it would have looked to Sir William. Except, of course, the electric light there," the woman pointed at the sconces, "would have been real candles."

There were appreciative noises from the tourists as they gazed around the hall. One of them walked to the wall for a closer look at some restoration work on the plaster mouldings.

"We frequently hold Tudor banquets ourselves, with authentic costumes, food and entertainment," continued the woman. "Very popular in the corporate entertainment market. If anyone is interested, I can let you have a leaflet on the way out."

She turned and noticed Justine and Mrs. Warburton. "Justine Parker? Here for the interview?"

"Yes."

"Good. This is the last room we're doing. I'll see you in my office in a few minutes; just to the right of the front door. Has Mrs. Warburton been giving you the tour?"

"Yes," said Justine, wondering if Mrs. Warburton actually had a first name.

"Good." She moved to the other end of the hall with her party and started telling them about the decorative plaster work above the large ornate fireplace, before leading them back out into the hallway. She could be heard saying goodbye to them, then a door closed and there was silence.

"I think that's your cue to go in for the interview," observed Mrs. Warburton.

"Yes," said Justine. "Thanks for the tour. The house is so lovely."

"Indeed it is," agreed Mrs. Warburton. Together they went back to the entrance hall, where Mrs. Warburton pointed to a door marked 'Office'. Justine took a deep breath to steady her nerves, and knocked.

"Come."

She pushed open the door and went in. The blond woman was sitting behind an antique oak desk holding Justine's CV. She gestured to the chair opposite.

"Hello. I'm Susan – general manager at Grangedean Manor," she said when Justine was seated.

"Hello."

"Look, I've read your CV – looks fine. Events co-ordinator at university, events administrator at your last place, promoted to events manager – blah blah blah. Fine. Just fine." She tapped the CV on the table a couple of times, as if considering her options, then deliberately put it face down on the table. "But I'm not interested in that – I'm much more interested in you, Justine – you as a person."

"Oh, right. OK." This was not how she expected the interview to start.

Or any interview, for that matter.

"I have one question. What is it about Grangedean Manor that appeals to you, and why?"

Fighting down the instinct to point out that that was two questions, Justine thought a moment and said: "My previous job was all about money. Events were purely about the numbers – numbers of people through the door, numbers of pounds profit made. And while I know that's important, for me it's about the event itself. Here at Grangedean Manor you can give people a taste of what it must have been like in historical times. I want to be able to make history come alive for them – that's really special." Justine's eyes sparkled as she went on, "Grangedean Manor is such a fantastic place – I mean, when the restoration is complete, we will be able to see the house just as people like Sir William de Beauvais would have seen it. How amazing is that? To look at a wall, or a window, or a fireplace, and to know that people 450 years ago would have seen just the same thing – it's like they just walked out the room and will walk back in any moment!" She stopped. Susan was looking at her with a quizzical expression. "Sorry – got a bit carried away there. Yeah – it's a lovely house. I'd love to work here…" she tailed off.

Susan carried on looking quizzically at her.

Justine thought she must have blown it.

"I see… When can you start?"

CHAPTER FOUR

It was 6 o'clock in the evening, the day after the big banquet. Justine had now been working at Grangedean Manor for over a year.

She finished some last emails and switched off her PC. The storm which had been threatening all day had now finally arrived. The rain was lashing down, with frequent rumbles of thunder and flashes of lightning that seared across the office with harsh white light.

She grabbed her bag, unplugged her phone from its charging cable and threw it in. She then grabbed her Bluetooth portable speaker and threw that in as well – she liked to have it filling her kitchen with its loud, pure sound while she was cooking and had even been known to do some serious karaoke, dancing round using her wooden spoon as a microphone.

The joys of living alone.

Something caught her eye in her bag and curiously she fished it out. It was an unopened box containing a solar charger for her phone and speaker. For a moment she couldn't think how it had got in her bag, then she recalled buying it on a whim when she'd last been in the phone shop – attracted by the thought of being able to charge her batteries even if there wasn't a plug handy. With a shrug she tossed it back in her bag and left her office.

She made her way towards the kitchens, with the sound of thunder echoing along the long basement corridor, then climbed the steps and went through the door into the Great Hall. Out of the windows she could see the sky was so dark it was almost as if it was a winter's night, as sheets of rain battered the ancient leaded windows.

A few of the electric candle lights were on in the Great Hall, and Justine's eye caught the picture of Sir William on the wall. As usual, she walked over and gazed up at the portrait. As she did so a flash of lightning lit up the room with a burning intensity that seared a negative of the painting into her brain. Immediately afterwards, there was a deep blast of thunder that made the windows shake and the whole room resonate like a giant drum.

At the same moment, the lights went out.

With the image of the picture dancing in front of her unseeing eyes, she turned and made her way by feel and force of habit to the main doors, as another roar of thunder shook the room and a searing flash of lighting lit it up as if it were broad daylight. She reached the main double doors and pulled – but they remained stuck. Starting to feel scared, she pulled again and again, as yet another flash of lightning illuminated the room, followed by another crash of thunder. This one was so loud, that Justine thought her ears had burst.

Now screaming, she pulled at the door again, but it remained stuck firm. She pummelled on it, shouting, but she knew it was no use. How would anyone hear her above the driving rain and roaring thunder?

Another bolt of lightning flashed and she ran to the door to the kitchens that she had come through only a few moments ago. She knew it couldn't be locked – it didn't have a lock on it at all. But like the main doors, it too was firmly closed. She beat on it screaming till her fists hurt, but no one came.

Another bolt of lightning.

Another immediate massive blast of thunder – the loudest yet.

After this came further loud secondary rumbles. They rolled on, one after another, but seeming to get louder and louder so that soon she was sure they were louder than the original crash...

Then she heard the voices.

At first they were indistinct against the lashing rain and roar of the thunder, but increasingly they became clear. Voices from the past, beating against the inside of her head: Queen Elizabeth's Annus Horribilis speech; Churchill's rousing call to 'fight them on the beaches;' Chamberlain's ultimatum that launched World War 2; snatches of speech referring to Queen Victoria, the American Civil War, Waterloo, the slave trade, the Fire of London, the Spanish Armada... with her head spinning and her eyes tight shut, Justine slid down the door and curled up in a foetal ball on the floor, wishing it would stop, sobbing for it to stop, becoming nothing more than a shrivelled bundle of anguish as the noise and the voices spun round and round in her head...

A crash of thunder – even louder than the last.

Then total, wonderful, silence.

Peace.

Justine uncurled herself slowly and opened her eyes.

The Great Hall appeared bright and fresh, as summer sunshine poured in through the great window. Carefully she got to her feet. Everything looked normal as she turned round and round, seeking some confirmation of the traumatic events of a few moments ago. But there was no sign of the storm or any physical evidence that it had ever happened. Just peace and quiet, with dust drifting gently down through the shafts of sunlight, birds singing outside and the soft sound of trees rustling in a light breeze.

She turned back to the double doors and reached out to try them again. At that moment they burst open.

A man strode in, in full Tudor clothing.

He was wearing a muddy doublet, muddier boots and a dusty cloak. His tousled blond hair fell over his forehead and was streaked with dirt, but there was no mistaking the trim beard and aristocratic bearing from the painting on the wall.

The man was every inch Sir William de Beauvais.

He stopped at the sight of Justine standing in the hall. Three more men were entering behind him, all dressed in similar clothes to his. One was in the middle of a conversation.

"So I said, 'Damn me, sir, if the horse founders under me, get me another!'" He laughed. "The scoundrel would have none of it, though..."

He and the other two stopped short at the sight of Justine.

"Well, well, well," said the man, "what have we here, Sir William?"

"I cannot tell, Dowland, except that it is a wench who is wearing the strangest garments I have ever seen." The blond man stopped and studied her closely, his expression one of amused curiosity as he walked all round her, staring at her short pleated skirt, plain sweater and soft leather boots.

"Do you pretend to be a man, wench? For if you do, you have the sorriest excuse for clothing. Your doublet has no shape, your breeches are unfinished and your hose is so thin you would sooner be barelegged."

He paused.

"Who are you and what are you doing in my house?"

CHAPTER FIVE

Justine had always felt that underneath her slightly fluffy exterior, there beat a reasonably rational heart. She wasn't superstitious; she made a point of walking under ladders and delighted in seeing a single magpie. These things proved how sensible she could be. Sure, she had a romantic streak as wide as an ocean, and often found herself disappointed when people she thought were nice turned out not to be, but no one could accuse her of believing in magic, or witchcraft, or even time-travel...

So there must be a perfectly rational explanation for this strange turn of events. What was the conversation she'd had the night before with Rick? He'd mentioned the local drama school providing actors – that must be it.

So she clapped slowly. "Very good! Love it! You're meant to be Sir William de Beauvais!"

"Aye, I am Sir William de Beauvais. And this is Master Dowland, Master Stanmore and Master Melrose." He indicated the three other men.

"Right. OK. Sir William de Beauvais, Master Dowland, Master Stanmore and Master Melrose. OK, guys, you can drop it now. I'm on the staff. You're very good, honestly. Who booked you? Why wasn't I told? I usually get the actors…"

"Actors?" Sir William barked. "By thunder, you think we are lowly mummers or strolling players?" He folded his arms. "I can assure you, we are nothing of the sort!"

"Yeah, right – so these beards are..." She grabbed Dowland's beard and gave a sharp pull. It stayed resolutely attached to his chin and he gave a wounded yelp. "...real, then. Sorry."

"By heaven, Sir William, turn her out! She is mad!" snapped Dowland, rubbing his chin.

"You are too easily frighted." Sir William chuckled at his friend's discomfort. "I feel she possesses an elfin charm. What is your name, wench?"

But Justine wasn't listening. She had just noticed the sconces had fat wax candles burning in them instead of light bulbs and flappy silk. And now she looked through the double doors, she could see that there was no literature rack, no suit of armour, and out through the open front door there was no driveway or gravel, just open lawns. 'OK, so maybe it's a dream,' she thought, 'a very vivid, very real dream. I must have banged my head during the storm. So that's all right then. Just a dream.'

She looked back at the men standing before her.

The man identified as Sir William, for all his muddy clothes and dusty cloak, carried himself with an easy, aristocratic charm, and it was clear to see that he was the man in the picture on the wall behind him. The man called Dowland was short and dark, with a swarthy, almost Hispanic look, and a gold earring in his left ear. Stanmore was tall and blond and was regarding her with a look of deep suspicion.

Justine looked at Melrose and saw that he was different from the others – a dry, cold man, with strange, almost lifeless eyes. He seemed to be dressed less for hunting than for a formal occasion; even his clothes were less dusty and muddy than the others. His doublet and breeches were dark grey, with slashes revealing a darker material beneath, and his black hose disappeared into boots that were stiff and shiny whereas the others were of soft brown leather. Yet, for all his formality, Justine thought he was actually less well off than the others, as if he was the poor relation allowed to tag along.

She became aware that Sir William was waiting his answer.

"Your name, wench?" he repeated.

"Oh, sorry, yeah. Justine. Justine Parker."

"Justine?" This was Stanmore. "Is that a French name? She is French? By heaven, turn her out, Sir William!

"Are you French?" asked Sir William.

"No, I'm from London. From Hammersmith," she added, feeling that a bit of extra geographical accuracy may help. Although as it was her dream, did that matter?

"Come, wench," said Dowland, "you cannot be from London and from Hammersmith. They are many miles apart."

"Give her to me, Sir William. I will put her to use in my house," said Melrose.

Sir William glanced at him, and Justine could see that this had touched a nerve. "No, Tom, I will keep her here. Martha has told me that we are short-handed in the kitchens. She can work there."

"If you please, my lord," muttered Melrose, his cold formality from a few moments ago briefly stripped away to reveal something more visceral under the surface.

"I do please, Tom," replied Sir William, seeming not to notice.

'I think I was right about Tom Melrose,' thought Justine. 'Definitely the poor relation – there's no doubt who is the lord and master in this house. Fascinating dream – very interesting.'

Sir William threw off his cloak and shouted out, "Martha! Martha! Here, I say!" Then he turned to the other men. "I think some hard labour in the kitchens should knock sense into this little madam, and teach her not to pull at men's beards."

The door under the gallery opened and a girl in her early twenties appeared. She was wearing a plain black dress and a simple cotton coif on her head. "Yes, Sir William?" she said with a warm smile.

"This girl is to be put to work in the kitchens, Martha. Cook can see to her tasks. Take her down."

Martha looked hard at Justine. "A strange girl, Sir William," she said with a confident smile. "I wouldn't have her in the house."

"By thunder, woman! I don't ask for your opinion, and I don't expect it!" barked Sir William. "Were you my wife, I would expect less of the carping concerns I get from you all day long. Now take her down!"

The smile froze on Martha's face. Justine felt that she had been put firmly in her place. "As you wish, Sir William," she said coldly. She grabbed Justine's arm and started dragging her to the door. "Now you come with me, missy, and we'll soon find out what you're made of."

The pain of Martha's grip on her arm was a shock to Justine. It was exactly the kind of pain which would normally make her wake up from a dream – but in this case it didn't; the pain, and the situation, continued.

As she was dragged to the door, Justine was forced to the terrifying conclusion – indeed the only conclusion.

This was actually happening.

This was real.

Martha pushed her through the door and down the stairs. In the flickering light of the torches on the walls, Justine could see that the stairs were completely flat, with no wear on them at all.

Oh yes, this was real all right. Somehow, time in Grangedean Manor had turned back hundreds of years and she was now a part of actual Tudor history.

'Oh Christ. Oh hell,' she thought, fighting down the panic that was starting to twist her stomach. 'I'm really back in Tudor England. What do I do now?'

---0---

Back in the Great Hall, Richard Stanmore settled himself with a deep sigh on one of the chairs at the high table, while Sir William sat at the head. Dowland and Melrose sat on the other side of Sir William.

"You are hard on your housekeeper, Sir William," observed Stanmore as he stretched his legs out to ease them after many hours in the saddle. "I think she has perhaps set her sights on you."

"My dear Stanmore," responded Sir William. "Martha is a housekeeper – a passable housekeeper – that is all. She should no more think to rise above her station than to fly over the chimneys." He paused and gave a broad grin. "Just because a man has known a woman in his bedchamber this very night past, it does not mean he has opened the door of his heart to her knocking."

On the other side of the table Dowland laughed loudly. "Will, you dog! Is there any woman of this house you do not 'know'?" He accompanied the word with an obscene gesture which gave Stanmore no doubt about its meaning.

"I'll admit the cook is not to my taste – that is all," responded Sir William. "Nor has this strange wench from Hammersmith been explored – as yet."

"And these girls have no cause for complaint?" asked Stanmore levelly, wanting to enter into the spirit of this humour, but not wishing to stoop to Dowland's levels of obscenity.

"My dear Stanmore – if by that you mean that the girls I employ do not object to my attentions before I carry them through, then I say I neither know nor care. If, however, you are referring to any concerns they may have afterwards..." Sir William paused for effect, "...then they are quite past caring!"

When the laughter had subsided, Melrose observed dryly, "Gentlemen, here you see the man with everything; good looks, good land, a fine house, wealth – and a form of droit de seigneur with all the women of his household. Except, of course, the cook. What more could a man ask for?"

"You do me proud," responded Sir William. He glanced at Melrose, then added casually, "it is too bad only one of us can enjoy such good fortune."

A chill suddenly descended on the room, despite the bright sunshine.

Stanmore could see instinctively that Sir William had touched the rawest of nerves in Thomas Melrose, although he did not know why these words had produced such a strong reaction.

Melrose's thin mouth was working and his eyes were narrowed as he struggled to contain himself. Stanmore found himself automatically looking down at Melrose's hand in case it went to his sword. Stanmore's own hand moved closer to his own sword, ready to draw it and spring to his master's defence if necessary.

Then the moment passed. Melrose smiled; a thin, humourless smile. "Indeed, my lord, it is too bad. But such is fortune."

"Aye," said Sir William, with a most guileless look. "Such is fortune." He turned and said to Dowland on the other side, "Come, we have all enjoyed a magnificent hunt. Shall we not have a pint of beer, some cake, and relive the glories of the chase?"

"My lord, I was sure you would never suggest it!" responded Dowland impishly, forcing Stanmore to conclude that neither Sir William nor Dowland had understood the depth of Melrose's anger just then. Maybe he'd imagined it? But then, over Sir William's shoulder, he caught sight of Melrose shooting a glance of pure loathing at his master, before composing his face into its more usual mask of urbane civility. 'No,' thought Stanmore, 'that was real.'

"Excellent," said Sir William and called out, "Martha! Here, I say!"

There was silence for a short while, then the door opened and Martha came in. "Yes, my lord?" she said coldly.

"Some cakes and ale."

"Yes, my lord."

"And the girl – she is put to work?"

"Yes, my lord." Martha turned to go back through the door. "And I don't warrant she's up to it, either, the little slattern," she muttered. She closed the door behind her.

"It pleases you to pull that woman along?" Stanmore asked.

"She is a servant," said Sir William. "And she cleaves to her position in life. There's no more to say on the matter."

"Indeed," cut in Melrose quietly. "But be sure to keep a watch on your back, Sir William, lest one who is in your service sees fit to attack it."

"Nay, Tom," responded Sir William, turning to him. "Upon my honour, no one in my service would attack my back. Not when I have such upright, steadfast and loyal bondsmen as yourself to look out for it." The challenge hung in the air between them.

"Indeed, my Master," answered Melrose. It seemed to Stanmore that his lips formed a thinner line and his eyes were even more lifeless than before. "You are fortunate in this matter."

"Excellent!" exclaimed Sir William. "There is no more fortunate knight in the county than myself." He spread his arms wide. "To have friends such as you – that is true wealth!" He smiled at each in turn. "I am indeed blessed!"

The door opened and a man in black breeches and a blue jerkin entered, carrying a wooden tray with a jug, four tankards and a large baked loaf. He set these down on the table in front of the four men and bowed low.

"Thank you, Simon," said Sir William.

"Master," muttered the servant in acknowledgement, then retired backwards through the door and closed it after himself.

CHAPTER SIX

At one end of the kitchens was a large metal spit, standing over head height. On the spit was the carcass of a boar and under it was a large brazier filled with blazing coals. The spit needed to be kept turning in order to ensure the boar cooked evenly, so it was linked by a series of chains and pulleys to a handle. And to work the handle, a dedicated person – known as a spit-boy – was needed.

Justine Parker, events manager at Grangedean Manor in the 21st century, was now its 16th century spit-boy.

Filthy with sweat and soot in the unbearable heat, Justine was sullenly turning the handle under the watchful eye of a small, shrewish woman called Margaret. When the servant Simon entered down the stairs from the Great Hall it distracted Margaret briefly, so Justine took the opportunity to rest. Immediately there was a shout from the cook.

"Hey, you girl! No stopping!"

Margaret looked up, saw what had happened, and as Justine pushed the handle round again, she stepped up and hit Justine in the side with a birch stick she was carrying.

"Oi, girl!" she shouted. "Don't you be stopping!"

Justine resisted the temptation to break the birch stick across Margaret's forehead. She had quickly learned that such defiance did not lead anywhere. This had been a lesson courtesy of the cook, a fearsome woman with teeth like an old graveyard and breath to match.

As she turned the spit, Justine recalled her introduction to the kitchens.

At first the kitchens had been a source of great wonder – her first glimpse of the reality of Tudor life, even blowing away her initial panic. She had simply stood and looked round in amazement, her mind almost exploding with the enormity of seeing at first-hand the lives she could only have imagined before.

People in smocks were chopping vegetables, pounding substances in pestles, kneading dough and rolling out pastry. They were all working at a large wooden table running the full length of the room. There was no natural light – some braziers on the walls and the fire under the roasting spit providing all the light and considerable heat.

Justine wanted to run up to each person and ask them what they were doing. What foods were they preparing? What tools were they using? She wanted to find out what they thought about the dishes they were making – dishes for the nobility that they would never be allowed to enjoy themselves. Did they like their jobs? What were their hours? What was the part of the job they liked best? What was the worst?

She wanted to ask them about their lives at Grangedean Manor and what life was like at their homes. How did they feed themselves and their families? Where did they get their own food…? So many questions – so many interesting facts to learn first-hand from real people in their very own words, instead of out of a history book…

But she hung back, because stationed at the centre of the table was a large, red-faced woman with straggly straw-like hair escaping from under a grubby white woollen cap, small, piggy eyes and a large nose covered in broken veins. The woman was attacking a joint of meat with a cleaver. Her air of authority and menace was palpable and Justine decided she must be the head cook.

Martha went over and leaned across the table, talking to the woman in a low voice. Justine couldn't hear the words, but there was no mistaking the meaning as the woman stopped chopping, and turned to stare at Justine.

"Where is this girl? Bring her here so I can see her better – me eyes ain't what they once were."

Martha pushed Justine up to the table in front of the woman, who put her cleaver down and peered myopically at her.

"I'll leave her to you, Cook," said Martha. "Menial tasks only, mind. Nothing better than scullion or spit-boy." She gave Justine a hard look and swept out, leaving Justine face to face with the cook.

"Ha!" exclaimed the cook and Justine got a full blast of the worst breath she had ever smelt. It was all Justine could do not to faint; instead she brought her hand up and rubbed her nose, trying to use the smell of her hand to mask the foul breath of the cook.

"A delicate little madam is this, I fear," the cook continued, addressing the room in general. "We shall have to knock some of the silk and lace out of her." The kitchen servants all nodded and made approving noises.

Justine decided to try a reasonable approach. "Look," she said "I'm sorry to bother you and all that, but I think there's been some sort of mistake…"

"Mistake?" responded the cook, in an ominously sweet-sounding voice. "Mistake?" she repeated softly. "I don't think my ears is gone." She inclined her head slightly at a small, weasel-faced woman standing next to her, while her eyes never left Justine's. "Margaret, is my ears gone?"

Justine noticed the kitchen servants now start to back cautiously away from the three of them at the centre of the table.

"Goodness, no, Cook," responded Margaret silkily, seeming to play along. "Better than those of a bat, they are. Begging your pardon, Cook."

"So, madam, think you my ears is gone?" the cook asked Justine, as the kitchen servants backed away further.

"Well, no, but..."

The cook gave a sickly smile and dropped into an even silkier voice. "And blow me," she purred, "if I didn't hear Mistress Martha say you was to work in the kitchens. That not so?" She paused. "Was I mistaken?"

The kitchen servants were now spread around the edges of the room, leaving Justine, Margaret and the cook quite alone at the centre of the table.

"Well, no, but..."

Then the explosion came, on a blast of stomach-churning foul breath.

"So you're to work! Hear me?" the cook bellowed, leaning forward so her face was inches from Justine's. "You're to work in my kitchen, doing work that I give you and thank me for it!" She paused to draw breath. "And if I hear so much as a whisper of complaint from you, you no good little piece of baggage, you'll find I'm not so reasonable no more, and you'll be begging me for mercy. You like that, girl?"

Justine tried to formulate a reply, but waves of nausea were making her feel she was going to throw up any moment.

"I don't like you, girl, I don't like you at all. But I've got you, so I'll use you. Margaret! Put her to the spit. And if she slacks a moment, sharpen her up with your birch."

Margaret ducked under the table and emerged next to Justine. She grabbed Justine's arm. "You come with me, missy," she said as she dragged Justine to the handle of the spit. A teenage boy was already turning it. "You, boy – go gather parsley from the gardens." The boy looked up and Justine caught a glimpse of white eyes in a soot-blackened face before he scampered quickly away. Margaret pushed her to the spit handle. "You'll be the spit-boy and turn that, missy, and don't you stop – or you'll have my birch here to smarten you up."

Justine put her bag down near the spit and started to turn the handle. It moved with difficulty and creaked loudly, but everyone had returned to their tasks and no one seemed to be particularly bothered as she got into a rhythm; turning the handle at the right speed to make the boar cook all round. In the searing heat of the fire, with a prize blister soon starting to come up on her thumb and an ache building in her back and arms, Justine watched them go about their work in wonder…

That was until the moment when Simon's entrance had brought her the birch stick in her side.

Maybe Tudor life wasn't quite as fun as she had originally thought? Maybe she had been a bit too enthusiastic, as Mrs. Warburton had pointed out? Maybe history was only fun when you looked back on it... Maybe, being stuck in history was actually rather scary…

Justine suddenly became aware of the foul reek of dead cat, and looked up to see the cook standing over her.

"You girl, stop now! The roast is done – can you not see?"

"But you said..." Justine started, then caught the look in the cook's eye and held her tongue.

The cook turned away and was bellowing orders. "You, you and you," she pointed at three of the servants, "come with me to the gardens to gather herbs. The rest of you can go up and start to prepare the Great Hall. Margaret, go up first and be sure the room is clear and the master is gone. You," she turned back to Justine, "dowse the fire and wait here."

Margaret immediately gathered her skirts and ran out. She could be heard pattering up the stairs to the Great Hall, as the cook gathered the three designated herb-pickers. When the cook was happy that everyone was in place, she marched out with them, like a mother duck with her ducklings in tow. Those who were to prepare the Great Hall were running around gathering up knives, wooden platters and pewter plates onto old blackened wood trays, and were making ready to take them upstairs.

Justine suddenly had a flashback to the night before; a line of actors playing at being Tudor servants, holding trays of food and preparing to go up into the Great Hall to serve...

...only this time the servants were real Tudors…

...the food was real Tudor food…

...and that fire was really blackening the belly of the roast...

Justine looked around in a panic for something to dowse it and saw an old earthenware jug standing by a tub of water. She ran over to it. The water was brown and smelt rank. She wondered if it might actually be the soup, but she filled the jug to the brim anyway and ran back to throw it on the fire. There was a whoosh of steam and a few sparks flew onto the flagstones. She stood back and looked at the remaining kitchen servants to see if there would be a shout of annoyance, but no one commented so she ran back, re-filled the jug and repeated the operation several times, with more steam and whooshing noises until the flames were gone and the fire was down to just glowing embers.

Breathing a sigh of relief she studied the belly of the boar and decided that it might, at a pinch, not be too obvious that it was burned – in the dark, with the light behind, perhaps. Relieved, she rubbed her hands over her face and through her hair, unaware she was leaving further black streaks on her already filthy face.

Margaret reappeared and announced that the Great Hall was clear. The remaining servants ran out with their trays and suddenly there was silence, broken only by the gentle hissing and popping of the fire as it died.

Margaret stood still and eyed Justine suspiciously. She still had her birch stick, which she held in one hand and tapped menacingly against the open palm of her other. "You, girl. You finished turning the roast?"

Justine nodded.

Margaret walked over and inspected it. "You burned it," she said coldly. "Cook will have to decide what's to be used and what's to be thrown to the dogs, as the Lord is my witness."

Justine remained silent, eyeing the birch stick suspiciously.

"You got a tongue in your head, girl?" demanded Margaret, an unpleasant sneer across her small face.

Justine didn't answer immediately – she was thinking hard. What would Mary Fox do now? Most probably she would snatch the birch stick with a defiant yell, give Margaret a few hard thumps with it – to pay her back for the earlier beating – then sprint across the kitchen and make good her adventurous escape, stealing the horse that just happened to be conveniently tethered outside. Yes, that's what Mary Fox would do.

But back in the real world, Justine Parker simply smiled weakly and said, "I am so sorry, Margaret. This is all a bit new to me, but I'm sure I'll get the hang of it soon. Is there anything else I can do to help?"

Margaret looked a bit taken aback but seemed to rally quickly. "If you cannot even perform duties as a spit-boy, why should you be given anything else to do?" She paused a moment. "You was only to do menial duties, anyhow." She glanced around the kitchens as if looking for the most unpleasant job she could find. "Yes," she said with a slow smile, "you can scrub the hearth."

Justine followed her gaze across to the blackened hearth under the arched stone chimney breast and her heart sank. The hearth was around six feet wide and three feet deep, with a black metal grate standing in the middle. All round the grate thick soot had piled up like black snow drifts, clinging to the legs of the grate, spilling over the front of the hearth, and streaking up the stone wall behind.

Margaret tapped Justine with her stick to walk her over to the hearth. "There, girl," she said when they were in front of it. "Clean that well – I'll be back presently to see how you have progressed." She turned to walk out, but then paused by a large tub full of a nasty-looking grey-green substance. "And when you have finished, you can empty out this tub of old tallow. It is no longer fit for anything but spreading on the land outside." She gave a small chuckle. "Fare thee well, girl," she said, and walked out, leaving Justine alone in the kitchens.

Justine stood in front of the hearth. "Welcome to Tudor England, Cinderella," she muttered to herself, then looked around for something to use on the hearth. After poking around the back of the kitchens for a few minutes, she came across a wooden broom standing in a wooden bucket. The broom looked just like the classic witch's broomstick, with hundreds of very thin pliable branches bound onto a long wooden handle and cut straight across at the end.

She took it back to the hearth and started sweeping, but the soot was so fine that all she succeeded in doing was stirring up great clouds of it, which then settled back onto the hearth – and also quite liberally onto her clothes and skin.

With a frustrated curse and some heavy coughing, she put the broom down and looked around for some other means of cleaning – such as maybe a damp cloth. Then her eye fell on the tub of rancid animal fat that Margaret had told her to clear. With an idea forming, she walked over and took a closer look. The fat smelt dreadful, but if her idea was good, it might just be what she needed. Gingerly, she put a finger into the fat to test the consistency. As she hoped, it was quite thick and glutinous – more so than one would expect from old animal fat. Goodness only knew what was in it.

She dragged the tub over to the hearth, as well as another empty tub she found nearby, then knelt down and, with an expression of pure disgust, scooped out a handful of the fat. She slapped it down onto a pile of soot, then rolled it around until as much soot as possible had been bound into the fat. With the same expression of disgust, she dropped the soot-filled ball of fat into the empty tub and looked at the grate. There was a clear dip in the pile of soot. The idea was working.

With grim determination, she set to work shifting all the soot by the same means; emptying the first tub and transferring all the fat and soot into the second.

Soon she had cleared the hearth completely. She managed to find a rough linen cloth to wipe down her hands and all the surfaces – leaving the hearth clean, if slightly greasy.

With a satisfied smile, she stood back and admired her work. 'Nice job, Cinders,' she thought, 'jolly nice job.' She picked up the now full tub of sooty fat and staggered with it along the corridor and out of the back door. There was a patch of dark brown earth nearby, so she upended the tub onto it, then carried the empty tub back into the kitchens.

She was just using the brush to sweep out the very last bits of soot when Margaret came back in.

Speechlessly, the serving girl took in the scene – Justine, her white eyes blinking guilelessly in a face blacker than a chimney sweep, standing with the brush by a clean and very shiny hearth. By her feet was the tub that had held the rancid fat, now completely empty.

"You done that, then?" Margaret asked suspiciously.

"Yes," replied Justine, and couldn't help adding, "it wasn't difficult."

"That's fine soot – no brush cleans that up."

"You asked me to clean the hearth and I cleaned it."

"But it's not a half hour passed..." Margaret fell silent and again looked suspiciously at the clean hearth and back at the sooty girl holding the broom.

"What's your name then, girl?" she muttered eventually.

"It's Justine."

"Justine? I ain't never heard that name before, as the Lord is my witness. What kind of name is that?"

"It's my name. It's not unusual where I come from."

"Where you from, then, strange girl?" Margaret looked at Justine's sooty sweater, skirt and boots. "Does everyone wear them strange clothes? Think you to dress like a man?"

"I'm from Hammersmith," said Justine.

"Where's that, then?" Margaret asked, suspiciously.

"It's in... it's near London," answered Justine.

"Out the parish, then." Margaret said, slowly. "I thought as much. Them's as out the parish is no good, my Ma says."

"I'm sure she does," responded Justine, slightly too glibly.

"You know my Ma, then?" Margaret said, her eyes narrowing, her voice sounding even more suspicious.

"Of course not."

"So how you know she says that, then?"

"I don't."

"But you said you were sure she does. You must have known that, else, how would you have known..." Margaret stopped, staring hard at Justine.

"You cleaned that hearth faster than a body could ever clean it…" she said slowly, as if starting to list out Justine's peculiarities.

"You claim to know what my Ma says when you've not met her yet… You wear strange clothes and you're from out the parish…"

Suddenly Margaret stepped back, staring wildly, then started to cross herself repeatedly. "Lord a' mercy – Lord a' mercy! I know you now! I know you, Satan! You're a... you're a... a witch!"

"Oh Christ! Hell, no..." Justine said, thinking fast as to what she could say to refute this dangerous allegation, but of all the things she could have said, this was possibly the very worst. Margaret immediately gave a small scream and put her hands to her ears. Her jaw dropped and her eyes opened so wide, Justine couldn't help but think they might pop out.

"Blaspheming the Lord?" Margaret said in a strangled whisper. "Invocation to your master the Devil? Oh mercy, mercy! I cannot tarry a moment in the presence of such evil!" She turned and made to run out of the kitchens, but stopped by the stairs. "I will fetch Master Hopkirk, the witchfinder. He'll know how to deal with you – witch!"

She ran up the stairs, leaving Justine staring after her, with the growing realisation that if time-travelling unexpectedly back to Tudor England was bad in itself, she had now made the situation considerably worse.

Almost immediately she heard the sound of heavy boots coming down the stairs. Quickly she looked around for somewhere to hide, but before she could conceal herself, a man appeared in the archway.

Could the witchfinder have been found so fast?

Then her heart gave a small jump of relief, as she saw that it was Sir William.

He had changed his clothes after the hunt and was now resplendent in a trim ivory doublet, with deep slashes over red velvet in his breeches and sleeves, grey hose and soft leather boots. He had a sword hanging from his left hip and a red silk cape on his shoulder.

"Ah, wench. There you are," he said with a broad smile. "Alone in the kitchens, I see. What did you say to that girl who would as like have knocked me over as she ran past me on the stairs?" He chuckled. "Ah, but 'tis no matter." He studied her in the dim light. "I see the soot of the kitchens has attached itself to you." He looked at her more closely. "By heaven, there is more soot here than girl!" He laughed. "Aye, you have a novel look about you – the look of a vagrant."

Aware that she cut more of a miserable figure than a novel one in her soot-blackened clothes and face, Justine couldn't think of a single thing to say. Frankly, she had to admit, not only did she look like a vagrant, but that was exactly what she had become – a stranger.

Out of place, out of time – and in a very dangerous, very frightening situation.

This wasn't a Mary Fox adventure. This was actually happening.

And with no guarantee of a happy ending.

"Come girl, why do you make sounds like a frightened mouse? And why do you pale beneath your soot? Am I a ghost?" asked Sir William genially. "Nay, withal – I am all too real." He put his hands on his thighs and pushed back his shoulders and roared with laughter. "Although parts of me are to be wondered at, as you shall discover ere too long!"

He grabbed her arm and started to pull her out of the kitchen. "Come now, girl, let me put you from your misery!" Justine's immediate thought was to get her bag from where she had put it near the spit, and she tried to get her arm free. "Do not struggle, girl, you're quite safe with me," said Sir William, still maintaining his jovial temper.

"My bag!" muttered Justine. "Let me get my bag." She broke free and grabbed it from the floor. After being accused of witchcraft, the last thing she wanted was curious Tudor eyes peering at its contents. Goodness knew what they would make of her phone, solar charger and Bluetooth speaker.

"Aye," said Sir William. "Take whatever you must." He laughed and grabbed her arm a second time. "I'll warrant that the sword of de Beauvais will cut and parry with honour tonight!"

He looked her up and down.

"Though we may need to have you washed first."

CHAPTER SEVEN

It was a quiet afternoon in the large taproom of the village tavern, situated on the edge of the green around two miles from Grangedean Manor.

A few villagers were sitting on stools or benches at the rough wooden tables dotted around the room. On every table was a fat tallow candle; each one pushed into the remains of the previous candle that had burned down to a hard yellow ring that was forever stuck to the table.

The only sound was the buzzing of two flies, darting in and out of the shafts of light from the small leaded windows. A couple of villagers waved them casually away if they got too close to their tankards of ale and crusts of bread.

The flies moved over to the corner and tried their luck with a small, dour man in grey, sitting on his own. They landed on his crust of dry bread and began to eat.

Unlike the other villagers, the man made no movement.

Growing bolder, the flies settled down to gorge themselves on the bread. Still the man made no overt movement, although an observant onlooker would have seen his eyes lower slowly and focus without any emotion on the flies.

They say that flies can see the approach of a threatening movement in two-tenths of a second, and their 360-degree vision means that they can fly directly away from the direction of attack. It was unfortunate for these two flies that while the hand that struck them came from behind, it was aimed at a point around one inch in front of them – so they flew straight into the path of its crushing blow.

The man flicked the bodies of the flies to the floor. Still without emotion he ate the rest of his bread and finished his tankard of ale. Leaving a silver three farthing coin on the table, he stood up, pulled his hat lower over his eyes, walked to the door and stepped out into the summer sunshine.

---0---

Margaret ran across the village green and arrived at the front of the tavern, just as the grey man was starting to walk away from it.

"Master Hopkirk?" she panted, running up behind him and grabbing at his cloak. The man stopped, but did not turn round. "Master Hopkirk?" she repeated.

"Yes?" he said, his voice barely rising above a whisper. "I am Hopkirk." He turned round slowly, then fixed her with a pair of cold grey eyes that seemed to suck every ounce of resolve out of her. "What is your business?"

Margaret swallowed and forced herself to look away from the eyes. "I was told you are to be contacted if a w... if a wi..." She could not bring herself to say the word.

"If a witch is found?" asked Hopkirk. She nodded. "Indeed. I am not only the magistrate, but am also charged to identify those who practice the work of the devil in witchcraft." He paused to let Margaret's breathing slow down. "Do I take it from your agitated state that you have identified a witch?"

Margaret nodded again.

"Then we will go inside the tavern and you may tell me about this witch, that I may know better who she is and how she may be identified."

Hopkirk led her inside the tavern and indicated a table. Margaret sat down. "But first," he whispered, "you will regain your breath and have some ale, so we may converse more easily."

Hopkirk sat opposite Margaret, raised his hand and clicked his fingers. A large, heavily-bearded man in an old white smock appeared out of the shadows at the far end of the taproom and approached the table. "Yes, Master Hopkirk?" the man asked in a deep, coarse voice.

"A pitcher of ale and a pair of tankards, Jake." He put another three-farthing coin on the table.

"Yes, Master Hopkirk." The innkeeper Jake padded back to the shadows, and could be heard pouring ale into an earthenware pitcher from a barrel. He reappeared with the pitcher and two pewter tankards, which he put down and filled. Then he slid the three-farthing coin off the table into his pocket and padded away.

Margaret forced herself to slow her breathing, while Hopkirk's cold grey eyes never left her face. Margaret found this deeply uncomfortable, particularly as he never seemed to blink.

Gradually her breathing slowed to normal levels. She gulped down some ale while Hopkirk maintained his silent stare. Margaret felt sure she should say something, but decided to wait until spoken to.

Eventually Hopkirk cleared his throat. "We'll start with your name," he said.

"It's Margaret, sir," she replied, with a weak grin. This seemed to have no effect whatsoever on the man opposite. She continued, "I work in Grangedean Manor – in the kitchens, mostly, and in the hall when there's a banquet."

"I see," he replied. "Then pray, good Mistress Margaret, tell me your tale."

Now that the moment had come to tell her story, Margaret felt very nervous. It had seemed so clear to her as she had run from the manor to the village – a witch had been identified, so the proper authorities must be informed. But now she was here it didn't seem so clear-cut. What if this grey man with his air of menacing power didn't believe her? What if he thought she was covering up her own satanic practices by pointing the finger at another woman? The risks of her position were now becoming clear to Margaret, and her resolve was weakening. The strange girl had blasphemed – there could be no doubt about that. But had she really known what Margaret's mother would say? Was that really evidence of the dark arts? And what about the fast work in cleaning the hearth – was that in itself proof of witchcraft? Silently Margaret offered up a prayer, 'Sweet Lord, oh Lord Jesus, guide my tongue to speak the truth and this man's heart to receive it.' She gulped and crossed herself, then finished in her head with a silent 'amen'.

"Oh, Master Hopkirk," she began, "a strange girl from out the parish comes to work in the kitchens at the manor. She wears clothes that are like a man's and she was able to clean the hearth faster than is natural, and she knows things she shouldn't know..." She faltered and stopped. Even to her it sounded thin. There was a silence as Hopkirk's grey eyes bored into hers.

"I will need more proof than this," he whispered. "Do you have more?"

Margaret felt her stomach knotting in tension. This was what she had feared the most; that she would have to repeat the girl's words – her blasphemy – in order to provide the unassailable proof that the colourless man in front of her was seeking. Would this make her a blasphemer too? Could she risk her immortal soul by repeating such words?

"Oh, Master Hopkirk," she blurted, crossing herself again and again, "I can give you such proof of this girl's wickedness, but I cannot say it! Such blasphemy will be to endanger my own immortal soul!"

"I shall be the judge of that," said Hopkirk, some colour coming unexpectedly into his cheeks. He licked his lips. "Blasphemy, you say? This is your proof?" Margaret nodded, wide-eyed. "Then I must hear it. I must."

"Oh, Master Hopkirk. She said... she said..."

"Yes?"

"She said... when I accused her of being a witch, she said..." Margaret's voice dropped to a hoarse whisper and again she crossed herself repeatedly. "She said... 'oh Christ in hell, no' – oh sweet Lord forgive me!"

The colour in Hopkirk's cheeks deepened and he licked his lips again. "She said that?"

"Those very words, Lord forgive me."

"And she dresses as a man, and can use magic to clean things and knows things she couldn't have known?" asked Hopkirk.

"Yes!" Margaret was relieved – it seemed like he was believing her. Jesus had heard her prayers!

Hopkirk's next words confirmed this thought.

"Then you were quite right to tell me – this is an envoy of Satan and we must be rid of her. Her name?"

"It is a strange name – not one I had ever heard."

"And it is?"

Margaret took a gulp of ale to steady herself, then another longer one that drained her tankard. She reached for the pitcher to top up, but it was empty. "Maybe it is a devil name?" she said. "Maybe if I say it, I'll conjure up her familiars, her evil spirits?"

"That I doubt. I'll need a name," answered Hopkirk, his grey eyes boring into hers.

"It is… it is… Justine," whispered Margaret. She paused and looked around, fearful for some evil spirits to materialise out of the shadows.

At that exact moment, a large white figure appeared and silently floated towards them.

Margaret gave a little scream and clutched at the edge of the table.

Then she realised it was only Jake the landlord in his white smock, padding towards them with another pitcher of ale.

"And how can she be known?" asked Hopkirk, ignoring Margaret's little drama. Margaret got her breath back, poured some more ale and took a drink. "She is tall, with dark red curly hair and bare head, and can easily be known by the strangeness of her dress."

"Which is?"

"She wears a badly-finished doublet, unfinished breeches, thin hose and man's boots."

Hopkirk considered this for a moment. "Aye, then we will work on this information, and we will find her and we will test her."

He gave a thin smile that didn't seem to reach as far as his eyes. Margaret felt the tension leave her body. A great weight lifted from her mind.

Hopkirk's voice dropped to the softest whisper, but there was no doubting the strength of his intent.

"We will test her," he repeated. "And if we find she is indeed a witch, then we will submit her to death by fire."

CHAPTER EIGHT

As Sir William de Beauvais led the girl out of the kitchens and up the stairs to the Great Hall, he was pleasantly surprised to find that she was accompanying him most willingly. Indeed, she was almost unseemly in her haste to get quickly away from the kitchens. Conveniently forgetting that it was he who had sent her there in the first place, he saw himself as her rescuer; a dashing knight saving the girl from the heat and the soot.

'Aye, they all submit in the end,' he thought happily, anticipating the afternoon's pleasures to come. 'No matter that their dress is bizarre, their speech is outlandish and their face...' he glanced back at the girl behind him and was rewarded with a nervous sooty grin '...their face is blackened with grime – they all submit in the end.'

They reached the top of the stairs and he looked back at her again, lit by the sunlight bursting through the door from the Great Hall. 'A comely face, despite the soot,' he thought as he led her into the Great Hall.

There they were greeted by the sight of the kitchen servants sent up by the cook, laying the tables for the evening meal.

To Sir William's surprise, the girl gave a sharp gasp and muttered something which sounded like "can't let them see me", then let go of his hand, shot past him in a cloud of soot and darted out through the main doors into the hallway.

Sir William ran out after her, just in time to see her cannon full tilt into his mother, who had just stepped into the hallway from a side room.

The force of the girl's impact made his mother stagger back; a large sooty mark appearing on the front of her beautiful red silk gown. The girl bounced off in the opposite direction, straight out of the open front door and onto the steps above the lawns, her hands waving like windmills as she tried to keep her balance. In this she was unsuccessful; she lost her footing, tripped down the steps and disappeared from view.

Sir William and his mother rushed out to stand on the top step, staring in amazement at the dirty figure lying spread-eagled on her back on the lawn below them.

Lady de Beauvais turned slowly to her son and asked, "Who..." she paused, staring hard at him, "...or what... is that extraordinary creature?"

"New serving girl, Mother," replied Sir William, with what he hoped was a sufficiently casual tone.

"And why, pray, was she running around the hallway in that dangerous fashion, knocking into me, leaving much soot on my gown and flapping her hands like a duck learning to fly?"

"High spirits, Mother?"

"High spirits indeed, William. You must take more care about the serving girls."

"Yes, Mother."

"What are her tasks?"

"I was going to have her... er... clean my chamber."

"I see. Clean your chamber? Is that indeed so?"

"Indeed."

"Let me see her." Lady de Beauvais stepped carefully down to the lawn, lifting her skirts to avoid the trail of soot. "Why does she dress like an unfinished lad? And she is filthy. You could not possibly allow such a girl in your chamber. Certainly not for cleaning, nor for..." a further pause, "...any other reason."

"I'm not sure what you mean, Mother."

But Sir William knew exactly what she meant. He also knew that his mother was very different to most Tudor nobles in the very important matter that was his love life.

Most noble families would have promised a first-born son like him to the daughter of a suitable family while both were just children, with the marriage taking place while they were teenagers. Not so his mother, Lady de Beauvais. Her own marriage had not been arranged. She was in fact the daughter of a merchant, and had married his late father, Sir Henry de Beauvais, for love. This had been despite the opposition of Sir Henry's parents, who thought she was beneath them, and her parents, who thought she was too ambitious.

As a result she had become convinced that arranged marriages were wrong. She had insisted that William should be allowed to meet a girl in his own time and to his own liking. As she had explained many times to the nobility of the county, she was only following the example of the Princess Elizabeth – now the Queen – and it was only right to let her son make his own choice.

So he had been encouraged to meet as many young girls as possible, in order that he should find one to his liking. Most of the really eligible girls had been promised to others and were now married, but there were still enough for Lady de Beauvais to arrange meetings so that love might take its course. But the only part of love that did take its course was his insatiable carnal appetite, followed by his immediate boredom with each of the girls once he had conquered them.

So there had been an unending procession of girls, from those of noble families down to Martha the housekeeper, who made the journey to his chamber – but so far not a single one had made it twice.

---0---

Justine groaned and slowly sat up. Immediately there was a sharp pain in her hip, which made her yelp. She felt it would ease if she could move it around and maybe put some weight on it, so she struggled to her feet and stamped around on the lawn, alternately bouncing her weight on her leg then shaking it out, while mother and son watched her speechlessly.

After a few moments the pain subsided, and Justine knew there was nothing broken.

She turned to Sir William's mother and said, "I am so sorry, Lady de Beauvais." She guessed that this aristocratic and beautifully-dressed woman would have such a title. "I was totally at fault. I was stupid and clumsy. Please," she added what she hoped was a winning smile, "will you forgive me?"

Lady de Beauvais stared at her. "You are no serving girl," she observed. "No serving girl would talk that way, or look me in the eye like that. Where are you from, girl?"

"I come from Hammersmith," answered Justine.

"And your name?"

"Justine Parker."

"Justine? Eh bien, vous êtes Française?"

"Er, no," answered Justine. "I'm English."

"Indeed. And you are obviously of a good family. Does your family have land? Are they at Court?"

"My father is... he, er... was... a doctor."

"An apothecary? A noble profession and an educated one. It would account for your own intelligent speech. He is dead, I assume, from your use of the past tense?"

"Yes, sort of."

"And your mother?"

"Much the same."

"You poor child." Lady de Beauvais considered her a moment in silence. Then she asked, "So how did you come to be in my house?"

Justine thought fast, trying to come up with a plausible story. In desperation she looked around, and in the distance she saw some horses in a field.

"I was out riding and I fell, and my horse ran off," she said, looking Lady de Beauvais in the eye with a maybe a little too much intensity. Lady de Beauvais gave a little snort. "A single girl out riding? Indeed, very independent. I have not heard of such a thing. Hmm. And what of your strange clothing?"

"I, er, ruined my gown when I fell, so I borrowed these from an empty cottage I found. I don't know what sort of clothes they are." She smiled rigidly at the older lady, as if to make her believe this by sheer force of will.

"Hmm," murmured Lady de Beauvais, "maybe some woodman's wife has made them." Justine couldn't help recalling that she had actually bought the skirt from a major department store only a few weeks ago.

Or in roughly 450 years' time.

She continued to smile, although now it was starting to feel very uncomfortable.

"And how came you covered in soot?"

"I was in the kitchens."

Sir William walked down the steps to join them and spoke up. "We were a girl short, Mother."

"This is an educated girl, and you put her to work in the kitchens?" asked Lady de Beauvais, turning to look at him in surprise. "Shame on you, William."

"Now look, Mother..."

Lady de Beauvais ignored him and turned back to Justine.

"Well, we cannot have you running around the house in such a state. It is not seemly." She turned to her son. "William, this girl will come with me. We will bathe her and dress her in proper clothes. She is a rather comely under the soot. You would do well to mark it."

"I have marked it, Mother," he replied.

"Aye, William, mark it well. And her spirit. Mark that well also."

"That, too, Mother."

She turned and swept up the steps into the house. "Come, girl," she called to Justine.

Justine started after her, then stopped and looked back at Sir William. She raised an eyebrow in enquiry, seeking his reassurance that she was now under his mother's charge. He smiled and made a small movement of his hand, indicating she should follow his mother, so she turned and loped up the steps into the house after the retreating figure of Lady de Beauvais.

CHAPTER NINE

The afternoon sun streamed in through the main doors of Grangedean Manor as Lady de Beauvais swept inside. Justine, who had stopped outside and had been studying the façade of the building, stepped in after her.

Lady de Beauvais rang a bell standing on a table. After a few moments a serving girl appeared from a side door.

"Prepare a bath upstairs immediately," ordered Lady de Beauvais.

"Yes, madam," said the serving girl, curtseying with her eyes down. She disappeared again through the same door.

Lady de Beauvais started up the stairs without looking back. Justine assumed she was supposed to follow and limped up after her.

There were pictures of worthy-looking family members all the way up the stairs. At the very top was a stern, uncompromising-looking man in his sixties with short-cropped iron-grey hair under a felt cap. His long luxuriant beard offset a plain black doublet and fur mantle round his shoulders. A magnificent gold chain was hung across his chest. Justine felt this was the most important portrait – not only was it at the top of the stairs, but there was something about the man that suggested both raw power and unquestioned authority.

"Sir Thomas de Beauvais," said her hostess from behind her shoulder. "He came here from Brittany with Henry Tudor and fought with him in the Battle of Bosworth against the usurper Richard of York. This land was his reward."

Justine stared at Sir Thomas de Beauvais – a man who had fought a historical battle a mere seventy years before. 'Am I mad?' she thought. 'This can't be real. It really can't.'

She winced as the pain in her hip flared up again, making it clear that this was all too real. Instinctively she shook her leg out to try and clear the pain.

There was a snort of amusement from behind her and she turned. "You perhaps have an ague," Lady de Beauvais observed, "that you must dance like you are possessed by St. Vitus?"

"It's my hip," said Justine. "I hurt it when I fell. Shaking it out helps"

"Indeed. I trust it is so, and not some madness or the plague."

Lady de Beauvais then did something sudden and unexpected. Frowning, she reached out and grabbed the bottom of Justine's sweater. In one movement she pulled it up, pushing Justine's arm above her head and leaving her armpit exposed. Lady de Beauvais studied Justine's armpit a moment, then looked down her side and across her stomach.

"What in God's name is this garment?" Justine felt her bra strap being tugged but said nothing. "Most unusual."

Thankfully Lady de Beauvais then lost interest in her bra and let her sweater fall back. She peered at Justine's face and neck, then crouched and looked intently at her legs.

"Hmmm," she muttered. "No buboes." She stood. "No sneezes?"

"Certainly not," answered Justine.

"Good. No plague. You'll do. Very well." Lady de Beauvais turned and walked briskly down the gallery towards the door at the end.

She turned and looked back at Justine, who had not moved from the spot. "Come, girl, do not tarry," said the older woman. "And do not touch anything until we have removed the grime of the kitchens from you."

They walked along the gallery and through the door at the end, into the long wood-panelled corridor which ran the length of the East Wing. Justine recognised it from her time; there were four bedrooms off to the right and on the left there were windows overlooking the front lawn. She glanced out of the leaded window. The view seemed at first familiar as she looked down at the lawns, but then she looked up and gasped.

There was nothing beyond the rolling Grangedean lawns but thick, green trees as far as the eye could see, swaying in the summer breeze with rooks circling and calling above them; covering the distant hills like a cloth of deep green velvet. Where were the big, ugly electricity pylons on the horizon, with the thundering lorries running along the dual carriageway, past the long, low warehouses and on to the sprawling estate of little box-like houses?

Now, Justine suddenly felt faint and put a hand down to the windowsill to steady herself.

The pylons, the lorries – they were all part of a familiar world; her world. Would she ever get back to it? Would she ever get back to the Grangedean Manor that was a museum, not a home? Would she ever see Mrs Warburton again, or Susan, or even Rick the grumpy catering manager? Did they even know she'd gone? Maybe she no longer existed in their world, as if she'd never been born…

"Come girl, I said not to tarry." Lady de Beauvais' voice brought her back to this world; the one where she did exist and was covered in soot.

The older woman was waiting for her in the doorway of one of the bedrooms.

Taking a deep breath, Justine straightened her back and walked into the room.

In the 21st century these rooms were open to the public and each was decorated as it was believed they would have been in the Tudor age – with a four-poster bed, a wooden chair and table and an oak clothes chest at the foot of the bed. True, the furniture had all come from various different houses and not Grangedean Manor, but it had been assumed that as it was authentic Tudor furniture, this would be acceptable.

So Justine was pleased as she walked in, to see that they had got it pretty much correct. A large four-poster bed stood against one wall; at its foot was a large clothes chest. An oak table and chair were placed under the leaded window, with a fireplace on the opposite wall. Even though it was a warm afternoon, the fire was lit. Suspended on a hanging frame above the flames was a copper tub and Justine could see there was water starting to boil inside.

Justine took off her bag and put it on the bed. She realised that in one respect they had got it wrong in the future – the bed was a mass of bright gaudy colours – from the painted wooden carvings through to the glorious tapestries hanging along the side of the tester at the top. In the Grangedean Manor of the future, they had assumed that wooden furniture would have been unpainted natural colours – but as Justine studied the bed she could see carvings of human figures, animals and foliage, all painted riotous reds, golds, greens and blues. It was a magnificent sight.

A large bow and a quiver of arrows was propped up in a corner. Justine smiled to herself – this was the Tudor equivalent to a set of golf clubs that had been left there for want of a better place. It made her realise the mundane normality of this historical way of life.

Next to the fire there was a copper bath, one that looked suitable for sitting in only, but a bath nonetheless. Justine smiled to herself; after falling back through time into the grime and heat of the kitchens, what she wanted now more than anything else in the world was a bath.

The door opened and the serving girl entered, carrying a similar copper tub to the one on the fire. She put it down on the floor in front of the fire, then took some rough sacking material from round her waist. Wrapping the sacking round her hands as mitts, she lifted the hot water tub off the fire and carried it to the bath, then tipped it in. She then hooked the new tub in its place over the fire.

Catching sight of Justine as she turned to leave, the girl's eyes widened and she put her hand to her mouth with a small gasp. Justine smiled warmly at the girl, but this just caused her to look even more alarmed and scurry out.

"She thinks you are a vagrant," observed Lady de Beauvais. "That makes her scared of you – you might carry the plague."

"I mean no one any harm – and as you said, 'no plague'" replied Justine.

"I know that, but they do not." Lady de Beauvais considered her a moment. "We will shortly bathe you and dress you in proper clothes. We will tidy your hair and cover your head. You will no longer look like a vagrant, but I think we need to be sure. You will need to change your name as well, so that no connection can be made with the dirty young woman who arrived here." She paused, staring at Justine intently. "Do you have any name you would like to be given?

There was only one name – only one possible name.

"Mary Fox."

Lady de Beauvais smiled. "Yes, good. So you will be Mary Fox. Let me see; you are the daughter of my old friend, Richard Fox, a London merchant. You are recently returned from France."

"Thank you, Lady de Beauvais," Justine said. "I will do my best to justify your faith in me."

"Indeed you will," said the older woman with a smile. "I shall see to it." She paused. "You will accompany my son, Sir William, to dinner tonight. He will escort you in, in sight of all our guests. You will do your best to please him."

"I will try."

Lady de Beauvais nodded and considered her a moment. "My son is a good man," she said. "He has taken on the estates and the house well since his father died."

"I can see that," answered Justine, not sure where this was going.

"Many, many girls have excited his interest, looking to be the next Lady de Beauvais. They enter his bed with that prize in front of them. But they do not hold his interest once they leave it. None have succeeded in entering his heart." She smiled again. "At least none so far."

Justine let the challenge hang in the air between them for a moment.

"As you say, Lady de Beauvais," she said carefully, "he is a good man. I will do my best to be worthy of him."

Lady de Beauvais nodded.

"But as to his heart," Justine said, "and as to mine – only time can tell."

Just then the door opened again and the serving girl came in with another tub of water.

"Sarah," said Lady de Beauvais, "this is Mary Fox, the daughter of an old friend. She has been lately in France and on her journey here has suffered a fall from her horse into a pile of soot. See to her bathing and dress her as befits the daughter of a merchant."

"Yes madam," answered the girl Sarah, looking at Justine, but now without fear in her eyes.

"Good. Go to it. She will accompany Sir William to dinner." With that, Lady de Beauvais turned and swept out of the room.

There was an uncomfortable silence, then Sarah said, "Begging your pardon, Mistress Fox. I had thought you were…"

"A vagrant?"

"I am so sorry."

"Please don't worry." Justine smiled. "Is the bath ready? I can't wait."

"Nearly, mistress." Sarah poured the hot water from the fire into the bath as before, then tested the temperature with her hand. "A mite too warm, mistress." She added the cold water she had brought, then tested the temperature again. "Perfect, mistress." She then produced a muslin bag from the pocket of her dress and opened it. Justine caught the scent of herbs – lavender, thyme and rosemary – as Sarah emptied the bag into the bath.

"There, mistress, that will restore your humours nicely."

Not sure quite what to make of this comment, and fearful of saying something to Sarah that would have the same effect as her earlier comment to Margaret, Justine limited herself to saying only "thank you Sarah, that's lovely." It seemed prudent to be as nice as possible to this serving girl.

And to avoid any references to Christ or hell.

Sarah fished around in the pocket of her apron again. She produced a small yellow ball, about the size of an egg. "The soap, Mistress Fox," she said triumphantly, as she dropped it in the bath, before going over to the oak chest at the foot of the bed and rummaging around. She selected a large piece of rough fabric that Justine assumed was a towel and handed it over.

Sarah then rummaged some more and lifted out a large green dress, something that looked like a wooden frame, and various other garments. She put them on the bed. Then she noticed Justine's bag and picked it up.

"Is this your bag, mistress?" asked Sarah. "Shall I sort out what is held inside for you?" She tried to open the bag, fumbling with the unfamiliar clasp.

"No," said Justine quickly, still fearful of letting anyone see her modern-day things. "Thank you." She held out her hand for the bag. "I'll sort it myself."

Sarah handed it over with a puzzled look. "My work is to help you, mistress," she observed, "but if you must sort it yourself…?" She left the question hanging.

"Yes, Sarah, if you don't mind. It's really nice of you to offer. I'll do it."

"As you wish, mistress," replied Sarah hesitantly. "You are being most kind, but I am only here to serve and to help you."

"And I really do appreciate it."

"Thank you, mistress – it is nice to be told that." Sarah turned and left the room.

For a moment Justine stayed stock-still, clutching the towel and her bag. The silence in the room was broken only by the crackling of the fire. Intently she listened out for the sounds of anyone coming down the corridor, but there were none. It did seem she was genuinely alone in this wing of the house.

She opened her bag and checked that the phone, charger and Bluetooth speaker were still there, then closed it and looked for a safe hiding place. She decided the best option was to tuck it under the deep layer of plump goose-down pillows.

Then she undressed and rolled her clothes up into a ball. She wondered what to do with them; they needed to be disposed of quickly – their very presence linked Mary Fox, the respectable merchant's daughter, to Justine Parker, the vagrant girl who was probably even now being sought for witchcraft. And if Lady de Beauvais thought her bra was unusual, what would anyone else make of it?

She looked at the fire, then back at the clothes in her hand. It seemed the obvious solution – but she hesitated. To burn these clothes meant she was severing her links with the future – denying who she really was – and maybe, reducing her chances of getting back again?

'Oh, come on,' she thought, 'it's only some clothes. Get a grip, girl. The real Mary Fox – or at least the real one in the books – wouldn't hesitate a second.'

With that, she stepped up to the fire and placed the ball of clothes onto it. For a moment nothing happened, except that the ball started to open out as it settled, then the flames took hold and the fire flared up as first her skirt, then her sweater, t-shirt, knickers, bra and tights caught fire. She watched as the fire quickly turned them to blackened, charred remains, except the wires from her bra which glowed bright orange before eventually bending and melting down into the coals.

She turned to the bath and was about to get in, when she noticed her boots were still standing by the bed. She picked them up and was about to throw them on the fire as well, when again she hesitated. 'My favourite boots,' she thought. 'I can't burn them, I just can't.' She put them back by the bed and climbed into the bath.

It was warm, not hot, but sheer bliss as she slid down into the bath and splashed the water up her body. She found the soap which smelled of olive oil, but she could not get it to lather, so she abandoned it. Instead she grabbed the towel, dipped one corner in the bath and used it as a flannel, scrubbing her face until the fabric was black with soot. She then used another corner to wipe her face until it was clean.

She wished she could wash her hair, but the bath didn't allow her to slide low enough and anyway the soap wouldn't work as a shampoo. She decided to let that one go for now – although her head did feel dry, sooty and a bit itchy. 'Oh, golly – I hope I don't have lice,' she thought, and spent a few minutes picking at the roots of her hair and examining anything that felt suspicious. Apart from some grass seeds, probably from her fall in the garden, there was nothing that could be cause for concern.

She wriggled her bottom a bit so she could slide further down the bath and get more comfortable, then she gave a deep sigh, relaxed her head back and stared up at the white plaster ceiling with its dark oak beams.

'I am lying in a copper bath in a Tudor house in Tudor times, and I have absolutely no idea how on earth I actually got here,' she thought. 'If it wasn't so definitely real, I'd never have believed it possible.' She wiggled her toes absently, finding herself starting to come to terms more with her situation. 'It must have been some kind of magic.' She stopped wiggling her toes. 'But that would be thinking like a superstitious Tudor; like Margaret. If you don't understand something, it must be magic – that's just a cop-out.'

Then she noticed a spider running along one of the beams and watched as it scuttled along. 'That spider might think everything is magic, because he probably doesn't understand anything. That's fine for him, but not me.'

The spider stopped, then scuttled along a bit further, then suddenly it disappeared.

Justine gave a small gasp. One second it was there; the next it was gone.

She studied the beam closely, and spotted a small dark patch around where the spider had disappeared. 'Maybe that's a hole,' she thought, 'and he just popped inside.'

A sudden thought hit her.

"That's it!" she said out loud. "That's jolly well it! A wormhole! I fell into a wormhole!"

Of course! It must have been a freak wormhole caused by the electrical storm – that for a split second linked the Grangedean Manor of 2015 with the Grangedean Manor of its Tudor heyday. She'd just happened to have been in the wrong place at the wrong time, and she'd fallen through it.

This seemed to make good sense. She'd seen plenty of episodes of sci-fi programmes like Doctor Who, Red Dwarf and Star Trek, where that sort of thing was accepted as perfectly rational. She'd also read A Brief History of Time and while she couldn't remember much because it seemed a bit jumbled in her memory (although it had seemed quite understandable when she was reading it), she thought there might have been something there about wormholes.

'I wonder if I'm the first person to fall through a wormhole?' she thought. An amazing thought occurred to her. 'Probably not – people disappear all the time and the police search for them for years and never find them; maybe they haven't actually been murdered or gone to Spain or something. Maybe, they've simply gone back to another time.'

This seemed to make excellent sense. Except for one thing. 'Then why don't they tell all when they get back?'

A sudden thought hit her, like a cold wave of inevitability crashing in. 'They don't come back, do they? Or we'd all know everything there is to know about wormholes and time travel…'

Justine sat up and put her arms round her knees as the wave of realisation made her head spin. She stared blankly into the distance.

'I'm never going back to my time, am I? I'm stuck here for the rest of my life…'

Slowly, she unclasped her knees, deciding she was not going to give in to despair. 'There's always hope,' she thought. 'If I got here, then surely I can get back again? Yes – there's always hope.'

She sank back into the bath and looked up at the ceiling, just as the spider emerged from his hole and started to scuttle along the beam again.

"Hello again," she said aloud with a smile. "You're a persistent little bugger, aren't you? Looks like I'll need to be as well."

A few minutes later she stepped out of the bath. Thankfully now the pain in her hip had gone.

'OK, so I'm Mary Fox, and a fine Tudor woman,' she thought. She towelled dry, then stood by the bed, looking at the clothes Sarah had laid out. 'No Velcro here. This time, it's the real deal.'

She put on the cotton stockings first, then the chemise – a sort of shirt. Then she put on the red petticoat, and was starting to try and put on the farthingale – a willow frame that would allow the skirts to be pushed out, when the door opened and Sarah came in.

"I thought you would want some help getting clothed, mistress," she said.

"Thank you Sarah, yes please," answered Justine.

Sarah helped Justine secure the farthingale, then laced her into a stiff corset that made her waist appear tiny and almost completely stopped her breathing.

Then Sarah tied a rolled-up piece of padded material around Justine's waist. "Got to get the bumroll right, mistress. Not sure how they do this in France," she said as she pulled it tight and did up the laces. Justine didn't answer – that would be wasting precious breath.

Sarah then pulled a grey skirt over Justine's head and down onto her waist. "Kirtle, mistress. I thought grey would look nice with the gown."

Again, Justine didn't answer. She was too busy focussing on breathing from her upper chest in short, shallow breaths.

Sarah lifted the heavy green velvet gown over Justine's head and pulled it down into place. Justine couldn't believe the weight of all this material and wood she was carrying. Suddenly the fake Tudor gowns she'd worn at the modern-day banquets didn't seem so bad – she'd give anything to be able to wear one now, with its soft padding and Velcro fastening…

Finally Sarah produced two grey velvet sleeves with delicate lace trimming and pulled each one up Justine's arm; lacing them under the shoulder of the gown. She stood back, looking Justine up and down, then nodded with approval. Justine wondered how she looked, but as there was no mirror in the room, she had to assume from Sarah's satisfaction, that Mary Fox would do.

"Now mistress," said Sarah, "your hair. Wait while I get a comb and a hood for you." She turned and went out of the door, leaving Justine standing in the centre of the room, her breathing now starting to come under control. After a moment, Justine shuffled over to her boots and tried to bend over to pick them up. This proved very difficult; only being achieved by sinking down like a hovercraft coming to rest and grabbing them in one hand. Justine decided that she had no chance of getting them on, just as Sarah came back into the room.

"Boots, mistress?" she asked, seeing Justine standing with the boots in her hand. "Oh, no – I have the prettiest slippers for you." She went to the oak chest and produced a pair of ivory coloured shoes, which she placed on the floor in front of Justine. Justine tried to step into the right shoe, but it was far too small. She nearly made a comment about Cinderella, but stopped herself just in time.

"No matter, mistress," said Sarah, and went back to the chest. She came back with another pair – with no better luck at getting them on. A further pair were tried with as little success.

"Maybe those boots are a better fit," said Sarah reluctantly. She picked one up and studied it closely. It had a flat heel and was made of brown leather. The pair had cost Justine over £60 from a leading high street store and she loved them. "A man's boot, mistress," Sarah said disapprovingly, before getting on her knees in front of Justine and holding it out. Resting her hand on Sarah's shoulder, Justine got her foot into the boot and wriggled it on. The other boot followed and Sarah stood back. "I suppose they cannot be seen under the gown," she observed after a moment. "Make small steps and they will stay hidden."

"I'll try," whispered Justine.

"Come mistress, we will do your hair and your hood." Sarah led Justine to the chair, and indicated that she should sit. 'How can I sit in this get-up?' thought Justine, but she did her best and managed to get her bottom onto the chair. It wasn't easy; the bumroll pushed her towards the front edge of the chair, while the farthingale dug in sharply.

Sarah produced a narrow comb with long teeth and started working through Justine's russet hair, pulling at the ringlets until it was all but straight, then pinning it back. She fitted a cotton cap over Justine's head and tied it at the back with laces. Then she produced a green velvet hood studded with fine pearls and trimmed with black ribbon, which she fitted over the cotton cap and secured with a pin.

Sarah then produced a small wooden pot containing white paste, which she rubbed all over Justine's face as a form of foundation, before applying some rouge powder to Justine's lips. 'I'm being made-up,' thought Justine. 'Goodness knows what's in this stuff.'

Finally, Sarah produced a fine silver necklace with a single pearl pendant and fastened it round Justine's neck.

"There, Mistress Fox. You are made truly beautiful. The master will no more resist you than fly across the heavens. He is waiting for you at the foot of the stairs."

Sarah then pressed something into Justine's hand. Looking down, Justine saw it was a hand mirror, made of polished metal. Slowly, and with some trepidation, she brought it up to her face.

She gasped. There, looking back at her, was a face she simply did not recognise. It was not even the face she was accustomed to seeing when she had put on Tudor costume in her own time – no, this was the face of a true Tudor beauty – and not one that could easily be connected with the grubby girl in the 21st century clothes who had been shown up to the room a couple of hours earlier.

Justine stood up. "Thank you, Sarah. You have done magnificent work," she said and smiled warmly at the serving girl.

"You have a wondrous beauty, mistress," said Sarah. "I have just made it known."

Justine took some small steps towards the door, and Sarah opened it for her, curtseying as she went through. 'Now I'm a Tudor lady, she curtseys,' thought Justine. 'Just remember, I'm now Mary Fox, who is a merchant's daughter from London.'

Justine walked carefully down the corridor, then opened the door out onto the gallery.

As she walked down the gallery, she saw Sir William at the foot of the stairs, his blond curls glowing in the evening sun, his beard trimmed and neat.

Justine admired his fine doublet, the deep slashes over red velvet in his breeches and sleeves, the grey hose and soft leather boots. He had a sword hanging from his left hip and a red silk cape on his shoulder.

She passed along the gallery and turned to walk down the stairs. As she glanced at the portrait of Sir Thomas, it seemed to her that he was a little less stern, and maybe even had a twinkle of approval in his eye.

She turned her gaze onto Sir William standing at the foot of the stairs and slowly, deliberately, she stepped down towards him.

She reached the foot of the stairs and looked down demurely as she curtseyed low. She held out her hand and he took it, brought it to his lips and kissed it gently as he raised her up. She lifted her eyes and smiled at him.

As she took his arm, she saw his mother standing in the corner and caught her eye. Lady de Beauvais gave a tiny nod of satisfaction, as Sir William swept her away through the double doors and into the Great Hall.

CHAPTER TEN

Justine caught her breath as she entered the Great Hall; her hand tightening on Sir William's arm in delighted surprise. She stopped a moment and took in the beauty of the room.

The Great Hall was a sparkling sea of brilliant light.

It seemed like there were a thousand candles all ablaze – set in silver candlesticks on the tables, in black metal sconces on the walls and hanging from large iron fittings on the ceiling. There were even a couple of elegant braziers in the corners; tall barley-twist metal posts with a bowl on the top and fat yellow beeswax candles throwing light up the grey stone walls. Justine looked up; the candlelight cast black flickering shadows in the gaps between the stones that made them look very deep and mysterious.

"It's beautiful," she whispered to Sir William, and was rewarded with a deep smile. "Indeed," he answered. "As befits your own radiant beauty."

She smiled back and they proceeded into the hall together, followed by Lady de Beauvais.

There were about thirty people in the hall, all standing at their places waiting for Sir William, Justine and Lady de Beauvais to take their seats. The tables were arranged in a horseshoe shape, just as they would be in Justine's time, with the top table running under the large windows, looking back to the entrance and the gallery above it. That meant the three of them had to walk the length of the hall and round the side of the top table to sit down.

As they were walking down the hall, Justine heard music – and when she reached the other side of the top table, she allowed herself a quick glance up at the gallery. There were four old men playing instruments, just as she had for her banquets. Justine smiled to herself – she'd certainly got one thing right.

Satisfying though that was, it did not dispel the fear, as she took her seat on the right of Sir William, that she would be recognised by one of the kitchen servants. Would they connect the grubby, bare-headed, strangely-dressed girl who had been turning the spit in the kitchens with Mary Fox, resplendent in her green velvet gown and French hood; the elegant daughter of a London merchant and special guest of the master of the house?

Justine also savoured the irony of her situation. For many months she had been the organiser of fake Tudor banquets, creating an experience for her guests that would only ever be a pale shadow of the real thing. Now here she was, a guest of honour and about to experience it for herself.

A long, low gurgling noise from somewhere under her restrictive corset brought her back to this particular time. She realised she hadn't eaten since she'd had a sandwich at her desk at lunchtime, many hours before the storm.

That lunchtime may be over 400 years in the future, but according to her stomach it was way too long in the past. She hadn't given it a moment's thought while she'd been in the kitchens, with Sir William and his mother, bathing, getting dressed and made up – but now she could see the servants marching in with plate after plate of delicious looking roast birds, hams, vegetables, fruit pies and many other enticing dishes – she realised just how desperately hungry she was.

Beside her, Sir William picked up a cotton napkin and threw it across his left shoulder. She glanced around the room. Everyone else was doing the same, so she did as well.

Then a servant approached Sir William with a silver bowl full of water and held it out to him. He washed his hands in it, thanked the servant and wiped his hands on the napkin. Another servant brought a bowl to Lady de Beauvais, and she did the same. Finally, a third servant brought a bowl to Justine, so she washed her hands and wiped them on her own napkin. As she looked up to thank the servant, her blood turned to ice in her veins.

It was Margaret.

Justine forced a quick smile, then looked down, trying to seem unconcerned. She fiddled with the pewter plate in front of her for a moment, then looked up again. Margaret was moving off, but as Justine looked, the serving girl glanced back over her shoulder with a small frown, then turned and disappeared into the kitchens.

Justine let her breath out slowly, trying to calm herself down. It had been such a shock to come face-to-face with Margaret. Had she been recognised? Would Margaret make good her threat to call the witchfinder if she recognised Mary Fox, the grand lady at the top table, as Justine, the girl she'd called a witch?

"What ails you?" asked Sir William. "You look like you have seen a spirit."

"It's nothing," she replied. "Really, it's nothing." Even to her it didn't sound all that convincing.

He pulled a roast peacock on a platter towards him. It looked as if it had not been cooked; its feathers and magnificent tail plumage were still in place. He pushed his knife into its side and lifted the entire skin off in one move, revealing the roast body underneath. "Was it that serving girl? he asked. "Did she upset you?"

"Oh no," she replied, more to convince herself than him.

"Good." The matter settled, he applied himself to cutting off the leg of the peacock.

For Justine the matter was far from settled. 'Maybe Margaret didn't recognise me,' she thought at first. 'Why should she? She only saw me with a dirty face in the half-light of the kitchens, and even I didn't recognise me in this outfit.' But then the image of Margaret glancing over her shoulder and frowning came up, forcing its way into her mind like an unwelcome guest at a party. 'She looked back. She definitely looked back. She frowned. She must have recognised me.'

Justine looked round the room, searching out for Margaret, until she caught sight of the girl bringing a silver jug of wine to Lady de Beauvais. Justine stared intently at her, but after Margaret had poured the wine and put the jug down, she turned and went through the door to the kitchens without so much as a glance in Justine's direction.

Justine realised she'd been holding her breath, and she let it out slowly in relief.

"I would have an answer?"

Justine became aware Sir William was staring at her, the half-eaten peacock leg in his hand and one eyebrow raised. He must have asked her a question while she was so preoccupied with Margaret.

"I am sorry, my lord," she replied.

"I had asked if you would eat." He waved the peacock leg at her empty plate. "The finest meats and vegetables have been prepared for your pleasure. The finest wines, too. Are they not to your liking?"

"Indeed my lord, I am not hungry."

Just at that moment, another long, deep gurgle came from under her corset. Sir William couldn't fail to hear it, even over the noise of the banquet.

"Verily," he observed drily. "Your stomach tells a different tale."

Yet another gurgle; this one even louder.

He smiled and took a bite of his peacock leg. "It has much to say on this matter," he added out of the side of his mouth.

Justine blushed. "I am sorry, my lord. Maybe I will have a little something."

"Indeed," he answered. "A good appetite at the table bespeaks a good one in the bedroom." He cut some slices of peacock and put them on her plate, added some carrots and beans, then fixed her with a twinkle in his eye. "I would you feed yourself well."

Justine looked back at him levelly. "I will have a little of this peacock, my lord. And that is all." She gave him what she hoped was an icy stare, "For now."

He gave her a deep, warm smile. Her heart did a little somersault.

"Of course," he observed. "Time is our friend in this." But Justine sensed he didn't really believe it, confident he would get his way when the time came.

She was about to respond, when two elegant men came up to the table. One was tall and blond; the other shorter, dark and swarthy. Justine recognised Stanmore and Dowland from that morning.

"Good evening, my lord," said Dowland, bowing low.

"We have not had the honour of an introduction to this good lady," said Stanmore. He bowed to Justine. "Madam, I am Richard Stanmore, at your service."

"And Oliver Dowland, likewise." Dowland also bowed low, but as he stood up, his eyes didn't get any higher than Justine's chest.

"Mary Fox," said Sir William, indicating Justine. "Daughter of Richard Fox, a merchant of London."

"Delighted, madam," said Dowland to Justine's chest "You grace us with your bounteous beauty.

"Richard Fox is an old friend of mine," said Lady de Beauvais, who had observed the two men's approach and was leaning across her son to join the conversation. "Mary will be staying with us while he travels abroad."

Dowland acknowledged her with a nod of his head, his eyes still fixed.

Justine gave an icy smile. She said, with all the grace she could muster, "I am honoured to meet you, Master Dowland. And you too, Master Stanmore. I am sure I shall have a generous welcome here in Grangedean Manor."

"Most generous," said Dowland. "Sir William is well known for his attentiveness."

"We look forward to better making your acquaintance," said Stanmore.

"Are we to join the hunt on the morrow, my lord?" asked Dowland. Much to Justine's relief, he finally dragged his gaze over to Sir William.

"Yes," answered Sir William. "The white stag has once again been sighted near Briar's Copse. We will seek it out."

"Very good, my lord," said Stanmore. "We will attend."

Again he bowed to Sir William, then to Lady de Beauvais, and finally to Justine. Dowland did the same, appearing to use the bow to steal one last look down Justine's cleavage, then they both backed away from the table and resumed their seats further down the hall.

Justine took the opportunity to eat some of the meat and vegetables on her plate. Hungry as she was, she ate slowly, conscious of the restricted access to her stomach under her gown. When she had finished, she took a sip of wine and sat back as best she could.

"They did not recognise you," observed Sir William slowly. "Even though you would have removed Dowland's beard this morning with your hand, and you called us common players."

He took a draught of wine and considered Justine with a smile. "With the removal of your outlandish clothes and the proper attire of a lady, you have been rendered a different person. It is remarkable."

"As you say, my lord, I am now Mary Fox. It is better that I should be her, not Justine Parker."

"Why, what dark secret does Justine Parker have to hide?" Seeing her eyes widen momentarily, he added, "Nay, do not answer. As I said before, time is our friend. You can tell me your dark secrets – as you may have them – at your leisure."

Justine considered this.

"If I tell my story, it will be to you alone," she said.

"Aye," he answered, laughing. "Pray never share a secret with Dowland. It would be to tell the whole of the county." He raised an eyebrow. "Stanmore – you could tell him, but in truth he would probably have guessed it already." He took another drink of wine. "Now Thomas Melrose – the third man you met this morning – there is a man you should watch. A secret shared with him would stay a secret only if it does not further his ambition."

Justine remembered the saturnine man of the morning's hunt, who would have had her as his servant if Sir William had not intervened.

"Is Master Melrose not here?" she asked.

"Nay, he has gone home early, complaining of a gripe in his stomach. Though I warrant it is in his heart instead."

Sir William poured himself some wine and drank deeply, as if to put a full stop to the topic of Melrose, Dowland and Stanmore.

"Let us turn to you, Mistress Mary Fox," he said, putting down his goblet and stroking the stem with his finger. "What is your ambition?"

Justine slowly reached out to the bowl in front of her and scooped what looked like some fruit compote onto her plate, giving herself precious time to think. If the question had been asked earlier that afternoon, her ambition would have been quite simple – to avoid being tried for witchcraft and to somehow reverse the time-shift that had brought her to the Tudor era.

But now, things had begun to change. Now she had actually met the man in the picture. How could she want to escape back to the modern world, knowing she was leaving him behind? Seeing his picture every day on the wall? And how could she organise fake Tudor banquets, knowing how magical the real thing could be?

"Well?"

"My lord," she said, with what she hoped was the right amount of sincerity, "my ambition is to marry well, to be a good wife and to be a good mother to many children." She took a dainty mouthful of the compote to emphasise the point and was pleasantly surprised – it was raspberries, blackberries and apples, although maybe with a bit too much sugar.

Sir William smiled and touched her hand. "It is an honourable ambition, Mary, and one I would see you fulfil."

Lady de Beauvais, who had been leaning forward and listening attentively to this exchange, smiled and sat back.

Sir William stood up. Immediately the whole room fell silent and stood as well. Justine quickly stood with them. As she stood, she felt Sir William's hand seek out hers.

"Thank you all for your attendance this evening. I shall now retire to my rooms. Goodnight, all."

He kicked back his chair. Still holding Justine's hand, he led her out of the hall past all the standing guests. Justine tried not to catch anyone's eyes, preferring to look demurely down, although she did glance up briefly to see if Margaret was there. There was a line of servants along the wall under the gallery, but Margaret was not among them.

Still, she was glad when they made it out of the hall, before starting up the stairs towards the bedrooms.

CHAPTER ELEVEN

The evening shadows were lengthening as Thomas Melrose rode slowly along the narrow dusty lane towards his house.

He was tired, he was thirsty and he was very, very angry.

He was angry with Arthur, his horse, who would insist on this leisurely plodding pace. Despite frequent sharp kicks in the flanks, Arthur continued with his head down and heavy hooves, seeming tired after the hunt. His pace was punctuated with an occasional snort, as if to show his master just what he thought of him and his boots.

'Even my horse will not bend to my will,' thought Melrose.

Yes, he was angry with his horse, but what was really working him up, what was really making his blood boil, was Sir William.

The casual arrogance of the man.

All the way home the scene in the Great Hall at Grangedean had been replaying in his head. Each time he relived Sir William's vile words, the wound they made had got ever bigger, ever more deadly, like a dagger probing ever closer to his heart.

"You do me proud. It is too bad only one of us can enjoy such good fortune."

"Yes indeed," Melrose muttered aloud. "It is too bad. By the Lord's wounds, it is too bad." He kicked at the horse again, but this achieved nothing more than a particularly contemptuous snort. If anything, Arthur slowed down a fraction, as if to make his opinion even clearer.

"Aye, well you may snort old fellow," observed Melrose. "But you have not been slighted every day by a man who is not worthy to clean your boots; a man who by his slightest action will blight the life of honest folk and lead them to their ruin."

Arthur curled his head back and looked up at his rider. It seemed to Melrose there was a look of enquiry in Arthur's large brown eyes.

"Every day I must endure these taunts and insults from this man," he explained. Arthur shook his head up and down and snorted again. "A man I once regarded as my closest friend – aye, a friend I held in the highest esteem since we were boys. Though he was the son of landed nobility and I was the son of a yeoman farmer." Melrose leaned forward and whispered in Arthur's ear, "A man whose life I even saved once, God forgive me."

Each lost in their own thoughts, the pair plodded slowly along the dusty lane.

---0---

It was a bright afternoon eighteen summers before.

Ten-year-old William de Beauvais was exploring a copse in the woods to the south of the Grangedean Manor parklands.

He was using a long branch as a beater's stick, trying to get conies out from their underground warren, so he could take a shot at them with his specially-made half-sized bow and arrows. This had involved pushing through the thick undergrowth and bashing the base of trees to try and startle the conies out of their burrows. He had been hitting trees in this way for more than half an hour, but had not released a single cony.

Getting bored, he started swinging his stick in a more casual fashion, in ever-wider arcs. Then he saw a dirty-looking brown log by the base of a tree. In his boredom and frustration, he gave it a particularly strong hit with all the backswing he had generated. He was surprised to find that instead of a solid 'thwack' as he would have expected, it made more of a soft 'thump' on contact. He was even more surprised, however, when it stood up and revealed itself to be a boy of his own age, yelling and clutching at the back of his legs in pain.

"What did you do that for?" yelled the boy, as William jumped back, startled.

William recovered himself.

"What were you doing hiding in my copse?" he asked in return, thinking that this was far more important than a mere tap with a branch. Besides, he could see from the boy's clothes that he was not from a noble family.

"You can't go round hitting people with a stick," responded the boy, who was trying to peer round at the back of his legs to assess the damage.

"Actually I can," said William, determined to stamp his authority on the proceedings. "I am William de Beauvais, son of Sir Henry de Beauvais, master of Grangedean Manor. Whereas you," he added, looking the other boy up and down, "are nobody."

The other boy paused in the act of lifting one leg for inspection. He slowly put the leg down and turned to fix William with a firm brown eye and defiant chin, as he said in a steady voice, "I am Thomas Melrose, and my pa farms them fields across the woods with wheat and barley. So if my pa didn't grow his crops, you'd not have bread on your table or beer in your cellar."

William felt this conversation needed bringing back to the key issue. "Doesn't mean you can go grubbing around in my copse, though. Hey," he said, as a thought hit him, "you were looking for conies weren't you? That's poaching. I can have you jailed for that. Or beaten," he added.

"You beat me already, ain't you? Then that's settled it," the other boy observed. Then he added quickly and with an edge of defiance, "Anyway, ain't caught no conies, so I've done no wrong."

"True," admitted William reluctantly. He decided to move on to something much more interesting. "See that tree over there?"

Thomas followed his pointing finger. "Yes?"

"See that large leaf under that branch?"

"Yes?"

"I bet you can't hit it with an arrow."

"I never used an arrow. Pa says I'm too young." Thomas studied the leaf, measuring distance. "But I can throw a stone and hit it, clean."

"Go on, then."

Thomas looked around the undergrowth, but there were no stones on the rough earth. Then he saw a small section of stick, about the width of his wrist and the length of his forearm. He picked it up and hefted it in his hand to test the weight. Then he pulled back his arm, took aim, and threw. The stick swung in a low arc towards the tree, spinning end over end. It just missed the leaf.

"Missed," shouted William. "My turn."

He pulled an arrow out of the small quiver on his belt and picked his bow out of the harness on his back. He slotted the arrow between his forefingers as he'd been taught, pulled back, took careful aim, held his breath, and fired.

The arrow flew straight and true, piercing the leaf close to its stem and detaching it cleanly from the branch.

William stood back; his triumph absolute, his mastery proven beyond doubt.

"I would have hit it, if I'd had a stone," observed Thomas casually.

"Never."

"Would so. I can hit anything with a stone."

"Look, that was the best shot I've ever done," said William, petulantly.

"Not bad, I suppose."

"Not bad? It was masterful. Say it was masterful, or I'll hit you again with my stick."

"I'll knock you down first."

"You'd never."

"Try me."

In response, William launched at Thomas, wrestling him to the ground. A fight ensued, involving punching and kicking. Eventually it ended, with no clear victor and two exhausted boys lying on the ground catching their breaths and rubbing their bruises.

After a short while, William stood up. After such an intense fight, his thoughts turned naturally to his stomach

"You want to come back to the manor for some food and drink?" he asked.

"Yes," answered Thomas, "I would."

And so their friendship, forged in battle, began that day.

---0---

At first, Lady de Beauvais was unsure about allowing William to mix with the son of a yeoman farmer, but she soon realised that there were very few boys of William's age in the area – and their friendship seemed genuine. So Thomas was allowed to come up to the manor regularly as a companion for William. At first he was only allowed up when William was not at his lessons with his tutor, a splendid old man from the village called Frobisher, who had a white beard so long he could almost step on it, and which he parted in the middle to make two separate beards that hung down either side of his ample belly.

After a couple of months, Lady de Beauvais decided that William's lessons would be more productive if he had another boy in class with him, and agreement was reached that Thomas could be tutored by Frobisher as well. So together they learned Latin, Scriptures, Greek and Mathematics; sitting at dusty desks while Frobisher lectured them for up to eight hours a day. By the time they were twelve, Thomas's quick brain and exceptional ability to learn meant he had caught up with William, and by the time they were fourteen, he had pulled well ahead. Frobisher was full of praise for the boy, continually remarking on his quick grasp of new concepts, and drawing unfavourable comparisons with William's lesser academic abilities.

Thomas loved to run home after lessons, to tell his father what he'd learned, and to see his father's eyes light up as he shared in his son's joy of learning.

"You're getting what few other men in this realm can boast, my son – an education," his father once said. "Use it wisely and maybe one day you'll make a fine gentleman."

"Don't give the boy airs," was his mother's reply. "Boys like Thomas have a place in life and must know it well."

"Nay, Jane, don't stop him trying to better himself," said his father. "Thomas has a talent for learning – and friends in high places. That's a powerful combination." He turned to Thomas and put his arm round his shoulder. "I know you'll make it son. I couldn't be prouder of you than I am today."

Thomas looked up at his father and smiled. "I'm proud of you, too, Pa, and I tell anyone who asks it."

Where Thomas had his books, William made up for his lower intellectual ability with athletic prowess. He could run faster, shoot straighter and fight better with a sword than Thomas, and would seek out any opportunity to take part in such pursuits.

More and more William sought to accompany his own father Sir Henry de Beauvais on his frequent hunts in the forests and fields, seeking out stags and wild boars.

As a yeoman's son, Thomas would not normally be considered eligible to join them – conies and hares would be all he would be allowed to hunt, but such was the companionship between the two boys, his participation was not only allowed, it was actively encouraged.

And so it might have continued – a friendship forged between boys in the hunting grounds, gardens and schoolroom of Grangedean Manor should have blossomed into a lifelong companionship of men. And indeed it would have done, had an unfortunate situation not occurred – a desperate tragedy that neither was responsible for, yet which led to a misunderstanding that left a deep scar on their youthful friendship.

It was after a fine hunt one golden autumn afternoon when William and Thomas, now in their late teens, were riding slowly back to the manor. They were highly elated following a protracted chase after a particularly fine roan stag, which had culminated in a momentous climax that neither could have predicted.

They had cornered the stag in a copse about a mile from the manor. It had stood just inside the copse, snorting and puffing with exhaustion after a long chase.

The two young men quietly dismounted upwind of the stag and crept slowly to the edge of the copse, William fitting an arrow to his bow as he went.

The sun was dropping behind the fine old elm trees, lengthening the shadows and creating dappled shapes that gave the hunters ideal cover as they moved.

They dropped to their knees into the soft undergrowth behind one of the elms, taking care not to snap a twig or make a noise to cause the animal to take flight. Keeping their breathing shallow and communicating only by hand signals, they carefully took position either side of the tree. Thomas hefted a short throwing spear in his hand and pulled it back, ready to throw. The plan was for William to aim an arrow for the sweet spot just above the foreleg where the heart could be pierced, and for Thomas to follow up with the spear if the animal was not killed cleanly.

Thomas watched as William pulled back on the bow so that the grey goose-feathered flight of the birch arrow drew level with his ear; the tension crackling in the yew wood and the tightly-twisted hemp strings humming under the strain.

William took a slow, careful breath as he stared down the shaft of the arrow, sighted it on the stag's haunch, then lifted it slightly to give it the arc it needed to find its target. He exhaled gently through his teeth to steady his nerve, paused a moment, then opened his fingers. It was the smallest of movements, but enough for the strings to snap forward as the tension unwound the bow in a fraction of a second, sending the iron-tipped arrow across the copse at over a hundred miles an hour to pierce deep into the stag's chest.

Enraged, the great stag lifted its head and roared in agony, its hooves carving deep gouges in the soft ground in front of it. The arrow had missed the heart by no more than a finger's width and it was still very much alive. It cast around, seeking the source of its pain, and its large angry eyes narrowed as they fixed on the two young men at the edge of the copse.

With an anguished bellow, it dropped its head, bringing its great pointed antlers down into position so they could inflict the maximum damage on the two young men.

Then it charged.

Thomas knelt and steadied himself, his spear pulled back over his shoulder ready to throw, as the great stag sped across the copse with William's arrow buried deep in its chest. It thundered towards them, snorting and roaring, clearly having every intention of skewering them on the points of its antlers. Then suddenly it clattered to a stop, just before it got in range of Thomas's spear and stood, pawing the ground and snorting great clouds of steam while its eyes flicked either side of the tree at each of them in turn.

It narrowed its eyes on William, then seemed to make up its mind. With a roar of pain and anger, it charged towards him.

"Die, damn you," shouted William, "die!"

Ignoring him, Thomas was totally focussed on throwing his spear as hard and true as he could. He held his breath, seeking out the ideal spot – on the chest just below the soft throat where the spear could fell the great beast in an instant.

He waited for his moment – when the stag would lift its head to expose the lethal spot. But the stag kept its head down as it closed the gap – until the last moment when it lifted it up to fix its aim on William – and Thomas snapped his arm forward with all his strength and let the heavy-tipped spear fly, straight into the stag's chest.

Dead before it even hit the ground, the great beast's momentum brought it crashing towards the pair, the great antlers gouging deep furrows in the soft undergrowth like a plough in a field, before coming to rest just inches in front of William.

Thomas found himself breathing hard and fast as the stag came to a stop, and it was some moments before he could bring his breath under control and turn to his friend.

William's eyes were wide, his cheeks red and Thomas was surprised to see him start to laugh; deep bellowing laughs of exhilaration and release of tension.

"Oh my friend, you throw straight and true indeed!" William stood up. "You must retrieve the spear that has done such noble work this day!"

Thomas stood up as well. "You also shoot true, my friend."

"Nay, my arrow failed to find the heart. But you found it, by God's good fortune, and I am not to be finding myself skewered on the antlers of that beast."

William looked at the twitching corpse before them. "On the day we first met, it was my arrow that was true, and your stick failed to hit its mark. Now we have changed sides completely!"

He laughed again. "Come, let us go back to the manor. We must send for servants to bring this beast back for the table – and we must tell the story of your bravery!"

---0---

Arriving back at the manor, they were still elated with the hunt and the stories they had to tell. Thomas was deeply happy – he had proven himself on the hunt and won the admiration of his friend, and he longed to return home to tell the tale to his father. Already he could see the old man's shining eyes and proud smile as he was taken through the tale of his son's bravery and skill with the spear in the face of such danger.

They rode into the stable courtyard and two servants ran forward to take their horses. They dismounted and strode through to the Great Hall.

As they got there, Thomas could see immediately that something was wrong.

Sir Henry and Lady de Beauvais we sitting at the table, with Jane Melrose, Thomas's mother, sitting by them. She was looking both uncomfortable and deeply upset at the same time.

"Oh, Thomas!" she said as he stopped in front of the table.

"Mother?" he asked. "What is the matter? Why are you here?"

"Your mother has some very bad news, Thomas," said Lady de Beauvais, her voice breaking.

Thomas looked at his mother, who was now in tears. "It's your father, Thomas. He's... he's..." The tears took over and she stopped, gulping and fighting for breath.

Thomas found his own breath catching in his throat.

"He's dead, Thomas. I'm sorry," said Sir Henry.

Thomas clutched at the edge of the table and dropped to his knees.

He stared up at his crying mother, then suddenly she seemed to disintegrate in front of him as his own tears flooded his eyes.

"It's not true," he whispered, blinking furiously. "If this is a jest, it is in the very poorest taste."

"It is true, Thomas," said his mother.

"Then how did it happen?"

There was a long pause.

"He has taken his own life," said Sir Henry, crossing himself.

Sir Henry and Lady de Beauvais looked briefly at each other, then at Jane Melrose. Thomas couldn't be sure, but it was almost as if they were confirming a previously-agreed story.

"We have no knowledge as to why he would do such a thing," Sir Henry finished.

Again, the look.

Thomas knew he was lying, but couldn't find it within himself to make the accusation. He stared at the man. Sir Henry had a look of pity carefully applied to his face, and Thomas, in that instant, despised him.

He turned to Lady de Beauvais. She too was looking back at him with a look of sad pity that made him sick.

He looked at his mother. She was looking down, with tears streaming down her cheeks.

"Come, mother," he said, finding his strength as he stood up, "we must go back home and make such arrangements as must be made."

He turned and made to walk out of the Great Hall. As he did so, he caught sight of William, who had been leaning against the wall behind him with arms folded. Their eyes met.

Thomas stopped with a jolt as a further dreadful truth was revealed in William's eyes.

"You knew," he whispered. "You knew all along."

William said nothing. Thomas shook his head, as if to deny the awfulness of this final revelation, and walked out of the Great Hall.

Once outside he quickened his stride into a run, as his anger took hold.

"My horse! My horse!" he shouted, running into the Grangedean stable yard. Arthur was produced and saddled up, while Thomas stamped with impatience.

As soon as he was ready, Thomas leapt onto Arthur's back, his anger communicating itself to the horse so Arthur reared up, neighing, before Thomas got him under control. Then he wheeled the horse round and together they thundered out of the gates. Arthur, who at that time was young and full of high spirits, shook his mane as he galloped down the forest paths towards Thomas's family farmhouse.

Clattering into his own courtyard, he leapt off Arthur's back and left the horse to trot into the stable alone, as he strode into his own small hall.

"Father!" he cried, "Father! Are you home?"

There was a silence.

"Father!"

Again, silence. No large comforting figure of the old man to throw his arms around his son and welcome him home.

"Father..."

Thomas sank into one of the high-backed oak chairs and let his head fall onto the table. Great, tortured sobs welled up and broke out of him as he grieved for his father, for his youth, and for the friendship he had come to value so greatly.

He sobbed until he felt he no longer had any tears left inside him; until he was as dry as an old, grey bone.

He was still slumped over the table when his mother entered.

"Oh, my son," she said "I am so sorry."

He looked up.

"So he is gone."

"Yes."

"But why, Mother?" he asked quietly, as she sank onto the chair next to him and put her hand on his arm. "What possessed him to do it? I mean, what pressure must he have been under?"

"Great pressure, my son," she replied. "He was facing ruin from the enclosure of the lands."

"Enclosure?" He turned and faced her. He felt his anger start to rise again, like lava in a rumbling volcano. "What enclosure?"

"Sir Henry. He has forced enclosure of your father's lands. It means we may no longer farm them."

"But that is our livelihood."

"Indeed."

"And this is why my father took his life?"

There was a small hesitation before the reply. "Indeed."

"And it is by Sir Henry's doing?"

Again, the small hesitation. "Indeed."

Thomas pushed back his chair and stood up. He could no longer contain his anger, and he strode to the fireplace, kicking aside the protective grass rushes on the floor. He turned back and faced his mother.

"Then we must starve?" he snarled.

"You will need to take service with Sir Henry's household."

"I shall not."

"You must." She paused and fixed him with a piercing stare, "or we shall surely starve."

"This is William's doing," said Thomas, softly.

He was exhausted; his anger had gone as quickly as it had come. "The man is as false a friend as has ever drawn breath," he said. "I shall never forgive him. Never."

---0---

And now it was seven years later, and Thomas Melrose and Arthur were finally plodding into the courtyard of the farmhouse.

Arthur's ears pricked up and he snorted at the familiar smell of his oat mash.

Melrose slipped off his back and tied him to a railing, then walked through into the hall to find his mother with some bread and ale on the table.

"How was the hunt?"

"As ever." He sat at the table, pulled off a piece of bread and ate. "The man must hunt so frequently," he said after a mouthful, "that he will lay waste to all the county if he can." His mother poured him a tankard of ale and he took a long draft. "But the arrogance of the man – that is what I cannot take. He must needle me at every turn."

He turned to his mother and looked her in the eye. "Isn't it enough that I must serve him – that I must attend him along with those imbeciles, Dowland and Stanmore, so he can maintain his lordly status?" He put his tankard down on the table. "I would do him to death, Mother, so help me God. I would do it without a moment's pity, as one kills a beetle."

"Shush, my son," she replied. "Do not suggest such a thing." She poured him some more ale. "And never in the name of the Lord."

"I would do it, Mother. Would I have the chance, I would do it."

"Nay – I would not lose my son as well as my husband. The justices would have your life for de Beauvais. I would not see you hang for him."

"Indeed, Mother." He smiled, a hollow smile. "It was a jest. He is not worthy, even of my hatred."

---0---

Jane Melrose stood up and walked to the door, not reassured in the least. "I will retire to my chamber. You may bid me goodnight shortly." He nodded to her, eating some more bread.

She turned in the doorway and looked back at her son.

'He does not know the truth of this,' she thought. 'Poor William de Beauvais is no more guilty in this than he is.'

She turned back and walked slowly to her chamber, her heart heavy.

'He must never know the full truth of his father's death,' she thought. 'For that would kill him as surely as the hangman's noose.'

CHAPTER TWELVE

Margaret had been watching as Sir William and the lady made their progress out of the hall. She had been hiding just inside the door to the kitchens and was confident that the lady had not seen her.

It had been a shock to realise that the master's dinner companion was actually the witch called Justine. She had seen it immediately when she approached with the silver water bowl – the shape of the face, the line of the eyebrows – it would take more than some make-up and a French hood to have fooled her. So she already had her guard up in preparation for Justine's guilty reaction, and was able to keep calm and not react herself. Thereafter, she was able to ignore Justine completely while serving Lady de Beauvais, before sending a kitchen boy down to the village to fetch Hopkirk.

She had also made some discreet enquiries from the other servants as to the name of this lady. The one named Sarah had told her that she was called Mary Fox, had come recently from France and was staying while her father was away at sea. "I helped bathe and wash her, and I clothed her," Sarah had said. "What a gracious lady. Not too sure what to do, mind, but most gracious."

Once the couple had left and the guests had all taken their seats again, Margaret ran down the stairs to the kitchens, to find Hopkirk had arrived. He was sitting bolt upright on a bench at the edge of the kitchen, staring unblinkingly at the hustle and bustle going on around him, his black cloak drawn round him despite the heat of the fires.

Margaret approached with caution; she was still wary of this small grey man with his power as a witchfinder and a magistrate.

"Master Hopkirk," she said. "You are welcome here."

He did not turn, but carried on staring at the activity in the kitchens.

"Mistress Margaret. I came when I was called." Now he turned and fixed her with his grey eyes. "You have identified this witch?"

"Oh yes, Master Hopkirk." She took a breath to calm her nerves. "She has been changed from a serving maid to a fine lady called Mary Fox. She must have enchanted the master as she was his guest of honour at the banquet."

"And she is still in the hall with Sir William?"

"Oh no – the witch has gone upstairs with the master."

"Upstairs? To his chambers?"

"Aye – I fear for him, to be alone and unprotected in her wicked grasp."

Hopkirk paused in thought, his eyes boring uncomfortably into hers.

"I will need to gather some people from the village; we must have numbers if we are to restrain her. It will take me a few hours so I think we must agree that we will come to arrest her in the morning."

At that point the cook came over, straightening her cap and running her hands down her apron. "Master Hopkirk, as I live and breathe."

"Madam Cook," he replied, slowly turning towards her.

"What a pleasure to see you in my kitchens, Master Hopkirk. Is there anything I can do for you?"

Margaret could not contain herself. "It's that girl from this morning, Cook. The one that was put to turning the spit. She's like as not a witch! Master Hopkirk is here to see her brought to justice."

"A witch indeed?" The cook scratched her cheek. "Aye, now I think on it, she was right strange, that one."

"She knows things she didn't ought to know," explained Margaret. "She made the hearth clean by magic. And she blasphemed something wicked, as the Lord is my witness."

"Blasphemed?"

"Aye. She said – oh Lord forgive me – she wished..." Margaret gulped and crossed herself, "...she wished Christ in Hell." Margaret crossed herself again several times.

"She never!" responded the cook, crossing herself also.

"And she enchanted Sarah to bathe her and clean her from the soot of the kitchens, and to make her into a fine lady called Mary Fox," added Margaret.

"Well, Master Hopkirk," said the cook, "this one is no good and that's the truth. You must find her and test her."

"I will," whispered Hopkirk. "Indeed I will." He fixed them both with his unblinking eyes, now burning fiery red in the reflection of the kitchen fires. "We will test her for witchcraft and if we find her to be a witch..." His voice rose to a menacing growl, "If she is found to be a witch, we will condemn her to the flames of eternal salvation."

"Amen to that," said the cook. "Tell us what we must do to help."

"You must gather up the servants, and be ready to help me hunt her down and arrest her. At present she is with Sir William in his room – we will arrest her in the morning."

"I'll have them ready."

"Good. I will return at dawn." Hopkirk bowed. "By your leave, Madam Cook."

"Master Hopkirk."

Hopkirk turned and went out along the corridor towards the door which led out to the herb gardens, leaving the cook and Margaret standing staring after him. The cook looked at Margaret. "I thought there was something not right about that girl. Her dress... Her speech... Not right at all"

"And from out the parish, too," added Margaret.

"Aye, from out the parish," agreed the cook.

Margaret gasped as a thought struck her. "Why are we not arresting her this very evening? Why wait until the morning? She's with the master on her own – maybe she's enchanting him." An awful vision came into her mind. "Maybe even now she has turned him into a cat!"

At that moment Martha came down into the kitchen, carrying a wooden tray with some plates on it. "There is more to clear; we need some servants up in the hall." She stopped, seeing the cook and Margaret standing together looking very worried. "Is there something wrong?" she asked.

"The girl you brought down here this morning – she's a witch," announced the cook.

"A witch?" asked Martha. "Are you sure? She was strange in her speech and dress to be certain, but a witch?"

"Aye," said the cook. "She knew things she didn't ought to know, and she used an incantation to clean the hearth, and she blasphemed something horrible to Margaret."

"She blasphemed?" responded Martha, appearing suitably shocked. "What did she say?"

"Terrible things," said the cook, as she and Margaret crossed themselves repeatedly. "She said…" the cook hesitated before uttering the words. "She said 'I would that Christ rots in Hell.' Oh Lord forgive me."

Martha crossed herself as well. "She said that?"

"Those very words to Margaret here – as true as life."

"And she's with the master in his rooms – enchanting him as we stand here!" burst out Margaret.

"No," said Martha, "that is Mistress Mary Fox, the guest of honour."

"One and the same," said the cook grimly.

"Mary Fox, the fine lady, is Justine the witch?" asked Martha slowly. "But surely I would have recognised her?" She stared at them a moment. "But now I think on it, there is some sense in the girl Justine being this Mary Fox. Both appear as if from nowhere and both have strange mannerisms – and both are tall and red-haired…" She slapped her fist into her palm. "By the risen Christ, I should have seen it myself."

"Maybe she enchanted you," suggested Margaret. "Maybe she thought I was of no matter, so she did not enchant me and I recognised her, but you, as the housekeeper were more important and she thought to enchant you not to recognise her." Margaret was very satisfied with this; it was clear logic. The facts were in order.

"So, what is to be done?" asked Martha.

"Margaret has called Hopkirk, the witchfinder," said the cook. "And he has said he will call together a band of villagers to take her, and to test her for witchcraft."

"He says he will take her in the morning, but she could have turned the master into a cat or a bat by then," said Margaret, repeating her earlier concerns. "I say we should go up to the master's chambers and take her now."

"No," said Martha quickly, surprising Margaret with the hard edge to her voice. "The master can take care of himself. We will take her when she comes down in the morning."

"Master Hopkirk said we should get the kitchen servants to help," offered the cook.

"I will tell them," said Martha. She moved to the other side of the kitchen and climbed onto a stool.

"Hear me all!" she called out. "Hear me!"

The servants started to put down their knives, pestles and other tools. After a couple of minutes they were all standing still, listening.

"The guest of honour this evening with the master, was in fact the serving girl who came this morning into the kitchens to turn the spit. We have reason to believe she is a witch, so we will need to arrest her and test her for witchcraft. We will take her in her room or when she comes down to break her fast in the morning."

"How do you know she's a witch?" asked one of the servants.

"She knows things she shouldn't know," said Martha.

"She used black magic to clean the kitchens," said Margaret.

"And she blasphemed," added the cook.

"What did she say?" asked another servant.

Martha crossed herself several times, then answered, "She said she rejected Christ and all his good works, and she wished he would go to Hell for all eternity."

Margaret watched the servants cross themselves repeatedly and mutter darkly to each other. One decrepit and elderly under-cook even dropped to her knees to pray feverishly for a few moments, then had to be helped back to her feet by those either side of her.

"We will meet here at dawn," said Martha. Master Hopkirk, the witchfinder, will come with others from the village. With him to lead us, we will take this witch and we will bring her to justice." She paused for effect, looking along the line of servants in front of her.

"And may the Lord have mercy on her soul."

CHAPTER THIRTEEN

As Justine left the hall after the banquet, her mind was racing.

It was obvious that Sir William would only be interested in one thing when they got upstairs to his rooms – sex.

He'd been perfectly clear on that at dinner and his suggestion that he could wait was scarcely credible. No, there was no doubt that he would expect to sleep with her tonight.

A battle raged between Justine's head and heart.

Her heart fired the opening shot.

'Go on girl, sleep with him,' it said. 'You know you want to. You know you want to be in the arms of a strong, handsome man. Grab it, relish it, enjoy it, love it!'

Then her head cut in. 'Don't be so foolish. Lady de Beauvais was clear that he loses interest in girls once he's had them. Don't kid yourself that you'll be anything different in that. Let him have you and you won't just lose his interest; you'll lose his protection and his mother's as well.'

Her heart could see this was a strong argument, but it rallied. 'You came here by some freak chance, maybe you could leave by the same means at any time. You always fancied him in the picture – now you've met him in real life. Better not let the chance go.'

That was an easy one for her head to counter. 'The freak incident that brought you here was just that – a freak. The chances of it happening again are so remote as to be virtually impossible. So it's likely that you're stuck here in Tudor England as Mary Fox for the rest of your days. And the natives are not friendly – they think you're a witch. So you need the protection of Sir William and his mother and you can't risk letting him lose interest.'

Her heart had to concede that this was the clincher. Her head pressed home its victory. 'And anyway, he's a hunter. Let him have his hunt. That's the only way to keep his interest.'

'OK,' said her heart, 'you win – for now.'

Her mind made up, she smiled at him as they went upstairs, and was rewarded with a deep smile back.

"You are radiant, Mistress Justine Parker – or as I must now call you – Mistress Mary Fox. Your beauty makes my humble home seem to come alive."

"My lord," she said, inclining her head in recognition of the full acceptance of her new name, as well as the fine compliment to her beauty.

Her heart put in an extra beat and told her head it had better watch its step.

They reached the top of the stairs and walked past the portrait of Sir Thomas.

"My grandfather, Sir Thomas," said Sir William. "He built this house in the reign of the first Henry Tudor."

"A fine gentleman," observed Justine. "I'm sure he would be proud of what you have achieved."

"I do hope he would."

With that they passed along the gallery and through the door to the bedroom wing.

As they walked down the corridor, Justine glanced through the leaded windows. Dusk was falling and the summer sky was a deep fiery red.

Sir William opened a door at the far end of the corridor, bowed and stood back to let Justine enter.

"My humble chambers are yours," he said.

Justine knew that this was the master suite and they had set it out as such in her time. It consisted of an ante-room for dressing and a bedroom beyond. Once again she was pleased to see they had got it pretty much correct – except that they had set out the ante-room as a museum exhibit, whereas this was a room that was lived in. And it was a total mess.

The room had three large chests for Sir William's clothes, plus a wooden chair and desk under the window.

The desk was strewn with papers and had a large ink pot with a jar of quills on it. There were ink spills on the desk and several papers on the floor. The chests were covered in discarded clothing – doublets lying on top of crumpled hose, with several pairs of boots on the floor near the chair. Clearly Sir William had sat in the chair, pushed off each boot and left them where they fell. A sword in its scabbard was propped up against the wall, near to where a burnished silver breastplate was lying.

Justine realised she must have been looking at the mess in the room with some disdain, as Sir William suddenly leapt forward, gathered up the discarded clothes, boots and armour and threw them into one of the chests. He then made a half-hearted attempt to sort the papers on the desk into a tidy pile. When he was done, he stood back with a weak smile, like a puppy who has sat on command for the first time.

"A thousand pardons, Mary; my servant has failed his duty. It is not usually such a mess."

"No, I'm sure it is not," she laughed. "Men," she observed. "They're all the same. Helpless. Always have been; always will."

"You have rendered me helpless, good Mary, with your beauty and your charms." He smiled and bowed deeply.

"Oh please, my lord," she replied, with a touch of amusement. "If you want to flatter me, you'll have to do better than that."

"Oh, I see," he replied with mock sternness, "I must first make love to you with words, like a Cheapside poet." He thought a moment, studying her intently.

Justine waited with high expectation for what she hoped would be some beautiful Shakespearean-style metaphors.

"Your lips are most wondrous," he began.

'OK start,' she thought.

"They are like… they are like…" He looked like he was running out of steam and Justine's hopes sank.

Sir William stared wildly out of the window for inspiration "Your lips are like… the um… red sky at night…"

She raised an enquiring eyebrow, interested to see where this was going and rather enjoying his boyish discomfort. "…as the… er… red sky betokens the promise of warmth and sunshine in the day to follow."

"Hmm," she responded, not wishing to hurt his feelings. "Not bad. Not great rhyme and meter, but I like the idea."

"Your eyes…"

'Wait up,' she thought 'there's more...'

"…are like cornflowers…"

"Cornflowers?" she enquired.

"Yes, cornflowers. Because…" again Justine raised an eyebrow and waited expectantly "…because… because I think cornflowers are the prettiest of flowers," he ended lamely.

Justine clapped her hands. "Thank you, that was a worthy effort," she said. "But I think the truth is that these Cheapside poets are safe just now."

He laughed, then started to unbutton his doublet.

"What are you doing?" she asked.

"I would not lie with you fully clothed," he answered. "Will you also remove your clothing so we can lie together?" He gestured the door to the bedroom.

"But I have not agreed to lie with you," she said, folding her arms decisively.

Sir William looked genuinely puzzled. "You truly would not wish to come to the bed of Sir William de Beauvais? Why would you not?"

"It's not you," she answered, thinking fast, "it's just that where I come from, it takes a bit longer. A man and a girl need more time with each other first."

He studied her intently for a moment, then burst out, "Poppycock! A wench is for the bed, no more and no less. It has always been so and always will be."

Justine considered this, then shook her head. "How can you say that? You might take a girl just because you can. But where's the satisfaction?"

"God's teeth," he answered, "I would show you if you'd let me…" He made a grab for her, but she dodged away behind one of the chests.

"But how much better to join with her in a warm loving embrace than to have to fight her every inch of the way," she answered, moving round the chest as he advanced on her. "Come on," she added, "I bet you've had to fight for a few of your girls, haven't you?"

"Aye, I might have," he answered, making a sudden change of direction to try and reach her from the other side.

"And there's hardly been much warmth afterwards has there?" she responded, making the opposite change of direction and keeping the large chest between them.

"So?" he asked, pausing a moment as he flicked his eyes left and right, judging angles of attack.

"So make her feel truly special… make her realise that she's the only one…"

For a moment, Justine thought she had scored a good hit with that shot. He stayed still, looking up and to the left as he did some quick mental arithmetic. "But if she is one of hundreds..?"

Justine groaned. "I know, but that is hardly what she wants to hear," she observed testily.

"In truth," he answered, ignoring her testiness, "what she wants to hear is of no consequence."

Justine could see she was getting nowhere with this. She decided to change her approach. "Listen," she said, "tell me what you like best in life."

"What I like best?" He looked nonplussed. "Why?"

"Because I want to know. Because I am asking."

"Yes, but why?"

"Tell me," she repeated "what you like to do best in life."

There was a moment's silence while he considered her thoughtfully. Then he seemed to make up his mind.

"That is easy," he answered. "The chase."

"The chase?"

"For the deer."

"And how do you feel when you've caught it?" she asked. "Do you marvel at its beauty, its nobility, its passion?"

"Nay, I kill it."

Again, Justine groaned with despair.

He laughed. "'Twas a jest! I respect the deer as a worthy foe, and I love it for its beauty, but surely you cannot draw comparison with a wench?"

"Yes, I can," she answered. "I'll demonstrate." She moved to the far corner of the room, turned away from him, then looked back over her shoulder with what she hoped was a 'noble deer' pose. "Pretend I'm the deer."

"This is unnatural."

"Go on." She shot him a look over her shoulder. "What happens now?" she asked.

"I laugh, because you look a fool." Again she shot him a look, challenging him to go with her on the pretence.

He sighed. "In faith, I see you across the clearing." He went down on one knee, then mimed selecting an arrow and fitting it to his bow, seeming now to humour her. "I kneel slowly, and prepare an arrow…"

His voice softened as he seemed to become absorbed by the scene.

"I slow my breath, because the smallest part of my scent in the still air could alert you to my presence... I draw slowly, looking for the spot where I can shoot true to your heart…"

She stared at him over her shoulder.

"I wait for you to be motionless, choosing my moment with care…"

He stopped; his breath as soft as the still morning air as he stared at her.

"…And then I wonder at your beauty, your nobility, as you stand proud in the morning mist, and I am sad for a moment to take such a life… but then I know that to make such nobility mine in conquest is… is a worthy pursuit… I steady my aim…"

He opened his fingers. "I let fly."

Justine fell back against the wall with a small cry.

He stood up and ran over to her.

"I run to her side, and I claim her as my own."

He took her hands in his and pulled her towards him.

"And now I look closely at her… I see how beautiful she is, how perfect is the line of her brow, the shape of her eye, the ruby softness of her lips…"

Still holding her hands, he dropped again to one knee in front of her.

"Mary Fox, the truth is you are the girl of my dreams and you have stolen my heart with your beauty and your charms. I have known you but a day, yet I feel I have known you a thousand years."

He raised her hands to his lips and kissed them.

"I cannot live another moment without knowing you are truly mine for all time," he whispered.

Justine's heart melted as she saw the sincerity in his eyes, and gently she raised him up until they were standing face to face.

She moved closer to him and he put his arms around her. "Oh my lord," she said, "kiss me."

Their lips came together and his mouth opened under hers. His tongue caressed hers gently.

She melted into his arms and into his kiss.

Time stood still.

Later, they broke off and stood back, looking into each other's eyes.

"Mary Fox," he said, "you are truly becoming the mistress of my heart."

"Sir William de Beauvais," she replied. "I think you have been master of mine for all time."

He took her hand and led her through to his bedroom. "Come, Mary Fox," he said, as he led her to the bed and laid her down, "I must know you completely."

Justine's heart went out to him. 'Oh yes,' it whispered 'I want this more than anything else in the world…'

And she would have submitted then and there, had not her head suddenly cut in.

'Just hang on one minute, young lady,' it said. 'Have you forgotten our agreement?'

'That's out the window,' said her heart. 'Were you not paying attention just now when he kissed you? That was a game changer. You won't get another kiss like that for oh… maybe 450 years. You can't ignore that kiss.'

'You can, and you will,' said her head. 'You must.'

Justine pushed him away and stood up.

"I am sorry, my lord," she said. "As I said before, this is too soon. We have been together for just one day." She tucked a stray lock of hair back under her hood and stood up as straight as she could, aware that her chest was now heaving right under his nose. "I am sorry. We cannot do this now."

'Well done, girl,' said her head. 'Good move.'

Her heart refrained from answering.

Sir William frowned. "But when we kissed… I thought that now we knew each other well?"

He looked enquiringly into her eyes, like a puppy who had sat on command but had not got a treat. "You would still refuse to lie with me?" he whispered.

"My lord," she replied. "My heart says I should, but my head says it is too soon."

He stood back, and stared at her for what seemed an eternity.

"I would have my way." He said finally. "With any other girl I would have my way. But you…" he leaned forward and touched her cheek, "…you are different." He stood back again, while she looked steadfastly at him, her eyes never leaving his face. "You have bewitched me; that I must bend to your will."

"My lord, this is not witchcraft," said Justine quickly.

"Nay, I have no time for such nonsense," he answered, much to her relief. "Witchcraft is most often born in the minds of the accusers, not in those they accuse. I see no proof of witchcraft in you – and without proof there is no basis for an accusation. And yet…"

He kneeled down in front of her and took her hand. "And yet, I am so enchanted by you, that I must bend to your will. No girl has made me do that before." He paused. "My lady, what would you have me do?"

She lifted his hand in hers, pulling him up from his knees till he was standing in front of her. "My lord," she said, looking up into his eyes "you are a huntsman. You must consider how to shoot your arrow true to my heart." She reached up and touched his cheek, stroking his golden beard. "And when the time is right, perhaps it will find its mark."

"Aye, I warrant it will," he replied, putting his hand over hers, holding it against his cheek. "But like as not the huntsman will be led a merry dance first."

She smiled. "Indeed, my lord." She was about to add something about it being a lively dance nonetheless, when she felt an involuntary yawn starting. Initially she fought to keep her mouth closed, but it was an unequal battle and very soon the yawn popped her ears and forced her mouth wide open. Sir William watched in amusement, waiting till she had finished, then gently took her hand off his cheek.

"My lady, you are most tired and must to bed this instant," he observed.

"Yes," she said, as another yawn, even bigger than the first, quickly followed. "It has been quite a day," she said. She hadn't realised till that moment just how totally exhausted she was.

"I shall call for Sarah to undress you and make you ready for bed," he said, moving to the corner of the room and pulling on a red cord. A faint sound of a bell could be heard in the distance. He turned back to her.

"You shall sleep in the room at the end of this corridor. It will be your room – for now."

"For now?" she asked.

"Aye, my mother's sister Katherine Mansfield comes from Nottingham on the 13th of August next. She is used to staying there. But it will be yours for the two weeks until then."

A small alarm bell rang in Justine's sleepy mind. Two weeks to the 13th August – that made this the end of July...

Suddenly she was wide awake again.

"My lord, what day is it?" she asked, trying unsuccessfully to keep her voice flat calm.

"Why, do you not know?" he asked, not seeming to notice the edge of panic in her voice. "It is the 30th day of July in the year of our Lord, 1565."

Justine felt her legs go weak. She staggered back with a small cry, as the realisation hit her like a steam train that she had found Sir William and was starting to fall in love with him – on the eve of the 31st of July, 1565.

The very day he was destined to die.

She remembered the leaflet that she had picked up, and even the words it had said; "Sir William de Beauvais - born 1539, died on the night of the 31st of July 1565 in a barroom fight. He was reputed to be something of a wild man."

"What ails you, my lady?" Sir William asked with great concern, dragging her back to the present. Justine shook her head, unable to speak and unwilling to explain. She stared at him with wild eyes, seeing him now, not as a future lover, but as a man with an imminent sentence of death hanging over him.

"Oh my lord," she lied, "I am tired, as you said. I feel faint." She fell back onto the bed.

The door opened and Sarah entered. She took in the scene – Sir William standing over Justine lying on the bed. "Shall I come back shortly, Master?" she asked with a knowing smile.

"Nay, Sarah, Mistress Fox is tired," said Sir William. "She must be undressed and made ready for her bed. Please go to it."

"Yes, Master," answered Sarah, the smile disappearing as quickly as it had come.

Justine stood up, nodded weakly to Sir William, and walked unsteadily over to the door. She turned and looked back at him standing by the bed.

"Goodnight, my lady," said Sir William.

"Goodnight, my lord," Justine whispered, then followed Sarah out into the corridor and along to her bedroom.

---0---

Once in the bedroom Sarah set to work; removing Justine's make-up and hood, unpinning her hair, helping her out of the Tudor gown, farthingale, kirtle and her boots, putting her into a nightdress and into bed.

Throughout this process Sarah found Justine to be a model of willing obedience; lifting up her face to have her make-up wiped off, raising her arms to have her sleeves removed, stepping out of the gown, farthingale and kirtle when asked and offering up her legs to have her boots pulled off – but Sarah could see that Justine wasn't seeing her, or the bedroom. Justine may have been like a willing child being undressed and put to bed, but mentally she was in a completely different place – her eyes focussed on dreadful visions that only she could see.

Sarah, who was a kindly soul at heart and who had developed an affection for this girl, tried to bring Justine out of it by engaging her in conversation.

"Did you enjoy the banquet, Mistress Fox?" she asked while unpinning Justine's hair.

Or, while pulling off Justine's boots; "Did the master have much to say? He is well practised in courtly conversation, so I am told."

But Sarah got no answer. With a sigh she tiptoed out of the room, leaving her mistress sitting up in bed, hugging her knees to her chest and staring blankly at the wall opposite.

CHAPTER FOURTEEN

As dawn broke the next morning and the first golden rays of the summer sun pierced the still mist of the forest, Matthew Hopkirk led a small militia of villagers along the path towards Grangedean Manor.

He was sitting on a small, grey, shifty-eyed donkey while the villagers followed on foot. There were just fifteen of them; Hopkirk had managed to recruit only those who were not working in the fields or in their houses, so his group mainly consisted of the elderly and a few of the young village girls.

The elderly men and women carried pitchforks, which they planned to use to make the witch keep her distance if things turned nasty. The young girls carried crosses as a shield against the malevolent power of the Devil.

The girls had been Hopkirk's easiest recruits; not only were they excited by the chance to cast a witch out of the village, but it was also an opportunity to prove how God-fearing they were in case anyone ever thought to accuse them of witchcraft in future.

One of the girls, a pretty fifteen-year-old with straw-blonde hair tucked up under her plain coif, hitched her skirts and ran up to Hopkirk as they walked up the lane.

"Master Hopkirk," she began, as she drew level with him. "How are we to know this witch when we get to the manor?"

Hopkirk turned his cold grey eyes and stared down at her without blinking. She swallowed nervously. "If she maybe turns into a cat, or a raven or suchlike?" she added.

"It is Agnes, daughter of Jake of the tavern, isn't it?" he asked coldly.

Agnes took a deep breath as she glanced back down the line of villagers to where her friends Ruth and Maggie were watching and giggling nervously. They had just now dared her to talk to Hopkirk.

"Yes, Master Hopkirk," she answered.

"We will know her, I assure you, Agnes. We are true God-fearing folk, so if she be a witch, we will see the blackness of her heart and the Devil that resides within."

Agnes shivered. She was a good Christian girl, to be seen in church every week and on all the saints' days. This talk of the Devil disquieted her greatly.

"But if she assumes a different form?" she asked, emboldened by the support of Ruth and Maggie further down the path behind her. Hopkirk seemed not to notice them.

"My child, we will have to hope she does not, so we may identify her and bring her to trial." Hopkirk paused and Agnes was surprised to see he went a little red in the face. "We will challenge the Devil by submitting her to a test. We will put her under water so we can see if she has the magic to save herself."

They walked a moment in silence, as Agnes pondered on this.

"But if she does not save herself, she will be drowned?" she asked.

"Aye."

"And if she does save herself, by magic or by turning into a fish or suchlike, what then?"

"Then we will banish the Devil with fire," he answered softly. "We will burn her."

"So she will be dead whatever happens?" asked Agnes.

"Aye. Such is God's will."

Agnes crossed herself. "Such is God's will, Master Hopkirk," she acknowledged, and ran back to tell Ruth and Maggie what she had learned.

---0---

A few minutes later the party passed through a gate under a brick archway into the stable yard of Grangedean Manor, just as Sarah the servant was walking along the narrow corridor in the top floor above, leading from her tiny bedroom to the main house.

Noticing the movement in the yard below, she stopped by a leaded glass window and pushed it open a fraction so she could hear what was going on. She bit her lip as she recognised the grey man on the donkey as Hopkirk the witchfinder. What could he be doing at Grangedean Manor with a collection of pitchfork-wielding villagers? Was there a witch to be found?

Sarah shrunk back into the shadows to watch and listen.

Hopkirk dismounted and a servant ran out and took the donkey's bridle, then led the angrily braying beast away to a stable.

Hopkirk placed himself squarely in the middle of the yard, as menacingly still as a stone gargoyle. He waited as the villagers gathered around him.

"We are here to arrest an alleged witch known as Mary Fox," he began, his voice carrying clearly up to the window above.

Sarah gave a small cry, then quickly shrank further back into the shadows in case she'd been heard. The witch was Mary Fox! There must be a mistake – the Mary Fox she had served the night before was a good and kindly girl. She was no witch – of that one could be quite certain.

Sarah crept forward again and looked down on the yard. All the villagers were listening to Hopkirk – by God's good grace her small cry had not been heard.

"We must proceed through to the kitchens, where we will meet with Martha the housekeeper, who will tell us where the witch Mary Fox is sleeping, so we can arrest her and test her by ducking."

The villagers growled and the elderly shook their pitchforks.

"Evil witch!"

"Cast out the Devil!"

"Mary Fox, servant of Satan!"

Hopkirk held up his hand and there was silence.

"We must proceed with caution; this witch may have the power of transformation and may escape arrest by changing her form to a cat or a raven."

"By what evidence do we have her accused?" asked one of the elderly women.

"By her blasphemy and her rejection of Christ and all his good works," answered Hopkirk. "She was heard to say this: that she would have Christ rot in Hell for all eternity." The villagers all gasped. "And that Christ is the Devil incarnate."

"Those words?" asked the elderly woman, sounding deeply shocked.

"Those very words," confirmed Hopkirk, "spoken to Margaret, a servant in the manor."

The villagers shouted, stamped their feet and worked up their righteous anger, then Hopkirk again held up his hand.

When there was silence, he said, "We will proceed now into the manor. Follow me." He turned and went into the building, followed by his enraged militia.

Upstairs, Sarah closed the window quietly and for a moment she stood rooted to the spot. Mary Fox accused of being a witch – it was not to be believed! But if Hopkirk were to arrest her and test her… oh, how could such a thing be allowed? Such a poor girl, so exhausted she could not speak or sleep, but who had been so kind and gentle… No – it cannot be allowed. She must be warned!

With a determined lift of her head, Sarah turned and ran down the corridor.

Soon she reached the bedroom door and knocked. There was no sound. She knocked again, louder.

"Hello?" came a sleepy voice. "Come in."

Sarah pushed open the door and peered in. Her mistress, the girl she knew as Mary Fox, was sitting up in bed, bleary-eyed and with tousled hair.

"Morning, Sarah," Justine said, yawning sleepily and stretching her arms out wide.

Sarah went quickly up to the side of the bed.

"Mistress Fox, you must fly now!" she blurted out. "Master Hopkirk the witchfinder is here to arrest you!"

Her mistress was wide awake in an instant.

"Hopkirk? Here? Now?" she asked, her voice coming out in a strangled squeak.

"Oh yes, Mistress," answered Sarah "I saw him enter the manor with some people from the village. They had pitchforks."

"Oh, Sarah, will you help me?"

"Yes, Mistress Fox," said Sarah. "Yes I will."

Justine looked searchingly into Sarah's eyes. After a moment she seemed reassured. "So what are we to do?" she asked.

"We must get you out of the manor to somewhere you can hide out."

"Oh, yes – but where?"

Sarah paused a moment, chewing on her lower lip. What she was about to suggest was highly risky – putting herself and her family in danger. But one look at the terrified girl in front of her, and she knew she was doing the right thing. She said, "My mother has a little cottage in the woods; I can take you there. You'll be safe a while."

"Thank you so much, Sarah," said Justine. "But I don't want you or your mother to suffer if I am caught."

"We can look after ourselves, Mistress, never you mind."

Sarah said the words, but in her heart she was not so sure.

Justine took both Sarah's hands in hers and said, "I cannot thank you enough. Really I can't." She swung her legs out of the bed and was about to stand up when suddenly she froze.

"What is it, Mistress?" asked Sarah, concerned.

"Sir William!

"The master – what of him?"

"I have to stop him going to the tavern this evening!"

Whatever Sarah might have expected her mistress to say, it was not that. "But the master does not go to the tavern, Mistress Fox," said Sarah, frowning. "He prefers to drink wine in the manor."

"Trust me on this, Sarah – he'll go today unless I can stop him," said Justine grimly.

Just then they heard some shouts from downstairs. Sarah stopped, listened a moment, then grabbed her mistress's arm. "You must come now, we have no time to lose!"

"I'll need to put my boots on!"

"No, Mistress! No time – not for boots!"

She pulled Justine to the door, then opened it a fraction to listen for sounds downstairs. She looked back with her hand to her mouth in a gesture of silence.

To her horror, Justine mouthed "wait" and slipped back into the room. For a moment Sarah thought her mistress would try and pull her heavy man's boots on, but instead the girl pulled a bag from under the bedcovers, swung it over her head and onto her shoulder. Then she grabbed the bow and quiver of arrows that still stood propped up in the corner and threw them onto the bed. Still barefoot, she ran back to Sarah at the door.

Sarah raised an enquiring eyebrow. Justine muttered, "It's a clue for William – best I can do," then slipped out of the room after her.

They crept quietly along the corridor towards the door at the end that led out to the gallery.

As before, Sarah opened the door a fraction, listening for sounds of Hopkirk and his posse of villagers. Almost immediately they heard the tramp of boots and a hissed direction to proceed upstairs.

Sarah quickly closed the door and looked back at Justine, her heart pounding fit to burst.

"We must go the other way," she whispered.

Together they ran back up the corridor, Justine's nightdress billowing around her; her bare feet making little sound on the wooden boards.

They reached the door at the end that led to Sir William's rooms. Justine looked at the solid door surrounded by wood panelling.

"We can't go in there, Mistress," Sarah hissed.

"Why not?" Justine squeaked.

"Those are the Master's rooms."

"But he could protect us."

"And have Hopkirk accuse him also?" Sarah shook her head. "Nay, Mistress, we'll not go that way," said Sarah. She glanced back along the corridor, expecting to see the door at the far end open at any time and the figure of the witchfinder appear.

"Then where do we go?" Justine whispered, the rising panic in her voice matching Sarah's.

"This way, quick!" said Sarah.

She pushed on an intricately-carved rose decoration at waist height on the wood panelling on the right side of the corridor. Immediately a small low doorway swung open below the carving to reveal a black opening behind. Without waiting for Justine, Sarah ducked down and disappeared into the dark space.

Sarah glanced back out and saw Justine's feet staying still, while the hem of her nightdress twisted round. 'The girl must be stopping to look back down the corridor,' she thought, 'when every moment is vital!'

Sarah was about to call out, when she heard the sound she had been fearing the most – the door at the far end start to open.

With a startled squeak Justine plunged head first past Sarah into the black opening. Sarah leaned back and pushed the door quietly shut, enveloping the two girls in total darkness.

Despite her thumping heart, Sarah stayed absolutely still, kneeling on the rough wooden boards. Then to her horror, she heard a board creak as Justine tried to get up.

"Easy, Mistress," she whispered. "Be quite still. It is dark and the roof is low at the start. We must gather our breath before moving."

"Where are we?" came the whispered reply.

"Old secret passage. It leads down through a hidden door in the courtyard. From there we can get out through the rose garden. I found it one day when I was cleaning."

"Oh. Right."

Then they heard the dreadful sound of boots marching along the corridor.

Closer they came; Sarah's heart thumping more and more as the boots got louder and louder. Then the boots stopped.

Right outside the door to the secret passage.

"The bed was still warm," came a menacing, sinister-sounding man's voice. "She cannot have gone far."

"She did not come past us as we walked along the gallery," came another voice, sounding like that of an old man.

There was the sound of several other people agreeing, accompanied by a noise like pitchfork handles thumping the floor.

"Sarah," Justine hissed. "We must move away!"

"Nay, 'tis too late – they will hear us. Best to keep very still, Mistress."

At that moment there was a slight scuttling sound from the floor inside the pitch-black hiding place.

Then the sound stopped, and Sarah heard Justine draw in her breath sharply. "Sarah," she hissed with unmistakable panic rising in her voice, "there's something crawling up my leg."

"By all that is holy, Mistress, you must stay still," breathed Sarah. "Belike, it is just a mouse," she said hopefully.

"Too heavy," came the whispered reply. "It's a rat… I know it's a rat… I hate rats…"

Sarah strained her ears to hear what was going on in the corridor outside their hiding place.

"She has disappeared, Master Hopkirk!" This sounded like an old woman. "She has used the Devil's magic to vanish into the air."

"Perhaps she has passed through this door here," said Hopkirk.

Sarah froze, her heart now about to jump out of her chest. She expected any second for light to flood in to the hiding place and a triumphant Hopkirk to bend down and drag them both out.

At that moment she heard Justine give another gasp and the tiniest cry. "It's moving up my leg," she breathed. "Oh God, oh God, oh God…!"

"Be still, please, Mistress…"

"Now there's another one! It's on my ankle…"

"In the name of Jesus, Mistress, please…"

"One's on my knee! What if it bites me?"

"Give your leg a shake, Mistress," hissed Sarah. "Just a small one, mind."

There was small grunt as Justine moved her leg, followed by a noticeable thump as the first rat jumped off and scuttled noisily up the dark corridor, followed by another thump and scuttling as the second rat followed.

"What was that?" said the sinister voice. "Quiet. I heard something."

Instantly there was quiet from the villagers in the corridor.

"Is there a secret passage here? A priest's hole or somesuch?"

The silence continued. Sarah prayed that none would know of the secret passage.

"There may indeed be one," said the sinister voice. This was followed by a sound that made Sarah's blood freeze in her veins and drew a small squeak from Justine.

It was the sound of tapping across the panels as Hopkirk searched for a hollow area.

The tapping started high and to the left, returning the dull thud of a solid wall. Then it moved across to the right, but just above their low doorway, so it still returned a dull thud.

Then it moved down and back across, getting closer and closer, till Sarah knew that any second it would return the hollow sound of an empty space.

Just when Sarah was convinced that all was lost, she heard another noise – that of a door opening.

"What is the meaning of this intrusion?" came the loud, indignant voice of Sir William de Beauvais. "Who are you, sir, that would trespass in my private rooms? And who is this rabble with you? What is your business in my house?"

The tapping stopped.

"I am Matthew Hopkirk, magistrate," came the sinister voice. "And I am charged to arrest a woman accused of the vile practice of witchcraft."

"Nonsense!" came the reply. "I am Sir William de Beauvais, and I do not entertain such fanciful notions."

"But I believe you have 'entertained' this woman," answered Hopkirk. "She is a serving girl, or the daughter of a merchant, and is known as Mary Fox."

There was a long silence. Sarah could picture the master going red with anger.

Eventually he gave out an explosive roar. "How dare you, sir!" he bellowed. "How dare you suggest that Mary Fox is a witch! Be gone sir, be gone this instant, and get your peasants and their pitchforks out of my house!"

There was a pause, as Hopkirk must have stood his ground.

"I warn you, Sir William, do not harbour a witch. For we will find her, and we will test her, and if she be found to be a witch, we will burn her to banish the Devil. And if we find you have been harbouring her willingly and defending her, as you seem to suggest, then we will test you too, and the Lord will have mercy on your soul."

"Get out!" bellowed Sir William, "get out before I have you arrested for trespass!"

"I go now, Sir William, but I shall return."

"You do that and I'll have you hanged for it! Out!"

The two girls heard Sir William's door slam, followed by the sound of Hopkirk and the villagers walking away down the corridor, then the door at the far end opening and closing.

Then – silence.

Sarah let her breath out in a long, low hiss of relief. "Oh, Mistress, that was ever so close," she said. "We must be away from here quickly."

"We can't go back out into the corridor," hissed Justine. "He might be hiding and waiting. He wants to drown me then burn me!"

"Nay," said Sarah. "We must be away to my mother's cottage. He'll not find you there. We go forward. Follow me. You have to crawl to start, but it soon opens out to a place where you can stand."

Sarah crawled forward and heard her mistress do the same. After they had crawled for a short while, the echoes of their hands and knees scraping the floor changed to a deeper, higher sound. Sarah said, "You can stand here, Mistress. Watch your head as you get up."

Sarah stood up and walked forward. Then she heard a rustle, a bumping sound and a small yelp behind her. "Watch your head there, Mistress," she repeated.

Sarah ran her hand along the rough wall beside her till suddenly it curved away. "And the corner here, Mistress," she said.

A little later she took a step out into empty space and nearly overbalanced. Recovering, she said, "The stairs here, Mistress." She trod carefully down the stairs, feeling each step with her toe before committing her weight to it. When she felt the last step, she reached her hand out, feeling for the old iron handle. Finding it, she twisted it round a three-quarter turn and pushed. A sliver of light appeared as she eased the door open an inch and squinted out through the gap.

After a moment, she opened the door some more and peered right round it. Satisfied that no-one was watching, she opened it fully and together they slipped out. Sarah pulled the door closed behind her. There was a click as the latch caught and locked – committing them to their escape.

---0---

Justine stopped and looked around her. They had emerged into a narrow shadowy passageway between two brick walls. She looked back at the doorway. It had been cut so cleverly into the brickwork that now it was closed it was virtually impossible to see where it had been – there were just some faint lines running down that followed the line of the mortar. You really had to look to see them.

Rubbing the bump on her head with her hand, Justine followed as Sarah crept to the end of the short passage, then stopped as the girl gestured for her to wait. Again Sarah peered cautiously round the corner. Appearing satisfied that no one was there, she turned back and gestured for Justine to follow her. They ran out into the courtyard.

The morning sunshine burned into Justine's eyes after so long in the dark, but she put this out of her mind – it was nothing compared to the thought of Hopkirk and his tortures lingering behind her.

She lifted her leg to look for marks where the rats had been, and was relieved that there was nothing to see. Thank goodness they had not bitten her; she'd have screamed for sure if they had – and it had been hard enough not to scream when they were on her leg. She shuddered at the memory.

"Come, Mistress!" urged Sarah.

They ran across the courtyard to a solid wooden gate. Sarah opened it slowly, and they slipped through.

They were now in a beautifully laid-out garden, with rose bushes set in deep beds, surrounded by well-maintained lawns. The roses were mainly red and white varieties. 'It's a Tudor rose garden – how beautiful,' Justine thought as they ran through it. 'If I'm not mistaken, we have a tea room here in the 21st century.'

"Come!" called Sarah. Justine followed her quickly across the garden and through another gate at the far end under a wooden pergola festooned with large, colourful roses.

Now they were in a garden with herbs laid out in narrow rows. Justine noted rosemary, basil and thyme, plus a couple of plants she couldn't identify, before they had crossed this garden and arrived at another wooden gate under a brick arch. Sarah pushed the gate and it opened easily. They ran through onto a narrow lane leading out to open countryside.

Justine would have loved to stop and enjoy the view of the Tudor fields, with occasional little cottages, dense green copses and burbling streams rushing down the hills. But instead she had to focus on keeping up with Sarah and trying – unsuccessfully – to avoid sharp stones with her bare feet as they ran. As the air started to burn in her chest, she tried to remember the last time she'd been to the gym. She wished it had not been so long.

After they had been running down the open path for what seemed to Justine to be hours, but must have been no more than a few minutes, Sarah slowed down to an easier pace and Justine saw that they were now approaching a dark wood. Soon they were trotting in among the trees; picking their way through majestic oaks and tall elms and getting deeper and deeper into the forest.

After a while Sarah slowed to a walk, allowing them both to catch their breath – and for Justine to realise just how much her feet were now hurting. Her initial attempts to avoid the sharp stones and sticks had proved ineffective and she had ended up just running as if she had shoes on and trying to ignore the growing pain in her feet.

Sarah came up to a twisted old oak tree and she stopped altogether.

"How do you fare, Mistress?" she asked.

"Fine," panted Justine. She hopped onto her left foot and pulled the right foot up so she could study the sole. There was a fair amount of blood trickling from a number of cuts, making red channels in the black dirt.

"I'm just fine," she repeated.

She gingerly set down her right foot, then leaned back against a low thick branch of the old tree and lifted the other foot to see the sole. It too was blackened with the dirt of the forest floor and running with rivulets of blood that were carving red tracks through the blackness.

"We will bathe your feet when we arrive at my mother's cottage." said Sarah. "It's not far now." She left the path and started walking through the forest.

Justine put her foot down gingerly and loped along, wincing, after Sarah.

They went deeper and deeper into the forest, till eventually they came to a small thatched cottage standing alone among the trees. It had tiny windows without glass that were no more than slits in the wall and a solid slatted wood door. Smoke was rising from the single central chimney. Justine was surprised to see the smoke of a fire on a summer's morning.

Sarah pushed open the door and they went in.

It was dark inside the cottage; with the weak beam of sunlight from the windows joined only by the orange glow of the central fire. There were no internal walls – just one room. The fire was in a grate in the middle; a table and a couple of stools stood against one wall and a low pallet bed against another. The bare earth floor was covered only with rough straw.

An old lady sat by the fire, watching a pot which was suspended over the flames from a metal frame. Inside the pot was some bubbling liquid, which she was occasionally stirring. She was wearing a rough woollen dress and apron, and had a simple cotton coif covering her hair.

She looked up as Sarah entered, and her face lit up with a broad smile, to be replaced by a frown as Justine then appeared in the doorway.

"Hello Sarah, dear," she said.

"Hello, Mother," said Sarah.

"Who is this that comes to call on us?" asked the old woman, pointing a bony finger at Justine.

"It is my mistress from the manor," answered Sarah. "Mary Fox, the daughter of a London merchant."

"Why does she wear only a night dress?"

"We had to run from the manor."

Sarah was silent a while, as she stared at her mother. Eventually she said, "Mistress Fox is falsely accused of witchcraft by Hopkirk, the magistrate."

Fortunately the old woman merely nodded, looked Justine up and down and said; "I have experience of Master Hopkirk – he is all too ready to see witchcraft in God-fearing folk and I'll have none of his false accusations here. You are welcome, my child."

"Oh, thank you," said Justine with some relief. "You are most kind." She wondered what the old woman's experience of Hopkirk had been and decided that there would be time enough for that story later.

She hobbled in across the straw, grimacing with the pain in her feet. Sarah's mother looked down at the trail of blood she was leaving.

"Oh, my poor child," she said, "your feet are cut to ribbons. 'Tis no wonder if you must run all the way from the manor." She looked up at her daughter. "Sarah?"

"Yes, Mother?"

"Fetch some water from the stream and we will see to these poor feet."

"Yes, Mother." Sarah grabbed an old tin pail and went out of the cottage. The old woman stood and picked up a small three-legged wooden stool, which she placed near the light of the fire.

"Now, sit down here and let me see."

Justine hobbled to the stool and sat down, putting her bag down on the floor beside her. She held up her right foot. The old woman lifted it and peered at the sole.

"Hmm. There are many cuts, but fortunately none too deep." She put the foot down and picked up the other, studying it closely in the light of the fire. "This too. The water will take off the dirt, then we will let God's grace take care of the healing. And if His grace does not do the work, we will apply a poultice of mouldy bread. You will need to rest a while till God's blessed work is done and the wounds have been closed over. Then we can dress you, and decide how you are to avoid the zealous Master Hopkirk.

She took another look at Justine's foot.

"Indeed," she observed, "your feet are otherwise unmarked – they are those of a young girl who has only ever seen the softest of shoes." She looked up, studying Justine intently in the firelight. "You are a merchant's daughter?"

Justine nodded.

"From London?"

Justine nodded again.

"Then you have truly led a charmed life, that you have not been made to wear rough, ill-fitting shoes. We are most blessed to receive such a fine lady in our humble dwelling."

"I am the one who is humbled, by your kindness and hospitality," answered Justine, grabbing this as a perfect cue to confirm her gratitude.

"Aye, you are welcome to stay a while." The old woman put Justine's foot down. "Let us hope the Lord is also welcoming, and chooses not to let these wounds become rotten with pus or canker."

Sarah returned with the tin pail full of clean, fresh water from the stream. Her mother took a piece of cloth from the table, sat down again and started cleaning the dirt from Justine's feet. Justine tried not to wince as the rough cloth rasped across the cuts, but as the water became blacker and her feet became cleaner the pain began to recede – to be replaced by a steady throbbing in the warmth of the fire.

Justine studied the woman who was cleaning her feet as she worked, bent over her task in deep concentration. A few tendrils of grey hair had escaped from under her rough cotton coif and were swaying with the rhythm of her movements. The sleeves of her brown woollen dress were pushed up to reveal bare arms that were surprisingly youthful – very much at odds with the calloused, working hands she was dipping into the water and sponging off the blood and dirt from Justine's feet. With a shock Justine realised that Sarah's mother must be nowhere near as old as she had first thought; the bony hands, grey hair and pinched face were more a result of unremitting hard work in harsh winters than of old age. Justine decided that she probably wasn't more than 45 years old – although she did briefly wonder if reaching such an age in the Tudor countryside was itself something of an achievement.

Sarah's mother finally took another cloth and tore off a strip. She used it to dry Justine's feet, then looked up.

"The wounds are not as bad as I first thought. The bleeding has stopped and with God's good grace you will be walking without pain in a short while." She smiled. "Although a pair of shoes would help."

"Thank you," said Justine.

"You will lie on the bed and rest a while. I will make you a hot posset."

"Lovely," said Justine, wondering what a hot posset might be. It certainly sounded like something comforting.

Sarah's mother then tore the remaining cloth into two strips and used each to bind Justine's feet, enabling her to hobble across to the bed and lie down.

"Rest a while," Sarah's mother repeated. "Sarah and I need to fetch some milk and ale from the farm a few miles hence. We will be back after noon."

The two of them left, closing the door with a creak.

Peace descended on the little cottage.

Justine lay back on the rough mattress, her hands behind her head in the absence of a pillow. She took a deep breath and let it out slowly, forcing herself to relax. Her feet were still throbbing, but the lack of pain made that easy to bear.

The weak shaft of sunlight that had been beaming in through the thin window suddenly disappeared as the sun went behind a thick cloud. The fire had subsided to a dull orange glow, and the cottage was now quite dark inside, with strange, unfamiliar shaped shadows thrown up by the old Tudor furniture.

In the peace of the dim, cool cottage, she became aware of the many sounds of the forest outside. She tuned in to the birds calling and singing in the trees; then she switched her attention to the breeze rustling the thick summer foliage, before idly noting the clip-clop of horse's hooves approaching…

Hooves?

Quickly she looked around, desperately seeking somewhere to hide, but the small, bare cottage offered no real hiding places, and anyway, it was too late, as there came the unmistakable sound of a man dismounting and heavy boots walking up to the door.

The door opened. A man's figure was silhouetted in the light of the doorway.

"Mistress Fox?"

She gave a little cry of relief as she recognised the deep voice of Sir William.

He closed the door behind him and approached the bed.

"Mistress Mary Fox. I have given chase and I have found my quarry," he said, his voice warm with the sound of a smile.

"And now my arrow must find its path – true to your heart."

CHAPTER FIFTEEN

Thomas Melrose stared at his mother open-mouthed across the table, his piece of bread frozen half way to his lips.

"You mean to tell me," he said very slowly and deliberately, "that the reason my father killed himself was not because of the enclosure of his land?"

Jane Melrose looked down at her pewter plate and poked at her half-eaten piece of salted mutton with her knife. She didn't answer. She was tormented with guilt – only the night before she had vowed never to let her son find out the truth of his father's death, and now here she was, at breakfast the very next morning, on the verge of stupidly revealing it all.

It had been a silly, chance remark, said without thought, which had begun this unstoppable cascade towards a truth she'd kept hidden for many years.

A truth she'd intended to take to her grave.

It had started when Thomas, still angry from Sir William's insulting remark of the previous day, had observed dryly over breakfast that Sir William should have been grateful that he, Thomas, had actually pushed him to study harder when they were boys.

His mother, chewing absent-mindedly on a piece of mutton, had answered, "Aye, and a shame for you that it led to the death of your father."

She might have been able to bluff it out; maybe to come up with some plausible explanation, but she had stopped, looking absolutely horrified. Naturally he had picked it up.

"My education?" he had asked, puzzled. "What had that to do with my father's death? It was the forced enclosure of his land that killed him, wasn't it?"

Her continued silence allowed him to deduce that this was not the case.

So now Thomas put down the piece of bread, leant across and pushed her plate away down the table, then grabbed her chin in his hand and lifted it up. After a moment she raised her eyes and looked deep into his.

He repeated the question that was still hanging ominously in the air between them. "The reason my father killed himself was not because of the enclosure of his land?"

"No, Thomas, dear, it wasn't," she said, with some difficulty. "Let me go, you're hurting me."

His eyes bored into hers, his hand still gripping her chin.

"Then – why?"

"Let me go, Thomas."

"You'll tell me?"

"Yes. Let me go."

He released his grip and took a sip of beer. "Tell me," he whispered, his voice unnaturally calm, like the still air before a storm.

Jane rubbed her chin. "It's not so simple."

"It never is."

"Your father loved you very much…"

"And I him," cut in Thomas. "To the point, woman."

"That is the point, Thomas." She paused, choosing her words with care. "It was because he wanted the best for you that he agreed to the enclosure."

Thomas stared at his mother with complete incredulity. "How could he begin to imagine that cutting me from my lands would be in my best interest?"

"He made a bargain with Sir Henry de Beauvais."

"A bargain?"

"Aye."

"With that man?"

She nodded.

Thomas pushed back his chair and stood up, his eyes burning.

Suddenly he brought his clenched fists down hard onto the table, making her jump.

"Why, in the name of the risen Christ, did he do that?" he shouted.

"He agreed to the enclosure so that you may be educated as Sir William's classmate, and for your inheritance," she whispered, looking up at him with wide, fearful eyes. "Sir Henry would never have agreed to such a thing normally." She stopped, then added, "And your father accepted a fair price for the land."

"He was paid for the land so I could be educated?"

"Aye."

"Then what became of the money? My inheritance?"

"Some was spent on clothes and Arthur, your horse. Your education was paid in full. The rest was…" she swallowed nervously "…it was – lost."

There was an uneasy silence as he thought hard. Finally he whispered, "Lost?"

"Aye. He… he gambled it away in the tavern mostly…" She swallowed again and looked up at him with eyes that were swimming with tears.

"It was the shame of that that drove him to take his own life," she said.

"Not the enclosure by Sir Henry?"

"No. Not that."

"And he agreed the enclosure so I could have an education? And some money to inherit?"

"Aye."

"And yet you say he was a gambler? My father?" Thomas thought a moment, "So how have we lived all these years? What money have we had in income if he gambled it away?"

"There was still some income from the lands that Sir Henry let your father work."

"But the money he received from the enclosure was gambled away? I will never believe the truth in that."

"I am sorry, Thomas," she replied. "The truth will be told by Jake, the landlord in the tavern. He saw your father in there many times."

"Then I must go to the tavern shortly and ask him – ask him to give the truth to your claim that my father was a gambler."

"I never wanted to tell you, Thomas. I know how much you loved your father."

"Aye, and you are so ready to tell me he was not the man I thought he was. That also hurts."

"Maybe it is good you know the truth of his death, Thomas." She paused. "My son, as I said, I would have kept this from you, but it was the truth, and maybe it is better for you to know it."

Thomas slumped back down in his seat with his head in his hands. After a few moments he looked up at his mother.

"William knew," he said. "When my father died I saw it in his eyes. He knew."

"He knew your father had made the bargain with Sir Henry," she answered. "But why would he have known your father gambled away the money?" She pressed her point. "He was your friend."

"A friend would have said something."

"What – that your father was a gambler? That would have been the worst thing to have said." Jane put her hand over his, stroking it gently with her thumb. "My dear son, I should not have told you this. I am sorry."

"Nay, woman. Do you know, I am glad you have told me," he answered, taking his hand out from under hers. "Now I value the truth in this."

He stood up.

"But I do not think Sir William de Beauvais is the innocent in this matter. He knew what my father was doing, and he did not share this news with me. I saw it in his eyes that day. He knew. And he has never forgotten it – every day he must remind me with his slights and his taunts."

"You read too much into his words," she said quietly.

"Indeed I do not," he snapped. "They are as plain as the nose on his face."

"You do, my son. You see slights where none are meant. You use them to stoke the fires of your anger but they are mere pebbles not coals, and they do not burn."

"You use a pretty turn of phrase, Mother," he observed dryly, "but you are not there each day to hear the words he uses."

"I know enough of life, and of the ways of men," she answered, "to know that Sir William is a good man and means you no ill will."

"But I know what I hear," he said, his voice rising again, "and I hear words that are the very driest of coals! They are very eager to burn! They turn my anger white hot!"

"My son," she said, trying to speak calmly and evenly to cool his anger. She could see that it was real and all too likely to become physical. "I would you listen to me. You imagine these slights – they are real in your mind but not in his."

"Again, I say, Mother, you are not there and I am. You must let me be the judge in this matter. He swallowed the remains of his beer. "Now, I must be away."

"Where?" she asked.

"I have business to attend to in the town. Then this evening, I will go to the tavern. I will ask the truth of Jake. A fool such as he will tell the truth in his eyes, whatever his mouth may say. And I will have the truth in this matter – I will not have anyone stand in my way."

"Be careful, son," she warned. "You must keep your anger in check. This is none of Jake's doing."

"Nay, indeed. It is Sir William's doing, and that oaf of a father of his. He is the cause of my anger," he patted the hilt of his sword, "and he will feel the full force of it if I chance to meet him!" He strode out of the room, calling for a servant to saddle his horse.

His mother sat silent, still and alone at the table, a single tear running down her cheek.

CHAPTER SIXTEEN

In the dim light inside the cottage, Justine looked up at William as he leant over the bed, his dark shape silhouetted against the meagre light of the window. At any other place and time Justine would have found this to be quite menacing, with echoes of some black and white horror movie she'd seen as a child – but this was William leaning over her and she could just make out the twinkle in his eye and the smile on his mouth – and she was not afraid.

"My lord," she asked softly. "How did you find me?"

"Ahh," he said as he sat down on the edge of the bed, his leather boots and belt creaking gently as he moved, "you are asking the huntsman how he follows the trail?"

She nodded, then realised it was probably too dark for him to see. "Yes," she said.

"Indeed," he answered, and she could hear the warmth of a smile in his voice, "I would love to tell you of the skill with which I picked up your scent; how I sniffed the wind and determined your direction; how I tracked you down by the smallest clues that would be all but invisible to any other person…" he laughed. "But, I cannot."

"Then how?" she asked, her curiosity raised.

Just then the beam of sunlight burst back through the small window and added enough light to the cottage that they could now see each other.

"'Twas not so difficult," he answered her, reaching forward and stroking her hair. "First, I noted the quiver of arrows on your bed, and I realised you had told me to hunt for you."

"It was all I could think of in a hurry," she said.

"And it was most effective," he affirmed. "It told me you had run from your bed in great haste and were seeking my help. Knowing that little grey man, that witchfinder, had come up the stairs, I understood that you could not have escaped that way. So I checked the secret passage behind the corridor…" She raised an enquiring eyebrow. "Ah yes – I have known of it since I was a boy and used to delight in escaping from my mother that way…" He chuckled, then became serious again. "But this morning I noted the dust disturbed on the floor. So I knew to check the hidden door out into the rose garden – and sure enough there were footmarks in the dirt leading from it."

He laughed. "You are most resourceful, Mistress Fox, but I quickly deduced you had no time to put on shoes, for the man's boots you wear were still by the bed, and when I looked at the other shoes in the chest, they were all half the size of the boots and none would have fitted you anyway." He chuckled softly. "So do I take it you were wearing those boots under your gown last night at the banquet?"

"Yes," she answered. "You're right; none of the shoes would fit."

"How amusing. My mother would have fainted had she seen them. So, I could only assume you had escaped barefoot from the manor." He turned to study her feet in their bandages, sticking out from under the thin blanket. "As I thought," he said, examining them closely, "there is blood in no small measure coming through the bindings."

"There were sharp stones."

"Indeed," he continued, "so it was not difficult to follow your trail."

"You're very clever," she observed, genuinely impressed.

"Nay," he answered, with what sounded like a touch too much self-deprecating modesty. "You left many spots of blood on the path. I did not need the nose of a hound." He paused a moment. "Although I'll warrant that peasant Hopkirk would have missed it."

"Lucky he didn't know where to start looking," she said.

"Aye," he nodded. "And in truth, I was lucky, too."

"How was that, my lord?" she asked encouragingly, wanting to help keep his tale moving along. She guessed that in a world with few books and no TV or cinema, listening to a story would be as much of an art as telling it.

He nodded in approval. "I lost the trail by an old twisted oak tree," he continued. "The spots of blood so kindly left for me stopped abruptly. I looked all around; I even checked the tree in case it was hollow and you were to be found inside, but there was no sign of you."

"So why 'lucky'?" she prompted.

"I had dismounted while I was looking at the tree, and my horse started to walk into the forest to find the sweeter grasses. So, once I had determined you could not be hiding inside the old oak, I chased into the forest after him. He had gone some way."

"I see." Justine smiled to herself as she had a mental image of William desperately crashing through the undergrowth after his horse.

"When I reached my horse, with luck I spotted some broken twigs with yet more spots of your precious blood on them, and I was back on your trail." He leant back with some satisfaction as his story reached its happy ending. "And here I find you, with your poor damaged feet bound up so they may be restored to good health." He patted her foot.

"Yes," she winced. "They are a bit sore."

"A thousand pardons. And did you wash them yourself," he enquired, "or is there an owner of the cottage who has performed this necessary task?"

"Well, it was Sarah who led me here," explained Justine. "This cottage belongs to her mother, and it was she who cleaned and bound my feet." Then Justine added, "They have gone for some milk. They said they'll be back in a couple of hours."

"They have given you great help," observed William.

"Oh yes. They have been so kind, helping me get away from that dreadful man," said Justine, the words catching in her throat as she remembered the sinister snake-like voice she'd heard on the other side of the wall while crouching in the dark of the secret passage.

"Then they shall be well rewarded," said William, reaching down to touch Justine's cheek. "They have done you good service, and by that they have done me good service."

Justine put her hand over his and held it against her cheek. Suddenly she felt an intense heat flow from his hand and she gasped as it started a hot glow that quickly spread to her whole body.

He leant down till his face was close to hers and she could see clearly into his eyes. She lifted her other hand up behind his head and pulled him closer, until their lips touched. His mouth opened on hers and their tongues came together in a gentle caress.

This time, there was no conflict between Justine's head and her heart.

This time, her heart was the winner, and she knew she was going to give herself to William completely, because she knew she had to.

Slowly she moved his hand off her cheek and started to guide it down her neck, then across the soft cotton of her nightdress towards her breast.

---0---

A couple of hours earlier, Hopkirk had slid into the kitchens like a grey-black snake, followed shortly after by his motley collection of young and old villagers.

Martha, Margaret and the cook had been sitting in a small huddle by the fire. They had been speculating on how long Justine would take to burn, especially if the authorities denied her the quick release of a bag of gunpowder round her neck. Martha had been of the opinion that Justine would allow herself a quick death, whereas Margaret was convinced she would try all manner of magical trickery to quench the flames, thereby delaying the inevitable for much longer. The cook, who was of a more practical disposition, compared Justine to a large boar – which she said could brown nicely in half an hour and cook through in two. But she did concede that the fire for a boar was smaller and further away than Justine's would be.

They turned as Hopkirk and his followers entered.

"Master Hopkirk!" exclaimed Martha immediately, jumping up. "Do you have the witch?"

"Nay," said Hopkirk. "She has disappeared like a wraith in the mist."

The villagers stamped and muttered under their breaths, knocking the handles of their pitchforks on the stone floor. "She used her magic to disappear!" blurted out Agnes, the pretty blonde daughter of Jake the innkeeper.

"Her bed was still warm, yet she was nowhere to be found!" added her friend Ruth excitedly. She turned to Agnes and whispered, "With God's good grace we'll not find her too soon – or the chase will not be half so much fun!"

Agnes, meanwhile, started to look around the kitchen. "I would we undo her magic and find her presently," she whispered back, "as I have not had anything to eat for this many an hour – and I will soon faint away." Her eye lit on a tray of cakes nearby. "There's my prize," she muttered, and started edging towards them.

"Your master, Sir William de Beauvais, was, let us say, most unhelpful," continued Hopkirk, the menace in his quiet voice leaving no doubt to Martha as to his sinister interpretation of Sir William's actions. "He stood in the door of his chambers with much anger on his face and in his voice, and he bade us leave immediately." He looked Martha directly in the eye. "Indeed, I would warrant that the girl may have been found by a simple search of his rooms."

Martha nodded in full agreement.

Just then Simon, one of the servants, came down into the kitchens.

"Some manchet bread and a flagon of wine for the master – he's riding out," he called. He stopped, taking in the strangers in the kitchens and the inactivity of the cook, Margaret and Martha, then shook his head as if to clear such irrelevant images. Again he called out, "Some manchet bread and a flagon of wine for the master! In a saddlebag, now! He's riding out and must have them!"

The cook nodded to one of the kitchen girls who had been nearby. The girl fetched a leather saddlebag, into which she put in a loaf of creamy yellow-coloured bread. She then took a costrel – a shaped leather pouch with twisted rope handles – and filled it with wine from a silver jug before stopping it with a wooden stopper and putting it into the saddlebag. She handed the bag to Simon, who grabbed it impatiently with a muttered "thank you!" and ran back out of the kitchens.

There was a moment's silence, then Martha said casually "If the master is gone, I would suggest I see to the tidiness of his chambers…"

"Indeed," agreed Hopkirk with equal casualness. "Such a task is onerous in the extreme. I would warrant you'll need the help of myself and these good villagers in this task. You can never tell what… ah… filth… may be found hiding in a dark corner…"

"Aye," smiled Martha. "It is well we search thoroughly in case we find such a… dirty… thing. Come, Master Hopkirk, we must be swift." She marched out of the kitchens towards the stairs up to the Great Hall.

Hopkirk swept his cloak around his dark grey body and followed, with the villagers jostling to get out behind. Agnes, who had got close to the cakes but not close enough, reluctantly gave up her quest and followed them out.

There was silence. Margaret looked at the cook. The cook looked at Margaret.

"Like as not the girl will be found," said the cook.

"Aye," said Margaret. She reached for a carrot, a chopping board and a knife.

"Like as not she'll be tried," added the cook.

"Aye," said Margaret with satisfaction, as she lined up a carrot on the chopping board and poised her knife in the air above it. "As the Lord is my witness, like as not she will."

She brought the knife down hard, cleanly severing the top off the carrot.

"Like as not she will."

---0---

The still air hung softly in the cool dark cottage.

Justine and William were lying close together on the rough little bed, with William sleeping deeply. Justine gently stroked his hair as he lay with his head on her chest and his warm breath drifting across her breast. She knew she would have to wake him shortly, as Sarah and her mother would soon be back, but decided to let him sleep a few more minutes while she enjoyed the memories of their passion and the warmth of his body.

He had been a surprisingly gentle lover. She had been ready for him to be rough and demanding – interested only in his own pleasure – but she had been delighted to find he was in fact totally attentive to her needs above his own. He had spent what seemed like a lifetime exploring her body, finding where the softest touch, the lightest stroke or the warmest kiss would deliver her the most pleasure. Indeed, he was so skilful at applying this knowledge that the climax, when it finally came, exploded simultaneously for both of them with such depth and with such intensity that she thought she would surely die of happiness.

She stared up at the rough wooden beams, just visible in the darkness above her.

Making love with William had felt natural; completely, comfortably and totally natural.

They had been fully at ease with each other from the very first moment; there had been none of the shyness or awkwardness that you would expect from first-time lovers – none of the fumbling, the apologies, the mistakes…

Now she thought about it, it had been as if they had made love many times before, and William's explorations of her body had been more like him re-acquainting himself with her than if he were discovering her for the first time.

She moved her hand down to stroke his beard and was rewarded with the sound of his breathing getting even deeper as he slept.

'You've found your ideal man,' she said to herself. 'Don't lose him now…'

Her hand froze mid-stroke and William grunted softly in his sleep.

The unwelcome memory had suddenly come rushing back of the conversation she'd had with him the night before in his rooms in the manor.

"My lord, what day is it?" she had asked, to which he had replied, "It is the 30th day of July in the year of our Lord 1565."

So today was the 31st of July.

The very night that history had decreed he would die, stabbed in some fight in a tavern.

'Well, history has got to change,' she thought. 'It will have to, because I am going to do all I can to change it.' She stroked his beard again. 'If I can keep him here till tomorrow, then history will have to take a different course and he will not die.'

Justine smiled grimly. 'That's it. He has got to stay here tonight. Then I will have won and history will have lost. I will keep him with me and I will keep him alive...'

She let her mind follow the course that this would mean. If William did not die, then he would need a wife. And after their passion just now, perhaps she would be the one to secure his heart. 'Then I can become Lady de Beauvais, the very model of a Tudor wife.'

That happy picture danced in front of her eyes in the dim light of the cottage.

'I wonder what a Tudor wedding is like?' she thought. 'I bet it is absolutely beautiful.' Images of a magnificent wedding banquet in the Great Hall sprang to mind, with garlands of flowers, glorious wines, sumptuous dishes and many happy guests to welcome her to the life of a Tudor lady. She would look proudly at William as he made a warm, funny speech, and she would catch his mother's eye and receive a nod of approval in return. She would be wearing the most exquisite white gown and hood, with beautiful pearls in her hair and emeralds round her neck. There would be many servants moving round the tables; serving the food; pouring the wine; making sure the guests had everything they needed. In her imaginary banquet a servant approached her proffering a beautiful silver bowl of water so she could wash her hands, and as she washed them she looked up at the servant and the servant looked down at her and the servant was Margaret...

The banquet disappeared in an instant, like morning mist in a puff of wind.

It would never happen. It could never happen – because Hopkirk wanted to test her as a witch and burn her at the stake.

William grunted again and moved against her, as he started to surface from his deep sleep.

"I need to save you, my love," she whispered. "And then I have got to save myself."

She looked down at his head.

"And it's not going to be easy."

---0---

The search of Sir William's chambers and the bedroom used by Justine had been most thorough. Beds had been looked under, chests had been emptied and curtains had been pulled back, but no sign had been found of Justine. Some enterprising villagers had even opened the smallest of containers – such as jewelled boxes, desk drawers and china pots – in the possibility that Justine had somehow miniaturised herself by magic and hidden inside them.

There had initially been some reluctance to enter the chambers of the lord of the manor, let alone to search them thoroughly. Hopkirk had made it clear that his power as magistrate gave them full authority, enabling the villagers to overcome their feudal inclinations and enter into the search with increasing enthusiasm.

Their fear, however, was even more marked at entering the bedroom used by Justine. Someone observed that she may have left an enchantment on the room, so no one would touch anything in case they were suddenly turned into a weasel or a stoat. Again, Hopkirk had to provide reassurance, moving around the room and demonstrating that nothing he touched had the power to transform him into any particular creature.

Justine's room was then searched equally thoroughly, but again, Justine was nowhere to be found.

Finally the search was over and Matthew Hopkirk stood in the corridor outside Sir William's chambers. He addressed the disappointed group of villagers clustered in front of him.

"So the witch is not to be found." He licked his lips. "She has indeed vanished like a spectre, either by transformation into a cat or a crow, or by some spell of invisibility."

This raised many mutterings of deep concern.

"We have found no trace of her, save for these boots we found in her room." He reached down and held up Justine's worn leather boots. "They are as a man would wear; a sure sign she cleaves only to Satan in her worship."

There were deeper mutterings from the villagers and signs of the cross were made repeatedly.

"So, while we must follow due process and test her for witchcraft, we can be most assured we are dealing with a foul and evil witch in the person of the girl known as Mary Fox."

Cries of, "Burn her! Burn the witch!"

Hopkirk held up his hand for silence, and was about to speak again, when a voice came from the back of the group.

"Master Hopkirk? I'm hungry."

"Who is that?" asked Hopkirk. There was a further moment's silence, as everyone looked around curiously, then young Agnes shouldered her way to the front and faced up to Hopkirk.

"I'm hungry," she repeated. "I want to go home and eat."

Gasps of shock at such impudence gradually turned into mutterings of agreement from the villagers, as they each realised how hungry they were.

Agnes looked round at them and drew strength and confidence from their apparent support. She looked back at Hopkirk.

"I want to capture the witch as much as I want anything, Master Hopkirk. She's evil, right enough, and must be stopped. But just now I'm awful hungry, and I want to go back to my pa's tavern and have some bread and ale." She looked back at the villagers and got more encouragement to continue. "We've been on the hunt with you since dawn, and we ain't had so much as a morsel of rye bread to eat."

Hopkirk stared at her with unblinking grey eyes and said nothing.

"We can carry on with the hunt after we've had some vittles," she observed.

Hopkirk continued to stare at her, still silent.

Agnes felt an uncomfortable need to fill the silence.

"We'll hunt better with food in our stomachs," she added.

"Indeed," said Hopkirk quietly, appearing to have come to a decision. He looked at the group, fixing them each in turn with his piercing gaze. "Is this the opinion of you all?"

At first there was an embarrassed shuffling of feet and some close studying of pitchfork handles, accompanied by scratching of ears.

Then, one by one, the villagers agreed.

"It has been a while…"

"Now I think on it, I do have a hunger…"

"Can't hunt on an empty stomach…"

"Better if we have a little food and ale…"

Hopkirk held his hand up again for silence.

"Then we must return to the tavern," he conceded, and there was a relieved muttering from the villagers.

"Come," he continued, "we will take bread and ale and make our plans for resuming the hunt."

The villagers stamped and voiced their approval. Hopkirk walked past them, along the corridor and through the door onto the gallery. They followed him down the stairs and through the Great Hall to the kitchens, where they could exit through the vegetable gardens.

He may have been prepared to search Sir William's bedroom, but not even Hopkirk would dare leave Grangedean Manor by the front door.

---0---

William swung his legs out of the bed, and stood looking down at Justine. She returned his gaze directly and steadily into his eyes.

He put his hand on her cheek and looked deeper into her eyes, as if searching out her soul. "Mistress Mary Fox," he said, "your beauty is a joy to behold."

They continued to hold each other's gaze for a few long seconds, then he sighed. "But I fear I have to forgo the joy for now."

He turned away and rummaged on the floor for the hose he had discarded so hastily earlier and started to pull them on. "For you have sore feet and cannot walk, and there is the small matter of that odious little man Hopkirk, who has an unhealthy interest in your whereabouts." He pulled his chemise over his head, then his breeches and doublet, before putting on his boots and cloak. "So I suggest you remain here and enjoy the hospitality of Sarah and her good mother till no doubt Master Hopkirk tires of your search and finds some other unfortunate girl to accuse."

Justine wished she could share William's optimism that Hopkirk would let her go so easily. "I would be so pleased if that were true, my lord," she said. "For I am innocent of all his charges."

"Then as God is your witness, you have nothing to fear," he answered, buckling on his sword belt. "But now, I must be away."

"No, my lord!" she said quickly, reaching out to grab him forcibly by the leg, then, worried he might think she was being too weird, turning it into a gentle stroking action at the last second. "I do fear he will not give up the hunt so easily," she added softly.

She deepened her stroking in the hope that this would make him change his mind about leaving.

"Then you must let me persuade him," he said, moving slightly closer to the bed to give her better access to his upper thigh.

"And let yourself be accused as well?" she asked, moving her hand higher.

"Hmmm. There is that."

"We must make a plan," she purred. "Why don't you stay here tonight and we can talk?" Her hand moved even higher, easing up under the hem of his breeches.

"Aye, for sure, we must…oh Heaven," he breathed, as her hand found its mark. She applied some pressure through the thin cotton material of his hose, and felt him stiffen once again under her touch. "Indeed we must… oh my love… to the left but an inch…"

The door opened and light flooded in as Sarah and her mother returned to the cottage.

Justine quickly withdrew her hand and stuck it back under the thin blanket. William stood quickly away from the bed, a look of studied innocence on his face.

Sarah was carrying a wooden bucket containing some milk and her mother was carrying a pair of rough-looking shoes. They both looked tired after many hours of walking, and relieved to be home.

The two women curtseyed low. "My lord," said Sarah, acknowledging her master's presence with a completely blank expression; as if finding him next to the bed of a semi-naked girl was not an uncommon situation.

"Ah, yes, Sarah," responded William, looking as if he was trying to take back control of the situation. "And this, I understand, is your mother, who I must thank for taking in Mary and bandaging her wounds?"

"My lord," said Sarah's mother, curtseying again. "I am honoured to have you in my humble home."

"Yes, well, it was but a brief visit," answered William. He glanced down at Justine in the bed, "though most rewarding. But now I must be away."

"No!" exclaimed Justine loudly. Everyone looked at her in surprise. "I mean, you must stay, my lord." She tried to sit up, clutching the blanket up to her chest. "We were going to make plans…" she hissed quietly at him, imploring him to stay with her eyes.

"Aye, but it is best if you stay here for now." He smiled, oblivious to her pleading. "I will return in the morning and we can talk more about how to secure your future."

"No, my lord – you should stay here tonight…"

"Mistress Fox," answered William with another smile, although now slightly forced, "nothing would give me greater pleasure, believe me." He reached down and stroked her hair, then stood back. "You remain here with these good people for your safety. I have outstayed my welcome and must be away till the morrow."

"But that's too late…"

"Too late?" asked William, quickly. "Too late for what?

Justine sat up some more, thinking fast. "Too late for me, my lord. I cannot spend a single moment away from you."

"My sweet Mary," said William, firmly. "Nor I you. But I really cannot be with you tonight. You must know it is not seemly for me to stay here." Sarah nodded in agreement and looked enquiringly at Justine, as if she should have known that it would not be possible for the lord of the manor to stay in a worker's cottage. He bowed to Justine, then turned to Sarah and her mother. "I must bid you all farewell, good ladies." They both curtseyed low as William turned and strode out of the cottage. He was shortly heard mounting his horse and cantering away.

There was a long silence in the cottage after he had gone, with only the sound of the breeze in the trees and the insistent cooing of a wood pigeon outside.

"I will prepare the posset," said Sarah eventually.

"And I have secured some shoes for you in a large size," said her mother, putting a pair of rough leather lace-up shoes down on the floor. "It took us some time to find them."

"Thank you," said Justine quietly. "You must think me a poor guest…"

"Sir William is our lord and master," said Sarah, taking the milk over to the fire. She added some wooden kindling to the embers and stoked them with a stick, turning the wood till it blazed nicely. "We must all do his bidding," she paused and suddenly her face broke into a broad smile – "however 'hard' it may be…"

The tension broken, Justine flopped back on the bed. "It wasn't hard…" she paused. "Well it was, but it was… oh… you know… it was wonderful…" she started to laugh. Sarah joined in and soon they were both quite breathless.

"You are not a poor guest, Mistress Fox," said Sarah, when they had got their breath back. "It seems you have truly won the master's heart – and that makes you even more honoured than when we left you earlier."

Sarah's mother, however, was not joining in the laughter. She was looking curiously at Justine, clearly puzzled about something.

"But why 'too late'?" she asked slowly. "You were most concerned not to let the master go." She moved round the bed to look closely at Justine. "You wanted to stop him leaving because you knew something of his fate if he did not."

She leant over the bed and put her face closer to Justine's.

"Do you have the gift of second sight into things yet to happen?" she asked quietly. "Do you have the powers of witchcraft?"

Suddenly the atmosphere in the cottage turned very cold. The laughter of the moment before evaporated.

Justine stared at Sarah's mother, her mind racing as she tried to decide what to say. To tell the truth was the highest risk – she would be citing time-travel as her evidence that she was not a witch – which was hardly to be believed. Quite possibly she would be bundled off to meet Master Hopkirk quicker than you could say 'Abracadabra'.

Or she could deny everything and say she really was a merchant's daughter from London. But she could hardly back this up for much longer now that Sarah's mother was suspicious – there was simply too much she would give away through sheer ignorance. At best they would think her strange in the head.

But maybe, just maybe, the truth was a risk worth taking?

If she could find a way to get them to believe she was the innocent player in this amazing time travel saga, then at least she would have some allies to help guide her though the maze of Tudor England – and if that meant a better chance to save both William and herself, it was a risk worth taking…

As these thoughts rushed across Justine's mind, she became aware that there was a vital piece of missing information. It was just that she couldn't quite grasp it – it was sitting just on the edge of her consciousness, tantalisingly niggling away at her like an irritating little stone in her boot. She knew it was important, yet as she tried to remember it, it darted away just out of her reach…

Then suddenly in a flash of inspired revelation, it came to her.

Gift! Sarah's mother said 'the gift of second sight!'

Justine realised that to Sarah's mother 'second sight' was a positive thing! Maybe that was why she'd had a run-in with Hopkirk before! Maybe she was a witch herself?

Justine's heart leapt as another inspired thought came to her. 'Maybe there is a way I can convince these two women – with a reason that would actually make some sense to them…'

She took a deep breath and steadily returned Sarah's mother's gaze.

"I am not a witch," she said slowly and carefully. "I have no knowledge of any such powers. I cannot do spells or make anything happen by magic."

Sarah and her mother stared at her in silence.

"But I think that witchcraft was practiced on me, and that is why I am here."

Justine looked from Sarah to her mother to see how this was being received. From the alarmed looks on their faces, she could see that it was not going well.

"You are enchanted?" asked Sarah cautiously, starting to edge backwards.

"No," answered Justine. "But I think a spell was performed on me that made me travel to Grangedean Manor."

"So where did you come from?" asked Sarah. "What sort of witchcraft is necessary to make a girl travel to a house? Surely you could just be taken there on a horse or by foot?"

Justine knew she was committed to her story now – there was no going back. "It is not so much where I came from as when," she said.

Sarah's mother frowned, clearly not convinced.

"I think," said Justine, "that maybe a witch, or someone with magic, cast a spell on me that made me travel through time itself – even though I stayed in the same place."

"You have travelled across time?" asked Sarah's mother incredulously. Justine supposed that as a person who lived by the movement of the sun and moon and by the changing of the seasons, she would have no concept of time as an abstract thing – let alone a thing you could travel through.

"Yes," said Justine. She thought a moment, trying to construct an explanation of time-travel that would have meaning to these people. "It is as if you were to wake up one morning and find that instead of living in the reign of Queen Elizabeth, you were now living in the reign of her grandfather King Henry. You would be the same person, but time would have moved backwards around you, so that the world and the people and the events around you come from history."

"So you have done the same; you have come into our world – into our time," said Sarah's mother.

"Yes."

"But where – or when – did you travel from?" asked Sarah.

Justine looked at the two women in the dim light. She knew this was a make-or-break moment; that she had to make this work…

"I come from 450 years in the future."

There was a long silence. The woodpigeon cooed loudly outside. The breeze rustled in the branches of the elm trees. Justine looked at each of the two women in turn as they tried to take in what she had told them.

Then Sarah's mother stood up and walked across the cottage. She turned and looked back.

"You are telling me that some witch, or some magic, sent you back by 450 years to our time and place?"

"Yes I am."

"And you expect us to believe this?" asked Sarah's mother, shaking her head.

"Yes," answered Justine. "It is true."

Justine saw looks being exchanged between Sarah and her mother – looks that begged a thousand questions – of truth, of lies and of madness; of the wisdom of allowing such a strange creature into the cottage, of witchcraft and sorcery. It fell to Sarah to voice the one question that needed to be answered before all others.

"But…" she said in a quiet voice "…why?"

Justine knew this was where her story needed to be at its strongest. "I was working in Grangedean Manor in the year 2015. For us it is a historical monument to your time – which we call the Tudor period after the Queen's family. I organised special Tudor banquets in the Great Hall. One of the guests must have been a witch or had some magic – and maybe she wanted me to save Sir William from his fate." Justine paused, to see how this was going down. The two women were still looking sceptical. "But when I got here I didn't know what to say, or how to behave, so I ended up working in the kitchens and saying the wrong thing to Margaret, so she thought I was a witch myself, and accused me to Hopkirk."

Sarah looked round at her mother, then back at Justine.

"There was many things you did not know when I bathed and dressed you," she said slowly. "Just now, you were asking the master to stay, when that was not proper." She thought some more. "And you were wearing the strangest clothes…"

She went over to her mother and pulled her further away from Justine across the cottage. They went into a little huddle, whispering quietly. Justine strained her ears, but could not make out what they were saying.

Would they believe her? Could they believe her? If they didn't, how would she escape, with bandaged feet and in her nightdress? And how could she get to William in time…?

After what seemed a lifetime, they both came back to the bed.

"Sarah and I have thought hard on what you have told us," said the older woman. "And strange though it is, we find ourselves inclined to believe your tale."

Justine realised she had been holding her breath, and let it out in a long sigh of relief.

"But..." said Sarah, "we need more information on what will happen to the master this day, and what we must do to prevent it. This is the reason we will believe you; if you are right and we can save the master's life, then we must make every effort to do so. We cannot take the risk that you are not lying and then the master loses his life."

"It is the very unbelievable nature of the tale that leads us to believe it may be true," said Sarah's mother, cautiously. "If you told the same to Master Hopkirk he would take it as proof absolute of witchcraft." She stopped, and was thoughtful a moment. "Or at the very least, of stupidity."

"You would not tell Hopkirk?" asked Justine quickly, her voice catching in her throat.

"Nay," said Sarah's mother, much to Justine's relief. "I have evidence of the man's accusations in the past, and as much as I am not yet convinced that you may have been sent here from times yet to come, as I look at you I do not believe you have the sign of witchcraft on your face."

"You had knowledge of Hopkirk and his accusations?" asked Justine. "Did he suspect you of witchcraft?"

"Aye. It was said, but he never made an actual accusation. I do have some of the arts; I have knowledge to make potions which can cure ailments. But I do not use incantations and I do not worship Satan," she paused. "You'll find we're God-fearing folk here."

"My mother would help cure people with her potions," explained Sarah. "But a child in the village died of sweating sickness, and Hopkirk looked to my mother as the possible cause. But enough of the villagers had been cured by her, that they would not entertain any accusation and eventually Hopkirk looked elsewhere."

Justine considered this – Hopkirk reacting to pressure from the villagers. "Do you think Hopkirk would ever withdraw the accusation on me?" she asked.

"Not if it was made by Margaret," answered Sarah's mother. She would have to withdraw it, not him."

"The villagers know you only as the accused witch," added Sarah. They will not fight for you as they did for my mother."

"No, only the Lord Jesus himself would get Hopkirk to change his mind," said the older woman. "So we will need to make our prayers for that."

"Thank you," said Justine.

She decided to change the subject. "You said you would have put a poultice of mouldy bread on my feet," she observed. "In my time we know that mould is a fungus and it kills the tiny little creatures that cause infection. That is just what we all know. It's not witchcraft."

"I am glad that my potions and my arts become commonplace in the future," answered Sarah's mother. "But right now I will continue to believe in their magical properties." She walked back to the bed. "And we have a task ahead of us – to save the master. You need to tell us what the future says will happen, and how you have come by this information."

"It is well documented in my time that Sir William was stabbed while in a tavern on the evening of the 31st of July," said Justine. "To us, it is part of history."

"So that is why you would have kept him here tonight," said Sarah.

"Yes," said Justine. "I don't know who kills him, or why, or what he was doing in the tavern, but I know that if I could have stopped him being there, then I would save him."

"So we need to plan our actions," said Sarah.

"Yes, and we don't have much time," said Justine. "We know the stabbing takes place this evening, but we don't know when. We must get to the tavern as soon as possible."

"Aye, and avoid Master Hopkirk, who will test you and condemn you to death by fire if he catches you," added Sarah.

Justine rather wished she hadn't been reminded of that. Hopkirk needed to be removed as a threat – or she would end of saving Sir William for some other girl to marry.

She swung her legs out of the bed and gingerly put some weight on her right foot, testing it for pain. She was pleased that it did not seem to hurt. She put her left foot down and did the same. Again, it seemed to be pain-free. She stood up with all her weight on her feet and did some little jumps. She turned to Sarah's mother and smiled.

"Yes," she said. "We need to avoid the attentions of Master Hopkirk. But I think I may have a plan for that."

CHAPTER SEVENTEEN

Bright sunlight flashed between the tall elm trees as Sir William urged his horse along the emerald green forest path at a reckless gallop, past the low branches and the high roots that emerged suddenly out of the deep shadows. But he was oblivious to any danger – he was in love, and love was to be celebrated.

It was to be celebrated with this joyful gallop at speeds more suited to the open plain than to a hazardous narrow path through a dense forest.

It was to be celebrated by encouraging his horse to soar gracefully over a moss-covered tree trunk; to land with pinpoint accuracy beyond and gather himself to gallop onwards towards Grangedean Manor.

It was to be celebrated by standing in the stirrups and whooping with elation as he emerged from the forest by the gnarled old oak tree, because he had finally found the girl he'd been searching for all his life, and she was just perfect – totally, wonderfully and completely perfect.

William turned onto the path back to Grangedean Manor and slowed to a steadier pace to collect his thoughts after his initial burst of lover's energy.

'She is most beautiful,' he affirmed to himself. 'Truly, she has a sweet, comely face, with a nose that wrinkles just so, and eyes that would make the fair Helen of Troy green with envy…' He chuckled. 'She does not defer to me, as all other girls do – and acts as if she is my equal. I should be repelled by this, but…' his mind went back over their passion in bed, and her hand running up his leg '…but to be sure, it is most refreshing.' This thought made him realise how thirsty he was. Rummaging in the saddlebag beside him, he found the costrel given to him by Simon earlier. It was empty. Now he thought about it, he remembered finishing it while he was tracking Justine's trail of blood spots through the forest. And anyway, it had been filled with wine – what he wanted for his thirst was beer – some refreshing beer.

He trotted into the stable yard at Grangedean Manor and leapt off his horse, as servants came out to take it from him.

He entered the building and strode through the corridors into the Great Hall.

"Martha! Martha, I say!" he shouted loudly, as he threw off his cloak and crashed down into his chair at the head of the table.

After a while he heard her leisurely and slow footsteps on the stairs from the kitchens, before she appeared through the door. There was once a time when she would have run up the stairs and arrived out of breath in her eagerness to serve him. He frowned. That time appeared to have passed.

"Sir William?" she asked, her voice and her expression staying just on the right side of insolence.

"Some beer!" he demanded, deciding to ignore both her attitude and her slow appearance – a man in love should not give mind to such things, however thirsty he may be.

"Yes, Sir William," she answered, giving a perfunctory curtsey and disappearing back down to the kitchens.

He relaxed back in his chair with a deep sigh and closed his eyes, letting his mind drift back on a wave of warm contentment to the little cottage buried deep in the woods. He was kneeling on the bed, looking down at Mary Fox as she lay smiling beneath him, her legs either side of him. Slowly, gently, he was stroking the warm, velvet-soft skin of her waist; feeling her moving in perfect time with the touch of his hands. She smiled as he broadened his strokes out so that his hands started to travel further and further up towards her firm, round breasts with their hard, red…

"Good day, my lord."

William opened his eyes, to find Dowland and Stanmore standing in front of the table.

"Well met, my lord" said Stanmore. "We are come for the hunt today."

"The hunt? What hunt?" asked William vaguely, much more interested in chasing after his memories as they slipped tantalisingly away.

"My lord," said Dowland. "Have you forgot? There is talk of the white stag up at Briar's Copse. We are keen to give it chase."

"I have no stomach to hunt a stag today," said William with finality.

"My lord?" asked Dowland, sounding confused.

"No stomach, my lord?" asked Stanmore. "Are you well?"

"Quite well, I assure you," answered William. "But I shall not hunt the white stag today. Another time, maybe. Good day, gentlemen." He relaxed back into his chair again and closed his eyes, seeking out the little cottage once again in his mind…

"But my lord, another time it may not be so easily found," spluttered Dowland. "It is a wily stag that we have oft chased but never caught." There was a silence, and William started to drift through the door of the cottage and towards the pallet bed. Then Dowland's voice pulled him back. "It has been seen at Briar Copse, my lord. This is our chance at last! We can approach from the west and push it back onto the woods."

William opened one eye and stared at the two men. "Nay, let it be," he said. "I have other things on my mind than that stag."

"But my lord, it is ours for the taking!"

"But my mood is not to take it today, Dowland," answered William curtly, opening the other eye. "So there's the end to the matter."

"As you wish, my lord," said Dowland, finally seeming to recognise that he was beaten. Then he sniggered and grinned in devilment. "Is it perchance a 'Fox' you are hunting instead, my lord?"

There was a heavy silence. Stanmore shifted uncomfortably from foot to foot. Dowland stared at William uneasily; his grin now starting to become more like a grimace.

William returned his stare, turning over the options in his mind as to how to respond to this insolence and intrusion into his private love. Anger was always an option – he could switch it on at will, and had been known to have men and women running for cover from his magnificent rage. But after a moment, he decided it would not be prudent. Anger would indicate that there was some truth to the suggestion made by his grinning friend in front of him, and while Mary Fox was still being sought for witchcraft by Hopkirk, he did not want to be accused by association. No, what he needed to do was wear a mask of innocence – and wear it until such times as she was no longer accused.

"Indeed, Master Dowland," he observed levelly, "I would hunt any creature I could give chase to."

Dowland let out his breath and un-fixed his grin. "As you say, my lord," he answered, sounding relieved. "Any creature indeed."

Just then Martha appeared at the door from the kitchens.

"Oh, Sir William," she said with a snide little smile, "the beer is spoiled – some rats have got inside the barrel and it has a most rank odour. I cannot serve it to you."

William stood up. "What?" he asked, dismayed. "But I have a raging thirst and must drink some beer now!"

"I am truly sorry, Sir William," answered Martha, not sounding sorry at all. "Some wine instead?" she suggested.

This was the last straw for William and he snapped.

"Nay, I have a thirst, woman!" he barked. "Wine does not satisfy my thirst – I need beer to quench it! By the Lord's wounds, is that too much to ask?"

"I am sorry, Sir William, but the smell is most rank. I truly cannot serve it." Then she added, "And the colour is, well… it is…" she looked down at her feet to cover her smile, "…it is green."

"My lord, why do we not repair to the tavern in the village?" suggested Stanmore. "There is beer to be had there." He laughed, then added, "Of the correct colour."

"Aye," said William. "That is the most welcome idea you have had today." He turned to Dowland, "Come, you also. We shall go to the tavern and drink our fill!"

CHAPTER EIGHTEEN

Agnes, the landlord's daughter, looked at Hopkirk as his grey eyes bored into hers from across the table in the dark, noisy tavern.

"I have known many witches," he said, in answer to a question from Maggie beside her. "And I have tested them all by putting them under water to see if they have the magic to save themselves."

Ruth, who was sitting on the other side of Agnes with wide, shining eyes, asked breathlessly, "Have any of them had that magic, Master Hopkirk?"

Hopkirk drank some ale and fixed the girl with his unblinking stare. "None chose to save themselves," he answered. "They may have decided to confound me by choosing to die instead."

Agnes considered this, her enquiring young mind spotting a flaw in Hopkirk's logic. "But what if they weren't witches at all?" she asked. "The outcome was the same in either case."

"Nay," answered Hopkirk. "They had the darkness in their eyes. You can always see the mark of darkness in their eyes." He broke off a crust of bread and ate it slowly, as they shivered with delicious fear. "The testing must be done, but in truth, I always know when I have a witch in front of me."

The three girls looked suitably impressed. "We'll find this witch, won't we Master Hopkirk?" asked Agnes. "Then you'll know when you see her in front of you."

"Yes, we'll find her," he answered.

"And will you test her by ducking?" asked Ruth. "Even if you can see the darkness in her eyes?"

"Indeed," he said, his tongue darting out of his mouth to lick his lips. "We must follow the process. She must be put under the water so we can be sure if she is able to save herself with magic."

"Aye," agreed the old men and women of the village, who were seated at a table next to them and listening intently. "She cannot have gone far," added an older man hopefully.

"The Lord will not guide her steps away from us – if she has rejected him and embraced the Devil then she will make mischief here," said an old woman.

"Indeed," said Hopkirk as he looked around the tavern. It had filled up considerably since he and his party of villagers had come in earlier, hungry and thirsty after their hunt. There had been much ale drunk and bread eaten, and the talk had all been about continuing the hunt in the evening – but Hopkirk had said they would resume it in the morning instead. He had suggested that the witch had clearly found a secure hiding place so she was unlikely to break cover before nightfall. A rough, cold, uncomfortable night, possibly without shelter, could well bring her out into the open and they could take her more easily in the morning. She would be tired, hungry and most likely unable to fight back with any spells or incantations when she was taken.

So he had bought ale and bread all round, and agreed to let his group of villagers have a relaxing summer's evening in the tavern before resuming the hunt at dawn.

He finished the ale in his tankard and beckoned to Jake, who was padding around with two pitchers, one in each hand.

Jake came over and refilled Hopkirk's tankard, then looked down at Agnes. "Come girl," he rumbled, "we are most full in the tavern this evening. You have sat with Master Hopkirk and these good men and women long enough. You will help me serve all these people."

"Yes, father," answered Agnes. She nodded to Hopkirk, got up from the table and joined Jake.

"Take this pitcher and serve those men over there," Jake said, handing her one of the jugs of ale and indicating a table in the corner.

Agnes looked where her father had indicated and saw four men sitting around a small table preparing to play cards. She went over and filled each of their tankards. Three of the men looked old and boring – she was not concerned with them – but one was younger and looked quite nice, so she decided to linger a moment and listen to their conversation.

"How is your good fortune?" asked the grizzled old man dressed in brown who was dealing the cards. His question was addressed to the younger man who was sitting opposite him. "We want no lucky man at our game."

"No lucky man? Why then you invite me to play but you expect me to lose?" responded the other. Agnes thought this was quite a good answer.

"Certainly. Do you take us for fools?" asked a fat man in a green doublet next to him. "You are a stranger to us – we would not have asked you to play if we thought you would win."

"In truth," responded the younger man, "I take for a fool any man who cannot use his wits in a game of cards." Agnes watched him pick up his cards and study them carefully, then take one out and put it back further along the fan in his hand. "You want only an unlucky man to play?" he continued equitably. "Well show me a lucky man, and I will show you a fool who lives upon his luck and never troubles to use his wits. Such a man can rarely win at any game."

The grizzled older man looked up from his cards, no doubt impressed by the younger man's quick mind. "Ah, but is not an unlucky man a fool also – for if he never troubles to use his wits, then he has only himself to blame for his luck!"

The younger man placed a card on the table, then looked up and winked at Agnes, drawing her into this verbal swordplay. "I say there is no such thing as an unlucky man – only a fool." She smiled back.

The fourth man, dressed all in black, looked at his hand and appeared to consider his options carefully. He had long grey hair and a trim beard, with bright blue eyes looking out from under a deep brow. Agnes thought he was probably the leader of the three older men. After a moment he calmly placed a card next to the first one on the table. "Aye, and a fool to say it," he observed, sitting back. "This taproom philosophy is as well in its place, sir, but I fear it is misplaced here."

"And what philosophy brings forth that conclusion?" asked the younger man crossly. "Or are you a knave in search of a fight?"

The challenge hung in the air a moment, as each of the other two players placed their cards on the table. The fourth man considered the cards a moment, then scooped them up and placed them face down by the edge of the table in front of him.

"Neither a knave, nor seeking to cross swords with any man," he observed calmly. "I say only that you presume too much. It is possible to have a man who is both wise – and out of luck."

The younger man then started to let his anger show, leading Agnes to think he may not be so nice-looking after all. "Show me such a man, knave," he growled as he slapped down a card to open the next round.

The man in the green doublet said, "We have an example here today. Are you acquainted with our esteemed magistrate, Master Matthew Hopkirk?" He inclined his head in the direction of Hopkirk and his villagers.

The younger man looked round, then nodded.

"Well, he is most decidedly a wise man who is out of luck."

"How so?"

"He is wise – he has identified a cunning witch who would kill us all with her wicked incantations. But he is out of luck," he paused as the grizzled older man in brown studied the card on the table, "for he has not found her so he can test her and if she is a witch, burn her."

"And drive out the devil that possesses her," said the man in brown. He placed his card down then drained his tankard, looking confident that he could not be beaten on this round of play.

The man in black, who had been mysteriously silent throughout this last exchange, placed his card down. The man in the green doublet barely glanced at it and reached out to scoop up the pile, only to find that the man in black had beaten him to it.

"Mine, I believe," the man in black said, and put the cards next to the first pile on his side of the table. Then he beckoned at Agnes to refill his tankard.

"I saw you earlier with this Master Hopkirk?" he asked her.

She nodded. The other three men paused to listen.

"And you have been with him this day, hunting for the witch?"

She nodded again. "Tell me," he said, looking her in the eye, "how was she known as a witch? Was she seen preparing a charmed circle, or brewing potions, or muttering incantations?"

"Nay, she blasphemed most foully," said Agnes, wide-eyed.

"She blasphemed?" The man looked at his companions with a raised eyebrow, then back at Agnes. "It must have been a foul blasphemy indeed for her to be so actively pursued."

"Yes, sir," answered Agnes earnestly. She put the jug down and crossed herself, then took a breath and said, "The witch was heard directly to say that she rejects Christ and all his works; that the good Lord should rot in Hell for all eternity, and that her one true lord is the Devil." She crossed herself again. "And that she would spit on the Host in Communion," she added.

The other three men crossed themselves. Agnes was pleased to see that the younger man visibly paled. "Aye, a most foul blasphemy indeed," said the man in black. "If she said that, then she should certainly be questioned thoroughly." The others nodded. "But," he continued, "as our Queen herself has observed, we should not make windows into the souls of men." He considered a moment. "Or, in this case, women. I believe we as a society are, in truth, more tolerant than this Master Hopkirk would allow." He got up from his chair. "Excuse me a moment, gentlemen."

Agnes followed him as he crossed over to Hopkirk's table and touched the grey man's shoulder. "Master Hopkirk?" he enquired.

The magistrate looked up without expression.

"Yes?" he answered quietly. "Who asks?"

"I am Master Robert Wychwoode, lawyer." The man in black paused, as if expecting some glimmer of recognition from Hopkirk, but only got a blank stare. "I am staying with my good friends here," he gestured back towards his table, "on my way to the Oxford Assizes." Hopkirk remained silent, so Wychwoode continued. "I could not help but overhear that you are in pursuit of a woman accused of witchcraft, but the evidence against her is for the sin of blasphemy. A strong blasphemy, I'll admit, but nonetheless, blasphemy."

Hopkirk stared at Wychwoode. "Are you suggesting that a blasphemer cannot be a witch?" he asked.

"Not at all," answered Wychwoode. "I am simply suggesting that the one does not necessarily lead to the other."

"Then you would need to conduct a trial to ascertain the truth?" asked Hopkirk.

"Indeed I would. That would conform to the principles of law and justice that I and my brothers in the law hold dear," Wychwoode said with apparent satisfaction.

"Then you and your brothers will be comforted to know that I will hold such a trial," said Hopkirk quietly. "Good evening to you, Master... Wychwoode, is it? Good evening." He turned back to Ruth and Maggie, who had been hanging on every word of this exchange.

Wychwoode stood a moment, his mouth working. "Master Hopkirk," he said firmly. "I understand you are a magistrate. You must have a care for the law and those who have reached greater positions of authority within it."

Hopkirk turned back slowly and looked Wychwoode up and down.

"I have such a care, believe me, Master Wychwoode," he observed. "But I have a greater care for the eradication of witchcraft. And if I find those who practice witchcraft, or those who appear to me to seek to protect them…" he paused, "…I will stop at nothing to destroy them. Whether they are a lowly maid or even a great lawyer."

Wychwoode's hand went to the hilt of his sword; his neck blotching to the colour of one of Agnes's prize red roses. "Do you threaten me, sir?" he barked.

Hopkirk stood up and faced the older man. His face was pale and grey, but there was no doubting his strength and power as he answered.

"I do, sir," he hissed. "I am the magistrate here, and my word here is the law. And I will not have it challenged by any man, least of all by a fancy lawyer from London. So, sir, leave me to my work and I will leave you to yours. Unless," he said, with a slight raise in his voice, "you seek to protect a witch, in which case…" he paused for effect, "…you become my work."

Wychwoode said nothing, but his mouth worked and more red blotches appeared on his neck.

Then he took a deep breath and very deliberately took his hand off the hilt of his sword. As he let the breath out slowly, Agnes noticed the whole tavern had become silent, watching this drama playing out in front of them.

"I can see you are a most determined man, Master Matthew Hopkirk," Wychwoode said slowly. "And I respect that determination." He looked around the room. "But I shall remember this conversation, Master Matthew Hopkirk, and I shall watch with great interest how you go about your work, and I shall be particularly interested in your respect for the law, and how effectively you cleave to the principles of justice." He bowed formally. "Good evening to you, sir." Then he turned and walked away.

Agnes watched as he walked back at his table, but did not sit down. He said something to the fat man in green, who nodded, then Wychwoode tossed a coin onto the table, turned and walked straight past Agnes and out of the door without looking left or right. The villagers, who were now crowded into the tavern in some numbers, watched him go in silence. His companions stood up, bowed to the young man they had invited to join their game earlier, and marched out also.

There was a silence in the tavern once the men had left, as the crowd of villagers looked at Hopkirk with increased admiration. Agnes could see they were deeply impressed that he had stood up to such a fancy London lawyer, and that it had been for a cause they held dear – their protection from an evil witch.

They turned to each other and there were mutterings of support for Hopkirk.

"He's right to be out seeking the witch," she heard one say.

"Can't be having meddling by London lawyers. He had no right to be telling our magistrate what's the law."

"Master Hopkirk won't be pushed off the hunt for this evil witch, for sure."

More and more villagers joined in, all of the view that Hopkirk had been right to send Wychwoode packing. Soon the hubbub was back to its earlier level.

The young man left at the card table gathered up the cards and sat idly dealing himself hands. Hopkirk and his villagers picked up earlier conversations. Agnes went back to circulating round the tables serving ale.

At one point she stopped by the table of a woman with two young boys who were not yet old enough to grow beards.

"Such excitement," she said with studied casualness, as she filled their tankards.

"Oh yes," said the woman. "My sons thought they might see a fight."

"As did I," said Agnes, with a smile.

She looked at the two boys, both dressed in the basic lace-up smock and open breeches of the field worker, with rough woven caps on their heads. They both seemed shy, looking down rather than catching her eye.

"I'm sure they'll see fights a-plenty in times to come," she observed, before moving on to the next table.

CHAPTER NINETEEN

Thomas Melrose walked up to the door of the tavern just as Wychwoode and his companions were leaving. He stood aside to let them out, then went in.

He was dusty and tired from the ride back from the town, and he was very thirsty. He caught sight of Agnes holding a pitcher of ale and gestured her towards him as he dropped heavily into a chair at an empty table.

"Some ale, girl, and presently," he ordered.

She fetched him a clean pewter tankard and filled it to the brim. "My thanks, girl," he said. He studied her a moment, thinking he recognised her from the last time he had been in the tavern. "You're Jake's daughter, aren't you?"

"Yes, sir," she answered. "Is there something you want?"

"Send your father to me," said Melrose. "I would talk with him."

"Yes, sir."

Agnes moved off round the tables towards her father. A few minutes later, Jake padded up to Melrose.

"Master Melrose, isn't it?" he asked in his deep voice.

"Aye, it is," said Melrose, studying the man closely. He noted the big, rough face with close-set eyes under bushy brows, and the fleshy nose criss-crossed with broken veins. "Sit down, Jake," he said. "I must talk with you."

Jake pulled out the empty chair opposite Melrose and eased his large bulk down carefully into it. "How can I be of service, Master Melrose?" he enquired.

"You saw my father in here by chance?"

"Aye, many times," answered Jake, settling back in his chair with a smile, as if he'd been expecting this line of questioning.

"And what was his purpose here?"

"As anyone's, Master Melrose," said Jake. "Good ale to drink and vittles to eat."

"For sure, for sure." Melrose took a deep draught of ale, and prepared to ask the question he needed to ask. And to hear the answer he would have preferred not to hear.

"And did he play, perhaps, at cards or the like?"

"Aye, that he did," was the unwelcome answer. "Cards, backgammon, draughts; he even would challenge others to a trial of strength – where he would sit opposite a man and they would each place their arms on the table, grasp hands and attempt to push the other man's hand to the table." Jake stared into space with a half-smile as if he was re-living the scenes of bravado, laughter and drunken merriment. "He was not a strong man, your father. He challenged many men and was beaten by most of them. But he was a man of great charm and ready wit." Jake laughed softly at the memories.

"But not for money?" asked Melrose earnestly, ignoring Jake's laughter. "He challenged for the fun and for the sport, not for money?"

Jake looked at him a moment, the smile dying on his face. "No, Master Melrose," he answered seriously. "Your father loved to wager on the challenges and games he played. He wagered big, and when he lost, he wagered again twice as much to try and get it back."

"He lost?" whispered Melrose. "Are you sure?" he asked, as if challenging Jake to say he'd made a mistake and that in truth his father had continually won.

"I am sorry, Master Melrose, he lost," confirmed Jake. "Near on a hundred pounds."

"A hundred pounds?" asked Melrose in total disbelief, blood draining from his face. "A hundred pounds, you say?" He sat back in his chair, quite beyond understanding. How could his father have squandered so large a sum?

"Aye, sir." Jake scratched his nose thoughtfully. "I know it was a lot, but he was a driven man. It was as if he would push himself always to his own downfall. I was saddened to hear he'd taken his own life. Deeply saddened."

Melrose fought down the sudden urge to jump up and strike this lumpen barkeeper. 'Were you really so saddened?' he thought furiously. 'My father must have put much of my money in your pocket too!'

Instead he leaned forward, put both his hands over Jake's large, rough, calloused paw on the table and said, "Thank you Jake, for telling me how it was. We were all saddened – he was a good man."

"That he was, sir, that he was."

"Tell me," said Melrose casually, keeping his hands over Jake's, "did Sir William de Beauvais ever play at cards with my father?"

"Sir William?" Jake asked. "Why no, sir. Sir William only came in once, as I recall." He thought a moment. "It was the day before your father took his life."

"Oh," said Melrose in surprise. He had been expecting to hear tales of William gambling with his father and pushing him on to lose ever larger sums. "So he saw my father here the day before he died?"

"That he did, sir." Jake nodded his big head, making his beard flap like a flag in a breeze. "They were talking quietly – at this very table as I recall – but I was not privy to their talk."

Melrose took his hands away from Jake and sat back to absorb this news. So William had been talking to his father at this very table – and a day later he was dead by his own hand. What other conclusion could there be than William was inciting him to suicide? That was how he knew! The day of the hunt when the stag had charged them and William's father had told him of the suicide, William had known. He'd seen it in the man's eyes; how could he ever forget the image of William leaning against the wall, with the look that said he knew?

"Thank you, Jake. You have been very helpful." Melrose finished his ale and stood up. "What do I pay for the ale?"

"That's not necessary, sir. I am pleased to have been of use," said Jake, heaving his bulk out of the chair. "Good evening, Master Melrose. You are always welcome here."

"Thank you again, good Jake, and well met."

Melrose made his way to the door and opened it, then walked straight into a man coming into the tavern.

It was William.

Melrose reeled back, and stared wide-eyed at his master.

William rubbed his nose and laughed loudly. "Hello, Tom," he said. "You must look where you go with more care. Have you been enjoying too much of our friend Jake's finest ales?"

CHAPTER TWENTY

Melrose took a step back and William marched past him into the tavern, followed by Dowland and Stanmore.

"Come, Tom, you must join us," said William jovially, turning and clapping Melrose on the back with good-natured but somewhat excessive force. "We have abandoned today's hunt in favour of slaking our thirst with some of Jake's good ale and we shall make merry with the good company in this place. Although I may say," he leaned in towards Melrose's ear conspiratorially, "we would sooner have made merry on the beer from my own kitchens, but it seems the rats have been pissing in it!" He roared with laughter at his own joke. "So here we are!"

Melrose fought back the urge to find a cutting retort; a pithy put-down that would have shown his master just what he thought of him. Instead he gave a small formal bow and said through gritted teeth, "Nothing would give me greater pleasure, my lord."

"Good." William marched over to a table and sat down, followed by the other three men. Catching Agnes's eye, he smiled and beckoned her over.

"Four of your finest beers, girl!" he ordered.

"Yes, Sir William," she answered, her eyes down, and went off to fetch some tankards.

William watched her retreating back for a moment, with a puzzled expression. Turning to his companions, he said, "I have not been down to this place in many months, but that girl is familiar to me. I would swear I have seen her only recently. How can this be so?"

"Maybe she has been up at Grangedean for… some purpose," suggested Stanmore with a lewd smile.

"Nay," said Dowland, watching Agnes's bottom with serious consideration. "She is a comely wench, and buxom with it. I would have recalled seeing her."

"You are not at Grangedean every moment of every day," said Melrose quietly. "She could have been there and yet have avoided your," he paused, as if searching for the right word, "your most thorough inspections."

"I would certainly have recalled her," observed Dowland. Melrose couldn't be sure if he was choosing to ignore the insult or simply did not understand it.

Agnes returned with four tankards and a jug of beer. She put down the tankards and filled them for the four men.

William stared intently at her, then banged the table making Melrose jump.

"I have it!" he cried, triumphantly. "I know I have seen you recently. You were in the party of that impudent magistrate Hopkirk, that would have trampled across my rooms this morning in search of the unfortunate girl he accuses of witchcraft!"

"Aye, my lord," she replied, her hand shaking slightly as she poured the last of the four tankards of beer. "We were charged by Master Hopkirk to seek out a most evil witch, that would enchant us all."

"Nonsense!" barked William testily. "I said this to Hopkirk this morning, and I say it again now; the girl is no witch!" He turned to his companions. "But this impertinent fellow would have her tested for witchcraft – and if she were found to be a witch, he would burn her at the stake!" Dowland and Stanmore made appropriate noises of shock and disbelief while Melrose held his peace. William turned back to Agnes, who was looking very uncomfortable to be in the presence of the master in full flow of his anger, and in defence of the witch Mary Fox as well. "You, girl!" he barked, and she flinched back, almost spilling some beer from her jug. "By what reason is she accused?"

Agnes curtseyed deeply and stayed down low. "Begging your pardon, my lord, but she was heard to blaspheme most foully," she said, finally looking up at him with wide, scared eyes.

"Get up, girl," he ordered. "Blasphemed most foully? What did she say, that has so offended the sensibilities of the precious Master Hopkirk and half the village?

"Oh, Master, she said..." the girl paused and crossed herself, then took a deep breath and let the words tumble out. "She said that she rejects Christ and all his good works; that the Lord should rot in Hell for all eternity; that her one true lord is the Devil; that she would spit on the Host in Communion." She paused, then added, "And she would condemn all who cross her to the everlasting torment."

"Blasphemy indeed," observed Stanmore drily.

"If it is true," snapped William. He seemed to compose himself a moment, as if letting his anger wash away like a retreating tide on the beach. "It does not have the ring of truth about it to me," he said. "I have sat with this girl at the banquet last evening, and have spoken much with her after, and I would not see it in her to hold such thoughts, least of all to express them in such a way."

"I swear upon my mother's grave she was heard to say this, Master," volunteered Agnes, with surprising boldness.

"An oath indeed," observed William. "But it was not to you that she said this diabolical litany?"

Agnes hesitated. "No, Master, not me. It was to Margaret that these words were spoken."

"Margaret? That little shrewish woman who works in my kitchens?" Now William laughed. "I doubt she is a reliable witness." He turned away from Agnes and back to his companions. "This is a frail case indeed," he said dismissively, the matter closed in his mind. "I give it no credence."

---0---

Agnes lingered for a brief moment, staring at William's back and coming to the conclusion that her audience with her master was over. She made her way back through the crowded room to Hopkirk's table, put down her empty ale jug and sat down, looking at Hopkirk with the bright eyes of one bursting to tell a desperately important story.

"Well met, girl," said the witchfinder absently. "Have you finished your serving duties already?"

"No," she answered. "I have been talking to Sir William de Beauvais."

"Sir William?" Hopkirk's attention was suddenly focussed very closely on her.

"Yes, Master Hopkirk," she answered, breathlessly.

"So what ails you, girl?" he asked. "You look as if you are sat on a burning coal."

"He says he gives no credence to the witch's blasphemy," she exclaimed. "He called it a frail case!"

"On what grounds?" Hopkirk leaned in and fixed her with his staring grey eyes. "What was his reason?"

Agnes hesitated. Deep down she knew she should not be telling tales against the master – it was not her place and it was against the natural order of things for her to be so bold. But there was something about the unblinking stare of the man across the table that mesmerised her, like a mouse before a snake about to devour it. She felt powerless to resist. "He said he has met her," she answered. "He said he knows her well." She paused. "He said she is under his guardianship."

Hopkirk leaned back and smiled. "Then he is indeed protecting her. I was correct in my assumption." He pushed back his chair and stood up. "He may be the lord of Grangedean Manor, but in this, I am his master."

Pulling his cloak around him, he pushed his way through the crowd, until he was standing at William's table.

---0---

William was talking to Stanmore as Hopkirk approached from behind. Seeing Stanmore's attention drawn to something over his shoulder, William stopped and turned round. Slowly, he looked the man up and down.

"Master Hopkirk," he observed drily. He found the sight of this grey man offensive, but decided to hold his temper. For now.

"Sir William de Beauvais," said Hopkirk, his sibilant voice grating.

"I warned you this morning to stay out of my affairs," William said. "They are none of your business."

"I believe they have now become my business," answered Hopkirk.

William's eyes narrowed. "How so?" he asked carefully.

"Because I have heard that you claim to protect the woman called Mary Fox, that we would test for witchcraft."

"I know her, that is all," answered William. "I do not deny it."

"So she is under your protection?" hissed Hopkirk.

"You mean, do I allow you to drown her for your perverse abomination of a trial?" growled William. "Then no, I do not."

"So, you do protect her." Hopkirk gave a small smile of triumph. "Then I must perhaps try you as well…?"

William let Hopkirk's question hang in the air, as he stared into the man's cold, expressionless eyes.

He became aware that the room had now fallen silent. Slowly he wrenched his eyes away from Hopkirk's and looked around him at the villagers' faces. They were staring intently at him to see how he would react; to see if the legendary de Beauvais temper would finally be unleashed by this monumental challenge to his authority and position.

As he looked from face to face, he considered his options. Would the villagers support him if he pulled out his sword and ran this impudent magistrate through? He may be lord of the manor, but in a tavern fight you could never be sure who would be for you and who against. That burly yeoman and the red-faced farmer – they looked as though they could be Hopkirk's men. The peasant woman with her arms around her two young boys – she may be for him, but neither she nor her boys would be of any use in a fight; indeed William could not even see the boys' faces – their heads were bowed, staring down at the rough dirt floor. The villagers now standing behind Hopkirk holding pitchforks – they may be elderly and young, but with those pitchforks they could be dangerous.

He decided he would try words and reason. For now.

He became aware that Hopkirk was looking with unhealthy interest into his eyes, as if looking for some sign or mark. Then the magistrate gave a cold smile and stepped back, as if he had found what he was looking for.

"Sir William?" asked Hopkirk, breaking the silence. "I would have an answer."

"You are asking if I practice witchcraft?"

Hopkirk gave a small nod of his head.

"Because I would not give up Mary Fox to your twisted justice?"

"Have a care," Hopkirk whispered softly, although his voice carried clearly to every person in the tavern. "It is God's justice I practice. To counter me is to counter God himself."

There was a murmur from the crowd in the tavern. William looked carefully round at all the faces. Many were nodding in approval and exchanging looks. William could see he was losing them to Hopkirk – they may have feared him as lord of the manor, but these simple folk feared God even more. William's blood turned to ice in his veins. If Hopkirk had the crowd, his cause would be easily lost.

He decided it was time to try and take God out of the equation.

"Nay, Master Hopkirk," William answered, slowly and deliberately. "I am as God-fearing as the next man, but right now…" he paused for effect "…I counter you alone."

There was a gasp from the assembled crowd.

Behind him, William could hear swords start to be drawn from scabbards, and he assumed it was Dowland, Stanmore and Melrose preparing to defend him.

He was only partly correct.

"You would deny my authority from God himself to test for witchcraft?" asked Hopkirk, his voice thick with assumed outrage.

"Yes, I would," William responded levelly.

"Then you give me no choice," snapped Hopkirk. "Take him!"

William's hand went to his sword hilt almost faster than the eye could follow, but even that was too slow. He had barely got his sword halfway out of its scabbard, when two strong hands gripped around his upper arms from behind and pulled him back. His sword dropped back into its scabbard. Someone unbuckled the belt straps and pulled it off him.

Hopkirk produced an evil-looking dagger from under his cloak, which glinted as it caught the light of a flickering candle. He thrust it up towards William's throat. William pulled his head back away from it, but could not move far enough, and he felt a sharp pain as the tip pierced the skin.

Hopkirk's eyes were grey and expressionless as he moved in closer. "So, you would deny my authority from God, Sir William?" he repeated softly. "You would deny God himself? That is the word of a witch indeed. The word of a man who would worship Satan." He pushed the knife a little deeper into William's throat. William squirmed and tried to lift his head further away. "And that must be tested, because, Sir William, you may reject God, but I do not, and neither do these good people, and God's justice must be served."

The crowd murmured their approval. William knew he'd made a terrible mistake – and had given all the momentum to Hopkirk.

Hopkirk looked past William at the man who was holding his arms and barked out an order. "Seat him. Bind him."

Hopkirk stood back and William saw there were bright red drips of blood on the blade of the knife. His blood! Seething with impotent rage, William was thrust down into a chair and his hands held down onto its arms. Two leather straps were produced and these were lashed several times around his wrists and buckled tight, securing his arms to the chair. William noticed with anger that they were his own leather belt straps that had, until a few seconds ago, held his sword and scabbard.

Hopkirk studied the man who had bound William to the chair. The man who had decided in a split second to grab William's arms and prevent him drawing his sword. "I must congratulate you for choosing to be on the side of God in this matter," he said.

"I do God's bidding," came the distinctive voice of Thomas Melrose from behind William.

For a moment William was totally speechless. He strained to look over his shoulder to see the man he had thought of as one of his closest friends, as Melrose tested the tightness of the straps, then moved round to stand next to Hopkirk, a look of quiet satisfaction on his thin features.

"Thomas?" whispered William, shaking his head in total disbelief. "Thomas? What, in the name of all that is holy, are you doing?"

Melrose said nothing; his thin mouth tightly shut.

"Dowland! Stanmore! To my aid!" William called out.

"They cannot help you," said Hopkirk.

"They are my men, and they must," answered William.

There was the sound of chairs scraping back and boots dragging on the floor, as Dowland and Stanmore were marched round into William's line of sight. Each one was held by another man, with a knife to his throat. They were both looking away, unable to meet their master's eye.

"Seat them and bind them also," ordered Hopkirk.

The two men were thrust down into chairs and held while some rope was sought. William noted with anger that neither man struggled, nor made any move to escape. The knives were being held loosely against their throats; their arms were being held down without much force onto the arms of the chairs – they could easily have made a bid for freedom and created a chance to fight for him. He was about to shout to them to fight back and escape, then he realised the hopelessness of their position. He could see the whole crowd was for Hopkirk, and without fresh loyalist fighters, the odds were against them.

With a sigh he sat back; waiting to see how this would play out and determined to seize any chance, however slim, to turn the tables on Hopkirk.

A couple of lengths of thin rope were produced and a sturdy yeoman bound Dowland and Stanmore's hands to the arms of their chairs. He pulled the rope as tight as possible – William could see it was cutting into Stanmore's wrists most cruelly. Stanmore winced but held his silence as the knots were made firm and tested by Hopkirk.

William looked the yeoman up and down. He had been right that this man would side with Hopkirk, but he was disappointed. "Geoffrey Smitheson, is it not?" he asked. The man avoided his eyes. "I helped you with a lowered rent last year, when the harvest was poor. Yet you are not for me in this matter?" Smitheson said nothing and stood back from the two men he had bound.

Dowland looked up at William with a defeated expression in his dark Hispanic eyes, like a guilty hound caught with the remains of the roast. "I am so sorry, Sir William," he muttered. "They were too fast for us, and..."

"Silence, fool!" screamed Hopkirk, suddenly stabbing his knife down into the wooden chair arm, just a hair's breadth away from Dowland's fingers. Dowland went white as he stared at the knife quivering upright in front of him, clearly imagining it slicing into his hand or severing the sinews of a finger...

"For the love of Jesus, man! What possesses you?" shouted William.

Hopkirk pulled his knife out of the arm of Dowland's chair and sheathed it carefully beneath his cloak. Then he turned slowly to William.

"What possesses me?" he asked, dropping his voice down so quietly that the crowd around would have had to strain their ears to hear him.

"What possesses me?" he repeated, this time louder, as he put his hands on the arms of William's chair.

"What possesses me?" he repeated a third time, winding up the volume and casting little glances to the crowd on each side as if to make sure he was pitching the anger at just the right level. From their rapt and horrified attention, it was clear that he was.

He leant forward and put his face close to William's. "It is not I that is possessed, is it Sir William?" he screamed.

William recoiled from Hopkirk's sulphurous breath as the magistrate's gaze flicked unblinkingly from one eye to the other, holding him in his mesmeric stare.

"It is not I," Hopkirk said, bringing his voice back down to its more usual hiss, "that has the darkness that I have seen clearly in these eyes; the darkness that speaks of sorcery and magic. The terrible darkness that possesses a man to worship not the risen Lord, but his eternal enemy, Satan!"

The crowd shivered and there were murmurings of shock and sorrow at the revelation that their lord and master – a man they had looked up to and respected – could now be so clearly exposed as a satanic witch.

"We must test him now, by immersion in water," commanded Hopkirk. He turned and saw Jake standing in the crowd. "Landlord, fetch a barrel or water butt. We will put his head under and see if he has the magic of witchcraft to save himself."

Jake turned and gestured with a flick of his head towards a couple of men, indicating that they should follow to help him fetch a barrel. The three of them went through a door at the back of the room.

Hopkirk turned back to the crowd.

"And if he does have that magic, then we know what action we must take!" He lifted his arms and spread them wide above his head. "We must let God's justice take its course!"

The crowd roared their approval.

"We must not suffer a witch to walk this earth!"

The crowd roared again.

Hopkirk picked up a candle and lifted it high over his head, where it flickered and cast deep shadows across the faces of the villagers. "And we will put him to death!" he shouted. "Death by fire!"

The crowd roared and chanted "Death to the witch! Death by fire!"

Hopkirk turned and looked down on Sir William de Beauvais, bound in the chair. As he caught William's eye, his face became quite expressionless – as if the rabble-rousing of a moment ago was no longer needed.

"You played by the rules, Sir William," he said quietly, leaning in. "And I respect that in a man."

Hopkirk leaned in closer.

"But, Sir William, do you know what? I have you now. I have you in my power." He moved closer still and whispered in William's ear. "So in the end, my lord, it was the rules that gave the game away."

He shook his head, almost in sorrow, then straightened up and once again addressed the crowd.

"Bring the barrel! We test him now!"

CHAPTER TWENTY-ONE

William stared into the oily black depths of the water as it rippled slowly to and fro across the top of the barrel in front of him. It stank of rotten eggs, dead fish and pond weed, but he knew that was now the least part of his problems. Standing before the barrel with his hands bound behind his back and his feet bound together, it was only a matter of time before he would be forced into the stinking water head first and be drowned in the name of Hopkirk's perverse justice and the satisfaction of the hostile villagers all around him.

Hostile villagers? What in God's name had he done to cause them to turn so easily against him? Had he not been an honest landlord, charging fair rents and avoiding the enforcement of widespread enclosure of common land? Had he not supported the church and provided a living for the priest? Had he not often attended services in the village instead of restricting himself to the chapel at Grangedean Manor as his father had done? Had he not provided much employment for servants and staff in his house, and for labourers on his land?

Yes, he had demonstrated himself to be a good and beneficent master to many, if not all, of the villagers who had happened to be in the tavern this night – yet Hopkirk had managed to turn them so completely against him so that not one had come to his aid, or that of Dowland and Stanmore, who were still bound to their chairs beside him.

And Thomas Melrose – what had he done to explain the man's abominable treachery? They had been friends since they were boys – they had learned their Latin together, learned to hunt together. Damn it all, they grown up together virtually as brothers – so what had caused Tom to turn into a murderous Cain? William searched his memory but could not settle on any particular instance or sign that could justify Tom's change towards him. For sure it could not be down to his relationship with Mary Fox; Tom had not been at the banquet last night and seen them together – in fact he had not seen Mary since yesterday morning, when he offered to take her as a servant but William had refused…

Was that it? Was it that refusal that had turned his friend against him? Surely not – no man could willingly turn traitor for the refusal of a strangely-dressed girl as a servant…

A strangely-dressed girl indeed, and yet – such a beauty.

Despite his situation, William smiled as he saw again her lovely face looking up at him in the gloomy darkness of the forest cottage, breathing softly through parted lips as he moved slowly inside her, reaching her arms up behind his head to pull his mouth down onto hers…

The image faded, and now he saw her running out into the grounds after she had knocked into his mother, flapping her hands and crashing to the grass in such a comic and endearing fashion…

Then she was beside him as they walked into the Great Hall for the banquet; her face glowing in the light of a thousand golden candles as she took in the scene with such a look of joy and wonder that he knew, then as now, that he would love her for all eternity…

An eternity that was about to begin very soon.

In truth, he would not see Mary Fox again in this life. Although he hoped that maybe, eventually, he might see her again in the next one. By God's good grace she would have a long and happy life first – oh, how he wished for that with all his heart.

With luck she would be well away from the village by now, helped by Sarah and her mother to seek good fortune in some new place; somewhere where she could be at ease without the threat of a trial for witchcraft.

He imagined her arriving at some new village, settling herself into a small cottage somewhere; maybe finding a new man she could love – a man whose love would be worthy of her; who would make her happy. Would he make her as happy as he, William, would have done? Would he look after her, care for her, make sure she felt loved and valued till the day she died?

As William stared into the dark waters that would shortly take him to eternity, he again hoped with all his heart that this would be so.

Then slowly, reluctantly, he looked up.

Hopkirk was in a corner conferring with Jake, Tom Melrose and the yeoman Smitheson. As William watched, the witchfinder came over towards the barrel and held his hand up for silence.

Looking around the expectant crowd with a grim face, he called out, "Are we all ready?" There was a murmur of assent. "Then let the trial begin!"

"I do not recognise the competence or the authority of this court to try me," said William levelly, hoping to take the momentum away from Hopkirk. "Nor do I recognise that there are any grounds." He lifted his chin and added a hard edge to his voice. "By what right do you dare to hold me prisoner and threaten me with drowning?"

"I do not need to justify myself to you, de Beauvais," answered Hopkirk with a thin smile. "I am appointed witchfinder in this parish, and I will do my duty by these good, honest, God-fearing people."

William shuddered. It was 'de Beauvais' now, was it? Did he no longer have sufficient respect from this dreadful little magistrate that he deserved to be called 'Sir William'?

"What are the charges? Who speaks against me?" he asked belligerently.

"I myself will prosecute," said Hopkirk.

"That does not surprise me," said William. Some people in the crowd laughed.

"And who speaks for you?" asked Hopkirk.

"Since you seek to open mine own heart and soul to your examination," said William, "then I will have to speak for myself." He looked at the hostile faces crowding in around him in the candle light. "And to be fair," he added, "I doubt if any of these good people would risk their own necks to speak out for me." He gave a little snort of derision. "That would not be bravery – it would be reckless foolhardiness."

"Have a care, de Beauvais," hissed Hopkirk. "Your fate rests with these good people – they will judge whether or not in truth you must face the test by ducking, once they have heard the case for you and the case against you. Do not presume upon their judgement."

"I presume nothing, Master Hopkirk," answered William, glancing down into the black waters awaiting him. "But I recognise when a decision is already made."

"Then let us see if you are correct," answered Hopkirk. "I will begin my questions."

He pulled his cloak closer around his grey body and advanced right up to the barrel, positioning himself opposite William.

"I shall seek to understand whether you are protecting the witch known as Mary Fox, and by doing so, are complicit in her own evil-doing." Hopkirk leaned his hands on the edge of the barrel as if he were standing at a pulpit. He stared at William. "I shall seek to prove that there are strong grounds to believe you are yourself a witch – and that we must submit you to the test of ducking for final proof."

"You are already making the assumption that Mary Fox is a witch," said William, seeing his opportunity to undermine Hopkirk's argument. "You have not yet tried her. What if she is not a witch? Then your case against me folds like a paper castle."

"She was heard to blaspheme most foully," said Hopkirk. "Such ungodliness cannot be ought but worship of Satan – and that is next to witchcraft."

"This is a tired argument," countered William. "She was heard by one person only, and that person a most unreliable witness who is not even here tonight to attest to it. I give her testimony no credence whatsoever." He looked at the faces around him to see how well this was being accepted, and was rewarded to see some beginning to look a little doubtful.

But Hopkirk countered swiftly. "I have heard tell of the witch's behaviour," he said, "and it endorses the accusation that has been made." He turned to the crowd. "This girl is from out of the parish. She uses unnatural magic powers to clean a hearth, she dresses as a man, she wears man's boots and she goes by different names – I have heard that she calls herself Justine and yet she also calls herself Mary Fox. These things are not in dispute." There were nods of heads and mutterings of assent – even those who had looked doubtful earlier were now nodding vigorously. "Such facts may be evidence enough, but then we have an accusation of blasphemy – an accusation made by a woman of our village of exceptionally good character." He put strong emphasis on the last three words, as if to counter William's earlier dismissal of Margaret's reliability as a witness. Then he looked across the crowd, holding the gaze of each man or woman in turn. "That is enough for me, and it should be enough for you as well!"

The crowd cheered and Hopkirk turned back to William with a silky smile.

"So I think we can all agree that the witchcraft of this woman Justine or Mary Fox, or whatever her name might be, is not in any doubt," he said.

William decided to try a different approach. "But you have no possible evidence of satanic arts on my part," he countered, "even if I am protecting her as you say, that is not witchcraft or anything close to it."

But Hopkirk didn't answer as William would have expected.

Instead he stayed silent, drumming his fingers on the edge of the barrel and appearing to be lost in thought as he stared down into the dark waters.

William was wondering whether Hopkirk had even heard him, and was about to repeat the point when the magistrate looked up and said, "I call on Master Melrose to come forward."

William watched with anticipation – and barely concealed loathing – as the gaunt figure of Thomas Melrose picked his way through the crowd and came to stand next to Hopkirk on the other side of the barrel.

Hopkirk turned to Melrose and said in his most polite and conciliatory tone, "You are Thomas Melrose, son of the late Walter Melrose, yeoman farmer?"

"I am."

"And you have known Sir William de Beauvais since you were both small boys?"

"I have," answered Melrose, looking at Hopkirk and not catching William's eye.

"You were schooled together at Grangedean Manor?"

"We were, by Master Frobisher."

"Master Frobisher?" Hopkirk feigned mild surprise. "A worthy pedagogue. You were both well taught."

"We were," agreed Melrose.

"So you know how de Beauvais thinks, and how he conducts himself?" Hopkirk paused and looked across the crowd for effect. "The values he lives by?"

"I do," answered Melrose.

"Tell me about these things." Hopkirk said, his voice now like flowing honey. "Tell me how Sir William conducts himself."

Melrose considered his answer carefully. "He has always had the ability to shoot straight with an arrow," he said, sounding as if this was a great wonder, rather than a skill patiently learned. "Even as a small boy, he could split a leaf off a branch by shooting through a stem no bigger than a few human hairs."

"And this is a trick…" Hopkirk let the word hang in the air a moment… "a trick born perhaps – of magic?" he purred.

"Of magic!?" shouted William. "Have you taken leave of your senses? It is the result of many hours' practice!"

"But Master Melrose has stated that you demonstrated this ability even as a small boy," suggested Hopkirk with what sounded like disarming reasonableness. "You cannot have had sufficient hours to practice by then."

"Maybe it was luck the first time," said William. "But I can swear to you, on my oath, it is the result of much diligent practice." He added, "It is a skill that any man here could perfect!"

"Indeed?" said Hopkirk. "These men are well practiced in archery." He looked across the faces of the men in the crowd. "Can any man here do the same thing?"

The men looked down and shuffled their feet uncomfortably. William stared at them in disgust. No man would boast of their prowess, lest they ended up joining him at the side of the barrel.

Hopkirk looked round the room with satisfaction, then back at William. "None of these men would claim the same level of skill. Truly, it appears your 'talents' are not of the natural world, de Beauvais."

"This argument is spurious!" shouted William. "I give it no credence!"

"The credence you give it, or don't give it, is of no consequence," snapped Hopkirk. "It is the one that these good men here give it that matters."

He turned back to Melrose. "And I believe you have further proof of Sir William's powers?" he asked, with an encouraging raise of his eyebrows.

"Aye," answered Melrose. "He commands beasts."

There was a collective gasp of shock from the crowd at this allegation. William clenched his fists behind his back. This could put him in the highest jeopardy if it were proven to the satisfaction of the crowd; the charge of witchcraft would be beyond question. He waited to see how this charge would be made.

Hopkirk kept silent a moment, watching the crowd and waiting as the groundswell of shock started to build the volume and intensity of their mutterings.

He raised a hand and after a moment the noise of the crowd settled back to a low rumble. "How is this so?" he asked softly.

"Yes, how is this so?" burst out William. "I too am keen to hear how this can be claimed!"

"Quiet!" snapped Hopkirk. "I am certain Master Melrose can clearly explain his statement."

"Aye, that he can – because you and he have collaborated on this nonsense!" muttered William, loudly enough for the crowd around him to hear. One or two laughed nervously.

Melrose looked directly at Hopkirk, and said, "We were out hunting a great stag, and William shot an arrow that failed to kill it…"

"So maybe my powers are not so magical, if I failed to kill it?" demanded William. "How is that, then?"

"Silence!" barked Hopkirk at him. "Your supernatural skill with bow and arrow has already been proven." Hopkirk turned back to Melrose. "So what happened then?"

"The stag was charging us, and would have gored us both on his antlers. I threw a spear but I was scared, and my aim was off." Melrose, paused and swallowed hard, as William snorted in disgust. "I knew we would both be killed the next instant," continued Melrose, "but Sir William called out to the beast."

Again, there was a gasp from the crowd.

"He called out? What did he call out?" asked Hopkirk encouragingly.

"He called out, 'Die, beast, die!'" answered Melrose.

"And then what happened?" asked Hopkirk.

"The beast was dead in an instant, and crashed to the ground in front of us."

"Dead in an instant?" said Hopkirk, sounding surprised.

Melrose nodded. "It crashed to the ground and such was its speed that it carried on moving towards us. The tips of its evil antlers stopped but an inch from Sir William's chest."

"Indeed? That is most… shall we say… fortunate." Hopkirk gave a little smile. "And how did Sir William react then?"

"He laughed and joked, as if this was the greatest sport," answered Melrose.

This was too much for William. He had held his anger in check during this exchange by further clenching and unclenching of his fists behind his back, but now his blood was up and his heart was racing. "By the Lords Wounds!" he shouted. "This is arrant nonsense! It was your spear that killed the beast, and I laughed in relief! The rest is wicked lies and misinformation!" There was silence. William took some deep breaths and tried to calm his wildly beating heart.

He looked at Melrose, who finally met his eye for a second, then looked away – as if the sight of William sickened him.

"Why, Tom?" he pleaded. "Why are you conspiring against me this way?"

"This is no conspiracy, de Beauvais," cut in Hopkirk before Melrose could respond. "This is just a seeking after the truth."

"The truth?" asked William. "The only truth I am now interested in, is the truth of why this man has turned traitor." He looked again at Melrose. "What have I done to you, Tom? What could I possibly have done that turned you so deeply against me?"

Melrose looked back at William. "You caused my father to die," he said softly.

"I? What had I to do with it?" William asked, genuinely confused. "He took his own life."

"You encouraged him. You spoke to him the night before in this very tavern, and the next day, when I was told, you knew. I saw it in your eyes."

"Tom, please, believe me," pleaded William. "If I never speak another word, know that this is God's honest truth." He paused, collecting his thoughts. He knew this was his main opportunity; if he could turn Melrose back to his side, there was a chance – albeit a slim one – of maybe winning round the crowd.

"Your father was a good man," he said firmly, "and I was trying to stop him taking his life. I was trying to talk him out of it. He had lost a lot of money, and he was full of guilt for you and your chances in life. I was telling him that I would help where I could."

Melrose opened his mouth to respond, then appeared confused and closed it again. Some in the crowd looked puzzled. William pressed his advantage. "I was trying to make him see he had everything to live for – in you. That's how I knew the next day. I knew that he was planning it, and I was only sorry I had not been successful in stopping him."

"A pretty speech, de Beauvais," cut in Hopkirk quickly, as again Melrose appeared about to speak, then again stopped, looking unsure. "But this is not to the point. The point is that Master Melrose has affirmed that you have an unnatural skill with the bow; that you command beasts and they act upon your command, and that you have been protecting a known witch." He signalled to Smitheson and a couple of his men who were standing behind William. "Prepare him for the trial!"

Smitheson and another man positioned themselves either side of William and at a signal from Hopkirk grasped his thighs and lifted him up.

"We will test him!" shouted Hopkirk, raising his hands above his head.

"Test him! Test him!" responded the crowd, turning it into a chant that built and built, echoing off the rafters of the old tavern.

"The people have delivered their verdict! We will put his head under the water! We will see if he has magic!"

Smitheson and the other yeoman lifted him higher over the barrel.

"For the love of God, Hopkirk!" shouted William against the din "What kind of man are you?"

Hopkirk leant across the dark waters of the barrel and looked deeply into William's eyes. "I am the soothsayer of your darkest fears, Sir William de Beauvais," he said quietly, so quietly that only William could hear against the shouting of the crowd. He put his hand on William's chest, as if to draw out his heart. "Let me reach out and touch your deepest dreams. Come to me, I must deliver your soul to the people before me who chant and cheer."

He stood back, leaving William suspended over the edge of the barrel, then he signalled to Smitheson.

"Duck him!"

The crowd roared as Smitheson and his companion started to tip William face first into the barrel. William fought with all his might, but having his feet and hands bound, he could only wriggle and flap like a fish in a net, and against the combined strength of the two burly yeomen, it had little effect.

As he struggled, he saw one of the two young peasant boys start to run forward – he assumed to help the yeomen drown him in the stinking water, but he quickly dismissed them from his mind as he saw the water rushing up towards him and knew that in a few seconds it would fill his mouth and his nose and then be drawn down into his chest and cause him choke and suffer an agonising death…

"Stop! Stop I say!"

The shout rang out loud and clear against the sound of the crowd. With a sense of shock and relief William felt the yeomen check and his movement towards the water stop.

"Stop now! Set him down!" The voice had such authority that William found himself being lowered to the floor again. The shouting died down and silence descended on the tavern.

Everyone, including Hopkirk, turned to look at the man who had shouted.

It was Melrose.

He was standing with his hands on his hips, his thin face flushed red and his eyes wide and staring.

"Master Melrose?" said Hopkirk. "What is the meaning of this?"

Melrose took a gulp of air as if to steady himself, then said quietly, "I was wrong. Sir William does not command beasts – my spear was thrown true and it was that that killed the stag." He looked at William. "I am sorry, my lord, for doubting you. You are no more a witch than is Master Hopkirk." He turned to Hopkirk. "Release this man, who I now believe has spoken true. He is my oldest friend, who tried to help my father and would have helped me if I had but let him. Let him go – he is innocent of your trumped-up charges."

"Thank you, my friend," said William, a glimmer of hope in his voice. He tried to shrug off the yeomen's grip. "You heard the man. Let me go."

But Smitheson and his fellow yeoman held him firm. "Let me go, I say!" demanded William.

"Not so fast, de Beauvais," said Hopkirk. "Keep him tightly held." He put his hands on the edge of the barrel. "This changes nothing. The case is sufficiently proven for the ducking test to take place!"

There was a muttering from the crowd and Hopkirk glanced quickly around. William could see that the mood had changed with Melrose's change of heart and that many of the villagers in the crowd were now looking shocked. He hoped that it was because they had been about to do something which went deeply against the natural order of things – they had been about to kill their lord and master. Hopkirk must have seen this as well, and he raised his arms.

"Listen, good people..." he began, then stopped.

There was a commotion at the door of the tavern, with loud shouting, heavy boots thumping and armour clanking. Then there was the unmistakable sound of swords being drawn.

There was a gasp from the crowd as they stared towards the door. Then they began to part as men forced their way into the tavern and advanced towards Hopkirk, William and the barrel.

Finally the crowd around Hopkirk parted and a man in black with long grey hair appeared, accompanied by a dozen militiamen with drawn swords.

The man stopped in front of Hopkirk and slowly looked at the tableaux in front of him – William held by two yeomen and bound hand and foot by the barrel; Hopkirk standing on the other side like a grey statue; the crowd all around with their faces eerily lit by the flickering yellow candles.

"This is ill-judged, Master Hopkirk," he said. "Ill-judged indeed." He looked at William. "This is Sir William de Beauvais, I believe, and I take it you would have drowned him in your pathetic search for your proof of witchcraft?" He paused but got no answer from the furious Hopkirk, who didn't look capable of speech.

The man nodded. "It is as well I decided to follow my instinct that you were planning something like this and return with these militiamen," he said. He gestured towards William. "Release this man immediately!"

Hopkirk turned to Smitheson. "You will do no such thing!" he shouted, then turned back to the man in black. "Robert Wychwoode, by whose authority do you presume to defy me?"

"By the authority of Her Majesty the Queen, in whose service I practice the law," answered Wychwoode. He turned to Smitheson. "Now release him!"

Reluctantly, Smitheson and his yeoman colleague set William down and stood back.

"No!" shrieked Hopkirk, his voice rising to a strangled scream. "Duck him! Duck him now! See if he has the magic!"

Smitheson hesitated. He looked at Hopkirk, who was mouthing and screaming with spittle gathering in little white strings at the corners of his mouth; then he looked at Wychwoode, standing solidly in the middle of the room and backed by armed militiamen. It was clear that the power now lay with the lawyer, so he reached round and started to undo William's hands.

"No!" screamed Hopkirk again.

Then everything happened very fast.

Hopkirk reached inside his cloak and suddenly the evil-looking knife appeared in his hand.

Before Wychwoode or a militiaman could stop him, he was running round the barrel towards William with the knife raised up in in his hand, clearly intending to stab him.

As Hopkirk ran, one of the young peasant boys suddenly darted out and flung himself at the magistrate, knocking hard into him and throwing him off balance. Hopkirk fell into the side of the barrel, causing foul-smelling water to slop out over the other side. The knife clattered away under a table as Hopkirk sprawled out beside the barrel, and the peasant boy, carried on by his momentum, lost his balance and crashed into the legs of the table himself.

The boy struggled to his feet. William saw he was now holding Hopkirk's knife, which he must have retrieved from under the table.

The boy rushed to William's side and quickly cut through the straps binding his hands and feet, then turned and grabbed Hopkirk. Forcing the magistrate to stand up, he held the knife up to Hopkirk's throat.

Hopkirk stood unsteadily, straining his head back away from the knife, his eyes staring wildly around the room for help. But the boy was standing with his back against the barrel, making it difficult for anyone to come at him from behind.

"What would you do, boy?" snarled Hopkirk over his shoulder. "Would you kill me? Would you kill a man of godliness and purity? Have a care for your immortal soul, boy!"

The boy didn't answer, but pressed the knife harder against Hopkirk's throat, drawing a little blood.

"Is that your reply, boy?" Hopkirk demanded hoarsely. "Then if you would dispatch me, do it now." The boy didn't move. "You do not have the will to do it..." said Hopkirk; a calculating edge creeping into his voice.

William wondered why the boy did not answer or make any further movement. He had Hopkirk under his control, but if he did not make a move soon, Hopkirk would take advantage. Sure enough, Hopkirk then made his own move, driving back with his elbows into the boy's ribs.

The boy let out a high-pitched scream, dropped the knife and staggered back against the barrel, causing his head to flick backwards over the black water. The movement made his cap come off and fall into the barrel. It lingered on the surface a moment, then filled with water and disappeared into the depths.

But William could see that no one was looking at the water in the barrel.

They were looking at the boy's long, russet-coloured ringlets that had been tucked up and hidden under the cap and now fell freely down to his shoulders. They were looking at the soft curves of a face that was not that of a young boy, but of a woman in her twenties. They were looking at the heaving chest pushing against the rough lace-up farm-worker's smock.

There was a gasp from the crowd.

"Oh my Lord," said one of the villagers. "It's her! It's the witch!"

CHAPTER TWENTY-TWO

For a brief moment everyone in the village tavern was frozen still, like a tableaux in an oil painting.

Justine took in the scene; Hopkirk standing beside her at the edge of the barrel with a look of amused satisfaction on his grey features, as if he'd known all along that she would eventually appear; Wychwoode and his men standing a few feet away with their hands ready on the hilts of their swords; William standing just behind Smitheson, his eyes flicking down to the sword hanging at the yeoman's hip; Dowland and Stanmore still bound in their chairs, with the tall, thin figure of Melrose just by them; the crowd of villagers all around, staring at Justine with expressions ranging from horror to fear to fascination. And at the back of the crowd, she could just see Sarah and her mother slipping quietly towards the door.

The silence was broken by Hopkirk.

"Mistress Fox," he said silkily, massaging his shoulder where he'd hit it on the barrel, then putting his finger to his throat and examining closely the fresh blood he found there. He rubbed his finger and thumb together to remove it. "What a pleasure it is to see you properly."

"So you're Hopkirk," Justine said. "I have heard so much about you."

"And I you, Mistress Fox," he replied. "I have so much I want to ask you."

"And none of it to the point, I'll warrant," said William.

"Now then, de Beauvais," said Hopkirk, still watching Justine like a snake watches a mouse, "we are asking questions of Mistress Fox, not you." William snorted in disgust and edged a little closer to Smitheson's sword.

Hopkirk continued. "So, you have been here all evening, masquerading as a farm worker, as a boy?"

"Certainly," replied Justine. "I wanted to hear what was said about me."

"No doubt you did. You were here with another farm worker and a woman," Hopkirk looked around for them. "Are they also not what they seemed? Another girl dressed as a boy, perhaps? A man dressed as an old woman?"

Justine smiled sweetly. "I don't know what you mean, Master Hopkirk."

"'Tis no matter," said Hopkirk, "we will catch up with them later. For now, more important matters concern us." He touched his throat again and examined the amount of blood on his finger – appearing satisfied that it was less than before. "Yes, we have much more important matters. Like the list of blasphemous oaths you have been heard to utter."

"A list?" asked Justine. "I don't recall more than saying the words 'Christ' and 'Hell' one after the other and not in a connected way at all. I certainly didn't mean any harm by it, although Margaret did seem rather shocked."

"So you deny saying that you would have Christ rot in Hell for all eternity and that He is the Devil incarnate?"

"Of course I do," answered Justine. "Deny it, I mean. What an incredible thing to suggest."

"But you would not deny that a Satan-worshiping witch may hold such foul and despicable views?" continued Hopkirk.

"If such a person did exist, I suppose she might," answered Justine carefully "but…"

"So, as such a proven witch, we must therefore assume that you do hold such views." interrupted Hopkirk, with a hint of triumph in his voice.

"No," said Justine, "I never said…"

"Silence!" cut in Hopkirk, fixing her with his basilisk stare. "We must now turn to the matter of your dress. Is it not true that when you were first seen yesterday, you were wearing a badly-finished doublet, unfinished breeches and man's boots?"

"A jumper and a skirt, if that's what you mean."

"The names of the garments are unimportant. It is the purpose behind them that is of most consequence – disguise and confusion to ordinary folk."

"I did not mean to confuse anyone," said Justine, then stopped. "I mean…" she hesitated, realising that the evidence of her disguising herself as a boy was now overwhelming.

"Indeed," said Hopkirk. "I think we have all the proof of disguise and confusion in front of us. So we'll move on…"

Just then Wychwoode cut in. "I am not happy with you questioning the girl in this manner, Hopkirk," he said tersely. "I do not recognise this line of questioning about clothing and blasphemy and suchlike. I warrant she has attacked you with a knife, but she was justified as you were attacking de Beauvais. I would prefer that both these matters were dealt with through the proper legal channels."

Hopkirk gave a deep sigh. "Master Wychwoode," he said, "I am quite weary with your constant interference in my business." He turned slowly and faced the lawyer directly. "I would have you remove yourself and your men from this tavern, before I have you removed myself."

"You talk as if you have a militia of your own," answered Wychwoode confidently. "Whereas you have a rag-tag collection of villagers with pitchforks. I would suggest you have a care when you make such claims."

"The only care I have now is to see these good, honest folk here free of the threat of sorcery and incantations," said Hopkirk. "Which is why I was following the line of questioning before your unwelcome interruption."

He turned back to Justine and again he stared at her, his eyes narrowed as if he was looking for something in her face. She stared levelly back, wondering what he was doing and if he was ever going to blink. Eventually he gave a small grunt and stood back. "The mark of darkness," he said, "as clear as I have ever seen."

He turned to the crowd. "The mark of darkness is there!" he said "She is proven to be an evil witch!" The crowd gasped at this revelation.

Hopkirk walked quickly to some women a few feet away and stopped just before them. "Do you fear for the lives of your children if there is a witch present in the village?" The women nodded vigorously. "Oh yes, we do indeed Master Hopkirk!" one of them confirmed.

He turned to some men standing further along and asked in a raised voice, "Would you fear your sons and daughters won't work in the fields and mills if there is a witch among them? A witch casting spells to make them sick?" The men nodded their heads and shouted that they would.

Hopkirk went over to Agnes and Ruth and asked, "Would you suffer a woman to live if she clearly has the darkness of evil in her eyes?" They shook their heads violently. "No, sir, not if she has the mark!" Ruth shouted back.

Despite her rising terror at the situation she had put herself in, Justine couldn't help thinking that Hopkirk was certainly showing his skill at working the room up to fever pitch; he would probably have made a good game show host if he'd been born 450 years later.

Hopkirk then leapt up onto a bench and addressed himself to all the villagers crowded into the tavern. He lifted his arms and turned to each part of the room, shouting, "Do we now test this woman, who has been proven a liar and a deceiver and who has the mark of darkness in her eyes?"

"We do!" returned the crowd, clapping their hands and stamping their feet.

"And do we test her now?" roared Hopkirk, clapping his hands in time with the crowd, encouraging them; goading them on; keeping the temperature red-hot to get the crowd ready to do whatever it took to kill Justine. "Do we duck her in the water and see if she has the magic?" he yelled.

"We do! We do!" shouted the crowd. Hopkirk jumped back to the floor and they started to surge forward.

In terror, Justine looked to William. But William was focused on Smitheson; she saw him casually drawing the sword at Smitheson's belt as the yeoman went past him, then, when the man was ahead of where William was standing, she saw the silver sword tip emerge from the front of the man's chest, then disappear again.

She saw Smitheson's face go ashen white, cough a gobbet of bright red blood down his chin, then he disappeared from her view as he dropped to his knees.

Oblivious to Smitheson's fate behind them, the crowd continued to surge forward, shouting and yelling, buoyed up by Hopkirk's rhetoric and full of bloodlust to get to Justine and duck her in the barrel; their pitchforks raised and their snarling, hate-filled faces behind the evil-looking points.

Justine was desperately hoping that now William had a sword, he would fight through and rescue her, but then she was shoved to one side by a man drawing his sword and in panic she screamed – until she saw it was Wychwoode himself putting his body and his sword between her and the crowd. She looked quickly to one side then the other and saw his militiamen now taking up positions around the barrel, their swords drawn and points facing the crowd.

With rising relief, she realised that William was not going to have to save her single-handedly; she was now inside an effective ring of steel formed by Wychwoode and his men.

Hopkirk and the crowd faced the ring of swords.

"Let us through, Wychwoode!" shouted Hopkirk. "This is our matter, not yours!"

"Go home, Hopkirk!" said Wychwoode calmly. "You have had your say, now I have mine. You have no authority here and this 'court' is a travesty of true justice. I am a servant of Her Majesty the Queen and in her name I tell you to desist from this nonsense! Leave this girl to me and the proper authorities."

Hopkirk shook his head. "No, I will not. We outnumber you many times – we will have our way."

"Not if I have ought to do with it," came a strong voice from behind them.

"Or I," confirmed another voice.

"And I," said a third

"And I, too," said a fourth.

Hopkirk turned and let out an oath. William, Melrose, Dowland and Stanmore were standing in a wide line behind them with drawn swords.

Hopkirk looked at the four swordsmen, then he glanced down and checked as he saw the sprawled body of Smitheson in front of them; a pool of blood spreading out from under the chest and soaking into the sawdust on the tavern floor.

"He must have got in the way of a sword in the rush," observed William casually. "Most unfortunate – he really should have been more watchful."

Justine was gratified to see Hopkirk go white and lick his lips nervously as he stared at the body, then look up wide-eyed at the four swordsmen. Then Hopkirk looked across from these four to the thirteen armed men in a ring around Justine. He could clearly see that his rag-tag army of elderly men, women and children were surrounded by men prepared to kill.

"Come, my friends," he said grimly. "It seems we are not going to complete our trial this evening. These men, who would protect witches, do not allow justice to be served." He turned to Wychwoode. "You have not saved these evil-doers, lawyer. You have but delayed the inevitable. For one day soon I will test them and if their evil is proven, as the Lord Jesus is my witness, I will send them to Hell by fire!"

"As you say, Hopkirk, but not tonight," answered Wychwoode. "Goodnight to you."

With that, Hopkirk marched towards the door. The villagers looked at each other, unsure of what best to do. One or two went straight out after Hopkirk. The others milled around for a moment, muttering and enquiring of each other, then they too drifted to the door and left into the night. Only Jake and Agnes stayed; Jake dragging Agnes to the serving table and stationing her there, while he stayed by the door to see the final villagers out.

Eventually there was just Wychwoode and his militiamen, William and his three friends, and Justine.

A blessed peace descended on the tavern.

Suddenly Justine felt the room start to spin. She gave a little cry as her legs gave way and she found herself slipping down into an all-enveloping darkness.

---0---

William sheathed his sword as Justine fell and ran over to her. He picked her up in his arms and carried her like a child over to a table. He swept aside some tankards, then laid her tenderly onto the table.

"Some ale, landlord, for the love of God!" he called out to Jake. "She has fainted!"

"I'm not sure I like her being here, Master," began Jake, "she being a witch and all…"

"By the Lord's Wounds, man," snapped William, "you cannot give credence to that nonsense after all that has passed tonight!" He touched Justine's cheek tenderly. "She is a mere girl, which is all and has had some adventures this night. She is now safe and has fainted from relief. Some ale, man, and presently!"

Jake nodded to Agnes, who filled a tankard with ale and carried it over to the table where Justine was sitting. Agnes stopped before she got to the table, stretched out her arm to its fullest length and gingerly put the ale down on the bench, then picked up the fallen tankards and ran quickly back to her station.

William put his arm under Justine's shoulders and lifted her into a sitting position, then held the tankard to her lips.

The feel of the cold liquid seemed to bring Justine back to a hazy consciousness, and her eyes fluttered open. She looked up at William with wide eyes.

"It's the 31st of July," she said in wonder. "You would have been stabbed by that man and died. But I was in the right place at the right time. I have saved your life." Then she shook her head and smiled slowly.

"I have changed history."

"Aye, my angel, so you did," answered William, thinking this was indeed a strange thing to say. "I shall forever be in your debt for that." He held the ale back up to her lips again. "Come, my sweet Mary, drink some ale."

Justine had a few more sips.

"I would have killed him – that Hopkirk," she said quietly. "I wanted to push that knife into his throat and..." She trembled as she relived the moment, as if staring at the dreadful scene again in her mind's eye. "I couldn't do it. When it came to it, I just couldn't do it."

"I know," he answered. "It is not easy to kill a man. You were most brave to attack him at all."

"I didn't think about it – I just ran at him."

"And I am still here because you were in the right place at the right time." He gave a little chuckle. "And well-disguised, I warrant. I had seen you a number of times before you revealed yourself, and I took you as we all did – as a young peasant boy."

He stopped at a sudden memory. "You would have tried to save me the first time they made to put my head under that stinking water. I recall now – you ran forward."

"Yes," she answered. "I wasn't sure what I was going to do, but I had to try and do something. When Melrose stopped them, I just shrank back into the crowd. I think people thought I was just a rash young boy running forward in the heat of the moment."

"A rash young boy!" He laughed. "'Twas a disguise well made."

"It was easy to do."

"Aye, but why?" he asked. "Why put yourself in Hopkirk's way, even with a disguise? Not that I am complaining, mind," he added.

Justine took some further sips of ale and looked away in deep thought, as if she was choosing what version of her story to tell. Eventually she seemed to have made up her mind.

"We have a saying where I am from," she said. "Know your enemy. I wanted to see what that man was doing. I wanted to understand him better – to find his weakness so I could defeat him." She looked up at William and shook her head. "But when I had the chance to defeat him – to kill him – I couldn't do it."

"Then we must find another way, and that we will when the time comes," he answered, trying to sound reassuring. "Come, finish this ale." He held the tankard back up to her mouth and she drained it.

"You have more colour," he said, putting the tankard down. "We must get you back to the manor" he added. "My mother can see to your well-being. She will be most concerned for you."

"Yes, I want to go to bed."

Melrose came over. "I must away, Will. I have much to think on this night."

"Aye, Tom." William stood up. "I must apologise if I ever gave you cause to doubt me. You have been my truest friend since we were boys, and my soul is tortured to think I gave you reason to turn against me. I can only thank the Lord he saw fit to show you the truth before it was too late."

Melrose did not answer immediately; he put his hand on William's shoulder and nodded. "We have had good times together," he said after a moment. "Good times indeed. I would have done well to have thought more on that, but I was blinded by my own thoughts on my father. When they made to drown you, I realised it was wrong – I was wrong. If they had carried their purpose through, I could not have made that a burden for my immortal soul." He nodded to Justine, then turned back to William. "Goodnight, my lord," he said, then walked out of the tavern.

William watched him go, then turned to Wychwoode. "I must thank you, sir, for your integrity and foresight in this matter," he said. "I owe you much. I would you and your men come to Grangedean Manor this night and enjoy some wine and some food, and a well-earned sleep as my guests."

"I must away to the Oxford Assizes on the morrow," replied Wychwoode. "But I will take up your kind offer this night, and I will make these men available to you for your protection for the next few days – or weeks if needed," he paused, then, like Melrose, he also put his hand on William's shoulder. "You are a lucky young man, possessed of a brave and loyal woman," he said. "But I fear this troublesome magistrate will not let the matter rest here. I fear he will shortly return and try once more to test your woman and yourself. You must be ready for him." He continued grimly, "For next time he may have more than a rag-tag army of ill-matched peasants with him."

"Aye," answered William. "I have had the same thought. But I will be ready – and I thank you for the loan of your men. They too are welcome to my house."

He turned to Dowland and Stanmore. "Will you come to my house too, my friends? We must drink some wine and relive the glorious rout this night of Master Hopkirk and his rag-tag army. For though he may return, for now we have sent him away with his tail between his legs, whining like a miserable cur! And that is worthy of a barrel of my finest wine!"

He paused and gave a rueful chuckle.

"Although in truth I'll not want to see a barrel again, as long as I may live."

CHAPTER TWENTY-THREE

It was very late one night around two weeks later, that Martha the housekeeper hobbled stiffly into the kitchen, put down the tray of empty wine goblets she was carrying and collapsed with a groan onto a small wooden stool in a dark corner. The cook and Margaret were already there, sitting on a couple more old stools, talking quietly and drinking ale. Other than these three, the kitchens were dark and empty; the usual bustle and noise gone for the night. The only light came from a couple of fat old tallow candles sinking softly into clay plates, plus the eerie glow of the previous day's fire as it smouldered gently in the grate – ready to be stoked back into life in the morning.

Martha reached down and pulled her shoes off, then rubbed her toes to ease the pain from running up and down the stairs over the last few hours with wine for the men in the Great Hall.

"They have been drinking so much," she said, shaking her head bitterly. "Master Dowland, Master Stanmore, Master Melrose and Sir William. It will soon be morning and they show no signs of stopping or retiring to their chambers."

"It is more than a fortnight since they sent Master Hopkirk about his business in the tavern, and still they celebrate wildly each night," observed the cook, lifting her head as the sound of raucous laughter drifted down from the Great Hall.

"And that woman – that witch – is all but mistress of this house now," muttered Martha. "They say she felled Master Hopkirk in the tavern with just the power of incantation." She stared into the fire. "He was cast down to the floor before he could attack the master."

"An incantation?" asked Margaret, "By the Lord's good grace I was not there, or maybe I would have been felled also."

The cook considered this. "Does an incantation thrown at one body work on another also?" she queried. "I would have believed an incantation is made for one body alone."

"Nay, it is like an arrow fired through a cotton sheet; it could fly on and hit any number of others," said Martha, pretending confidence. "That is a well-known fact of incantations."

"Aye, and now she is living among us as bold as you like, as the Lord is my witness," said Margaret bitterly.

"She is all so sweet and full of kindness, and she acts like she would be mistress of my heart, but I can see that she is but masking her evil ways and biding her time to cast a spell of sickness on me." Martha rubbed her feet absently, still staring into the settling embers of the fire. "She would have me believe she knows nothing of the ways of a great house – she asks me at all times of day how this must be done or how that must be done; she says it is not how they do things 'where I come from', then she smiles at me like a soft-headed child and thanks me over and again," Martha gave a soft bitter laugh. "Truly I would slap her in the face if I could."

"She came to my kitchens and offered to help with kneading the marchpane," observed the cook. "A girl not capable of turning the roast a few weeks past, now she comes to help knead the marchpane."

"What did you say?" asked Margaret.

"I smiled, right enough, and showed her what was to be done," answered the cook. "As you have said, she is all but mistress of the house now."

"And what is more, two days ago she offered to help me organise the next banquet," said Martha indignantly. "She said she had some experience of that 'where I come from'. Naturally I thanked her but refused. She appeared defiant and made some spiteful remark about only wanting to help."

"She cannot have come from a great house," said Martha, "or the fine expensive sugared foods she would have eaten would have blackened her teeth."

"She is most particular to keep them white," observed Margaret, looking down at the circles she was making in the dusty floor with her toe. "Simon says she asked him to make her a tool for cleaning them. She had him take a stick and whittle a flat end, then push in many pig hair bristles to make a small brush. Then she took some chalk, mint leaves and some oil and beat it into a paste, which she keeps in a jar. He says she will spend much time in cleaning her teeth with this concoction on the brush, two or three times a day."

Martha and the cook sat in silence, pondering this behaviour.

The cook shook her head. "They say it is only a matter of time before the master takes her to be his wife," she said bleakly.

"The Lord help us," said Margaret, crossing herself. "The witch will be the next Lady de Beauvais." The three of them stared desolately into the glowing embers of the fire; each considering the dire prospect of life under Mary Fox as their mistress.

The cook eventually broke the silence, saying out loud what the other two were thinking. "We must do all we can to stop that happening," she said. "Has Master Hopkirk been heard of these past two weeks? He must be pressed back into the downfall of this dreadful witch."

"I have heard tell that he is moving about the county," said Martha. "Maybe he is seeking support and will return with forces behind him."

"Aye," said the cook, nodding. "There is much to hope upon."

"He will have to call the witch and the master out, and there are still the militiamen here to guard them," said Margaret. "They will defend the witch."

"Perhaps we can find a way to let Master Hopkirk in?" suggested the cook hopefully.

"All the gates are secured daily," said Martha. "No person is allowed in or out of the estate without one of the militiamen agreeing it. I myself have to ask permission." She gave a derisive snort. "The mistress's sister, Alice Mansfield, is expected to stay shortly, coming all the way from Nottingham. How will we allow her in if the gates are all barred? I cannot imagine Lady de Beauvais will suffer her to remain outside. It is quite ridiculous that we must have such measures."

"There must be a way to get Master Hopkirk and his men in unseen," said Margaret thoughtfully. She paused a moment then looked up with bright eyes. "Maybe out of the woods to the south?"

"It is possible, for sure," said Martha. "It is a long stretch of land for the militiamen to guard and I believe there is a path through the trees into the parklands." She leaned forward and stared into the glowing embers of the fire once again as she considered all the options. Then suddenly she leant back and slapped her leg, causing the other two to jump. "I've been a fool!" she exclaimed. "There is no purpose in finding a way for Hopkirk and his men to gain entrance to the estate, unless we can tell him what it is! We must first get ourselves out – or one of us must – to find Hopkirk and show him the way back in!"

Martha turned to Margaret. "It must be you!" she said. "Tomorrow you must go to the south side woods and see if, or where, they are guarding it, then find the path so you can lead Hopkirk in."

"And if they are guarding it?" asked the cook.

"Then we will think on ways we can disable the guard," said Martha, practically. She turned back to Margaret. "Take the path yourself, then you must go to the village to wait for Hopkirk so you can guide him back."

Margaret was silent a while, staring into the fire. "I might have to disable a guard – oh Heaven, will that need some sort of seduction? What if he is pig-ugly or has foul breath? What if he makes to kiss me and I can do nothing but submit? How would I then disable him? Would I have to kill him – or just tie him up?" She turned to Martha. "Can it not be you that goes to the village?" she asked, with a forced-looking smile. "You could ask permission and be granted leave."

"As housekeeper I would be expected back presently," said Martha, "and we do not know how long Hopkirk will be. No, it must be you."

"Maybe you could find the path first?"

"No," answered Martha, "how would you lead Hopkirk in, unless you knew exactly where the path was to be found? And the best person to do that is the one who found it."

"Oh." Margaret swallowed hard, then straightened her back a little and said in a small, but brave voice, "Yes, I suppose it must be me."

"Good," said Martha. "We must act swiftly. Explore the south side tomorrow. Tell no one what you are doing – especially the witch or her tame handmaiden Sarah – and make sure you are not seen. Look particularly for a path out of the forest where Master Hopkirk can lead many men into the estate – by God's good grace he has been able to raise sufficient."

She paused as another roar of laughter was heard from upstairs, followed by the sound of chairs being pushed back, then boots tramping unsteadily out of the Great Hall and up the stairs.

"Then by the will of God this evil witch will be banished from Grangedean and gone from our lives for ever."

CHAPTER TWENTY-FOUR

Justine sat bolt upright, her eyes wide with the shock of a sudden awakening.

Slowly she looked around her, expecting to see the sight she had woken up to every morning for these past two weeks; her room in Grangedean Manor. She looked for the deep red velvet drapes on the magnificent four-poster bed, the metal-bound oak chest of Tudor gowns at its foot, the carved and painted fireplace with the welcoming fire dancing in the grate…

Instead she saw something she was not expecting – the grey plastic steering wheel of her little Ford car in the flickering orange overhead lights.

Above it she could see dark cedar trees at the edge of the park through the now cleared windscreen. She looked down at her lap; her phone was lying there in its battered old case, with a Mary Fox story still showing on the screen.

In panic she felt the wheel – it felt solid enough. She became aware of a low rumbling noise; it was the little engine chugging away, powering the whirring demist fan.

Justine gave a small cry of anguish.

It had all been a dream – a very vivid, very real dream, but in the end, just a dream.

She was still in her car – on the night of the banquet for the Americans.

She must have dropped off to sleep while reading on her phone, waiting for the windscreen to clear. And she'd been reading a Mary Fox story, so it was not surprising she had become Mary Fox in her dream, having a wild, exciting, Tudor adventure...

Desperately she put her head back in the seat, trying to drop back off to sleep so she could get back into the dream again. But it didn't work – after a few minutes she was still wide awake.

And what was worse, the dream was now starting to fade.

As she tried to remember what had happened, it all became confused and jumbled. People and conversations started to drift out of her mind, and when she tried hard to reconstruct them, she couldn't be sure if she had them correct, or if she was just making them up. What had William said at the banquet? Was it at the cottage or at the manor that they had made love? Why was Wychwoode disguised as a peasant boy in the tavern?

Justine turned to her side in the seat, put her elbow on the armrest and leaned her head on her hand to get more comfortable. But sleep now seemed further away than before.

What was that horrible man called? Hopkraft? Falkirk? Why was he chasing her?

Was she even being chased? If she was, surely William would have protected her?

William? Was that William de Beauvais, the lord of Grangedean Manor? The one who had been killed in a fight in a tavern in 1565?

But hadn't she saved him…?

For a moment she clearly remembered knocking into a grey man trying to stab William, so she'd saved his life. Or had she? That was silly – it was all just a dream – you don't change history in a dream. He was stabbed in a fight; historical fact.

She stared out of the windscreen at the cedars in the distance, hoping to buy herself a few more minutes to try and remember the dream. A barrel flashed into her thoughts, and a knife. She knew they were important, but why? It all seemed further away than ever.

A man… a lover..?

Then her phone started ringing; the opening bars of The Phantom of the Opera.

Justine looked down at the screen. There was a caller ID picture on the screen.

It was her mother.

Justine looked at the clock on the dashboard – 1.33am. In amazement she swiped to take the call.

"You all right, Mum?" she asked cautiously. "It's really late. It's past half-one in the morning."

"Hello Justine, dear." Her mother's voice was as bright and chirpy as ever.

"Why on earth are you calling me at this time?"

Her mother did not acknowledge the sharp tone. "I just wanted to say, don't forget you're coming down for the weekend."

"You wanted to remind me of that at half past one in the morning?" Justine was incredulous.

"You weren't in bed."

"How did you know that?"

"You had a banquet. You're never in bed before two after a banquet."

"How did you know I had a banquet?"

"I'm your mother. I know everything about you." Her mother sounded smug. "I know you had forgotten you're coming for the weekend."

"I hadn't forgotten," Justine lied. She must have agreed to the visit at some point, but she couldn't for the life of her remember having done so. "Any special reason?" she asked cautiously.

"Just that we like to see our little girl occasionally," replied her mother, shifting into her 'I'm trying not to be wounded by my daughter's indifference' voice. Justine suspected there was a big 'and…' still to come.

"And… it's your father's birthday."

"Of course." Damn – she'd completely forgotten that.

"So we're having a party." That, too.

Her mother paused. "Are you bringing anyone?" she asked, casually. Too casually.

The loaded question hung in the air.

"I mean," her mother continued sweetly, "it's been quite a while now since you last brought a boyfriend down."

"No Mum, I'm not bringing anyone," Justine said with finality.

"OK dear, just asking."

"Well don't. I'll find someone when I'm good and ready."

"OK dear." There was a pause. Justine could virtually hear her mother choosing her words with care. "Actually, one of my friends has a nephew she thought you might like to meet…"

Justine sighed. Her mother was so predictable. "Your friends always seem to have nephews," she snapped. "And they always seem to want to meet me. Only, they all turn out to have buck teeth, a squint and terrible personal hygiene."

"Yes, but apparently this William is absolutely charming and very good-looking. He has land in the country, and he farms and he hunts. Mary says you'll love him."

"William?" A picture of a smiling man in Tudor clothes suddenly appeared in front of Justine's eyes, holding out his hand to her as she descended the last step of a magnificent stairway. She shook her head as the image faded quickly. "He hunts in the country?"

"Yes. And the way my friend, Mary Fox, describes him, he sounds very handsome."

Justine's breath caught in her throat. Mary Fox? How did her mother know about Mary Fox…? Another picture jumped into her mind – an elegant Tudor lady. Then some words; the lady was talking "…you will be Mary Fox, the daughter of my old friend, Richard Fox, a London merchant…"

"No!" Justine gave a strangled yelp.

"What is it, dear?" asked her mother, sounding concerned.

"But I'm Mary Fox!"

"Mary Fox? You're Mary Fox?" Then, completely unexpectedly, her mother sniggered.

Justine had never known her mother to snigger, but there was no other word for the strange sound that she had just heard.

"That's funny!" her mother snorted. "That's unreal!"

Justine looked at the phone. Somehow, the normally static caller identification picture of her mother had come to life. It was actually laughing.

"Stop it, Mum, you're freaking me out…"

"Mary Fox? That's the funniest thing I've heard in years!" As she laughed, her mother's voice started to change; it became deeper, harder and yet more sibilant – in fact it started to sound more and more like… then the name jumped into Justine's head, accompanied by a dreadful sick feeling in the pit of her stomach… it was the voice of Hopkirk.

Justine's eyes opened wide as a series of images suddenly crowded unbidden into her mind.

A terrible storm, resolving itself into a bright summer's day…

A cook with foul breath making her turn the spit…

A dark passageway with a rat crawling up her leg while Hopkirk tapped on the other side of the wall…

A beautiful man smiling at her in the dim light of a humble cottage in the forest…

Planning to be at the tavern with Sarah and her mother – and disguising themselves as a peasant woman with two young sons…

Coming back to the manor on horseback – so tired that she would have fallen off had William and Wychwoode not ridden on either side of her horse…

Being put to bed by Lady de Beauvais and sleeping a deep, dreamless sleep…

Now, she remembered everything – it all came flooding back as if it had never gone away. As if the dream were absolute reality.

And now Hopkirk was forcing his way back into her life, his horrible hissing voice coming out of her phone.

As Justine looked at the screen with sick fascination, Hopkirk's laughter was clearly coming out of her mother's mouth.

Then the laughter stopped and the picture of her mother started to change; it melted and shifted; the nose started filling out, the brow jutting, the hair shortening – until it was the grey, unblinking basilisk face of Hopkirk himself that looked triumphantly out of the screen at her.

As she watched in horror, Hopkirk gave an unpleasant smile.

"Oh, Mistress Fox," he hissed. "You know I will not be defeated again – not by you, or that self-opinionated lawyer Wychwoode, or by de Beauvais. You know that I will find a way to get to you and de Beauvais, and try you both for sorcery!"

"No, Hopkirk!" gasped Justine, staring at the screen in horror. "No!"

"So why did you not kill me when you had the chance?" sneered Hopkirk, his face now coming out of the rear-view mirror as well as the phone. "How long will you regret not pushing in that knife..?"

Justine swung round to see if he was sitting behind her, but there was no one there. "I couldn't do it!"

"You are weak. You are useless!" said Hopkirk, now looking in at the side window as well. "You and de Beauvais will never be together! I will hunt you down and I will not stop until I have you both in my power. I shall test you both under water and then I'll burn you both for sorcery!"

"No!" shrieked Justine. "Leave me and William alone! Leave us both alone!"

The phone slipped from her nerveless fingers. Then she felt the car seat was no longer supporting her weight; it was becoming soft and liquid, like chocolate melting in a hot pan. She grabbed at the steering wheel but it too seemed to melt in her hand and then the seat gave way completely and she felt herself falling and falling, as if down a long dark liquid tunnel, slipping and sliding with nothing to hold onto, dropping down faster and faster, then her mother's voice came back and could be heard, saying "Mistress Fox? Mistress Fox?" over and over, while Hopkirk's laughter filled her ears, and she was sliding and falling faster and faster, then her mother reached out and grabbed her shoulder and shook it, repeating "Mistress Fox?" only now it wasn't her mother's voice any more, now it was Sarah's voice, and her shoulder was being shaken harder and harder...

"Mistress Fox?"

Justine opened her eyes.

"Oh Mistress, you were having ever such a nightmare – you were calling and crying – I had to awaken you."

She was in her four-poster bed in Grangedean Manor.

Justine sat up slowly and tried to gather her wits; trying to comprehend where she was and what was real.

"Sarah?" she asked, nervously. "Where am I?"

"You're safe in your room here at Grangedean Manor, Mistress."

"Am I? Am I really?" Justine looked desperately around the room. The four-poster bed looked solid enough, as did the clothes chests. She reached out and felt the nearest post of the bed, hung with a red velvet drape. It definitely felt real as she stroked the soft, thick material. Out of the diamond-paned window she could see the tops of the trees swaying gently in the summer breeze. The regular morning sound of the wood pigeon coo-cooing could be heard from outside.

"Are you sure this isn't a dream?" Justine asked in a small voice.

"Nay, Mistress, not a dream," answered Sarah. She reached down and shook Justine's shoulder again. "There, Mistress," she said. "That felt real enough, didn't it?"

Justine flopped back onto the bolster.

"Oh, Sarah," she said, staring up wide-eyed at the serving girl. "I had such an awful dream. I'd gone back to my original time and although it was good to talk to my mother again, I felt I had abandoned William and you and everyone."

"Oh, Mistress, no."

"Yes – except Hopkirk – he came after me to taunt me for not defeating him."

"I did think you were dreaming of Master Hopkirk, Mistress," said Sarah. "It sounded like he was attacking you – you said 'No, Hopkirk, no!' I heard you quite clearly. I hope I did right to wake you."

"Thank you, yes," said Justine. "Just knowing he's still out there and wants to try me and Sir William..." Justine shuddered. "Such a horrible man."

"Well, he's not here now, Mistress," said Sarah with a reassuring smile, "but the master and Lady de Beauvais are down in the hall, and they would have you join them presently to break your fast." She started rummaging in one of the oak chests. "Which means I must have you dressed and have your hair set and your face lightly painted; so you can make your entrance this morning and stun them all to silence with your natural beauty."

She produced a blue velvet gown and held it up for inspection. "Here Mistress," Sarah said, "I'll warrant this will be just the thing."

"The master and his mother are in the hall?" asked Justine.

"Aye, Mistress, although I cannot answer as to how Sir William has managed to be awake and in control of his humours this hour – he was drinking again with Master Dowland, Master Melrose and Master Stanmore till but a few hours since. I saw him going to his bed just as I had risen from mine for the day's labours." She chuckled. "Any other man would have stayed abed till sundown with the amount of wine he looked to have had."

"Then I had better get up," said Justine.

She swung her feet out of the bed and stood up, taking a deep breath in and out – to clear her head of Hopkirk and put the nightmare out of her mind. "Right, Sarah," she said, forcing herself to be bright and cheerful, "let's get dressed!"

A short while – and much tight lacing – later, Sarah was finished. She stood back to admire her handiwork. "There, Mistress, you are truly a beauty. I'll warrant your friends in your future time would not even know you! Stay here withal and I will let the master know you are ready to come down to the hall." With that she curtseyed and trotted out of the room.

Justine stood still, trying for a few minutes to adjust her breathing to the tight corset of the heavy gown. She had found that if she focussed on relaxing her shoulders and straightening her back, she could maintain some sort of control of her breathing. But she still hadn't got used to the way the clothing pinched in her waist and prevented her from eating more than the tiniest amount of food. 'If I do ever get back to 2015,' she thought, 'I'll make my fortune with the Tudor Costume diet. "Look great and lose weight!" – I'll clean up.'

There was a knock on the door. "Come in," she called.

The door opened and William strode in.

"My sweet Mary," he said, looking her up and down. "Each morning these past two weeks I have marvelled how you grow ever more beautiful." He bowed. "I would be honoured if you would accompany me back down to the hall to break your fast."

"Good, my Lord," answered Justine, then winced as she realised she sounded like a bad Shakespearean actor, "I would be most honoured."

He held out his arm and she slipped her hand onto it. They stepped out of the room and made their way down the great stairway and into the hall.

Lady de Beauvais stood as William led Justine to her place at his side. As they all sat down, servants ran out from the kitchens with plates of bread, meats, cheeses and cups of beer.

William immediately set about loading his plate with as much of the food as he could fit on it. Justine watched in wonder – she and Lady de Beauvais were both much more restrained, taking only as much as they could manage in their tight gowns.

"I would have you accompany me on a tour of the estate this morning," said William between mouthfuls of bread and cheese. He gave a small sidelong glance at his mother as he said it, giving Justine the distinct feeling that there was some unspoken message passing between them.

"That is a fine notion, William," said his mother. She smiled at Justine. "I am sure Mary will appreciate seeing more of the lands you own." She took a small piece of bread and a sip of beer. "Although I would have you keep a close eye on Mistress Fox, my son, lest she once again loses her horse."

Justine glanced at the older woman to see if this was a joke or if she was serious, and was relieved to see a twinkle in her eye.

"I would like very much to see more of the lands, Lady de Beauvais," she said, feeling that, as ever with this fine older lady, humility was probably the best policy.

"Good. I shall see to it that you have a steady mount for the ride." Lady de Beauvais turned to her son; her voice taking on a more business-like tone. "Now, my son; you still have men placed at all ways into the manor and the lands?"

"Aye," he answered, equally business-like. "Wychwoode has made them available to us for as long as we need them."

"But this matter needs to be settled for good, and presently," she answered. "Otherwise we are in a state of siege, awaiting the pleasure of that odious little magistrate to make his move."

"I am expecting Wychwoode back this day from the Oxford Assizes," said William, cutting a large piece of beef with his knife and putting it in his mouth. "We will consider our options and make our plans."

"Yes. We need a clear plan. I believe this dreadful little man will continue to chase after you and Mary whatever we try to do to stop him. He will not be diverted."

Justine had a flashback image of Hopkirk's face coming out of her phone and the rear-view mirror, as well as the side window of her car. "You and de Beauvais will never be together! I will hunt you down and I will not stop until I have you both in my power. I shall test you both under water and then I'll burn you both for sorcery!"

"What say you, Mistress Fox?"

"Eh?" exclaimed Justine, quickly putting the image out of her mind. Lady de Beauvais was looking expectantly at her. She paused a moment to gather her thoughts. "I was thinking that we should find his weaknesses and use them against him." That sounded good – she even impressed herself.

"Go on," said Lady de Beauvais. "What are his weaknesses?"

"He is an arrogant peacock," William suggested, "so sure of himself and his mission from God."

"Yes," said Justine, her mind racing. "He is arrogant and sure of himself. He also needs to command respect from his followers – he cannot bear to be made to look a fool. If we want to beat him, we have to discredit him completely."

"Indeed," said Lady de Beauvais, "that is very sound thinking." She glanced at her son, as if to ensure he had noted that Mistress Mary Fox had brains as well as beauty.

An idea started to form in Justine's mind – an idea of how to exploit the chink in Hopkirk's armour. She considered it a moment and decided it definitely had potential, although it was only a rough idea. She decided to park it for further consideration later.

"We will make plans later today when Wychwoode returns," said William. "I have also asked Tom Melrose to join us. I value his council."

"Even after he has betrayed you?" asked his mother.

"Aye," answered William, "but we have talked much on that. He was angry and Hopkirk recognised it. That is how Hopkirk was able to turn him against me."

"In the tavern you said his father had lost money," prompted Justine, keen to get more of the background. Even though she'd been hiding among the villagers in disguise, like everyone else in the tavern that night she'd followed the exchanges between Melrose and William with great interest.

"He had gambled it away," answered William. "It was the money my father paid him for the enclosure of his lands. It was Tom's inheritance, and his father lost it at gambling." He paused a moment, considering. "I know it was hard for Tom to understand – his father was a great force in his life.

"How much land was it?" Justine asked thoughtfully.

"It was enough for a man to plough and earn an honest living."

"And how much compared to your lands?" she asked.

"Around one tenth part of one tenth," he answered cautiously.

"Only one percent?" Justine looked at him in surprise. "Then you must return it to him! It is the best way to secure his loyalty. It means nothing to you, but everything to Tom."

"You would have me give away my lands?" William asked incredulously.

"If it secures his service to you, then yes, I would," she answered. "It seems to me to be a small price to pay."

"Yes, perhaps I could offer him a good price…" suggested William thoughtfully.

"No," Justine said firmly. "You must give the lands to him for free. It's the right thing to do."

William opened his mouth to try again, then seemed to think better of it. He turned to his mother. "What say you?" he asked.

His mother looked from one to the other as she considered her reply. "Mary makes an interesting suggestion," she said, "and not one I would have thought of myself. But you would do well to heed it, my son. With the house likely to face attack, you need to know you can count on the loyalty of all your men. Thomas Melrose has betrayed you once before and could do so again. Giving him one tenth part of one tenth still leaves you nine and ninety."

William looked like a man who knows he is outvoted by two strong women, but one who would not want to back down too easily. "I will think on it," he said eventually. "In time, I'll think on it."

"Good," said Justine brightly. "Then let's go for that ride in the park!"

CHAPTER TWENTY-FIVE

The militiaman watched idly as the steady stream of urine splashed around the base of the tree, spraying off the side of the trunk and sending a lazy plume of steam into the morning air. He raised the stream high to see if he could hit one of the leaves, and was pleased to see it buffeted in the arc of liquid. After a few moments he gave a final shake, pulled up his hose and breeches and walked back a few steps to where he had left his halberd. He picked it up and resumed his position, guarding the entrance to a path that wound through the forest towards the village.

It had been an uneventful morning, just like every other morning in the two weeks since he had been placed here on duty by Master Wychwoode. His orders had been very clear – no one comes into or goes out of the parklands. Just like every other morning, he had arrived at dawn to relieve the previous guard and had then stood – or sat – at the edge of the forest until dusk, before handing over to the next guard.

It was a lonely watch – no one to talk to and nothing to do except observe the birds in the sky and the occasional coney or squirrel in the forest. Once he had nearly managed to kill a coney as it ran out in front of him; his aim with the sharp tip of his halberd had been close, but not close enough. That was a shame – a coney would have supplemented his meagre rations nicely. He licked his lips at the thought of how he would have skinned the coney with his dagger, then built a small fire and roasted it on a stick. Much better than the few cuts of cold ham and a hunk of rye bread that was all he was given each day, along with a flagon of ale.

He wondered how long this guard duty would last – another week, another month, another year? All to keep that little grey magistrate and his forces out of the Grangedean estate. Quite right too; the man was obsessed and had to be stopped – just as, with God's good grace, they had stopped him that night in the tavern.

His mind drifted back to that eventful night. He could scarcely believe that Hopkirk had the presumption to try Sir William de Beauvais for witchcraft – that was going deeply against the natural order of things. Even if the plucky girl Mary Fox had not run out to stop Hopkirk stabbing Sir William de Beauvais, then he would have done so himself. Or at least he would have tried, even though he had been the other side of the barrel at the time…

Ahh, Mary Fox – now there's a girl…

Despite being accused of witchcraft, she hadn't run away; instead she had disguised herself as a boy and put herself right in the lion's den, like the prophet Daniel – and just like Daniel, God had saved her – He had shown that she was a good person and not an evil witch, for all Master Hopkirk had accused her.

So if he had to stand guard here for a year, or even two, to keep Mary Fox from the grasp of Master Hopkirk, then that's what he would do.

He looked briefly to his left across the parklands. The east wing of Grangedean Manor could just be seen among the dark cedars. Nothing out of the ordinary caught his eye, so he turned to the right and looked along the edge of the forest. Again, nothing.

He resumed his guard position.

---0---

Margaret ran silently out from behind a tree a few yards from the militiaman's back and darted lightly to the cover of the next one. Her shoe scraped slightly on the soft earth as she ran, and it made the smallest of sounds.

The militiaman glanced round, his small eyes staring suspiciously into the forest, but nothing caused him to raise the alarm. He did not appear to see or hear Margaret hiding behind the tree in the dappled shadows; she was breathing as quietly as she could, despite having run from tree to tree all the way from the manor. After a few moments she peered out and saw the militiaman shake his head and turn back to look across the parkland.

Checking again that his back was definitely turned, she darted like a small flickering shadow towards the next tree. This time she was less fortunate – a dry twig snapped under her foot with the sound of an exploding firecracker in the quiet morning air.

The militiaman was up on his feet in an instant, turning towards the forest; the wicked tip of his halberd dropping into the ready position.

Margaret froze between trees, camouflaged by the confusing patterns of light and shade in the forest.

"Stand, ho!" shouted the militiaman, his eyes scanning from tree to tree. "Who's there?"

Margaret held her breath and stayed silent.

"Who's there?" he repeated and advanced cautiously into the forest, his halberd sweeping in front of him. Then he spotted her. With a grunt of satisfaction he walked forward until the sharp steel tip of his halberd was at her throat, while the curved axe-head blade pointed down at her feet.

"'Tis I, Margaret," she answered quickly, stepping back with her gaze fixed on the tip of the halberd. "I am a servant at Grangedean Manor."

"What is your business out here?" he demanded.

She looked anxiously around for inspiration and saw some mushrooms growing on the forest floor.

"I am, er, collecting mushrooms," she answered.

"Step forward so I can see you fully and walk out into the sunlight."

"Raise your halberd first," said Margaret, with more strength in her voice than she felt. "I cannot walk further or I will impale myself."

He grunted in acknowledgement and pulled the point back. She walked forwards while he backed away, his halberd held in the ready position in case she made any sudden moves.

She stepped out of the forest shadows into the sunlit parklands, and stopped.

"Margaret – a servant?" he said, studying her. "Collecting mushrooms?" She nodded.

He looked her up and down. She was wearing a simple dress and plain woollen apron. "Then why do you not carry a basket?" he asked suspiciously. "You would need a basket to pick mushrooms."

"I would carry them back to the manor in my apron?" she suggested.

He shook his head. "That is too great a distance," he said. "I will not credit that."

She was silent, considering him.

So the moment had arrived; the moment she had been dreading, when she must do whatever must be done to get Master Hopkirk into the manor.

This coarse peasant stood between her and the success of that plan – so he must be removed.

And if it must be done, it must be done this moment.

Margaret straightened her back. "Oh, good sir," she said with what she hoped was her most alluring smile, "you are indeed a most observant guardsman." She put her hands on her hips and pushed her small chest out towards him. "You have found me out."

"Found you out?" He sounded deeply suspicious. "What have I found out?"

"That I am not in truth picking mushrooms you are quite right." She moved closer to him and smiled up coquettishly. "That I have come out here for a much larger prize."

He looked down at her and laughed. She caught a whiff of his sulphurous breath and forced herself not to recoil. "What prize is that, Mistress Margaret?" he asked, chuckling.

"Why," she said, moving closer "it is you, you big ninny."

"Me?" The smile froze on his face.

"Yes, you. I have seen you in the manor, so big and strong, and I thought 'that is the man for me'..." She looked carefully at him to see how he was taking this nonsense in. "So I asked the sergeant and found out you were on guard duty here each day, and I thought I would come out to see just how...

big..." she moved closer still and pushed her chest virtually into his stomach "…and strong… in truth you are."

He stepped back. "You have seen me and wanted to meet me?" he asked incredulously.

"Aye," she answered, moving closer again and putting her hand on his cheek. She stroked it up and down against his coarse beard.

He reached up and removed it. "I am on duty," he said. "I am to guard this path through the forest. We can meet and talk about this later."

"So you are minded to meet with me?" she affirmed, then reached up again and ran her finger gently along his lip.

"Aye," he answered, his breath catching as she pushed her finger into his mouth.

"Then why wait?" she said, in her softest and silkiest voice. "We are alone. We can get to know each other here…"

"Nay…" he muttered, but this time he did not remove her hand.

Margaret moved even closer still and put her left hand up to stroke the side of his chest.

"Good sir," she purred, "we must take our chances while we can…"

That was when his resistance crumbled.

He put his hands on her tiny waist, and pulled her into a close embrace.

It was the move Margaret had been waiting for. Her left hand moved smoothly down his side and her fingers wrapped around the hilt of the dagger at his belt…

---0---

Justine urged her horse to a gallop to try and catch William as he thundered across the Grangedean Manor parklands, his challenge to out-ride him still hanging in the air behind them.

"William!" she called out. "You started before I was ready!"

"Come, Mary!" he called back over his shoulder. "You must catch me!"

Justine gripped harder with her knees and urged her mount on, her hair flying out behind her, moving as one with the magnificent animal as it strained to catch up with the rider ahead. William was on a big, heavy war horse; Justine's lower weight and nimble, eager mare meant that she had a speed advantage, and soon she drew level.

For a few exhilarating moments they rode side by side at full gallop. Justine couldn't help but laugh out loud with joy as the horses flew along together in the morning sunshine.

William looked across at her and laughed as well. "Bravo!" he called out. "You have skill at riding a horse!"

"Aye, my lord!" she called back. "It was as well I took the mare and not the sumpter!"

It had been earlier that morning in the stable yard that the choice had been made. William's mother had been as good as her word and had produced what looked to Justine like a steady old cob horse, together with a primitive-looking side-saddle. Lady de Beauvais called the horse a 'sumpter', which Justine took to have been the Tudor name for it. She must have looked surprised, for Lady de Beauvais asked if she were not happy with the choice.

Justine hesitated. She didn't want to offend Lady de Beauvais, but the thought of riding out side-saddle on an old plodding horse on such a fine summer's day made her feel like someone's aged aunt.

At that moment a beautiful young mare was brought out for exercise, skittishly prancing across the yard with her groom hanging onto her like grim death. On a sudden whim, Justine asked if she could take the mare instead.

"You would ride out on this one? asked Lady de Beauvais in surprise.

The mare pulled her head back, nearly pulling the groom's arm from its socket. "She is indeed quite difficult to manage," Lady de Beauvais said doubtfully.

"I have ridden lots of horses, many just like her," said Justine. She approached the mare and reached up to stroke the soft velvet muzzle, making 'shhh' noises to reassure the animal. The mare whinnied, but brought her head down and kept it still, so after a moment, Justine moved her hand up the side of the horse's head. She carried on whispering to the mare – more 'shhing' noises and 'there, there' – which seemed to have the calming effect she wanted. Soon the mare was quiet and still.

"What is her name?" asked Justine, still stroking the horse's cheek and muzzle.

"Juno." Lady de Beauvais paused a moment, considering. "You have a way with a horse. That is good."

Justine cast her mind back to Pony Club camps as a child; how she'd always found that ponies responded to her calm voice and touch, while the other children were often told 'that pony is too hard to handle; leave it to Justine Parker'.

"She is beautiful," she said.

"You may ride her," said Lady de Beauvais, suddenly and decisively. Then she turned to the groom. "Fetch a saddle for Mistress Fox, she will ride astride."

Justine looked at her, surprised. "You may have a way with a horse, but not even you can control Juno from sitting aside her."

"Thank you," said Justine, with a big smile.

"And you must change your clothing. We cannot have you trying to ride with full skirts. I will have you dressed in something more suitable."

Which is how Justine came to be riding Juno at full gallop alongside William, dressed in a special split skirt. She also had men's hose on underneath – mainly to maintain her dignity, but also to help avoid chafing against the high backed wooden saddle.

William sat up in his saddle and started to rein his horse in; they were approaching the edge of the forest.

Justine pulled up as well, and soon they were trotting gently alongside each other, their horses snorting, whinnying and throwing their heads around in appreciation of the gallop; steam rising from their sweaty flanks.

"You ride well, my sweet Mary," said William, when they had both got their breath back.

"I was well taught, my lord," she explained. "We had a club for young children and their ponies, and I rode every day as a young girl."

"What an interesting notion," he observed. "You are ever full of surprises."

He pulled his horse to a stop, so she did likewise. He turned to her, and looked her deep in the eyes. "And I have a surprise for you, too," he said softly.

She took a deep breath, smiled and replied "A surprise? What is that, my lord?"

"It is more that I have something I would ask of you…"

She looked into his eyes, searching behind them – trying to see if he was being serious, or if this was the build-up to some joke.

He leant across and took her hand in both of his. She realised he was trembling. He took a deep breath. "I have met many women, and none have had your beauty, your charm or your ready wit. In truth, I have never met a woman such as you, sweet Mary, and I would have you with me for all time. Mary Fox, will you…"

But he never finished the sentence. Instead he was cut off by a chilling sound in the still morning air; a long, drawn-out, blood-curdling shriek from the forest ahead, that ended in a terrible gurgling death-rattle – then silence.

William gave Justine a brief look of shock – and was that also a small amount of relief? – then he kicked his horse into an immediate gallop and sped off towards the place where the sound had come.

"Yes… oh yes…" breathed Justine. "Of course I will…"

Then with a sigh she kicked Juno into a gallop and once again chased after William across the parklands.

She arrived at the edge of the forest to see that William had dismounted and was on the ground, bent over the body of a man. He looked up as she reined in and dismounted.

"It is one of the guards," he said. "He has been stabbed." He stood up and moved back; Justine could see the man had the hilt of a dagger sticking out of his chest.

She knelt down beside him and studied the dagger. It looked as though it had gone in deep, just below his breastbone. She put a finger to his neck. The pulse was there but it was weak. The man was still breathing, but only just, and with great difficulty.

She wished she could do something for this poor man, who had been guarding the estate for her protection. She wished she could get him to A&E

at a 21st century hospital – with immediate surgery he might possibly have a chance. But out here, with no real medical practices, there was nothing she could do – except give comfort.

She lifted his head onto her lap and stroked his cheek. The man looked up at her with pinprick black eyes and coughed. A fine spray of blood hit her skirt.

"Mistress Mary?" he whispered. "Is that you?"

"Yes," she said.

"I have failed you."

"No, of course you haven't."

"I would have protected you. No one is to leave the park, Master Wych…" he coughed again and gathered what little strength he had left. "…Master Wychwoode said, but that bitch has got out. I let her go. I failed you." His eyes closed.

"Not at all." She stroked his cheek again as his breath got weaker. "I'll be fine. Who got out?" she asked.

He was quiet a moment, then his eyes opened and he looked up at her. "I'm cold," he said.

"Shh. We'll get help and you'll be fine."

"Nay," he answered, so quietly she had to lean right in to hear, "that bitch has killed me."

"Who's that?" she asked.

"She said her name was Margaret," he coughed again. "A serving wench at the manor."

"Margaret?"

"Aye, she said she loved me…"

The man gave another cough, then his breathing slowed and stopped. As she watched, his eyes lost focus, then rolled up into his head.

Justine looked down at the body and felt regret for the waste of this man's life. But then she frowned.

Why was it only regret she felt? There was a dead body on her lap – why was she not feeling fear and revulsion? With a start she realised that her attitude was becoming much more Tudor – she was becoming hardened to death as an ever-present part of life. The old Justine – the one from 2015 – would have been sick, or would have screamed at the man's death. Mary Fox, the Tudor adventuress, on the other hand, simply laid the body on the ground and stood up, smoothing down her skirts.

William looked at the body. "Who did this?" he demanded. "Who has killed one of our guards?"

"It was Margaret," she answered calmly. "The serving girl who first accused me of witchcraft. She stabbed him and got out of the park."

"That shrewish little woman?" he asked. She nodded.

"I should have cast her out before now!" he muttered. "I should have cast her out the moment we returned from the tavern." He walked away, thinking hard. Then he turned back. "I'll warrant she has gone to fetch Hopkirk – to lead him in on this path!

Justine could now see clearly what had to be done. This was the moment when she had to take charge. Whatever happened, Hopkirk could not prevail; the memory of Hopkirk's challenge from her dream came back to her and she wasn't prepared to let him defeat her now.

She mounted lightly onto her horse, then wheeled round to face William.

"We have to get back and prepare ourselves," she said firmly. "We have men to organise and plans to put in place."

Then she wheeled Juno round towards Grangedean Manor and kicked her into a gallop. "Come on!" she called over her shoulder. "No time to lose!"

William walked over to his horse, who was calmly eating grass a few yards away.

"By the Holy Cross," he observed softly to the animal, "she is as much a leader of men as is our own glorious Queen." He mounted up. "I would I had completed my offer of marriage, for now I fear she'll not spare me the time!"

He kicked his horse into action and galloped off after Justine.

CHAPTER TWENTY-SIX

As William and Justine rode back to the manor, Margaret was running blindly along the dark path, picking her way through the deep forest under low branches and over high roots by instinct alone. In her conscious mind there was only one aim – to get as far away as possible from that awful thing back there – that awful thing that she had done.

Her breath punched in and out of her chest in great racking sobs as she ran; every breath accompanied by a fractured prayer to God or to Jesus for forgiveness.

She had killed a man. She had committed the most heinous of mortal sins – murder.

Suddenly a massive wave of nausea hit her. She stumbled to a large tree for support and leaned against it, waiting for the nausea to pass. But it didn't pass; instead her body contracted as her gut went into spasm and she leant over and she retched, again and again and again. Even when there was nothing left inside her, still she continued to retch. She thought she would surely die.

Eventually the nausea passed and the retching stopped. Wiping her mouth with her apron, she stumbled on a few more yards and collapsed down onto the forest floor with her back to the trunk of another tree.

She stared across the forest.

But the scene in front of her eyes was not the trees, branches and woodland path; it was the scene that had played continuously in front of her, without mercy, ever since it had happened.

She was looking at the militiaman as she grasped the dagger at his waist.

She was mouthing 'I love you' as he smiled at her.

She was staring into his eyes as she eased the dagger out of its sheath and in one smooth movement, thrust it deep into his chest.

She was seeing his eyes widen as the dagger went in; the smile turning to disbelief and then to shock; his eyes contracting and his knees giving way as dropped.

She was hearing the long, chilling shriek as he then flopped over onto his back and writhed on the ground with blood soaking into the front of his tunic; eventually ending when he lay still, staring hopelessly up at the sky.

She was recalling her panic as the full realisation of what she'd done thundered into her, the realisation that she had committed the mortal sin of murder.

After that, she did not recall, except that she must have run into the forest and started her headlong flight along the path, before the nausea made her stop and retch.

After many minutes sitting against the tree, her head started to clear. She looked about her, as if seeing the forest for the first time.

The path, barely more than a track between the trees, ran in front of her, winding its way from the parklands through to the road to the village.

She remembered now what she had to do – to get to the safety of Hopkirk's protection and lead him back along the path towards the manor. That was why she had to dispose of the guard; it was for the greater good.

Margaret gasped as the realisation hit her. In truth it was actually God's good work she was doing! She was helping Hopkirk to get to the witch and to burn the Devil! If she was doing God's work, then God must have wanted her to kill the guard! Maybe the guard had been a sinner – she had seen him shamelessly pissing up into the air towards the Heavens, which must surely be a sin – maybe he had sinned greatly in other ways too!

That was it! She was not the sinner – no – she had in truth been a tool of Lord Jesus, being used by Him to cut out the canker of sin by committing a mercy killing on an evil man who deserved no better…

Margaret stood up, put her shoulders back and took a deep breath.

She was God's chosen servant, and she had His important work to do.

She looked up at the morning sun as it filtered down through the trees and used it to get her bearing, then she turned and set off south along the path towards the village.

---0---

It was a long walk, and the sun was nearly overhead when Margaret staggered, dry and dusty, into the cool, dark tavern.

Jake was padding around with his pitcher of ale so she asked him, as she sank onto a bench by an empty table, if Hopkirk was anywhere to be found.

"Right enough, Mistress Margaret," said Jake as he filled a tankard for her, "he's expected back this very afternoon."

"Where has he been?"

"'Tis said he has been around the county seeking men to join his cause."

So Martha and the cook had been correct – Hopkirk was recruiting forces. Margaret permitted herself a moment of quiet satisfaction. God was most assuredly looking for her help in His work!

"They say he has gathered some four dozen men," continued Jake.

"Four dozen? Does that mean he plans to attack the manor?" she asked.

"I'll warrant it does," replied Jake. "He's talked of nothing else since that night when the witch was revealed right here in my tavern."

"I have heard much about that night," said Margaret. "They say the witch threw an incantation at Master Hopkirk and he fell down to the floor."

"An incantation?" Jake did not look as if he was bothering to hide his surprise.

"That's what I have heard from folk who were there."

Jake let out a deep guffaw. "Nay, she threw herself bodily at him, and struck him with some force, like she were a ball from a canon."

"Oh." Margaret considered this doubtfully. "Are you sure?"

"I was one of the folk who were there. I was as close to her then as I am to you now." Jake chuckled. "I'll warrant she may be a witch, but I know what I saw with my own eyes – and it was no incantation. She hit him with her body, with the force to knock ten men off their feet!" Still chuckling to himself, Jake padded off to serve others, leaving Margaret sitting alone with her thoughts.

So the witch had not used an incantation to fell Hopkirk – that much was clear. Did that mean she was supposed to think that maybe, the witch was not such a powerful sorceress as everyone was saying? Or was God testing her; deliberately trying to sow doubt in her mind, so He could see whether she had the strength of will to resist?

Well, if that was so, then she would prove to Him that her will was as strong as iron. She would prove she was resolved to carry through her mission. After all, God had commanded her to commit murder in His purpose – and she had risen to obey His command.

Margaret straightened her bony little shoulders and stuck out her chin.

Let the witch do her worst. With Hopkirk – and God – on their side, Margaret knew absolutely that the righteous would prevail.

---0---

At about the same time that Margaret was sitting nursing her pitcher of ale and contemplating a long afternoon waiting on the arrival of Hopkirk, Sir William de Beauvais was striding into the Great Hall at Grangedean.

He had decided to change out of his riding clothes and was now resplendent in a blue doublet and breeches, grey hose and black boots. On his head was his favourite grey velvet cap with a peacock feather protruding from the brim.

Justine and Lady de Beauvais were sitting at the long table. Melrose was standing opposite them, along with a man in black with long grey hair that William recognised as Wychwoode.

"Ahh, William," said his mother, "good of you to attend our council."

"Mother," he acknowledged, with a little bow. He then turned to Justine and bowed again. "Mary." She inclined her head at him, then broke into a mischievous smile. "What were you going to ask me when we were out riding, William?" she asked, her voice as innocent as a child asking for a comfit.

His mother looked at William and raised an eyebrow. "You have not…?" she began.

William gave a warning cough. "Um, no – we were disturbed..."

"Oh really, William!" said his mother, "Could you not at least…?"

"Has anyone thought to call for some beer?" asked William quickly, wanting to cut her off. "A council such as this cannot be run on a dry throat." He stood and shouted "Martha! Martha! Here I say!" then he sat down again.

"Really, William," scolded his mother, "must you bellow like an enraged bull in my ear?" He noticed her catch Justine's eye momentarily, and they exchanged a small but knowing smile. William sighed inwardly – what must a man do to keep the women of his house in control?

Wychwoode cleared his throat, bringing the meeting back to order. "I understand one of my guards has been murdered?"

"Yes," said Justine. "And by a forest path that may lead from the village to the estate."

"This is a clear sign that we are soon to be under attack," Wychwoode grimly. "Who has done this? Do we know?"

"Aye," answered William, relieved to be back on more important matters. "He named his assailant before he died. It was one of our serving maids – the one who first accused Mary of witchcraft and called in Hopkirk."

"Then she is most assuredly in league with that man."

"She has run off; we think to the village," said Justine. "It is most likely she has gone to find Hopkirk and show him the way in."

"And he will come stealing in like a wolf in the night," said the lawyer. "We will need to be ready for him."

Martha appeared through the door from the kitchens.

"Yes, Sir William?"

"We will have some beer and some manchet bread."

"Yes, Sir William." She turned and disappeared back through the door to the kitchens.

"We must put men by…" began Wychwoode, but stopped in surprise when Justine raised her finger to her lips and shushed him quiet. Everyone turned to look at her. "Martha," she whispered, indicating the door to the kitchens.

William could see it was still slightly ajar.

Justine got up and walked carefully and very quietly over to the door, then wrenched it suddenly open. Martha was revealed standing behind, the expression on her face alternating between shock at having been discovered listening, and pretend innocence.

Justine kept her composure. "And a flagon of wine, if you would, please Martha," she said levelly – as if the housekeeper had been correct to hang back in case of further orders.

William saw Martha shoot a look of the purest loathing at Justine, before assuming her customary mask of subservience. "Yes, Mistress Fox," she muttered. Then she deliberately turned her back on Justine and walked slowly down the stairs.

Justine waited until Martha's footsteps could be heard reaching the corridor below, then she closed the door fully and returned to the table.

Wychwoode, Melrose and Lady de Beauvais were staring at her open-mouthed. William, however, was smiling with quiet pride. Truly this Mary Fox was a remarkable and ingenious girl.

"We can't be too careful," Justine observed as she sat down. "I have my doubts about Martha's loyalty."

"It looks as though you have good reason," observed Wychwoode dryly. "We must be most diligently on our guard."

"Aye," agreed Melrose. "This man Hopkirk is full of cunning. He will use whoever he can to further his ends."

William looked at Melrose and nodded. "He used your anger to turn you against me, Tom. You, who was schooled alongside me from a boy."

"I was angry – that is true," agreed Melrose, with a rueful shake of his head.

"And I am truly sorry, Tom," said William. He paused a moment as he considered his next move. Mary Fox had suggested he should return Tom's lands. Without payment! It went against his every instinct – but look how Mary Fox truly seemed to understand the minds of others. She had seen so clearly how Martha would behave – she knew the housekeeper would be listening at the door. If she was right in this, he must give her other advice much credence.

He took a deep breath and looked up. "If we get through this, Tom, I will restore your family lands to you and yours. In perpetuity. It is the least I can do."

"My Lord…" exclaimed Melrose in surprise. "Are you sure?"

"Aye," said William. "You have come back to me and shown your loyalty. I value that above all else."

"My Lord!" Melrose touched the hilt of his sword and bowed. "You have my loyalty indeed!" William thought that as he stood up again, he stood a little taller; his eyes looked less hooded and his shoulders more relaxed. 'Good,' he thought, 'Mary Fox was right in this matter also. And it has secured Melrose for our cause.'

Once again, William observed a small glance between his mother and Justine, as if he had passed a test and the two women were now ready to move on.

Justine stood up.

"How many men do we have?" she asked, her voice sounding so business-like that Wychwoode briefly glanced up at her in surprised admiration. "I still have eleven of my militia," he answered.

"Plus Melrose, Dowland, Stanmore and you, Master Wychwoode," added Justine. "So we have fifteen men."

"And I, my sweet girl…?" said William with a small smile. "I also have a sword – and the wit to use it…"

"Yes, William, but you're a marked man," answered Justine. "If it comes to a fight, Hopkirk will target you directly, and if he kills you, he has won. We can't let that happen."

"You speak the truth, Mary," acknowledged Lady de Beauvais.

"And I would that I am not killed, more than I have a concern for Hopkirk's victory," pointed out William.

"Which is why we have to plan properly," answered Justine. "You and I will conceal ourselves in the secret passage and emerge only when Hopkirk is defeated. That way his whole cause is compromised – if he cannot take us both and try us for witchcraft, he has failed in his mission."

William stared at her in amazement. "You would have me skulking in the dark like a thief, while my own house is under attack?" he asked incredulously. "While my comrades fight on my part?"

"It's not skulking," answered Justine. "It's…" she paused a moment "…it's a tactical withdrawal."

"What if we are discovered?"

"We shouldn't be, but I suppose you should have your sword with you, just in case."

"Most assuredly!" exclaimed William, nodding sharply, so that the peacock feather danced wildly on his cap. "I will have my sword so I can burst forth and skewer that troublesome magistrate like the scoundrel he is."

"Nay, William" said his mother. "You will do as Mary commands in this matter. I will not have you killed by that vile little man. You know he would have stabbed you himself had it not been for Mary's brave action in the tavern. She is trying to stop history repeating itself."

"In any event, we will not let him get as far as the manor, Sir William," said Wychwoode, leaning forward with his hands on the table. "We will place men each night near the path where my man was killed, concealed in the trees. Then we will have the element of surprise when Hopkirk and his men come upon our ambush."

"We had best start this very night," said Melrose.

"We will," said Wychwoode. "Each night from now we must be ready for an attack."

"And must Mary and I sleep each night in the secret passage?" asked William, attempting to make this sound like a joke.

"No, William," said Justine. "But we must be ready to run to the passage the moment we hear a sword being drawn."

"But if Hopkirk comes in the dead of night…?"

"I will set a guard on the door from the gallery," said Justine. "Hopkirk cannot get to the bedrooms unless he comes along the gallery, so a guard will see him in good time to slip through the door and alert us."

"We cannot spare any of the men," said Wychwoode "Who will you use?"

"I will use my maid Sarah," answered Justine. "She has already agreed to help us in this way."

"Then that is settled," said Lady de Beauvais.

The door from the kitchens swung open, and Martha appeared with a tray of beer, wine and bread. Everyone was silent, all eyes on her as she walked across the room towards them. Martha placed the bread on the table and poured each person a tankard of beer, apart from Justine. She took a fine silver goblet off the tray and presented it to Justine with exaggerated deference, before filling it with wine from a small pitcher. She then put her nose in the air, turned and walked out of the room and slammed the door behind her.

The silence continued after she had gone, until eventually it was Lady de Beauvais who spoke.

"When we have removed the threat of this odious magistrate, we must look to our household staff," she observed carefully. "I would that we can rely on their unquestioned loyalty."

"I would do it now, Mother!" challenged William, scraping back his chair and leaping to his feet. "I will turn her out this instant for disloyalty and insolence!"

His mother raised her hand to calm him down. "Nay, my son. Now is the time for planning and preparation, not for concerns about servants. Let us settle the bigger matter first."

"But I will not have such behaviour in my house…"

---0---

While the argument continued between Sir William and his mother on the merits of removing Martha, Justine was definitely of the opinion that William was right. Keeping Martha in place was more of a risk than throwing the girl out; she had seen enough spy thrillers to know that as an 'inside person' Martha could be very valuable to Hopkirk in an attack.

So, once the argument was settled in Lady de Beauvais' favour – and William had stopped sulking – Justine decided to have a word with Martha. She slipped quietly down the stairs and made her way into the kitchens.

There were servants bustling all round; stuffing joints of meat, rolling pastries, slicing fruits and preparing dishes. Justine spotted Martha chopping some herbs and walked over to her.

"Hello Martha," she said pleasantly.

Martha carried on chopping, giving no indication she'd heard.

Justine tried again. "I wanted to thank you for bringing me the wine." As conversation-starters Justine knew it was lame, but it would have to do.

Martha scraped the choppings into an earthenware bowl. "'Tis no matter, Mistress Mary Fox," she said without looking up. "I serve the master and Lady de Beauvais, and they have ordered that I serve you also – so that I do."

"And I am grateful."

"Are you?" Martha finished scraping the chopped herbs and suddenly looked up with cold blue eyes.

"Of course."

"I should like to think you were, but I can scarce credit it, Mistress Mary Fox." Martha paused, studying Justine carefully. "Or should I call you Mistress Justine Parker – for is that not also your name?"

Justine was silent, shocked at hearing that name spoken aloud after so long.

"I recall that was your name when you arrived here, some two weeks since, as a vagrant who should have been turned out." Martha reached for some more herbs and started chopping, her blade moving almost faster than the eye could see. "But you weren't turned out, were you, Mistress Parker? You were put to service in these very kitchens as a scullion to turn the spit, which was no better than you deserved – and yet here am I, these two weeks later, ordered to serve you as the master's consort." Martha stopped chopping and stabbed the knife brutally into the wooden board, then looked up again. "And you would tell me there is no witchcraft in this?"

"No, Martha," replied Justine as steadily as she could, "there is not."

"Well, I do not believe that, Mistress Justine Parker, truly I do not." Martha pulled the knife out of the board and started chopping again. "And when Master Hopkirk catches you, do you know what he will do? He will take you to the fine brick well in the courtyard close to this place and he will try you there by ducking. And if you are proved as a witch, he will burn you at the stake."

"Then I will do all I can to stop Master Hopkirk catching me," said Justine levelly.

"Nay. He will catch you, and he will try you," said Martha with full confidence, "because he has the Lord Jesus on his side." She put down her knife and again stared at Justine with cold eyes. "His authority comes directly from God and from Jesus, whereas yours comes from Satan, may the Lord forgive me for uttering that name." Martha crossed herself. "With God and Jesus behind him, Master Hopkirk cannot fail, and your destruction is most definitely assured." She smiled coldly.

Justine, however, was staring wide-eyed at the housekeeper. Martha's words had brought back the idea she'd had that morning at breakfast for the downfall of Hopkirk – only now Justine knew in a flash exactly what she had to do to make it work.

The plan was clearly highly risky, but if she could pull it off, it would spell the end of Hopkirk's dogged pursuit.

Justine smiled back at the housekeeper.

"Thank you, Martha. You have opened my eyes to the truth," she said, and turned to run out of the kitchens and up to her room to put her plan into action.

Martha watched Justine go, then resumed chopping. "The truth will be your downfall, Mistress Justine Parker," she said aloud.

"Master Hopkirk will see you find it in the very fires of Hell."

CHAPTER TWENTY-SEVEN

Margaret yawned as she swilled the dregs of ale around the bottom of the tankard and chewed on her last crust of bread. The long, slow afternoon had dragged by; the sun was moving lower in the sky and the shadows outside the tavern were starting to lengthen – but there had been no sign of Hopkirk. The only highlight of the afternoon had been a conversation with Agnes, the young daughter of the landlord Jake.

"It's Mistress Margaret, isn't it?" Agnes had asked, as she stopped by to refill Margaret's tankard and give her a crust of bread. "I recall you from the day we searched Grangedean Manor for the witch."

"Yes, I am Margaret."

"You waiting for someone? I see you sitting here a while."

"Yes," Margaret replied, glad of some conversation. "As it happens, it is Master Hopkirk himself I am waiting for."

"Master Hopkirk? You're not a moment too soon. He is expected back this very afternoon."

"So your father has said." Margaret studied the younger girl and decided she would be a useful source of information – if the past looseness of her tongue was anything to go by. "I am told he has been about the county, gathering men."

"That's what he said he would be doing." Agnes sat down and made herself comfortable opposite Margaret. She poured herself a tankard of ale and leaned forward, bright-eyed, ready to tell her tale. "He came back in here the next night after the witch revealed herself and he vowed on all that is holy that he would find the witch and destroy her. And Sir William too, for being her protector." Agnes took a deep draught of ale. "But he knew he could not take them without some good fighting men, so he set off to go round the county, pressing men to his cause."

"But why not recruit men from the parish?" asked Margaret. "Why recruit outsiders?"

"Lord love us, Mistress Margaret!" exclaimed the girl. "He needed men who could not possibly be loyal to Sir William! So he must seek them from further afield."

"He is certainly dedicated to his task," observed Margaret thoughtfully. "It cannot be easy to recruit men to a stranger's cause."

"That is no matter to one such as Master Hopkirk," answered Agnes, with the fervour of a true disciple. "He can persuade any God-fearing man to his cause because it is the Lord's work he does."

"Then the Lord must have blessed his endeavour, for your father said he has gathered some four dozen men," said Margaret.

"Yes! We had word back from his party that he has been greatly successful, and that we should expect him back any day now with the men. There is much excitement in the village – nobody likes the thought that the manor is a godless place with a witch in residence." Agnes looked serious. "We pray for deliverance from her wicked grasp."

"She is all but mistress there now," said Margaret eagerly. "They say the master will have taken her to wife soon – or at least before All Saints Day is out," she added. She was rewarded with a gasp of amazement from the younger girl.

"The witch has enchanted him for certain," Agnes said breathlessly, "there is no other way of it."

"It does seem that is so," agreed Margaret. "I am come here to meet with Master Hopkirk and offer help to him and his men."

Agnes stood up. "Then you are well met here, Mistress Margaret. As I said, we expect him here soon, so you can offer your help to him directly." She took her pitcher and moved off to serve at other tables.

But there had still been no sign of Hopkirk by the time Margaret had finished her bread. She was just deciding that Agnes had been wrong and he would definitely not be coming this day – and was preparing to ask Jake for a room for the night – when she heard the sound of marching boots and jingling sword-belts outside.

Her heart lifted as the door opened and the familiar – although rather dusty and travel-weary – figure of Matthew Hopkirk walked in, followed by what seemed a never-ending procession of armed men.

"Master Hopkirk!" Margaret exclaimed, jumping up from her bench, "You are come!"

But Hopkirk did not respond, as his attention was focussed on seeing all his men into the tavern and seating them. He did not even seem to notice the excited Margaret leaping up from her table in the shadows.

Margaret ran over and tapped him on the arm, causing him to turn in annoyance.

"Well met, Master Hopkirk!" she said breathlessly.

"Who asks?" he snapped, barely glancing at her

"'Tis I, Margaret, from Grangedean Manor!" she answered with a smile. He looked blankly at her. "That first called out Mary Fox as a witch!"

"Oh, aye. Now I recall."

She gestured to all the men, who were seating themselves at tables while Jake and Agnes were running out with tankards and pitchers of ale for them. "You have gathered forces to take the witch?"

"That I have," he said, "and I must see to them." He started to turn away.

"Good," she said, reaching out and taking hold of his dusty sleeve. "But the manor is well guarded. I have come to help guide you in."

He stopped and turned slowly back, his unblinking grey eyes now boring into hers. "You have information on the defences?" he asked carefully.

"Oh yes, I do, Master Hopkirk!" She let go of his sleeve.

"Then you will share this information." He gestured to a table. "Sit and tell me what you know."

Margaret's heart swelled with pride as she sat down opposite Hopkirk. God must be pleased with her work, that he had put her in such a position of trust to this powerful man.

"The manor is well guarded?" he prompted her, once she had a fresh tankard in front of her and he had paid Agnes to fill it with ale. She took a sip to steady her nerve. "Aye. There are militiamen provided by Master Wychwoode posted at all the main entrances to the parklands."

"Master Wychwoode? That meddling lawyer?" Hopkirk made an annoyed hiss between his teeth. "I will take great pleasure in dealing with him in the course of this action." He considered Margaret. "How many men does he have – is it all that were here in the tavern?"

"Yes," Margaret paused for effect. "All except one – who is dead."

"Dead? That is convenient. How came he by that happy state?"

Margaret gave a slow smile. "I killed him," she said quietly.

Hopkirk looked at her in genuine amazement. "You?" he asked.

"Yes, it was me!" she said proudly. Then she added seriously, "But I was doing God's work, Master Hopkirk, God's good work."

"But how in Christ's holy name did you accomplish this deed?" he asked, looking Margaret up and down, clearly trying to imagine how this tiny woman could overpower a well-armed guard.

"I gave him to believe I was in love with him, so I could get close enough to grasp the dagger at his belt – then God guided my hand and gave me the strength to plunge it deep into his chest."

Hopkirk shuddered at this, but then stared at Margaret with a look of new-found respect.

"That is great work," he said. "I am… that is, God is… well pleased with you."

"God was looking for me to make a way open for the forces of righteousness to come in to the manor and take the witch," she answered. "The path that the man was guarding – it is now open to you and your men." She sat back, pleased that she had done her work.

"A path is open?"

"Yes, I have cleared a way in for you – through the forest." She was shocked when Hopkirk did not thank her for this critical action.

"But Wychwoode will undoubtedly know what you've done, assuming he's found the body. You did not hide it?" he snapped.

Margaret felt a cold dread – not only was Hopkirk not praising her, but he appeared to be chastising her instead. "No, the moment the deed was done I came straight here to tell you all, and to offer my help."

Hopkirk considered his options. "So they will know that we know of the path. They will expect us to use it. They will most likely conceal men about the end of it to ambush us." He looked up and gave a cold smile, making her heart sing. "You have done well, Margaret. They are expecting us to take the path." He paused. "So perhaps that is what we will not do."

"What will we do?" she asked, her pride in her deeds now fully restored. Truly God had heard her prayers. She added, "All the other gates are guarded."

"They won't put their best fighting men on the main gates," he answered thoughtfully. "They'll need them for the ambush. The main gates will only be guarded by servants. We need to find a reason to get them to let us in."

A thought occurred to Margaret, remembering something Martha had mentioned the night before. "Lady de Beauvais's sister is expected any day soon, from Nottingham. She will demand to be allowed in."

"Perfect," said Hopkirk, looking like a man with plan taking shape. "Absolutely perfect. We will attack them with all our force."

He drained his tankard.

"And we will attack when they least expect it."

---0---

Robert Wychwoode paced along the edge of the forest, studying each tree carefully in the deep orange glow of the evening sun. In particular, he noted the trees that lined the entrance to the path as it wound its way out of the parklands and into the depths of the forest.

The militiamen standing in a line behind him watched, as Wychwoode's strategic mind calculated the best position for each one; the best angle of crossbow fire; the best shadows for a man to melt into and become invisible.

There was a palpable air of anticipation as the men waited to be given their positions for the ambush – excitement crackling like an approaching electrical storm. Two weeks of uneventful guarding had made them bored and listless; it had dulled their wits and left their spirits dampened. But the murder of their comrade in cold blood at the hands of a serving woman had deeply enraged them and now, like fighting dogs about to be released from their cages, they were eager to be at the throats of their enemy.

Wychwoode turned and started issuing his orders.

"You," he said, pointing to the first man, "station yourself behind this tree here." The man moved quickly into position as directed. Wychwoode walked over and stood beside him, scanning the section of path visible from his cover, then stepped out onto the path. He looked back to see if the man could be seen, then grunted to himself in annoyance, returned and pushed the man deeper into the shadow of the tree. Then he walked back out onto the path and looked again at the man's position. Satisfied that he was now invisible, he said, "You stay in this position. Cover this section of the path and be ready to bring down anyone moving along." The man nodded briskly, cocking his crossbow, selecting a bolt from the pouch at his belt and slotting it onto the breech of the weapon.

Wychwoode walked back to the line to select the next militiaman, and placed him in the next ambush position.

Eventually all the men were in their places.

Wychwoode walked thirty yards along the path into the shadowy depths of the forest, then turned and walked slowly back out to the parklands, looking carefully about him as he went. A couple of adjustments were made to the position of some men, before he declared himself satisfied.

"Note the position of the shadows," he ordered. "When the sun sets you will have deep cover, but if they attack at dawn, the shadows will be on the other side of the trees. Make sure you move with them." The men nodded, studying the tree they were using as cover; looking to see where the shadow would most likely appear at dawn. "Now, prepare for the night, and stay alert. I want no man to fall asleep on this watch."

The men grunted their agreement and settled themselves by their trees. Like the first man, the others with crossbows made sure their weapons were cocked and ready. Other men had halberds which they leaned carefully up against the trunks next to them, ready to be snatched up the instant feet were heard approaching. The men whose main weapon was the sword gave a few practice draws of their blades from scabbards, thrusting into the air in front of them as if visualising how their blades would punch deep into the bodies of the enemy.

Wychwoode took a roll of wire from his belt and tied it between two trunks, one foot above the forest floor, as a tripwire. He tested it for tautness, re-tightening it until he was satisfied. He then tied a second one between two trees around ten feet further along the path. The nearest militiaman raised an eyebrow in enquiry.

"They will be expecting a tripwire," explained Wychwoode as he crouched down and squinted at the two wires to ensure they were all but invisible, "so they'll be proceeding carefully, feeling ahead." He stood up. "When they find the first one they'll think they have outwitted us – so they'll cut it and rush forward. That's when the second one will bring them down." The militiaman nodded, but said nothing.

Wychwoode walked back out to the parklands, to where William and Justine were waiting patiently on their horses.

"The ambush is secure, my lord," he said. "No man will pass through unharmed. If they attack in the night or at dawn, my men will stop them."

"You have done well," said William. "We are most thankful for your diligence in this."

"My men are pleased to have this chance to avenge the death of their comrade."

"And I, too, would have that magistrate stopped. For good, if possible," said William. "He is a thorn in my side that annoys me, with his fanciful notions of witchcraft and the like."

"There is no arguing with the man's conviction that he is on a mission from God," answered Wychwoode. "The only point he will accept now is the point of a sword." He patted Juno's muzzle, causing the mare to raise her head and whinny. "You and Mistress Fox should return to the manor and rest for the night."

He bowed. "My men and I will receive Hopkirk if he comes this night. We will put an end to this matter."

Chapter Twenty-Eight

It was the darkest hour, just before dawn the next morning, when a lone hooded figure on a dark horse trotted up to the main gates of Grangedean Manor.

The clip-clopping sound of the hooves alerted Simon, the servant on guard duty, who had been dozing beside the gate inside the grounds. He staggered to his feet and picked up the heavy halberd resting against the wall. Lifting the point with some effort, he poked it though the gate and stammered out a challenge. "Who… who goes there?"

The rider made no move to rein in the horse – perhaps they had not heard him. He challenged again, trying to put a little more authority in his voice. "Halt now and show yourself!" He lifted the point of the halberd a little higher to show how serious he was, as he could hear the horse and rider trotting ever closer.

Just when he thought the horse must soon run onto the tip of the halberd, it clattered to a stop of its own accord.

As he stared hard, Simon could just make out the horse standing outside the gate, with its rider as a black silhouette against the night sky above.

"Identify yourself!" he demanded.

The rider spoke in a muffled voice. "Alice Mansfield."

"What is your business?"

"My sister, Lady de Beauvais, has invited me to stay at Grangedean Manor."

"Alice Mansfield?" asked Simon dubiously. He recalled being told that Lady de Beauvais's sister might be arriving, and that if she did, he was to let her in. He had naturally assumed, however, that she would arrive during the daytime.

The first light of dawn started to appear, softening the harsh night sky with a pale glow creeping upwards from the east.

Simon scanned the path leading up to the gate. There was no one else to be seen – just the line of hedges and bushes casting long shadows in the gradually emerging light. He decided it must be safe. Cautiously he unhooked a great metal key from his waist and unlocked the gate, then pushed it open. It swung heavily on its hinges with a creaking sound that was unnaturally loud in the still air, causing several pheasants to whir noisily up from nearby trees. He stepped through, pushed the gate back behind him and walked up to the horse and rider, still holding his halberd.

"Alice Mansfield?" he repeated. He could now see that the rider's face was hidden inside a deep hood. "Why do you not show yourself?" Another thought struck him. "And why are you alone?" he asked. "Why do you not have cases and servants and suchlike?"

"I became separated from them."

"They did not stay with you?" Simon asked in disbelief. He stared at the figure on the horse above him. There was something decidedly odd about this woman…

A cold flush of fear suddenly flowed through him. Now he thought about it, perhaps opening the gate might have been a mistake. He glanced back nervously – he could see in the strengthening dawn light that it was still slightly open behind him.

"Why do you not show yourself?" he asked again, raising the halberd.

There was a pause, then the voice came from within the hood. "I am tired with a long ride from Nottingham. I need to paint my face before I would have people see me, as the Lord is my witness."

Simon started. That phrase, 'as the Lord is my witness' – there was only one person who often said it in that way…

Suddenly he recognised the voice.

It was not the voice of a rich lady from Nottingham – no, it was the voice of a servant at the manor. A servant missing since the foul murder of a militiaman in the parklands…

"Margaret!" he exclaimed. "It is you, isn't it? What are you…?"

But he never finished the sentence. As he spoke, the bushes along the path seemed to erupt, spewing forth armed men. Where there had been only Simon and the horsewoman, alone in front of the gate, now there were upwards of fifty men, all brandishing swords and daggers, surrounding the poor bewildered servant. Simon spun round in surprise, and in doing so, he dropped his halberd. With rising panic, he scrambled to pick it up, but a well-aimed boot from the nearest man sent him flying back towards the brick wall next to the gate. He landed with his back to the wall, his head hitting it with a bone-jarring thud that sent stars spinning before his eyes. As he slumped against the wall, dazed and confused, he became aware of a man in a grey cloak approaching.

The man crouched down in front of him and a pair of unblinking eyes stared into his.

"A poor guard indeed," said the man. "To open the gate on such slender evidence. Truly the Lord has guided my hand in this deceit."

The man took out an evil-looking knife and held it up in front of the dazed servant's face. "I would let you run free, but I fear you may raise the alarm when we have passed into the manor to do the Lord's good work." The man studied the blade, appearing to consider his options. "So the Lord will forgive me for what I am bound to do now in His name…" He shifted his grip on the handle, then thrust it forward.

Simon felt what seemed like a heavy punch in the throat. Then he found he couldn't breathe.

Then he felt nothing.

---0---

Margaret stared in horror as Hopkirk pulled his knife from the neck of the lifeless body and wiped it clean on the rough woollen jerkin. He stood and turned to address his men.

"The Lord has blessed our plan with success thus far," he said. His voice was soft, but his words still carried clearly to all the men gathered around him. "Your silence in concealing yourself before Margaret rode to the gate was enough to ensure that this simpleton," he gestured to the body of Simon slumped against the wall, "did not hear your approach. And Margaret," he looked up at her, "you played your part well."

Margaret pushed her hood back as she stared white-faced at Simon's bloody body. 'It must have been necessary,' she told herself. 'He had to die. It is truly God's work we are doing here.' But in her heart she was remembering what a friendly companion he had been since they had started working together in the manor as children. She remembered the good times they had shared, how they had laughed and joked as they worked in the kitchens; how they exchanged stories in the servants' rooms; how they giggled and whispered together behind the cook's back…

Maybe he did have to die in God's name – but maybe God was being unbearably harsh in demanding his sacrifice.

"He was a good man," she said sullenly.

Hopkirk glanced up at her sharply. "Aye," he answered. "But a man who may have endangered our mission. God's mission." He considered her a moment, appearing once again to be calculating his options. He gave a small grunt, as if he had reached a decision. "You can dismount now," he said. "I will take the horse."

One of the men reached up and lifted Margaret down. Hopkirk climbed up into the saddle, adjusted the leathers, then leaned down and said something quietly to the man that Margaret couldn't hear.

The man nodded, then suddenly he grasped Margaret by the waist and lifted her bodily off the ground.

"What are you doing?" she yelped. "Put me down!"

Hopkirk leaned down again, and addressed the struggling serving woman. "You have been of use to me. Yes, to God, even. But your usefulness has passed. Go with the Lord, Margaret. We must be away."

"What?" she cried in total disbelief. "You would discard me now, when I have helped you this far?"

"Aye, that I would. We have the Lord's battle to fight to rid us of witchcraft. You are no longer part of that fight, Margaret. You have killed a man," he observed, without a trace of irony. "Now go and make your peace with the Lord." He nodded at the man holding Margaret, then turned the horse and headed through the gate, followed by all his company.

The man holding Margaret let her down, then quickly put his hands round her throat and squeezed hard, until she stopped struggling and her body went limp.

He let her body fall to the ground and hurried through the gate after his companions.

---0---

Sarah came awake with a start, nearly falling off her stool at the end of the gallery corridor. She knew that some sudden sound had caused her to wake up, but she wasn't sure if it was real or part of a dream. She thought it might have been the sound of pheasants whirring up from the trees, but she couldn't say for certain.

Anyway, it was no matter – she could only have been asleep for a few moments since Mary and Sir William had gone to their rooms after bidding her goodnight, and she had settled down at her guard post to keep watch for Hopkirk's potential attack.

She shifted to get more comfortable on her seat. It was a wobbly three-legged milking stool that she had pushed hard up against the wall to stop it falling over – which was useful as it meant she was hidden in the deepest shadow at the end of the corridor, just beside the main door through to the bedrooms.

She yawned and stared at the nearest portrait painting – of a stern-looking old lady in a fine green silk dress.

She looked idly down at her own dress – an old woollen one in a dull brown colour. She scratched her leg, wondering what it would be like to have a fine silk dress to wear that didn't itch so...

Suddenly she stopped. Was it not the middle of the night – only a few moments since she had started her guard duty? So how could she see the painting when the gallery should be in pitch darkness? How could she could make out the colours of the woman's dress in the picture and her own?

She looked to the window – and then under her breath she uttered a short, sharp curse.

The first glow of dawn had started to lift the total blackness of the night. There was no doubt – the sky was glowing orange when it should have been pitch black.

Which meant it was now the morning.

Which meant she had actually been asleep for many hours on her watch.

Sarah's hand went to her mouth as an awful thought hit her. What if Hopkirk and his men had crept past her while she slept and murdered the Master and Mary in their beds?

With a growing sense of dread she stood up, took a large black key from the pocket of her apron and unlocked the door to the bedrooms. The key turned sweetly and silently in the lock, thanks to the oil that Mistress Mary had insisted was poured into the old iron mechanism the night before.

With her heart pounding, Sarah crept as quietly as she could along the corridor to her mistress's room. Slowly she opened the door and looked in. The curtains were still drawn around the large four-poster bed, and if she stood very still and listened intently, she could just hear the gentle sound of her mistress's deep and regular breathing.

With a long sigh of relief she closed the bedroom door, then padded back along the corridor and slipped through the main door to resume her guard.

She sank gently down on the stool, taking comfort in a small prayer of thanks to Jesus for keeping guard over her mistress while she had been so wantonly asleep. The night-time silence of Grangedean Manor once again settled around her.

The image of her smiling mistress hovered in front of Sarah in the dim light.

Such a strange, but warm-hearted girl, this Mary Fox – appearing at the manor these two weeks hence and making such a mark that now she was all but the mistress of the house. So full of ideas – like the quiver of arrows to help the master come after her, or the disguise in the tavern. Could she truly be from times yet to come – times so distant that it was beyond the capability of a simple soul to understand? Sarah thought of the strange things that Mary had described to her mother and her, as they had all sat together in the gardens one evening. She recalled the images that Mary had conjured before them, to try and help them understand the things of the future world.

"Imagine a large covered cart made of iron, like a beetle's carapace, that can travel at twice the speed of a galloping horse, yet without a horse to pull it!"

"But why would you want that, Mistress?" Sarah had asked, confused.

"To get to somewhere else – somewhere you want to be."

"But I don't want to be anywhere else. I'm happy here."

Then there were the large flat black stones, shining and smooth like the surface of a still pond, yet which were hung upon a wall and lit up brightly with moving pictures of people in other places and at other times.

This idea had fascinated Sarah. "You would see on one of these stones what other people were doing? Belike you were spying on them?"

"I suppose so, yes. But most times they know they are being watched. Sometimes they might put on a play for you to see, or show you events that are happening in faraway lands."

"And you say that this is not done by magic?" Sarah's mother had asked suspiciously. "It is as a crystal ball that a mystic might use."

"Not at all," had been the reply. "They work because clever people have understood how to make them, and other people have assembled them using special machines." Mary had thought a moment, as if considering how best to explain. "You make bread, yes?"

"Yes," they answered.

"You know that if you grind the wheat into flour then add yeast and cook it in the oven, you get a loaf of bread?" They nodded. "Then turning wheat into bread is not magic?"

"No, that it is not," Sarah's mother replied.

"So the people who make the black stones know that if they take all the right pieces, and put them together in the right way, then the stones will show the pictures. That is not magic." Mary sat back, satisfied.

There was silence while the Tudor women digested this information.

"Ah," Sarah said, spotting the flaw in Mary's argument. "But if you can see what others are doing by staring into a flat stone, why do you need the covered carts? You can see other places without having to go to them."

"But what if you simply have to be somewhere else? Like if you're having a baby, or if you're sick? Then you need to go to a large building where sick people are healed by trained apothecaries."

"There are special buildings full of apothecaries to cure the sick?" Sarah's mother asked, intrigued.

"Yes, there are," Mary said with a smile.

"But not the common people? These buildings must be only for the nobility?"

"No – every man in the country, even ones with no money at all, can go there and the apothecaries will do all they can to cure him."

Sarah could not accept this. "But surely not a beggar?"

"Absolutely – every man can get help."

"But why would they do that?" Sarah exclaimed.

"Because we believe every man deserves help in their time of need…"

Sitting alone in the dark corridor with these memories, Sarah smiled to herself. 'Maybe Mary is just a great storyteller,' she thought. 'Although Mother seemed to accept that such strange future things could happen.' Mother had even said to Mary that she dearly wished she could see one of these black stones – which had made Mary smile in such a strange way…

A stair creaked.

Sarah froze.

With fear turning her stomach to ice and blood starting to pound in her ears, she forced herself to hold her breath and listen. Maybe she'd just imagined it…?

It creaked again.

This time there was no mistaking it, nor the muffled whisper of command that followed, nor the soft brushing sound of leather sword belts against woollen breeches.

These were the sounds of men entering the hallway and starting up the stairs.

Despite legs that felt as wobbly as a fruit pudding, Sarah stood up as quietly as she could and slipped back through the main door, quickly locking it behind her. She then ran along the corridor to Justine's room.

"Awake, Mistress! Now! Please!" she hissed in Justine's ear, as she shook the girl's arm through the sheets.

Justine grunted and turned over.

"Awake, Mistress! Oh, in the name of sweet Jesus, awaken!" urged Sarah, shaking harder.

Justine opened her eyes, unfocussed and vague in the dim light. She looked sleepily up at Sarah.

"They're here, Mistress!" hissed Sarah. "Oh my Lord, they're coming up the stairs!"

Now Justine was wide awake.

"They're here?" she squeaked.

"Yes, Mistress! You must hide now!"

Justine threw back her sheets and stood up. "We must get William!" she whispered.

Together they ran to the door and peered cautiously along the corridor, now bathed in an orange glow as bright beams of dawn light shone through the leaded squares of the window panes.

As they looked, the handle of the door at the far end started turning.

Justine gasped and was about to retreat back into the bedroom, when Sarah put a hand on her arm and shook her head, holding up the key to show she had locked the door. Justine smiled grimly and nodded, and together they ran out of the bedroom and along to William's rooms.

---0---

Justine opened the door carefully and peered round. At first she thought William had been abducted after a struggle – there were clothes strewn all about the room, armour pieces on the floor and papers fallen off the table. Then she remembered that this was just the usual mess. She signalled to Sarah and together they went to the door to the bedroom.

Justine carefully opened it and peered round

The curtains around the magnificent ornate four-poster bed were pushed back and it was quite empty.

Justine ran to the bed in panic. Had Hopkirk somehow got in already and taken William?

"'Tis no matter," came William's voice.

Justine turned with a squeak of relief, to see him standing behind the door, already dressed and buckling on his sword. She threw her arms around him. "I thought they had taken you," she said, taking comfort from the feel of his hard chest on her cheek and his strong arms around her.

"I was awoken by the sound of someone putting up pheasants," he explained. "Then I heard you two running around, so I knew something was amiss." He unclasped Justine and looked down at her. "Are we under attack?"

"Yes, Master," said Sarah. "I heard them coming up the stairs so I locked the door. We must hide immediately!"

At that moment there was the unmistakable sound of an axe thudding into the door at the end of the corridor.

There was a brief moment as they all looked at each other in shock, then they turned as one and ran out of William's rooms. They emerged into the corridor just as another blow was heard and the silver head of an axe suddenly appeared next to the black iron lock.

William quickly put his hand to the intricately carved rose decoration on the wall. The low door to the secret passage swung open by their knees, revealing the dark dusty space within.

"In, Mary, now," he commanded.

For a split second Justine hesitated. The memory of the rat on her leg was all too clear, and she had no wish to renew its acquaintance – but then she saw the axe head disappear with a grinding sound from the protesting wood of the door as the man wielding it prepared to make another blow, and she popped down into the void like a rabbit down a hole, quickly followed by Sarah.

Justine stopped once they were far enough inside for William crawl in after them. But there was no sound of him coming in. She wriggled round and looked back out of the hole, then yelped in fear.

William's boots could be seen planted squarely, facing down the corridor. Then there was the sound of his sword being drawn.

"Oh, for goodness' sake!" she hissed as she poked her head back out. "Get in here, you silly man!" She reached up and grabbed his hand to pull him in.

"Nay!" he said, pulling his hand away, "I'll not hide like a coward when there's a fight to be had!"

"Get in here and don't play the hero!"

The axe came down again by the lock and the door start to bend inwards.

"Get in!" she yelled.

William hesitated only a second longer, then sheathed his sword, dropped to his knees and scrambled through the door. Justine leaned back and pulled it shut, just as another axe blow could be heard, followed by a crash as the door was thrown open.

The three of them froze as boots came running along the corridor, stopping right outside their hiding place.

Justine fought to control her breathing as a very familiar and most unpleasant voice spoke in a commanding tone on the other side of the wall. "You there, and you – search the bedrooms." Justine pictured Hopkirk in his grey cloak singling out the men for this task. "Make sure you search most thoroughly – leave no corner unchecked. Look in every chest, right to the bottom; under each bed, check even above the canopy of each one."

There were grunts of acknowledgement as the men split to search both rooms.

"You," Hopkirk must have indicated some further men, "guard the corridor. They may try to flee from the search. If so, take them as they come out." Justine heard the sound of boots moving back towards the door and swords being drawn.

There was a short silence, broken only by the sound of Hopkirk pacing up and down outside the hiding place. The three fugitives stayed as quiet and still as they could, scared to move a muscle in case it made a creaking sound to alert Hopkirk. They could hear the sound of his boots getting louder as he paced towards them, then fading as he paced away.

Then there was the sound of boots coming out of William's room.

"Nothing, Master Hopkirk. We have searched most thoroughly."

"He must be there. He must!" Hopkirk's voice was starting to sound pinched and high. "Go again and seek him out! I want him found!"

"Yes, Master Hopkirk," said the man, with a doubtful edge to his voice. The boots went back towards William's room and a door slammed.

A moment later more boots were heard, this time coming out of Justine's room.

"There's no sign of the witch, Master Hopkirk," said a voice, "for all we have looked in every place it is possible to hide a body."

"She's there! She's there!" Hopkirk was screaming now. "I know she's…"

Suddenly he stopped. There was a moment's silence, then he spoke more softly. "She's here, isn't she? She's right here. There's a priest's hole or suchlike – I knew it before…"

He started tapping the wall.

Tap tap tap. Tap tap tap.

Tap tap…

Thud.

There was no point worrying about making a noise now. "Quick!" Justine hissed. "Get to the door outside!"

The three of them scrambled onto their knees and started crawling quickly away from the entrance to the priest's hole. Sarah led the way, with William and Justine crawling behind.

Immediately Hopkirk heard them. "Quick!" he screamed. "Quick! They're in there!" There was a thumping sound as he frantically prodded and pushed at the carvings, and by luck he quickly hit on the correct piece. The door swung open and light flooded into the hiding place and along the passageway.

Hopkirk bent down and peered in triumphantly, just in time to see Justine crawling along the low passage, then standing as she reached the place where it opened up to full height.

"Get them!" she heard Hopkirk yell. "Get in there and get them!"

The man who was with him immediately dropped to his knees and shuffled into the hole.

"Men here, men here!" screamed Hopkirk, his voice rising almost to a falsetto. A man must have appeared from the bedroom. "In there!" Hopkirk shouted, pointing down at the hole. "They're in there! Get them!"

The man scuttled into the hole and started shuffling along behind his fellow.

Sarah, William and Justine ran along the passageway, then round the corner. Immediately the light from the open doorway was cut off, and they were back in pitch blackness.

Justine slowed down, feeling her way cautiously along the wall with one hand, and listening out for Sarah and William to start down the stairs ahead of her.

Then she heard footsteps closing up behind her.

Finding herself making small cries with each step, she tried to increase her pace – but the total darkness meant she couldn't go much faster for fear of falling.

The footsteps got closer.

Now she could hear heavy breathing as well.

She tried to run faster, but it was too late.

A hand suddenly clutched at her nightgown from behind, forcing her to a complete standstill.

"William!" she screamed, trying unsuccessfully to push the hand away. "They've got me!"

Another hand grabbed her around the waist and held her tight. She heard a throaty chuckle behind her shoulder. "Yes, we got you, witch!"

"William!" she screamed again, just as she felt the man release her nightdress and instead clamp his rough, calloused and foul-smelling hand over her mouth.

"Hold your tongue, witch!"

Then he started dragging her backwards; her bare heels trying to get grip on the rough wooden floorboards.

Justine did the only thing she could think of doing in the heat of the moment. Hoping desperately that she wouldn't catch something nasty, she bit down as hard as she could on the man's hand.

It was like biting on a rotten stick. There was a foul taste and she felt warm, metallic blood flood her into mouth, but she had the satisfaction of hearing the man yelp in pain and release her. She spat the disgusting substance out and started to run forward.

She didn't get very far – the man reached out and managed to grab her foot. She fell heavily with a shriek, just managing to put her hands out blindly in front of her at the last moment to break her fall.

Then she felt the man tighten his grip on her foot and start to drag her backwards. She heard his menacing voice from above her. "Best not to have done that, witch," he growled.

"William!" she shrieked again, as she scrabbled with her fingernails to find some purchase on the floorboards.

Then she heard William's voice. "Here, my love," he said quietly. "Stay low."

There was a whooshing, swishing sound above her, followed by a grunt from the man. Then her leg was released and she heard him make a long drawn-out groan. A moment later, she screamed as she felt his body – presumably now dead – flop down hard across her back and pin her to the floor.

"Get him off me!" she yelled in uncontrollable panic, trying to crawl forward but unable to move from the dead-weight on her back. "Get him off!"

"Hold still," came William's voice, and she felt the man being rolled slowly off her.

"Oh God, William!" she exclaimed "Is he dead?"

"I truly hope so." He grabbed her hand and helped her stand up. For a moment he paused, listening. Footsteps could be heard coming fast down the passageway.

"Come," he said, "let us get out of this place before his companions arrive to finish his task." He quickly pulled her away from the body and they started running forwards. "With luck he will cause them to trip and fall in the dark," William said.

Almost immediately they heard steps coming round the corner, then a shout of surprise, and a loud thud as a man hit the floor hard. William chuckled. "As good as a trip wire," he observed.

They ran a few more yards, then William spoke again. "Here are the stairs," he said.

Together they clattered down, then out through the secret door into the shadowy corridor leading out into the courtyard.

William pulled the door closed behind them, hearing the lock click shut. Almost immediately the faint sound of a man hammering on the other side of the door could be heard.

William smiled at Justine. "Are you well?" he asked.

"Oh God, William!" she looked at him wide-eyed. "I bit him! I bit the man and tasted blood!"

"Aye – you do have some blood on your chin. Here..." He took a handkerchief from his sleeve and carefully wiped it away.

The banging on the door behind them got louder.

"Come, my love," he said, "we must run for the cottage before they discover the way to open to door."

They ran together across the courtyard, making for the wooden gate out into the rose garden. William reached it a pace or so ahead of Justine, threw it open and ran through.

They ran across to the rose-covered pergola, then through the gate into the herb garden. The wooden gate out to the country lane was just ahead, promising escape and freedom.

Triumphantly, William threw open the gate and ran through.

Straight into the arms of two of Hopkirk's men.

---0---

As he struggled to free himself from their grip, William saw Justine run past him. Before he could shout a warning, another man appeared and grabbed her from behind, holding her tight around the arms.

A third man appeared from behind an ornamental bush. He pulled Sarah out from behind it with a look of triumph, then started tying her wrists behind her back.

"Let me go, you impudent fool!" shouted William, struggling to free himself from the men holding him. The men said nothing, and William could feel his wrists being bound behind his back; the ropes cutting deep into his skin. "Do you dare bind me?" he yelled. "Do you not know who I am?"

At that moment Hopkirk himself slid into his line of sight with a thin triumphant smile that did not reach his unblinking grey eyes.

"Aye, we know exactly who you are, Sir William," he said. "A man accused of harbouring a known witch and suspected of witchcraft himself on firm grounds. A man shortly to be tested alongside her, and this serving girl, for magical powers." He sniffed. "A man to be tested by ducking in the deep water of his own well to see if he has the magic to save himself." Hopkirk gave a small, hollow laugh. "We have no need of a barrel this time, de Beauvais." Then he turned and walked slowly up to Justine.

He studied her closely a moment, his grey eyes boring into hers. Then, as she watched in terrified silence, he reached up and touched her hair. William could do nothing to stop this sickening act; he could see that Justine was fighting the urge to scream, as Hopkirk's cold, reptilian hand rasped down her ringlets. Despite herself, she let out a small gasp of revulsion as his hand touched her cheek, then started moving slowly down towards her neck. "Nay," he said. "Do not flinch from me, my pretty. You are being touched by the hand of God this day and I will see his work done through to its conclusion." He stared deeper into her eyes. "Such a sweet face, but I see the mark of evil, as clear as a bolt of lightning crosses the night sky."

He let his hand drop and turned back to William, his voice taking on a more business-like tone. "Such a fortunate chance that I had men stationed at all the side gates for just this opportunity," he said. "Although I do believe that the lawyer Wychwoode had himself put a man here to stop me." He glanced over to a bush where a pair of feet in rough leather boots could be seen protruding. "'Tis a pity he did not choose one with the capacity to fight, though." William glanced down at the feet and with some difficulty, managed to hold his tongue.

"And where is this precious Master Wychwoode, I wonder?" continued Hopkirk. "Busy waiting to ambush us on the far side of the park, I'll warrant." He laughed. "Aye, a fool's errand. But he and his men are too great a distance away to hear us, and nor will they ever come to your rescue. I have detailed a handpicked group of my best fighting men to march out and engage them directly. I'll warrant we will outnumber them considerably – so you can expect no help from that quarter." He paused. "Nor from your mother, in case you were wondering. She is even now being guarded in her rooms by a couple of my ablest men – and as she is a lady of such fine standing, I have told them to be on their best behaviour at all times. Of course," he continued with a sickeningly innocent expression, "I cannot guarantee they will obey me in this. Your mother is still a magnificent woman for her age…"

William struggled against the ropes binding his wrists and fixed Hopkirk with a burning stare of hatred. "I'll see you in chains for this, Hopkirk!" he snarled.

"Nay," said Hopkirk. "You no longer have any chance to make good on that threat. For all you tried to evade me, my plans have run exactly as I expected. I wasn't sure of which direction you would come, but I was sure you and your companions would be flushed out somehow. Indeed, it was just like picking fish from a barrel!" He gave a dry chuckle. "My apologies, Sir William. There – I have once again talked of a barrel! I know you are not greatly enamoured of these. Just my little jest."

Hopkirk turned and looked in satisfaction at the two girls; Sarah standing with her hands tied behind her back and Justine grimacing as one of his men tied her hands also. He turned back to William.

"So now I have you. I have the witch and I have a serving girl as well. What a perfect start to a summer's day." He turned to the men holding the captives.

"Take them to the well."

---0---

Martha turned over on her pallet bed in the dormitory room above the courtyard that she shared with the cook, Margaret and a few other servants.

She settled on her back, folding her arms under her head, and looked up at the rough wooden roof beams rising up to a sharp point high above, festooned with cobwebs. The dawn sun was streaming in through the single open window, throwing deep shadows behind the beams. Martha sought out one particular shadow – her 'morning sundial'. It had nearly reached a particular broken slat in the roof that would mean it was an hour after dawn; time to arise and begin the day's labours.

Another day under the cruel regime of the witch! How was this to be borne by anyone of goodness and purity?

Martha offered up her regular morning prayer. 'Sweet Jesus, you who are forgiving, kind and gentle, make this the day that the evil witch vanishes from my life; make her go away, or better still, gentle Jesus, make her meet a truly unpleasant death. Please, Jesus, as you love me, make it happen. This very day. Amen.'

She rolled out of bed and stood up, yawning and stretching her arms.

Just then she became aware of a commotion in the well yard outside the window – some shouts and cheers, with the words "Witch! Witch!" coming through. With sudden hope rising, she ran over to the window and peered out to see what events were taking place in the yard below.

Hopkirk (she recognised the top of his hat) was leading three bound prisoners towards the well; one was Sarah, one was the master, and – oh glory to God! – the third was the witch herself! Bareheaded and in her night gown, there she was, being led towards the well!

Jesus had heard her prayer! Truly, he had heard her!

With an excited squeak, Martha leapt back from the window and ran to the cook's bed. She shook the sleeping woman's shoulder.

"Awake, now – they are about to try the witch at the well!"

The cook stirred sleepily and gazed bleary-eyed at the housekeeper.

"What is to do?" she asked, her voice still thick with sleep.

"Hopkirk is here! He has the witch and the master and Sarah. He has them by the well! My prayers are answered! He is to try them for witchcraft!"

The cook sat up, now wide awake. "Hopkirk is here to try the witch? You are sure?"

"I'm sure!" Martha grabbed her dress and threw it over her head, sliding her feet into her shoes. "Come – we must go down there now!"

The cook heaved her bulk off her bed and started to dress also. Martha, meanwhile, was running round waking the others. She stopped a moment by the one empty bed and smiled – it looked like Margaret must have been successful in getting Hopkirk into the manor. With luck they'd shortly have her back with them – particularly now that it looked like the witch's time at Grangedean was coming to an end and everything would be back to blessed normality.

Soon everyone was up and dressed. Martha led them down the narrow wooden stairs at a run, almost tripping and falling at one point in her haste to get down.

Emerging into the yard, she ran across to the crowd that was now starting to gather around the well. She recognised several of Hopkirk's original followers from the search of the manor two weeks before, some of whom had again brought their pitchforks. Agnes and Ruth were there, giggling excitedly. Martha supposed Hopkirk had sent word to the village that the witch was found, and they had all come up to see her tried. Jake had even brought a cart with some casks of ale up from the tavern, which he was selling to the thirsty crowd at a farthing a pint.

Martha elbowed her way through to the front of the crowd to get a better view.

As she emerged she saw Hopkirk standing on the raised dais in front of the well talking to one of his men. Next to him, in the shadow of the large tiled roof above the well, were standing the master, the witch and Sarah the serving girl, each with ropes binding their wrists and the ends tied to one of the roof posts.

Martha looked at the witch. The girl was still in her nightdress and Martha thought she must be freezing. If so, she gave no sign of it. Martha tried to catch her eye, but the girl steadfastly refused to look at the people in front of her. In fact, Martha thought she was searching the faces in the crowd, trying perhaps to see if a particular person was there? Maybe she was expecting someone to rescue her? Martha sniffed. That was definitely not going to happen – particularly after the Lord Jesus has so clearly answered her prayer.

"Mary Fox!" Martha called out to get the witch's attention above the noise of the crowd.

Slowly the girl lowered her gaze and met Martha's eye.

"I told you this would come to pass, did I not?" Martha shouted. "I said that Master Hopkirk would come for you and would try you by ducking at the well! Did I not tell you?"

The girl remained impassive.

"And what is more I prayed to Lord Jesus for this to happen, and he has heard my call! Truly he has forsaken you!"

At this, the girl smiled and slowly shook her head.

"Nay, you cannot deny me this," Martha responded. "You are forsaken and will burn in Hell!"

Sir William shot an angry look across at Martha. "Hold your peace, woman!" he shouted. "This is as much your doing as anybody's. As soon as I am able, I will have you turned out of my house!"

"You will be in no position to do that, Sir William," responded Martha triumphantly. "Soon you will no longer be the master of this house – you will be a witch condemned to burn or you will have perished by drowning in the well."

William shook his head sorrowfully. "What have I done to make you hate me so, Martha?" he asked.

"There was a time when I would have done all for you, Master," she answered. She stepped up to the dais next to him, and her voice became warmer, more reflective. "A time when you took me to your bed and made my heart feel so alive. Then this witch came and enchanted you and took you from me."

"Martha," he said. "Are you deluded? You must know your station. I would never take you to wife."

"Yet you took her," Martha pointed at Justine, "a mere scullion girl! You must have been enchanted to take her and not me!" Her voice rose. "You knew happiness with me in your bed, yet she took you by magic!"

"Martha, for the love of Christ, hold your tongue!" snapped William. "I am sorry if you thought I might have cared for you, but…"

At that moment he was interrupted by loud shouting from the other side of the yard. As one, the crowd turned to look. There were gasps and growls as they saw three men with drawn swords running into the yard, howling like wolves and making straight for the well. They were being pursued by two of Hopkirk's men, also with swords out.

---0---

Justine strained over the heads of the crowd to see who these men were, as Martha ran back into the crowd and started elbowing her way towards the action.

Justine heard William groan, just as she also recognised the bright silk doublets of Dowland and Stanmore and the more sober clothing of Melrose. They were running for the well, appearing intent on fighting their way through and rescuing the accused captives.

As they approached the well, three more of Hopkirk's men emerged from the crowd, drew their own swords and started running to meet them. Within seconds, Justine could see that the would-be rescuers were completely surrounded. Clattering to a stop, they quickly arranged themselves defensively back to back, each with their sword facing out towards the ring of armed men now encircling them.

"The damned fools," muttered William. "They have not even had time to put on armour. What did they mean to accomplish by getting themselves killed or taken?"

"They are brave – and loyal," said Justine, then added under her breath, "Athos, Porthos and Aramis – to the life."

"Eh?" asked William.

"Nothing, my lord."

She saw Hopkirk push past and march out towards the unfolding drama on the edge of the crowd.

"Well met, good sirs," he announced in a brusque tone, as he elbowed his way into the circle of swordsmen and faced William's three friends. "What mean you to achieve here?"

Melrose looked at the magistrate with what Justine thought was a very determined expression on his thin face.

"You have trespassed on Sir William's land and have unlawfully restrained his person and two of his household," he said defiantly, jabbing the tip of his sword towards Hopkirk to emphasise the point. "We would free them and restore the natural order."

The men either side of Hopkirk stepped forward half a pace, raising their swords towards Melrose's neck.

"Then you and I share the same sentiment," observed Hopkirk silkily, waving his men back to their places.

"How so?" Melrose asked dubiously.

"I would free them also," said Hopkirk levelly, "but only if they be not witches."

"Which you will test by drowning them in yonder well?" This was Stanmore, looking briefly over his shoulder, giving the man opposite him the chance to step in closer.

"That is the correct way of these things."

"Thereby rendering them quite – dead," snapped Stanmore, forcing Hopkirk's man back with a few warning sweeps of his blade.

"Unless they are indeed possessed of magic," said Hopkirk.

"In which case you will burn them at the stake, you piece of carrion!" shouted Dowland.

"Tsk tsk," admonished Hopkirk. "Their immortal souls must be freed of the Devil." Hopkirk waved his men forward one step, closing the ring tighter.

"So," said Melrose, raising his sword so it was almost touching the sword of the man opposite, "they die in either case."

"Indeed they do." Hopkirk shook his head regretfully. "Such is the way of these things."

"Then we will not allow it," said Melrose defiantly. "While we have breath in our bodies and swords in our hands…"

"Fie!" cut in Hopkirk suddenly "You waste my time!" He stepped out of the ring and marched back to the well.

"You have loyal friends," he snapped to William and Justine as he stepped up onto the dais beside them. "But their loyalty is misplaced."

"They have right on their side," answered William. "God will guide their hands."

"No!" shouted Hopkirk, turning and facing William, and now Justine could see the mask of civility stripped away to expose the zealotry that drove him. "It is I! It is I who has God on my side! It is I who fights for truth, for purity and justice – a fight you could not hope to understand! I am the one whom God favours, not you, nor her, or her!" he pointed at Justine and Sarah. "And certainly not them!" he shouted, pointing at Melrose, Dowland and Stanmore.

"In the name of God!" he screamed at his men. "End this nonsense!"

As the crowd yelled and whooped, his swordsmen moved in and started to engage with the three would-be rescuers.

Justine held her breath as she watched the fight over the heads of the crowd, seeing it quickly develop into a desperate melee with Dowland, Stanmore and Melrose circling back to back as the attackers came in and pressed them hard with their relentless swords.

She could see Stanmore's blond head above the fray; a look of grim determination on his face as he fought desperately against repeated attacks.

"Come on, Stanmore!" she yelled, forgetting her own predicament for just a moment. "Oh, do come on!"

She watched as he parried sweeps from two attackers, before turning a third on his hilt. Then he stepped to one side and let the man's own momentum carry him past, giving him the space to pull back his sword and thrust it deep into the man's side. The man went down like a sack of corn. William yelled "Huzzah! Well done, Richard!"

"Silence, imbecile!" snarled Hopkirk over his shoulder. Justine noticed he was gripping the upright well post with knuckles that were bloodless white.

As Stanmore turned to face his next attacker, Dowland was locked in fierce hand-to-hand combat with another. It was clear to Justine, even with her experience of sword fighting limited to cautious re-enactments, that he was coming off worse in the encounter. The attacker was pressing him hard with a sword that moved almost too fast for the eye to follow, driving him back towards the edge of the crowd with fierce cuts across the chest, great lunges towards the head and wide sweeps across the legs. It was all Dowland could do to defend himself against such a fierce onslaught – let alone make any attacking move of his own.

Then Justine saw his attacker make a feint with his sword to the left, which Dowland swung to his right to parry – leaving his chest wide open. Justine screamed as, with a vicious smile, the attacker lunged forward and buried his sword in up to the hilt.

Dowland dropped to his knees, then his head fell forward and he slid from view.

At this there was an agonised roar from William. "Oh my God, Oliver! No!" He rounded on Hopkirk like a wounded lion. "By all the Heavens, Hopkirk, I'll see you pay for that!"

"Strong words, de Beauvais," snapped Hopkirk, "for a man in your position."

Justine could see William struggling against the ropes that bound him, his face red and his eyes fixed on Hopkirk's neck.

A sudden roar from the crowd brought their attention back to the fight.

They saw that Stanmore was now standing still, face to face with one of Hopkirk's men. The two of them were staring deep into each other's eyes, almost as if they were lovers. Justine bit her lip, uncertain as to whether they had just locked swords or one had run the other through; hoping against hope that it was not Stanmore who had taken a mortal hit. The two men stared at each other a moment longer, then, to Justine's horror, Stanmore gave a little cough and a trickle of blood appeared at the side of his mouth. Like Dowland before him, he too dropped slowly out of sight.

William's head fell forward with a deep groan of despair and Justine saw his shoulders shaking as he tried to control the great sobs that racked his body.

"Courage, William," she said, as much to reassure herself as him. "It's not over yet."

"Richard and Oliver, both dead in my cause," he muttered bleakly. "I am truly cursed."

Then Justine became aware once more of the sound of clashing blade on blade and the roar of the crowd, and she looked back at the fight.

"Not totally, my lord," she said. "It looks like Thomas Melrose is holding his own."

"Thomas?" William's head came up in surprise.

Looking across the crowd, Justine saw the most magnificent sight.

Melrose was not only holding his own against the four remaining men, he was dominating them. His blade was moving lightning fast, with practiced sweeps, cuts and parries against those who came at him from all sides – he was keeping them away from his front, turning and protecting his back, and when openings occurred, he was exploiting them ruthlessly.

"Belike Oliver and Richard will be avenged," William said, "Tom will send them all to hell." Justine noticed just a tinge of pride in his voice. "I taught him well, eh?"

But Justine was remembering the promise that William had made the day before to return Melrose's lands – and she thought that perhaps this was what was also spurring Melrose on to ever greater feats of swordsmanship.

And there was no doubt he was fighting like a man possessed.

As Justine and William watched, one of the attackers left his chest unguarded and Melrose unerringly picked his spot at the point where the man's breastplate was buckled, thrusting his sword deep into the chink. Turning and withdrawing his blade as his opponent went down, Melrose parried a sweep from behind him, turned this man's sword on his hilt and pushed it away to expose the man's neck. Justine quickly screwed up her eyes in horror, as Melrose flicked the tip of his sword down. When Justine opened her eyes again, the man was clutching at his blood-covered neck, his eyes wide in shock, before he fell forward out of her sight.

"Oh golly, William, I feel so sick," she muttered.

"Be brave, my love," said William. "Thomas has fight enough for us all just now."

"I can't watch," she said. "They'll kill him like the others." She turned away. "Then they'll kill us."

"Nay," he said, with the smallest note of triumph in his voice.

Justine heard the crowd give a sudden gasp, then a deep roar of appreciation, followed by booing and hissing. It reminded her of a pantomime crowd.

If only this was just a pantomime…

"Thomas has felled one more man!" yelled William, breaking into her thoughts. "And the other has slunk away like a miserable cur. He has triumphed!" William stamped his boot. "God speed, good Thomas! He has run to get help!"

Hopkirk stepped across and slapped William across the face with his open palm. "Be quiet, dolt! Your foolhardy friend may have escaped but there is no help for miles."

Justine looked across at the six bodies lying dead on the cobbled stones of the yard. Most were dressed in the drab woollen uniform of Hopkirk's militia; but two were clearly distinguished by their brightly coloured silk doublets, expensive ruffs and fine boots.

"And your other two friends will be of no help to you now."

---0---

William rubbed his jaw where Hopkirk had hit it, but even Melrose's triumph could not mask the pain he felt at the sight of his friends lying dead, their foolhardy bravery come to naught.

No more would he hear Oliver Dowland's drunken boasts of the magnificent chest size of his latest conquest, or witness Richard Stanmore's unerring ability to locate a hidden stag as if by smell alone. William could see them now, sitting across the table with goblets of wine, Oliver in full flow on the latest girl he'd found, while William and Richard laughed so hard at his use of his hands to describe her assets that they would nearly choke on their wine; or out on the hunt with Richard pointing at a patch of forest and swearing blind there was a stag in there – and his quiet satisfaction when proved right.

William looked back at the grey man standing next to him. "My good friends Richard Stanmore and Oliver Dowland fought this day with great courage and honour," he said firmly. "Each one of them had more goodness in the smallest part of their smallest finger, than you will ever have in your heart, Master Hopkirk." He took a deep breath. "But what is done is done. If you must have this travesty of a trial, then let us begin."

---0---

Hopkirk stood squarely on the dais and looked down at the sea of faces around him. Despite William's resigned agreement to start, he did not want to begin until the crowd was sufficiently fired up to become the single-minded mob that he needed to drive his trial to a satisfactory conclusion. His life's mission – to seek out and destroy witchcraft wherever it lurked – always required the support of a mob; to make sure that the fear of witchcraft was kept alive at all times, but also to ensure that more witches could be identified later by individual members of the crowd who had been present.

So he waited, letting the momentum build after the excitement of the sword fight.

"Witches! Evil witches!" called out a voice at the front.

"Burn them!" came another voice in response.

"Worshipers of Satan!" came a third.

This was picked up by more voices; more angry shouts and cheers of support.

Hopkirk spread his hands out wide in front of his body, his open palms facing the mob. This generated even more shouts and louder roars – but now they became incoherent, with no single words being clearly heard.

He crossed his fists up high in the sign against witchcraft and the mob went wild – screaming, waving their arms and pitchforks.

He uncrossed his hands and punched the air: the mob gave a mighty, tumultuous roar that could have been heard in the next county – a roar of hatred born of fear coming from hundreds of throats but from a single collective mind.

Hopkirk punched the air twice more, each time producing the same momentous roar, before he decided the mob was ready. He made a sweeping motion with a flat palm and in response, the crowd fell silent.

Every eye was on him. Every man, woman and child, waiting expectantly for the show to begin.

"Good people!" he began. The mob roared its appreciation. He let them shout a moment, then held his hand up for silence.

"Good people – you who worship the Lord Jesus, and who fear God – we are here today to seek God's truth about these three." He waved at William, Justine and Sarah. Again the mob roared, and again he let them a moment, then held his hand up and waited for silence.

"These three are accused of witchcraft and we must test them to see if they have the magic powers! The powers of Satan himself!"

These words worked the mob into its loudest screaming frenzy yet. When silence was eventually restored, Hopkirk continued.

"We will tie each one by the feet and hands and lower them into this well, until they are fully under the waters. If…" he paused for emphasis, "if they have the magic to save themselves, then we will know them truly for a servant of Satan! And what does the Lord Jesus want us to do with the servants of Satan – his bitterest enemy?"

"Burn them! Burn them!" responded the mob.

"Aye, we will burn them! We will banish the Devil with fire!"

Hopkirk turned to some of his men standing nearby and pointed at Justine. "She will go first. Prepare her for the trial!"

---0---

Justine tried hard not to shout out in fear and pain as the men tied ropes around her, binding her arms close to her chest, then secured the free end of the rope that usually held the bucket onto them. Then they tied her feet together with another length of rope, before lifting her up and carrying her over the lip of the well – so she was hanging just above the edge of the well, swaying over the waters far below.

The rope supporting her went up to the capstan in the roof which was attached to a pulley that could be turned by a handle at the side of the well. Justine looked up; there was many yards of rope wound around the capstan – plenty to drop her all the distance down the deep well. It was held by a pin that stopped the pulley wheel from turning.

She looked down at her feet swinging over the black void and tried to fight down the terror of the cold dark waters waiting for her down below.

She heard William's voice from over her shoulder.

"Courage, my love – we will meet again this day in heaven and have all of eternity together."

"I'm not ready for that just yet, William," she muttered, but was not sure if he heard her.

Hopkirk leaned down and picked up a stone from the cobbles, then he held it by Justine.

"Let us see how far down to lower you," he said quietly to her, and let go of the stone.

There was an agonising few seconds as it fell, then they both heard it splash into the dark waters far below.

"Quite a fair way down, my pretty one," he said with a sickening smile, "before the waters test your purity. We will make sure you have sufficient time down there for the test to be most effective."

He stood back and addressed the crowd.

"This woman has blasphemed the Lord, has dressed as a boy in order to confuse, and has caused alarm and fear amongst good, honest God-fearing folk. We will test her now…" he paused and turned to Justine, "unless…" he said quietly.

"Unless what?" asked Justine querulously.

Hopkirk smiled. "Unless you are prepared to confess your witchcraft, and that you worship the Devil."

"What then?" Justine asked, although she knew exactly what his answer would be.

"You will be burned at the stake as a witch."

"As I thought. Well, you know what, Master Matthew Hopkirk," she said, with much more strength than she really felt, "I wouldn't give you the satisfaction."

"Aye, well – I thought not," Hopkirk sighed. Then he turned back to the mob.

"She will not confess! Then let the trial begin!" As the crowd roared, he gestured to a man standing by the handle. "Let her go!"

The man knocked the pin out of the pulley wheel.

Justine screamed, "No, wait!" But it was too late. She felt a sickening lurch in her stomach as the capstan started to spin and she dropped just like Hopkirk's stone, plummeting towards the deathly dark waters below.

With her screams echoing off the black slime-covered walls and the circle of light above her shrinking quickly to a small disc, she fell so fast that she hardly had time to prepare herself. The water came up and hit her with an almighty splash, punching her in the soles of her feet, then knocking the air from her lungs. Immediately, the weight of the ropes pulled her down and the freezing black waters closed over her head.

She felt the water trying to force its way into her nose and mouth and found herself grunting in the back of her throat as she flopped and writhed on the end of the rope like a fish on a line, her chest starting to burn and stars starting to dance in front of her eyes, as the effort to hold her breath became harder and harder, but still she hung on, her grunts ringing louder and louder in her ears until she started to think there really was no hope and maybe she should just let the water in and end it all, and surely it wasn't death that was scary – but rather it was the process of dying that petrified her – and anyway, she'd been dead for all eternity before she had been born, so how hard could it be to do it again – except that she hadn't been dead for all eternity before her birth, she had been alive 450 years before, for two glorious, exciting, momentous weeks, and she'd met William and could have been the next Lady de Beauvais, if only she didn't have to die, if only, if only – oh, sod it, sod it, sod it, sod it, just open your mouth, and end it now, girl…

There was a sudden tug on the rope.

Then another. And a third.

Then the rope started moving jerkily upwards, and then, wonderfully, her head broke clear into the air – the beautiful, glorious, life-giving air that Justine sucked in by the lungful as she found herself being winched slowly up the well, gasping, coughing, retching…

And alive.

She looked above her. The circle of light was becoming larger and larger as she was winched slowly and jerkily up the well shaft, until the light was strong enough to make out the green glistening slime-covered bricks lining the top of the well. Finally she had to screw up her eyes against the bright sunlight as her head emerged over the edge.

Into a scene of stunned silence.

Hopkirk was staring at Justine with a look on his face that she could only interpret as total shock.

William was staring at her open-mouthed, while Sarah looked at her pale and wide-eyed.

Even the man operating the pulley wheel was paper-white as he made the last few turns, then replaced the pin and reached over to pull her back over the side.

It took some time to get the sodden ropes undone, but eventually Justine was standing free by the side of the well, shivering in her soaked nightdress.

"By the Risen Christ, man!" barked William at Hopkirk, as he and Sarah were being untied. "Do you not see how she shivers?"

Hopkirk tore his gaze from Justine and turned slowly to William, as if seeing him for the first time. "Eh?" he muttered.

"She is cold!" said William. "And she is – wet." He indicated her chest. Justine looked down and realised in shock that her soaked nightdress was virtually transparent.

"Aye, aye… indeed," said Hopkirk vaguely. It was clear he had not registered Justine's condition at all. He looked to the silent crowd. "Someone – a cloak or… somesuch." A woollen cloak was found and passed up to Hopkirk, who carefully wrapped it round Justine's shoulders. She pulled it tight to re-establish her modesty – as if her heaving chest had not just been on show to the whole crowd.

She turned to William. "Thank you," she said quietly.

"'Tis no matter." He was equally quiet.

"William," she asked, "what has happened? I nearly drowned down there."

"My love – it was without doubt the strangest thing I – or I believe any man – has ever witnessed. As you descended, a voice was heard.

"A voice?"

"Aye. It was as loud and as clear as the voice of the finest orator – but no man could be seen speaking." He studied her closely, then he whispered, "My sweet Mary, it was the voice of our true Lord Jesus Christ."

"Christ?" She was suitably shocked.

"Aye. Christ himself."

"What did he say?"

"He said – and I'll remember these words till the day I die – he said, "Matthew Hopkirk – I am the Lord Jesus Christ and I say before these people that you do not act in my name. Mary Fox is my loyal handmaiden – she is not now, nor has she ever been, a witch. Matthew Hopkirk, you are a servant of Satan and I call upon you in the name of God my Father, to end this trial now."

"He said all that?"

"Those very words, in front of me, Hopkirk and this whole crowd."

Justine smiled. "That was nice of him."

They became aware that Hopkirk had started to address the people gathered round the well. "The trial is over," he said. "We have heard from the Lord Jesus himself that there is no witchcraft here. Go to your homes, go to your church, and worship him who has spoken to us this day."

But the crowd did not move. Instead Justine could hear some angry murmurings starting amongst them.

"Go now!" commanded Hopkirk. "The trial is over."

The murmurings swelled and became louder. Angry exchanges were starting within the crowd. Justine watched as the anger built amongst them and within them, growing and building, feeding on itself as more and more heated exchanges took place. All it needed was a spark and the crowd would once again turn ugly.

It was Hopkirk himself who provided that spark.

He raised his hand to try and silence the crowd, just as he had before Justine had gone down the well. But the power he had wielded earlier was gone – stripped away by a divine accusation of Satanism – and instead of placating and silencing the crowd, it reminded them of the hold he'd had over them.

And they didn't like it.

"You are a worshipper of Satan!" shouted a voice.

"We thought you were a man of God!" said another. "You had us for fools!"

"You would lead us on the path to Hell!" said another.

Hopkirk tried again. "Good people…" he began.

"We'll not be called good by you!" shouted a further voice, which was followed by a cheer from the crowd.

Once again they were starting to become a single-minded mob – but not one that Hopkirk could control.

And as a single-minded mob, they surged forward towards the dais.

"Stop them!" screamed Hopkirk to those of his men who were nearby. But they, too had heard the voice – and they too held their positions.

The crowd surged further forward and several sturdy-looking peasants ran up onto the dais with their pitchforks held forward as weapons. Hopkirk was pushed quickly backwards against the side of the well.

Justine, William and Sarah stood to one side, watching. "I fear Master Hopkirk now knows what it is to be the accused," observed William with a smile.

"Aye, Master," said Sarah. "But why do they not skewer him now? He is in their power."

"Belike they will shortly," said William. "Have patience."

They saw Hopkirk retreating from the pitchforks as far as he could, then it looked as if he was going to try to get in a position to address the crowd again. Keeping a close eye on the pitchforks, he reached up with one hand and grasped the roof post of the well, then used it to pull himself up, until he was standing on the edge of the well itself with his back supported by the roof. The pitchforks were raised up accordingly, to keep him under threat.

"My people…!" he began.

At that moment a loud, piercing scream came from within the crowd.

It was a long, drawn-out scream of pain, rage and anguish, and it made Justine shiver despite the cloak drawn around her shoulders.

Hopkirk stared into the crowd from his vantage position up on the well, and his face paled as he watched.

The screaming continued, and it was getting closer.

Justine saw the crowd turn to look at the screaming person, then part like the Red Sea before Moses to let them through.

A small hooded figure emerged out of the crowd.

She thought it was incredible that such a small person could make such a noise, but there was no doubt where it was coming from.

Then the screaming stopped. The figure stepped up onto the dais, pushing pitchforks aside to get to where Hopkirk was perching on the side of the well. The figure stood in front of him a moment, looking up, before pushing back the hood to reveal itself.

It was Margaret.

Hopkirk went even whiter than before.

"You would have killed me, Master Hopkirk!" she said, her voice carrying clearly across the silent crowd, "when I had done all for you."

"Margaret!" Hopkirk managed a watery smile, blinking furiously. "How good it is to see you well!"

"Aye, and no thanks to you – it is thanks to Lady Alice who found me on the road and gave me care and water after I had all but died at the hands of your man."

"Lady Alice – indeed – how wonderful…"

"And now we have heard the word of God himself, that tells us that you follow Satan!" Margaret reached across to the villager next to her, snatched the pitchfork out of his hand and brandished it at Hopkirk.

"So Matthew Hopkirk, I would you join your master!"

She thrust the pitchfork violently forward. It caught Hopkirk squarely in the stomach, forcing him to double up and his head to drop down below the edge of the well roof, so that he had nothing now to support him.

He lost his balance.

For a moment he scrabbled at the roof of the well above him, but he could not get a grip and with a despairing yell, he dropped backwards like a felled tree.

His head hit the far wall with a sickening crack that drew a collective gasp from the nearest villagers, before he slid down into the hungry black mouth of the well.

For a split second he appeared to be suspended there, then, with a swirling of his grey cloak, he disappeared from view.

The crowd held its collective breath as the body plummeted down the long well shaft, thumping and bouncing off the walls.

Then a loud splash echoed up from the depths.

Shocked, no one made a sound.

Then a lone voice shouted out, "Hopkirk is dead! The servant of Satan is gone to meet his master!"

Another voice responded "Yes! Christ has saved us!"

"The Lord has blessed us!"

"Now we are freed from Satan's grasp!"

Then a cheer went up, and soon everyone was shouting, throwing their hats and pitchforks in the air and shaking their fists. There was much congratulating and clapping of backs, as well as some dancing round in jubilation. Many villagers ran over to Jake's cart and started filling their tankards with celebratory pints of ale.

William turned to Justine and Sarah and shouted, "This is a most welcome outcome! We are well rid of that monster!"

"Indeed, my lord," yelled Sarah, "he has truly gone to meet his master!"

"I warrant Satan will welcome him with open arms, even while devising some eternal torture," yelled William.

"Yes, Sir William, I warrant he will!"

"Christ has forsaken him – and this we have heard in his own voice!" William shook his head in wonder. "That I have lived to see this day – that is the true miracle." He looked at Justine. "What say you, Mary, my love?"

But Justine was not listening to him, instead she was staring across to the far edge of the crowd.

Sarah's mother – whose name she now knew was Ruth – was standing apart from the rest of the villagers and was studying something in her hand that looked like a small, rectangular black stone. As Justine watched, Ruth dropped the object into her apron pocket.

Justine smiled to herself.

The plan she had devised to humiliate Hopkirk had worked out spectacularly in the end, even if not exactly in the way she had envisaged.

The plan had required some preparation, as well as the phone, speaker and solar charger she had kept securely hidden in her bag. It had also taken all her powers of persuasion on her secret accomplice – Ruth.

They had met the evening before in a quiet corner of the rose garden. Justine had shown Ruth the phone and Bluetooth speaker, both on full power thanks to the solar charger, and had explained her plan.

At first it seemed that for all her earlier interest in seeing a 'black stone' – and her general open-mindedness – Ruth was still very much a woman of the 16th century.

"This thing, that you call a 'phone' – you are telling me it is not magic?" Ruth had asked dubiously, as she turned it over and over in her hand.

"No," said Justine. "Because it can only do what it has been made to do, and it only responds to set commands. Many hundreds and hundreds of these phones are made every year in my time, and each one is the same – each one does exactly the same thing if you give it the same command. That is no different to the bread that rises if it is made and baked correctly, or the gown that looks the same as another gown, if you cut it to the same pattern and sew it the same way. As I said before, these things are not magic."

"And you want me to command this stone to speak in the voice of the Lord?" Ruth looked up at her with worry written into every line on her face.

"Yes, I do, if it will make Hopkirk look a fool and stop him doing his trial, assuming he does get past our defences and into the manor.

"And if I touch the stone in a special sequence, as you say you will instruct me, then the voice of our Lord Jesus will issue forth from this other thing?" Ruth gestured at the speaker. "That is surely blasphemy and I will suffer eternal damnation."

"It is not the real voice of Jesus," said Justine, thinking fast. "As you say, we could not command Him to speak. But we can make Hopkirk think it is Him, which is not blasphemy if we're doing His work, is it?"

"Perhaps." Ruth studied the phone. "Perhaps not. Show me how it makes pictures that move."

Justine took the phone and found a music video. "There." She handed it back.

Ruth watched in amazement. "And these are not people as small as beetles who inhabit the inside of this phone?" she asked.

"No, look." Justine turned the phone horizontally and the image resized bigger. "There – it makes the picture bigger when you turn it. The people are not there, their actions were captured once before and can be shown on any phone like this one, whenever you command it." She pressed the stop button and sighed briefly, as Howard, Jason, Gary and Mark disappeared from the screen.

"Hmmm." Ruth looked up. "So how then, do I command the voice of our Lord?"

Justine took the phone and patiently instructed Ruth on the sequence of swipes to open the voice app, find the text file she'd previously written, and play it through the Bluetooth speaker.

"And you will have secretly placed this thing you call a 'speaker' in the roof of the well?"

Yes, I'll secure it up in the roof out of sight. I'll do it tonight and check it again each day in case Hopkirk gets in."

"And I am to make the voice of the Lord speak out when Hopkirk is about to start his trial?"

"Yes." Justine smiled nervously. "Please don't leave it till William or I go down the well – that will surely be too late."

"I will try," answered Ruth. She looked up with a frown. "But I must remember the sequence of commands with my finger, and start to perform them in good time. How should I know when to begin? And I must not be seen tapping on this black stone by honest folk, or they will think I have taken leave of my senses and carry me away."

"Ruth, I am really grateful that you are helping me," said Justine.

"Aye, well, you are a good woman, or at least my daughter tells me so," said Ruth, then she added with a sly smile, "and as I have seen with my own eyes, very much enamoured of the master. 'Tis enough for me."

"Thank you," said Justine. "I hope we never have to put this plan into action, but if we do, I know you'll get the timing just right."

'And she very nearly didn't,' thought Justine, as she stood on the dais the next morning, watching Ruth drop the phone in her apron pocket and hurry away from the celebrating crowd in the well yard. 'One more second – just one more second fumbling with the phone and it would all have been too late.'

She turned to William.

"You spoke, my lord?"

"Aye. I would know your thoughts?"

"My thoughts, my lord?"

"On how it is a miracle that I have lived to see this day."

Justine looked at Sir William de Beauvais and suddenly it was as if she were seeing him for the very first time.

This handsome, charming, strong, sensitive man from history, whose portrait she had so often gazed at in the Great Hall, who she now loved and who truly loved her back; this man had been destined to die some two weeks before.

It was not a miracle that caused him now to be standing in front of her, very much alive.

He was here now because of her; because of Justine Parker.

Because she had somchow fallen through a freak time portal and abandoned her own time in favour of his.

Because she had known what would happen to him on that fateful night, and was there in disguise to try and do something to save him.

Because she was able to use her 21st century technology to convince a murderous mob to switch their anger onto the very man who would have killed her and William.

"No, my lord," she said with a shake of her head, "it was not a miracle."

She smiled warmly, with love dancing in her eyes.

"I think it was fate."

CHAPTER TWENTY-NINE

The wedding of Sir William de Beauvais and Mary Fox was celebrated on a glorious October Saturday, eight weeks later.

The ceremony took place in the little chapel at Grangedean Manor that sat a hundred yards away from the house down a path through the gold and brown autumn trees.

It was along this path that the bride and her entourage processed towards the chapel to the sound of its pealing bells, past cheering crowds of well-wishers who had come up from the village to see Mary Fox become the next Lady de Beauvais.

Her entourage consisted of the ten-year-old twin sons of Alice Mansfield as page boys and three small girls as her bridesmaids. She had picked them specially; Amy and Elizabeth Stanmore aged five and seven, and eight-year-old Olivia Dowland. Their job was to hold up the hem of Mary Fox's gown and stop it dragging in the dusty track, and it was a job these girls performed with great enthusiasm and rather too much giggling.

Walking nervously alongside was Sarah, once Mary Fox's maid and now elevated to the position of her lady-in-waiting. Sarah looked uncomfortable in an elegant pale blue velvet gown with blue and white patterned sleeves and matching underskirt. Her long dark hair flowed down to her waist and round her head was a thin wooden band garlanded with lilies of the valley.

Without a break in her stride, or in her smiling and waving at the villagers, Justine inclined her head towards her lady-in-waiting and whispered, "Keep your chin up, Sarah, you have every right to be here and to be looking so lovely in that dress."

"Mistress Mary, you are most kind," answered Sarah, her cheeks starting to flush. "But I cannot help but wonder if every villager's eye is on me, asking how a lowly maid has been so elevated that she wears such finery and walks by the side of such a noble lady as yourself."

"Nonsense," replied Justine. "They are very happy for you, and rightly so." She smiled at the cheering crowd. "It seems to me, Sarah, that they are as pleased to see me wed today, as they once were to see me drowned."

"Aye," replied Sarah. "They know you are favoured by Jesus, and revile Hopkirk as a servant of Satan."

Justine spotted Jake and Agnes, who were serving tankards of ale off their cart by the side of the path. She gave them a cheery wave, then chuckled to herself as she thought she must look like minor 21st century royalty. Agnes waved back, dancing round on the tips of her toes with joy.

"Truly, Sarah," said Justine from the side of her mouth, "now they wish us well."

"You are a vision of beauty, my lady," answered Sarah.

"Thanks to you. This dress is magnificent – and I would not have known how to go about having it made if you had not been there."

"You have learned so much these last two months, my lady. You've not once mentioned 'where I come from' this many a week."

Justine stopped and turned to Sarah. "No, I don't suppose I have," she said slowly. Then she turned and pointed back at the manor house still visible beyond the cedar trees behind them. "I suppose that is where I come from now."

"Yes, my lady," said Sarah firmly. "It is."

They walked on a few more yards and stopped at the door of the chapel.

"Let me check the dress, my lady," said Sarah, and made some small adjustments. After a moment she stood back and looked Justine up and down.

Her mistress was clothed in a gown of the finest ivory silk, made by the best team of seamstresses in London that Sarah could find. The bodice was bordered with silver thread, embroidered with a thousand tiny seed pearls and lined with white sable fur. The underskirt was visible from the front and was of pale blue satin and embroidered with intricate floral patterns in silver. Her sleeves were of ivory silk, slashed to show the pale blue satin lining beneath. A single pearl on a silver chain hung at her throat and on her head was a simple, elegant French hood in white velvet surmounted by a double row of pearls.

"Perfect, my lady," said Sarah. "Just perfect."

---0---

Sir William and Thomas Melrose were standing together in the front pew of the small whitewashed chapel, with the curate standing holding his prayer book in front of them.

William looked round towards the door.

"My lord, you will strain your neck if you keep turning so every minute," muttered Thomas. "She will be here soon, upon my oath."

"Aye," answered William. "But I would catch sight of her the instant she appears."

"You will see her shortly, then you will have a whole lifetime to gaze like a love-struck youth upon her fair face," said Thomas with a smile.

"Aye. And I would it would begin soon," said William, staring down the chapel.

Every row of pews was crammed full of guests. He picked out Robert Wychwoode, Jane Melrose and Sarah's mother Ruth, who was now excelling herself as the manor's new housekeeper.

An ancient man hobbled in, leaning heavily on a stick, almost doubled over so his forked beard trailed on the flagstones. He pushed in to sit at the end of one of the rows.

"Dr. Frobisher! I had no idea he was still alive," said William.

His gaze moved to the row directly behind him, and he caught sight of his own mother. She gave him a teary smile as she played with the diamond on the chain around her neck.

"My mother is so pleased to see me wed at last," said William as he turned round again to Thomas, "that she would cry like a babe."

"She is pleased to see you settle yourself as a husband, and no doubt soon a father," answered Thomas. "Or maybe she is crying because she fears your beautiful bride may choose not to arrive here today."

William heard some sounds coming into the chapel through the slightly-open door and lifted his hand to silence his friend.

"I'll warrant from the sound of cheering outside, that she is arrived now," he said.

There was movement as the door was pulled open, then suddenly he saw his bride standing at the end of the chapel, silhouetted against the autumn sun so that she looked like a ghost with a golden halo. Then she stepped forward a couple of paces and the door was shut behind her.

Beams of light from the high windows shone down on her. William caught his breath. "By all that is holy," he whispered, "there is not another girl in the whole of England more fair."

"She is a true beauty," agreed Thomas. "You are a lucky man indeed, my friend."

The bride glided slowly up the aisle, with Sarah beside her and her attendants following behind. As she drew level with William, she held up her hand, and he took it, then stepped out beside her, facing the curate.

---0---

Justine held her breath a moment, resisting the urge to gaze up at William. Instead she gave a little squeeze of his hand and was rewarded with a squeeze in return.

The curate looked at each of them and nodded.

"Dearly beloved friends," he read from his prayer book, "we are gathered together here in the sight of God, and in the face of his congregation, to join together this man and this woman in holy matrimony, which is an honourable estate, instituted of God in Paradise, in the time of man's innocence, signifying unto us the mystical union that is betwixt Christ and his Church: which holy estate Christ adorned and beautified with his presence, and first miracle that he wrought, in Cana of Galilee, and is commended of Saint Paul to be honourable among all men; and therefore is not to be enterprised, nor taken in hand unadvisedly, lightly, or wantonly, to satisfy men's carnal lusts and appetites, like brute beasts that have no understanding: but reverently, discretely, advisedly, soberly, and in the fear of God, duly considering the causes for which Matrimony was ordained. One was the procreation of children, to be brought up in the fear and nurture of the Lord, and praise of God. Secondly it was ordained for a remedy against sin, and to avoid fornication…" the curate looked up and gave both bride and groom a significant stare, "…that such persons as have not the gift of continence might marry, and keep themselves undefiled members of Christ's body. Thirdly, for the mutual society, help, and comfort, that the one ought to have of the other, both in prosperity and adversity; into the which holy estate these two persons present come now to be joined."

He paused and coughed loudly, as if to make sure the congregation were aware he was coming to an important bit. "Therefore if any man can show any just cause, why they may not lawfully be joined together: let him now speak, or else hereafter for ever hold his peace."

The curate looked up and glowered at every member of the congregation in turn, but thankfully no one spoke.

"I require and charge you," he continued, "as you will answer at the dreadful day of judgment, when the secrets of all hearts shall be disclosed, that if either of you do know any impediment, why ye may not be lawfully joined together in Matrimony, that ye confess it. For be ye well assured, that so many as be coupled together otherwise than God's word doth allow, are not joined together by God, neither is their Matrimony lawful."

He turned to William. "Sir William de Beauvais, wilt thou have this woman to thy wedded wife, to live together after God's ordinance in the holy estate of Matrimony? Wilt thou love her, comfort her, honour, and keep her in sickness and in health? And forsaking all other keep thee only to her, so long as you both shall live?

William looked at Justine, then back at the curate.

"I will," he answered firmly.

The curate turned to Justine.

"Wilt thou have this man to thy wedded husband, to live together after God's ordinance, in the holy estate of Matrimony? Wilt thou obey him, and serve him, love, honour, and keep him, in sickness and in health and forsaking all others keep thee only unto him, so long as you both shall live?"

She took a breath, knowing that the next two words she uttered would mean her life could never be the same again.

No more Justine Parker, the girl from 21st century Hammersmith.

Now she would forever be Lady Mary de Beauvais, the loving wife of a Tudor knight. Maybe the mother of his children.

She said, "I will."

---0---

The rest of the ceremony passed in something of a blur for the new Lady Mary de Beauvais.

She remembered Sarah stepping forward to give her away and the vows being exchanged with her and William agreeing to 'have and to hold from this day forward, for better, for worse, for richer, for poorer, in sickness and in health, to love, and to cherish, till death us depart'. She thought how little the service had changed in over 400 years – and with a small tinge of sadness – what a shame it was that her parents were not there to see it.

But the future that her parents inhabited was now firmly in her past; her role now was to live her life to the full as the new Lady de Beauvais, and to make a new family with William. Her old family from 2015 would have to be kept secure in the hidden recesses of her mind, just like the phone, charger and Bluetooth speaker that were safely locked away in a little jewelled box in her room.

So when William put the ring on her finger, she thought it was so beautiful she could not stop looking at it, all through the dull prayers that followed and which seemed to go on for hours.

Eventually the prayers were over and she and William emerged together from the chapel into the glorious autumn sunshine, and were greeted by the sound of the villagers cheering them to the tops of the golden brown trees.

CHAPTER THIRTY

The CEO stood in the middle of the hall, his hands thrust deep into the pockets of his jeans, looking around him. He looked in his mid-forties, tall with short grey hair and small round glasses. His gaze stopped on the picture of the blond knight with the white stag.

"Who's that guy?" he asked

"That's Sir William de Beauvais, the owner of Grangedean Manor from the 1560s," said Mrs. Warburton. "A very interesting man indeed."

"Why so?"

"He married late by Tudor standards, after he had been accused of witchcraft and nearly drowned in a ducking trial."

"The guy was the lord of the manor? Why was he accused of witchcraft?"

"It's unusual, I agree. He was accused by implication, trying to protect a girl. The girl that, in fact, he later married."

"A romantic, huh?" The CEO looked at the picture. "Did they give witches a rough ride in Elizabethan times?" he asked. "I thought that was later – in the 1600s. Salem and all that."

"Salem was in America, but we had our fair share here as well. But you're right – in Elizabeth's reign many people didn't believe in witches; there was none of the mass hysteria of the later Puritan era. Witchfinders would have to whip up the hatred and fear in order to get the mob on their side."

He moved to the next picture, a portrait of a handsome smiling Tudor woman in her mid-50s. "Who's this dame?"

"That's Lady Mary de Beauvais, Sir William's wife. She, too, was a remarkable woman. She was accused of witchcraft and tried by ducking in the well – but it is said that the heavens opened and Jesus himself appeared, claiming she was his chosen one and not a witch at all."

"That has gotta be mass hysteria."

"For sure. The interesting thing is that there are several accounts that corroborate the story, so it must have been a mass hallucination that felt very real to the people who were there."

The CEO studied the picture of Lady Mary. "She was a fine-looking woman."

"Indeed – she was known as a real beauty in her youth." Mrs. Warburton moved closer to the portrait and gave it deeper inspection. "But she was also known as a very progressive, forward-thinking woman – and prepared to fight for what she believed was right."

The CEO walked on, his Converse sneakers squeaking on the flagstones. He stared at each of the tapestries and the leaded windows in turn.

"Place like this has gotta be haunted?" he demanded.

"Certainly," said Mrs. Warburton. "An old house such as this has to have its ghosts."

"Cool. What's the ghost here? A headless woman?"

"Oh no. It is the ghost they call the Grey Man. He is sometimes seen in the bedroom wing; people have seen him standing in the corridor as they come through the door from the gallery, but as they get closer he disappears through the wall." She paused a moment. "But most often he is seen out in the car park by the old well. They say that every year just as the sun goes down on the 14th of August, the Grey Man can be seen standing by the well in the courtyard and holding his hands out as if addressing a crowd. Then he turns and glides through the side of the well and disappears. The local people will tell you that if something bad is going to happen around here, then it invariably happens on the 14th of August." She shook her head ruefully.

"They say it is always the fault of the Grey Man."

---0---

It was early the following evening as Rick the catering manager stamped up the stairs from the kitchens and into the Great Hall. A massive storm was coming and he wanted to get home before it hit.

He was also in a foul mood. The night before he had had to fire one of the actresses hired as a serving girl for the banquet, and now she had put in a formal complaint.

The girl had come down the stairs carrying too many pewter plates and had missed her footing on the bottom step; she had fallen headlong and thrown all her plates into the air, so that they had crashed down to the flagstone floor causing breakages and mess everywhere.

Rick had let his annoyance show, barking out, "Oh effing hell! What the frigging heck was that?"

The girl had been insolent, saying. "Sorry, Rick," like she didn't mean it in the slightest.

"Sorry?" he had said grimly. "Sorry? You'll be effing sorry if you don't clear up that effing mess. You'll be out on your effing ear!"

"Sorry," repeated the girl, and went forward to pick up the first plate. But then she had clutched at her leg, muttered something about being hurt, and had just started to walk out of the kitchen, leaving him to clear up.

So he'd stopped her and told her she was fired, and to get out for good.

Now he'd had an email from the agency telling him she'd complained and saying he was out of order. They were threatening to withdraw all their staff before the next banquet.

Rick went through the low door and into the hall. Out of the windows he could see the sky was so dark with the approaching storm, it was almost as if it was a winter's night. It looked like he was too late – it was going to hit any second.

A few of the electric candle lights were on in the Great Hall, and Rick's eye caught the picture of Lady Mary de Beauvais on the wall. He glanced at it, and as he did so a flash of lightning lit up the room with a burning intensity that seared a negative of the picture into his brain. Immediately afterwards, there was a deep blast of thunder that made the windows shake and the whole room resonate like a giant drum.

At the same moment, the lights went out.

With the image of the picture dancing in front of his unseeing eyes, he turned and made his way by feel and force of habit to the main doors, as another roar of thunder shook the room and a searing flash of lightning lit it up as if it were broad daylight. He reached the main double doors and pulled – but they remained stuck. He pulled again and again, as yet another flash of lightning lit up the room, followed by another crash of thunder. This one was so loud, that Rick thought his ears had burst. He pulled at the door again, but it remained stuck firm. He pummelled on it, shouting, but was sure no one would be able to hear above the sound of the rain and the echoes of the thunder.

Another bolt of lightning lit up the room and he ran to the door to the kitchens that he had come through only a few moments ago. He knew it couldn't be locked – it didn't have a lock on it at all. But like the main doors, it too was firmly closed. He beat on it till his fists hurt, but no one came.

Another bolt of lightning.

Another immediate massive crash of thunder – the loudest yet.

After the massive crash came further loud secondary rumbles. They rolled on, one after another, but seeming to get louder and louder so that soon he was sure they were louder than the original crash.

Then he heard the voices…

END OF PART 1

PART 2

THE ALCHEMIST'S ARMS

CHAPTER ONE

Southwark, November 1574

The waterman shipped his oars and let the little boat drift slowly up to the dark jetty. As the bow bumped against it, he clambered out and secured the line to a small rusty cleat.

He turned to the two sodden men still hunched in the stern of the boat.

"Southwark, sirs," he muttered. "As bidden."

At first the two men seemed stuck to their seats, as if pressed down by the cold, unrelenting rain that had accompanied them across the Thames from the little wharf at Queenhythe. The waterman stared curiously at their dark shapes silhouetted against the shimmering water, as if unsure how he was going to get them out of his boat. Then he gave a barely perceptible sigh and held out his hand to the nearest man. The man looked at it in disgust, but then grabbed hold and used it to step safely onto the glistening planks of the jetty.

While the first man was shaking the rain out of his hat, the waterman held out his hand to the second.

"I am perfectly capable of disembarking from a wherry!" the second man snapped, and the waterman moved back. With a grunt of annoyance, the man stood up and stepped carefully onto the jetty.

"Wait here," said the first man. "We will be in need of a return to Queenhythe later."

"The bear pit is closed at this time of night," observed the waterman. He gave a small snigger. "If that is why you are here, of course."

There was a heavy silence, punctuated only by the gentle rhythmic thump of the boat against the jetty and the patter of rain on the water. The men stood as still as statues, and the waterman started to wonder if they had even heard him. He cleared his throat and tried again. "Because if it is girls you want…" then suddenly he found himself staggering backwards, propelled by the point of a dagger pushed up into the soft base of his jaw, and ended up pressed hard against a slimy wooden post. "Oh, we are not here for the stews of Southwark, knave," came the voice of the second man, with soft but unmistakable venom. "If that is what you are suggesting."

The waterman said nothing, but pressed his head further back on the wooden post, his eyes fixed on the blade that was just visible in the darkness.

"Nay, knave, we are not here for whores." The blade pressed a little deeper and the waterman winced as he felt it break through the skin. "We are on private business – and if you have any sense you will wait here to carry us back to Queenhythe, then you will most assuredly forget that you ever saw us."

The dagger pressed a little deeper.

The waterman remained silent, unable to speak.

Then the dagger was pulled back, and the man turned away. Immediately the waterman put his hand to his throat to stem the hot blood that started to ooze out.

"Or belike I will seek you out and let my blade here finish the task. Do I make myself clear?"

"Indeed you do, good sir," the waterman answered, his voice coming out as an unnatural, guttural croak. "I will be here to take you back across the river." He rubbed his throat. "No matter how long that might be," he added with an attempt at a thin smile."

"Good. Make sure you are." The man sheathed his dagger then stepped off the jetty and onto the street beyond. "Or I will find you, be assured of that."

---0---

The two companions walked the Southwark streets in silence a few moments, their leather shoes squelching in the mud and filth.

Suddenly the first man stopped. "Why did you threaten that man so, Frances?" he asked sharply.

The other man stopped also. "Nay, Tom, had I not been clear on the consequences, he would be back in his boat and rowing for his life the moment we had stepped away from the jetty. Then we would have been stranded in this hellish mud pit for the night, forced to wait for the bridge to open in the morning. Besides," he added, "a small threat to secure our easier return to civilisation is a fair trade."

"Aye," answered Tom, following close behind, "and raising a hue and cry for the murder of a wherryman would help our cause better?"

"Do not give him the dignity of an honest trade, my friend," snapped Francis. "Did you not take offence, as did I, at his suggestion that we were here for the Southwark stews? Why else, he was suggesting, do gentlemen steal across to Southwark at dead of night?"

"We gave him no better reason." Tom was silent a moment as he trudged through the street; the dark, oppressive houses looming overhead against the night sky. "Perhaps we should have let him think we were here for a couple of whores. 'Tis a better reason than the truth."

"Nonsense. What if his next passenger was someone who knows us? A knave such as he would be sure to boast of the two fine gentlemen he carried across to the brothels of Southwark."

Tom snorted in disbelief. "Now it is you who is talking nonsense." He stopped as his foot sank deep into a puddle, and foul brown water slopped up his ankle. "By the Lord's Wounds, Francis, curse this God-forsaken place! My shoes are ruined! This is my best pair!"

"Stop your whining," snarled Francis. "I will have reason to have a better pair made for you if we succeed in our venture." He marched on through the mud. "And a fine pair for myself as well," he added.

"Aye, but no need of a new hat if it fails," muttered Tom, shaking the muddy water off his shoe and trudging after him through the dark.

---0---

Tom caught up with his companion at the next street corner. Francis had stopped and was scanning each of two possible alleys that forked away in front of them.

"I do not recall which of these I was to follow in the instructions I was given," he muttered.

Tom studied each in turn. "They look much the same to me," he said.

"That does not help."

"Let us try the left first," Tom said reasonably. "Then if that is not correct, we can always re-trace our steps back, and try the right."

Half an hour later they stopped again.

"By the Risen Christ," snarled Francis, peering around in the dark. "I warrant we have been at this corner at least twice before. We are now completely lost."

"At least the rain has stopped," Tom pointed out, trying to sound reasonable.

"Small comfort," Francis snapped back.

"I was sure we were tracing our steps back to the fork in the road."

Francis gave a dismissive snort. "We will walk that way," he muttered, pointing along an alley. It was darkened by oppressive timber houses with their 'jetty' upper stories leaning in towards each other, like giants squaring up for a fight.

It was not long before they came upon a tavern sign swinging in the night air, bearing the name 'The Blue Maid' and a picture of a girl milking a cow. "See here," said Tom, pointing up. "I say we step inside and ask the good men of Southwark if they can help us."

Without waiting for Francis, he walked down a short dark passageway that opened out into a courtyard, brightly lit by several flaming braziers. A half-open door to one side revealed more light and the sound of voices. Tom pushed it open and Francis followed him into the tavern.

As they made their way through the warm fug of candle smoke, Tom spotted a table with two empty seats next to a couple of elderly labourers. He sat down.

Francis sat opposite him and looked round in distaste.

The room held around fifteen wooden tables and benches, each with several men sitting at them nursing tankards of ale. They mostly wore the rough clothes of labourers and peasants, although there were a few better-off yeomen. A couple of peasant girls were travelling round the tables with pitchers of ale, filling tankards as they went.

One of these girls appeared with two tankards and thumped them down on the table. Tom gave her a three-farthing coin, which she bit carefully then pocketed, seeming satisfied with its authenticity. Then she slopped ale into each tankard and moved away. Francis stared down coldly at some solid object floating in the brown liquid, then picked it out and flicked it away.

One of the labourers at their table put down his tankard and stared suspiciously at the two newcomers, then touched his cap in a gesture of servility that seemed to Tom to be only just short of insolence.

"We do not often see fine gentlemen such as yourselves in the Blue Maid," he said, his eyebrow raised.

"Filthy night," answered Tom levelly. "We sought shelter from the downpour."

"Aye, that will be the reason," replied the labourer, with a small knowing smile on his face. "For it is sure not the ale that draws you in." He looked pointedly at Francis.

"Now listen, fellow…" snapped Francis, "mind your ton…" He stopped sharply as Tom kicked him under the table. "By Christ's Wounds, Thomas…?"

The labourer laughed. "Your companion is a sensible fellow, sir, as is his foot," he said.

Francis said nothing, but his mouth closed like a trap and Tom noticed a red flush start to creep out from under his ruff and spread up his cheek.

"You are right, sir," said Tom, with a faint, and he hoped, conciliatory smile. "This is not our usual place to drink." He paused a moment, choosing his words carefully. "But the truth is that while we were indeed seeking shelter, we are in Southwark to find a particular man who lives hereabouts."

"He must be a special fellow," observed the other labourer.

"Or he owes you money," said the first, and gave a great roar of laughter which ended in uncontrolled coughing and gulping of ale.

Tom waited until the paroxysms had died down, then said, "No, we have heard tell of his powers and we sought to meet him."

"He has powers?" asked the first labourer. "Does he practice sorcery?"

"No, no," Tom said quickly. "I do not think his powers come from sorcery. They say he is known as…" he paused, "the Alchemist."

If he was hoping for an awed reaction, he was disappointed.

"Plenty of folk round here known by that name," the labourer said matter-of-factly. "Thriving trade by those who will tell you they have the secret of turning base metal into gold."

"They say," cut in Francis with a tight-lipped smile, "that he can be known by the pictures painted onto his arms." He placed his own arms on the table. "He has two muskets in the form of a cross, on this one," he pointed to his right forearm, "and on the other, a single short-barrelled piece, but which has no lock or other visible sign as to how it could possibly be loaded."

"Ah, that Alchemist." The two labourers exchanged a significant look.

"You know this man?" Tom looked at each in turn, his eyebrows raised.

"Aye."

"And you can direct us to where we might find him?"

"Aye."

"Then please be good enough to do so."

There was a moment's silence. "He is not far from this place," said the first labourer.

"Mighty close," said the second.

"You will soon find him," added the first.

They both drained their tankards, taking their time.

"By thunder!" exploded Francis, rising from the bench with his hand reaching for the dagger at his belt, his face now deep red all over. "Will you tell…?" He sat down abruptly as Tom again kicked him hard under the table.

Tom waited until Francis' face had started to fade back to its more usual colour, then asked quietly, "Where is this Alchemist?"

"That table over there," said the first labourer with a smile. He pointed across the tavern to where a thin man with no hat and dark spiky hair was sitting, talking to two yeomen.

"Over there?" Francis sounded incredulous.

"The very man, sir."

"Christ's Blood, you could have said…"

"Nay, good fellow," Tom held up a restraining hand to Francis, "these worthy men of Southwark have had some sport at our expense – we should leave it at that." He drained his tankard and stood up. "Come, we have business with the Alchemist." He gave a small nod to the two labourers. "Good evening, sirs." Without waiting for Francis, he started threading his way across the tavern to the Alchemist's table.

Francis stood also, gave a hard-eyed stare at each of the labourers in turn, then stepped over the bench and hurried off after Tom. He joined his companion in front of the Alchemist's table.

The three seated men looked up at them, their eyebrows raised in enquiry. "I am told you are the one known as the Alchemist," said Tom, to the spiky-haired man.

The man looked them both up and down in turn, then gave a barely-perceptible nod.

"I am," he said slowly. "Who's asking?"

Tom said, "One who would talk with you in private."

The Alchemist stared at them for what seemed an uncomfortably long time, then he glanced at the two yeomen at his table.

"Leave us."

The yeomen said nothing, but both stood up and made their way to another table.

Tom and Francis sat down in their places, opposite the Alchemist. Tom glanced at the man's arms, which were sleeveless. There were the pictures as had been described; the strange hand-gun on the left and the crossed muskets on the right.

"What do you want from me?" the Alchemist asked.

Tom took a deep breath, glancing around to ensure that in the hubbub of the tavern, their words would not be overheard.

"It is just possible you can help us," he said quietly, "in a matter of the greatest importance to the future of England…"

CHAPTER TWO

Grangedean Manor, February 1575

Lady Mary de Beauvais leaned forward towards her son.

"You will do well to stop looking like you have bitten on a lemon," she whispered, "and start being thankful for these people's kindness."

She stood back. There was a long moment of silence.

"Yes, Lady Mother," the boy muttered.

She leaned forward again. "I mean it, Ambrose," she whispered, this time putting a little more steel in her voice. "The Grenville family are being most kind in taking you into their house and having you educated with their son – it is a real privilege."

"Yes, Lady Mother." The boy's head dropped and he seemed to be studying the hem of her voluminous skirts.

"So would you prefer your father and I sent you to the grammar school instead?" She put her hand under his chin and lifted it up, searching his eyes for some recognition of the sacrifice she was making.

She was sending him away from Grangedean Manor, and it was breaking her heart.

Yes, it was only for one year, but even a few days without her son by her side seemed almost unbearable.

She forced a smile.

"They will teach you better hunting and archery skills, and you will make great friends with Richard Grenville." She stood back again, still holding his chin. "There will be jousting and swordsmanship, too."

"I just want to stay at home, Lady Mother." His big, liquid eyes looked up at her – and that was when the hardness in her heart melted – like butter in a hot pan.

"Oh Bambi," she cried softly, as she pulled his small body into her arms, "I will miss you dreadfully – but I know it is the right thing to do." She kissed him on the forehead and once again stood back. "One day you will be Sir Ambrose de Beauvais, the head of our family and you need to know what it is to be a leading member of society. What better way to learn, than to have your schooling with the Grenvilles and see how it is done?"

"You could teach me."

She shook her head slowly. "No, Bambi, I could not. Because..."

She paused a moment. Because the truth was, she simply did not have the background or the knowledge to prepare him fully for his life in 16th century society – but that was something she could never explain to him.

She turned back to her son.

"Do not worry," she smiled reassuringly. "You will soon find the Grenvilles are like a second family. I wager that by the end of the year you will be just as upset to be leaving them, as you are to be leaving your father and me now."

He did not reply.

"Do you know," she continued, her voice becoming strangely flat, "I understand what it is like to leave home, to leave your mother and father, to leave everything that you recognise and hold dear." She shivered, and not just from the cold winter air in the Great Hall. "But you have to learn to accept it. To get on with life – to make the best of it even, and to come to love it." She paused, her eyes looking through him as she stared at visions that only she could ever see; visions of a world she had known that was lost to her forever. Then, with an effort, she pulled herself back to the boy. "I do understand what you are feeling, Bambi, believe me I do." She touched his cheek tenderly. "You will have such a lovely time there."

"But Mother," he whispered urgently, shaking his head. "I will not." He swallowed hard, struggling to get the words out. "They are Catholics, Mother! Kat told me."

Lady Mary resolved to have a word with Kathryn, her middle child. Goodness knows how she had found this prize nugget of information, and yes, the Grenvilles were Catholic. But as her husband Sir William had pointed out, some of the most noble families came from the old faith, and anyway, one doesn't ask too many questions when a family as noble as the Grenvilles agrees to take your son in and start him on the path to a first-class education.

William himself had been quite sanguine about the arrangement.

"I have had a word with Sir Nicholas," he had said when they had first discussed the matter of faith. "He says they follow the law and attend the Protestant church in their village."

"Good," she answered. "I do not want our son getting into any trouble, William. It is dangerous being Catholic right now. Every day they say there are plots to kill the Queen and put Mary of Scotland on the throne." She stared hard at him, her mouth set in a thin line. "Are you sure you are not leading him into danger by putting him in a Catholic household?"

"Of course."

"Well, if you are sure."

"He is an eight-year-old boy, Mary, my love." William patted her arm with a smile. "He is hardly likely to start plotting against the life of the Queen."

So Ambrose already knew. The original plan had been for his father to tell him once they were on the road to the Grenvilles' palatial Hetherington Hall, hundreds of miles away in North Yorkshire.

Mary held up a hand to her son. "Ambrose, please!" she said. "We have to respect other peoples' beliefs."

"No, we do not," he hissed back. "The Queen…"

"The Queen does not want us to fight with the Catholics," his mother cut in quickly. "She wants us to live together in peace."

"That is not what Nicholas Stanmore says," muttered Ambrose. "He says the Queen wants to rid the land of every last Catholic. He says she wants to hang, draw and quarter every one of them for being a damned traitor." He looked up at her with troubled eyes. "And Nicholas said the Pope has told every Catholic it is their duty to kill the Queen."

"Ambrose!" she cried. "Do not say those dreadful things!" She put her hands on her hips. "Nicholas Stanmore is eleven years old and should not be saying such words." She paused. Despite his tender years, Nicholas was factually correct. In the five years since the Pope had issued the *Regnans in Excelsis* bull, excommunicating Elizabeth and exhorting her catholic subjects to commit regicide, she had managed to avoid any assassination, mainly due to the network of spies run by the Secretary of State Lord Burghley and Sir Francis Walsingham. "The Queen is a very great lady," she continued, "who I am confident will rule this land for many years to come, and one day will protect us from our enemies when they try to conquer England."

"You do not know that for certain. You cannot."

"I do…"

Mary stopped herself. The truth was, that she did know that one day Elizabeth would defeat the Spanish Armada, and that her reign would last for forty-four glorious years, but one thing was for sure – she could not tell her son this.

"I do…" she repeated, "*not* know this for certain. But," she continued, "I have every faith in our Queen's best intentions, and I know that she is a very great lady who deserves our respect – and I know she will only execute Catholics, or anyone else, if they are proven to have plotted against her life." She put her hands on his shoulders. "Come now, little Bambi," she said, her tone softening. "It will all be alright, I promise." She squeezed him gently. "Your father and his men-at-arms are waiting to ride with you to Hetherington Hall and it is a very long way."

He stared at her a moment, then gave a weak smile. "Yes, Lady Mother."

He ducked away from her hands and ran to the doors of the Great Hall.

"Oh wait!" she called out suddenly. He skidded to a stop and turned.

"I had forgotten something. I have a small gift for you. I almost let you leave without it." She walked back to the high table, picked up the small jewelled box she had put there earlier and opened it. "Do you want to see it?"

Ambrose was about to answer, when there was the sound of heavy boots along the flagstones and the doors were thrown open.

The man who strode in was tall and athletically-built. He carried himself with an easy grace; and although the trim beard and blonde hair cascading out from under his velvet cap were both peppered with a little grey, his face was remarkably unlined – giving him the look of a man much younger than his thirty-six years.

Sir William de Beauvais was carrying a thick fur cape draped over his arm, similar to the one he wore himself.

"Come, son," he barked, as he draped the cape over the boy's shoulders, "put this on against the cold. We must be away if we are to reach the first stop before nightfall. It is many days' ride to Hetherington."

Ambrose pulled the cape tight. "Yes, Father, but Lady Mother has a gift for me."

"What is that?" There was a twinkle in Sir William's bright eyes. "What does your mother have for you?" He marched across the room and peered at the object that lay on her open palm. "Aha – it is a fine thing this; a golden frame with a perfect painted illumination of your mother's fair face for you to remember her by…" In one quick move he picked it off her hand and tossed it high in the air to his son. "Here, catch it, boy!"

"William, no!" Mary snapped, as the small picture spun lazily across the room, throwing out golden beams of morning sunlight.

Ambrose held out his hands, his eyes fixed on the little object spinning towards him.

He very nearly did catch it – and surely would have done were it not for an unfortunate flash of light from the golden frame that seemed to momentarily distract him.

As it was, the frame caught the edge of his hand, bounced up over his shoulder and dropped onto the top of a large oak chest behind him. William and Mary watched with open mouths as it landed with a thud, then skittered across the top of the chest and dropped quickly out of sight down the back.

There was a moment's silence.

"Oh, William!" Mary gasped. "What on earth did you do that for?"

William gave her a weak smile and a small shrug of his shoulders, for all the world like a guilty schoolboy saying 'sorry', but he said nothing. This was a tactic he had tried many times in their ten-year marriage and usually it melted Mary's heart. Most times she would laugh, punch his shoulder and call him her 'dear, silly man'.

But this time she stood still as his charm bounced off her, much like the golden frame had bounced off Ambrose's hand.

"William!" she barked. "That was a totally, completely and utterly stupid thing to do! It might have caught his eye!"

"But by God's good grace, it did not, my love." He tried another smile, then let it drop.

"No," she answered, "but it was delicate and made of gold – at best it will be bent or scratched!"

"Let us see, my love," said William and strode over to the oak chest. "Come, Ambrose," he said, as he started to pull the chest away from the wall, "help your father."

"Shall I call Simon or another servant?" Ambrose asked uncertainly.

"No son, come and help me now. We must retrieve your gift and set off without waiting for servants."

The boy scampered over to the wall and started to push at the chest, his little muscles bunching and his face quickly reddening. As William pulled and Ambrose pushed, the heavy chest moved slowly away from the wall. Once a sufficient gap had been opened up, Ambrose dived down and retrieved the painting.

"See Lady Mother!" he exclaimed, his eyes sparkling as he held it out to her. "It is wholly undamaged! God has protected it for me to treasure while I am away!"

"There, Mary, my love," said William, with undisguised relief in his voice. "No harm done." He turned to Ambrose. "Come son, we must be away. Say farewell to your mother."

The boy ran into Mary's outstretched arms, still clutching her gift. She kissed the top of his head, savouring the fresh, boyish smell of his hair and wanting so desperately to preserve it in her memory, so she would never, ever forget it…

"Fare thee well, Lady Mother." Ambrose tilted his chin and met her gaze. She could see the tears welling up in his eyes and knew it was a mirror of her own tears. "Fare thee well."

"Take care, my sweet Bambi." She kissed his head again. "Do as you are told and do not get into any trouble."

"No, Ma, I will not."

Sir William came up and put his hand on Ambrose's shoulder. "Come on, son, we must be away."

"Take good care of him on the journey, William," she said.

William looked quickly at her, clearly noticing the catch that she could not hide in her voice. "For sure, Mary."

"And how long will you be gone?"

"A month or two. The snow is fair thick here, and is likely to be thicker in the north – so I warrant we will not make a fast pace."

She nodded. "Well, go safely, keep warm both of you, and William – hurry back."

"Yes." William pulled at the boy. "Come, we must make Reading by nightfall."

Ambrose wriggled out of his mother's arms.

"Fare thee well, Ma," he repeated, then suddenly he was gone, running out with his father to leap on his pony and ride away from her for a year, or maybe more…

---0---

As the doors closed behind William and Ambrose, Lady Mary went over to the high table and flopped down onto one of the benches.

Hot tears started to roll down her cheeks.

You told yourself you wouldn't cry. You promised yourself…

She sniffed loudly and wiped her tears with her handkerchief.

He'll be fine with William and the men-at-arms on the journey, and he'll have the time of his life at Hetherington Hall…

The door from the kitchens opened and an old woman came in, wearing a plain black woollen dress and a white cap. She carried a wooden tray containing a silver goblet and a pitcher, together with some bread and a clean, folded napkin.

"A little draught of wine and some manchet bread to restore your humours, my lady?" she asked softly.

Mary pushed her handkerchief back into her sleeve and looked up with a watery smile. "Oh, thank you Ruth. Perfect timing as always. Just what I needed."

The old woman set the tray down on the table, poured a goblet of wine and handed it over. Then she sat beside her mistress.

"As your housekeeper, I know it is not my place to ask how you are faring, my lady," she said. "But as your friend and confidant, and even the one-time saviour of your life, I feel I have the right to ask and be answered."

Mary took a sip of wine and a deep breath. "Of course." She picked up the napkin and unfolded it carefully, then dabbed her eyes with it, playing for time.

"Dearest Ruth, I know I am doing the right thing by Ambrose, but deep down I keep thinking I have failed him." She dabbed her eyes again. "I am his mother. It should really be me that teaches him how to be a nobleman and a credit to his family, but I cannot." She turned to the housekeeper. "I just do not know enough, even after ten years here…"

Ruth put her hand on Mary's arm.

"As the Lord is my witness, I do understand, my lady. In truth, these ten years you have barely set foot outside Grangedean Manor, and certainly not ventured further than the village. I understand well that you have made a life for yourself here, but it has very narrow boundaries."

Mary shook her head slowly. "Ruth, you know that I once stood accused of witchcraft." She shivered. "When you have every soul shouting at you, calling for your death…"

"I know, my lady, truly I do." Ruth nodded. "And I see how you have built your life here in Grangedean – a life that is comfortable to you and keeps you protected from the unfamiliar outside world that tried to do you harm." She smiled. "If I were in your position, I am sure I would do the same. But you cannot keep Ambrose forever with you,
locked inside this house. By sending him to a noble family, you are indeed making sure he steps outside your boundaries and is taught by the very best means possible." She looked directly at Mary, her steady blue eyes clear and certain. "So how can you be failing him? He will come back from the North a

better educated child and a future head of the family. Where is the failure in that?"

"I suppose you are right."

Ruth gave a small laugh. "And if you ever want to teach him of the wonders of the world yet to come, you can tell him of the polished stones called 'phones' that talk with the voice of Our Lord, or the covered wagons that travel without a horse to pull them."

"Goodness, no!" Mary exclaimed, her eyes wide. "That would be a disaster – he can never know about those, or the truth about where I am really from!" She paused to gather her thoughts once more. "Ruth, that is our secret – yours, mine and Sarah's. No-one else must ever know how I travelled here across time itself from the distant future."

"No, Lady Mary, it is our secret, my oath upon it. I have not breathed a word to a soul, and nor has my daughter, Sarah."

"Thank you, Ruth; I know you and Sarah would never betray me."

It was a secret the three of them had managed to keep for ten years – and amazingly in all that time no-one else had ever questioned Mary's claim to have been the daughter of a friend of the de Beauvais family.

No-one had subsequently seen through the beautiful gowns, the carefully-applied make-up and the noble bearing of the elegant Lady Mary de Beauvais, to the real, frightened girl that had been kept so painfully hidden for so long.

That girl was called Justine Parker of Hammersmith, West London, who was born in the late 20th century, and who found herself in the wrong place at the wrong time – when an electrical storm opened up a freak wormhole in the fabric of space-time and deposited her, bewildered and alone, in 1565.

Accused of witchcraft by a superstitious serving girl, she had been relentlessly pursued by the witchfinder, one Matthew Hopkirk, determined to try her by ducking her in the Grangedean Manor well. With the help of Ruth and her daughter Sarah – who had been one of the servants – she had managed to thwart Hopkirk.

From there she had married Sir William de Beauvais to become Lady Mary, and ultimately mother to Ambrose, Kathryn and her youngest daughter, little Jane.

Ruth had been given the post of housekeeper and Sarah was made her lady-in-waiting. But it was not just out of loyalty that the secret had been kept – although Mary liked to believe that this was the strongest cause – but practical reasons also. For who would believe such a strange tale? Who in the 1560s or 1570s would even grasp the concept of time travel? To tell the tale would be seen as madness at the very least – just as it had been touch-and-go when Ruth and Sarah had first been told.

And now Justine was Lady Mary de Beauvais, a well-established Elizabethan wife and mother, mistress of Grangedean Manor.

Once she had come to accept that time-travel was a one-way trip and there was no going back, she had found herself embracing Elizabethan life – although without 21st century technology she had to rely instead on 16th century manpower. Fortunately, that was plentiful, and she had soon organised an army of servants to help her run the house.

But it wasn't just the daily tasks that she felt could do with the modern touch; it was the quality of life as well. As Justine in Hammersmith, she had had the radio on at all times, living her life to the sound of chat, banter and music. Now she only had the mobile phone she had brought back with her, carefully hidden in a small locked casket in her bedroom. It was taken out and charged with her solar charger when she was alone – allowing her a few precious minutes for a nostalgic wallow in the few music videos stored inside. The joy of connecting with her previous life through the phone was tempered by the torture of the ever-present 'no signal' message – as well as the fear that despite the charger, one day the precious phone would die completely and sever her last link with the 21st century.

"You look sad, my lady," said Ruth, breaking into her thoughts, and as ever, seeming to read them. "Do you grieve for the life you once led?"

Mary nodded with a rueful smile.

"It must be hard, when you are the only one who knows about the times yet to come, to have no other body to talk to. No one who understands about such things as wagons called cars and polished stones called phones."

"I suppose it is." Mary forced a smile. "But then I think that Kat needs a new kirtle and Ambrose must go to the butts to practice his archery, and maybe the rushes need changing in the bed chamber, and I forget about my old life and I get on with this one."

"Quite right, Mistress."

Mary looked up, and her eye caught the oak chest, still pushed away from the wall.

"Come Ruth, we have to put the oak chest back in its place. Call a servant to help."

Ruth stood and picked up the tray. "As you wish, my lady. Again, I am sorry to have upset you."

Mary stood also. "I am fine, Ruth. My oath upon it."

She even sounded like an Elizabethan!

As Ruth disappeared down the stairs to the kitchens, Mary went over to the chest. There were black marks along wood panelling, showing it had stood close to the wall for many years. She ran her fingers along the back edge and examined the deep dust left on them.

It is filthy! Why did no-one clean behind it? How on earth did I miss this?

A sudden flash of something glinting in the shadows on the floor caught her eye, and she bent down behind the chest to have a look.

She could just make out a small recess in the darkness, caused by the curved edge of a worn floor board not quite touching the panelled wall.

Bending further, she could see there was a metallic object lying deep in the dust. She reached down closer and put her fingers into the hole. She could feel the object – it was cold and very smooth; so smooth that her fingers could not seem to get a purchase.

Bending still further, she pushed her whole hand slowly into the space, and very carefully felt for the edges of the object. Once she had these, she was able to get a grip between her thumb and forefinger. Triumphantly she eased it out.

Standing straight, she went over to the window and examined her trophy. Blowing away the dust, she could see that it was a square brushed steel box. It was not big – it fitted snugly into her palm, and it was made of two parts fitting closely together. She turned it over. On the larger part was a black oval, surrounded by a relief pattern of scrolls and whirls. In the centre of the black oval was a white moulded skull.

Then her heart missed a beat.

It was a 21st century cigarette lighter.

She picked it up with her other hand and flicked the lid open. There was the lighter mechanism. She ran her thumb slowly down the strike wheel a few times, fearing to try lighting it; fearing to be proved that it was what she thought it was.

Then suddenly she found herself pushing hard on the wheel and flicking her thumb down.

A flame shot out of the nozzle.

With a small cry, she snapped it shut again, as she stared, mesmerised, at the little object.

There was only one person she knew who carried such a lighter – she had often seen him use it in the kitchens at Grangedean Manor when it was a modern-day visitor attraction, right up to when she'd got caught in the electrical storm and transported back to 1565.

It belonged to Rick, the spiky-haired catering manager.

Which could only mean one thing…

If the lighter was here, then Rick was here, too.

CHAPTER THREE

Ruth came back up into the Great Hall with a servant in de Beauvais livery.

"Simon will put the chest back, Mistress," she said.

The man went over to the chest and started heaving it back into place.

"Wait!" commanded Mary. He stopped and looked back up at her in surprise at the urgency in her voice.

"Ruth," she asked, "tell me how long this chest has been here against the wall? I do not recall."

Ruth thought a moment. "I believe it was when you were preparing for the birth of little mistress Jane." She nodded to herself. "Yes, I believe the master had some craftsmen make it and install it while you were in your confinement."

Jane was nearly four – which meant that the lighter must have been dropped into the hole at least four years ago, before the oak chest had covered it up. At the time Mary had been preparing for childbirth by being confined to a dark room and resting – as it was believed that the chances of miscarriage were reduced by avoiding any sort of stimulation. It seemed that she had not registered the new chest after emerging from confinement – no doubt with the birth of her third child she had other things on her mind.

So Rick must have been living in Elizabethan England for at least four years.

Four whole years!

What stories could they have shared if she had been able to chat to him? What memories of the future had they in common?

Ruth was wrong – there *was* now another living soul in Elizabethan England who knew what a phone was supposed to do; who understood how cars worked. Another living soul who would truly understand how she felt.

Had it been an electrical storm like hers, that had opened up the wormhole in time and transported him here? Had he been as petrified as she had been when falling into the past – and as surprised to find himself in such a strange time, even if in the same place?

Then suddenly Mary's heart missed a beat.

Rick wouldn't just know about phones. He would also know the answer to her burning question...

He would be able to answer the question that kept her awake at night, the one that had *really* kept her confined to Grangedean and the village, the one that had first forced itself into her head like an unwelcome stranger just after she and William had emerged from the little church as husband and wife all those years ago…

It had started as just a little niggle; a feeling of mild unease, but it had grown stronger and more corrosive with each passing year and with the birth of each child…

Rick was out there somewhere. Somehow, anyhow, she *had* to find him.

Because it was not just their shared experiences she had to discuss. It was also because Rick was the only person alive who could give her one other crucial piece of information…

"Ruth," she asked as casually as she could, nodding to Simon to push the chest back into place, "did you ever see a stranger leaving the Manor at that time? A man with short dark hair that stuck up from his head in spikes, like a hedgehog? A man wearing the strangest of clothes?"

"No, Mistress," Ruth answered slowly, with a sideways look that said she had picked up on the casualness in Mary's voice, and was calculating what it might mean. "What sort of man might that be?"

"No-one. No-one at all."

Ruth looked unconvinced. "Marry, my lady, I do not recall such a man, although I warrant I would have done from your tale of him." She paused. "I can ask the rest of the servants if one of them has seen him?"

"No, it is no matter."

"Indeed, Mistress? 'Tis no matter?"

"None at all, Ruth, believe me." Mary recoiled at the thought of the servants gossiping about the strange spiky-haired man that so interested her. "It is certainly not a matter I wish to have discussed with any other soul in this house."

Ruth nodded, clearly accepting of her mistress's occasional odd behaviour. Then her eyes slid over to the servant Simon. Mary followed her eyes and saw Simon had his back to them, with his hands remaining on the chest. His body was very still; a stillness that plainly said he was straining to hear every word passing between the two women behind him.

"Simon?" They saw him flinch slightly at Ruth's tone, then he slowly stood up and turned to them, a look of studied innocence carefully applied to his face. "You will not talk of this day's dealings with anyone else. Do I make myself understood?"

He gave a sly smile, as if he now had a secret he could not wait to share with all the serving women. "Yes, Mistress Ruth," he answered, although it was plain he did not mean it.

Ruth stared coldly at him. "I am most serious, Simon. If I hear you have talked of this, you will be cast out and will be left to vagrancy."

He swallowed hard and visibly paled. "Yes, Mistress Ruth," he muttered.

"You may go, now."

"Yes, Mistress Ruth." He scurried over the door leading down to the kitchens and was quickly gone.

There was a long, long moment of silence. Then Ruth spoke. "As your sometime saviour and close confidant, I would know the truth." Her voice became steely hard. "I warrant that you asked this question for a reason. This hedgehog man means much to you."

Mary let her breath out slowly. "Ruth, we have known each other many years?" Ruth nodded expectantly. "So I cannot hide from you that I found this." She opened her hand to reveal the lighter. "It belongs to the man with spiky hair – a man I once knew from my own time. And if this is here, then he will be, too."

Ruth picked it up curiously and studied it.

Then suddenly she gave a small cry and the lighter dropped from her hand, falling heavily to the floor.

"Lord a' mercy, my lady!" she gasped, crossing herself several times. "Lord a' mercy! 'Tis the work of the devil!"

Mary picked up the lighter. The white skull shone out starkly against the black enamel. "No, Ruth, this is not the devil's work – it is the work of men, just like all things made in my time."

"Then what of the devil's mark?" Ruth had turned as white as the skull itself.

"It is…" Mary stopped, suddenly unsure. The 21st century iconography of a skull in this context could surely be explained without ironic reference to hell, but in the moment she couldn't think how. "It is the work of men," she said lamely. "Look." She opened the lid and flicked the wheel. A flame shot out. "It has only one purpose – to light fires."

Again, Ruth gasped and crossed herself as she stared at the bright flame dancing in Mary's hand. "A tinder box! 'Tis a miniature tinder box!"

"Yes, and it works the same way, too." Mary flicked the lid shut, putting out the flame, then opened it again and flicked the wheel once more. "Turning the wheel strikes a spark, which lights the oil stored inside."

Ruth looked slowly up at her. "You make polished stones called 'phones' that talk with the voice of the Lord," she said, shaking her head, "and tinder boxes no bigger than a pebble – these are truly wonders." She held out her hand. Mary flicked the lighter shut and put it on Ruth's palm. Ruth studied it carefully a moment, then tried to light it as Mary had done. It took a few goes before she too had the flame dancing off it. "Ha! 'Tis not natural, that would have a fire lit without a normal tinder box."

She closed the lighter and handed it back.

"Your friend that would be a hedgehog – he will be concerned to find this wonderful thing again. He must have lost it when he came here like you did, on a witch's curse."

Mary had forgotten she had concocted the story of a witch sending her back in time – as she believed this would actually be more credible to 16th century women than the space-time wormhole she believed was the true cause.

"Yes, and I would like to give it back to him."

And to ask him the question…

"I warrant you would." Ruth smiled. "And talk together of the times yet to come, but which for you both are but memories."

"Yes, Ruth, I would like to talk with him." Mary said, then paused. "But…"

"What ails, my lady?"

"Oh, Ruth, I know it sounds stupid, but…" She faltered to a stop.

Ruth sat slowly on the bench seat. "Pray tell, my lady. There is something that troubles you." She gestured to Mary to sit beside her. "I can see you are deeply a-feared of something."

Mary was about to sit down, when a heavy yawn overtook her. It started deep in her chest and quickly reached up till it popped in her ears, forcing her mouth open and her eyes to screw tight shut. She put her hand up to try and cover it, but there was no hiding it, it was so all-consuming.

"God's truth, my lady, you must a-bed this instant" said Ruth. "I had not seen it before, but now I see that you are as tired as a stag running from the hunt."

"No, I am fine," answered Mary, once she had regained the power of speech. "I'm fine." She flopped down next to Ruth. "I have been very worried about Ambrose," she said. "And in truth I have not slept much these past nights thinking of his journey."

"Pray sit, my lady." Again Ruth patted the seat beside her. "Tell me what troubles you."

Mary sat, and looked into her housekeeper's eyes. Then she sighed and shook her head. "Ruth, I have been worried about Ambrose, but there is something else that has been troubling me for many years – and finding this lighter means I may get the answer."

Ruth stayed silent, as if she were giving Mary the space to speak when she was ready.

"I know it is stupid, Ruth," Mary said after a moment, "but I need to find this man. I want to ask him a question. I want to ask him if… if…

Mary swallowed hard. This was the question that had been eating her from the inside for these last ten years, and now she was about to say it out loud. What if it sounded completely stupid?

She looked at Ruth.

"I want to know if I will still exist in the future!" she blurted out.

There was a silence. Then Ruth frowned. "I know not what you mean, my lady," she said slowly.

"I mean, I need to find out if I have changed history so much that I have endangered my own existence." Mary paused. Ruth was still looking confused. "If this man does not know who I am, then maybe it is because I do not exist in the future; the future that he knew before he came back in time himself.

And if I do not exist for him, then at some point I must stop existing at all," she paused again, searching the housekeeper's eyes for acknowledgement that this was so very difficult, "because I will have changed history."

Ruth stared at her, wide-eyed, with her mouth pursed. "But you lived in your time, did you not? And you were transported here on a witch's curse – so what is to think on?"

Mary put her hand on Ruth's arm. "Dearest Ruth," she said, "I know. But what have I done since I got here?"

"You have married the master and become established as a fine wife and mother, beloved of all."

"That is lovely to hear, but what I have really done is to change everything." She leaned in towards Ruth. "I saved Sir William when history said he was to die, and I had three children, who will grow up and have lives of their own."

Ruth nodded slowly, as understanding started to show in her eyes. "And you fear that all five of you, who were never here in the original history – the one that led to your birth – will create new consequences…" she said slowly.

"Exactly. Consequences that may mean that events will go this way and that way – until one day, something happens that means that maybe my grandparents are not born at all, or never meet each other…"

"…And so you will not be born either." Ruth shook her head.

"You see?" Mary said. "If the man who owns this lighter knows who I am, then I still exist in his time – the future that runs on from where we are now, with me, William and the children all existing."

"And if he knows you not?"

Mary sighed deeply and grimaced. "Then at some point perhaps I will just… disappear."

Ruth stroked Mary's cheek. "My dear lady," she said softly, "I am sure that cannot be. You are a good person, who goes to church at all times required by God and by the law. God will not let you disappear, my word upon it."

"That is good, I am sure," Mary answered, "but I need to know." She shook her head and stood up again. "So I want to go to the village this evening and start asking if anyone has seen this man."

"You can be away in the morning," said Ruth, her eyes narrowing and her voice becoming firmer. "I will have your horse Juno made ready for you to ride out, after you break your fast."

Mary gave a small inward shudder. To spend the rest of the day and all night trapped in Grangedean Manor, thinking on what she had found and not doing anything but trying to sleep – that would be unbearable!

"I cannot wait until morning, Ruth; truly I will not," Mary said firmly. "I must go to the village now and start asking. I can be back by nightfall."

"But the hedgehog man has been here four winters or more – belike he can wait one more day to be found?"

"No, my mind is firm on this, Ruth." Mary drew herself up and lifted her chin. "I will go to the village this hour and see if I can find out more."

"Alone?" Ruth fixed her with an accusing eye. "That is not seemly. You must take a servant or some men-at-arms with you."

Suddenly Mary was a teenager again, standing in front of her mother being told not to go out 'dressed like that.' She wanted to stamp her foot and shout "I am a 21st century woman – I can go wherever I please!" But instead she took a breath, smiled and said, "No, Ruth, please have Juno saddled now."

Ruth observed her silently a moment, then seemed to try a different approach. "My lady," she said, "you will fall from the very saddle, you are so very tired." The old woman's expression softened as she put a hand to her mistress's sleeve and looked up at her. "Your eyes are like the tiniest flakes of coal deep in the snow," she said softly. "Please, let it rest, let *you* rest but a few hours, and go a-freshed in the morning."

Mary smiled. "Ruth, you have always looked after me like you were my own mother, and I respect you for it, but on this matter, I will not be swayed."

"Then take Simon to look out for you."

Mary glanced across at the door where the servant Simon had so sheepishly departed a few minutes before. "Right now, Ruth, I would rather not. I will go alone."

Ruth bowed her head. "As you wish, my lady." She looked up and nodded briefly. "As you wish."

She turned and walked slowly to the doors.

CHAPTER FOUR

The low winter sun was already turning the sky from grey to red as Lady Mary de Beauvais pushed open the heavy wooden door and stepped into the village tavern.

Although she had been inside once or twice over the years, the sight of the stark room with its blackened wooden tables and spluttering tallow candles never failed to give her a sickening shiver of fear, as she re-lived the events of that fateful night ten years before. It was the night when William had been accused of witchcraft by the snake-like magistrate, Hopkirk, and so nearly drowned in a barrel in a witch-trial. When that had been thwarted, Hopkirk had tried to attack William with his wicked knife.

Mary shuddered again.

Historically, William should have died that night. All the 21st century historical records had told how he was killed in a tavern brawl on the 31st of July 1565.

But this time she had been there too, in disguise. When the moment came – a split-second moment when history would have taken its course and William's life would have been brutally cut short – she had acted instinctively.

She had rushed at Hopkirk and knocked him down, stopping him from stabbing William.

So it was the night when history had been changed forever. Sir William de Beauvais, far from dying as a young man, was now very much alive. And instead of dying childless as history had ordained, he was the father of Ambrose, Kathryn and Jane.

So history had been set on a new path – a path that could lead to Justine Parker, now Lady Mary, no longer existing.

What would happen if she were to disappear? Would it be as if she had never existed at all? And what of William, Ambrose, Kat and Jane – would they too disappear? Would history re-establish itself as if she had never travelled back in time? But then the events that led to her birth would re-establish themselves as well! So then she would suddenly reappear… and maybe end up bouncing between existence and non-existence like a paradoxical tennis ball…

Mary shook her head. This was ridiculous.

Life – real life – must go on. And right now, that was in Elizabethan England.

She looked around the tavern.

It seemed nearly empty, with just a couple of village men at one table. She sat down away from them, and looked round for the innkeeper Luke, or his wife, Agnes.

Luke and Agnes had taken over the ownership and management of the tavern some five years before on the death of Agnes's father, old Jake. He had been quite the village character, padding around the tavern in his dirty smock like a grey ghost; his grizzled beard so long that it would have reached the floor, had it not had to pass first across his enormous belly. But Jake could not go on forever, and one day he had been dispensing his customary pearls of wisdom to a group of villagers, when he had suddenly turned bright red, made a noise like the hiss of steam escaping a boiling kettle, and, as the villagers stared transfixed, had toppled slowly forward face-first like a felled tree. He was apparently dead before he hit the floor, according to the tales that spread like wildfire among the villagers after the unfortunate event.

Mary and William had attended the funeral in the little village church, sitting calmly in the front row of the pews reserved for them, while the rest of the village were crammed noisily in behind them. Mary had wanted to buy Jake a coffin, but as William pointed out, Jake had been a willing associate of Hopkirk on the night he was nearly killed, and it was hard to forgive that, even in death. So Jake had been buried in just a shroud. The village had paid their respects – and Elizabethan country life carried on. Agnes and Luke were established as the new owners of the tavern, and they had done well to maintain the warmth and atmosphere established by Jake.

Only that warmth appeared to be lacking this evening, as the two men sitting across the room suddenly noticed Mary. Immediately they stopped talking and stared at her with dark, hostile looks.

In that moment, she felt very exposed.

These men were clearly finding it unacceptable to come across a single woman in the tavern. Mary shifted uncomfortably on the bench as a cold flush flooded through her like a tidal wave. What on earth had she been thinking, to come to the tavern unaccompanied? She should have listened to Ruth instead of being so headstrong…

She dropped her head and stared down at the table, wondering whether she should get up and go, scurrying back to her little bubble of comfort in Grangedean Manor like a naughty schoolgirl...

No. She could look after herself.

A chill wind blew across the back of her neck as the door opened.

She glanced behind her and saw some more villagers shambling in, clapping and blowing on their hands to get some heat into them after the cold outside. As they started to make themselves comfortable at the next table, one of them looked her up and down, then nudged his companion, muttering something. His companion laughed.

"Art all alone, lady?" the first man asked, his mouth twisted into a sneer. "I think 'tis a bit late for you to be out without your husband."

Mary looked at the man. He was a red-faced labourer with few teeth and little hair, dressed in a moth-eaten woollen jerkin and filthy breeches.

Suddenly Mary knew what she had to do. She was a 21st century woman and she was lady of the manor. She was not going to be told where she could go and when – and certainly not by a man as filthy as this.

Very slowly and carefully she stood up, then lifted her chin defiantly.

"My husband," she said firmly, "is your master, Sir William de Beauvais, and he is away at this moment." The man looked surprised – clearly he had not known who she was. "And I will not be told by you, or by any other man, where I can go." She lifted her chin a little higher. "Do you understand me?"

The man looked down. "Yes, my lady," he muttered.

"I did not hear you."

He looked up. "Yes, my lady," he repeated. "Begging your pardon, my lady."

"What is your name?"

"Simeon, my lady."

"Well, Simeon, I thank you to keep your opinions to yourself in future."

"Yes, my lady." He sat down and there was silence in the tavern.

"Good." Mary sat also, trying to look calmer than she felt.

Gradually conversation resumed.

As if this was her cue, Agnes appeared with a full pitcher of ale in one hand and a fistful of tankards in the other. She was a small, plump woman with a pinched face, eyes that seemed too close together and mousy hair hanging in straggly tendrils round her face. Mary was put in mind of Mrs Tiggywinkle from the Beatrix Potter books of her childhood; a look which was reinforced by the plain brown woollen dress and white ale-stained apron.

"Ale, my lady?" she asked. Mary nodded, and Agnes put a tankard down, filled it with a flourish, then stood back, pushing a tendril of hair behind her ear. "There," she said. "A fine ale just for my lady. The first of a new barrel."

"Thank you, Agnes," said Mary, putting a three-farthing coin on the table. Agnes scooped it into a pocket on the front of her apron.

"I wanted to ask you a question, Agnes," Mary said, quite levelly. "If you have a moment."

Agnes smiled; a thin, shallow smile that didn't quite manage to reach her small eyes. "For sure, my lady. But by your leave, I would first attend to these folk." She gestured over to Simeon and his friends.

"Go to it."

Agnes gave a small nod. "I will return most presently." She moved over to the villagers' table and started serving, laughing quickly at some quip by one of the men and responding with a comment of her own that drew a great roar of laughter in return.

Mary couldn't help wondering if she had been the butt of their joke, and decided she probably had been. She sighed. Elizabethan England was such a strange land – and it was clear that even after living in it for ten years she knew so little of how it worked. But now that Rick was out there somewhere, she was going to have to step out of the safe, comfortable world of Grangedean Manor and explore it…

Agnes sat down opposite Mary and folded her arms under her ample bosom.

"You wanted to ask me a question, my lady?"

"Yes, Agnes, I did." She took a sip of her ale.

"About four years ago, did a stranger come into the tavern? A strange man in strange clothes, with no hat and hair that stuck up in spikes like a hedgehog?"

As she said it, she knew how slim her chances were of Agnes remembering one customer from such a long time ago – however strange he might have been.

But never in a million years, could she have imagined the reaction she would get from the little woman across the table. The colour drained from Agnes's face, and she stared open-mouthed at Mary. After a while, small intermittent mewling sounds started coming from the back of her throat.

"So you knew this man?" Mary hazarded.

Agnes nodded, wide-eyed but still said nothing. Mary pushed her tankard across the table, and Agnes drained it in a single gulp.

"Tell me about him, Agnes." Mary said gently.

Agnes pushed a tendril of hair behind her ear and took a deep breath.

"My lady, how is it that you know of him?

Mary frowned. "Tell me what you know, first."

Agnes leaned forward. "My lady," she said, pleading with her eyes. "This is not a good man. He is godless and Heaven knows he lacks a soul. What e're your business be with him, please, I beg you to think again on it."

"Tell me how you came to know him."

Agnes leaned further forward. "It was not more than ten or twelve months since my father had died, God rest his soul," she began. "I was alone in here one morning, when this man staggered in. He looked frightened, like he had seen an evil spirit, but I was a-frighted also when I saw him."

"Why was that?"

"As you said, he had no hat, and his hair was in spikes like giant thorns. Or a hedgehog, yes." She nodded to herself as she stared at the images in her head. "He was wearing loose blue breeches with yellow stitching, that I had never seen on a man before." She suddenly fixed her gaze back onto Mary. "They reached right down to his ankles! Would you believe it?"

Mary shook her head. "No," she answered.

"His unshaped jerkin had only the smallest of sleeves," Agnes continued, her eyes glazing over as once again she was lost in her memories, "and on his arms were painted pictures of muskets."

Mary nodded. Rick had had tattoos of guns on both arms – she remembered now. He was always talking about guns, and had once showed her the tattoos as they sat outside the Grangedean Manor visitor café having a coffee. "The ones on my right arm, these are AK47s," he had told her. "Over a million of them around – developed after the war and still going strong. Very reliable. On my left arm, a .44 Magnum. You seen *Dirty Harry* or *Taxi Driver*? .44 Magnum," he had sniggered, holding his two fingers to her temple as if they were a gun. "Go ahead, make my day!"

She had found the whole thing a bit sickening, and had said so.

"Yeah, well, it's good to have a hobby," he had answered. "One day I'll have a .44 Magnum, or an AK47. Or a sniper rifle, like in *Day of the Jackal*. Awesome killing weapon, that."

Mary said to Agnes, "You must have found him frightening."

"Aye." Agnes nodded again. "He begged me for a pint of ale, though he had no coin upon him that I recognised."

"Did he offer coin?"

"He did – smooth silvery tokens bearing the head of a queen, but not a queen I knew. I told him we only accept Queen Elizabeth's coin here."

"What did he say to that?"

"He insisted that it was Queen Elizabeth – but I refused to accept it, saying it was not. But he was so desperate for vittles and ale, that I took pity and gave him some."

"Where did he go after he had eaten and drunk?"

Agnes shook her head slowly. "Oh no, my lady, he never went to any place! No – he stayed here."

"He stayed here? In the tavern?" Mary asked. "For how long?"

"A few months. He told me he had some experience of preparing food, so I gave him work in my small kitchen, and a truckle bed to sleep on at the day's end."

So Rick had been living and working only a couple of miles from Grangedean Manor for a few months – and Mary had had no idea! She might even have come in to the tavern after Jane had been born, and been completely unaware that someone she knew – someone who also came from the 21st century – was there as well.

She could have found out already if he knew her. If she still existed in his time…

"So what happened after a few months?" Mary asked. "Why did he go, and where?"

"Oh, my lady!" Agnes stared at her as a tear suddenly appeared and started to roll down her cheek. "He had to go. We had to turn him out."

"Why?"

Agnes swallowed hard, and a second tear appeared. "Because he tried to force himself upon me while I were a-bed," she whispered, "and Luke came in and caught him in the attempt."

"Oh, how awful!"

"Aye." Agnes sniffed loudly and wiped her eyes on her sleeve. "Luke cast him out that very night."

"Luke cast him out? Where did he go?" Mary asked again.

"I cared not, but I heard tell he fetched up at Master Melrose's house, and worked for him a while." Agnes sniffed again. "Had I been asked, I would have warned Master Melrose against the man, but I was not told where he had gone until after he had moved on again."

Mary paused, as Agnes wiped her eyes and sniffed once more. Then she said, "Thank you, Agnes. You have been most helpful."

Agnes looked up at her with pink eyes. "He was a godless man, as I have said, my lady. A godless man. And God willing you will not find him, for if you do, I warrant he will only bring you misery."

CHAPTER FIVE

Reading, February 1575

Ambrose de Beauvais lay back on the thin, hard bed and studied the gold-framed picture clutched tightly in his small hand.

Slowly he traced a finger down his mother's face.

"Good night, Ma," he murmured. "God save thee well this cold night."

He let out a slow breath. "Pa and I – we have ridden far this day, and I am so tired Ma, truly I am. I would sleep this moment like I were dead to the world, only it is all so strange here, and there are such loud noises of the men drinking downstairs that I could not sleep. I would be in my own bed at home, Ma, with you to tell me a story so I could lay my head to my pillow and feel your hand on my brow and hear one of your wondrous tales." He blinked away a small tear and sniffed. "Will you tell me again of gentle Cinderella, Ma, or the tragic Princess Diana?"

His mother's picture smiled up at him, staying resolutely silent. "But I have a story to tell you, Ma," he murmured, "about what happened to me and Pa on the road this day." He shifted his position to get more comfortable, and began his tale.

"We were some hours in the saddle after we took our leave of you this morn, and I said to Pa that I was sore and hungry. Pa said he was hungry too, and we stopped and dismounted our horses in a clearing, where some other travellers were also stopped. I tied my pony, Thelwell, up, and Pa and the men tied up their horses, and we had just sat down with some bread, cheese and wine when a man galloped past us as fast as the wind. He was riding well, Ma, like you have taught me, with his head close to the horse's mane and his bottom in the air..." Ambrose paused and let out a small giggle. "I beg your pardon, Lady Mother, you always tell me I should not say such words." He took a breath. "...Anyway, he was riding well. But as he passed us, one of the other travellers' horses took fright at the sight, making a great neighing and standing on his hind legs, and this caught the eye of the running horse, causing him to shy most suddenly and toss the man from his back. The man fell so badly and his head hit the ground so hard, that it would not be possible that he would survive. Pa and I ran to the man and Pa felt his neck, but then shook his head and closed the man's eyes, so I knew the man was dead even though Pa did not say it."

Ambrose paused a moment, and swallowed to clear the lump in his throat. "It was terrible, Ma, so terrible. One minute the man was riding hard, the next he was dead. I asked God what had this man done so wrong, that he must be struck down so? And God told me in his own way. Because a moment later some more men rode by, pulling up their horses sharply when they saw what had come to pass. Pa told them the rider was dead, and their leader, an old man with long white hair, got down from his horse and checked the body for himself. Then this leader said how it was a shame that the man was dead, as he may not now be brought to justice. He said the man had 'cheated the hangman'. I was expecting Pa to ask what the man had done, but instead Pa gave a great shout and ran over to the leader, calling him Wychwoode and embracing him warmly. It seems you and Pa know this Master Wychwoode well, as he was part of some adventures you had before you were married and I was born."

Ambrose touched the picture softly. "You never told me anything of these adventures, but the way Master Wychwoode talked of them, it seems they were most dangerous. Why have you not told me, Ma? You tell me many exciting stories, but not those ones. I asked Pa but he would not tell. He said they were stories for another time. Then he asked Master Wychwoode what the unfortunate dead man had done, and Master Wychwoode said the man was part of a papist plot on the life of our Queen. He said the man was called Francis Alleyne, and that spies had found out that he was part of the plot, so Master Wychwoode, who works for a man called Walsingham, was chasing this Alleyne to bring him to justice."

Ambrose put the picture carefully under his pillow and tried to get more comfortable on the hard bed. "And now Pa and this Master Wychwoode are drinking in the tavern downstairs and I am commanded to sleep, but I cannot, for the noise and the hard bed, and for not having you to stroke my head and call me your 'little Bambi', and because this talk of papist plots makes me so concerned, Ma..."

The door swung open and Ambrose looked up, to see his father standing in the doorway.

"Art not yet asleep, my boy?" asked William, swaying slightly and grabbing the door frame for support, before coming over to the bed and staring down on Ambrose, his face looking flushed. "What shall I tell thy mother, sirrah?" he demanded. "Shall I tell her you were falling asleep in the saddle on our travels because you would not sleep in your bed?"

Ambrose shook his head solemnly. "This is not my bed, Pa," he said. "My bed is soft and warm but this one is cold and hard." He sniffed quietly. "And I cannot sleep with the shouting from downstairs."

"Nonsense, son…" began William, then stopped as a loud crashing sound came from below, accompanied by a great roar of laughter. "Yes, well, 'tis but occasional, and you must be so tired after our strange adventure this day, that…" Again he was interrupted, this time by the sound of a heavy punch being thrown, followed by an even louder crash. Father and son then listened as Wychwoode's authoritative voice barked out commands, clearly trying to restore order.

Ambrose waited till there was relative quiet again, then said, "and my Lady Mother is not here to stroke my head and tell me her stories."

William took a deep breath and sat down heavily on the side of the bed. "You would have me tell you a story, son?" he asked, then put out a hesitant hand to his son's head. "What would you have me tell?" he asked, stroking Ambrose's hair cautiously, as if it were too hot to touch.

"No, Pa" answered Ambrose, moving his head away slightly. "Perchance another time."

William quickly withdrew his hand with a barely disguised expression of relief. "That is good, my boy. Another time then." He stood up. "Sleep well, son. We have an early start in the morning." He walked over to the door, then turned. "I will be up to bed myself presently. I trust you will be asleep when I return."

He was just about to leave when Ambrose sat up.

"Pa?" he said, his voice catching. "There is something else…"

William paused, his hand on the door knob. "Yes, son?"

"That man who died today. Master Wychwoode said he was a papist, who would have been hung for his part in a plot to kill the Queen?"

"Yes. But what of it?"

"The Grenvilles are papists, and I am to spend a year or more with them." Ambrose looked at his father with an ashen face. "What if they are also plotting against the life of the Queen?"

William returned to the bedside and again sat down.

"Ambrose, my son," he said, looking into the boy's wide eyes. "I know the Grenville family of old, and they are too well established, and too secure in their position, to let old papist beliefs lead them into treason." He gave a small smile. "I would not take you into danger, I promise."

"You swear, Pa? On Ma's life, and on Kat's and Jane's? You swear?"

"Yes, Ambrose. I swear it." He ruffled the boy's hair. "I swear it, truly I do." He took a deep breath.

"I promise – you will be in no danger at the Grenvilles."

CHAPTER SIX

The sun had barely risen over the white, snow-frosted parklands of Grangedean Manor, when Lady Mary de Beauvais swung herself up into the saddle and wheeled her mare, Juno, round to face the gate. The groom who had been holding the mare's head bowed and retreated to the warmth of the stables.

"I will be back well before sundown," Mary said to her lady-in-waiting, Ruth's daughter Sarah, who was standing close beside Juno and was huddled in her cloak, blowing on her hands to keep them warm. "Please make sure Kat and Jane attend to their needlework, and Ruth has the month's accounts ready to review when I am back.

"Yes, my lady," muttered Sarah without raising her head. There was something in her tone that made Mary look at her sharply.

"Come now, Sarah, be of good cheer!" she said. "What ails you?"

"Naught, my lady."

"Nonsense." Mary pulled back on the reins and Juno's hooves clattered with impatience on the cobbles. "You look as though there has been a death in the family."

"Nay, my lady."

"Then what?"

Sarah looked up slowly. "My mother has told me that you have found out that there is another here, a man from your time."

"Yes! It is amazing news!"

"Nay, my lady," Sarah answered. "I am much a-feared."

"Why?"

Sarah hesitated, clearly wrestling between her sense of propriety and voicing her deep concern. Eventually propriety lost. "My mother says you intend to seek him out – alone, if necessary." She paused again. "It is not seemly, my lady, for you to be searching the land alone, looking for a strange man, while the master is away. And it could be most dangerous." She looked up and stared at Mary, her face pinched and red; her breath misting in the cold morning air. "I do not like it."

"I appreciate your concern, Sarah, truly I do." Mary leaned down and touched her friend's shoulder. "But I do not intend to go chasing off after this man today – just to visit Master Melrose to hear what the man
did when he worked there, and where he might have gone afterwards. I shall be back later, and we can decide then what is best to be done."

"But you go alone to Master Melrose?"

"I do, Sarah." Mary answered. "In my time, women would go alone wherever they please. I have hidden myself away for ten years in Grangedean. Now I need to get out and experience England."

"But this man could be anywhere in the land by now."

"Then, yes, I will seek him out."

Sarah frowned. "But my lady, in truth, what do you know of this land? In the time since you came here from the far future, you have not once gone further than the village. You are as much a stranger today as you were ten years ago. You have always said it is best for you not to travel away from Grangedean Manor."

"I know, Sarah, but if Master Melrose can point me in the direction that this man has gone, then I will find him. I must, and I will go on my own if necessary, because it is my quest and no-one else's." Mary put a little steel in her voice. "Last evening I faced a villager down who questioned me being out alone, and if I could do it to him, I can do it again." She smiled. "And as I say, I come from a time and place where women can go as they please, without needing a man to guide them."

She dug her heels into Juno's flanks and headed for the gate. Then she added over her shoulder, "So how hard can it be?"

---0---

Thomas Melrose stared at Mary, his mouth hanging open like a piece of loose sacking. He closed it with what seemed an effort, but his thin face stayed as white as the rolling snow-covered hills outside his pebble-thick leaded windows.

"I do not see you outside Grangedean Manor these past ten years, yet now you plan to travel the land in search of that man, Richard?" Mary nodded. "But why? The man is poison."

"I would ask him some questions which only he can answer."

"Well, I am sure you have your reasons, Lady Mary, but I would not be in that man's presence again for all the silk of the Orient."

"Why?" she asked. "What did he do?" Although from other reports of Rick's behaviour, it wasn't hard to guess.

Melrose shook his head. "I trusted the man. I took him in. I gave him shelter and an honest workman's wage. And how did he repay me?

"How?"

"He tried to bed my daughter, my sweet Olivia." Melrose drained the goblet of wine in his hand and refilled it from the pewter flagon in front of him. "I stopped the man in time, but if I had not been so fortunate to be passing her chamber and hear her cries, he would have succeeded."

"Then he would have been arraigned on a charge of rape?"

"Belike." He took another sip of wine. "But how to prove it?"

"By the word of your daughter." Mary said indignantly. "If the crime was against her, she would be the accuser and witness."

Melrose stared at her with a half-smile. "Lord a' mercy, Mary, you have hidden yourself away from us all these last ten years, but even so, you should know that this is not how such things work."

"How so?"

He paused a moment, regarding her over the top of his goblet. "I have no doubt Sir William treats you most kindly, and does not beat you as he is entitled to do, but…"

"He would not dare," she interrupted.

"…quite so – and in truth I cannot imagine him wanting to do so, either. But the law permits it, because the law is always on the side of the man. So the outcome of any arraignment and trial for rape is almost always that the word of the man is believed." He gave a hollow laugh. "Unless, of course, a child ensues and it is conclusive that it is his. But even then he may claim consent, or choose to marry the girl – in which case it becomes a case of fornication before marriage rather than rape."

"So even if Richard had raped Olivia, the chances of him being found guilty…" she began.

"…would be very low," he said. "Yes. And I would certainly not have allowed a marriage."

"But that is awful." Mary bit her lip. So Rick had tried it on with Agnes, then with Olivia Melrose, and who knew who else besides? The man had clearly decided to let his basest nature loose once he had arrived in Elizabethan society; once he was freed from the norms of the 21st century. And this was the man she wanted to have a cosy fireside chat with, reminiscing about the joys of 21st century life? She felt sick at the thought; the man was clearly a monster. And one with a very short fuse as she now remembered – such as the time he'd bawled out a temporary waitress for tripping on the stairs and dropping some plates.

But being a bad-tempered sex maniac didn't alter the fact that she had to see if he knew her in the future.

"As may be, Mary," continued Melrose, "but that is very much the world we live in. A man is generally presumed innocent if the victim of his crime is a woman."

"And that is acceptable to you?" She fixed him with a firm stare. Thomas Melrose might be an Elizabethan, but surely even he could see that was wrong?

He inclined his head. "I do not say that it is acceptable to me that this man would bed my daughter against her will. Certainly not." He paused. "But I do accept that men have dominance over women, for that is the natural order of things, ever since Eve submitted to the serpent and so tempted Adam to eat the apple and fall from grace."

Mary almost bit her tongue.

Better to stay silent than decry a social order favouring male dominance – based on a fantasy text written by men.

She took a breath, then forced a smile. "But what if a woman refuses to accept male dominance?"

"Then she is both brave and foolish." He narrowed his eyes. "And are you that woman, Mary?"

"If necessary, yes."

"Ever since you took charge of the fight against Hopkirk and his men," he said, "you have been the controlling force in your family." He took another sip of wine. "And when the Lord Jesus himself spoke to all assembled, telling them that you were a virtuous woman not a witch, it gave you an unassailable authority for such behaviour."

"But I have never, ever referenced that, not even to William in private," she observed. And that was true, because she knew it had actually been an app on her phone that produced the voice and nothing to do with Jesus at all. But that didn't mean it wasn't the elephant in the room whenever they were together, making William somewhat wary of her, so she could sometimes play on it to get her way. Poor William – unknowingly married to a headstrong, modern time-traveller, and emasculated because of his own religious beliefs.

"I know," Melrose answered. "William has been clear that you have always behaved with virtue, so nothing needed to be said."

"But you feel I should still play the subservient wife?"

He nodded slightly. "Yes, but not because it is an act. Because it is how things should be. The natural order."

"Well, it is not natural to me."

"That is clear."

"And you do not approve?" she asked.

"No."

"And even if Richard attacked your daughter, you would accept it is the natural order?"

He paused, eyeing her thoughtfully. "As a father, no. But as a man, yes."

"Well, I am sorry, Thomas, but I simply do not agree."

"That is your prerogative. But I would still take a stick to this man Richard and beat him close to death for what he did."

"As would I."

He smiled and drained his goblet. "You would indeed? Although he is strong, and determined?"

"You mean that as a woman, I would not be a match for him?"

He laughed. "As a woman, no. But as Mary de Beauvais, beloved of God and one I saw ten years ago as a brave, strong woman, then maybe."

"Then maybe one day I will," she laughed back. "But I have to find him first."

"And ask him your questions?"

Mary hesitated. "I know that part of it makes no sense," she said eventually, "but I have to. I really have to find him."

"Aye," he said, "if you insist, then I am clearly powerless to stop you."

"So will you help me by saying where he went?"

"It was some time ago – he will doubtless have moved on by now."

"He may well have done, Thomas," Mary was unable to keep the edge of irritation from her voice, "but I would know where he went initially, so I can continue my quest."

Melrose stared at her a moment, his eyes searching across her face as if trying to see inside her and understand her true motives. Eventually, he said, "He said he was going to London."

"A big city."

"He mentioned Southwark – a place he had known as a child." Melrose sat back, clearly unsure if he should give the further information in his possession.

Mary waited.

"He said he wanted to see what it was like today."

Not sure if there was more to come, Mary waited further. Talking of Rick was clearly painful for Melrose, but he looked as if he would probably volunteer more information. Eventually her patience was rewarded.

"I recall asking if Southwark was but a small village in his youth, that would now have grown in size," he said eventually. "It was most strange. He laughed as if I had made the funniest joke, and when he had regained his breath, he said that it was more likely that Southwark had substantially shrunk." Melrose gave a weak smile. "I did not understand the man. I thought at the time that he should perhaps be better held in Bedlam." Melrose shook his head. "Marry, you are like to get just such nonsense yourself when you find him. That is if he is still living this day," he added. "A man such as he would surely have found the sharp edge of another's sword by now. Another father or husband who took great exception to the man's behaviour."

Mary shook her head, although she could not prevent a broad grin appearing. Southwark had *shrunk*? That could only mean that the Rick she sought was from the future like her. It was definitely the right man.

"Thank you, Thomas," she said. "I will see if I can follow the trail you have given me." She looked him in the eye. "I will set off for London tomorrow."

Melrose was about to answer, but stopped as a girl swept into the room and came up to touch his shoulder. She looked around eighteen, had long black hair, the brightest hazel eyes and was dressed in the simplest of pale blue velvet gowns. She had a dark, almost Spanish look about her, in marked contrast to Melrose's thin, drawn features and grey hair.

Melrose put his hand on hers and his face lit up in a beaming smile. "Ahh, my sweet child!" He stood and took the girl's hand across the table. "Lady Mary de Beauvais, allow me to present my daughter, Olivia."

Mary smiled at the girl. "I believe I made Olivia's acquaintance ten years ago," she said. The girl paused in front of her, one eyebrow raised in enquiry.

"We have met before?" she asked. "I do not recall."

"I believe you were a bridesmaid at my wedding." Mary remembered three small, excited, giggling girls holding her train and frequently having to be shushed by Sarah as her maid of honour. "But were you not Olivia Dowland at that time?"

"Ahh, yes." This was Melrose. "When Olivia's father was sadly killed in the defence of your honour and your integrity in the face of that dreadful magistrate, Hopkirk, I took in Olivia and her mother." He smiled warmly. "And I found that in return they both stole my heart. I was married to her mother for four happy years until she was cruelly taken from me by a dreadful chill…" he shook his head, "and I have raised her child as my own."

"I am so sorry for your loss," said Mary.

Olivia was staring at Mary, seeming bound in her own thoughts. "Of course – Lady de Beauvais," she said. "I think I remember your wedding. It was such a beautiful day and I felt like you were a lovely princess marrying your prince. I was very young, though, was I not?"

"It was some ten years since," agreed Mary.

"I am eighteen now," said Olivia. Then she blurted out, "And I am bidden to serve in the household of Lady Burnham! She has a town-house on the Strand in London and a magnificent estate in Essex! Is that not such a wondrous honour?" Olivia giggled, then added, "And so much fun to be had in London, I am sure!"

"Olivia is required to attend on my Lady Burnham at his lordship's house on the Strand on the first day of March," said Melrose proudly.

The girl turned sharply to her father. "Did I not hear as I came in, that Lady Mary is setting off for London tomorrow?"

Mary answered for him, "Yes, that is my plan."

"Why then, Papa, that is perfect! I am to go to London in but three days! I can travel with Lady Mary and her retinue. She can see me safely to the Strand in good time!"

Melrose looked down at the table. "I would not want to impose on Lady de Beauvais, my dear."

"But it would be such fun to travel together!" Olivia turned to Mary and took one hand in both of hers. "Please, Lady Mary, please say you will!" She turned on Mary, challenging her to agree.

Mary could see that Melrose was looking uncomfortable, and, being mindful not to challenge his authority after their earlier conversation, she said, "I would you let your father decide on this, my dear."

Olivia turned to Melrose, dropping her head in a gesture of supplication, then looking back up at him. Mary could not see Olivia's face in full, but she could see Melrose was struggling under the full force of his daughter's eyes.

"We agreed, my dear," he stammered. "I was to take you myself and keep you safe. You cannot ask the same of Lady Mary." Then he hesitated, and muttered, "Although I can think of no other woman who could do the task better."

"You are handy with a sword, Father, I will admit," answered Olivia, then her head lifted as a thought seemed to hit her. "But I have the perfect answer! We can all go together! Lady Mary would be better with another man to look out for her, and you will still be taking me as we agreed!" Olivia clapped her hands. "It is perfect! We shall set off in the morning!"

"Now wait, my child," Melrose countered, with a small, pained smile and a hastily raised palm, "but a moment, please." He looked first at his daughter, beaming with the brilliance of her idea, then at Mary, who found herself unable to meet his eyes. There was a silence which went on a bit longer than was comfortable, then Melrose said, "This is all to presume greatly on Lady de Beauvais's goodwill. I say we must travel separately as we had originally planned, and not impose upon her – nor upon her quest to find this… this man she seeks."

But Olivia was oblivious to the discomfort in the room.

"Nonsense, Father. It makes perfect sense for us to travel together." She turned, and the full impact of her large eyes now landed on Mary. "What say you, Lady Mary? Would it not be such fun?"

"It may be, my dear," answered Mary, forcing herself to look away, "but your father is perhaps not so keen on the idea as you are, and…"

"Father will come round – he always does," interrupted Olivia. "And we will have so much to talk about on the journey, you and I, that I simply cannot let this opportunity pass!"

"But…" Mary tried half-heartedly – although this cause seemed all but lost.

"I must ask you all about fine households!" continued Olivia, as if Mary had not spoken. "You can tell me what is to be done by ladies-in-waiting. What should I wear each day? May I paint my face and wear my finest silver, or must I be as a nun, all chaste and plain?" She put her hands together as if in prayer and her lips moved silently. Then she smiled and said, "I am most observant in my prayers and worship, Lady Mary, truly I am and God knows this well, but I do so love to wear the finest gowns and jewels!" She leaned forward and whispered, "In truth, I would make a perfectly awful nun!" She leaned back, then she drew a sharp breath. "My hair! How must I wear my hair? Can I let it fall to my waist or must I braid it each day?" She turned to her father. "You see?" she said seriously, "I have so much to ask of Lady Mary – so many questions! I could not possibly travel without her." She leaned over and took his hand in hers. "You would be failing in your duty as a kind and loving father if you were not to allow this."

But Mary's blood was running cold as Olivia excitedly set out these topics of conversation. How could she possibly answer a single one of these questions? In truth, Olivia at eighteen would know far more about

Elizabethan society than she ever did – and that meant there was no way she could let this girl accompany her.

"Well, perhaps, but…" Melrose began.

"Good, then that is settled." Olivia took Melrose's goblet and drained it in a single gulp. "Hmmm" she said with a knowing smile at Mary, "we will need to take some finer Rhenish than this on the journey, or we will die of thirst!" She refilled the goblet from a pewter tankard and tried it again. "Ahh, but perhaps it improves with each sup. We shall see. Who is the man you are chasing and why, Lady Mary? It sounds so mysterious. You must tell me all."

Momentarily wrong-footed by this sudden change of subject, Mary wasn't able to think of an answer immediately, and Melrose cut in. "Lady Mary seeks Richard, the man who behaved so badly that he must be turned out."

"Oh him." A ghost of a smile flickered quickly across Olivia's face, passing so fast that Mary wasn't sure she had actually seen it, before the girl's expression hardened. "That dreadful man," she said. "Why in Our Lord's name would you want to find him?"

Mary was about to give a bland explanation about just wanting to ask Rick some questions, when Melrose spoke sharply. "We should not be asking Lady Mary such things, my dear," he said. "It is her business, not ours."

"But it was our business when we took him in, and when he … he tried to use me so harshly." Again, the briefest of smiles. "You turned him out, yet Lady Mary seeks him now." She spread her arms wide as if to emphasise her point. "That is most definitely our business, Father. Come Lady Mary," she said, "tell me all."

But Mary didn't answer. Instead she stood up quickly, causing Olivia to step back. She announced, "I do apologise, but it is getting late and I must be back at Grangedean Manor presently. I am so sorry, my dear Olivia, but I feel it is best for you and your father to travel to London in a few days as planned. I, meanwhile, will make my way there tomorrow. Alone." She took both of the girl's hands in her own and gave her warmest smile. "I am sure you will have a splendid time in the household of Lady Burnham, and I wish you all the very best of fortune there." She turned to Melrose. "And I must thank you, Thomas, for your information on Richard's movements, and I will trouble you no more on this matter." She nodded at both of them to signify that she had made her decision and would not be turned, then she walked calmly out.

CHAPTER SEVEN

The early morning snow lay thick on the ground as Sir William and Ambrose de Beauvais, together with their two men-at-arms, stumbled bleary-eyed out of the inn to saddle up their horses. The dark, freezing air numbed their fingers despite thick leather gloves, and made their breath turn to clouds of steam in the light of the burning braziers.

Ambrose's pony, Thelwell, skittered and shied as the boy struggled to get the heavy saddle on its back; its hooves clattering on the cobbles. William finished saddling his horse, checked the men-at-arms were mounted, then tethered his own horse and came over.

"By the Lord's Wounds, son, this beast of yours is making a din," he muttered, a pained expression on his face. "The sound is passing through my head like a red-hot poker."

"He will not stay still so I can saddle him, Pa" said Ambrose.

"Here, let me." William took the saddle from his son and placed it on Thelwell's back, stroking the pony's neck and making 'shh-ing' noises. Thelwell settled after a moment, and William stood back. "There, son. Now, let us be away."

Ambrose looked around for a mounting step, but did not see one. With a sigh William picked the boy up by his waist and lifted him easily into the saddle. "Come, we have no time to tarry. We have many miles to cover this day."

Ambrose was just settling himself in the saddle and gathering his reins when the door of the inn opened and Robert Wychwoode strode out.

"Good morrow, Sir William" he said jovially. "And to you also, young Master Ambrose."

"Good morrow, Master Wychwoode," William answered.

"Which way are you headed?" asked Wychwoode.

"Did I not say last evening?" said William. "We are headed for Stratford-upon-Avon – we hope to make it there tomorrow."

"Stratford?" Wychwoode exclaimed. "I am also on the same road; I am bidden there to question a man."

"Some legal case?" inquired William.

"Nay." Wychwoode seemed to wrestle with his conscience a moment, as if he was making up his mind whether or not to reveal some nugget of information. He cleared his throat. "'Tis concerned with that man who fell from his horse yesterday, and met his untimely end."

Ambrose gripped his reins tightly. "Does this man in Stratford know more of the papist plot to kill the Queen?" he asked. "Will you make him tell you all?"

Wychwoode smiled slowly. "I know not, young Ambrose," he said, "but I will know more when I have questioned him."

One of Wychwoode's men led a horse out of the stable, ready saddled up. Wychwoode swung himself up and settled into the saddle, as his other men emerged and all mounted up around him. He turned to William. "Come de Beauvais, let us ride together, at least until Stratford. It will be good to have your company."

William nodded and mounted his own horse.

"But what of this man?" Ambrose urged. "What of the papist plot?"

"In good time, son," cut in William. "We will ride together, and I am sure Master Wychwoode will tell us what he can, when he is ready."

"But Pa…"

"Nay, shush, son." William turned his horse's head in the direction of the gate at the far end of the inn's courtyard and encouraged it to a brisk walk. "Do not put pressure on Master Wychwoode."

The party filed out of the courtyard, with Ambrose bringing up the rear, his head down and the cold starting to bite into his bones even before he made it out onto the frosty track.

----0----

As the pale wintery sun struggled to show itself above the black skeletal trees, Ambrose allowed himself to contemplate the possibility that maybe, just maybe, he would at some point start to feel a little warmer. Even a bit warmer, just a little bit, would be so good. But until that point, there was nothing for it but to huddle into his coat, grip the reins in his numb fingers, and concentrate on… on what?

On the horse in front.

Left leg forward. Right leg forward. Left leg. Right leg.

Tail swish!

How stiff is a horse's leg? Why does it not bend as a man's leg does as the horse moves? Ambrose clicked his tongue. Of course! Because its knee is facing backwards.

Left leg. Right leg…

What would Ma be doing now?

Would she be rising from her bed, and waking Kat and Jane? Would she be chiding Kat for not seeing to her hair? Or picking up Jane and giving her a big hug because she had had another bad dream?

Left leg. Right leg…

Tail swish.

She would be taking Kat and Jane to the Great Hall to break their fast. There would be bread, and cake and ale, and Kat would eat too much because she was but a small pig who lived for her stomach, while Jane would cross her arms and say 'no' and Ma would have to make a game of the food to make her eat it. Ma would say the piece of bread was a wondrous bird, that would fly into Jane's little mouth, so she must catch it before it would swoop away again…

Left leg. Right leg.

Biting cold.

Tail swish.

----0----

"Francis Alleyne was a very bad man. A very bad man indeed."

Robert Wychwoode leaned back and stared at William and Ambrose in turn, his eyes flickering orange in the firelight as if there were sparks shooting out of them. "He was part of a plot against the life of the Queen, and would have put Mary of Scotland in her place."

"How did you know, Master Wychwoode?" asked Ambrose. "What led you to him?"

"Ahh, young Ambrose – straight to the point." Wychwoode leaned forward and stoked the fire with the black poker so that more sparks flew up from the glowing logs. "You are truly your mother's son." He smiled. "She has the clearest mind I have ever seen in a woman. Calculating and sharp."

"Aye," said William with a small nod, "I do not dispute that. Especially if I am late to bed after a flagon of wine." Both men laughed.

"Do not talk of Ma in such a way," said Ambrose, then realised he was talking to grown men. "Please," he added, somewhat lamely.

There was a moment's silence. "Well spoken, young man," observed Wychwoode. "Well spoken." He looked across at William. "He has her spirit, too, I see. You must watch your son, my dear de Beauvais, lest one day you find he has got the better of you."

William smiled. "I do not fear that day. What father would?"

"So what led you to this man Alleyne, Master Wychwoode?" Ambrose repeated, determined to get an answer and feeling emboldened by his father's approval. "Please tell me, sir."

"Yes, young man, I will." Wychwoode glanced behind them, but it was clear they were alone, sitting by the fire in the parlour.

The evening had come eventually, and they had stopped at a small inn for the night. After some boiled ham and ale, Ambrose had felt much better, and was starting to feel the warmth of the parlour fire work its welcome way into his bones.

"Francis Alleyne was a name that my master, Walsingham, had heard from two or three papists that he was…" Wychwoode hesitated, as if searching for the right word, "…interested in. So I was tasked with locating him, and putting one of my men close to him to see if he was indeed a plotter."

"You had a man spy on him?" asked Ambrose. "Pretend to be his friend, when all the time he was planning to betray him?" Ambrose could not believe grown men could do such a thing, for betrayal of friendship was surely the basest of behaviour?

"Aye, for that is the best way to find out information."

"If my friend Nicholas Stanmore betrayed me, I would never forgive him."

"Indeed you would not, and nor should you." Wychwoode shook his head slowly. "But Alleyne was plotting the life of the Queen, which would have put England in the hands of the papists. This would be worse than a friendship betrayed, much worse. So we must take equally strong measures to stop this happening."

Ambrose tried to imagine what it would be like if Nicholas were to give up a secret they shared – not that any of their secrets were anywhere near as big as this man Alleyne's. But it would still be a dreadful thing. How could you trust someone if they might betray you? Ambrose decided that the world of men was not a pleasant place. He shivered, despite the heat of the fire.

"How goes it, son?" asked William, putting his hand gingerly on Ambrose's shoulder. "Art tired and ready for bed?"

"No Pa," he answered quickly. "I am well, but I do not like to hear of a friend's betrayal."

"For sure, Ambrose," said William, "for I know how much betrayal can hurt." There was a long silence while he stared unblinking into the fire. When he spoke again, his voice was strange – hoarse and guttural. "Aye, and when it is from a man I considered a friend since we were your age, it hurts all the more."

Again there was a long silence. Ambrose was trying to understand who had betrayed Pa, and how anyone could do such a thing, when Wychwoode spoke.

"But all was well in the end," he said. "Your wife's good council prevailed and the friendship was made strong again."

Ambrose looked from his father to Wychwoode and back. Suddenly he had understood. "These are the tales of your adventures with Ma!" he exclaimed. "I would know more of these tales! Pa, please tell me!"

"Another time, son." William patted Ambrose's shoulder before withdrawing his hand. "Another time."

Ambrose crossed his arms and stared angrily into the fire. William put his hand on his leg. "Nay, son, do not frown and cross your arms so. The tales of your mother's and my adventures can surely wait. For now I say we would hear more of this tale from Master Wychwoode." He turned to the older man. "So your fellow let the plot continue till there was enough evidence, then came to you?"

"Yes, indeed. Our man, Tom Cobham, followed the plot until contact was made with a mysterious man in Southwark known as the Alchemist, and a large sum of money was offered to this man, that he would kill the Queen."

"Did you capture the Alchemist, too?" asked Ambrose, reluctantly switching his attention back to Wychwoode. Ma and Pa's story might have to wait, but he would definitely hear it. That was for sure.

"Nay, he has slipped though our hands and we have lost him." Wychwoode shook his head. "In truth, we do not know where he has gone."

"But now you have Alleyne dead, belike the plot is over?" asked William. "It has lost its leader so it is like a headless corpse. The Alchemist is cut loose and has no direction, so we have naught to fear from him."

"Unfortunately not." Wychwoode drained his cup and poured more wine from a pitcher on the table next to them. "We believe there was someone else behind the plot – another, more active leader than Alleyne – someone who we believe Alleyne himself was working for. We do not know for sure who this man is, nor do we know where this Alchemist has gone. And with Alleyne dead, we have lost our best source of information."

"But what of Tom Cobham? asked William. "Can he not make a guess where the Alchemist has gone?"

"No, the meetings with the Alchemist were held in a tavern or, I understand, in the street behind it to avoid overhearing, and Tom was not able to learn any more about him."

"So the plot is still alive, and the Alchemist is still at large, planning to kill the Queen on behalf of an unknown papist plotter?"

"Yes," said Wychwoode drily, "that is a fair summary of the situation."

"And the man in Stratford?" asked Ambrose suddenly. "What of him?"

"Aye," added William, "what of this man?"

Wychwoode looked at them both in turn. "I trust you, de Beauvais, and this is to go no further." He nodded, as if convincing himself to continue. "Cobham told me he had heard brief mention of a John Tyler of Stratford, so I must follow every lead. I have no great expectation of this Tyler of Stratford, but I will seek him out." He leaned back in his chair and again drained his cup. "I will find this man and see if he gives me any clue on the identity of the true leader of the plot."

"But what if he will not tell you?" asked Ambrose.

Wychwoode put his cup down carefully and fixed the boy with a stern, steady gaze.

"Oh, if he knows anything of this plot, anything at all," Wychwoode nodded very slightly, as if he were reassuring himself as much as Ambrose, "then he will tell it to me. As the Lord is my witness, he will tell it to me."

CHAPTER EIGHT

Lady Mary held the piece of bread high above the mouth of her youngest daughter, Jane. "A beautiful, magnificent bird, flying high above you!"

The little girl's eyes followed it closely as it swooped and dived above her. "Ickle bird, ickle bird!" she chuckled, as the bread passed close to her mouth, then climbed high again, out of reach.

"Please Ma, just give it to her," sighed Kathryn. "Must we do this every morn?"

The bread came to roost in Jane's mouth, and the four-year-old started to chew on it happily.

"Yes, Kat, if it gets your sister to eat."

"You do not play such games with me, Ma."

"No, and I do not have to, as you will eat any food put in front of you." Mary eyed the seven-year-old girl with a warm smile. "Which is a good thing, my sweet child."

"Jane eats well enough when Ruth is with her. Last night when you were away, she ate the whole leg of a pheasant."

"Did she? Did she really?" Mary's warmth turned to mild suspicion. "This is not you telling one of your tall tales?"

"No Ma," Kat stared back with the clearest, widest blue eyes. "She ate the whole leg, and Ruth did not need to make a game of it, or pretend it was a bird."

"But it was a b… no matter." Mary smiled again. "Then she will eat well for the next few days, as I have to go to London shortly, and Ruth and Sarah will be looking after you."

There was a silence as Kat stared at her.

"You are going away?" she asked eventually.

"Yes, my sweet."

"Without me, or Jane?"

Mary smiled gently and nodded.

There was another moment's silence. "But… how long will you be gone?" Kat asked, her lower lip now starting to tremble slightly.

"No more than a week or so, I am sure," answered Mary, smiling inwardly at Kat's swift transition from petulance to dependence. "I will be back soon, I promise."

"Will you take Sarah, too?"

"No, it will just be me – I have said that Sarah will help look after you and Jane while I am gone."

"Take Simon."

"He is needed here – I cannot spare him." Simon was the only serving man left in the Manor now that William had taken his men-at-arms, so it was important he stay to help Ruth and Sarah. Also, Mary could still not forget the man's rather sickening sly smile on hearing of her interest in Rick.

"So you will be on your own?"

"Yes." Mary put her hand on Kat's shoulder. "I will be fine on my own. I can take care of myself." She knew as she said it, that it was as much to reassure herself as Kat.

Then she squared her shoulders.

She had hidden away for too long! Now it was time to get out and prove she could look after herself.

"But a bad man might attack you."

"I can take care of myself, Kat. Really."

"But what if a bad man creeps up?" Kat's lower lip was trembling more. "What if he creeps up when you are not looking?"

"Then I will make sure I am always looking out for him."

Kat changed tack. "Why do you need to go anyway, when Pa and Ambrose are gone too?"

"It is just something I need to do. Someone I need to see."

"Why?"

"It is what I need to do, Kat. I will be back soon, I promise. Really."

"You promise? Really, really, really?" Kat looked at her solemnly. "Cross your heart and hope to die?"

Mary leaned over and gave Kat a hug, pressing her daughter's head into her chest. "I promise," she whispered into the little girl's ear. She sat back and crossed herself. "Cross my heart..."

But very much hoping not to die.

The main doors swung open and a serving girl came in and bowed.

"There is a Mistress Melrose here to see you, my lady."

The girl had barely stepped back when Olivia swept majestically into the hall, her fur travelling cloak sending the rushes on the floor scattering behind her like waves in the wake of a boat.

"Ahh, Lady Mary!" she said, taking off her hat and shaking out her long dark hair. "I am so pleased to find you still here, and not yet set off for London!"

"Mistress Melrose, Olivia, what a surprise," answered Mary, putting an edge of polite coldness into her voice. "No, I will be setting off shortly, but for now I am breaking fast with my children."

Olivia studied each little girl for a moment, seeming quite oblivious to Mary's disapproval.

"Such sweet children" she said. "What are their names?"

"This is Kathryn, and this is Jane."

"So lovely. What a credit they are to you. Are they yet betrothed?"

"At four and seven?" Mary shook her head. "Certainly not."

"'Tis no matter." Olivia said dismissively, reaching for a cup and pouring herself some ale. "Time a' plenty for that." She drained the cup and poured some more.

Mary stared at her, not quite believing that the girl had the gall to help herself to ale without so much as a 'by your leave'. "It is indeed a pleasure to see you again so soon, Olivia," she began, although she could hear the flatness in her tone that said the opposite. "May I ask…?"

"For sure," Olivia cut in. She was clearly expecting the question, and gave Mary the full force of her most dazzling smile. "You want to know why I have called on you this frosty morn?"

Mary nodded slowly and deliberately. "Well yes, I did wonder." Although now she was beginning to have an inkling.

"I have come to beg a small favour."

"A small favour?" Mary prepared herself to say once and for all that she was not going to have Olivia as a travelling companion to London. The thought of having this spoiled girl tagging along – no doubt asking unanswerable questions on the ways of Elizabethan nobility – put a cold shiver up her spine.

Olivia took a breath and put her cup down on the table. "Aye. My dear grandmother, my father's mother, has been taken unwell with a fever. My father is loathe to leave her, and has bade me come hither to ask if I may accompany you to London."

And there it was.

There was a moment's silence.

"Accompany me?" asked Mary, her voice frostier than the cold drifts of snow outside the Great Hall.

"Aye." Olivia paused. "To London."

Another silence. Then Mary leaned forward. "Now, listen, Mistress Melrose, I…"

"Can you make sure a bad man does not attack my Ma?" interrupted Kat suddenly.

"Kat!" snapped Mary in annoyance. "This is grown-up talk."

But Olivia moved over to the wide-eyed little girl and sank gracefully down in front of her until their faces were level. "It is Kathryn, is it not?" she asked sweetly.

"Yes, Livia. But my Ma and Pa call me Kat."

"Kat." Olivia stroked the girl's head. "Such lovely hair you have, my sweet child. So soft and so pretty. Well, Kat, my little puss, do you want me to go with Ma to London?"

"Yes, if you promise to keep her safe."

"Of course I will, my sweet one. Your Ma will be as safe as safe can be, if she is with me."

"You promise?"

Mary frowned at her eldest daughter. "Shh, Kat. I said I can look after myself."

Kat looked up at her. "But Livia says she will make sure you are safe. She promised."

"Well, it is very kind of Mistress Melrose," said Mary, with a forced smile. And yes, it was lovely that Kat was so concerned to stop her going to London alone, even if her concern was misplaced. "But I am not sure it is necessary…"

"But she said!" Kat looked hard at Olivia. "You said!"

Olivia put her hand over Kat's in a sickeningly sweet gesture. "I did, little puss."

"So you go with my Ma, then. You keep her safe."

"I will." Olivia stood up. "For you, Kat." She turned and gave her dazzling smile to Jane, who was clutching a last piece of bread and watching with big eyes. "And you, little Jane, do you want me to keep Ma safe?"

"Please, Olivia," Mary cut in, alarmed that this charade was going on forever. "I am sure Jane will agree with you. She is only four."

"Good." Olivia's smile disappeared immediately and her expression became firm as she put on her hat. "When do we set off?"

Mary had one last try. "It is awfully kind of you, Olivia, but I really would prefer to travel alone…"

"But Ma!" squeaked Kat. "Livia said she would keep you safe!"

"I know she did, Kat, but…"

Kat stared at her, and Mary saw the tears well up and spill over her cheeks, like a tap had been turned on. "I want you to be safe, Ma…"

That was when Mary knew she was beaten.

She gave a deep sigh. "You will need to go home first," she said to Olivia, "to gather your belongings and tell your father."

"Nay, I have all I need with me, now, and my father has already given his blessing." Olivia produced another of her bright smiles. "He holds you in high regard, and has spoken at length of your courage and resource."

"He is most kind."

"My horse is ready," continued Olivia, "and I have a small box-cart tethered to it with all my clothes inside."

Mary looked at her two daughters, their little faces staring up at her. Jane still clutched her last piece of bread, which would need to fly like a bird before it could be eaten. "Then allow me to finish the meal with my children and prepare myself. We will leave within the hour."

---0---

Mary and Olivia urged their horses up a small slope, to be faced with a fast-flowing stream crossing their path just ahead.

"I would we rest a while, Lady Mary," muttered Olivia. "I am tired to my bones and sick with cold."

Mary looked at the stream in the flat afternoon light. Although it looked deep and at least fifteen feet wide, the path ran straight up to the nearest bank, then emerged immediately opposite on the far side. "It looks like we can ford the stream on this path," she said, taking out and studying the map that Luke the innkeeper had drawn for her. "This is most likely the Black Bull Ditch, which means that over there," she pointed to where some dark smoke could just be seen on the horizon against the grey sky, "is the village of Hammersmith. We can be there in half an hour, then we can rest up and get warm in an inn."

The village of Hammersmith. Mary had always known that the suburb where she had once lived as Justine had started life as a small village, but to be on the verge of seeing it – of walking the streets that would be one day become her familiar landmarks – that was a wonder indeed. It was not surprising that Rick had headed for his own home of Southwark – the fascination with seeing how it looked way back in history was utterly compelling. And how great to be able to swap notes with Rick when she actually met him...

"But the box-cart, my lady."

"...Eh? What's that?"

"The box-cart." Olivia turned in her saddle and pointed back. "It will get water inside and my best gowns will be ruined if we ford the stream. We must find a bridge."

Mary looked at the troublesome object. It was a wooden box of about four feet square, with a large wheel either side on a single axle. Two long handles came out of the front and each was tethered to a strap behind Olivia's saddle.

Mary sighed.

They were three hours from Grangedean Manor, and should have been much further on by now. But their progress had been slowed considerably by this box-cart trundling along behind Olivia's horse. It should not have caused any problem if the roads had been well-made, but on the rough snow-covered paths they had travelled, its axle had frequently seized up with ice, caught on large stones or got stuck on hidden roots. If anyone was tired it shouldn't be Olivia, who had remained resolutely in her saddle each time the axle jammed, but Mary, who had to dismount and free it.

"For sure," Mary muttered. "We will find a bridge."

It took half an hour and directions from a couple of labourers, before they came across a small wooden bridge within a tiny hamlet of rough cottages. Mary crossed the bridge then headed in the direction she thought would take them back towards Hammersmith.

"I would still like to rest, Lady Mary," Olivia called after her. "It has been a half hour for sure. Maybe we should have seen if one of those little houses could have taken us in?" Mary did not turn round, or answer. "They all had smoke from their roofs," continued the girl, "so they would have had a fire for us to rest by and warm ourselves."

Mary stopped and turned back with a pained smile. "We have no surety of a warm welcome, though. We need to find a proper inn at Hammersmith." She turned back and was about to walk her horse on, then shifted round again in her saddle and added, "We would have been there by now if we had used the ford to cross the stream."

Olivia did not answer, and their slow progress resumed, the atmosphere between them as cold as the snow draped on the bushes and the surrounding fields.

The journey had started well enough, with Olivia chattering happily as they made slow progress along the path, asking questions about noble living that Mary had deflected as best she could, until the chatter turned to speculation on what life would be like with Lady Burnham.

Mary then found herself tuning out Olivia's voice, and instead started wondering how she would find Rick when she got to Southwark. Could you just go up to someone and say, 'Do you know a man with spikey hair and tattoos of guns on his arms?' She suspected a tavern would be the best place to start; 21st century Rick had always liked his beer, and it was likely that 16th century Rick would be no different. She could imagine him standing on a table with a tankard of ale in his fist, singing drunken songs, to the amusement – or perhaps bemusement – of his 16th century companions. Yes, she'd start in a tavern and see where that took her.

But her wandering thoughts were interrupted by the first tortured screech of the wooden axle of the box-cart as it iced up, followed by her eventual dismount and fumbling with freezing fingers to free it – once it was clear that Olivia was not going to get off her horse and free it herself.

Many similar stops had then occurred, leading to the gradual cooling of relations with Olivia as it became clear that this spoiled little girl could not – or would not – do anything to help.

The light had become very grey as they eventually rode into a village of squat black and white houses, each with smoke coming from their roofs.

As large flakes of snow started to drift down, Mary took a brief glance at Olivia. The girl had snowflakes caking up her eyelashes, making her look as if she had aged twenty years. Mary assumed she herself looked much the same.

"We are in Hammersmith, I believe," Mary said, trying to sound more confident than she actually felt, "and we are sure to find an inn here." But unfortunately, none of the buildings looked like an inn, and in the flat light and increasingly heavy snow, it would soon be hard to make out any buildings at all.

Mary was debating whether to knock on the nearest door and beg for shelter, when she just made out a long, low building ahead that looked different to the surrounding houses. Moving closer, she could see a painted sign on the wall announcing itself as 'The Cock and Magpie'.

"Here we are," she said, trying to put a cheery note into her voice.

They rode under a low arch and emerged into a courtyard, under the watchful gaze of several horses in stables to one side. They found a couple of empty stalls, and once the horses were comfortable, made their way into the inn.

Inside, Mary could see that the Cock and Magpie was not much different to the village tavern at Grangedean – just bigger. There were plenty of blackened oak tables with brightly lit tallow candles and bench seats. Mary started towards the nearest empty table and was about to sit, when she noticed Olivia had already walked up to two well-dressed gentlemen sitting by the fire.

"Good sirs," she heard Olivia say, "we are two ladies travelling to London and the snow has chilled us to the bone. May we join you at the fire?" She indicated a couple of spare chairs. "We shall be no trouble, and glad of good company." Mary could not see Olivia's eyes, but she knew that these two gentlemen, both of whom were fine-looking men, one in his late twenties and one nearer forty, would be powerless to resist them.

"For sure, mistress," said the younger man, standing and bowing. "We would be glad of the company of such fine gentlewomen as yourself and..." he turned and bowed at Mary, "your delightful companion."

"Good sirs," said Mary, with a stern glare at Olivia, "we should not impose upon you." She forced a smile, despite her annoyance. "Please excuse..."

"Nonsense, my dear," interrupted the older man, also standing and bowing, "we should be most offended if you were to abandon us now. Please," he waved at the two spare chairs, "be seated. The fire has warmth enough for us all."

With another angry glance at Olivia – which was rebuffed with a bright, innocent-looking smile – Mary pulled off her travelling cape and sat down.

The men insisted on ordering large glasses of mulled wine all round. While they waited for the drinks to arrive, Mary stretched her toes out to the fire, starting to let the delicious warmth flow through them like the sunrise advancing across the fields at dawn. She had not intended to interact with anyone other than when absolutely necessary – for clearly it was foolish to risk showing her ignorance of Elizabethan life – but as the warmth enveloped her, she found herself starting to relax.

"Have you come far?" asked the younger man.

"From Grangedean," answered Olivia. "And we are on our way to London, where I am to serve in the household of Lady Burnham."

"Indeed," said the older man. He paused a moment "I am sorry, mistress, we do not know your name?"

"Olivia. Olivia Melrose."

He nodded. "Honoured to make your acquaintance, Mistress Melrose." He turned to Mary. "And are you to serve in the same household?"

"Oh no!" exclaimed Olivia, before Mary could answer. "This is Lady Mary de Beauvais, of Grangedean Manor." She gave a silvery laugh, making Mary wince. "She is not to serve in any household, but to be served in her own! For now she is on her way to London to seek out a man."

The older man raised an eyebrow. "That is most forward, Lady Mary." He shook his head slightly. "What would Sir William have to say?"

"You know my husband?" Mary was surprised.

"Sir William de Beauvais of Grangedean Manor? I know of him, but by name only." He regarded her quizzically a moment. "Allow me to introduce myself. I am Sir Robert Standing of the City of London, and this is my good friend Lionel Shelton. We are on our way from London to Birmingham."

Shelton bowed his head briefly. "Delighted, my lady, delighted."

"How wonderful!" laughed Olivia. She put her hand on Shelton's arm. "We are like ships that pass in the night," she said conspiratorially. "One evening to make merry, then never to see each other again!"

Shelton put his other hand over hers. "Indeed, Mistress Melrose, we must make merry if we can."

"Olivia, please. Call me Olivia!"

Just then the drinks arrived. Mary took a cautious sip of hers, and found it to be rather pleasant; full-bodied and spicy. She settled back in her chair and stared into the flames, letting the heat of the fire and the richness of the wine wash over her. She was vaguely aware that Olivia was chattering away brightly, and that Sir Robert and Shelton were hanging on every word and each musical laugh, but she really wasn't listening. Olivia had the admiring male audience she so clearly relished – Mary was resigned to letting her get on with entertaining them. The warmth enveloped her, and her eyes began to close…

"You must tell me of the man you seek, Lady Mary."

Mary opened her eyes. Sir Robert was smiling at her. Beyond him, she could see Shelton carefully brushing a stray lock of hair back from Olivia's forehead.

"Oh," she murmured, "it is just an old friend. I have not seen him for many years, and have heard tell he is now living in London."

"An old… friend?" He smiled again, but this time there was a more quizzical edge.

Mary shook her head. "I fear you misjudge me, Sir Robert. I am the wife of Sir William de Beauvais, and like to remain so. My interest in seeking this man is purely in renewing a very old friendship, nothing more. And anyway," she fixed him with her steeliest stare, "with respect, sir, it is no business of yours."

"You are right, Lady Mary. It is no business of mine. Please forgive my impertinent curiosity."

"'Tis no matter."

Sir Robert stared into the flames a moment, then drained his glass. "So you are escorting the delightful Mistress Melrose to London, so she can find her place in society?"

Mary nodded. Sir Robert glanced across at Shelton and Olivia, who were now giggling together, oblivious to anything but each other. "Such a charming child, is she not?" asked Sir Robert. "She and my companion Master Shelton, seem to have formed a close bond in such little time."

"I think that is her way. She has a character that men find attractive."

"And she is most fair of face as well…" he murmured.

Now it was Mary's turn to look quizzical. "That is very forward of you. The grey in your beard suggests you are old enough to be her father." She sat back in her chair and eyed him over the rim of her glass. "Is there not a Lady Standing who would object to that remark?"

"There is, aye." He paused a moment. "You are right. And anyway," he glanced across to where Olivia was now stroking Shelton's beard, "I fear I have lost out to a man who is much closer to her age than I."

---0---

The winter sun struggled weakly through the rough sacking covering Lady Mary's bedroom window. She opened her eyes and stared blankly at the chipped plaster ceiling, unsure for a moment where she was. Then it came back to her: yesterday's snow; stopping at the Cock and Magpie in the village of Hammersmith; drinking mulled wine with the two strangers by the fire; Olivia flirting shamelessly with one of them, before Mary had insisted they take their leave and had dragged the unwilling girl away and up to their room…

She sat up and looked across at the other bed – Olivia's.

The covers were flung back and it was empty.

Mary got up, and with muttered curses under her breath, started getting dressed as fast as she could. She was about to head out into the narrow passageway to start searching for Shelton's room – where no doubt she would now find the wayward Olivia – when she heard a thud against the door, followed by a small sob.

She pulled the door open, and had to step back as Olivia fell into the room at her feet, wearing nothing but a dirty and bloodied undershift.

"Oh, my goodness, Olivia!" she exclaimed. "What has happened to you?"

The girl squinted up at her through puffy red eyes, one of which was starting to blacken with a dark purple bruise. She tried to speak – but her mouth was too swollen, and all that Mary could hear was another sob.

"Come, we must get you on the bed this instant." Mary took Olivia by the arm and started to pull the girl up, but this caused an agonised howl, so she quickly let the arm drop back again. "Come, you need to be on the bed in more comfort." With a hard stare through her slit eyes Olivia held up her other arm. Mary grabbed it, and after much struggling, cursing and many yelps of pain from both of them, she finally got Olivia onto the bed.

Once the girl was laid out, Mary stood back and assessed the situation.

The rapidly blackening red marks around Olivia's eyes and mouth suggested she had been punched in the face. The undershift had streaks of dirt down one side, as if she had been pulled along the floor. But it was the blood staining the garment lower down that spoke of the worst part of this attack. Mary gently pulled at the undershift, easing it up to reveal the tops of Olivia's legs, but the girl shrieked and pushed it down again.

"By Christ, Olivia," said Mary quietly, "what has happened to you?"

As Olivia stared again at Mary her eyes started to brim with tears and she gave another great tortured sob. Mary immediately dropped to her knees and put her arms round the girl, hugging Olivia's head to her chest, rocking her back and forward as the sobs grew louder and more pained.

"Oh, my child, my poor, poor child," Mary whispered, stroking Olivia's hair, "my poor sweet child...."

The sobs continued, each one racking the girl's whole body in a convulsion of pain. Mary held her tight throughout, continuing to stroke her head and soothe her with soft shushing sounds, until the sobs started to die down, and eventually stopped altogether.

Mary eased Olivia's head down onto the pillow and slid her arms gently out from underneath. Olivia's head lolled sideways and her breathing became regular as she fell into what seemed like a deep sleep.

Mary stood up slowly. She stretched her arms out wide, feeling her back and shoulders cracking as they protested at the strain of holding the girl for so long.

At least Olivia looked peaceful as she slept – were it not for now blackened bruising on her face and the blood at the base of her belly… Mary again pulled the bottom of the shift up, exposing the girl's groin, but this time there was no howl from Olivia. Instead, just the evidence that Shelton – and it had to have been Shelton – had cruelly robbed Olivia of her innocence...

Mary eased the shift up further, to reveal the grazing down Olivia's side where she must have been dragged along the floor. Mary could imagine her fear as she tried to get away from the man, only to be dragged back and flung down on the bed, before…

Mary stood back.

This man Shelton must be made to answer for this brutal attack – an attack made on an innocent girl by an opportunist stranger with not a care for anyone's feelings but his own. The words of Thomas Melrose came back to her. "A man is generally presumed innocent if the victim of his crime is a woman." Well, this man Shelton *must* be made to answer for this crime.

Leaving Olivia asleep, Mary marched down the stairs to the main tavern. A middle-aged woman was scraping the used candles from the tables and putting out fresh ones.

"Tell me," Mary said, "are Master Shelton and Sir Robert Standing to be found? I would talk with them."

The woman paused and shook her head. "Nay, mistress. They have been gone this half an hour." She started putting out candles again. "They seemed in a fair haste to be away, despite the snowfall." She thought a moment. "The younger man in particular. Could not be away fast enough, though he was laughing and jesting with his older companion as he went."

Mary had to force herself not to kick over a nearby bench seat in her anger.

"Art well, mistress?" asked the woman, with concern in her voice. "Your face is flushed redder than a beetroot."

"I am well, thank you," Mary answered, breathing deeply.

"You look as if you have just seen a spirit," observed the woman.

"I am fine, really I am." Mary repeated. She took a couple more breaths to calm herself. She was about to make her way back upstairs to the room, when she stopped and turned back to the woman. She said, "My companion has been taken unwell. We were expecting to continue our own journey today, but I now think we will need to stay a week or maybe two while she recovers."

The woman froze, then looked at Mary with wide eyes. "She has not a fever?" she asked, her voice rising up to an unnatural-sounding level. "She has the sweating or sneezing?"

"No, she does not," Mary answered. "She has taken a bad fall and will need time to restore herself."

The woman let out her breath and once again resumed putting out fresh candles. "Then if she needs to rest, let her rest," she said over her shoulder. "I have precious few travellers stopping at this time of year, so the room is yours to stay as long as you want."

---0---

"But I must be with Lady Burnham's household on the Strand by the first day of March!" cried Olivia, when Mary told her later of the decision to stay a while in Hammersmith. "She is expecting me and I cannot disappoint her!"

She started to sit up from the bed where she was lying.

"My dear girl, lie back," said Mary, pushing her gently down again. "Do you really think you can attend Lady Burnham while your face looks like that? She will refuse to accept you."

"Like what?" Olivia asked. "What is wrong with my face?" She fingered her eye and mouth, then winced at her own touch.

Mary fetched a polished metal mirror from her bag and offered it over. Olivia took it and held it up gingerly to her face – then gasped and dropped it, as if it had suddenly become white hot. "By the Risen Lord, Lady Mary, look at me!" Olivia picked the mirror up and stared into it again. "I am disfigured! I shall never again be able to turn a man's head with my looks!"

"I should think after this night, that is the very last thing you would want to do," muttered Mary. "And anyway, a couple of weeks and you will be back to your best again, I have no doubt."

"Then yes, we must stay here until my face has healed. Until I am fully healed…" Olivia stopped suddenly, staring at Mary. Once again her eyes filled with tears and she gave another sob. "But I shall never be
healed, shall I? Because I can never be wed!" She stared at Mary, her eyes as wide as they could go with the bruising. "I can never be wed for I am no longer a maid…"

"My dear child, that is not going to be a problem unless we let it be a problem." Mary smiled at her. "Not every man who thinks he has married a maid is correct. Many are fooled by a small bag of pig's blood judiciously applied to the bedding in the morning."

Olivia looked cautiously hopeful. "Oh!" she said in a small voice. "You are sure?"

"I am indeed." Mary handed her a lace handkerchief.

Olivia wiped her eyes and gave a watery smile. "Then there may be hope?"

"I am sure that when the time comes, we will find a way."

Olivia paused and put the mirror carefully down beside her on the bed. "I have been something of a nuisance to you, have I not?" she said slowly. She looked up at Mary. "I was content for you to fix the box-cart each time it froze up, and to go out of your way to find the bridge…" There was a moment's silence, "and now I have been a silly girl, and we must stop our journey for one or maybe two weeks because of my stupid, wilful behaviour…"

Mary dropped to her knees by the bed, and clasped Olivia's hand in both of her own. "My dear sweet child," she said fiercely, "you must never, never, *ever*, blame yourself for the actions of a man – do you hear me?" Olivia gave a small but hesitant nod. "It is never a girl's fault if a man decides to act like a coward and a beast!" She stood up. "If Lionel Shelton forced himself upon you, then it is for his conscience, not yours, to answer for it."

"But as a girl, I must submit to a man's will. It is as God has ordained," said Olivia in a small voice. "My conscience must answer for refusing to submit, so that is why he has need to become angry, and to strike me, and to…"

"No!" snapped Mary, so loud and so sudden that Olivia gasped in fright. "I will not accept that!" She paced away from the bed, then turned back, her hands on her hips. "If society tells you that men may use a girl as they please, then society is wrong – and this subservience has got to stop! Do you know," she continued, "there was a time when I lived in a land where a woman's worth is measured equal to a man's, and I will respect no man unless he earns it, and nor should you!" She paced away again, then turned back and fixed Olivia with a stern look. "No man has the right to attack a girl, or to force himself on her." Then she added in a quieter voice, "And I am sure God will understand that."

"You do have the strangest way of seeing things, Lady Mary." Olivia tried to smile, although it was hard to tell with her bruises. "So you say I must not blame myself for this?"

"No, Olivia, you have been badly used by a cruel, selfish man. You should direct your anger at him, not yourself."

Olivia was silent a while, as she took this in. "Then I do that," she muttered. "I blame Lionel Shelton." She paused again. "And I do apologise to you, Lady Mary, for being a wilful girl, and for using you so thoughtlessly."

Mary smiled. "I thank you for your apology – which I accept." She paused, considering her words carefully. "And I too, apologise, for I wanted to be alone on my journey – such that I did not value your company, and did not stop you going to that man, Shelton…"

"You were asleep." Olivia observed.

"But I should have stayed awake…" Mary answered. "I have failed you my child – failed in my duty of care." Mary wiped away a small tear with her sleeve. "And for that I am truly sorry."

"So we can be friends now? asked Olivia in a small voice.

"Yes," said Mary, "we can. And now," she continued, "we must help you recover from this dreadful attack and get you better as quick as we can. Then we can get you to Lady Burnham, fully restored to your health and beauty."

"And no more talk of Lionel Shelton?"

"None at all." Mary nodded. Then she gave a small chuckle. "No more mention of Master Lionel blasted Shelton."

"Or Lionel cursed Shelton?" suggested Olivia, with as much of a smile as she could manage.

"Nay. Nor Lionel fopdoodle Shelton!" said Mary. This was a word she had heard Ruth using about the servant Simon, when he had apparently done something particularly foolish.

"A filthy yaldson!" laughed Olivia. "For his mother was a whore!" She put her hand to her mouth in sudden shock. "By Heaven, Lady Mary," she gasped, "we are using words that no lady of standing should ever utter!"

Mary took Olivia's hand. "It's good to curse this man, Olivia. For he has used you so badly, that if I ever see him again, I swear to you, he will live to regret it."

CHAPTER NINE

March 1575, North Yorkshire

Ambrose, William and the men-at-arms emerged from the dark forest into the grey afternoon light and found themselves on the edge of a high ridge.

The ridge was sliced through the middle by a deep wooded ravine, as if giant hands had pulled the sides apart and left an ugly, gaping wound. To get across, they would have to descend to the base of the ravine, then climb up the far side.

The wind drove heavy snow into their faces.

William pulled up his horse. Ambrose and the others stopped beside him.

"There, my boy, see that?" William pointed across to the far side of the ravine. Ambrose peered through the misty air, squinting against the wind and snow.

"No, Pa. What is it?"

"There. You can just see the chimneys. That, my boy, is Hetherington Hall."

Ambrose stared hard across the ridge, till he thought he saw what looked like some trees that were straight, and unlike all the others around, had no snow-laden branches.

Chimneys!

"Is it there, Pa?" he asked, "is that really it? Where the Grenvilles live and I am to make my home?"

"Indeed it is." William smiled at him – or at least he might have smiled: it was hard to tell when his beard was so caked with snow.

"Then come, Pa," Ambrose said, as he turned Thelwell onto the narrow path that disappeared down the side of the ravine into the mist. "We must make haste. My feet and hands are as cold as they ever were, and I would get to the house and warm them quickly." He rode on, following the path, and disappeared over the edge.

---0---

William indicated for the men to follow him, then urged his horse on and soon caught up with his son. Ambrose and Thelwell were picking their way carefully down the path, keeping close to the bleak rocks to one side in order to avoid the sheer drop on the other.

"Have a care, son," called William.

"I am, Pa," Ambrose replied over his shoulder, as he steered Thelwell round a hairpin bend and continued on down. "The path is wide enough for two." He let Thelwell speed up, so that William had to increase his own pace.

"I said, have a care, son!" he repeated, torn between a sudden feeling of pride in his son's horsemanship, and concern for his safety.

"Do not fret, Pa," Ambrose chuckled, as he urged his pony on. He looked back over his shoulder again. "Thelwell is as keen as I am to reach a warm stable!"

"Ambrose!" yelled William, suddenly seeing his son heading into real danger. "For Our Saviour's sake, have a care! The path narrows!"

Ambrose turned back and must have seen what William had seen – that the path in front of him curved around a rocky outcrop, and as it did so, narrowed to a single horse's width. He tried to pull his pony up, but the packed snow underfoot had become icy, and Thelwell's hooves could not find grip.

Together the pony and rider slid towards the edge of the path, and William could see that it was only a matter of moments before they must disappear over and be dashed to death on the trees and rocks below.

Urging his horse forward, he grabbed at a thick branch that grew out of a fissure in the rock, then leaned forward as far as he could and at the last possible second, grabbed the back of Ambrose's saddle with his other hand.

The weight of the pony and its forward momentum meant that it was a slim chance he would be able to stop them sliding over, but he had to try. As the muscles in his back and shoulders screamed in protest, he hung on with strength he did not know he possessed, fighting as he felt his arms being torn from their sockets.

Ambrose and Thelwell came to a stop just inches from the edge.

There was a moment as they both gathered themselves, then the pony and rider backed carefully towards William.

Feeling that he had just been split into two on the rack, William slowly released his grip on the branch and then on Ambrose's saddle.

"Oh Heavens, Pa," said Ambrose over his shoulder, "that was close!" He turned slowly in the saddle and William could see that even against the snow on the ground and the flat, colourless skies, his face was a sickly white.

"Come, son," said William quietly, "let us continue carefully to the valley floor. I would not be on this ledge a second more."

Ambrose nodded, and encouraged a reluctant Thelwell to start down the path once more.

William turned to the two men-at-arms. They had stopped just up the path, the shock on their faces no doubt a mirror of his own. He nodded to them to follow on.

A short while later they were riding through the wild sycamore trees that populated the floor of the ravine, picking their way over roots and branches that lay in soft-edged mounds under the thick carpet of snow.

"What is that, Pa?" asked Ambrose, pointing ahead. Now it was William's turn to squint through the trees, seeing nothing but brown and white shapes all the way to the far side of the dark ravine floor. Then he saw it – a small hut with a thatched roof, sitting alone in the middle of the forest.

They approached it with caution; William dismounting and walking up first. He could see no light through the window, nor smoke from the hole in the roof.

"Stay back son," he warned. Then he tried the door. It opened easily, and he peered inside. Then he reappeared.

"Come Ambrose," he ordered with a smile, "there is no one here."

There was nothing inside except a bed, a small table and a wooden chest. There was a small grate to one side, with logs piled beside it.

William sat on the bed and indicated for Ambrose to sit as well. William put his arm around the boy. "Art well?" he whispered. Ambrose nodded and looked up at his father. Suddenly his eyes were full of tears.

"I would have perished in that instant, Pa."

"Nay," said William, brushing his son's tears away. "Not while I was there to look after you. I would never let harm come to you, my boy. Never."

Ambrose snuggled deeper into his father's embrace, and then put his head down onto William's lap. William started gently stroking his soft hair, and after a few minutes he could tell from the regular breathing, that his son was fast asleep.

William laid him gently down on the bed, then went outside to where the two men-at-arms were waiting, their horses pawing the snowy ground and their breath steaming in the cold air.

"My son is exhausted, and has suffered some shock at nearly falling up there," he said. "I would he stays here tonight and tomorrow if needs be, until he has recovered himself." The men nodded. "I will stay here with him, and we will have a fire for warmth and food from our packs. You two head on up to Hetherington and we will meet again tomorrow."

The two men wheeled their horses round and started riding towards the far side of the ravine, and the path that led up towards the house, as William went back into the hut and prepared to light the fire.

---0---

The snow was still falling the next day in the flat afternoon light, as William and Ambrose arrived in the stable yard of Hetherington Hall.

Ambrose slithered off Thelwell's back and his boots crunched as they landed on the snow-covered cobbles.

A liveried servant ran out from the stables and held out his hand to take the reins.

"Welcome, young Master de Beauvais. We have been expecting you this many a day," the man said. "Let me take your pony while you go inside and warm yourself." Ambrose stared at the man, surprised at a total stranger addressing him by name.

"Give him your reins, son," said William.

Ambrose handed them over. "Thank you, young master," said the servant. "Your pony has got himself warm coming up the valley – I will rub him down and give him water and mash before he catches a chill." The man started leading Thelwell away, then turned back. "And the same for you – you run into the house with Edgar here, and warm yourself by fire."

Ambrose looked round, to find another servant had suddenly appeared beside him, like a ghost in the grey light.

"Welcome, Master de Beauvais," the man said and took Ambrose's arm. "This way, please. Let us get you inside, and in front of the fire."

Ambrose looked back at William, who nodded his approval to go with the servant.

Together they went through a side door and into a long, echoing corridor paved with flagstones. It was lit by burning braziers mounted periodically along the walls; the orange light of the fires flickering off the arched ceiling and making the bricks seem to dance brightly. Just being out of the cold wind made Ambrose feel a little warmer, and by the time they reached the Great Hall with its magnificent roaring fire, he was starting to feel the familiar throbbing of the warmth coming back into his fingers and toes.

"Stop here, and I will fetch the Master," said the man Edgar, and left them alone in the hall.

"How do you fare, son?" asked William softly, as he lifted the thick fur coat off Ambrose's shoulders. "Here, let me see your hands." He pulled each of his son's gloves off. "Aye, they are more white than pink right now, but that will soon be mended. Hold them to the fire, and let us get the heat back into them."

Ambrose held them as close as he dared to the dancing flames. The throbbing got worse, as it always did when he warmed his frozen hands, then started to get a little better.

"There, son. You will soon be warmed through." William took off his own gloves and held his hands to the flames as well. "We do not want you to catch a chill, either."

"No, Pa."

"You are strong, though." William said. "This weather is worse than I have ever seen, and we have been over three weeks on the road. Yet you have kept riding on, and never a sneeze or even a cough." He looked his son up and down a moment. "You are a fine boy, Ambrose, and will make a fine young man."

"Thanks to you, Pa," replied Ambrose with a smile.

---0---

As Ambrose knelt to warm himself by the fire, the doors swung open and William saw a large, red-faced man with a full beard stride in, followed by a slim woman with grey hair. She seemed to glide effortlessly across the floor like a serene ghost.

"God save you, good Sir Nicholas," William said, bowing to the man. "And God save you also, Lady Grenville," he added, taking the woman's arm and giving her hand a brief kiss.

Sir Nicholas and Lady Grenville returned the greetings, as a servant entered with a tray of silver wine goblets and a matching jug, then proceeded to pour the wine and hand round the goblets.

"It has been many months since we last met, my dear Sir William," boomed Sir Nicholas, "when we agreed that your fine son could be tutored in Latin, Greek and suchlike with my own Richard." He drained his goblet in one gulp and thrust it out beside him for a refill without taking his eyes off William. "The boys will have a fine time together, believe me, for it is not just classes they must attend, but their archery practice in the butts will be daily once the snow clears, and there will be hunting and other such pastimes for them!"

He beamed jovially at William, then frowned. "But by the Lord's Wounds, my dear fellow, I forget myself as a host! You must be chilled to the bone!"

"Aye, but it is not my bones that matter," said William, gesturing to Ambrose. "It is my son who needs to be made warm again, after so many weeks in the cold and wind."

"Indeed," said Lady Grenville, gesturing at Ambrose, "come hither, child – let me see you."

Ambrose stood up, but stayed close to the fire.

"Oh my, how could I be so thoughtless!" she cried. "You must not leave its warmth until all the chill is gone from you." She wafted over and took his hands in hers. "Your hands are as blocks of ice, are they not?" She took each in turn and rubbed it between her own. "There, child, we will soon have you restored!"

"Thank you, my lady," Ambrose muttered.

"I want you to think of this as your own house, my child," she said. "Is that not so, Nicholas?"

"That is so," he answered.

Ambrose looked carefully up at Lady Grenville. "And what of worship?" he asked. "Are we to attend Catholic mass?"

There was a brief pause, and William thought he saw a look pass between Sir Nicholas and his wife, then she smiled sweetly and said, "Good heavens, no! Queen Elizabeth has forbidden such things. What a forward young man you are, Ambrose de Beauvais!" She patted his head and William saw him flinch slightly. "There is a fine little church in the village and we attend services there, exactly as the law says we must."

Sir Nicholas drained his cup again.

He turned to the servant who was refilling it. "Have Richard brought in," he ordered. "He can meet our young guest who is to be his companion in the schoolroom and the butts."

"And Master Topsham, also," added his wife, "who is to provide their schooling each day."

"Then we will eat," said Sir Nicholas. "My wife tells me that a boar has been well roasted and will certainly warm us all!"

---0---

That night, Ambrose lay in the soft, warm bed and studied the gold-framed miniature of his mother. The frame was looking a little faded and scratched, but the smiling face was as bright and as colourful as ever.

"We have arrived, Ma," he whispered softly to her. "I have been cold, and I have been hungry, but we have finally arrived, Pa and me. We have had some adventures on the way, Ma, like I told you before, with the man Alleyne falling from his horse and being killed, and Master Wychwoode joining us till he turned off at Stratford to question a man called John Tyler about a Catholic plot to kill the Queen – which I know would upset you so much, Ma, because you have said what a great lady the Queen is, and what she will do to make England the best nation in the world one day."

He stroked the side of his mother's face. "And I all but fell off the side of a ravine, Ma, but Pa was there and he hung onto me and stopped me from falling." He took a deep breath to clear the memory of sliding towards the edge of the icy path. "Then Pa and I found a small hut and we slept there the night and through the morning as well as we were tired and it was warm under some blankets we found there and with the fire." He smiled at the little picture. "And now we have arrived, Ma, we have actually arrived. Hetherington Hall is a fine house. So far I have only seen the Great Hall and my bed chamber, for they said I must rest after supper, but I feel sure it will be good here." He stroked his mother's face again, and she smiled back at him.

"I have met Sir Nicholas and Lady Grenville, and they have said I am to imagine this is my own home, although it is not, is it, Ma? My home is Grangedean Manor with you and Pa – but I will do my best to be part of their family while I am here, and be a credit to you and Pa, and to the Grenvilles." He wriggled down the bed to get more comfortable, enjoying the feel of real bedsheets and a soft mattress; so much nicer than the rough blankets and hard pallet beds he had endured in the taverns on the journey.

"And I have met Richard Grenville, who is nine, and I must be assured we will be good friends, although he has a slightly mean look, and Master Topsham, who is to be my tutor in classes with Richard, who seems to be a kindly man." He paused. "Also I have met a man called Lambert Moreton, who is Sir Nicholas's nephew and is staying here for a few weeks. He came in when we were eating our supper of roast boar, but he would not eat with us, and instead he was much pre-occupied with some important matters. He would not discuss these where Pa and I could overhear, so he demanded Sir Nicholas to come out of the hall with him to carry on the conversation, which I thought was not polite, and if I had done that, you would have scolded me for it, Ma, I am sure you would." Ambrose smiled drowsily. "Although I would rather have you here and scolding me, Ma, than hundreds of miles away at home. Are you thinking of me, Ma, like I am thinking of you?" He shook his head. "I am sure you are too busy with Kat and Jane to think of me, aren't you? But maybe you do." He looked up and across to the glowing embers of the fire, then back at his mother. "I have asked Pa to tell you how much I love you and I miss you, when he gets back home, and he says he will, and he ruffled my hair and said I am a fine boy. But Pa has said he will not yet set off on his homeward journey as the snow is already so thick and it falls heavily. But when he does, and he gets home, he will tell you, because I asked him too… because I asked… because…"

The miniature dropped out of Ambrose's fingers and onto the bed, as he slipped gently into a deep sleep.

CHAPTER TEN

The Strand, London, late March 1575

Lady Burnham stared down her nose as Mary and Olivia were ushered into her presence in the Long Gallery.

"Mistress Olivia Melrose?" she demanded with an audible sniff of disapproval. "You are two weeks late. I should refuse now to take you in."

"We do most humbly beg your pardon, my lady," said Mary. "But we were unavoidably detained in the village of Hammersmith. The snow was so thick we could not leave the village, nor find any messenger able to get word to you."

This was mostly true – the snow had fallen heavily ever since they had arrived at The Cock and Magpie and it would have been foolish to try and travel while it lay so thick on the ground. But it had thawed enough to travel a good few days before Olivia's face and outer scars had healed enough to be concealed under make-up. By then Mary thought it too late to send a messenger; as he would only be a day or two ahead of them. So, once Olivia was fully restored to health, they had pressed on into London and were able to present themselves at Lady Burnham's magnificent riverside house, hoping she was there and still disposed to see them.

"Indeed," said Lady Burnham to Olivia, "and who is this who has brought you here, Mistress Melrose, and speaks for you while you look to the floor?" She glared at Mary, then back to Olivia. "Is this Mistress Melrose, your mother?"

"Oh no, Lady Burnham," said Olivia, "my mother has sadly passed away. This is Lady Mary de Beauvais of Grangedean Manor, who has very kindly brought me here."

"Lady Mary de Beauvais?" Lady Burnham appeared to attempt a cold smile, "I have heard of your husband, of course – Sir William. Yes, I have heard of him…" She left it there, seeming to imply that not having heard of Mary as well was somchow Mary's own fault

Then Lady Burnham rang a small hand bell, and a few moments later a liveried servant appeared.

"Take Mistress Melrose to her rooms and ensure she is settled in. Introduce her to Mistress Tyndall, who is to share rooms with her. They will join me and my other ladies at supper."

The servant bowed and showed Olivia to the door. Olivia followed him with her head still down, and was almost out of the room when she suddenly turned and ran back to Mary, flinging her arms around Mary's neck and hugging her tightly. "Fare thee well, dearest Lady Mary, I shall miss you so, truly I will!" She pulled back and looked at Mary with tearful eyes. "You have been so good to me, and I am sure I did not deserve your patience and love – I have been such a foolish girl!"

"Nay, child," whispered Mary, "you may have been wilful to start, but I warrant you have learned some valuable lessons these few weeks. I would you mark them well."

Olivia nodded.

"So remember what I told you," Mary said quietly, taking a silk handkerchief out of her sleeve. Then she dropped her voice so Lady Burnham could not possibly hear. "What that man did to you was wrong, and unforgiveable, and if you ever have the chance, you should find a way to make him pay for what he did." She wiped Olivia's cheeks where the tears had fallen, then cupped the girl's face in her hands and looked deep into her eyes. "No man has the right to take you against your will," she whispered fiercely, "and you must never, ever, ever blame yourself for a man's weakness. As I told you when we were in Hammersmith, I once lived in a land where a woman's worth is measured equal to a man's, and I will respect no man unless he earns it, and nor should you." She leaned forward and kissed Olivia on the forehead, then let the girl go and stood back. "Now my beautiful child," she said aloud, "hold your head high, and be the brilliant person that I know you can be."

Olivia nodded, then gave Mary one last watery smile, and was gone.

There was a long moment's silence after the door had closed, then Lady Burnham observed drily, "If you were that girl's mother you could not love her more. I warrant she has gained much from having you as a travelling companion."

Mary nodded slowly. "Aye. She is young and I will admit I thought her very foolish and self-centred when we first met, but the time we spent together has made me grow to see her as a young woman with a good heart, and maybe I saw something of myself as a girl in her. She is both willing and able, and I am sure she will serve you well." Then Mary fixed the older woman with a firm eye.

"And I trust, Lady Burnham, that you will do the same for her."

---0---

A few minutes later, Mary stepped out of Lady Burnham's house and paused on the step, looking down into the hustle and bustle of the Strand, trying to pick her moment to join the mass of people that were progressing in both directions in the slush and mud.

Some were on horseback, some on foot, and many were pushing wooden carts laden with produce. These enterprising merchants had either stopped and were selling to the rest of the crowd, or were pushing on, seeming desperate to get somewhere else.

A gap opened briefly in the crowd and Mary grabbed her opportunity. She lifted her skirts clear of the mud and stepped briskly into the flow of people and carts. As she started walking she could see a cart just up ahead loaded with bread in baskets, and a sudden rumble in her stomach reminded her that she hadn't eaten in many hours.

It was not easy to get through the crowd, but finally she caught up and grabbed a rough-looking loaf from one of the baskets.

"One farthing, lady," the man called out, stopping his cart.

She paid and he was about to push on, when she said, "Pray tell me, sir, how may I get to Southwark from here?"

"Southwark, lady?" He paused a moment, considering. "You can walk across the bridge, but that is a long walk, or you can just step down to the riverside right there," he indicated a gap between two houses close by, "and take a wherry across." He looked her up and down. "Hath not a husband to tell you this and to take you?"

Mary forced herself to smile sweetly and said, "My husband is not with me now, but we shall soon be re-united."

The man grunted. "Fare thee well, mistress," he said, and pushed his cart back into the stream of people.

Clutching the loaf, Mary turned down some steps to a small landing stage. A waterman was sitting in a boat tied to the stage, as it bobbed gently up and down on the brown waters of the Thames.

"Would you take me to Southwark?" she asked.

He nodded and she stepped down into the boat, arranging her skirts as she sat on the worn leather-covered seat in the stern. The waterman cast off, settled himself on the thwart and started to row.

As they headed out into the Thames, Mary took a few small bites of the bread. It was dry and tasteless, but at least it was reasonably filling.

The river was teeming with hundreds of boats, large and small. Some were crossing in the same direction as them, but there were also many boats coming up or down river across their path. The waterman seemed oblivious to the danger and steered safely past every possible collision without ever once taking his eyes off her loaf of bread, which made her feel quite uncomfortable.

Twenty minutes later he was helping her up onto a landing stage.

Mary thanked him and handed him the agreed coin, and after a moment's pause, the rest of her loaf.

"Thank you," he muttered, and was about to climb back into his boat, when Mary had a sudden thought. "Excuse me," she said. "But I need to find a particular man. I am told he lives in Southwark, but I do not know his address."

The waterman stared at her blankly and she immediately regretted asking. It had been a spur-of-the-moment thing – almost as a return favour for the remains of the bread – but now she could see how very odd it sounded.

"I am sorry," she said, "it is no matter. I should not have asked…"

"This man you seek – belike it is not your husband?"

"Well, no, but I do not see…"

"Hmm." The man shook his head slowly. There was a long silence. Mary was about to thank him anyway and walk off, when he said, "You have a name?" before breaking off a large piece of bread with brown teeth and chewing on it slowly and noisily. She nodded, mesmerised by the sight and sound of the chewing. It reminded her of a cement mixer she had once seen as a child.

He continued chewing for what seemed like forever, then eventually he swallowed and said, "Start at the Blue Maid." He looked about to break off some more bread, and Mary stole herself for another long bout of chewing, but thankfully he muttered instead, "The men in there know everyone. Tell them what your fellow looks like and happen they will know where to find him." Then he turned without any further word, stepped back into his boat and pushed off for the northern bank.

Mary paused a moment, trying to get the image of the waterman's chewing out of her mind, then cleared it with a shake of her head and set off through the streets. It seemed she'd had the right idea herself to start at a tavern, so she walked with her head high and hope rising that she would soon be able to meet Rick – and ask him her all-important question.

But the Blue Maid wasn't easy to find at first. After several wrong turns, many double-backs and a series of confusing directions from locals, she was starting to believe that maybe the waterman had been playing with her – deliberately sending her on a fool's errand. Had he been put out by her being a woman alone, or by the way she had stared at him when he was chewing the bread? But she had given it to him, after all… Then she spotted the sign of a girl milking a cow swinging lazily on a building up a side road.

With a small sigh of relief and a mental slap on the wrist for being paranoid, she hurried along to the sign and was relieved to see that it bore the name 'The Blue Maid'.

Mary entered the tavern and stood a moment in the doorway, adjusting her eyes to the dim light coming from the candles stuttering on the tables and the warm fire in the chimney breast close by. She started to make out the throng of men laughing and shouting at the blackened wooden tables; men dressed in the sombre colours of yeomen or the dirty smocks of peasant land-workers; also a few in fashionable doublets. Women in ale-stained aprons weaved round the tables with trays of tankards or wooden platters of food, leaning across the tables to serve the men; getting their bottoms slapped or having to push away hands that tried to stroke their hair.

At first no-one seemed to notice her. The noise of laughter and conversation continued unchecked, ebbing and flowing around the room. Then one man in a rough leather jerkin sitting at the table nearest the door happened to look up and stopped talking abruptly. His companion followed his gaze and stopped with his tankard raised part-way to his mouth. This aroused the curiosity in the men at the next table – and from there the next – until within half a minute the whole tavern was staring open-mouthed at her in stony silence that went on for an uncomfortably long time.

Mary shivered, despite the warmth of the fire.

What seemed like a hundred dirty, bearded faces were staring at her; their eyes boring into her with expressions ranging from idle curiosity through to unhealthy interest. Suddenly she was back in the Grangedean tavern on the night ten years before, when she stood accused of witchcraft and knew that behind the eyes of every man, woman and child in the place was a desire to see her burned to death.

Now it was clear why everyone had been so concerned that she should not travel alone.

Mary cursed inwardly. What had she been thinking – to assume that just because she came from the 21st century, she was immune to the basest instincts of 16th century men? Had she learned nothing from Lionel blasted Shelton?

A moment later her worst fears were confirmed.

"Art alone, mistress?" called out the man who first noticed her. "Or is your husband to be found presently?" The men around him sniggered.

Before she could think of a suitable answer, another man spoke up. "The stews are closed down now, mistress, if that is the home you seek." There was laughter from a few of the men. "Although," he continued, "there are plenty of new brothels in their place."

"Art well dressed for a whore," said a small, swarthy man with a scar down his cheek. "But I have a good purse and," he stood up and thrust his hips forward suggestively, "a hearty appetite!" There was much laughter and he came over to where she stood. "I shall take a piece of this in the back room!" he announced to the rest of the tavern. Then he grabbed her sleeve. "Come my lovely, and earn your keep!" She recoiled from the man – from the foul smell of his breath and his body. Desperately she tried to pull away, but he had a firm grip on her sleeve and was not about to let go. He rounded on her, his rough, scarred face close to hers and the stench of his ale-laden breath filling her nose and mouth. "I said to come my lovely, so come," he growled.

"Get away from me!" Mary snapped, then added in the firmest voice she could muster. "I am no whore!"

Unfortunately this revelation did not result in him releasing her sleeve and apologising for his dreadful mistake.

"I care not," he said, pulling at her again. "I want a piece, and it is all the better if I do not need to pay."

Mary was just drawing breath to scream as loud as she could – however futile that might be, when she heard a firm voice say, "Unhand her, Jake!"

Another man had stood up. With hope rising, Mary could only assume that these words meant he was on her side. She recognised him as the first one to have noticed her just now.

She and Jake watched as this man came over.

"I said, unhand her," the man repeated.

"Nay, Ned, she is to be my fun this afternoon," Jake snarled. "You wait your turn."

"Leave her, Jake," said the man called Ned. Then he smiled at Mary. She smiled back, and was about to thank him profusely for rescuing her, when slowly and deliberately, and with his eyes fixed on hers, he licked his lips.

Her blood ran cold.

His next words confirmed her worst fears. He said, "I saw her first, so I have her first. You wait your turn."

But Jake was not going to give up easily. "She is mine, Ned!" he snarled. "So be gone before I make you!"

"Nay, she is mine, I tell you!" answered Ned, and suddenly an evil-looking knife appeared in his free hand. Jake took a step back, staring at the blade, which allowed Ned to grab Mary and start pulling her towards a door at the back of the room.

"Let me be!" she cried, looking around for someone – anyone – to help her. "I am Lady Mary de Beauvais!" But all the faces seemed like stone, all watching impassively as she was dragged past them. Desperately she looked for the higher-ranking men she had seen initially – anyone in a fine doublet who might come to her rescue, but those she saw had their heads down, although one did look up as she passed, and she saw him shake his head sorrowfully.

Ned flung her through the door, then he closed it behind him.

"Get away from me," she yelled as she backed into the room, "or you will regret it!"

"I think not, mistress," he said with another evil grin, advancing on her with the knife raised. "I too have an appetite, and you are just the wench to fill it."

"Did you not hear what I said? I am Lady Mary de Beauvais," she repeated, trying to keep her voice steady, "and my husband is Sir William de Beauvais. Perhaps you have heard of him?"

"Nay. Never."

"If you do this, he will find you and he will kill you."

"I care not if you are cousin to the Queen herself," he answered. She bumped up against the far wall and heard herself whimpering in fear.

He came right up to her and put his knife to her throat.

As she tried to shrink from the blade, he reached down with his free hand and untied his breeches. As they dropped to the floor, she felt his hand grasp her skirts and work its way under them, then she felt him position himself closer to her body.

So, this was how she was to learn the lesson not to go out alone in Elizabethan London. What were all her fine words to Olivia worth, if she ended up walking into a situation where it happened to her?

Mary screwed her eyes shut and held her breath. Nothing happened.

She opened her eyes.

Ned's coarse face was burning bright red in front of hers; his eyes bulging and his tongue sticking out between blue lips.

A pair of hands were around his throat, throttling him.

With a gurgling sigh his face dropped out of her sight – to be replaced by that of the man who had been standing just behind him.

It was the well-dressed man who had shaken his head as she had passed by a minute earlier.

She stared at him, struggling to find any words appropriate to the situation.

The man flexed his fingers, with a grimace of pain. Then he smiled.

"Lady Mary de Beauvais, eh?" he said. "I have heard of your husband Sir William, of course, but have not had the pleasure of making your acquaintance before now."

Mary took a deep breath to steady her nerves, and waited a few moments for her heartbeat to get back to something like normality. "You shook your head as I passed," she said slowly. "Yet now you come in and stop this man?" She paused. For all his fine clothing, this man might be no better than Ned and Jake. "Or are you merely going to replace him yourself?" she asked with an edge of resignation in her voice.

He gave a small barking laugh. "Nay." He shook his head. "You need have no fear on that score. No. I could not countenance such a fine lady being so ill-used." He paused. "I could see that all the men in the tavern back yonder were on the side of Master Ned here, and that to deny those of them who wanted to take a turn at you, as I fear they were planning, would make rescuing you at best difficult – and at worst suicidal."

"So why…?"

"Ahh. Then I remembered that this room has a side entrance from the street, so giving me a way in unseen and us both an effective escape route." He looked down at Ned, who was groaning and coughing at their feet. "And I think we should effect that escape before Master Ned here recovers sufficiently to raise the alarm, or anyone else comes in for their turn."

He took her arm and guided her across to the far corner of the room, where there was a wooden door partly obscured behind some stacked beer barrels. He pushed it open and led her out into the street.

"I found this when I was here a while ago and needed to conduct some private business away from the tavern," he said conversationally. "A useful thing to know."

He took her quickly along the street and through several turns before she found herself stepping down onto the same small jetty where she had originally arrived in Southwark. Another wherry was tied up and bobbing alongside, and her rescuer helped her down into it. They settled themselves side by side on the seat at the back.

"Queenhythe as fast as you can, sirrah," he snapped. The waterman cast them off and started to row.

Mary glanced back at the Southwark jetty, but there was no sign of pursuit, so she turned back and studied the man next to her.

He was clearly a gentleman. He was well dressed, with a fine embroidered doublet, well-fitted hose and soft leather shoes. His beard was trim, and the hair that curled back over his ears was thick and dark.

Mary realised that in all the drama of her rescue, she had not shown this man her deep gratitude. "I must thank you, sir," she said, "for your action today. You have saved me from dishonour by that foul brute of a man."

"Aye." He turned to her and smiled. "But I must ask what in heaven's name you were doing entering a Southwark tavern alone? Did you not know that men such as Jake and Ned would see you as fair game?"

Mary paused, staring across the river and trying to decide what her story should be. The only sound was the waterman's oars splashing rhythmically as she considered her options. Eventually she decided that this man had an honest, open face, bright blue eyes, and should be trusted.

"I was looking for an old friend, and I had heard he was in Southwark. I wanted to ask if anyone could help me find him."

"An old friend?" She sensed an edge of humour in his voice and turned to him. He had an eyebrow raised.

"Yes. Is that so bad?"

"No, but it raises more questions than it answers."

"Well, I am not prepared to answer them right now. And anyway," she said carefully, "I do not even know your name."

He removed his cap and made a small bow from the waist.

"Tom Cobham at your service, Lady de Beauvais."

CHAPTER ELEVEN

Hetherington Hall, late March 1575

Sir William and Ambrose were standing at the edge of the woods, looking out over the misty ravine.

It had become their habit to meet there every morning, despite the cold wind and driving snow. It was good to spend a few minutes alone together; time when they could share stories and observations about their lives at Hetherington Hall without being overheard.

William huddled into his thick fur coat. "Art well, son?" he asked.

"Yes, Pa."

"And becoming friends with young Richard Grenville? You said yesterday that he was spiting you occasionally."

"We are good friends."

Something in Ambrose's voice made William look hard at his son. "You are sure?"

Ambrose was silent a moment, then said, "He called me a name, Pa." He paused while a strong gust of wind howled around them. "So I knocked him down."

"What name?"

"It was nothing."

William put his arm on Ambrose's. "What name, son?" he repeated.

Ambrose was silent and William waited. After a moment Ambrose said, "He called me a heretic."

"A heretic?"

Ambrose nodded.

"I suppose he knows no different with his Catholic upbringing," said William. "So you knocked some sense into him, eh?"

"Yes Pa." Ambrose paused. "And now we are friends, truly."

"Belike he respects you now, for standing up to him."

"Yes, I think he does."

William waited while another gust of wind howled around them. "And what learning have you had this past day?" he asked.

"Latin mostly – we have been learning how verbs should be declined."

"And divinity? Have you been learning the true faith?"

"Aye, Pa. I have my divinity lesson each day at the same hour of the afternoon."

"But no papist heresy?"

"No, I am instructed about the true faith by Master Topsham."

William turned to him. "And Richard? He called you a heretic, but he should not call you that name. Does he not baulk at learning how faith should be practiced according to God's true wishes?"

"He is never there for my divinity lesson. Master Topsham and I are always alone."

There was silence as William considered this. "And this is the same time each day?" he asked slowly. "Is it by chance," he swallowed, "at five in the afternoon?"

"Yes, always at the same hour. Always five in the afternoon."

"And you are sure Richard is never there?"

"Never." Ambrose looked at his father. "Why?"

William shook his head. "No," he said slowly. "'Tis no matter" He looked at his son with a weak smile. "No matter at all – I am mistaken."

But that was just to protect Ambrose, for he was not mistaken. Five in the afternoon was when he too was always left alone. Whatever was happening, whether he was talking to Sir Nicholas or Lady Grenville, or even to Lambert Moreton, just before five they would always make some excuse and leave him alone – not to re-appear for at least an hour.

William stared across the ridge; the harsh edges of the ravine softened by the snow.

What would be the one thing the Grenvilles might do as a Catholic family all together, which they would want to keep secret from him and Ambrose? A Catholic family that were making an outward show of conformity by attending the Protestant church in the village – but in truth, could not let go of their heretical practices?

It would be to hold a secret Catholic mass somewhere in the house, every day at five.

William resolved to find out if he was right. He would try to follow them and see where they went.

Because if they were holding mass, it was treason – and not only were they putting themselves in danger, but he and Ambrose could potentially be implicated too.

His words to Ambrose came suddenly back to him, cutting into his head like the wind howling across the ravine.

Son, I promise you will be safe at the Grenvilles.

William felt sick. Here he was, not a couple of weeks into his son's time at Hetherington Hall – and already these words had become a hollow, empty promise.

He cursed his stupidity for ever taking Grenville at his word. But Grenville had been so convincing; so open and honest when they had met in London, that although the family were Catholics in the past, they had accepted the new laws and moved on. But now he thought on it, Grenville had been at such pains to explain how the family were conforming to the law and attending Protestant church, that perhaps he had been just a little too eager.

But why? What purpose would it serve to have Ambrose in the house if their mass was discovered?

If indeed they were holding mass.

He had to find out, so he could decide what action he must take to protect his son.

And it would have to be this afternoon – he could not wait another day with this uncertainty.

----0----

"Good Sir William, I would you give me leave just now – I have matters I must attend to in the kitchens regarding the evening meal." Lady Grenville gave thin smile. "I am sure you can devise some entertainment of your own?"

"Indeed, my lady," William answered with a smile that was as thin as hers. "I have my bible to study and my prayers to make – I pray God will cause this snow to melt so I can soon be on my way home and no longer be a burden on your kind hospitality."

"It is no burden, my dear Sir William." She floated gracefully over to the door; her skirts gliding across the floor without any rise and fall. "It has been a pleasure to have you as our guest and I know it is a comfort to your charming son." She paused with her hand on the door. "You are welcome as long as God sees fit to keep the snow from thawing."

She wafted through the door and closed it sharply behind her.

William waited around ten minutes, hoping this would give the family enough time to make their way to their secret mass, then he slipped off his shoes and padded silently to the door.

Where would they have gone? There were a number of possibilities he had considered since the morning meeting with Ambrose – and the one he felt most probable was the east wing, where he knew there were some empty guest rooms on the upper floor which were locked for the winter.

He emerged into the narrow corridor and checked left and right to make sure there was no one else in sight. Then he crept softly along until he came to the main stairway. Again he checked he was alone, then stepped as quietly as he could to the top of the cold stone stairs. There he stopped, listening intently, trying to ignore the sound of his heart thumping like a galloping horse. After some minutes, he made his way slowly along the corridor towards the east wing, checking each floorboard before committing his full weight to it, in case of tell-tale creaks.

He arrived at the door to the first of the three closed-up rooms on the corridor. He put his ear to it, but there was no sound from within. The same was true of the second, and also of the last. He was about to walk away, when suddenly he thought he heard a distant male voice.

He stopped, every nerve on edge, straining to hear it.

Nothing. He was about to leave when – there it was again.

Distant. Faint. But definitely a male voice.

Perhaps it was someone talking elsewhere in the house? There was no reason to suppose anything sinister if it was just two servants talking…

Then it came again. Louder. Clearer.

And now he could hear the words.

"Benedictus qui venit in nomine Domini."

William gasped. "Blessed is he who comes in the name of the Lord."

So it was true!

The Grenvilles were indeed committing treason by celebrating the Catholic mass in secret.

He moved closer to the door of the third room, and put his ear gently against it. He could still hear the voice, but if anything, it was slightly less clear. Very slowly he eased the latch up, then pushed the door open by no more than an inch. Still the sound remained faint, forcing him to conclude that wherever the mass was taking place, it was not in this particular room.

But where? Stepping back into the corridor he looked at the wood panelling that closed it off at the end. He tried to recall what was below this corridor – some formal rooms for receiving guests? And the main receiving room at the end of the wing, with windows on all three sides and magnificent views over the snowy gardens and parklands? If it was, and William was pretty sure it was, then why was this corridor above it blocked off short? There had to be a room beyond.

He went up to the wood panelling and gingerly put his ear to it.

"*In nomine patris et filii et spiritus sancti, Amen*," came the man's voice, much clearer now and sounding like it was only a few feet away on the other side of the panelling. It was followed by an "Amen" from the congregation.

William pulled back as if the panel had suddenly become white hot, then stood still a moment. So there was a room beyond the panelling – which presumably the Grenvilles accessed through a secret door in this corridor or in the third room.

William hesitated, unsure whether to run and risk being heard, or to creep slowly away and risk being spotted.

Then there was a louder sound – one that made his heart miss a beat.

It was the sound of chairs scraping back.

"The mass is ended. Go in peace to love and serve the Lord."

He only had seconds to get away before the family would emerge from their secret mass.

Throwing caution to the wind, he ran back down the corridor as quickly as he could and almost fell down the stairs, then sprinted across to the room where he had left his shoes. He put his head round the door – thankfully there was no one there – and slipped quietly inside.

He ran softly to the place where he had left his shoes.

They were not there. They had gone.

In rising panic, he looked everywhere around the room.

They were nowhere to be seen.

With a stream of muttered curses, he headed back up the stairs and made for his rooms. He would have to get another pair as quickly as possible before he ran into any member of the family and had some explaining to do.

Arriving at his door, he glanced around to check he was still unseen, then slipped inside.

With a sharp intake of breath, he spotted his missing shoes immediately.

There was no mistaking them; they had been placed clearly in the middle of the floor.

So someone had found them in the room downstairs, and brought them up to his rooms.

Which could only mean that someone – presumably a servant – had seen them, knew they were his, and had taken them to his room.

Which, in turn, meant that a servant knew he had been creeping around the house with no shoes, at precisely the time when the Grenvilles were attending their secret mass.

And if a servant knew, then how likely would it be that the Grenvilles would soon know as well?

William sat on his bed and looked blankly at the drapes hanging around it.

If the Grenvilles knew that he was aware of their treasonous masses in Hetherington Hall, then he had suddenly become a significant threat to their security. They could hardly risk him leaving the Hall.

And if they knew, then it was not just discovery by the authorities that put him and Ambrose in mortal danger – now it was the Grenvilles themselves.

CHAPTER TWELVE

Tom Cobham's eyes were fixed unwaveringly on Lady Mary's over the rim of his glass. He stared hard at her as he swilled his wine round.

"My dear lady, let me understand this," he said, as the wine spun lazily in the glass. "You have left your home and your children to come to London to seek this man you call Richard?"

She nodded.

"Yet you have nothing more to go on than you know his name and the possible chance that he lives in Southwark?"

Again, she nodded.

"And this is because you knew him ten years ago, and you would like to see him again?"

"There are questions I would ask him that only he can answer."

"Marry, I trust there are. He had better have answers that the Lord himself could not give, for you to have put yourself in the gravest danger in seeking him out."

"It seemed the right place to start looking."

"Aye, and look how it nearly ended." He continued to swill the wine around his glass. She smiled.

"Again, I owe you my thanks."

"That man Ned was acting as a wild beast, which was according to his nature. I used the only force he would understand."

"And I am deeply grateful."

There was a silence as Tom continued to stare hard at her. She wasn't sure which was the easiest thing to look at – his piercing blue eyes or the mesmeric circular movement of the wine. She chose his eyes.

"How would you have recognised this man – even if you had managed to find him?"

Mary thought a moment. She had decided in the boat across from Southwark to trust Tom. He had saved her honour, and possibly her life. And now he had taken her to the safety of his small house near Blackfriars, made her comfortable, fed her and given her some wine.

Maybe he could help her find Rick. He certainly seemed to be confident, resourceful and knowledgeable. She leaned forward.

"Last time I saw this man, he had spiky hair like a hedgehog."

"As do many men. You would have needed more."

"He had two tattoos – pictures – on his forearms. They were of guns… of weapons that look a bit like small muskets."

Mary was totally unprepared for the effect that this had on Tom.

The glass froze so abruptly in his hand that wine slopped out and splashed across the table. But Tom ignored it, his face suddenly turned ashen white as he stared at Mary with a look of total horror.

"By the Risen Lord," he whispered slowly. "You seek the Alchemist?"

Mary raised an eyebrow. "If that is what you call him. I knew him as Rick, or Richard."

"No, no, this is not possible…" Tom shook his head fiercely. "This cannot be – it is too much of a coincidence."

"Why?"

"Because I, too, seek the Alchemist." He frowned, his blue eyes searching hers. "But I cannot find trace of him." He poured himself more wine and drank it in a single draught. "He has not been seen for many days. Something caused him to disappear – it was around a week ago."

Now it was Mary's turn for a sudden shocked reaction.

"A week? No!" She banged on the table with her hand, making him jump. "No! If only Olivia had not…" She stopped herself.

"By the Lord's Wounds, if only Olivia – who e're she might be – had not… what?"

"No." She shook her head. "It was not her fault…"

"But...?" he asked.

Mary paused, waiting for her ragged breathing and racing heartbeat to subside. Eventually she said, "I agreed to take a young girl with me from Grangedean Manor to London, as she had been offered a position in the household of Lady Burnham in her place on the Strand. We were in Hammersmith when she was… when she was…"

Suddenly Tom's room disappeared and she was once again in the back room of The Blue Maid. She flinched as the foul pockmarked face of Ned appeared in front of her again and she could feel his hands fumbling at her skirts, smell his evil breath in her face; feel the sharp point of his knife pricking at her throat. She gave a small cry and put her hand to her neck as if to protect herself from him.

She heard a voice say, "Lady Mary! Art unwell?"

She stared at Ned, recoiling from the rough touch of his hand on her leg… then she felt a hard shake on her shoulder, and as she looked at Ned, his twisted, evil features slowly faded and were replaced by the open, honest and very worried face of Tom Cobham.

"Lady Mary," he repeated. "What is it?" He put his hand over hers. "Were you back in the Blue Maid just then, with that wretch Ned? You looked as if you were re-living his attack."

She nodded, wide-eyed.

"My dear lady." He pushed a glass wine towards her. "Drink this – it will restore you."

Mary took a small sip, and felt the wine fill her head with a warm glow.

She forced herself to breathe normally. "I am fine," she said, as much to reassure herself as him. She could feel Ned slipping back into the shadows of her mind again.

Tom gave her the time she needed to recover.

"Olivia was…" she began again.

"Nay, tell me not," he said, "if it once more brings back your memories of the Blue Maid."

"No, it is right that I tell you," she said. "And I can control my memories now." She took another sip of wine, then a deep breath. "Olivia was attacked by a man called Shelton, who left her bloodied and bruised so she could not be seen in polite society. We had to wait two weeks in Hammersmith before she was fit to travel to London." She paused. "Two weeks that meant I missed Rick." She shook her head, her eyes closed tight. "I would have found Rick if Olivia had not…"

"If Olivia had not led this man Shelton on?"

Mary opened her eyes. "No, that's not…"

"Not what you would say to Olivia?" He smiled thinly. "But it is what you were thinking."

"If Olivia had not been attacked," she corrected him. "He hit her in the face and dragged her roughly across the floor. It was certainly no fault of hers."

"He was clearly not a true gentleman, this Master Shelton."

"No more than Ned – for all he dressed as befitting a much higher rank."

Tom stood and fetched some rags from a bucket in the corner, then mopped up the spilled wine. Mary waited until he had thrown the rags back in the bucket, then asked, "And why do you seek Rick, or the Alchemist as you call him, Master Cobham?"

Tom sat down and poured himself some more wine, very slowly and deliberately, as though he was giving himself extra time to think.

"Let us just say that he is a person that some very influential men of my acquaintance would like to speak to. They too have questions that only he can answer."

"Oh." She thought a moment, then said, "Is he mixed up in a Catholic plot or some such thing? He is not a Catholic as far as I remember."

Tom stood up again. "Lady Mary de Beauvais," he said, "I must tell you that the man you call Richard, and I know as the Alchemist, is indeed part of a Catholic plot against the life of our sovereign lady Elizabeth. And the fact that he has disappeared is extremely concerning for me and my master, one Robert Wychwoode, as it is highly likely that the one man in this realm who can truly succeed in taking the Queen's life, is this Alchemist."

He looked as if she should be impressed with the gravity of this pronouncement, but instead she squeaked, "Robert Wychwoode?" He nodded. "But I know a Robert Wychwoode! Is he tall with long grey hair, and a lawyer by profession?"

"Yes, that is my master in this matter."

"Oh yes! I know him! Ten years ago he helped me and my husband William defeat a dreadful man called Hopkirk. He saved us both, in a way." She smiled. "How can I help?"

"Lady Mary, it is most fitting that you know my master, but I must ask you to consider this from my view." He leaned forward with his hands on the table. "Through the oddest of coincidence, you and I seek the same man. We came together by chance encounter. In my line of work I view such apparent randomness with the deepest suspicion. I must ask you this – and I demand a straight answer on pain of your eternal soul. Did you engineer this meeting? Are you part of the plot I seek to foil?"

A hundred different responses flashed through Mary's mind, ranging from flippant to sarcastic. She paused a moment. Surely the best was response was to treat the question was with the gravity it deserved?

"No, Master Cobham," she said slowly and deliberately. "Everything I have told you is God's truth. I swear it on the lives of my husband and my three young children."

He continued to stare at her silently for some time, then he whispered. "Even though you have not told me everything? Oh, I can see that what you have told me is true – I believe you on that, but if I am to trust you completely, I must know that you will tell me all." He paused, then said, "Why did you withhold from me the rape of Olivia?"

Now it was Mary's turn to stare in silence. "How did you know?" she asked eventually.

"I guessed, from what you said, and what you did not," he answered. "And now I know. Why?"

Mary took a deep breath. "It was our secret. She has to be seen a maid or she will never be wed. Surely you would have guessed that was the reason?"

"Aye." He stood up, and looked down at her. "But I have to trust you if we are to seek the Alchemist together, and any secret must be between us, not setting us apart."

----0----

It was later that evening and they were settled in front of the fire, both with full glasses of hot mulled wine from a large pitcher warming by the flames.

"I promised to tell you the reason I am seeking the Alchemist," Tom began, "so I will tell you all."

Mary sat back in her chair and took a sip of her drink, letting the warmth flood through her. It was surprisingly good, much like the wine she had had in front of the fire in Hammersmith. At least she was with Tom, so she was safe; not like that piece of vermin, Lionel blasted Shelton.

Shelton was nothing like Tom. She studied him as he talked. The way his mouth turned up at the corner as he spoke showed he was honest... The way his eyes crinkled just a little bit – making him look like he was smiling all the time – that spoke of trustworthiness. The way his Adam's apple bobbed in and out of his beard…

Focus.

"…when I was drinking with some acquaintances in a London tavern and one of my companions had too much to drink. So much so, that he was making disparaging remarks about the Queen."

"Oh!" She took a sip of her wine, then gulped down the rest of the glass. It really was delicious. "What did he say?"

"He cast doubt upon her purity, questioning if she was truly a virgin, or some such. He cited Thomas Seymour and the Earl of Leicester as possible lovers, but as I say, he was much taken with drink."

"What did you do?"

Tom refilled her glass from the pitcher. "I told him that what he uttered was nonsense as best, and in truth would be seen as treason. I said that had he made the same remark when sober, he would have been arrested. After that no more was said on the matter, till I was leaving the tavern and this tall, white-haired old man pulled me to one side."

"Wychwoode?"

"Yes. He had overheard what had passed, and asked if I took pride in defending our Queen's honour. I told him that I did. So then he asked me if I would do so again, for him. After a brief hesitation, I said I would consider it." Tom looked up. "In truth I was finding life somewhat tiring, and I was intrigued by the possibility of some excitement. Wychwoode suggested that I come to his chambers in Lincoln's Inn to discuss this further. When I was there, he asked many questions about my upbringing and religious beliefs. When he had assured himself that I was to be trusted, he told me that there was word of a Catholic plot to take the life of the Queen and to put Mary of Scotland on her throne. He knew from other spies that it was afoot, but he had no knowledge of the master plotter behind it. So he had devised a plan that would reveal who this was."

Tom paused a moment, and refilled his glass.

Mary realised she had been staring at him again. Now she was seeing the way his blue eyes seemed to glow, and the way his hair curled back over his ear. His strong hands with their fine down of dark hair. Hands that had closed around Ned's neck; hands that had saved her honour…

Focus.

Plots. He had been talking about a Catholic plot…

"But are there not many such plots?" Mary asked, brightly. "What made this one different?"

"For sure there are many, and most are not worthy of the name 'plot' – they are simply gatherings of self-righteous Catholics who discuss their fanciful ideas with no real means of carrying them out. But this was different, and it was different because of the Alchemist." He paused. "The Alchemist was rumoured to have spent many months using tools he had constructed himself, to make a special form of musket that only he knew how to make. This musket was as thin as the width of a sword, and could be loaded with a singular metal capsule containing both powder and ball, and could be discharged many hundreds of yards from its target, but yet it would hit such a target with unerring accuracy. This meant that a plotter would not need to get close to the Queen in order to have any chance of striking her with a fatal shot – and thus be pulled away or run through with a guard's sword – but could remain hidden at great distance and strike with impunity."

"A sniper!" Mary blurted out.

"A sniper? What is that?"

"Oh, it is a name I once heard for such an assassin."

"A sniper? A killer who strikes in secret from a distance? I have learned a new word, eh?" Tom smiled. "Well, whatever name you give him, we understood him to be called the Alchemist."

Mary considered this a moment. "So the man I know as Rick is a dangerous assassin?"

"It would seem so."

"And you know him as the Alchemist?"

"Aye."

"But why do you call him that?" Mary paused, trying to remember what she had once heard about alchemy. "Is it not all about finding the Philosopher's Stone or turning base metal to gold or some such? What is that to do with Rick making a weapon?"

"I admit that he is not what you would call a traditional alchemist. But he was heard to say that his special musket was made of base metal, and he would accept only gold in payment for using it. So in a sense he was turning base metal into gold, and the name stuck."

Mary sipped her wine, letting this news sink in. So Rick, the catering manager with a passion for guns, had landed in Tudor England like her, but unlike her, he had decided to use his future knowledge – and his lack of morality – to make himself a rich man. She could imagine him working quietly away in some back room in Southwark on the tools he needed to construct his gun, then maybe when he'd made it, taking it to a forest to practice, like in *The Day of The Jackal.* Then letting it be known that he had such a weapon, to flush out a master plotter with enough gold to make him very rich.

"You said there was a plan to find the person behind the plot?" she asked.

"Aye," he said, refilling her glass again from the pitcher. "We knew that there was a man involved by the name of Francis Alleyne. We also knew he was planning to seek out the Alchemist and pay gold for the man to use his special musket as a – what was it?

"A sniper."

"A sniper – that was it. But we needed to know who was providing the gold to Alleyne. In order to gain his trust, I pretended to be an ardent Catholic and persuaded him to let me join him on his planned trip to Southwark to seek out the Alchemist. We found him, in The Blue Maid as it happens. We offered him many hundreds of gold sovereigns; the condition being that he would take a shot at the Queen with his special musket, and kill her."

"But how would this give you the name of the master plotter?"

"I needed Alleyne to trust me enough that he would reveal the name – either in casual conversation or by reference that I could interpret." He shook his head sorrowfully. "And I believe Alleyne would have done at some point, had he not been suddenly killed."

"Killed?" Mary asked in surprise. "How did that happen?"

"Wychwoode and some of his men were secretly following him, but somehow Alleyne spotted them and took flight. In the ensuing chase, Alleyne's horse shied at some other travellers. He was thrown to the ground and died on the spot."

"So you do not know who is the mastermind behind the plot?"

Tom refilled her wine, then shook his head. "Unfortunately, we are no nearer to finding him." He paused, staring quietly at her over the rim of his glass. "However, there is still one man who we believe is part of the plot that may hold the key – a man in Stratford-upon-Avon called Tyler. Wychwoode has gone there to find him and see what he knows, and I think we should go there too, and find Wychwoode. You must tell him all you know of this Alchemist."

"We must," Mary said, putting her glass down on the table. "We must go at first light tomorrow."

Tom raised an eyebrow, then smiled. "'Tis short notice indeed, but if you wish, Lady Mary, then we will."

"I do," she answered. "Because Rick is out there with the most powerful sniper musket in existence, and we do not know where he is or when he will strike. The life of Queen Elizabeth is in our hands and we have to do whatever it takes to stop him."

"I admire your fervour," he observed.

"I am concerned for the Queen's safety," she answered.

But it wasn't just the Queen that was her primary concern – it was also preservation of her own life and her family's. For what had just become clear was that Rick now presented a new and horribly credible threat to the life of Elizabeth. Which meant that there was a very real possibility that the Queen would die now – and not in 1603 as history originally decreed.

Mary shuddered inwardly. If Elizabeth died now and Mary, Queen of Scots came to the throne, England would revert to Catholicism. And there was every chance that Mary of Scotland would be just as vindictive against Protestants as her namesake Mary I had been. So Protestant families such as hers would be in very real danger. Indeed, it was only three years since the massacre of the Protestant Huguenots on St. Bartholomew's Day in Paris – and who was to say that the accession of Mary II would not lead to the same outcome in England?

But that was not the only threat. For if Elizabeth were to die now, then the changes to history – the history that had led to the birth of Justine in the 1980s – would be cataclysmic. The possible alterations to the historical timeline caused when she had saved William and given birth to her children would pale in comparison.

So if Elizabeth were to die now, then what would be the chance of her being born at all?

Mary looked up at Tom with wide eyes.

If the Catholics did not kill her, then history most likely would.

CHAPTER THIRTEEN

Hetherington Hall, mid-April 1575

William leaned forward and glanced to his right along the high table. Sir Nicholas Grenville was deep in conversation with his wife. William listened intently, but was unable to catch any part of their conversation over the hubbub of supper in the Great Hall.

Did they suspect him of knowing about their daily mass? There had been no outright accusations in the few weeks since his shoes were found, but that had not stopped him behaving like a guilty schoolboy, nervously examining every word said to him by Sir Nicholas or Lady Grenville for signs that they knew.

Lady Grenville turned suddenly and stared at him, as if he were the subject of their conversation.

William smiled weakly at her, and she smiled back.

Was her smile forced? Was it proof she knew that he had discovered their treasonous and heretical secret? That despite their outward conformity to the law by attending Protestant services in the village, they were also attending clandestine masses in a closed-off room every afternoon? And presumably, therefore, hiding the priest somewhere in the house?

William sat back and stared around the magnificent Great Hall. If there was a priest living here, then he would have to eat. So maybe he was in the hall, brazenly and openly sharing supper with the other friends and hangers-on who always seemed to be present at Grenville's meals? William studied the men at the two side tables running down either side of the hall. Perhaps it was the elderly white haired man in the high ruff at the side table on the right? Or the middle-aged man on the left, smiling serenely as he broke a small loaf of bread?

William leaned forward again, as a man seated at the far end of the high table caught his eye. He was a young man with thick brown hair in a gaudy doublet that seemed at odds with his sombre face. Despite the doublet, something about him suggested an otherworldly air. Yes, this young man was the most likely the priest.

If so, then they were brazenly hiding him in plain sight, openly treating him as a guest or a member of the family. William bit his lip. Maybe it was not even a secret – maybe everyone else in the room knew it – and only he, William, was the one supposed to be in the dark.

Except that now he did know.

Maybe the servant who had found the shoes had casually mentioned this to one of the family, and conclusions had been drawn? Maybe even now Sir Nicholas and Lady Grenville were deciding what was to be done with him – and with Ambrose.

"Sir William, you look quite pale. Are you well?"

William glanced to his left at Lambert Moreton, who appeared concerned.

"I am quite well, I assure you," William answered. He looked at Moreton, as if seeing him for the first time. The man was very thin – almost to the point of emaciation – looking as if a breath of wind would blow him down. His sandy hair fell across one eye and his beard was so wispy that it needed some shadow across his face to see it was there at all.

"I am glad to hear it." Moreton pulled a plate of roast goose closer, then held a sharp knife up to William's face. "Can I cut you another slice of goose flesh?"

"Thank you, yes, indeed, that would be very kind of you." William cringed at this answer; he sounded like a nervous maid at her first banquet.

Moreton cut a couple of slices, then put them on William's plate. "Are you enjoying your stay at Hetherington Hall, Sir William?" he asked, his voice conversational and quite neutral. "Are you being treated well while the weather continues to force you to stay these many weeks? I have never known the snows to stay so long, although now that we are half-way through April, I am sure the Lord will see fit to start the thaw and bring spring at last."

"Yes, indeed," William answered, trying to match Moreton's conversational tone. "Being here as Sir Nicholas's guest gives me more time with my son, and the unexpected pleasure of being in his company for a while longer."

"Of course." Moreton cut some goose for himself. "And plenty of time to explore Hetherington," he added casually.

William felt as if a bucket of cold water had been emptied over him. He stared at the man, unable to think of a single thing to say.

"Is it as big or as grand as your own Grangedean Manor, I wonder?" Moreton continued, seemingly unaware of the effect his words were having. "My uncle has some magnificent rooms, do you not agree?" William found himself nodding weakly. "Indeed," Moreton continued with a small smile, "there are many interesting rooms just waiting to be discovered, are there not?" Again, William nodded. "It will be such a shame when the thaw does finally come and you wish to leave us. So many more interesting times we could have enjoyed in your company. And your charming son will be disconsolate, if his father is not there to keep him safe."

'Keep him safe?' Was that an open threat to Ambrose?

William took a deep breath and squared his shoulders.

He could not give anything away – he had to be assured, confident and strong. For Ambrose.

He cleared his throat. "Ambrose will be happy with his studies, and his swordsmanship lessons, and his archery," he said. "That is what Sir Nicholas and I have agreed for him."

"Of course, but Sir Nicholas would want to be sure he was quite safe. Swordsmanship and archery can be quite a danger for a young boy such as he."

There it was again! A threat that Ambrose could come to some harm, no doubt if William revealed their secret. He turned round and faced Moreton directly.

The man's thin features were open and his eyes were clear.

Perhaps William was misreading this conversation? Maybe it was all just innocent chatter?

He smiled slowly. "Indeed, Master Moreton, but I have entrusted the care of my son to Sir Nicholas, a man of honour who lives by his word. And Sir Nicholas has given his word that Ambrose will be safe in his care."

"My dear Sir William," Moreton said, "the Grenvilles are an ancient and honourable family. I am sure no harm will befall your son, particularly while you are here to keep watch on him."

Was Sir Nicholas using this feeble-looking young man as a mouthpiece; making it clear what would happen if he were to bring the attention of the authorities to their secret Catholic practices and hidden priest? But surely they realised he would be putting his own son in danger if he brought such an accusation – for all in the house would be implicated.

"Ambrose's safety will always be my prime concern," he said. "I would never do anything that places him in a position of danger."

"I am sure you would not, Sir William. You are a cautious man I am sure – one not wishing to take any unnecessary risks."

"Indeed so," answered William. "Which is why I shall be pleased to stay as long as I am welcome, and avoid the treacherous snow and ice that lies thick on my path to the south."

"Oh, you are welcome to remain here as long as you feel able." Moreton took a drink of wine. "If you are willing to stay beyond the thaw, you would be an honoured guest."

"That would be most pleasant," William replied, "but I am keen to get back to my wife and other children as soon as I can."

"A pity. But I am sure Sir Nicholas will be most understanding." Moreton stood. "Now if you will excuse me, Sir William, but I have some business to attend to." He gave a small bow. "By your leave," he said, and walked out of the Great Hall, pausing only to exchange a few quick words with Sir Nicholas. After Moreton had gone, Sir Nicholas leaned forward and jovially raised his glass. William returned the gesture with a weak grin.

Was the broad smile on Sir Nicholas's face a sign that he thought his secret was still safe?

Or that his suspicions were confirmed?

As William saw it, he had three options – none of which were particularly appealing.

He could escape now with Ambrose, but that would be as good as an admission of knowledge of the mass and the hidden priest – or why would he need to escape? The Grenvilles would realise the danger this put them in; they could not risk that he would reveal their secret. They would no doubt give chase with dogs. He had met their two large mastiffs and did not fancy his and Ambrose's chances of outrunning those fierce creatures in the heavy snow and across that deep, wooded ravine.

But if he stayed at Hetherington Hall once the snow had thawed, then he would again be giving a clear signal that he knew of the secret worship – for why would he stay if not to protect his son from danger?

And finally, if he left as soon as the thaw came, he was abandoning his son in a treasonous house. What if the house was raided and the priest discovered? Ambrose could be implicated, or at least questioned, and that was not something he could willingly contemplate for his son.

William's hand trembled as he took a drink of wine.

CHAPTER FOURTEEN

Stratford-upon-Avon

The Alchemist drew back into the shadows, pressing himself against the wall and hearing the footsteps getting louder.

They stopped at the end of the passageway.

He held his breath and waited for what seemed like eternity, his head turned away from the street so his pale face would not stand out in the darkness. Then he heard the sound of a shoe scraping on the rough cobbles – the sound of someone turning.

If the man walked even a few steps into the passage, then all would be lost.

The footsteps started again – and quickly faded into the distance.

The Alchemist let out a sigh of relief.

He waited a few more minutes just to be sure, then moved out of the shadows and peered slowly round the corner onto the street.

It was empty.

He walked quickly in the opposite direction to the footsteps. A few turns later he came across a small tavern. Without hesitating, he pushed open the door and went in, found a table in the corner near the fire and sank into the seat.

That was close – too close. If he had arrived just five minutes earlier at John Tyler's house in Stratford, he would have been taken. He had just been approaching the house when the door had opened and a tall man in black with long grey hair had emerged.

Wychwoode.

He had recognised the man from Francis Alleyne's description. And Wychwoode worked for Walsingham, the Queen's recently appointed spymaster.

The Alchemist shuddered at what had happened next. Wychwoode had stood back to let three men out of the house. Two were clearly his own men – rough looking and dressed in black like their master. But it was the sight of the one that they supported between them, wearing only a blood-stained shirt and torn hose, that made the Alchemist's own blood run cold. It was Tyler – clearly wounded and being led away, no doubt for further questioning. And there was no possibility Tyler would stay silent – Wychwoode would make sure of that.

The Alchemist ordered a tankard of ale, and when it arrived, drank most of it down in one go.

Now Wychwoode had Tyler, it would only be a matter of time before the whole plot would be blown wide open. Tyler knew too much – and when they got him to London and that infernal Tower, he would no doubt tell all. In which case the Alchemist, as the lone assassin, would be a hunted man.

Unless he could stay one step ahead... He gave himself a wry grin. Considering his pursuers were nothing but medieval dimwits, with no means of communicating faster than a man can ride a horse, that shouldn't be too hard a task.

The Alchemist beckoned a serving girl over, and she refilled his tankard.

Idly, he slapped her bottom as she turned and she gave a satisfyingly indignant squeak.

So now he would have to change his plans.

He had been due to stay in Stratford with John Tyler, keeping safely out of sight until the arranged time to travel to the agreed place, set up the gun and take the shot at the Queen. But that was no longer an option, so he would need to find somewhere else to stay.

He finished his ale and stared into the fire.

Was he being realistic, planning to keep this plot going? Now they had Tyler and would make him talk, maybe the leader would then want him to abandon it?

The Alchemist hoped not. The opportunity to change history – no, no, to *make* history – was too appealing to abandon. To kill Queen Elizabeth would make him famous throughout the realm; throughout history. And rather than go to the gallows for it, he would be hailed as a hero by the new regime under Mary, Queen of Scots. He would be feted by royalty and probably knighted too.

Oh yes. Sir Richard Hornby – it had a good ring to it.

Hadn't he come a long way from doing the catering at Grangedean Manor in 2015 – working with a bunch of misfit actors and corporate guests, all living in fantasy-land and pretending to be high and mighty Tudors? Well now he would be the real thing – a real Tudor noble. Books would be written about him, films would be made of his exploits and generations of school kids would have to learn his name! Serve the little pests right.

So he would see this thing through; he would kill the Queen and he would change history.

Whatever that meant.

But there was no doubt he would have to do this alone. He would have to stay low; keeping out of sight, living off his wits and trusting no-one until the job was done. Then he would make contact with the leader and claim his rightful due – his riches and his title.

If he was going to have to live in this dreadful medieval time, then he was not going to live as a peasant labourer. He might as well live in as much style as he could.

The Alchemist reached down and patted the long bag made of rough sacking at his feet. This was the gun that was going to make it happen. All the hard work in creating it was finally going to pay off. The months spent making rudimentary tools, perfecting them until they were fit for purpose, then seeking out raw materials and spending further months working them. The rejects thrown away or melted down and used again and again, the long days and nights spent covered in soot and sweat to make something that could be factory-made with ease in the 21st century – all this would be worth it when he got that famous pale red-head in the cross hairs and gently squeezed the trigger…

The Alchemist ordered a third tankard of ale and some bread. When he had finished, he picked up his bag and slipped quietly out of the tavern.

---0---

The little cottage stood alone in a forest clearing around a mile out of Stratford, with smoke drifting lazily out of a hole in the wood-tiled roof. It had no windows and just one blackened oak door with a large key-hole and handle.

The Alchemist circled cautiously round it several times, using trees to shield himself from any possible view. Once he was satisfied that no-one was observing him, he walked up to the door and knocked.

It was opened by an old man with unkempt grey hair and beard, dressed in a rough woollen smock and wearing a filthy woollen cap.

He stared suspiciously at the Alchemist.

"What do you want?" he asked.

"I am traveling north and need a bed for a few days to break my journey. Can you let me stay?"

"You are not a vagrant?"

The Alchemist smiled. "No, I have a house in Southwark, but I have come through Stratford on my way to meet my brother in York." The invented brother was the simplest story he could think of.

"No pox or sneezes?"

"No, and not near anyone with those these last few weeks." The Alchemist had heard the same question enough times, starting with the dumpy little landlady at the Grangedean tavern, to know that fear of strangers in these times was mostly fear of the spread of plague.

"Hmm." The man continued to stare at him suspiciously. "You will not stay in an inn?"

"No."

The man stood silent.

"I have some coin," offered the Alchemist. "If that would help?"

"You can agree the payment with my daughter," the man said eventually, then called over his shoulder, "come here, lass."

A moment later, a dark-haired girl of about twenty appeared in the doorway. She looked the Alchemist up and down. "What is it father?" she asked.

"This man would stay with us a few days," the man said. "Name a fair price."

The girl stood silent a moment, then gave a small nod and stood back from the doorway. "Ha'pence a day and you will sleep on the floor."

"Thank you," the Alchemist replied, then picked up his bag and stepped into the cottage.

It was dark inside, with the only light coming from a small fire in a free-standing grate in the middle of the single room – which itself seemed no bigger than an average 21st century double garage. A small pot was bubbling on the grate.

The Alchemist stood a moment while his eyes adjusted to the darkness. Gradually he made out a few more pots and pans and a couple of wooden plates on a small table in the corner, two truckle beds against the walls, and two wooden stools by the fire.

"That will be your corner," said the girl, pointing to the opposite side of the room from the two beds. The Alchemist went over and put his bag down, pushing it as deep as possible into the shadows.

"My name is Richard," he said. "What is yours?"

"I am Ursula," she answered, "and my pa is Walter."

The Alchemist reached into his purse and took out two coins. "There are two pennies," he said. "I will not be more than four days."

She took the coins with a small smile and quickly pocketed them in her apron. "I have some broth," she said. "Art hungry?"

He nodded. The meagre bread and ale he had in the tavern was a while ago.

Walter pulled the table out and put the two stools by it, as well as another he produced from underneath. The men sat while Ursula served the broth, and Walter poured ale from a pitcher.

"York, you say?" he asked. "That is a long way to go from Southwark to see your brother."

"Yes. I have not seen him for some years."

Walter acknowledged this with a grunt and carried on eating.

Ursula, however, was still curious. "Was that when he moved to York – when you last saw him some years ago," she asked, her eyes twinkling in the firelight, "or were you split at birth?"

"Have a mind, lass," snapped Walter. "You will not be prying into Master Richard's affairs – he is our guest."

"He has paid me tuppence for four days – so he is a paying guest. I got a right to ask."

"It is no problem," said the Alchemist. He smiled at Ursula and was rewarded with a smile in return. "I have not seen my brother in over four years."

"There is the answer, lass," muttered Walter. "Now leave the man be."

Once the meal was over, the Alchemist retired to his corner, pushing the sacking bag deeper into the shadows as he sat down. He had just got comfortable sitting on the floor with his back to the wall, when he looked up to find Ursula standing over him.

"Here," she said, "a blanket to sleep under."

"Thank you." He opened up the rough woollen blanket she offered him, then put it over his knees. She sat next to him. "Tell me of your life in Southwark," she said.

"Have you been there?" he asked.

"Nay," she said quietly. "I have never been further than Stratford. I go there often – for the market." There was a silence for a moment. Then she said, "Is it a big place?"

"Big enough."

"Bigger than Stratford?" Her eyes were wide.

"Yes – and it is just across the river from the City of London."

"London?" She bit her lip. "I have heard tell of London. They say the streets are paved with gold?"

He smiled. "Are the streets of Stratford paved with gold?"

"Nay." She shook her head. "Of course not."

"Well, neither are the streets of London."

She smiled hesitantly, searching his eyes as if checking to see if he was teasing or serious. He laughed and after a moment she laughed back.

"You are a naughty man," she said, punching him softly on the shoulder, "to jest with me so." She smiled again, winding a lock of hair thoughtfully round her finger as she looked at him. "I shall have to watch my words, lest you turn them into something I never meant."

The Alchemist was about to reply, when Walter appeared in front of them.

"I go out to catch a coney or a hare for supper," he muttered.

The Alchemist started to stand up. "I can come and help."

"Nay," Walter answered, "I hunt alone."

The old man went to the door and took a slingshot off a hook, then put some small rocks from a pile into a bag and hefted it over his shoulder. He picked up a large cudgel, which looked a bit like a baseball bat. "I will be back presently," he said, and was gone.

There was a silence in the little cottage, as the two of them sat together. Then Ursula got up and walked over to the table. "You can tell me of London and Southwark," she said over her shoulder, "and tales of the folk that live in such places."

"They are ordinary folk, like you and me."

"Are you ordinary, Master Richard?" She turned. "You seem not like any of the folk I know."

"Why is that?"

She studied him as he sat on the floor of the dark cottage. "You come to our cottage that is away from other dwellings instead of stopping at one of the inns you must have passed to get here... you carry no clothes save a rough bag with shiny iron sticks within, that you hide away with much trouble..."

He raised an eyebrow. "Have you looked in my bag?"

"I would not have done so. But I saw inside just as you came in the cottage, for all I was not meaning to do so."

The Alchemist thought quickly. "It is a gift for my brother."

She smiled. "Yet you hide it away?"

"It took me many weeks to make. I do not want any harm to come to it."

"For sure." She seemed to lose interest in the bag and its contents. "But still you have not answered my question."

"I do not remember you asking a question."

"That I did. Why you did not stop at an inn?"

"I do not like inns." She raised an enquiring eyebrow. "I worked in one for a while, so I know what kind of places they are." He stood up and went over to her. "I prefer honest folk and honest food."

She did not move. "What if my pa and I are not honest folk?"

"Oh, you are." He moved closer. "You are both honest as the day is long." He put a hand up to her cheek and stroked it softly. For a moment she let his hand caress her skin, then she took it gently and moved it away. "Have a care, Master Richard," she said quietly. "You have paid for bed and board – no more."

He stepped back and smiled carefully. "For sure, Mistress Ursula, that is understood."

There was an uncomfortable silence, then suddenly the door opened and light flooded in. They moved quickly apart; the Alchemist returning to his corner and Ursula busying herself with pots and pans at the table.

Walter entered the cottage, closed the door, then threw a rabbit carcass onto the table. "A coney in the first few minutes," he announced. "I saw it at first but a few yards from the door. A good hunt, for all it took every stone I had to hit the thing as it ran. But I had him eventually." He took his bag off and hung it back on the hook. "Plenty there for a rich stew, lass. Do you have vegetables?"

"Yes," Ursula answered. "Enough for today. I will get more in a day or two from the market."

She picked up the rabbit. "A fine beast." She handed the Alchemist a sharp knife. "You can help me skin it."

The Alchemist picked up the rabbit and started skinning and gutting it, working quickly and with precision. Ursula stopped and stared.

"By Heaven, Master Richard, you have some skill with the knife!"

"I told you, I worked in a tavern," he answered, separating the skin from the flesh. "Preparing a rab… I mean a coney, for the stew was everyday work."

"It was a trade well learned," she said. "You are a man of many parts."

Walter came over and watched as the Alchemist finished preparing the meat, cutting it into cubes ready for the pot. "The lass is right, Master Richard," he observed. "You have a talent. Use it well and you will never go hungry."

---0---

The Alchemist woke with a start the next morning. Walter and Ursula were already up, and were moving around the cottage, making plenty of noise with spoons and plates as they prepared breakfast. He lay on his back and stared up at the hole in the roof that served as a chimney. There was no sunlight coming through.

"Art awake?" asked Ursula, coming over to where he lay.

"Yes."

"'Tis nearly first light. We shall eat shortly, then my pa is going into Stratford – he has some business there for the day." She studied him as he lay. "What would you do?"

"I do not know – what needs to be done?"

"Bread to be made," she said. "You can help."

"Aye." He stood up and pushed the blanket into the corner.

Walter was already at the table. The Alchemist sat and stared bleakly at the food. What he wouldn't give for a proper 21st century breakfast of bacon, eggs, sausage and tomato, all washed down with a large orange juice and a steaming mug of black coffee… He sighed. Instead he was marooned in the 16th century, with nothing but blackened bread and watery ale, in the company of two uncouth, unwashed peasants…

At least when he was Sir Richard, he would eat as well as anyone in this appalling era.

"…Amen."

Richard looked up. Ursula and Walter were staring at him expectantly – waiting for him to speak.

"Yes, yes, sorry… Amen."

Walter grunted in approval, then tore off a hunk of bread and poured himself some ale. Ursula did the same, so the Alchemist took a small piece of bread and tried it. It was dry and sooty, with a heavy taste of rye and something bitter, which he decided was very similar to the taste of the ale. Not only was it nothing like 21st century bread, but it was even drier and harder to swallow than the pale bread he bought from the market in Southwark.

"You do not like it?" Ursula was staring at him, and he realised he had been making his dislike obvious.

"It is different from what I have been used to, that is all."

"It stops us from starving, lad," said Walter firmly. "And the lass makes it well. That is all there is to be said on the matter."

They ate on in silence, then Walter drained his mug of ale and stood up. "I will be gone till nightfall, lass," he muttered, and left the cottage.

The Alchemist and Ursula finished their meal.

"Now is the time to make more bread," she said. "As you would have done when you worked in a tavern?"

He shook his head. "That was a task I was never given."

She gave a small smile. "Then mayhap if you see how it is made, you may like it more." Reaching down under the table, she brought up a hessian sack, about the size of a 21st century box of cereal, and a large wooden plate.

She opened the sack and scooped out a handful of dark brown flour, which she poured into a pile on the middle of the plate. Then she added a small amount of ale from the pitcher and worked the mixture with her hands until it was a sticky-looking dough. Then she added some more flour and ale and worked those into the mixture. The Alchemist watched, fascinated, as her long slim fingers moved deftly through the ball of dough, quickly working more flour and ale in until it was roughly the size of a large potato.

"Here," she said, looking up from her work, "you can do as I have done until you have doubled this in size." She pushed the plate towards him. "I shall make ready the bread oven outside." She walked out of the cottage, leaving the Alchemist with the dough.

After a moment, he reached for the flour and poured a small amount onto the board next to the ball of dough. Then he did as Ursula had done, adding a few drops of ale and working the mixture with his fingers. He soon found it to be unpleasantly sticky, so he added a bit more flour to try and dry it out. Unfortunately, this was too successful, and soon the resulting piece of dough was horribly dry and flaky. More ale just made it sticky again, so he decided to try folding it into the main ball. This seemed to work – the new larger ball was not too different in consistency, so he repeated the process.

By the time Ursula came back into the cottage, he was sitting in front of a ball of dough of the right size and, he felt, pretty good consistency.

"There," he said, pushing it towards her. "Done."

She picked it up and studied it, kneading it gently. Then she nodded and put it down. "Good. You have done well. We will prove it by the fire."

She took a piece of grey cloth and wrapped the dough inside it, then put it on the plate next to the fire. "Come, this will need some time. You can help me tend the oven."

He followed her outside, then round to the back of the cottage. There was a small extension off the back wall built of rough bricks, with a wooden door set near the top. Ursula opened the door and a blast of heat hit the Alchemist.

"Pass me some faggots, please," she said. He glanced around and saw some tied bundles of twigs in the corner. He grabbed one and passed it over. She threw it in the oven, then held out her hand again. He gave her another bundle, then a third, and she threw each one in. She closed the door and stepped back.

"Thank you. We have some time to wait until the dough has proved."

She sat against the wall of the cottage and stretched out her long legs. She patted the ground next to her, inviting him to sit as well.

"How long will you stay with your brother?" she asked.

He shook his head. "I have no fixed plans." He stared at the forest, squinting at the bright sun flashing through the trees as it rose.

"Does your brother have a trade?" she asked.

The Alchemist thought about this. What might this mythical brother do for a living in York? Suddenly Shakespeare came to mind. "He is a writer of plays."

"Oh." It was a good answer – she had no knowledge of the theatre.

"Has he a family in York?"

"Yes." Again, this brother's fantasy life needed fleshing out. This was getting a little tiresome. "He has a wife and… er, two sons."

"Is that all? Only two?"

He shrugged. "He may have more by now."

"And you?" she asked. "No wife waiting on you in Southwark?"

He turned sharply to look at her. "No."

She was silent for so long that the Alchemist almost drifted off to sleep. "Why so?" she asked.

"What?"

"Why so – that there is no wife waiting on you?"

"I do not know. I have not yet found a wife."

The truth was, after he had arrived in the strange world of 1571 from 2015 by freak accident, his first thought had been that this was only temporary – so he might as well have some fun without worrying about the consequences. He had quickly started to eye up the girls. The squinty-eyed pub landlady had been giving him all the signs – hands on hips, winking at him, calling him 'my sweeting' – so it was hardly surprising he thought she was looking for a real man for a change, and had crept into her bed chamber when he thought her husband was away for the day. Only it turned out that not only was she totally frigid, but the man had come home early, and together they had thrown him out.

Then there had been that stunning young gypsy-like girl, Olivia Melrose. At first he'd trod warily around her – she was very young and treated him like dirt, but he'd softened her up eventually with flattery and compliments – until he was sure she was about ready to submit. He'd cornered her alone and was just making real progress when her sallow, humourless father had poked his long nose in and stopped them. It was not surprising that he got thrown out again – the girl had accused him of forcing himself upon her, when in truth she'd been giving him all the signs as well.

So when he had finally come to the conclusion that time-travel was a one-way trip and he was stuck in the 1570s – and had settled in Southwark – the thought of finding a wife had rather lost its appeal. Instead he had thrown himself into making the sniper rifle.

The rifle was his ticket to fame and fortune. And once he was Sir Richard, he'd have his pick of the women. They would be falling over themselves to be his wife.

That was for the future. For now, this peasant girl was warming up nicely…

A few minutes later, they went back inside the cottage. Ursula partially unwrapped the cloth bundle and peered inside. The ball of dough was clearly bigger. "Good," she said, opening it fully. She placed it on the wooden plate and looked up at him. "Work it some more."

He started kneading it again. It was less sticky now and warmed his fingers. He continued a minute or two longer, until his fingers started to ache, making him stop kneading and stretch out his hands with a small wince of pain.

She moved round the table to stand close to him, her hip and shoulder touching his. "But you have still to build strength in your fingers." She pulled the plate towards her and started working the dough herself. "You must work it so," she said, "with slower movements, thus."

The Alchemist found himself staring at Ursula's hands as they caressed the dough, watching as she squeezed it in her fist so it grew longer, then folded it on itself and pushed it out, before pulling it back again and squeezing it once more…

She turned to look at him. Their faces were almost touching. "You see?" she said. "It is but a slow, gentle movement."

His head started to move forward, his lips seeking hers, his hand starting to come up behind her back.

She put the bread down and stood back quickly.

"Nay," she whispered. "Bed and board – I have said that is all."

She picked up the dough and again wrapped it in the cloth. Then she placed it back by the fire.

"Come," she said, "we must keep the blaze burning in the bread oven at the back." While he stood motionless, she went outside once again.

He found her by the oven, poking the glowing embers inside with a stick.

"The dough will soon be ready and the fire is hot," she said, with her back still to him.

"Yes," he said, "the fire is hot."

There was a heavy edge to his voice that caused her to turn quickly.

He was standing close behind her. Again, their faces were almost touching. This time he gave her no chance to pull away, but put his hand behind her head and pulled her towards him.

Their lips met and her mouth opened, her tongue darting out to meet his, and for a brief moment she kissed him with real passion. Then suddenly she drew away, her eyes locked onto his, and she shook her head.

"Bed and board is all," she murmured. "Bed… is all…"

Then their lips came together again and she kissed him hard, kissed him with a hunger, as if she could not get enough of him, with small mewling noises in the back of her throat as she kissed.

His hand moved down from her head, and fastened on her bottom, pushing her onto him, so she could not fail to feel his hardness. Then his other hand started bunching up her skirts, lifting the thick layers of material until it was resting on the bare skin of her upper thigh, before starting to make its way up and inward…

She broke off and stood back, her skirt dropping heavily down again.

"The bread…" she muttered. "We must put it in to bake." Leaving him standing once more, she hurried into the cottage, before reappearing a few minutes later carrying a small metal bucket. She showed him that the dough was inside, then she put it in the oven.

He had not moved a single muscle since they had broken off.

She took his hand. "Come," she said. "There is some soft heather in that clearing over there, and while the bread bakes we have time to know each other better…"

---0---

It was a while later, and the Alchemist and Ursula were lying naked on their backs on the heather. She had her head on his left shoulder, and he was stroking her belly.

She picked up his right arm and studied it. "What are these pictures?" she asked.

"They are called assault rifles," he answered.

"Salt rifles?" She studied the tattoos closely. "I know not what this means. To me they are like muskets…" She twisted his arm round. "What is this curved piece in the middle?"

"It is where the…er… balls are stored."

"Oh." She was silent a while. "Why do you have pictures of such muskets on your arm?"

"Because I am interested in them."

She dropped his arm and twisted to look at him. "Is that what the shiny iron sticks in your bag are? Are they pieces of a musket like this one?"

"No, they are… for decoration in my brother's house."

"Oh." She was silent again. Then suddenly she jumped up. "The bread! It will burn!" She ran round the clearing gathering up her clothes, struggled quickly into them, and ran off towards the cottage.

The Alchemist stayed where he was for a few more minutes, enjoying the peace of the forest, then dressed and walked slowly back to the cottage.

As his eyes became used to the darkness inside, he saw the bread on the table. He picked it up and studied it – but it looked largely unburned. As he put it back on the table, some movement in the corner caught his eye.

It was Ursula, and she was sitting in his corner with his bag open.

She was lifting out the metal tubes that formed the sniper rifle, and was studying each piece.

He hurried over. "What the heck are you doing?"

"This is no decoration," she said slowly. "It is a salt rifle like the ones in the pictures on your arms." She held up the stock. "See, here is the part where your finger fits and pulls on this lever to make it fire." She looked up at him. "Why do you bring such a thing into my home?"

He squatted down. "It is for my brother."

"What does he want with it?"

"So he can hunt coneys better."

"You will show me."

Just then the door opened and Walter came in. "My business in Stratford is done early," he announced. Then he saw Ursula. "What hast there, lass?" he asked. "Sticks that shine like the moon."

"It is a salt rifle that belongs to Richard," she answered. "For hunting coneys."

"Aye?" Walter moved closer and peered at the rifle barrel. "How does it do that?"

"Richard will show us."

The Alchemist sighed deeply. He hated to be forced to show the gun, even to these two peasants, but he couldn't see an alternative right now. He reached into the bag and took out the two steel tubes, the scope and the butt, and took the breech block off Ursula.

As they watched mesmerised, he screwed one tube into the breech block to create the barrel, and the second, shorter tube into the other end of the block, then screwed the wooden butt onto this tube. Then he fitted the scope to the top of the block, and presented the weapon to Walter.

The old man picked it up and held it with one hand on the barrel and the other on the breech, with his finger on the trigger. "A musket, this?" he breathed. "Though not like any musket I saw when I was a lad fighting the French." He studied it in the glow of the fire, then went over to the door and opened it to get the better light. "How do you load and prime it?"

The Alchemist reached into his bag for one of the twenty or so cartridges he had made, then took the gun from Walter, snapped open the breech and slipped the cartridge inside. Then he stepped out of the cottage and said, "Find me a coney."

Walter scanned the undergrowth for a moment, then pointed wordlessly at the base of a tree about twenty yards away. The Alchemist followed the man's finger, and saw a small brown shape just beside the tree. He lifted the gun to his shoulder, took careful aim through the scope and squeezed the trigger. There was a crack like the breaking of a branch, a puff of smoke from the barrel, and the rabbit disappeared from view. As the gun went off, both father and daughter jumped, and Ursula gave out a small cry of alarm.

Walter was the first to recover. "By heaven, you made the coney disappear! What art of Satan is this?"

"None," said the Alchemist. "As you said, it is a musket. I have simply hit the coney with the ball."

"From this far?" Walter shook his head. "To hit from this far in one shot is sorcery indeed."

"You made the creature disappear, I swear to it," Ursula said.

"Wait here," the Alchemist said, and walked over to the tree. He soon found the remains of the rabbit a further ten yards back. The bullet had passed straight through its chest, killing it instantly. He picked it up and carried it back to where the others were standing.

"There," he said, handing it to Ursula, "shot through the chest."

There was a silence, as Walter looked from the gun to the rabbit, then to the Alchemist. He appeared to be trying to make a decision – then he said quietly, "Be gone from my house this instant. Whatever piece of musketry you have there, I want it gone. And you. Right now."

Ursula said, "But, Pa…"

"Nay, lass, I want this man gone, and that is the end of the matter." He pushed Ursula into the cottage. At the door she turned and looked back longingly at the Alchemist before Walter pushed her again and she disappeared inside.

The door slammed, and the Alchemist heard the key turn in the lock. With a sigh he dismantled the gun, put it in the bag and hefted the bag over his shoulder.

Then he set off through the forest.

CHAPTER FIFTEEN

Stratford-upon-Avon

Mary looked around her in wonder in the early spring sunshine, as she and Tom rode into the centre of Stratford-upon-Avon. The snows in the fields had melted fast as they had journeyed up from London, and now the only sign that the winter had finally departed was the occasional mound of slush remaining in the deep shadows.

The streets were full of timber-beamed houses, leaning into each other across the cobbled street, their tall upper storeys periodically blocking out the sunshine. But it was the very normality of the houses that caused Mary to stare about her and catch her breath as she rode. Stratford was the town that embodied Tudor England to the people of the 21st century. As the birthplace of William Shakespeare, Stratford had a magic about it that connected you directly to the Tudors – and now here she was, riding into Stratford behind a real Tudor man, and seeing it in its real Tudor splendour.

Not that it was particularly splendid. The stench of human waste and rotting food was indescribable, and she held her lavender nosegay close to her face to block it out as much as she could. Best not to look down, either. A sewer channel running along the centre of the cobbles was clearly the source of the smell, with things floating in it that did not bear close inspection. Instead she focused on Tom's broad back and the thick dark hair escaping from under his cap.

Maybe sensing her gaze, Tom turned his head slightly and she caught sight of his profile and a half-smile.

Then, just for a moment, it was William's profile she saw; strong, open and honest, and she felt a small stab of guilt.

But no. She shook her head to herself. She had nothing to be guilty about. She and Tom had just got a little tipsy that night in his house – that was all.

There had been a moment after Tom's explanation of the Alchemist's plot when the conversation had faltered, then stalled completely, and then they were left in silence, each searching the other's eyes…

God, he was handsome…

And kind, and gentle, and he'd saved her from Ned, so he could be a man of action when he needed to be…

Then the moment when their heads had moved naturally together, and he had started to lean to one side as he moved in, which was nearly the point of no return, and if she didn't do anything or say anything then she would be helpless and it would be too late, and William would never, ever forgive her, and she would never forgive herself, and it would be too late, too late…

So she had pulled back.

"Nay, Tom," she had muttered. "This is not seemly."

And he had nodded, and smiled, and sat back, and said, "For sure, my dear Lady Mary, for sure," and they had got on with planning the trip to Stratford, as if this had never happened, which of course it hadn't, so she had nothing to be guilty about…

Suddenly a small boy appeared as if from nowhere and ran across the road in front of her. No sooner had she realised he was there, than she saw his foot catch on the edge of the sewer channel and he started to fall. With a shrill squeak of alarm, she realised he was falling directly into the path of Juno's hooves. Just when it seemed certain he would be killed or maimed, he pushed off the ground with both hands and emerged unscathed, seemingly from right under the hooves. With a laugh and a brief wave, he ran off down an alley.

Tom stopped and turned in the saddle. "Art well?" he asked, a concerned frown on his face. "I heard you cry out."

"I am well, Tom," she answered. "A boy nearly ran under my horse, but no harm came."

"Good," he said, and turned back in his saddle. He was about to ride on, when Mary called out "Wait!"

Tom turned back again. "What is it, Lady Mary?" he asked, then paused and added, "You are as pale as a bed sheet. What ails you?"

"That boy," she said. "I might have killed him."

"Aye, but you did not, so as you say, no harm done." Tom walked on.

Mary stopped a moment to catch her breath, then nudged Juno in the flanks and followed.

Sure, that boy might have died. And maybe his death would have had no consequence for the world.

But what if that had not been just any small boy? What if it had been William Shakespeare himself?

He was about the age that Shakespeare would have been, and this was Stratford… She had been day-dreaming and not looking where she was going. It would have been her fault if he had died. Let alone any official punishment, she would have had to live with the knowledge that she had killed Hamlet before he'd even been born. How could she have lived with that loss? Or Macbeth? Or Lear…

For a brief moment, the future of the English language could have been in her hands – and she would have changed it forever.

Mary sniffed on her nosegay. She had to protect the future. It was her future and it needed her to be on her guard – to protect it from threats that only she could see.

Mary shivered, then gave Juno another nudge with her heel and trotted closer to Tom.

"Come Tom," she said, "let us make haste to Master Tyler's house, and see what we can learn that will help us stop this man, the Alchemist."

Tom stopped and turned again in the saddle. "I realise that we do not know where he lives. But I am sure he will be known hereabouts. We must find someone who can tell us."

Just then a man pushing a cart laden with baskets of bread went past them and turned down a side alley. Tom stared at him a moment then laughed and said, "The market – of course! We will ask there – someone is bound to know."

They turned down the lane after the man, and soon found themselves in the noise and the mayhem of the market square.

Mary gazed about her in wonder. There were stalls selling bread, vegetables and ales, as well as stalls with all types of clothing, from hats, shoes and hosiery, to basic doublets, plain breeches, woollen skirts and grey dresses. Several stalls were selling meat such as pig and goat – where the animals were still alive and running around in pens. Mary saw a small goat being pulled from the pen. The stall holder then cut its throat, skinned and butchered it on a wooden slab, before handing over fresh cuts of meat to a woman in a woollen dress.

Where 21st century Justine Parker would have been sick, or fainted; 16th century Mary de Beauvais merely shrugged, and nudged Juno to walk on.

It was then that she realised that while she had been looking around, she had lost sight of Tom.

Desperately she scanned across the square, trying to make out his distinctive hat among the various men on horseback. Then with relief she spotted him making for a long, low fence at the far end of the square. She saw him dismount and tether his horse to it, alongside others already tethered there. 'A car park,' she thought, as she made her way over to the fence and dismounted from Juno, 'or at least the Tudor equivalent.'

Juno neighed and lifted her head. Mary stroked her muzzle. "There, old girl, I will be back soon." She tied the reins to the rail. "Do not worry." Juno gave a small neigh in response, and Mary caught a look in the horse's eye that said, "Don't leave me here among these strange sights and smells…"

"You will be fine, old girl," she answered, "I will not be long, I promise."

Fighting through the crowds, she caught up with Tom. He had made his way to a stall selling vegetables, and was bawling at the man.

"John Tyler! Do you know a John Tyler?" The man nodded and Tom stood back, looking pleased. Then the man said, "Yes, master, we have turnips."

"Not turnips, for Heaven's sake! John Tyler!" The man shook his head. With a muttered curse that Mary didn't hear – but guessed it was about deaf idiots – Tom stamped off to the next stall, and from there to the next and the next again.

After twenty minutes of fruitless search, they stopped at the edge of the square, close to three women who were talking amongst themselves.

"By thunder," admitted Tom, "it was madness to think we could find someone here who knows this man. I would we take a few minutes rest, then be on our way."

Mary nodded, and was about to add a comment, when she overheard what one of the women beside her was saying.

"It was sorcery, I tell you! He pointed the stick at the coney, and it disappeared in a puff of smoke!" The woman mimed lifting a rifle to her shoulder and made a sound like gunfire. "Like sorcery, I tell you! It just disappeared!"

Mary and Tom's eyes met and they shared a knowing look. Maybe coming to the market might help them in their search after all – but for the Alchemist rather than Tyler.

Mary put a hand on the woman's shoulder. "Excuse me," she said, "but I could not but help overhear. What did the man point at the coney?"

The woman looked her up and down, taking in the travel-worn but elegant style of her clothes, clearly deciding that Mary was of the nobility. She made a small curtesy. "Beg pardon, mistress, but it was a thin shiny iron stick. He pointed it at the coney and the stick made a cracking sound and the coney disappeared."

"Was it like a musket?" This was Tom, who had stepped over.

"Aye, a bit like a musket, except it was very small and thin. He called it a 'salt rifle'. And it worked by sorcery."

"And what was this man's name?" asked Mary, her breath catching in her throat.

"Richard was his name, mistress."

Mary gasped. "And did he have pictures painted on his arms of similar looking muskets?"

"Aye, that he did."

"And he had spiky hair, like a hedgehog?"

"Aye, that also, as you mention it." The woman smiled, as if to herself, "Fine hair, I thought it."

"And how did it come about, that he used his thin musket to make the coney disappear?" Mary asked.

"My pa and I live in a cottage in the wood. He knocked on our door and asked for a bed for a few nights." The woman gave a concerned look at her two friends, as if seeking reassurance. They nodded, so she continued. "My pa and I let him in for two pennies, as he said he would not stay in an inn."

Mary nodded. No doubt he wouldn't want to risk staying in an inn, in case he was spotted by one of Wychwoode's men.

"What is your interest in Master Richard, mistress?" the woman asked.

"What is your name?" asked Mary.

"Ursula, mistress."

"Well, Ursula, we believe this man Richard is very dangerous, particularly with his special musket. We want to catch him and stop him before he causes any serious trouble."

Tom asked, "How did he come to show you the musket?"

"I asked him what were the sticks in his bag, and he showed how they were put together to make a small musket – only it was sorcery, the way he disappeared that coney, so we…" she swallowed hard, then continued, "we threw him out."

"And when was that?" asked Tom.

"It was last evening, sir."

"And did you see which way he went?"

"Nay, sir – my pa and I went back in the cottage and he said that was the end of the matter."

Tom paused, tapping rapidly on the hilt of his sword as he thought.

"Can we see your cottage?" he asked.

Ursula nodded slowly. "If it pleases you sir, of course."

"Now?"

"It is about a half hour's walk."

"Good," said Tom. "Then let us start now."

---0---

They approached the cottage with Ursula leading them. There was no sign of movement, other than a small wisp of smoke drifting lazily into the clear sky from the hole in the roof.

"This is where you left him?" asked Tom.

"Aye."

"He has a full day's start on us, but he is on foot." Tom looked around at the trees and undergrowth. "We can see if we can track him on horseback, and catch him up. But we need to take the same path from the start."

Tom crouched down and silently studied the ground around him, but seemed to see nothing that interested him. Then he moved on to another patch of ground, and then another. Then suddenly he let out a low exclamation of triumph and carefully picked up what looked like a small piece of twig. As Mary and Ursula watched, he leaned down and picked up another, similar twig, and studied both carefully.

"See here," he said, showing them to the women, "broken clean in two by a man's foot, and not long ago by the look of how white is the wood inside." He stared at the trees around the spot where he had found the twigs. "And judging by the lie of these on the ground, I would say he was heading that way." He pointed towards a gap in the trees, then moved slowly towards it, studying the ground as he went. Suddenly he stopped again, and pointed at something they couldn't see at his feet. "Another broken twig. We have his direction," he said, with a satisfied smile. "We must ride."

As Tom and Mary mounted up, Mary looked down and said, "Thank you, Ursula. We will track Richard down, and stop him from making trouble."

"God speed, my lady," Ursula replied. She curtseyed again, then went into the cottage.

Mary trotted on. "We must take care," she said when she reached Tom.

"Aye. This Alchemist is…" he looked back at her, "what was the word you used? A sniper?"

"Yes." Mary shivered despite the warmth of the spring sun as she looked around the forest. "He could be watching us even now."

Desperately, she scanned the trees around them, looking for signs of movement or a glimpse of Rick's spiky hair.

"Marry, we are being too alarmed. He does not know we are following him," Tom said. "So he is unlikely to be watching us now. My thought is as I said – he has nigh on a day's start on us, and is already many miles ahead."

But Mary was not reassured as they headed deep into the forest and the trees closed in around them, cutting out much of the sunlight and enclosing them in a cold, dappled world where shapes were difficult to define; a world where every shadow could be Rick standing by a tree, and every brief flash of sunlight could be a home-made telescopic sight trained on them…

She forced herself to try and breathe calmly; to observe each shadow dispassionately as she rode, noting how its shape changed exactly as you would expect if it was indeed a shadow, and not a man with a gun…

Suddenly there was a loud cracking sound. Mary squeaked in alarm.

Tom stopped and smiled. "My horse snapped a branch," he said. "You have naught to fear."

He walked on, and Mary followed. A few minutes later he stopped and dismounted. "Wait," he said, as he crouched down and studied the path. "As I thought." He looked at it some more, "the mark of his foot in the earth. We are still on his trail."

"He could be just ahead," said Mary, as Tom got back on his horse and started forward again. Mary stayed still a moment, listening intently – but all she could hear was the breeze rustling the tops of the trees and birds chirruping softly. There was also a harsh rasping sound that she couldn't initially place, until she realised it was her own laboured breathing. Telling herself not to be so panicky, she squeezed Juno's side and trotted up behind Tom.

A few minutes later they came to a small clearing. Almost immediately Tom stopped, dismounted and went quickly to a small black mound in the middle of the space, crouching down to study it closely and poking at it with a stick. Then he turned with wide eyes, and before Mary could ask what it was, he held his finger to his lips to indicate silence. He looked all round the clearing, before pointing to a nearby tree and indicating that she should dismount and join him there.

With her heart in her mouth, Mary did as he wanted.

"It is a fire," he whispered, "and only recently covered over. He may be close by, even watching us now."

"Oh my Lord," she hissed. "What do we do?"

Tom paused a moment. "If this weapon of his is as good as Ursula says it is, then we are in real danger." Mary said nothing more – her mouth had suddenly become too dry to speak. "So I suggest we mount up slowly," he continued, "and turn back down the path. Then when I give the word, ride as fast as you can back to the cottage. We can seek shelter there while decide our plan."

Mary nodded, and walked slowly over to Juno. Again she listened to the sounds of the forest, but again she could hear nothing untoward. She glanced at the trees around her, but again, no tell-tale flash of sunlight bouncing off metal or glass…

She mounted Juno, and turned to face the way back to the cottage. She heard Tom mount up behind her; heard his horse's hooves start to move, and she walked slowly on herself.

The rasping sound of her own breathing now sounded deafening, as the sounds of the forest died away, until her breathing was the only sound she could hear, then Tom shouted, 'Now!' and suddenly all the sounds of the forest came back as she dug in her heels and Juno leapt forward into a gallop as the path and the trees started to fly by, then a fallen tree trunk appeared in her way so she gathered Juno's reins and muttered, 'Come on old girl,' and Juno took off in a perfect jump and was still in the air when there was a sudden sound like a breaking branch from one side and Juno screamed as a red cloud burst from her neck and she landed on the other side of the trunk and carried on down in a sprawling fall that sent Mary clean over her head and into the undergrowth…

---0---

Mary lay looking up at the sky between the trees for a moment, unsure of where she was and what to do next. She closed her eyes, trying to stop her head from spinning.

When she opened them, there was a man with a gun standing over her.

The gun was pointing right into her face. She could see that the man silhouetted against the sunlight had spiky hair like a hedgehog. She couldn't see his face against the sun, but she could hear his voice.

It was Rick's voice.

"Get up," he ordered. "Get up now."

Then she heard Tom, as if from far away. "You, Alchemist. Leave her."

"Hello, Tom Cobham." The gun did not move an inch. "It has been a while since we last met in the Blue Maid, when you invited me into your little plot. But now it is you chasing me. So which side are you on exactly?"

Tom said nothing, staring at the Alchemist in disgust.

"So am I to take it you are no longer in league with your hot-headed friend, Alleyne?" The Alchemist nodded to himself. "I thought as much. You did not seem to be one of those firebrand Catholics – so perhaps you are actually working for Wychwoode?" Again, Tom was silent. "Fair enough," said the Alchemist, as if answering for Tom, "so even if Tyler talks, the plot is blown open anyway. Thanks, Cobham."

Tom lifted his chin and stared at the barrel of the gun. "Right now, I take only Lady Mary's part, Alchemist. Leave her."

"Lady Mary, eh?" Still the gun didn't move. "I wondered if I would bump into you one day, Justine, after the storm when you disappeared so mysteriously – just like the one which landed me in this fucking fairy-tale country." He paused a moment. "You've done well, haven't you, Justine? Lady Fucking Mary now?" There was that arrogant sneer in his voice that she remembered now, only too well.

Too late.

She got slowly to her feet, testing her weight on each knee and hip to make sure nothing was broken. Everything seemed in order.

She should be scared – but in one heart-stopping moment, she had the answer to her question!

He knew her.

He called her Justine!

So she still existed in his future!

She wanted to sing and dance with joy! Saving William and having her family had not changed anything – she still existed in Rick's future!

Then the reality of the situation hit her.

She still existed for now...

Unless he succeeded in killing the Queen…

She stared at Rick across the barrel of a gun – a gun made to a 21st century design which he was planning to use to kill Queen Elizabeth.

And he seemed to have no qualms about using it. She looked over at Juno. Her faithful companion of ten years was lying on the ground completely still, except for the tiniest flaring of a nostril and an almost imperceptible rise and fall in the chest.

Suddenly Mary knew that there was nothing more important right now, not even having her own existence confirmed, than to comfort her dearest friend. Ignoring the gun, she ran to Juno's side and lay down beside the horse's head, then stroked the soft, velvety muzzle.

"There old girl, there, it will be alright…"

There was a flicker in the dark liquid eye and it fixed on hers.

"There, there, shh, my sweet," she said, and suddenly all she could see was that first day when Juno had been presented to her by Lady de Beauvais, William's mother, with a stern warning that this feisty young mare would be too much for a girl like Justine to handle... But she and Juno had bonded immediately; a pairing that had lasted ten years, until Juno was her stately 'old girl' and she was the matronly Lady Mary de Beauvais herself... Ten years of friendship and understanding that this monster of a man with his dreadful home-made gun had ended with a single shot...

'There, there, old girl," she whispered. "We will soon get you home and have you tucked up in your stable with a nice warm blanket and some of the oats you love..."

But the eye that looked into hers started to cloud over, until it became completely opaque, and the nostril stopped flaring, and the chest was still...

Then, in a sudden moment, her mood turned to anger.

Mary stood up and faced the Alchemist, ignoring the gun that was still pointing at her.

The elation of a few minutes ago had disappeared like morning mist.

"You filthy little man," she snarled. "You filthy, evil, monster of a man. I will make sure you pay for this..."

"Brave words, Justine, or should I say 'Lady Mary'?" He paused. "You really must tell me your story some day." He briefly waved the barrel of the gun towards the path. "Only it will have to wait, because right now I need your undercover lover-boy here to tie up his horse, then join you."

He turned and pointed the gun unwaveringly at Tom.

There was a moment while Tom tied his horse to a sturdy tree, then he appeared beside Mary. They exchanged a quick glance, and Tom gave her a grim look that seemed to say, 'Play along with this and we'll find a way out.' He took and held her hand, giving it a small squeeze.

"Now," continued the Alchemist, "walk down this path side by side, and I will walk behind you with my gun so I can stop either of you trying to run. And as you have seen from the old nag just now, this gun works." He chuckled. "Touching scene back there, by the way, 'Lady Mary'. Remind me to put you up for an Oscar. You almost had me there." Again, he chuckled. "But the fact is, I have you both, and I have you covered. At this close range, I could blow your heads off your shoulders – so do not try anything silly. Now walk."

---0---

As they walked back down the path, Mary could see that there wasn't any real opportunity to run. If either of them tried to make a break for it, she had no doubt that the Alchemist would shoot them immediately – and she was not prepared to take the risk for Tom or for herself. So she held on to his hand

and walked slowly down the path. She also took extra care stepping over roots and fallen branches, in case she inadvertently tripped. She did not want to give the Alchemist cause to think she was about to try something 'silly'.

It was not long before they were once again outside the cottage door.

"Open it," the Alchemist ordered. Mary pushed it open and they all went in.

As Mary's eyes grew used to the gloom, she could see that Ursula was tending to the fire, while an old man that she assumed must be Ursula's father was at the table skinning a rabbit. They both looked up as Mary and Tom walked in, then Ursula gave a small cry when the Alchemist walked in behind them holding his gun.

"Hello again, Ursula," the Alchemist said cheerfully. "I found these two on the path, and I thought I would bring them here for safe keeping." He waved the barrel of the gun towards the corner where his blanket still lay. "All of you, get in that corner and sit with your backs to the wall."

Reluctantly they complied, except Walter, who stayed by the table. "You," he growled, "leave my dwelling now."

"I said sit!" barked the Alchemist and pointed the gun at the old man. With a scowl, Walter went over to the corner and sat. "Now," said the Alchemist when they were all in a row, looking up at him. "There's a few things I need to do first. But then I will be gone, and will leave you all… resting in peace."

Mary felt her blood turn to ice. "So you're going to shoot us all?" she muttered.

The Alchemist shook his head. "Certainly not. I only made a few cartridges, and I'm hardly going to waste four of them on you lot."

"So what do you want with us?" asked Tom.

"I am heading up north, to finish the job that you asked me to do, Master Cobham," replied the Alchemist. "Even if you are no longer willing to see it through, I find it suits my own plans to finish it. So I will need the horse which you so conveniently left for me on the path, together with some food and some drink for the journey." He took the sacking bag off his shoulder and grabbed the rabbit, some knives, a pot, a costrel for carrying drink and Walter's slingshot, and threw them in. Still pointing the gun at them, he stood in the middle of the room by the fire.

"I must bid you all farewell," he said. "I doubt we will meet again."

"What you are doing is so wrong!" cried Mary. "Have you no thought for the future?"

"What fucking future, Justine?" he replied with a sneer. "The future that you and I know – the one that has not actually happened yet? Well, now it probably never will. Do you know what? The only fucking place it actually exists is as memories in your head and mine. And the truth is, I do not particularly care about it, and shortly, neither will you."

"You are a monster!"

"Sure, but soon I will be a rich monster, and a hero." The Alchemist kicked the pot away from the fire. "Pity you will not be around to see it."

Then as Mary watched in horror, he took another kick at the grate itself. It flew across the room, scattering burning embers as it went. One ember landed at the foot of the table, and the dry wood caught quickly. Soon flames were licking up the table leg.

The Alchemist waited until the flames reached the table-top, then he grabbed a blanket from Ursula's truckle bed and held it to the flames. When it too was alight, he tossed it back onto the bed, spreading the fire to the other side of the cottage.

Walter stood up, his face red with anger. "What do you think you are doing, you filthy cur?" he yelled. The Alchemist pointed the gun squarely at him. "Be seated again, old man, or I will kill you!"

"I am as like to die anyway!" yelled Walter, and Mary saw him start to run at the Alchemist and his gun.

Immediately there was a cracking sound and a puff of red smoke burst out of Walter's back.

She saw the Alchemist smile as the old man dropped to his knees, then fell forward face-first onto the floor, and was still.

Ursula screamed, and Tom started to get up, but the Alchemist had reloaded the gun and was pointing it at them, snarling, "I do not want to use any more bullets, but I will if I have to."

Tom sank back, his face contorted with rage. Mary leaned across and put her arm round Ursula. The girl buried her face in Mary's shoulder, and Mary felt her whole body shake as she sobbed.

"Right. I am off now," said the Alchemist. He backed to the door, grabbed the key off the hook and let himself out. The last thing Mary saw was the barrel of the gun disappearing through the door as it closed.

Just then the other truckle bed caught fire with a whoosh of sparks. The whole cottage was now burning.

"We have to get out!" yelled Mary.

Tom ran around the burning furniture and over to the door. He pulled and pushed on the handle, but the door remained resolutely closed. He turned back to Mary and Ursula. "He has locked it!" he yelled over the roar of flames. "We are trapped!"

CHAPTER SIXTEEN

The Strand, London

Olivia Melrose put down her sewing and stood up, smoothing her skirts and patting her hair in place.

"Lady Burnham wants to see us now?" she asked.

The elderly steward nodded. "Yes, Mistress Melrose. She has asked for you and Mistress Tyndall to attend on her presently."

Olivia glanced at Maggie Tyndall. The other girl laughed nervously. "What can she want, do you think?"

"I know not, Maggie," Olivia said. "It is unlike Lady Burnham to call us back so soon after we were dismissed for the afternoon." She walked to the door and nodded her thanks to the steward, who was now holding it open. "But I am sure she has her reasons. Come."

Maggie Tyndall also stood up. Her friend was a small, blonde-haired girl of eighteen with bright blue eyes that seemed too large for her face, but which Olivia knew could have a mischievous twinkle in them that men found irresistible.

The two girls made their way to their mistress's presence chamber and pushed open the door. Lady Burnham was seated in her usual high-backed chair by the fire. A man was standing beside her with his back to them. Olivia thought there was something vaguely familiar about the shape of the hair under his cap, but she dismissed the thought. No doubt all would be explained shortly.

"You asked to see us again, my lady?" she said, after both had given a low curtsey.

"Yes, Olivia, I did." Lady Burnham gave one of her frosty smiles. "I have some news for you both that I think will delight you."

Olivia glanced once more at the man, and wondered why he remained turned away. There was definitely something familiar about him, and now it was starting to make her feel a little uneasy. Lady Burnham continued, "Yes, I have some wonderful news." Again she gave a smile. "I have been asked to accompany Her Majesty the Queen on her forthcoming progress in the North, and I have decided to take the two of you to attend on me."

Maggie made a small jump. "Oh, my lady! We are to go on progress with the Queen?"

"Yes, dear, you are. I have chosen you both as I believe you have shown me good service." She looked pointedly at Olivia. "Even though you have been with me for only two weeks, Mistress Melrose, I have seen much good in you. You have a wise head on those young shoulders." She paused. "I believe you will be fine ambassadors for my household in the royal presence."

"Ohh, how wonderful, my lady!" squeaked Maggie. "Are we to meet the Queen?"

"Indeed you will, which is why I have asked this gentleman here to school the two of you on royal protocol. He is with the Queen's staff and will accompany us on the progress."

The man turned round slowly and smiled at Olivia.

Suddenly the room seemed to spin and she clutched at Maggie's arm for support.

Lionel Shelton!

She stared in shock as he came up to her. "Hello, Mistress Melrose," he said. "It has been a while since we last met."

Olivia did not answer; she could think of nothing to say.

"Come," barked Shelton, "and submit!"

"I wouldst not, Master Shelton! Please no! Do not raise your hand to me again! I beg you!"

"You are a wayward child, that I would teach some manners now!"

"I beg you, no!"

"You already know Master Shelton?" demanded Lady Burnham, glancing suspiciously at each of them.

"Indeed, my lady," Shelton answered easily with a sly grin, removing his cap and bowing to the girls. "Mistress Melrose and I met by chance on a snowy night some weeks ago in the little village of Hammersmith. We passed a most pleasant evening in the bar of a tavern, as I recall."

Olivia continued to stare at the man, still unable to find any words.

"No, Master Shelton, no! By Heaven, do not strike me again!"

"Then do not make me, you wilful girl! Submit now and it will be better for you!"

"Master Shelton has said he has already made your acquaintance, Olivia," said Lady Burnham with a small sniff of displeasure. "Please do him the courtesy of an acknowledgement."

Olivia took a deep breath. She knew what she had to say – '*Indeed, Master Shelton, how nice to see you again…*', but how could she trust herself not to blurt out – '*How dare you come into my presence once again, you filthy monster?*'

She took another deep breath. "Indeed, Master Shelton," she whispered, "how nice to see you again."

"Good." Lady Burnham nodded, seeming oblivious to Olivia's inner distress. "We are to join the Queen's entourage at Greenwich in three days. Until then you will be in Master Shelton's charge; he will school you on how to behave at Court and in the presence of the Queen." She waved her hand in casual dismissal. "Schooling will begin in the morning. Meanwhile, you are free to your own activities until supper."

Olivia and Maggie curtseyed, then walked out of the room.

Lionel Shelton!

As Olivia followed Maggie down the endless corridors back to their rooms, it seemed like the wood-panelled walls were closing in on her, crushing the air out of her body and stopping her from breathing.

Lionel blasted Shelton!

When they eventually reached the sanctuary of their room, Olivia could do nothing except sink down onto the bed and lie immobile, staring up at the ceiling. Maggie, however, was like an excited kitten, unable to keep still for even a moment.

"We are to see the Queen!" she cried. "Oh my, whatever shall I wear at Court?" She threw open her clothes chest and started taking out garments. "I will need new gowns and shoes, of course – these old things will never do..." She stopped a moment. "I shall have to ask Master Shelton what is worn at Court! He will know." Then she jumped onto the bed and leaned over Olivia, her face suddenly filling Olivia's entire field of vision. "I say, Livvy, that Master Shelton is quite a catch, is he not? Quite the handsome man." She frowned. "His eyes, were they blue or grey?" She shook her head. "No matter – I shall observe them most carefully next time we meet." She looked up. "I liked his beard though – well cut and trim. I wonder if he has a wife already? I might make a play for him, Livvy. You do not mind, do you?" She moved closer, so a tendril of her hair hung down by Olivia's nose. "You mind not, do you Livvy dearest, if I make a play for him? You know him already – from some snowy evening – you have no designs on him yourself?" She paused expectantly. "Do you, Livvy? Livvy?

Lionel Shelton! Dear God, no!

It seemed to Olivia at that moment that it was not Maggie Tyndall above her, but now it was Lady Mary, grabbing her shoulders and staring fiercely down at her, saying once again the words spoken so passionately in Hammersmith.

"My dear sweet child, you must never, never, ever, blame yourself for the actions of a man – do you hear me? It is never a girl's fault if a man decides to act like a coward and a beast. If Lionel Shelton forced himself upon you, then it is for his conscience, not yours, to answer for it."

Then it was Maggie once again, looking at her expectantly, waiting for an answer.

"What was that, Maggie?" she muttered.

Maggie squeaked in exasperation. "Oh, Livvy, you have not listened to a word I have said! I am thinking to make a play for Master Shelton. I think his beard is most becoming, and his grey eyes – or perhaps they are blue, I shall have to check – are quite piercing. I asked if you were of a mind to make a play for him yourself."

Olivia stared up at the girl's face.

Such a pretty face.

So how would it look if Shelton punched it as hard as he had punched hers?

Olivia shuddered. Would it change Maggie's bright, innocent personality as much as it had hers, if Shelton also dragged her across the floor, threw her down on the bed, and… and…

That was not going to happen.

"Maggie," she said firmly, "Master Shelton is here to coach us on royal protocol. He is not, I am sure, seeking a wife. I would advise you most strongly to end these silly thoughts of romance, and concentrate on learning how best to behave at Court."

Maggie climbed slowly off the bed and looked down at Olivia.

"And you are not saying this because you want him for yourself? she whispered. "Because you have met him before, drinking in some tavern?"

Olivia stood up and held Maggie's face in her hands. "Maggie Tyndall," she said, "I love you as my best friend in all the world, so please believe me when I say I have no interest in this Lionel Shelton. None whatsoever. And believe me also when I tell you that I know this man, and I know he will not make a good husband – for you, for me, or for any girl." She moved her hands down to Maggie's shoulders. "So let us do no more than learn from Master Shelton how we should behave at Court; let us conduct ourselves properly as befits our station, and let us put aside any thought of romance with him."

There was a long silence as Maggie digested this, then eventually she nodded. "Marry, Livvy, I see you are most sincere in this, so I suppose I must take your advice on the matter."

"Good. Now, let us get dressed for supper, and tomorrow we shall learn how best to attend my lady at Court."

---0---

"When the Queen enters a room, you are to sink to a curtesy – and you must be sure never to raise your head to a level that is higher than hers – although," Lionel Shelton paused and studied both girls, "I doubt either of you is taller than Her Majesty anyway."

"Are we allowed in her presence chamber?" asked Maggie.

"Aye, the Queen likes to have many people around her at all times."

"How exciting!" Maggie breathed. "And what if she speaks to you?"

"You address her as 'Your Grace' and you answer her question succinctly and truthfully."

It was the following morning and the three of them were gathered in the long gallery, bathed in the sunlight that flooded in from the diamond-paned leaded windows overlooking the Thames, making rippling patterns on the opposite wall as the light reflected off the water.

Maggie and Olivia had finished their duties with Lady Burnham after breaking fast, before making their way to meet Shelton in the gallery. Olivia had done all she could to delay the start of the meeting; lingering at breakfast, deciding to change her sleeves, then her shoes, until Maggie could no longer contain her impatience and had dragged Olivia into the room where Shelton was pacing up and down. After pleasantries between Maggie and Shelton, the session had begun, and now it was in full swing.

"And what about the Queen's courtiers?" asked Olivia. "How are we to behave if we meet them?"

"A fine question, Olivia." Shelton gave a slow smile. "I know how like you are to turn a man's head, so..."

"I have learned where such behaviour leads, believe me Master Shelton," Olivia cut in. "And I am not the same girl that I was. Now please, answer my question."

Shelton pursed his lips. "I would say that if you meet one such as The Earl of Leicester or Sir Christopher Hatton, you should be polite and ladylike – and aware of courtly manners."

"What are those?" asked Maggie.

"Such that they may well pay you compliments, or profess love, but such wooing is all part of the game at Court – you are not to act as if it were real."

"Oh." Maggie considered this carefully. "But what if it really were real? What if they really were wooing you? How would you know the difference?"

"It would not be real, believe me," said Shelton. "For the Queen does not approve of her courtiers having romances."

"Then why do they do it, if it is not really real?" asked Maggie, with a frown.

"Because it is how the Court works," he answered. "Compliments and poetry and courtly love are what makes the whole system function. Especially," he added, "in relation to Her Majesty herself."

"But she has now said she is married to England, and will never take a husband," Olivia observed. "So what does it benefit the courtiers to profess love to her?"

"It is the game she likes to play – and she has them play along with her." He gave a small laugh. "And it trickles down to all the ladies at court."

"So how does it work, exactly?" asked Maggie. "Show us."

Shelton looked slowly at each of them in turn. "You would have me show you?"

Olivia shot a furious glance at Maggie, but it rebounded like an arrow off a shield. The girl was staring intently at Shelton, her lips parted and her eyes wide. Olivia heard her say under her breath, "Grey – I knew it."

Shelton walked over to Maggie and bowed. "Mistress Tyndall," he said quietly, taking both her hands in his, "may I say how radiant you look today, as lovely as a soft-petalled rose…" He brushed a stray lock of hair back over her ear. "Nay, for that is to do a disservice to your wondrous beauty for you are a thousand times more fair, my dearest Maggie…"

Maggie smiled sweetly and was about to answer, when Olivia cut in. "Such wooing would not fool a simple child, Master Shelton. Surely they do better than that?"

"Oh, but do go on, Master Shelton," breathed Maggie. Then she shot a stern look at Olivia, before turning back and whispering, "You were saying?"

"Master Shelton was giving you a valuable lesson in the shallow, meaningless tittle-tattle that passes for conversation at Court," snapped Olivia. "And you would do well to heed how shallow it is." She turned and stared out of the window at the boats making their way up, down and across the Thames, trying to control her ragged breathing. When she turned back, Maggie and Shelton were standing just apart, with a studied air of innocence on both their faces.

"You will continue the instruction of us both, Master Shelton," Olivia ordered, "so we may be fully prepared for our life at Court. The instruction will be here each day and," she added, with a furious look at both of them, "I need hardly say that outside of these sessions of instruction, we will not engage you in discourse of any kind. Do I make myself clear?"

---0---

It was two days later that the barge pulled slowly away from the Strand jetty, then made its way up the centre of the river.

Olivia sat quietly in the stern, looking out as the city passed by, watching the hundreds of other barges, wherries and sailing boats criss-cross the Thames. There was the occasional large ship amongst the crowd of smaller vessels, majestically making its way towards the port of London with just one or two sails unfurled; men lining the decks as the vessel slipped through the water. The river was a mass of sounds as well as movement; boatmen shouting for way as others came too close to their wherries, passengers greeting each other as they passed; pilots shouting the depth as they manoeuvred their barges towards the dock – and all accompanied for Olivia by the rhythmic splash of oars from Lady Burnham's rowers.

Olivia glanced back over her shoulder. The house she had called home these last couple of weeks had blended into the mass of buildings along the bank and could no longer be picked out. She turned forward again and looked along the length of the boat. Lady Burnham was close by, seated under the canopy to protect her from the sun and keep her complexion pale – staring down her nose at the rowers, just as one could imagine the Queen might do.

Maggie was sitting up at the front of the boat, talking to Shelton and smiling most inappropriately at him.

Olivia frowned. God knew well enough that she had tried her hardest to keep them apart – but it seemed the more she tried to warn Maggie off the man, the more the silly girl seemed to want him. Olivia had therefore switched her tactic to one of total indifference to see if that worked, but it seemed that Maggie was drawn to Shelton like a moth to a flame, and continued to behave in a way that was guaranteed to get the man's interest.

Not that there had been much time when the two of them could have been alone. It had been a frantic few days since Lady Burnham's announcement. There had been Shelton's sessions of instruction – which Olivia got through by concentrating fiercely on the information he was providing and trying to ignore her rising bile every time she looked at the man. Then there were clothes to be selected, trunks to be packed, and Lady Burnham's own travelling wardrobe to be managed. So the time had passed quickly, and now they were on their way to Greenwich to join the Court as it set off to begin the summer progress.

What would Court be like? Shelton had made it sound most strange; a constructed society where false flattery was required in public – especially towards the Queen – but in private the conversation was mainly tittle-tattle and idle gossip. The Olivia of a few weeks ago would have revelled in such artifice – indeed that would have been her natural style – but the Olivia who had suffered at the hand of Shelton was altogether different. Since that dreadful night when she had lost her innocence – no, when he had forced it away from her with unspeakable violence – she had left her childhood pleasures behind, and entered reluctantly into the adult world. But it was not just Shelton's attack that had been responsible – that had only been the start of her transition. In truth, it had been Lady Mary's unexpected kindness that had completed the journey. To have been so caring and understanding, even after Olivia had been as manipulative as she had been on the way to Hammersmith, showed Olivia that other adult behaviour could be kind, selfless and confidence-building. Indeed, Lady Mary had been very clear with her strange notion that a girl had the right not to have to submit automatically to a man.

But then, why should such a view be strange? Was there not a Queen on the throne? Perhaps things were going to change, as Lady Mary had said. Olivia prayed that one day girls would be able to own property in their own right, marry whoever they chose and take part in the government of the land, as Lady Mary had told her with such great confidence.

Lady Burnham leant back and fixed Olivia with a hard stare. "Master Shelton seems remarkably familiar with Mistress Tyndall," she observed. "I would you take the girl aside and tell her not to lead him on in this way."

"I have seen this also, Lady Burnham," answered Olivia, "and I have told her she must be more considered in her behaviour."

"Well, she has either not heard your wise words, or she has rashly chosen to ignore them."

They both viewed the flirting going on at the front of the boat.

"If he decides to act on her inappropriate ways," said Lady Burnham, "then she must accept the consequences. And I do not feel she is suitable marriage material for him, should it get that far."

"He could always restrain himself," muttered Olivia. She did not think she had said it loud enough to be heard, but the breeze must have carried the words to her mistress. "By the Lord's Wounds, Olivia," Lady Burnham exclaimed, her eyebrows almost disappearing under her hood, "what a strange notion!" She stared at the girl a moment. "He is a man – if he decides to act upon her flirtation and take it further, then that is his right – and she must accept that it is her own fault."

Olivia stayed silent, and Lady Burnham turned away.

Again, the image of Lady Mary came unbidden in front of her. "*You must never, never, ever, blame yourself for the actions of a man – do you hear me? It is never a girl's fault if a man decides to act like a coward and a beast.*"

Olivia nodded to herself.

One day, Lionel Shelton, you will pay for your actions that night.

Not long after, they rounded a bend and Olivia caught sight of the royal palace at Greenwich, its magnificent brick towers and chimneys rising above the surrounding trees.

The barge drew up alongside a set of stone steps that descended into the river in the middle of a long waterside wall. A footman in the Queen's livery took hold of the gangplank, then folded it back so that it rested on a step. Shelton jumped down first, then held out his hand to help Lady Burnham off the barge and up the steps. Then he came back for Maggie, and escorted her off as well.

Olivia waited as he turned back and held out his hand to help her down.

"I am perfectly capable of stepping ashore, Master Shelton," she growled.

He shrugged his shoulders without a word, then went over to Lady Burnham and made an exaggerated show of offering her his arm. Together with Maggie they started out towards the palace.

Olivia stepped carefully off the boat and followed them up the path.

CHAPTER SEVENTEEN

The fire was now raging out of control, and there was no way out.

Mary, Tom and Ursula moved ever closer together, until they were huddled in the centre of the cottage, each staring out at the advancing flames.

Tom unsheathed his sword and poked it at the timbers and rushes that blazed around them, pushing them back to try and create a break in the fire. Mary could see that this would only delay the inevitable, as she found herself coughing uncontrollably.

"The smoke!" she gasped. "It is the smoke that kills! We must cover our faces!"

Ursula ripped off a piece of her skirt and tore it into three strips. They each bound the material as masks around their faces, which made breathing a bit easier.

Then Tom turned to Mary. "I would not die from burns or smoke," he said, his eyes narrowed above the mask. "It is not how I choose to go and meet my maker." He put the tip of the sword up to his ribs. "I must end it shortly, then you can do the same."

Mary looked at the shining blade, flashing with orange in the light of the fire.

Was this it?

Justine Parker, the time-travelling adventurer who survived drowning in a well, married a knight, had three kids and – and what?

She pushes a sword into her own heart because there's no hope?

And then what?

She had been so frightened of suddenly disappearing because she had changed history – that she hadn't particularly thought about what would happen if she died anyway.

Rick would have won – that was for sure. He would assassinate the Queen. Then it would be as she had originally feared. The future – her future, the one with cars and phones and planes and TVs that existed only in her memory – might now be very different.

Mary looked up.

Would it disappear, just as that smoke disappeared through the hole in the roof?

If it were not for that hole drawing the smoke and heat upwards to escape into the air, they would surely have been consumed already.

The hole in the roof!

"Tom, quick!" she screamed, pointing up at the hole. "Lift me up!"

Tom looked up and understood immediately. He re-sheathed his sword and yelled to Ursula, "Help me!" Together they grabbed Mary's legs below the knee and lifted her bodily up to the roof in one swift movement. Mary grabbed at the shingles surrounding the hole, then screamed as the heat in the smouldering wood scorched her hands.

Tom and Ursula brought her back down quickly.

"Too hot to hold!" she shouted. Tom and Ursula both took the masks from their faces. Mary wrapped them round her hands and held her arms up ready. Again they lifted her up, and this time she was able to hold on to the shingles. With her arms in agony as she hauled up her full weight, she was able to get her head, then her upper body through the hole. Gasping for breath in the clearer air, she wriggled and squirmed until she was out of the hole and rolling helplessly down the shingles and falling in an ungainly heap by the front door.

The Alchemist had left the key in the lock.

Quickly she turned the key and pushed the door open. A wave of heat and flames blew out, catching her in the face and sending her staggering backwards onto the earth. She struggled to her feet, her breath coming in gasps as she ran back to the door. Inside she could see Tom and Ursula, their faces blackened and their eyes staring. Fierce flames burned between them and the door, making their escape seem impossible.

There was a loud cracking sound over the roar of the flames.

The roof was starting to collapse.

A large burning beam began to fall. Tom leapt out of its way, but Ursula was not so lucky. Mary saw it catch her legs and knock her to the ground, then it fell on top of her and pinned her down across the waist.

Quickly the flames transferred to her clothes and within seconds her skirts were alight.

Tom started trying to lift the beam off her, but it was clear it was too heavy.

Then Ursula yelled something Mary couldn't hear to Tom. He shook his head and tried again to lift the beam. Ursula shouted again and again, but he continued to shake his head and kept trying to free her.

Mary could see that it was a matter of seconds before flames would reach Tom and she screamed "Tom!" at the top of her voice. Then Ursula screamed at him as well. It sounded like, "Please!"

Tom glanced at the flames that were starting to lick at his feet, and made one more attempt to move the beam.

Ursula screamed again, and finally Tom stood up. He stared a moment at Ursula, then at the flames between him and the door. He said something to her, briefly touched her cheek, then ran through the flames towards the door.

He emerged into the open, smoke-blackened and wide-eyed, gasping for air.

As he and Mary watched, another beam started to break away from the roof, and it seemed to Mary it was coming away directly above Ursula. For a moment it hung above the unfortunate girl, but she was trapped like a fly pinned to a board and could not roll away.

Then it started to move again.

As Ursula struggled and Mary screamed, it fell.

At first it seemed to fall in slow motion, then it increased its speed and came down with sickening inevitability.

There was nothing Ursula could do – she did not stand a chance.

It fell with all its weight and a dreadful crash that could clearly be heard over the flames, directly onto her head.

There was a single convulsive spasm, then no further movement in her body.

After that, it seemed that everything happened very fast. The rest of the roof collapsed with a sound like thunder and a whoosh of sparks. The whole cottage was now alight, with heat so intense that Mary and Tom were pushed back, able only to stare helplessly in silence as the fire quickly consumed what was left of the little building. Then it died down almost as quickly, once everything that could burn was finally consumed. Mary was reminded of a modern-day cooker being turned off.

Tom turned to Mary, his face black except for two tear lines down his face. "No more than a few minutes," he muttered, "since that man kicked over the grate." He shook his head. "No more than that to destroy a cottage and kill a good woman."

"And her father."

"Aye." Tom nodded. "And him too." He was silent a moment. "At least it was quick for her. She would have known very little when that second beam took her life."

Mary put her hand on his arm. "What did she say to you?" she asked quietly.

He turned slowly away from the fire and stared at her. Fresh tears rolled down his cheeks.

"She said…" he stopped, his mouth working. "That I must not save her, she wanted to die."

"But why?"

He took a deep breath. "Because she said she was not worthy to live after what she had done." Mary stayed silent, letting him find the words in his own time. Eventually he said, "Because she had lain with that man. She could not suffer herself to live, knowing what sort of a man he was."

"She had lain with him?"

He nodded. "She said that. She begged me not to try and save her, but to save myself." He stared at the cottage, now a blackened and twisted hulk with small fires still burning here and there, then turned back to Mary. "I would have saved her, as God is my witness – I would have done. I would have moved that beam if I had had just a little more time…"

Mary gently brushed away another tear as it ran down his cheek. "I know, Tom. I know."

"She was a good woman." He gave her a watery smile. "She was honest and true. She did not deserve to die."

"She did not."

Tom suddenly grasped her hand. "We must stop that man, the Alchemist," he said. "We must find him and turn him in to Wychwoode. He cannot succeed in this plot." Tom gestured at the smouldering cottage, "and he must be made to pay for what he has done." He nodded, as if to himself. "He is not too far ahead; we must track behind him, unseen and unknown, until we can find a way to capture him." He nodded again. "The sooner we send him to Hell where he belongs, the better."

"I would we wait until the fire is totally out, so we can get to the bodies of Ursula and Walter," said Mary. "They should be taken out of that place and buried with dignity."

"Aye," he answered, "they should. The flames may have died down, but it will take many hours – days even – before it is safe to enter, and we cannot let the Alchemist have such a start on us."

Mary turned sharply to stare at him. "You would leave them there unburied?"

"If it means we have a better chance of catching the man who did this to them, and bringing him to justice, then yes." He looked steadily back at her. "If that is acceptable?"

"Yes, I suppose you are right." Mary stood up. "Then we had better start now, had we not?"

He stood also. "Good. We will go to where I left my horse."

They started walking along the path towards the forest. Mary stopped by the body of Juno, still lying where she had fallen earlier. "Wait," she said, then knelt beside the horse's head and stroked the soft cheek and velvet muzzle, still slightly warm. "Goodbye old girl," she whispered. "Rest in peace, my lovely." Then she put her head onto Juno's neck and lay a moment staring up at the mare's ear, as if she expected it to twitch like it used to. But it stayed resolutely still.

She felt Tom's hand on her shoulder.

"Come, Lady Mary," he said quietly, "we should keep moving."

But with a sudden sob, Mary knew she could not leave Juno, and clung even more tightly to her horse for a few minutes more, feeling the hot tears roll down her face and dissolve into the soft brown coat.

When she finally let go and stood up, Tom was patiently waiting a few feet away.

She nodded, acknowledging that he had left her alone to mourn her friend, and dried her tears on her sleeve. "Thank you," she added, as she walked past him and into the forest, although she could not stop herself continually looking back, until the still brown body had finally disappeared behind the trees.

Tom trotted after her, and together they walked to where he had left his horse. As expected, it had gone.

"Look." He pointed down and she could see the hoof tracks in the soft earth of the path, heading away from them.

Mary was about to march on, when a terrible thought came into her head.

"What if he is waiting for us again with his sniper musket?" she asked, shivering despite the warm air filtering through the trees.

"Surely not," answered Tom. "He will want to be as far away as possible from the fire, now he is on his horse – or rather, on my horse. And besides," he chuckled, "he thinks we are both dead."

They walked further into the forest. Occasionally Tom would stop and study signs on the path or on the trees close by. Mary didn't know what he was seeing that helped him track Rick, but once or twice he darted into the undergrowth to study something Mary couldn't see, then he nodded to himself, and headed on back onto the path.

They were walking on in silence after one such time, when Tom said, "Can I ask you something?"

"For sure," she replied.

He stopped and looked hard at her. "Why did that man the Alchemist call you a different name? What was it; Justine or somesuch?" He narrowed his eyes. "And just before he started the fire, he said something about the future being but a memory for you both. What did he mean by that?" He looked up at the trees around him, as if he was seeking inspiration from their branches and leaves. "What exactly is your connection to the Alchemist, Lady Mary?"

Mary studied her hands, still wrapped in the rough strips of cloth from Ursula's skirts, and realised just how much the burns were hurting. But that was nothing to the painful consequences if she gave the wrong answer to this question. Clearly, the truth was not an option – however much Tom wanted to help her, the risk that he would abandon her or hand her in to a witchfinder if she tried to explain she was a time-traveller, was too great.

"Tom," she said, taking his hands in both of hers and trying not to wince with the pain. "There is indeed some history between me and Rick." He raised a blackened eyebrow and she quickly added, "I always said I was trying to find him to ask him questions." She searched his eyes but he was giving nothing away. "But there is nothing sinister in it, and that is God's honest truth." He stayed silent for so long that she felt compelled to continue, "I swear I will tell you when this is over, but until then I want you to trust me that I am on your side and the Queen's – and I want that man to stop the task you set him, and to pay for what he is done." She gestured back down the path. "I had Juno from when she was not much more than a foal – and more than anything she was my friend. He killed her, and he killed Ursula and Walter." She let go of his hands and stood back. "And for that I want to make him pay."

"There is nothing sinister?" he said eventually. "You swear on your oath?"

She nodded. "I swear."

He was silent again for what seemed an uncomfortably long time. "Then I will trust you on this, because I know you are an honest woman, and I respect you greatly." He nodded. "And when this matter is over, I want you to respect me too, and tell me all."

"I will."

"Good." He smiled. "And let us find a stream to wash ourselves quickly and clean your burned hands, for I am tired of being blackened with soot on my skin and my clothes, and I see from the pain in your face that your hands are raw under those rags."

---0---

Eventually they came across a stream. It was about ten feet wide, with clear water running over clean rocks and stones. Mary thought it looked three or four feet deep, which was perfect. She suddenly felt very dirty, and had to fight the urge to throw off her filthy clothes and jump straight in. But first Tom made her kneel on the bank and dangle her bare hands in the cool water, which made the pain in them subside to a dull throb.

He made her keep them there for what seemed like ages, then he took them out of the water and examined them.

"They are still red and raw," he said. He studied them further, then added, "You will need to bind them with a poultice of goose or pig fat, but for now these needs must suffice." Still holding her hands he looked up into her eyes. "So, Mary, how does it?"

"I will live," she answered. "I can manage."

"Good." He let go of her hands and stepped back, still staring into her eyes. "Now I must undress and wash my body and my clothing in the stream." There was a silence, then he added, with a raised eyebrow, "I will be fully unclothed, Lady de Beauvais..."

Mary forced her gaze away from the bright eyes in his blackened face. "Yes," she muttered. "Unclothed. We cannot be seen together in such a state." She gave a small smile. "I will bathe elsewhere…" She backed away, then followed the stream round a bend to the other side of a thick bramble hedge. There she undressed fully, before taking her torn and tattered gown down to the water and using a rock to scrub the soot out of it.

As she scrubbed, the downstream water ran black, as the dirt and smoke washed out and splashed away across the stones. But just as she thought it was nearly clean, she noticed that the water upstream was black as well, and she wondered for a moment how the dirt could travel the wrong way… Then she realised she must be getting the soot from Tom's washing coming downstream, so after pulling out her gown and laying it on the bank to dry, she peered round the brambles to see if he had finished.

There was no sign of Tom upstream, just his clothes also laid out on the bank to dry, and the winter sun glinting off the surface of the water. She could see both banks and the trees in the distance, but Tom had disappeared.

With a gasp, she started to splash her way towards the spot where his clothes were. Maybe he had drowned? Or someone had taken him while she had been washing her gown…

She was nearly at the spot, when there was a sudden eruption of water that sent her staggering back, and Tom emerged like Neptune from the deep, water flying off him as he stood up and shook his head, his well-shaped body shining in the sunlight as if it had been carved from oiled teak.

Mary stopped transfixed at the sight of his muscled chest and defined abdomen, with its dark streak of hair running down his stomach towards the thick curls of his…

Mary gasped again, and Tom opened his eyes.

At first, they fixed on hers. Then she felt her blood run cold as they moved slowly down, stopping on her breasts, before moving lower to fix on the base of her own belly.

Mary knew she had to move; to turn and wade back round the brambles and out of his sight, but her legs seemed unable to respond, and for what seemed like several minutes they both remained still, like two naked statues facing each other; silent, unmoving.

Then Tom waded forward until he was close enough to touch her. Slowly he reached out and stroked his hand down her cheek.

Mary knew she had to stop this now before it went too far, but instead she found herself leaning in towards his hand as it travelled down to her neck, trapping it briefly onto her shoulder, before it moved softly down over her collar bone and onto the top of her breast.

She heard someone moan gently, then realised it was actually her, as his hand slid down over her breast and cupped it.

Then he came in closer till their bodies were almost touching.

He moved nearer still, and she gasped as they pressed together, his hot skin burning her belly and her breasts as if they were on fire.

His hand moved off her chest and round her back, then down to her bottom, and his mouth closed on hers, his tongue finding hers and caressing it, playing with it, loving it.

She closed her eyes, as again she heard the moan.

As her eyes closed, she saw William.

He was smiling at her as he held out his hand to lead her to the altar in the wedding chapel all those years ago. Then the chapel faded, and now William was in Ruth's cottage, as they lay together in the little bed. Now he was smiling with pride as she handed Ambrose to him, gazing with adoration into the baby's wide blue eyes…

Mary jumped back and out of Tom's grasp.

She realised she was breathing deeply, as if she had just run a marathon.

"Nay Tom," she panted, "this is not seemly. I would not do this."

He said nothing for a long time. Eventually he nodded and stepped back. "Sir William is a fortunate man," he said. "I must respect your will in this, though I like it not."

"Thank you, Tom," she answered. "That is the honourable thing."

"Hmm," he agreed, then turned and made his way to the bank, before lifting himself out of the stream and returning to his clothes.

He dressed quickly while she was still wading back to her clothes, then strode off through the forest. Mary struggled quickly into her wet, clingy gown and set off after him as fast as she could, while trying not to trip over roots or turn her ankle in a muddy hole.

Finally she caught up and came level with him, panting hard.

He was striding purposefully along the path, staring straight ahead and no longer searching for hoof prints or other tell-tale signs of Rick's passing. When she asked why not, he just grunted, then muttered something about knowing where the Alchemist was heading anyway. Then he increased his pace so she had to keep running just to stay with him.

Suddenly she had enough.

She stopped abruptly in the path, planted her feet and put her hands on her hips, and waited for him to notice she was no longer there.

Unfortunately, he either did not notice, or chose not to, so she was forced to shout out after him.

"Tom!"

The call echoed around the still forest, bouncing off the tall elms and sycamores; putting up a couple of noisy rooks.

He stopped and turned, then strode back to her with a look of thunder.

"Hush your noise, woman!" he hissed. "What if that murderous friend of yours is near? We would not let him know we still live!"

"Then do not run off and leave me, so I must call your name!" she hissed back. "And anyway, you said he would be miles ahead on his horse..." She thought a moment, "…your horse."

"Aye, but there is a risk he is near, and your calling could be heard in Oxford. Indeed, I have not heard any person shout so loud as you in all my days." He regarded her a moment. "That is some power you have in your chest, Lady Mary."

He turned away and started walking again, so she called out – more softly this time – "Wait!"

He stopped again, this time with his back to her.

"Listen, Thomas Cobham," she ordered, advancing right up behind him and hissing into his ear. "In case you have forgotten, we are following this man so we can stop him trying to kill the Queen, and to make him pay for the killing of Juno, Ursula and Walter." He didn't move. "I am a married woman, Tom," she whispered, "and would not cuckold my husband." She saw him stiffen his shoulders. "So I suggest you stop behaving like a spoiled little boy, and start behaving like a man, because we need to get this Alchemist, and we are not going to do that by behaving like children."

He turned slowly round to face her.

"Hmm," he said slowly. "Then as a man, I suggest we make all haste to the next town, which is Henley-in-Arden. There we can eat, sleep, change our clothing and avail ourselves of a couple of horses so we can make good speed up north…"

---0---

It was only ten miles to Henley-in-Arden; a journey which should have taken them no more than a few hours. However, despite Tom's urgency, Mary found it impossible to make good speed. The forest path was hardly a path at all; more a rough track with frequent obstacles – so she was continually having to lift her heavy, sodden skirts and step over roots, as well as duck under low branches. There were also many thick muddy puddles that were covered in leafy plants and hard to make out, so she was constantly stopping to check the ground before committing herself to the next step.

There were a number of times when Tom, who seemed to have the sure-footedness of a gazelle, was striding so far ahead that she was fearful of losing him altogether. Each time she had to call out to him – not too loudly – so he would stop and wait for her to catch up.

At one point she came to a small fallen tree with a large puddle just in front of it, on a narrow section of the path. The trunk crossed the whole path and disappeared into thick gorse bushes on either side. There was no way round – so she would have to go over. She stopped and studied it carefully, trying to decide if she could get over in one leap, or if she was going to have to risk stepping in the puddle first, before clambering over. As she studied it, she decided that the puddle was just too wide, and the tree trunk too far in front, to be cleared in a single leap. She looked up and saw Tom making his confident way along the path many yards ahead. He must have got over this obstacle with ease.

"Wait!" she called.

She saw him stop and turn, then stand waiting. She picked up a piece of broken-off branch that was lying nearby and used it to test the depth of the puddle. It hit something hard without going too deep, so she decided to risk it.

Lifting her skirts, she put her right foot gingerly into the puddle, letting it down gently till she felt it hit the bottom. The water was cold and glutinous, and she let out a small involuntary yelp as it closed over the top of her shoe.

She looked up. Tom had moved back towards her, and was now watching as she carefully put her left foot in the puddle. This time there was no hard stop, and she felt her foot sink deep into the mud.

"Could'st not have jumped across, like a mountain goat?" he called.

She regarded him with her hardest stare. "Are you calling me a goat?"

"Not if you are stuck in that puddle." Then he laughed. "You look more like a heron, standing on one foot."

"You may have been able to leap about like a goat, but I have heavy skirts on, and smaller legs." She scowled at him. "Are you going to help me?"

"What, and miss the chance to see you fall flat upon your face in the mud?"

"Oh right!" she muttered to herself. "That is how it is going to be, is it?" She looked down at her feet, then up at the tree trunk. "I shall do this myself without your help, Master Thomas bloody Cobham."

She reached forward and put her hands on the trunk, lifting her right leg out of the puddle and positioning her knee up next to her hand. Then she rocked forward in order to get her left leg up.

It was stuck.

She rocked again. There was a gloopy, squelching noise, but it stayed stuck.

"Art now a tree frog, my lady?" he enquired politely.

She chose not to answer, but instead rocked again, pulling at her left foot with all her strength.

It came free with an even louder squelch. With a strangled yell she fell forward, landing in a sprawling, muddy heap on the other side.

She looked up to see Tom above her, laughing uncontrollably.

Without a word she stood up, smoothed down her skirts, tried to pat her hair into place, then walked on past him with her head held high.

Which would have been fine, had she not then tripped over a root and fallen forward, landing flat on her face with a most un-lady-like shriek.

She lay there a moment with her cheek in a puddle.

Damn! That was not supposed to happen.

She felt strong hands grab her under the armpits and lift her easily to her feet. He stood her in front of him.

"There, my lady," he said with a big smile. "Now I have seen you fall flat on your face in the mud. We can continue our journey."

She stared into his eyes. He had splashes of earth all down his cheeks and caking into his beard – although goodness knew what she must look like.

"You are a cruel, heartless man, Thomas Cobham," she said. It was meant as a bit of a light-hearted quip but he seemed to take it seriously. He shook his head, his laughter gone in an instant.

"Nay, Mary. I am not heartless," he said quietly. "Far from it. I have a heart, and it would be yours if it could be." He brushed some mud gently off her nose. "But it cannot be, I know that. I have accepted it." He put his finger to her lips. "Say naught, sweet Mary." Then he touched the same finger to his own lips. "For there is naught to be said."

---0---

By the time dusk fell, it seemed they were still no nearer to habitation.

"We must stop," muttered Mary, as she stumbled over a root. "It gets too dark to walk this path."

"Aye," he answered, "we will have to rest for the night. He looked around. "There is a small clearing there – let us use that."

Mary went into the clearing, swept the undergrowth for sticks and rocks, then sat down. She took out her costrel and shook it. There was hardly any water sloshing around at the bottom, so she finished what was left. "We need to find an inn soon or we will die of thirst," she said. Then there was a loud rumble under her grubby gown. "And hunger," she added.

"My need right now is to keep you warm," he said, busily gathering some twigs and building them up to a conical pyre in the middle of the clearing. Then he picked some dry grasses and pushed them in the base of the pyre, before getting two flinty stones and striking them together to make a spark.

One of the sparks caught on the grasses, and he blew gently on it, until it was firmly alight. Then he piled more grasses and twigs on, until there was a good fire going.

Mary felt in her pocket and caressed the smooth metal and plastic of the 21st century lighter that she carried with her at all times for safekeeping. How easy it would have been to take it out and use it to light the fire – and how many difficult questions would she have had to answer as a result? No, the lighter stayed firmly in her pocket as she stared across at Tom, his face flickering orange in the light of the flames.

"I was thinking how we might get to the Alchemist before he gets to the Queen," he said.

Mary smiled carefully. "You said earlier that you knew where he is going?"

"Aye." Tom took a stick and poked the fire to stir up the flames. "I believe he is planning to shoot at the Queen when she passes through York on her progress."

"This is what you would have asked John Tyler?"

"Aye, although I doubt he would have given this information freely." He poked at the fire again. "I have been giving this much consideration, and I believe York is the place."

She raised an enquiring eyebrow, and he continued, "Her Majesty plans to ride the streets, accompanied by her chief courtiers, such as the Earl of Leicester. There are some streets that are long enough and wide enough for crowds to line them, and there are tall houses in many places that overlook these streets." He regarded her with a half-smile. "We saw how terrible this sniper musket of his can be, with your poor horse…" he shook his head sadly, "so we know he can be many hundreds of yards away from the Queen and still fire upon her with deadly accuracy. I believe that the long streets of York, with the Queen in the open and the Alchemist in a high window at a distance, give him a perfect opportunity."

She nodded. "So we must make haste to York, and search for him."

She pictured the Alchemist, with his high velocity modern-day rifle, taking aim at Elizabeth through his telescopic sight from a safe distance. No Elizabethan security would be effective against him. She shuddered. So they would have to find him and stop him themselves.

"Yes, we must," he answered, "but I warrant he will not be easy to find."

Mary thought a moment. "We know the route Her Majesty will take through York?"

"Aye, well enough."

"And we can see the houses that over-look the route, and the streets that are widest?"

"Aye," he repeated.

"Then, as you say, we must look not to the Queen, but to the top floor windows above her route. We must look for the sight of that musket appearing out of a window, and run up to the room where he has placed himself to stop him."

He observed her levelly. "But if we only see him when the musket appears, we may be too late," he said. "When he slayed old Walter, he had only to raise the weapon and pull on the trigger and the ball did its evil work in no more than a heartbeat. What is to say he could already have slain the Queen thrice over before we burst through the door of his room?"

Mary considered this. Of course, he was right – the Alchemist may only position his gun seconds before the Queen appeared. But somehow she doubted it. "I expect he will prepare well ahead of the Queen's appearance, so I suggest we work together thus." She gazed into the fire a moment while she got the plan clear in her head. "I will walk in advance of the Queen's procession by say five minutes, looking up at the windows. You will walk a couple of minutes behind me, so if the Alchemist does place his musket after I have passed, you may see it." She sat back and smiled. "Then we can be sure of seeing the musket with enough time to work out which house he is in, run in and then stop him."

He shook his head.

"What?" she asked. "I think it is a good plan."

"For sure," he murmured, "except for one thing."

"What?" she repeated.

"If you walk ahead of the procession, you will be walking towards every possible window in full view. I think it is a near certainty that the Alchemist will see you. He will then realise that you escaped the fire in the cottage, and will understand your purpose in an instant. He will slay you as you walk in the street."

Mary give a small sigh. "Indeed, Master Cobham. Then what would you have us do?"

He sat back. "I would walk the other way, so we cannot be seen approaching, and seek out the tell-tale silver musket from below." He paused. "As you say, I would have us walk apart, so that if one misses the sight of the musket, then the other may not."

"But what if we get all the way to the Queen without seeing the Alchemist?" she asked. "Do we then turn round and walk back in full view? It is no different to my plan."

He drummed his fingers on his thigh for a while as he thought. Then he said, "For sure – you shall walk forwards ahead of the procession, but wear a broad hat – and perhaps a boy's clothing – to stop yourself being recognised from above."

"And you?"

"I shall ride with the Queen, so that if you see the Alchemist readying himself to fire, you can make that loud fishwife call of yours, and I shall pull Her Majesty away."

"Good," she said. "Then that is settled. And there is one more matter that must also be addressed."

He raised an expectant eyebrow. "Which is?"

"Hetherington Hall is close to York, is it not?"

He nodded. "I believe so."

"My son Ambrose is there, being tutored with the Grenville boy. I cannot pass so near without seeing him. We will stop there on our way to York."

CHAPTER EIGHTEEN

"We will need some new clothing," Tom observed, as they sat together by the fire in a Henley tavern the following evening. "That gown of yours is no more than a sooty rag, and I do not doubt," he added quickly, before she could comment, "that my attire is not much better."

"We also need to buy horses," Mary added. "The Alchemist has yours, and mine…" She broke off as a lump came to her throat, "and mine," she finished, taking a deep breath to stop the tears that invariably started when she thought of poor Juno, "lies in the forest."

He put his hand on her arm. "I know, dearest Mary," he said. "I know how much she meant to you. If there was any way to bring her back, I would do so in a heartbeat."

She sighed. "No, what is done is done, and I can never have her back. But," she added after a moment, "if I ever get the chance to make that man pay for what he did," she looked hard into his eyes, "then believe me, as God is my witness, I will make him pay." She turned Rick's lighter over and over in her pocket, feeling the smooth steel and shiny plastic skull. Just holding it made her feel as if she held his life in her hand. She opened the lid slightly with her thumbnail, then snapped it shut.

"You say 'what is done is done'," he observed, "yet you have such a look on your face, Mary, that you make me almost frightened." He squeezed her arm. "I would not be in the Alchemist's shoes if you were in a position to do him harm.

---0---

The next morning, they explored Henley's meagre covered market. The only stall they could find that sold women's clothing was one that seemed to have nothing but the plainest dresses – the kind usually worn by serving women. No doubt the quality women of the town had their kirtles, gowns and skirts made by a seamstress, Mary decided, just as she would have done back at Grangedean Manor. Reluctantly she bought the only dress that fitted her; a plain brown one in rough wool.

"I shall be the only gentleman on the road to York this spring accompanied by his own serving maid," observed Tom with a smile, when she tried it on in the tavern.

"Then you had better find clothing as befits a gentleman yourself, Master Thomas Cobham," she responded, squinting into the hand mirror he was holding up and failing to find an angle where the dress looked acceptable, "or I shall be the only such maid on the road to York with her own manservant."

Fortunately for Tom, they found a stall selling more varied men's clothing, and later that day it was a gentleman in a grey doublet, cream nether-stocks slashed with brown, grey hose and black shoes who stepped out with his rather dowdy maid to find a horse trader.

They found one at the back of the market; a small, shifty-looking man with a cast in his eye and ill-fitting wooden teeth. He only had two horses – which, unlike their seller, looked in fairly reasonable condition.

Tom asked the price, and seemed happy to accept it. While he was fishing for coin in his purse, Mary stepped forward.

If Tom was this useless at negotiating, then he needed her help.

As Justine Parker, she had been to Marrakesh on holiday a couple of times – so she knew a thing or two about haggling…

"At that price you are robbing us," she stated firmly. "We will pay half that."

"The deal has been affirmed by your master," sneered the man, "there is an agreement."

"Well, I do not agree," snapped Mary. "No coin has changed hands, so the deal is most definitely not affirmed."

Tom slowly closed his purse and stared at Mary with his mouth slightly open. "I shall be riding one of these horses," she continued, "and I will not ride easy if I know we have been robbed."

"'Tis a fair price," said the man, looking at Tom for confirmation. Tom shrugged and waved his hand in Mary's direction, as if to show he was content to hand over the negotiation to her.

"My master," she said, ignoring the small snort of mirth this brought from Tom, "is a gentleman, and does not regularly buy horses, nor deigns to barter with tradesmen. Whereas I…" she flashed her eyes at the man, who was starting to look uncomfortable, "…I know the price of a horse, and I say again – at the price you ask for these two sorry creatures, you are robbing us."

"I have stated the price…" the man began, but some of his earlier conviction seemed to be ebbing away, and he faltered to a stop.

"And I have said we will pay half that, which as you well know, is fair for these horses."

"And if I say no?"

"Then we will find another trader."

"Ah," said the man, a glint of triumph appearing in his eye, "but there is no other trader within ten miles of Henley. I am the only horse trader here."

"Then we will walk on a further ten miles," answered Mary. "We walked here from Stratford, and we can walk on to the next town."

The man looked again at Tom, as if seeking an ally, but Tom remained silent.

"By the holy cross," the man muttered into his beard, then he looked up. "I'faith," he said, "I accept your offer."

"Good," said Mary. "It is a fair one." She turned to Tom. "Pay the man."

Tom silently opened his purse again, and took out Mary's offered amount.

"Who exactly is the master here?" asked the man, as he took the money, but Tom just smiled, took the reins of both horses and started leading them away.

"I think you know the answer to that," said Mary with a smile. "Fare thee well, good man." She hurried on after Tom.

They rounded a corner and Tom stopped.

"I would never have walked another ten miles."

"I know that," she answered with a small twinkle in her eyes. "You know that. But fortunately…" she patted the muzzle of the smaller horse, then looked over at Tom, "…he did not know that."

---0---

It is around one hundred and fifty miles from Henley-in-Arden to North Yorkshire – a distance that Mary knew would one day take only three or four hours by car on smooth, 21st century motorways. But in 1575 it took them nearly four weeks on horseback across rough tracks, poorly made roads and forest paths.

Not that the journey was without its benefits. As spring took a firm hold, the countryside around them burst gloriously into life. Wild daffodils poked their yellow and orange heads out of the undergrowth and stood to attention as they passed; carpets of bluebells spread out along the forest floors like a colourful welcome mat, and above them the trees started to turn green, softening the spiky canopy of the forest with their soft foliage.

But there was monotony too. Tavern after tavern came and went – all with their rough itchy bedding, homemade pies and ale, and their procession of fellow-travelling humanity. Every evening they found a new one, and every morning they paid and left – and by lunchtime each day, Mary could not remember the name of the tavern, the bedroom she had slept in, or the meals she and Tom had eaten.

And Tom. Tom was always friendly, ever the perfect gentleman, considerate of her needs, playful and irreverent, but never over-stepping the line she had set down for him. Just occasionally she caught him looking at her out of the corner of his eye with a sad, almost hungry expression, which he would quickly replace with a half-smile, then engage her with a new topic of conversation. This was presumably as a form of diversionary tactic, as if to pretend she hadn't seen or understood just how much he was keeping his true feelings in check.

And it was no different for her, either.

The effort it took to keep him at arm's length was eating her up inside. Every time he smiled, cracked a joke for her amusement, or deferred to her wishes when he would clearly have done something different – it was all she could do to stop herself from throwing her arms around his neck and crushing his mouth with hers… But she had made it clear that they were friends not lovers, and that would never change.

So their journey to the north continued in a spirit of companionship, until one fine sunny spring morning they emerged from a dark forest into the bright sunshine and found themselves at the edge of a steep precipice.

As Mary looked, she could see it was actually a wooded ravine, cutting deep through the land as if a giant hand had ripped it in two.

Tom brought his horse up alongside hers and pointed at some chimneys just visible above the trees on the far side.

"Hetherington Hall, I believe."

Mary stared at the distant house, trying to make out the shape of the building against the trees.

Hetherington Hall!

So this was the house where William had brought Ambrose all those weeks ago. Suddenly she felt a warm glow spread throughout her body. Just to see the house where he now lived made Ambrose feel close enough to touch.

To hold her son in her arms once again…

She squinted against the sun as she studied the house. Which one of those tall chimneys was above the room he was in right now? Maybe he was studying with his teacher in a schoolroom under that one on the right wing? Or maybe he was not inside the house at all – instead he was outside at the butts, practicing his archery…

Mary's horse snorted and pawed the ground, as if it was as keen as she was to finish the journey.

"Come," she said to Tom. "We must get there as soon as we can."

Now she switched her focus onto the ravine, looking to see how they could get safely across.

The path ran alongside the ravine for a few more yards, then it seemed to disappear over the edge. Cautiously, she walked her horse forward. As she got closer to the edge, she could see that instead of dropping away completely, the path sloped steeply down the rocky, almost vertical side of the ravine, before making a few hairpin turns lower down on its way to the bottom.

She leaned back towards Tom. "We can follow the path if we take it slowly," she announced.

Tom nodded and they set off in single file with Mary in the lead.

She let her horse pick its way down, trusting that it was sure enough of its way not to falter or slip on the loose stones. At first the horse was extremely careful, placing each leg slowly and testing the surface before committing itself, but after a couple of the turns, the way seemed to become firmer, and soon the horse seemed to gain confidence. Its head came up, its ears went forward, and with a little neigh of pleasure, it began to trot down the path at a good pace.

Soon they were out of the sunshine and Mary shivered as the air grew cold. The rocks beside them were jagged and harsh with only occasional shrubs or branches sprouting from fissures, and here and there some trickling streams of water ran down leaving brown stains in their wake. On her other side was a sheer drop to the floor of the ravine, so Mary stayed as close as possible to the left, leaving plenty of room between her and the edge.

Then they came to a narrow section that curved round a rocky outcrop, and the path reduced to just the width of one horse.

Mary could see that not only was the path frighteningly thin, there were also some patches of loose-looking stones as it curved round the outcrop. The horse's pace, which had been fine when the path was wide and firm, was now dangerously fast. It was clear that the horse thought so too, and it tried to slow down. Unfortunately, just as it passed a sturdy-looking branch growing out of a fissure in the rock, it hit the patch of loose stones and started to scrabble for a foothold.

For one awful moment, Mary was looking into empty space over the horse's head, its ears laid back on its neck in fear. But then the horse managed to regain its footing and carry on down the path, treading with more care and caution. She let it walk slowly on a few more yards, until it was on a wider section of the path and its ears had come back to their more relaxed position. Then she pulled it to a stop, making reassuring 'shh-ing' noises.

"That was close," said Tom from behind her. "That was a narrow and dangerous section of the path – it is most fortunate that your horse is sure-footed."

"Well, I am glad she was." Mary turned in the saddle and looked back into his concerned face.

As she studied him, suddenly her eyes flooded with tears, causing his face to dissolve in an instant into a thousand fragments.

"What ails, Mary?" he asked quietly. "Art quite safe."

"I know." She wiped her eyes with her sleeve. "But I just had a thought. What if a similar thing happened to Ambrose and William?" She sniffed and blinked a few times. "The winter snows have not been gone long, so it must have been icy when they came down this path. What if one of them lost their grip completely? What if we get to the bottom of this ravine and find they never even made it to Hetherington? What if we find them still there? What if we find them…" she could hardly bear to say the word "...dead?"

"I am sure not, Mary." He gave a weak smile, which looked like he was reassuring himself as much as her. "Sir William is a good horseman, I am sure, and had a care for his son also." He gestured at the far side of the ravine. "I am sure we will find Ambrose safe and well at Hetherington, and Sir William the same back at Grangedean Manor."

"Hmm," she agreed, and gingerly urged her horse to walk on.

As they continued down, the horse seemed to become more cautious, and Mary wondered if it had learned its lesson for itself, or was simply reflecting her own caution. Juno would have instinctively known what Mary was thinking.

They reached the bottom without further incident, and despite Tom's assurances, Mary insisted on them both tracking up and down the foot of the precipice, checking for any signs of William and Ambrose's bodies. Tom picked up a large branch and used it to poke at the mossy mounds and beds of early spring flowers, as well as levering up fallen branches to look beneath. When they had covered all the ground thoroughly – with extra care taken at the spot directly beneath the rocky outcrop – Tom led them back to the path.

"Art sure now, Mary?" he asked.

She wanted to say that they should cover the ground again, and maybe dig in any soft spots – but she could see this would be poorly received. Clearly, as far as Tom was concerned they had checked and found nothing – so she would be pushing her luck to continue. She straightened her back and nodded to Tom. As Tom had said, she should trust to Ambrose and William's horsemanship and expect to find her son where he should be – in Hetherington Hall, and her husband back at Grangedean Manor.

They remounted their horses, and were preparing to ride on, when a sudden pang of guilt made Mary stop.

In all this time, how often had she thought of the family she had left behind at Grangedean? Of Kat and Jane, of Ruth and Sarah? She had promised Kat that she would only be gone a few days – and how long had it been now? More than two months? What must the poor little girl be thinking? An icy chill went up Mary's spine. Would little Kat be wondering if a 'bad man' had got her mother, as she had feared, and had to be comforted by Sarah? And was Jane blithely eating her breakfast, even without her mother there to make it fly like a bird? Or maybe Ruth was working her magic touch and getting the girl to eat.

Mary bit her lip. Was William back home by now? And if so, was he looking after his girls? As a father he could be somewhat distant; so was he now being more attentive to his children's needs? Mary really hoped he was.

Unless, of course, he had left them with Ruth and Sarah, and had decided to go out looking for her. Was he even now scouring the land, anxiously following her trail?

Mary gasped. Had he followed her trail to Southwark? To the Blue Maid? Or to Hammersmith, with tales of his wife's cosy fireside chats with Sir Robert Standing, while Olivia flirted so dangerously with that monster, Shelton?

Mary bit her lip again. What would she say when she got back to Grangedean? How would she look William in the eye and make him understand that nothing had happened?

The stream! With Tom! What of that?

But nothing had happened – she had pulled away. So there was nothing to tell.

She glanced across to where Tom was sitting on his horse, regarding her with one eyebrow raised.

"You appear thoughtful, my dear Lady Mary," he said. "What ails you?"

"Marry, 'tis nothing."

"I doubt that," he answered. "I know that when you bite your own lip it means you are deep in thought about something that bothers you." He cocked his head thoughtfully. "Is it your concern for your son and husband? We have searched most thoroughly and found no trace. Would you have me search again?"

"No," she answered slowly. "It is not just William – it is the girls as well. They know not where I am."

"And you would have them know?"

"Of course, they must be worried sick. For ten years I have hardly set foot outside Grangedean – now I am two months gone with no word."

"For sure." He smiled reassuringly. "We will find a messenger when we can, and see if we can get word to them."

If only we could send a quick text – how easy would that be?

"Then let us continue," he said. "At least you can reassure your son of your safety." He started riding across the floor of the ravine towards the far side.

They had only gone a couple of hundred yards through the sycamores, when suddenly Tom stopped. "What's that?" he said, pointing at something in the distance.

Mary followed his finger, but could not make out anything but trees.

"What?" she asked.

"That," he repeated. She looked harder, and suddenly a shape that looked a bit like a thatched roof seemed to emerge from the jumble of the forest. After that, she could make out walls, a door, a window and the rest of the roof. Once she made it out, she wondered how she could possibly have missed it at first. "It is a hut," she said.

"Aye," he answered. "Let us explore it further."

As they approached it, Mary could see it was very small; no bigger than a 21st century garden shed. Tom tried the door, and it opened easily.

Inside, it was almost empty; the only pieces of furniture being a pallet bed and a small oak chest.

"It is a watchman's hut," said Tom. "That is all." Idly he opened the chest and peered in. "By Heaven!" he exclaimed as he reached inside.

"What is it?" she asked.

With a look of concern, he took out a black metal object that looked like a flattened oval ring with a central bar, with a substantial length of chain hanging off it.

"It is a manacle," he said, examining it and testing the chain. "Someone uses this hut to keep a prisoner." He peered again into the chest, and took out another, identical manacle. "Or two prisoners." Quickly he put them back and closed the lid. "Come," he said, "we must make haste away from this place, lest we suddenly meet the jailer."

---0---

Hetherington Hall was grander up close than Mary had expected, with two broad wings either side of the central house, all brick-built with diamond-paned windows and topped with magnificent twisted chimneys rising into the clear blue sky. The main entrance was up some stone steps, flanked by two balustrades that were themselves each finished off with a fine stone lion, as if guarding the house from intruders.

Mary walked up the steps and pulled on the bell-rope.

The door was opened by a sallow-faced man in what she assumed must be the Grenville livery. "Servants' entrance is at the back," he said, and started to close the door.

Mary stepped forward. "My name is Lady Mary de Beauvais," she announced, emphasising the 'Lady'. He still seemed unimpressed. "My son Ambrose de Beauvais is here under the care of your master, Sir Nicholas Grenville," she added. "I must see him."

"A moment, mistress," the man muttered, then disappeared back into the house, closing the door on her and leaving her standing.

She waited for what seemed like ages, wishing Tom was here to support her. But she had insisted on him staying by the top of the ravine while she went to the house alone – to spare Ambrose from any questions regarding the strange man accompanying her. Tom had pointed out that he was hardly a strange man, and that Ambrose was surely able to understand the idea of a travelling companion, but Mary was insistent, and he had remained behind at the edge of the forest, while Mary had gone on alone to the house.

Eventually the door opened again and the thinnest man Mary had ever seen came out. He had sandy hair that fell across one eye and a beard so fine that she had to strain her eyes to see it. If it were not for his fine doublet, nether-stocks and hose, she would have thought he were a woman.

He looked her up and down, and Mary was conscious that she was still wearing the plain gown that she had bought in Henley-in-Arden – and after nearly four weeks on the road and the occasional wash in a stream, it was not at its best. Not only did she look like a serving-girl-turned-vagabond, but she must have smelled fairly ripe as well. No wonder the liveried man who had first opened the door had thought she was a servant.

"Lady Mary de Beauvais?" the thin man said, in a disbelieving tone.

"Yes," she answered in her best 'Lady of the Manor' voice. "And I must see my son Ambrose, who is in the care of Sir Nicholas."

The man shook his head. "I am afraid that will not be possible."

"Why so?" she asked.

"Because," he said smoothly, "Master Ambrose has gone with Sir Nicholas and Lady Grenville to York to see the progress of the Queen." He looked her up and down again with barely concealed distaste. "And because I cannot believe for one moment that the vagrant serving woman I see before me is the wife of Sir William or the mother of Ambrose de Beauvais."

Mary took a breath and smiled sweetly. "I can see that it may be difficult to tell," she said, "but I can assure you that it is of necessity that I am wearing this garb, and I am indeed Lady Mary, and can verify it as soon as I see my son. I need to see him," she added.

"As you say." The man stepped back. "But I cannot alter the fact that he is staying at the Grenville town-house in York, and will not be back for many days, until the progress of Her Majesty the Queen has passed on."

"I see," Mary said. "But he is well?"

"He is well enough, I warrant, to satisfy a mother's concern."

Mary regarded the man for a moment. Clearly she was not going to get any more information from him.

"Thank you, sir," she said. Then she added with what she hoped was her most disarming smile, "You have me at a disadvantage. I do not know who I have the honour of addressing?"

The man was silent a moment, then he gave a small bow and said, "Lambert Moreton at your service. Sir Nicholas Grenville is my uncle."

"Well, Master Moreton, I am honoured to make your acquaintance."

Moreton gave a thin smile that failed to reach his eyes. "And I yours, Lady Mary, if that is who you are." He bowed again. "Now, by your leave, I have business to attend to in the house, and must repeat that Master Ambrose is not here. I suggest you return once the progress has left York, and he is back." He slammed the door shut in her face.

Mary walked down the steps and made her way to the edge of the ravine.

Tom was sitting with his back to a tree, while the horses grazed quietly nearby. His head was lolled over to one side, and he seemed to be asleep.

She went up to him.

"Tom, Tom!" She shook his shoulder. "Wake up!"

He opened one eye. "Hmm?"

"Ambrose is not here – I am told that he has gone to York to see the Queen."

"Oh." He stood up and put his hands on her shoulders. "I am sorry – I know you were keen to see him."

"Aye. Perhaps we will see him in York. But, Tom…" she paused. "Something was not right…"

"What?" He stood back and searched her eyes. "You have a concern?"

"Yes." She shook her head, as if to clear it of the sinister presence of Lambert Moreton. "It was Sir Nicholas Grenville's nephew who told me, and he was hiding something – I am sure of it." She shook her head again and looked up at him. "Tom, what if something has happened to Ambrose? What if he's not in York and they are covering it up?"

He moved his hands up to cup her cheeks. "My dear Mary, I am sure Ambrose is well and happy, and currently in York, excitedly awaiting the arrival of Queen Elizabeth." He let her go and stood back. "We should go there ourselves as fast as we can. We have our mission – to save the life of the Queen."

CHAPTER NINETEEN

The road to Wyvern Castle, North Yorkshire, early May 1575

Olivia Melrose looked out of the open carriage window at the bleak northern landscape as it rolled past in the warm sunshine. Beside her, Maggie Tyndall was silent, staring out of the opposite window.

Lady Burnham, sitting bolt upright opposite them, looked from one girl to the other. "I have held my peace these last few hours since we left Fambridge Hall," she observed, "but I can hold it no longer. What has happened, that the atmosphere between you two is colder than a December frost?"

Olivia looked at the back of Maggie's head, then at her mistress. "It is nothing, my lady, just a small misunderstanding."

"Well, I would advise you both to clear it up before we reach Wyvern Castle this evening. We are there three days before progressing into York, and I would not want to have all that time with the two of you acting like a couple of angry geese who spit at each other." Lady Burnham folded her hands on her lap. "Do I make myself understood?"

"Yes, my lady." Olivia went back to staring out of the window. Maggie said nothing.

"Mistress Tyndall?" Lady Burnham snapped.

"Yes, my lady," muttered Maggie.

Olivia sighed. The truth was, that Maggie was cross with her because she had been proved right about Shelton…

It had all started when Olivia decided that Maggie's flirtation with Shelton had now gone far enough. They were becoming quite blatant, and knowing Shelton as she did, Olivia was frightened that if it got too heated – and Maggie then tried to resist – his response would be to do to Maggie what he had done to her.

So the previous morning she had found him alone in the long gallery at Fambridge Hall, and it had been the perfect opportunity.

"Master Shelton," she said, "I must speak with you."

"Why, Mistress Melrose," he answered with a raised eyebrow, "this is a surprise. I had thought you were going out of your way to avoid me since we left London."

Olivia ignored this. "I must tell you of Maggie Tyndall."

"I rather think I know more on that topic than you at this moment." He started walking away from her down the gallery. "If we are to go by who is spending the greater time in Mistress Tyndall's company."

She caught up and walked alongside him. "She may spend time in your company, Master Shelton, but she has no real interest in you."

He stopped. "Really, Mistress Melrose? That is not my reading of her behaviour."

"I will not discuss how poor you are at reading a woman's behaviour, Master Shelton," Olivia retorted, then cursed inwardly. She had promised herself to keep this about Maggie and not let him get past her defences. Indeed, she knew that if she did not control the situation correctly, she could find herself once again in trouble from his violent temper.

She took a breath and continued, "I can assure you, she is but a young, inexperienced girl who knows not what effect her beauty has on men. There is no meaning in what she says or her behaviour towards you. She has no real interest in you."

"And she has told you this herself?"

Olivia gritted her teeth. "Of course," she lied. "We talk often."

"And yet she is but a young, inexperienced girl and there is no meaning to what she says?"

"Do not throw my words back at me, Master Shelton," she hissed.

"But I am listening to what you say, Mistress Melrose, and taking most careful note." He gave her a sarcastic smile. "And I do the same with Maggie Tyndall, and do you know what she tells me?" Olivia looked away, as if by not seeing Shelton she could also avoid hearing him. "She tells me that my eyes do please her greatly – both of them in fact – and that she finds my hair and my beard much to her liking, and that my…"

"Enough!" Olivia snapped. "Let me be most clear, Master Shelton. Maggie Tyndall is a sweet, innocent girl who has taken it into her head that you are an honourable man, worthy of her attention. I think we both know you are neither of those things. In fact, as I know to my lifelong cost, you are a thoughtless, heartless monster with no care for the feelings of any person but yourself – indeed I wonder if you deliberately sought the position with my lady Burnham because I told you that was where I was going when we met in Hammersmith, so you could taunt me further..." She thought she saw him flinch very slightly – and decided she had hit the mark. "So I would you leave Maggie alone," she continued, "and do not encourage her any further in her girlish fantasies. I trust I make myself perfectly clear, Master Shelton?"

"A pretty speech, Mistress Melrose. But not, I regret to say, 'perfectly clear'." Shelton assumed a sickly, thoughtful expression. "How is it that on the one hand Mistress Tyndall says to you that she has no interest in me, yet on the other hand, she thinks I am an honourable man, worthy of her attention?" Again he raised an eyebrow. "I merely ask so I can be perfectly clear."

"Do not twist my words, Master Shelton, and you leave Maggie alone," Olivia snarled, "or I will see to it that you suffer harm, just as you made me suffer harm back in Hammersmith."

Suddenly the mask of civility was stripped away, and Shelton once again raised his hand to strike her.

Olivia forced herself not to flinch and stared into his eyes with defiance. After a few seconds, his hand came down.

"Do not threaten me, Olivia Melrose," he hissed, "and know your place as a woman." He brought his face right up to hers, so their noses were almost touching.

Still she did not react, but carried on staring into his eyes.

"Or I will need to instruct you in manners as I instructed you once before."

She forced herself to keep still, and did not blink.

"Do I make myself 'perfectly clear' – *Livvy*?"

With that, he turned on his heel and marched away down the gallery, leaving Olivia standing. As soon as he had slammed the door behind him, she staggered to a bench seat and collapsed onto it, her breathing ragged.

'Livvy?' How dare he take Maggie's pet name for her and twist it into something sick?

She should never have let it get that far – she should never have let him make her angry. She had managed to avoid such a situation ever since London, but now it had happened, and it was her fault for starting it…

Olivia stood up and adjusted her gown. No, it was *not* her fault! Lady Mary had said that she should never blame herself for the actions of a man – and especially not Master Lionel blasted Shelton.

Olivia squared her shoulders and walked steadily to the door at the far end of the Gallery.

Just as she put her hand to the door, it opened.

She stood back, fearing that it was Shelton returning, and prepared herself to confront him once again. But it was not Shelton.

It was the Queen.

She was in conversation with a tall older man dressed in black, with long flowing white hair.

"…Let me assure you, Master Wychwoode," the Queen was saying, "I am placing my trust in your preparations for the progress through York, so the safety of my person is in your hands. But I must stress once again, that I do not want to be seen to be afraid withal. It is not in keeping with the picture I have created, to be as a weakened coward that hides behind her men. So there are to be no extra guards or such-like – do you understand?

"I do, madam," the tall man answered.

"I care not how you make sure I am protected, but I will not have it seen by the people…"

Suddenly the Queen stopped short. Olivia, who had dropped into the lowest curtesy she could manage, could only assume that despite being behind the door, she had just been spotted.

Olivia felt a hand come under her chin, and pull her up.

"Who are you, girl, that would listen to my private counsel with Master Wychwoode?"

Olivia stood as tall as she could. Fortunately her head was still lower than the Queen's.

"Olivia Melrose, Your Grace," she said, then curtseyed again.

"Stand up, girl," snapped the Queen. "Who exactly are you, Mistress Melrose?"

"I attend on Lady Burnham, Your Majesty."

"I see." The Queen considered her a moment with thoughtful eyes. "And how can I be sure you are not a Catholic spy, sent to learn my secrets and so use them against me?"

Then the man Wychwoode suddenly exclaimed, "Olivia Melrose?" Olivia nodded slowly, unsure as to how this tall elderly man could possibly know her.

He studied her face. "Then your father is Thomas Melrose, known to Sir William de Beauvais?" She nodded again.

He looked puzzled. "But I do not see your father in your face…?"

Olivia shook her head. "Nay, good sir," she said. "My true father was killed when I was but a small child. He fought most bravely in the defence of Sir William and Lady de Beauvais. His name was Dowland."

Wychwoode turned to the Queen with a look of triumph. "Your Majesty, I can vouchsafe that this girl is honest and true. I was acquainted not only with both her real and adopted fathers, but with the desperate battle that took Master Dowland's life, and with the honour and courage her new father showed in his own fight. He was a brave man who in a moment of madness made a grave error of judgment, but then he did all he could to right the wrong." He turned to Olivia. "So he took you in and raised you as his own?" She nodded. "Then he has remained a good and honest man. I trust he still lives?"

"He does, indeed."

The Queen smiled, a warm smile that illuminated her pale beauty. "Then child, you are most welcome to us, and we trust you will become better acquainted with us in the coming weeks."

Olivia bowed her head once more, then felt the Queen's hand brush her cheek. She looked up.

"Go, my child, and serve your mistress well. You have found favour in our eyes."

Wychwoode stood back, and Olivia walked out of the door, feeling as if she was floating six inches in the air.

When she arrived back at their rooms, Maggie was not there, so it was not until they met at the table for dinner, that Olivia could speak to her friend.

She decided to keep her meeting with the Queen a secret for the moment, and to concentrate on the other matter.

"I was able to converse with Lionel Shelton this morning," she said casually.

Maybe it was too casual, and Maggie was immediately on her guard. "Why, what passed between you?" She grabbed at Olivia's sleeve. "Is he happy that we are being discreet?" She glanced around the Great Hall to ensure they were not being overheard against the noise of dinner. "Has Lady Burnham said aught about us? Oh!" she put her hand to her mouth and looked across the hall to where Her Majesty was seated. "It is the Queen, is it not?" she whispered. "I knew it, Livvy!" Olivia winced at the name – now tainted by Shelton. "I saw her observe us only yesterday and noted that she did frown so!" Maggie's eyes widened. "Her Majesty has become aware that Master Shelton pays me such attention and she is concerned! We are being too obvious! And Her Majesty has noted this to my lady, has she not, Livvy?"

Olivia held up her hand to stem this flow. "No, sweet Maggie, she has not." Maggie's shoulders sagged in relief. "Nor has my lady said aught, either. But," she continued, "I have spoken with Master Shelton and asked that he pays you less attention, before my lady, or even Her Majesty, *does* say something."

There was a long silence as servants placed large plates of swan, pig and vegetables in front of them. Once they had gone, Olivia saw that Maggie's pretty face had clouded over, like a storm blocking out the sun. The girl spoke slowly and deliberately, as if she was testing a difficult theory.

"You have spoken with Lionel, and you have told him to pay me less attention?"

Olivia nodded.

Maggie's voice became even quieter, so Olivia had to strain to hear her over the noise of the banquet. "And you feel this is your business, Mistress Melrose?"

"I do, for I know Shelton, and I do not think him an honourable man." Then Olivia added, "And I have your best interests at heart, Maggie Tyndall."

Maggie stared at Olivia, then slowly, she shook her head. "I had thought better of you, Mistress Melrose, truly I did." Olivia said nothing. "I knew you disapproved of Lionel and me; oh, yes I did. But I thought you had accepted that we have feelings for each other, and in truth, I thought you were happy for us." Maggie shook her head again. "And now you tell me that not only are you not happy for us, but that you have interfered by asking Lionel to pay me less attention?"

Olivia nodded again.

Maggie stood up. "Then I must take my leave of you, because I cannot remain in your company a moment longer." With that, she flounced out of the hall.

Olivia remained seated, but she saw that Shelton himself had been watching this exchange, for he got up, shot her a look of pure loathing, then followed Maggie out.

Olivia found she had lost her appetite, and a few minutes later she nodded to Lady Burnham to excuse herself, and left the hall also.

She heard the raised voices as she approached their rooms – and it was clear they were the voices of Shelton and Maggie.

Quickly she threw open the door – to find Shelton standing over Maggie, who was lying on her back on the bed. His balled fist was raised, ready to strike her. Maggie had her arms held above her head in self-protection.

Immediately Olivia ran towards Shelton, shouting, "No!"

Shelton looked round, and lowered his hand.

"Be gone, Shelton!" Olivia snapped. "This instant!"

Shelton looked from Maggie on the bed, who was now sobbing, to Olivia, who was pointing imperiously at the door. After a moment, he walked out, without another word.

Olivia immediately ran to Maggie and put her arms around the crying girl. But if she had expected Maggie to cling to her and profess eternal gratitude, she was gravely mistaken.

In fact, Maggie started trying to beat her fists on Olivia's chest as she sobbed, causing Olivia to jump back and stand away from the bed in surprise.

"What did you do that for?" she asked. "When all I had done was stop that man from attacking you?"

"All you had done?" Maggie sat up, wiping her eyes and looking indignant. "All you had done, Mistress Melrose, was to give a sweet, gentle man cause to doubt me – such that he became confused about my feelings for him, and in his confusion, he knew not what he was doing!"

Olivia thought perhaps she must have misheard this – for if she had heard correctly, then surely the words made no sense. "Are you serious? He is a violent, controlling man, who was about to strike you! How was that 'confused'?"

"It is the natural order for a man to be controlling," answered Maggie. "And for a woman to be controlled. So what you told him this morning went against the natural order, and he was confused."

"But he was about to strike you!" exclaimed Olivia.

"And that was because of you!"

"I do not believe I am hearing this!" Olivia yelled, stamping her foot.

"Then do not hear it!" Maggie responded. "Be gone and do not ever talk to me again!"

---0---

Olivia continued to stare out of the open carriage window at the landscape rumbling past, conscious that beside her, Maggie was looking out of the opposite window. They had not exchanged a single word since Maggie had sent Olivia away that morning.

If only Maggie would not be so mutton-headed! Surely she could see that it was Shelton who was the villain here, not Olivia? Why could she not understand that a woman did not need to feel guilty for being attacked by a man – that it was his responsibility, not hers?

Suddenly Olivia shook her head.

No! That was to miss the point! The point was, that girls like Maggie thought it was the natural order of things for the man to be always right, whatever his actions, because the laws and rules of society said this was so. Had she, Olivia, not felt the same, before Lady Mary had opened her eyes to the truth?

If only Lady Mary were here, she would explain it to Maggie with the same passion and conviction that had caused Olivia to change her own mind. If Lady Mary were here, then Maggie would understand why it was no longer acceptable for a woman to be seen as the possession of a man.

Olivia sighed and focused once again on the landscape. Trees, cottages, forests and fields all appeared and disappeared, with the occasional yeoman, farmer or peasant standing with his family like statues and watching as the procession went by.

"We must be close to Wyvern Castle," observed Lady Burnham to no-one in particular. "The local townspeople are gathering to bid good cheer to Her Majesty. Were it not so warm, Olivia, I would have you close the window, for the common folk are apt to smell quite noisome." She reached down and pulled her travelling bag onto her lap. "Instead I will use my lavender nosegay." She started rummaging in the bag.

Olivia nodded politely, then resumed her vigil at the carriage window.

The carriage slowed and rolled to a stop. "The Queen must now be at the gates of Wyvern Castle," said Lady Burnham, looking up from her bag. Then she resumed her search. "I know my nosegay was in here before. Now, where is it?"

Olivia continued to look out of the carriage at the faces of the townspeople as they went by.

Suddenly she stopped and stared hard at one face in particular. She could swear it was a serving woman on a brown horse who looked exactly like Lady Mary!

Surely not? In truth, she had just been thinking of Lady Mary, so perhaps it was not surprising to imagine that some woman in the crowd was actually her.

She leaned out of the window, looking back and desperately trying to see the woman again, but there was no sign of her. Olivia sat back and shook her head. It had surely been a mistake – for Lady Mary was no doubt long since back at Grangedean Manor, and the possibility that she was even now dressed as a serving woman watching the Queen's progress towards York was arrant madness…

Just then they came to a halt.

Suddenly a face appeared at the open window. It was only there for the briefest instant, but now there was no doubt – it really was Lady Mary! She had her finger to her lips to caution for silence.

Despite the shock of seeing Mary again, Olivia knew she had to stay calm. She glanced quickly back at the others inside the carriage. Neither seemed to be aware of what had just happened. Lady Burnham was still rummaging in her bag and Maggie was staring out of the other window.

By the strangest good fortune, neither had seen what she had seen.

Olivia looked back at the window.

It was empty.

Pretending she was interested in the crowds now lining the road, she leaned out and looked back along the carriage.

Lady Mary was standing just behind, talking to a tall handsome-looking man who held the reins of two horses. Seeing Olivia, she moved forward and stopped by the back wheel of the coach.

"Meet me by the main gate this evening at seven," she hissed.

Olivia nodded, then sat back again, trying to control her breathing and appear normal.

Soon the carriage started to move forward again, and shortly after, passed under a magnificent brick archway and into the grounds of Wyvern Castle.

---0---

Mary waved her hand to ward off the evening midges as they swarmed around her.

She stared at the brick arch above the ornate iron gates to Wyvern Castle. It rose to around six feet above the top of the gates themselves, with a series of bricks standing proud of the wall to create a diamond pattern. At the top was a large stone shield with some form of spacer behind it, as it appeared to float clear of the wall by several inches. The image of what looked like a dragon was carved onto it; it had a dragon's head, body and wings, then a long tail curling round its body that ended in a diamond-shaped tip, but curiously, it had no front legs. She assumed this must be the coat of arms of the Wyvern family.

Strange that there was no guard on the gate, given the importance of the royal visitor and her retinue; Mary supposed that there would be guards by the door to the house itself. Olivia would no doubt have the ingenuity to slip out unseen for their meeting.

Mary looked at the house, just visible through the trees beyond the gates, then up at the tall elms surrounding the wall. If the Alchemist wanted to take his shot from up in one of those, he would have a good view of the house, and presumably a clear line of sight into the grounds. But would he want to risk Elizabeth not coming out, or coming out all too briefly to get the shot? And would he be prepared to wait in a tree for three days on the chance of getting sight of her in the open? No, most likely his plan was as they first thought – to assassinate her when she was more easily visible, passing through the streets of York. So, she would be safe in Wyvern Castle until then, and Mary could decide what she was going to have to do to stop the Alchemist.

There was a rustling of leaves the other side of the gate, and suddenly Olivia was there.

"Lady Mary, by God's good grace!" she exclaimed, peering through the ornate ironwork. "What is your purpose here?" She paused, then added with a smile, "For all that I am most glad to see you!"

"My dear, sweet child," Mary answered, putting her hand through the gate and clasping Olivia's. "Your face is well mended, I see. You are back to your full beauty, as I was sure you would be."

"Aye, and no thanks to that snake Shelton, who is here even now!"

"He is here?" Mary's eyes widened. "How is this so?"

"He is at Court, in the Queen's retinue."

"And do you manage to keep apart from him?"

"Not as much as I would like." Olivia swallowed and looked at her feet. "I have had furious words with him, over his behaviour."

"Why, has he again attacked you?" Mary frowned.

"No, he has not attacked me, but he has made to strike my friend Maggie."

"Is your friend Maggie hurt?"

"Nay," Olivia looked up. "I was able to stop him before harm was caused."

"Well done," Mary said. "And does she also avoid him now?"

"I wish so, but she is too enamoured of him," Olivia answered. "She thinks it is my fault for pouring poison in his ear."

"Then we must make Maggie see him for the man he is." Mary said.

"Yes, we must," answered Olivia. "And I would you talk to her the way you talked to me – you make it seem so clear, how a man should not hold dominion over a woman."

"Indeed," Mary said, nodding. "And we must also think how to make Master Shelton realise the error of his ways," she added. She paused, then said, "All in good time, but now, dear Olivia, I need your help."

"For sure. What can I do?"

"For a start, pray tell me why you are here with the Queen? Are you so soon elevated to a position at Court? I may say," Mary added, "that I was most shocked to see you in the window of that coach. When I left you in the house on the Strand all these weeks ago, I scarcely thought I would see you again in Yorkshire. I had to look twice to be sure it was really you."

"And I could not believe I was seeing Lady Mary dressed as a servant, either," said Olivia with an interested little smile.

"A long story – for another time." Mary answered, a little too quickly.

"Does it involve the fine-looking man you were talking to by my coach?" asked Olivia, her eyebrow raised.

Mary smiled, then shook her head. Trust Olivia to home in on the question she would prefer to avoid. "You have not told me why you are here," she repeated, trying to change the subject.

Olivia paused, her lips pursed. Clearly her interest was piqued, but it looked as though she was prepared to let the subject of Tom drop for now. She said, "My lady Burnham is in the Queen's party for this progress, and she has asked both Maggie and myself to attend her."

"Then that is great good fortune," Mary answered, "as I need the help of someone I can trust who is in the Queen's entourage." She put her other hand through the gate and grasped both of Olivia's firmly. "I have good reason to believe that the life of the Queen is in grave danger, and I need to prevent this attack from happening."

Olivia gasped. "How so?"

"I have been following a man who has both the will, and the means, to kill her. I believe he will make his attack in York, so I need to secure a position within the entourage myself, so I can get close to Her Majesty and stop this happening."

"Yes, you must!" Olivia thought a moment. "There is a man here that the Queen says she trusts to safeguard her person. You must tell your story to him, so he can help you." She paused again, as if deciding how much information to share. Then she said, "He told the Queen that he knew you and Sir William. He said he was part of the desperate fight many years ago that cost my true father his life. A tall old man with long, grey hair."

"Oh!" Now it was Mary's turn to gasp in surprise. "Wychwoode! Wychwoode is here?"

Olivia nodded. "Yes – that was his name."

"Then that is even better! He will be able to help us. Tom and I must see him."

There was a moment's silence. "Tom?" Olivia asked quietly. "Is Tom the man you were talking to?"

Mary smiled. "Tom is one of Wychwoode's men," she said. "We have journeyed together from London with common purpose – to save the Queen. He is even now waiting in the forest, and will join us in the Queen's party. If you and Wychwoode can get us both into the house, and allow us to clean and dress ourselves as befits a courtier, we can finish the task and stop the killer from making his strike."

"And this Tom," Olivia observed, "…he seemed a fine-looking man..."

The statement hung in the air for a moment – sounding more like a question. Then Mary smiled again. "Indeed, but I do not see what…?"

"There it is!" Olivia looked triumphantly at Mary. "Each time you talk of him, you smile. And when I questioned you a few moments ago, you changed the subject most quickly." She pulled her hands away from Mary's. "What is this man to you?" she asked.

Mary sighed. "The truth is, Tom and I have shared many adventures together and have become… close." Then she added, "But nothing has happened, and I have told him most firmly that it never will."

Olivia was silent a while. Then she asked, "And he feels the same?"

Mary was once again in the forest on the way to Henley-in-Arden; standing in front of Tom with his hair and beard full of mud. "He said to me these words... 'I have a heart,' he said, 'and it would be yours if it could be' – but then he accepted it was not to be."

Olivia reached for Mary's hands and took them in her own. "He is a man of honour, then."

"Yes." There was a silence. Mary wondered if she was going to get a lecture on propriety – which, in her heart she knew she deserved – or sympathy instead. Then Olivia burst out, "By Heaven, Mary, you bear this well! This is not easy for you! He seems a good man who cares for you, and you for him, and yet you must push him away! How can you cope with this? Were it me, I am sure I would not have pushed him away! You have such strength, Mary!"

Mary sighed. "Aye, well, I do have strength, because it is the right thing to do. But it is done, and now the most important thing is to get in and meet with Wychwoode."

Maybe a lecture would have been easier.

CHAPTER TWENTY

Hetherington Hall

William de Beauvais looked round as Lambert Moreton approached from the house. He was walking quickly, staring intently at William.

"A moment, son," William said to Ambrose, who was in the act of fitting an arrow to his bow, as Richard Grenville looked on. "Master Moreton comes, and I think he needs must talk with me. You keep practicing your archery." Then he whispered in Ambrose's ear, so Richard would not hear. "You are shooting true, and making your father very proud."

He stepped aside as Ambrose fired the arrow, and turned to face Moreton.

"How can I help you?" he asked.

"Sir Nicholas is requesting you ride out to meet him, on a most important matter."

"Sir Nicholas?" William raised an eyebrow. "We spoke only a couple of hours ago in the Great Hall. What has emerged since then?"

"He has had to ride out on a matter of the utmost importance, and is asking that you meet him presently." Moreton paused and looked over at Ambrose. William followed the man's gaze, to see that his son's arrow had hit the bullseye."

"Good shot, Ambrose!" he exclaimed.

Moreton did not offer any comment on the shot. Instead he said, "And your son, too. Sir Nicholas has asked that you both meet him."

"I will call for my men-at-arms – they are close by at the stables."

"Nay," Moreton seemed slightly flustered by this. "There is no time."

William looked at the thin man. "I would prefer to have my men with me and my son," he said firmly.

"There is no call for that," Moreton snapped. "This is but a short ride, and we shall be back most presently." He paused. "Do you not trust, me, Sir William?"

William did not, but felt he could not say as much. "And where is it that we are to meet?" he asked instead.

"I am to lead you to Sir Nicholas," Moreton replied. "I have had both your horse and Master Ambrose's pony saddled up and made ready." He gestured to the side of the house, where a groom was standing with Thelwell, William's horse and another horse as well. "If you will please accompany me?"

William shrugged casually. "I see no reason why not." He went over to Ambrose. "Come son, gather your arrows. We are bidden to ride out and meet Sir Nicholas on some important matter."

"As you say, Pa." Ambrose shot William a quick glance that plainly said, 'Where are we going and why?' William shook his head with a silent reply of 'I know not, but we must take care,' before turning and following Moreton.

Ambrose walked over to the straw target and pulled out all his arrows. Replacing them in his quiver, he trotted after the two men. Richard Grenville started walking back to the house.

William made sure to walk confidently as if he had not a care in the world, although nothing could be further from the truth. Since that fateful day when Moreton had threatened Ambrose's safety, William had been on his guard at all times. Unwilling to leave Ambrose in a traitorous household, he had stuck doggedly by his son's side, continually making excuses as to why he should remain at Hetherington Hall, rather than setting off back to Grangedean and Lady Mary. He had not even found a way to get a messenger to send her news that he was safe. Indeed, it now seemed to be accepted that he was almost a permanent guest; one who would stay as long as his son was being educated in the household.

Many times he had rehearsed the story he would tell Mary when he returned to Grangedean with Ambrose, no doubt to a barrage of questions and cries of "I have been sick with worry, here at Grangedean all these months!" and "I had believed you had perished!" Indeed, it was the thought of Mary, alone and concerned back at Grangedean, that caused him deep anxiety in his day-to-day life, catching him suddenly at times when he was least expecting it – such as when he rode out hunting with Sir Nicholas, or made small talk with Lady Grenville.

The anxiety he felt for Lady Mary was second only to the anxiety caused by the knowledge that he and his precious son were guests of a Catholic family – not a loyal, compliant Catholic family as he had naively assumed all those months ago when he had taken up Sir Nicholas's casual offer to educate Ambrose, but a militant, treacherous Catholic family. For the day before he had overheard a conversation between Sir Nicholas and Moreton that gave him grave concern.

He and Ambrose had just returned from an early ride in the park. His son had put Thelwell in his stable, then headed off to change for his lessons. William had been concerned over a slight heat in his own horse's foreleg, and was crouched down in the stable soothing it with cold water. So when he heard the voices of Lambert Moreton and Sir Nicholas in the yard just outside, he remained low and listened intently.

"I would travel to York to see the procession," Sir Nicholas was saying. "Lady Grenville is set on seeing the Queen. She wishes to confirm to herself how a bastard looks when dressed in finery – like a servant assuming the garb and airs of her mistress."

"And you would go with her?" This was Moreton.

"For sure," answered Sir Nicholas. "I would not have her travel to York alone."

"But is it wise for you both to go?" Moreton asked. "What if some accident or misfortune was to befall Elizabeth the usurper? As a Catholic you would automatically be under suspicion." There was a pause. William could imagine Sir Nicholas's florid face creased in thought. It sounded like Moreton was pressing his point. "Would you not prefer to remain here in Hetherington, and avoid any possible risk?"

"But Lambert, my boy, do you think some such misfortune may occur?"

"Naturally not. But it is a risk, and risks are best avoided. After all," Moreton added, "the sight of that woman encouraging cheering crowds of heretics to adore her will make you sick to your stomach."

Sir Nicholas grunted in agreement. "You are right, Lambert, as usual," he said. "I shall indeed remain here throughout the progress and any man of Walsingham's that cares to visit will find us living a blameless Protestant life."

"That is a wise decision, Uncle," said Moreton, "a wise decision indeed."

There was a long pause – so long that William thought that the men must have gone. With his thighs starting to burn with the pain of crouching, he decided he had to stand up. Just as he was preparing to raise himself, he heard a voice again. Quickly he dropped back down.

"Who was that at the door, that you must attend her?" It was the voice of Sir Nicholas.

"Naught but an itinerant woman," answered Moreton. "She was seeking a position of service."

"Ahh. Did you turn her away?"

"I did. She was most unsavoury."

"Good."

There was the sound of boots scraping across the cobbles as the two men finally walked off. William remained crouched down by his horse's leg a few minutes more, then cautiously he stood up.

The stable yard was empty.

So the Queen was coming on progress to nearby York? William recalled earlier talk of the summer progress, but it had slipped his mind.

Then an idea began to form.

York! It was the perfect opportunity for him and Ambrose to slip away! To make their escape from this dangerous household, with its threatening young upstarts like Moreton and the ever-present fear of being accused of Catholic practices. William gave a hollow laugh as massaged feeling back into his legs. He had led his son into this viper's nest of heresy, and now here at last was a way he could get the boy back to the warmth and safety of Grangedean Manor.

The more he thought about it, the better it looked.

It would be only natural for Ambrose to want to see the Queen, and only natural for his father to offer to take him. The Grenvilles would be hard-pressed to refuse. And even if they sent an escort of men-at-arms, there were bound to be heavy crowds in York. So it would be no trouble to manufacture a means to become separated, then ride out of the city and set off down south. It would be a while before their absence was noticed, giving them plenty of time to get well ahead of any potential pursuit.

William frowned. Ideally he would want the protection of his own trusted men-at-arms on the journey. But it would raise suspicion if he tried to take them to York. So they would have to be left behind, and he and Ambrose would have to travel alone through hundreds of miles of rough country.

He bit his lip. Could he travel all the way to Grangedean without them? The two of them alone?

He nodded to himself. Of course. The boy was strong. Had he not proved that on the way up to Hetherington? And the snows had gone, so it would be an easier journey.

Then it was settled. He and Ambrose would set off for York, slip away, and leave this hellish house behind them.

With a renewed purpose, William strode out of the stable and marched back up to Hetherington Hall.

---0---

And now he and Ambrose were following Moreton to where the three horses were standing saddled and ready. They mounted up and Moreton led the way out back along the path, with William behind and Ambrose bringing up the rear.

William remained silent as they rode through the parklands towards a side gate in the perimeter wall, waiting to see if Moreton offered any further explanation. As they passed through the gate in silence, there was a fork in the path beyond. One fork led to the village and open fields, while the other led directly to the ravine and on down the side.

Moreton took the path to the ravine.

William glanced back at Ambrose and could see his son's concerned face – which was no doubt a mirror of his own. Why would Moreton be leading them towards the ravine? William made a split-second decision. The York plan was perfect in every way, but it was too late.

This whole situation was now too risky and they had to make their escape right now.

He turned to look at Ambrose again, preparing to wheel his horse around, grab Thelwell's bridle and ride back to the fork in the path. Then they would turn for the village and make all speed away. With the element of surprise, they could get a start on Moreton and open up a good distance from any pursuit.

But as he turned, he saw a sight that made his blood run cold.

Four burly horsemen in Grenville livery were riding out from the gate and coming up fast behind Ambrose. Even as William watched, they reached the boy and surrounded him.

Moreton turned. "My dear Sir William de Beauvais," he called, "I thought you might consider leaving us, so I prepared a little escort. By all means ride off and preserve yourself, but please be aware that you must leave your son in my care." He gave a thin smile. "And I cannot guarantee that my care will be as…" he seemed to be searching for the right word, "…as loving as yours."

"Damn you, Moreton," returned William, all hope of escape now disappearing. "What is the meaning of this?" He decided to try innocent bluster. "Are we not to meet Sir Nicholas as bidden? Why do you threaten my son so?"

Moreton stopped and wheeled his horse round so he was facing William and Ambrose. The horsemen brought Ambrose up close, then stopped also. The small boy and pony seemed dwarfed by them.

"Oh come now, de Beauvais, Sir Nicholas knows nothing of this." Moreton growled, a deep frown appearing on his thin face. "But I am no fool. Did you seriously think I did not know about you creeping about the house back in the winter, spying on us?"

William gripped his reins hard as he tried to maintain a neutral face. "I have no idea what you mean," he said.

"Truly?" Moreton shook his head. "I doubt that very much. Indeed, I will have one of my men ask your son. I am sure he can tell me what you know." He nodded to the man beside Ambrose. The man drew his sword, then grabbed Ambrose's arm and put the point up towards the boy's chest.

"Damn you, Moreton!" snapped William. "He knows naught! You threaten a child?"

"If necessary. Now tell me."

William glanced at his son, whose eyes were wide with fear as he stared down at the point of the sword. William turned back to Moreton. "Devil take you, Moreton," he muttered. "Yes, I did do some quiet exploration. How did you know?"

Moreton smirked at his own cleverness. "An honest man does not leave his shoes behind when abroad in the house, nor does he look guilty later when the talk is of exploring the rooms." He gestured to the man next to Ambrose to sheath his sword.

William breathed a small sigh of relief as the blade slid into its scabbard. "An honest man does not hold Catholic mass in clear contravention of the law," he answered. "Nor, no doubt, does he hide a priest in the house to conduct such services."

Moreton looked at him as if he were the basest worm. "A man must worship almighty God in the way of truth, or he is neither honest to himself nor to God. But I do not suppose that means anything to you, de Beauvais, who is content to blow with wind and worship as ordered by a heretic bastard."

"You talk treason, Moreton," William said quietly. "Have a care."

"And who is to hear?" Moreton shrugged. "These men are good Catholics, who are loyal to me and to the Grenvilles." He smiled his thin, sickly smile. "And where you are going, neither you nor the boy will be able to tell."

"What are you planning to do with us?" William demanded, trying to put some authority into his voice.

Moreton stared hard at the bushes beside the path a moment, then he laughed, making his thin body shake like a branch in a storm. "My dear Sir William de Beauvais," he said after a moment, "please give no further thought to escape. For you are instrumental to my plans." He laughed again, then suddenly the laughter disappeared from his face as if it had never existed. "I have two plans. One is to keep you both safe – so do not fear. For now. You are my failsafe if aught goes wrong with my other plan."

"Your other plan?" William asked.

But Moreton said nothing more. Instead, he glanced again at the bushes, then he gestured to the men, wheeled his horse round, and set off along the path to the side of the ravine.

William and Ambrose were herded along behind him like a couple of unwilling sheep, as the group headed over the edge of the ravine and started picking their way down the narrow rocky path.

CHAPTER TWENTY-ONE

"How do I look?" asked Mary, as she and Tom prepared to leave their rooms and go down to the Great Hall.

"Magnificent," he answered with a smile. "You are no longer the dirty serving woman or ragged traveller I have known, but are now restored to your full glory." He swept off his cap and bowed low. "After all these weeks, I am honoured finally to meet the noble Lady Mary de Beauvais."

"Oh come now," she said, feeling her cheeks starting to burn, "you have known me in good times and bad. A bath and some proper clothes do not make a difference." Although there was no denying that it had been glorious to finally get out of the threadbare servant's dress and put on the fine pale yellow gown with grey underskirt and sleeves that Olivia had found for her.

"Well, madam," he said, straightening up again, "I beg to disagree." He put on his cap. "Shall we not go down and show the court your nobility and bearing, and see if they are of the same mind as me?"

"Let us go down, for sure, but you mind your tongue, Thomas Cobham, or it could get you into some serious trouble."

"Not just my tongue," he muttered, but just loud enough for her to hear. He opened the door and stood back. "You must lead, good lady, as I am worthy only to follow in your shadow." He gave her a cheeky smile, "and I want better to see the faces of those women you pass – for I am sure they will turn green with envy!"

"Nonsense!" she replied, although she couldn't hide a smile of her own. "And anyway, remember we are only here a couple of days, till everyone goes to York and we can stop the Alchemist."

The thought of that man out there with his awful gun, no doubt hiding in some inn or cottage until the Queen's progress came to York, caused a sudden icy finger of fear to run down her back. She stopped a moment. So much rested on her and Tom's shoulders – not just the safety of the Queen, but the future she remembered, and her own future too.

She shook her head to try and give herself the reassurance and strength she needed to face the challenge ahead.

We have a plan – and it has to work!

At least the first part had been easy – getting into Wyvern Castle and establishing herself and Tom as members of the Queen's entourage. Olivia had been as good as her word, and had gone straight to Wychwoode, who had pulled whatever strings he needed to pull to get them in. They had been sitting chatting idly by the gate for only an hour when Olivia had come back with a sombre-looking elderly man dressed all in black, who turned out to be the Wyvern steward.

"Come, my lady," said Olivia, with a poorly concealed sideways glance that was clearly intended to size up Tom. "You and Master Cobham are bidden to join the progress at the invitation of Master Wychwoode, who says he wishes to avail himself of your good council on the matter of the preparation of the Queen's route through the streets of York. He has made rooms available to you, and has servants ready to bathe and dress you both as befits a courtier."

The sombre man produced an enormous bunch of keys from a leather bag slung round his shoulder, then spent what seemed like an agonising eternity carefully surveying each key before selecting one and opening the gate. Finally, Tom and Mary were able to walk through, as the man locked up again behind them.

Mary looked back at the wall above other side of the gate while the steward was locking up, and saw it had the identical shield above, with the same legless dragon.

"What is that strange beast?" she asked the man.

He regarded her dolefully as he put the keys back in his bag, as if debating whether or not he could trust himself to impart such information. Then he cleared his throat and said slowly, "Madam, 'tis the Wyvern itself – an ancient beast that has been on the arms of the family for over two hundred years." Then he was silent again. Mary was just about to ask if it was chosen for the family name or the other way round, when the man suddenly carried on. "This is known as the hanging gate," he announced, "as it was the old Lord Wyvern's practice to use it to dispose of anyone who challenged or stole from him. He would order a rope to be thrown up behind the shield," he pointed upwards, "and hang the unfortunate by the neck. Indeed," he continued, "so many times has this occurred that the supporting stone behind the shield is worn quite smooth. Which," he added "makes it all the easier to haul a man up to his death."

---0---

Mary took Tom's arm, and they descended the ornate stone stairway with its magnificent wood panelling, together with pictures of the Wyvern family and their illustrious ancestors.

The stairs and the hallway below were crowded with nobility of all sorts; elegant women in gowns of every hue, dripping with emeralds, diamonds, rubies and opals, their hair loose and flowing or contained in different types of hoods. They were accompanied by men in embroidered doublets with slashed nether-stocks, rich coloured hose, and all topped off with a variety of decorative caps and hats. Everyone was talking, which meant they all had to raise their voices nearly to a shout, making a wall of sound that was almost painful to Mary's ears. She also noticed that there was none of the usual smell of sweat she had now grown used to with Elizabethan crowds; instead there were a variety of intriguing and quite pleasant scents. She identified lavender, rose, jasmine and cedar, as well as hints of pine and nutmeg, before she had even reached the foot of the stairs.

She could see the occasional man in the black garb of a lawyer or secretary standing out against the sea of colour, and searched across the crowd for the distinctive white hair of Robert Wychwoode. However, she reached the foot of the stairs without spotting him.

As they passed through a pair of tall oak doors into the Great Hall, she saw Olivia immediately, waiting just inside as agreed. Beside her was a small girl of about eighteen, whose striking beauty was marred by a fearsome scowl as she glared down at the floor.

"My dear Lady de Beauvais," said Olivia, when they had greeted each other with a kiss. "Allow me to present Margaret Tyndall, also in waiting to my lady Burnham."

The girl slowly raised her head and stared defiantly at Mary, who stared back with a slight smile.

"You must be Maggie, of whom I have heard so much," Mary said. Then she stood slightly to one side to let Tom through. "Allow me to present Master Thomas Cobham, who has been most kind and most accommodating on our journey here. We have been through many adventures."

Tom stepped forward, swept off his cap and bowed low to both girls in turn. "Mistress Melrose, Mistress Tyndall, you are both well met."

Olivia nodded her head in acknowledgement. "Indeed, Master Cobham, I am most indebted to you for keeping my friend safe on the journey."

"For sure, Mistress Melrose," Tom answered as he put his cap back on, "I would be well minded not to take the credit for keeping Lady Mary safe, but to say that on just as many occasions, it was she who did such service for me!"

"And the better man for admitting it," said Olivia, with a small sideways glance at Maggie.

"Mistress Melrose, you are too kind," Tom replied.

"Olivia, please! Call me Olivia. And she has done so much for me, too"

"Very well – Olivia – we shall share our tales of Lady Mary's courage and resourcefulness anon, over a glass or two of claret." He smiled, then put a hand on her sleeve. "And I have no doubt that the more claret we drink, the better will be our tales of Lady Mary's bravery and daring!"

Then Tom turned to the girl beside her. "And now, Mistress Tyndall, pray tell me what ails you, that you have such a look of pain on your pretty face?"

"Maggie is upset," explained Olivia, "as she accuses me of trying to end her relationship with one Lionel Shelton, who I do not believe is worthy of her."

"It is not for you to decide," Maggie muttered.

"As one who has experience of this man," Olivia continued, as if Maggie had not spoken, "I know that he does not share your amorous feelings."

Maggie rounded on Olivia, "And pray tell how you know this?"

"Olivia speaks the truth, Mistress Tyndall," Mary cut in quickly, before any argument could start. "I can vouchsafe that this Shelton is a base creature, and best left alone."

"Oh heavens!" cried Maggie, stamping her foot, "Does no one support me in my liaison with Lionel Shelton?"

"No," answered Mary, "and for good reason." She took Maggie's hand in both of her own, and said, "Come with me, child, I have something to tell you." Then she led Maggie away to a window seat where they could sit as far as possible from the crowds.

She indicated to the girl to sit down, which Maggie did by dropping inelegantly onto the seat with a deep sigh and her arms folded.

Mary ignored this. "I could tell you all the dreadful things this man has done to other girls just like you," she said. "Painful things. Selfish things. Wicked things. But I will not. Instead I will ask you to answer just two questions."

Maggie looked up. Mary pressed on while she had the girl's attention. "One, what is the best thing Shelton has ever said or done, and two, what is the worst?"

Maggie hesitated. "Go on," Mary encouraged her.

"The best – he has said my eyes are as the prettiest cornflowers and my hair is as the sunlight itself."

"And the worst?"

Again Maggie was silent, her eyes staring deep into Mary's.

"He made to hit me, because he believed I might have doubted him," she said eventually in a small voice.

Mary said nothing for a while, to see if Maggie would draw her own conclusions. After a moment, the girl nodded. "This is not the behaviour of an honourable man – a man who is in love – is it?"

Mary shook her head. "No, I do not think it is."

"Is it the behaviour of a seasoned courtier who professes love without meaning?" Maggie asked.

Mary nodded.

"But what of the cornflowers?"

"Pretty words do not make a lover," Mary whispered. "But it is the actions that make the man."

"But he was upset. I upset him. It is perfectly right and proper for a man to become angry if a girl upsets him."

"No!" Mary grabbed her shoulders suddenly, causing a couple of nearby courtiers to jump. "No man has the right to strike a girl," she hissed quietly, but with real force in her voice, "however angry he may be!" She let go and sat back. "I know that men have all the rights, but that has to change – and one day it will, I swear. One day women will be as equal to men, and the better for it."

"But…" Maggie looked at her with wide eyes, "no woman can be equal to a man – it is not natural, or as God would wish."

"Why?" Mary responded, leaning forward again and keeping her voice low in order to avoid drawing in any of the surrounding courtiers. "Why must God favour men over women?"

Maggie answered immediately, "Because Eve betrayed Adam."

Mary sat back. There was no point in trying to offer an explanation based on Darwinian evolution to this girl – she would have to take a more sideways approach. "And why did Eve do as she did?"

"Because of the serpent?"

"Indeed," Mary said in triumph. "And was the serpent male or female?"

"Male, of course." Maggie shook her head at Mary's apparent stupidity, then suddenly she stopped, as a light of understanding came into her eyes. "So…" she said slowly, "it was not the woman's fault, but a man's…" She stared at Mary, as she worked it out further. "It is men who tell us we must obey them – yet it is they who make the rules…" She looked in awe at Mary. "So we should recognise that it is not God's law, but…"

"Man's law, yes." Mary finished for her. "And as I say, one day this will change, and women will take their rightful place as men's equals."

"You are sure of this?"

"I am." Mary smiled. "Maybe not in our lifetimes, but one day." She stood up and held out her hand for Maggie to stand as well.

Maggie was silent for a long moment, as she thought it all through. Then she took Mary's hand and stood.

"You are saying that one day my daughters or theirs will benefit?"

"I am."

"Very well, Lady Mary," Maggie gave a small curtsey and smile, "That is a change I would desire."

"So if that is your desire, then you will change yourself now? You will have no more flirtation with Shelton?"

"No, none. He is as the serpent. I see that now, and…" She nodded, as if confirming it to herself, "…and I am quite cured of him." She paused, then added, "I think."

"What you must think, Maggie Tyndall," said Mary, "is that this is a vain, shallow man who is not worthy to kiss the hem of your gown, and you would do well never to forget it."

"I will," Maggie said again, only this time with a bit more conviction. "Yes," she said firmly, "I will."

"Good." Mary stood back to let Maggie go first. "Then let us re-join the others and tell them our news."

They weaved their way back to Olivia and Tom.

Olivia raised an eyebrow in enquiry. Mary said, "Maggie has something to tell us."

Maggie looked down a moment, as if seeking inspiration from the toes of her shoes, then looked back up. "I am no longer enamoured of Lionel," she said slowly. "Indeed, I have seen that he is not an honourable man."

Olivia looked hard at Maggie, as if to say, 'I told you so!' But instead she asked, "And this is how you truly feel?"

Maggie nodded and smiled weakly at Olivia. "I have been quite the little madam, have I not? I am so sorry. Will you ever forgive me?"

Olivia drew the girl into a tight embrace. "Of course I will, you silly goose!"

"I rather think Maggie is now fully cured of Master Shelton," observed Mary to Tom. "Shall we now seek Master Robert Wychwoode? You and I do have some pressing business with him." She looked around the room, and with relief, she finally spotted the tall white-haired lawyer on the other side of the Great Hall.

Together she and Tom pushed their way across the room until the crowds parted and she found herself once again in Wychwoode's presence. He was facing away from her as he was talking to a couple of men, but as Mary approached something made him stop and turn round enquiringly.

He had definitely aged in the last ten years; his face was more lined, and there was a droop to the corners of each eye, but the white flowing hair was as thick as before, and there was still no mistaking the power and authority that emanated from him like an aura. A large beaming smile spread across his face like the rise of the summer sun, then he bowed deeply.

"Lady Mary de Beauvais!" he exclaimed as he stood up. "You are indeed well met!. It must be all of ten years since we thwarted that appalling little witchfinder!" He kissed her in greeting. "Olivia Melrose told me you were here, and we should find space for you and Tom at Court. I trust the rooms we have secured suit you well?" She nodded. "Good." He looked her up and down. "And the clothes we have found do become you most excellently."

Tom pushed forward. "And here is Thomas Cobham, too!" Wychwoode exclaimed. "Art come to report on the matter we started all those months ago?"

Tom nodded, and Wychwoode became serious in a heartbeat. "Then come, we must take a walk in the gardens where we can converse in peace."

Together they made their way out of the Great Hall and through the main doors into the gardens. Soon they were able to talk freely without fear of being overheard.

"I questioned a man called Tyler in Stratford but was not able to get any information from him on the whereabouts of the Alchemist," Wychwoode said. "So I had him transferred to the Tower in London for further questioning." He shook his head. "Which means we have now lost track of this Alchemist. I take it that the reason you are here is that you have knowledge of the Alchemist after Stratford?"

Tom nodded. "Aye, we do. We went to Stratford ourselves to seek out this man Tyler, but we picked up the trail of the Alchemist himself – so we followed him instead." Tom answered. "We found him – or more to the point he found us. He then caused the death of Mary's horse, as well as an honest woodsman and his fair daughter by burning their cottage to the ground. We were also trapped, but escaped only by the greatest good fortune and the resourcefulness of the good Lady Mary."

Wychwoode turned to Mary and nodded. "I have remarked on your courage and resource in the past, Lady Mary," he said with a smile. "I am pleased to see this has not left you." He turned back to Tom, as Mary felt herself blushing for the second time that evening. Tom continued, "We believe the Alchemist is hiding out near here even now."

"Indeed?" Wychwoode raised an enquiring eyebrow.

"We believe he intends to take his shot when Her Majesty is on progress through the streets of York," said Tom.

"With this special musket of his," Wychwoode asked, "the one we heard he had fashioned himself, to find its target even from five hundred yards or more?"

"He has this, and some of his singular cartridges that contain both powder and ball," said Tom.

Wychwoode was silent a moment, deep in thought. "I have sworn to Her Majesty to keep her safe." He looked at each in turn. "We have to get to this man and stop him before he has his chance."

"We do have some thoughts on a plan to stop him," said Mary.

"Pray tell." Wychwoode said.

Mary explained their plan for her to seek out the Alchemist and for Tom to ride close by the Queen.

Wychwoode nodded. "It has the makings of a plan," he said slowly.

"Can you have some of your men available to help us?" asked Tom.

"Aye, Tom, I will," Wychwoode paused, "but all must be done in secret – in the shadows. Her Majesty has made it most clear that she will not be seen to be cowering in fear behind men – rather, she must be clearly visible to all."

"But that is what the Alchemist wants!" exclaimed Tom. "If the Queen is in clear view he can get his shot."

"She does not account for the accuracy of his special musket," added Mary. "This makes it different from every other attempt; the Alchemist can be many hundreds of yards away and still be sure to kill her."

"Aye." Wychwoode agreed. "But the Queen has been most explicit on this, and we cannot go against her wishes on the basis of a possible weapon about which we cannot be certain."

"I have seen it in action," Mary said firmly. "The Alchemist used it to kill my horse, and before he burned the cottage down, he shot the old woodsman dead right in front of us. It is real, believe me."

"I do believe you, my dear Lady Mary, indeed I do," answered Wychwoode. "But I cannot go against the Queen's wishes. This whole operation must be conducted in total secrecy." He looked from Mary to Tom. "I will support you both with a few men, but that is all I can vouchsafe. We will sit together tomorrow and plan this in more detail." He looked at Mary. "Does that meet with your approval, my lady?"

She nodded slowly. "Indeed, Master Wychwoode, it does – as long as we can be sure we can find the Alchemist before he can use his musket." Then she looked down. "But there is one other thing…"

He raised an eyebrow. "Which is, my lady?"

Mary took a breath. For all her concern to protect the Queen, there was something else that had been eating at her, ever since she had been turned away by that strange Lambert Moreton at Hetherington Hall. It was a mother's concern for her son, and knowing that he was here in York while there was a killer on the loose, was a worry that she could not ignore. It seemed only fair that Wychwoode, with all his influence and connections, should offer help in return for all she had done – and was prepared to do – to protect the Queen.

"I have been told that my son, Ambrose de Beauvais, is in York to see the progress," she said. "I am told that he is staying at the town-house of his hosts, the Grenvilles. I am concerned for his safety."

Wychwoode stared at her, chewing on his lip. "My dear lady," he said after a moment, "I am sure your son will be in no danger with the Grenville family. None at all." He gave a reassuring smile. "But I will send a couple of my men to the Grenville town-house to keep watch on him." He touched her on the arm. "Does that reassure you?"

Mary breathed a sigh of relief. "Yes," she said. "Thank you."

She looked at Tom. "Come on," she said brightly, "let us re-join the revelries, then tomorrow we can plan our campaign against this Alchemist."

But Wychwoode held up his hand. "By your leave, Lady Mary," he said, "I would speak alone with Master Cobham first. He has been working on my orders these past few months, and I would like to have his report in person."

Mary nodded. "Of course," she answered. "Tom. I will see you in the Great Hall shortly." Then she turned and walked alone back to the castle.

---0---

Tom waited until Mary was out of earshot, then turned to Wychwoode.

"I have a feeling this is not about me reporting to you, but perhaps the other way around?" he asked. "You have something you wish to tell me?"

"Aye, I do. What Lady Mary has said raises the gravest of concerns. I would not have this said to her face, but I have information which means that young master Ambrose is indeed in great danger."

Tom checked the retreating figure of Mary to make sure she was definitely out of earshot. "Go on," he replied.

"You may recall I said this man Tyler did not talk in Stratford and we sent him to the Tower for further questions?"

Tom nodded.

"Well, now he has talked."

"Willingly?"

Wychwoode shook his head with a grimace. "Nay, unfortunately not. Let us say that we had to… persuade him… to co-operate."

"Then the information is tainted, surely?" Tom said. "It is well known that a man will say anything he can to stop pain being applied."

"I agree, and I do not use such methods lightly," Wychwoode muttered, "but Walsingham was insistent. This Tyler was a strong man, and held out for nigh on two weeks, it seems, before he died. I have had a messenger only this morning. It seems that before he died, he revealed one piece of information which Walsingham believes is genuine. It may lead us to the man who controls the plot."

Tom thought a moment. If Wychwoode believed that Ambrose de Beauvais was in danger, it could only mean that the household who had taken him in were themselves implicated in the plot. Mary was right to be concerned. "Is it Grenville?" he asked.

Wychwoode nodded. "We think it is. Tyler said only one word that we could clearly define, in response to the question 'where is the plot centred?' He said 'Hetherington'."

"And York is less than an hour's ride from Hetherington Hall, home of the Catholic Sir Nicholas Grenville…" said Tom, finishing the thought. "Then why have you not arrested Grenville and taken him in for questioning?"

"We have no evidence linking him to the Alchemist or Alleyne, other than the word of Tyler."

"Procured under torture." Tom could see the problem. "Are you watching the house?"

Wychwoode nodded. "Indeed, I have now sent men to conduct clandestine observation round the clock from key vantage points. I have my first report due to me tomorrow morning on the current movements in and out of the house." He gave a hollow laugh. "As we get closer to the progress through York, it may be that something incriminating is seen."

"But it may be that the Alchemist is operating alone – under instructions not to make contact with the Grenvilles?"

"Indeed. But let us see when we get the report tomorrow."

"And will you send men to the Grenville town house in the meantime?" Tom asked.

"I will," answered Wychwoode. "I promised the same to Lady Mary, and I will do all I can to deliver on my promise."

Tom was silent a moment, deep in thought. If Mary still thought that Ambrose was in danger, she would not be focused on preventing the assassination of Elizabeth. So as long as she knew Ambrose was safe under observation at the Grenville town house, then that danger was lifted. "But we should not share any of these suspicions with Mary," he said slowly, "unless we have more solid proof."

"I agree," said Wychwoode. "For now she is determined to stop this Alchemist, and her courage and resource will be a key part of our success in doing so. We must keep her mind on that goal – and that goal alone."

CHAPTER TWENTY-TWO

As Mary made her way back into the Great Hall through the crowds of Elizabethan courtiers and hangers-on, the first person she recognised was Lionel Shelton.

He was standing just inside the door, scanning the crowds as if he was looking for someone. As Mary approached and their eyes met, she saw his expression darken as if a thunder cloud had rolled across his face. Then he deliberately turned away as if to carry on searching.

Ignoring the insult, Mary marched up to him. "Master Shelton," she demanded, raising her voice to be heard above the cacophony of noise in the room. She put her hand on his elegantly slit velvet sleeve. "I would speak with you."

He turned back slowly and looked her up and down, paying unnecessarily lengthy attention to her chest. "Yes, my lady?" he drawled, raising his eyes to hers with a sickly smile.

"What you did to Olivia Melrose was a sick, monstrous crime and should not go unpunished," Mary said. She knew it sounded weak when said out loud, and certainly not as good as it had in her head as she was walking over. She stared defiantly at him.

"Indeed, Lady de Beauvais," Shelton answered, seeming impervious to her glare. "And by what spurious authority do you intend to have me charged?" He shook his head. "I would deny any accusation, naturally."

"Yes, I am sure you would," Mary snapped back. "I doubt your conduct as a gentleman extends to honesty and repentance. Anyway," she continued, "an accusation and a trial would undoubtedly affect your reputation. Some would believe you capable of it, even if you were not found guilty."

"I very much doubt that," he said. "It would be the word of a young girl against a gentleman at Court – and a wanton, lascivious young girl at that. Few would give her story credence – even if she were prepared to admit she had carnal relations outside of wedlock." He smiled again, showing yellowing teeth. "For that would reflect poorly on her, such that she could never marry." He paused, "As well you know, my lady."

All Mary knew at that moment was that she was not prepared to let this arrogant, depraved man get away with his crime against Olivia. "I know a time and place where evil creatures like you get the punishment they deserve for raping an innocent girl," she muttered.

"Well, I suggest you go hence to that place, because here and now, I know I can act with impunity."

The look of smug triumph on his face caused a sudden thought to occur. "You would have no hesitation to do it again!" she exclaimed, and he grinned at her, confirming her worst fear. "With Maggie Tyndall!"

He stared over her shoulder into the distance. "She is indeed very comely, and I feel she may be more willing than Mistress Melrose..."

"Oh no, no, no..." Mary shook her head. "That boat has sailed, Shelton. Maggie Tyndall no longer has any regard for you."

He continued to stare into the distance. "So I must either win her back..." he paused, then snapped his head round suddenly and stared at Mary, "or I must disregard her affection entirely. I must have her. She has become an itch that I must scratch."

Then he removed his cap, bowed and said, "But that shall be for later, by your leave my lady, as I have some more," he paused, "important matters to attend to." Leaving Mary feeling sickened to her stomach, he threaded his way to the door, pausing only to bow briefly to Olivia and Maggie as they passed him on their way into the room.

The two girls came straight over to Mary.

"Were you talking to Shelton?" asked Olivia, her eyes wide. "What did you say to him?"

"He smiled at me in a way that I did not like!" complained Maggie. "As if I was but a foolish child who could not be trusted."

Olivia turned to her. "There," she said. "Now you have the measure of him – you see the kind of man he is. As I have told you, he has no real regard for you and he never has."

Mary put her hand on Maggie's sleeve. "We are only looking out for your best interests."

Maggie gave them a watery smile. "I know," she said slowly, "but I did think he had the nicest eyes," she paused, "and I liked his hands as well."

"Which he would have used to strike you," added Olivia. "Had I not come in."

"There is that, I suppose," Maggie admitted.

"Which no man should think he has the right to do," said Mary.

Maggie nodded. Then she said, "I think I will go to my rooms a while." She gave Mary a small curtsey. "By your leave, my lady."

"So," Olivia said, when Maggie had gone, "what did Shelton say just now?"

"That he would take her whether she wants it or not."

"The man is a monster – the very devil!"

"He said she is an itch that he must scratch."

"Then we must stop him, for sure. What are we to do?"

"We have to punish him – we have to teach him a lesson he will never forget." Mary took Olivia's hands in her own. "And I think I have just the plan we need." She paused. "But it will also need Maggie to play her part…"

---0---

A night owl hooted softly as two hooded figures, barely visible in the deep shadows, crept along the back of Wyvern Castle and slipped quietly in through a side entrance.

They passed silently along the dark passageway until they came to a heavy wooden door set into a semi-circular stone wall. The first figure eased the latch up as slowly as possible, then opened the door inch by inch. Suddenly there was a sharp screeching sound from the hinge; unnaturally loud in the still night. Immediately the figure paused, listening for any sounds of footsteps or a shout from someone alerted by the noise. After a minute or more there was no such response, so they resumed opening the door, but slower still. As soon as it was sufficiently open, both figures slipped silently through, then padded quickly up a set of circular stone stairs.

At the top, they paused in front of another door. One of the figures put their hands to their mouth and made a soft owl hoot of their own.

After a moment, the door was opened and candle-light spilled out, illuminating the two hooded figures, as well as the one who had opened the door.

"Is it safe?" hissed one of the visitors.

"Yes," came the answer, and the two entered the room.

Once inside, Mary and Olivia pushed back their hoods. Mary smiled at Maggie, standing back from the door and holding her candle. Her face looked unnatural in the flickering light and shadows. "Then it is done?" Olivia asked.

"Aye." Maggie gestured towards the bed, "He sleeps like an infant."

They looked across to where Lionel Shelton lay spread out on the bed, stark naked. A goblet lay on the floor, leaving red wine stains on the rushes.

"How much sleeping draught did you give him?" asked Olivia.

"As much as you said, and a few drops more for good measure."

"Good," Olivia answered. "That is more than it takes to put my lady Burnham to sleep when she asks for it – but 'tis well done, I see."

"And he had not tried anything untoward first?" asked Mary.

"Nay, I was fortunate that the potion did its work before he was able to," answered Maggie, "though he was most in haste to get unclothed when I said I would lay with him willingly. I had only to unlace my sleeves and he was throwing off his own attire like a man burning with a fever."

"Good." Mary became more business-like. "We need to carry him out to the place I have in mind quickly, in case the potion wears off. Blow out your candle, Maggie – between the three of us we can carry him in the dark."

---0---

The early morning sun beat down on the long column of horses and riders that snaked its way along the path from Wyvern Castle to the front gate.

At the front of the column was Her Majesty Queen Elizabeth, resplendent in white and gold, her red hair rising from her forehead and decorated with pearls and emeralds; her sharp dark eyes looking straight ahead as she rode. Beside her was the Earl of Leicester, more soberly dressed in a grey doublet, and beside him was a hawksman with the Queen's hawk on a leather gauntlet. The bird flapped its wings idly and the hawksman made soothing noises, before slipping a small leather hood over its head to calm it.

As the procession approached the imposing arched gateway, the Earl looked up and sniggered.

The Queen also glanced up briefly, then held up her hand and brought her horse to a stop, causing the column behind her to halt also.

The Queen turned to the Earl and said calmly, "Why is there is a naked man hauled to the top of the archway?" She glanced briefly up at the man. He had been tied with a rope under his arms and then been hoisted up above the gate, almost up to the shield with the legless dragon. The rope then passed over the supporting stone behind the shield, before being tied off securely at the base of one of the brick pillars.

The Earl sniggered again. As if on cue the column of riders behind him all started to laugh, until after a few minutes there was barely a single man who was not roaring with laughter.

The Queen herself did not crack a smile, but held up her hand again, and the laughter died down quickly. "Who is this man?" she demanded. "I can not see his face from this angle, as there are other parts of him which are more – prominent – in my view."

The Earl wheeled his horse round and rode back a few yards to get a better view, then returned to the Queen's side. "I would say it is Master Lionel Shelton, madam," he said.

"And why," the Queen asked quietly, "do you suppose Master Shelton has been pulled up to the top of the brick archway above these gates?"

"I have not a clue, madam," answered the Earl. "Although I warrant this is some form of punishment for bad behaviour – for I understand this is called the hanging gate."

"It is well named," observed the Queen drily. "Although I note he supports his weight with his feet on the brick lintel – so the organiser of this punishment does not wish him to perish by this act."

"Belike he has angered someone and they have simply sought to make him the laughing stock he now is?" suggested the Earl.

"I agree," answered the Queen.

"Shall I have this investigated, madam?" Leicester asked. "To have the perpetrator brought to justice?"

The Queen shook her head. "Nay," she answered. "No doubt this was deserved, and I would commend whoever devised this punishment for their ingenuity." She trotted through the gates without looking up, then stopped and turned back to the Earl. "Enough of this fool – we are set to hunt this morning. Have him taken down and banished from Court for life. I never wish to see him again." She thought a moment, then added, "I fear I have seen quite enough of him as it is."

The hunting party then followed her though the gates, each member looking up and laughing at Shelton, suspended naked in front of the arch above them, his eyes tightly closed – as if somehow by not seeing his tormentors, they could not see him.

CHAPTER TWENTY-THREE

"Master Ambrose *and* Sir William?" asked Tom, staring at the small, anonymous-looking man dressed in a jerkin and breeches that were a patchwork of green and brown. "Are you certain? Sir William was supposed to have journeyed back to Grangedean Manor these many weeks since."

It was later that morning, and Wychwoode and Tom were gathered in the far corner of the Wyvern gardens, behind a maze made of high green hedges. It was the perfect spot for a meeting with Wychwoode's spy.

"Indeed Master Cobham," the man answered. "I have seen with my own eyes the boy and a man of noble bearing addressed as Sir William de Beauvais by Moreton."

Wychwoode asked, "Where was Moreton taking them?"

"I know not, Master Wychwoode, but…"

"Go on," Tom prompted.

"But it was against their will, Master, that much was clear. Moreton had some men-at-arms who threatened the boy, so the father must go along with their orders."

"Did Moreton say anything?"

"He said, and I have this committed to my memory, 'you are my failsafe if aught goes wrong with my plan.' Then he led them away from the house, I know not where."

Wychwoode took out his purse and pressed a coin into the man's hand. "I thank you. Now go and resume your watch on Hetherington."

The man nodded and slipped away. He quickly disappeared into the hedges beyond the maze; his green and brown clothing blending him into the foliage.

Wychwoode watched him go. "He is one of my best men," he observed, "able to hide unseen in any hedgerow." He turned to Tom with a smile. "He could be a couple of feet from you, and you would never know."

"I shall watch my step, then, Master Wychwoode," answered Tom with a laugh, "in case he might be listening and reporting my words back to you."

Wychwoode laughed also. "Then say naught to give me cause for concern – and you have naught to fear."

There was a silence as each man became serious once more, considering the importance of the message they had heard.

"So, the master plotter is this Lambert Moreton," said Wychwoode. "Belike even Sir Nicholas is unaware of this."

"It would seem so."

"Then I am minded to arrest Moreton now…" the older man mused.

"And have Sir William and Ambrose de Beauvais killed?" Tom replied. "Is that not what Moreton meant by a 'failsafe'? And besides, if you arrest Moreton, the Alchemist is not prevented from carrying out his part of the plan."

"True."

"Perhaps..." Tom stopped.

"What?"

"Perhaps Moreton *did* see your man in the hedgerow..."

"Not possible."

"But if he did – maybe he spotted movement – particularly if he was expecting clandestine observers..." Tom shook his head, "then I think he was sending us a message."

There was a pause as Wychwoode considered this. "If so," he said, "if we *do* accept that my man may have been seen, then what Moreton was telling us... is that Sir William and Master Ambrose are his hostages."

"I think so." Tom kicked at a pebble on the path.

"Then we are in the hands of you and Lady Mary tomorrow in York, to find this Alchemist and stop him killing the Queen."

"And if we do, and Moreton hears that the Queen progresses unharmed through the streets of York – then I would not give a fig for the life of the hostages..."

Wychwoode put his hand on the younger man's shoulder. "I need hardly remind you, sir, where your duty lies," he said softly.

Tom kicked the pebble again.

For sure, his duty lay with the life of the Queen – that much was obvious. He must do all in his power to preserve her. But it could not be denied that if he did, then he would most surely be condemning the husband and son of Lady Mary de Beauvais to an untimely end – which did not bear thinking about. But if they were successful in stopping the Alchemist – and as a consequence Sir William met with an unfortunate end, then Lady Mary would become a widow and free to marry once more... To become Mistress Cobham. There was no denying it was an attractive proposition, though he felt sick to the pit of his stomach for even thinking it... No, no. The honourable thing to do as a gentleman would be to find a way to save Sir William... His feelings for Mary must be put aside. Mary would remain a happily married woman and mother. She would return to Sir William and his brief adventure with her would be over, so they would part... But then, how could he forget the vision of that magnificent body coming up the stream towards him? And the feel of her breasts against his chest, the soft touch of her cheek, and the eyes... the eyes that said they loved him, as sure as day follows night... How would it be to have those lovely eyes look adoringly into his every morning, every evening, every night? As adoringly as he would gaze into hers? And the truth was, it was the best option all round – not only to save the Queen but also win Mary as a prize...

Tom kicked the pebble hard, and it went skittering away into the bushes.

But that would not be the honourable thing to do…

Wychwoode again put his hand on Tom's shoulder. "Your duty lies with the Queen, my friend," he said softly, "for all your heart may lie elsewhere. I have seen the looks you share with my lady."

Tom gave a half-smile. Wychwoode was only seeing half the picture. "I will do all in my power to save the Queen," he said. "You have my word on it – my word as a gentleman."

"And we do not share this with Lady Mary..."

"That will not be an easy thing to countenance," Tom answered. "This is her family…"

"If we stop this Alchemist, I will send men to Hetherington immediately. They can seek out Sir William and Ambrose before word reaches Moreton of the Queen's deliverance from danger." Wychwoode paused a moment. "We also know now that Moreton deliberately deceived Lady Mary. Her son remains at Hetherington Hall, and is not at the Grenville house in York."

"Aye," answered Tom, "he would not have wanted her meeting her son and husband, or she would have upset his plans. He had to get rid of her, and quickly."

"Indeed."

"So you will send men to Hetherington?"

Wychwoode nodded.

"Your word upon it?"

"My word also." Wychwoode agreed. "So 'tis sealed. We have both given our word to do the honourable thing."

---0---

When the banquet ended, the revelries began.

Under the watchful eye of the Queen, a stream of entertainers were brought on to do their turn, then shepherded away again to applause from the gathered throng which matched exactly the Queen's own level of approval. So the jugglers who received a polite handclap and a bored yawn from Her Majesty got no more from the rest of the room, while the dancing girls who did intricate dances with fans and flowers and who got a more sustained clapping and a smiling nod from Elizabeth, received a more raucous reception from the rest of the audience.

As each act was presented, Robert Dudley, Earl of Leicester, made concerned side-glances at the Queen to see how she was taking them, showing visible relief whenever she smiled. On her other side, Sir Thomas Wyvern was looking increasingly horrified as each act came into the Great Hall. As the host, he was bearing much of the cost of the Queen's stay – and perhaps after putting up a couple of hundred voracious courtiers for three days, these performances were the last straw. By the time the last act was completed – a re-creation of the defeat of the French by the British fleet at the Battle of Saint-Mathieu in 1512 using actors wearing model ship costumes – Sir Thomas looked positively unwell. And when the French ship *Cordelière* caught fire and sank using a mixture of fireworks and red silk 'flames', he seemed on the verge of a faint. The only time he was seen to smile, albeit very slightly, was when two ships inadvertently collided, and that section of the dance had to be restarted.

Lady Mary turned her attention back from their unfortunate host, to Wychwoode beside her.

"Now the entertainments are concluded, Lady Mary," he said, "I would we once again talk through our plans for the morrow – for we will have no opportunity for a second chance like those unfortunate actors just now."

"For sure," Mary nodded.

"Now, I have attempted with as much force and vigour as I can to have her Majesty change her route, but Leicester, who is an infernal meddler in these things, has insisted we stick to the plan. He says that no other streets are as wide or as easy to pass along, and he has also had the entire route swept and cleaned, with fresh straw laid along every yard, in order to preserve Her Majesty from the common sights – and smells – of an English town."

Wychwoode paused, and pushed a small piece of bread around on his plate with his knife. "I have advised him that there might be an attack on Her Majesty's person, but have desisted from explaining about the Alchemist and his – what was it Lady Mary called it, Tom – ah yes, his 'sniper' musket. I think that our noble Earl will not believe me were I to try and explain about this fellow, so I have left it only that I have good reason for concern."

"And Her Majesty on her horse?" prompted Tom.

"Aye. I have made it clear that I would prefer Her Majesty to walk, as we can surround her with men and shield her from this dreadful Alchemist. However, Leicester has again insisted that she ride – as he says it not only makes her more visible to the crowds, but makes her also rise majestically above them. He believes it helps create the illusion of her being 'elevated' above her people – which is all of a part in her perception as their glorious monarch."

"Good PR," muttered Mary to herself. There were a few 21st century celebrities who could learn a thing or two from how Elizabeth created her mystique and the cult of 'Gloriana'.

"What was that you said, Lady Mary?" asked Wychwoode.

"Nothing. Please continue."

"So we have no option but to stop this Alchemist before he can strike." He turned to Tom. "Your original plan was workable, so you, Cobham, will ride alongside the Queen as agreed. Look always forwards and upwards to see if you can spot the would-be assassin – as we believe he will most likely be stationed at an open window at the highest point in a building, or possibly on a roof. If you see him, what is your immediate action?"

"I will take hold of Her Majesty's bridle and quickly pull her round out of the line of the man's sight."

"Indeed. But we hope it will not come to this, as Lady Mary will be walking a few minutes ahead of the procession and will be looking to see if the weapon can be spotted further in advance."

"And if I see him?" Mary asked. "I will be a single woman against a man with the most powerful musket ever made."

Wychwoode looked at her closely, as if he was studying her suitability for something. Then he nodded, and said, "I would have you dressed as a boy, with a cap to cover your hair, in case the Alchemist sees you first. As I recall, you disguised yourself as such when we conquered the witchfinder all those years past, and you still have the smoothness in your cheek to fool even the closest observer." He paused. "And two of my men armed with swords and pistols will stay close to you – but not too close, so they are spotted. When you see the Alchemist – and I trust to God you will – you can call on them to help you to disarm him."

"That is good," said Mary. "I need to meet them tomorrow when we get to York and confirm actions."

"That is agreed." Wychwoode stood up. "Now, I have other plans to prepare for tomorrow, so I will take my leave." He looked down at them. "I would you both retire early; we must all be refreshed and ready for the morning."

After Wychwoode had made his way out of the Great Hall, Tom turned to Mary and put his hand over hers. "Whatever the morrow brings," he said, "we have stories to tell, do we not?"

"Aye, Tom," she answered, putting her other hand over his, "but I feel that tomorrow's story will be the one to top them all."

CHAPTER TWENTY-FOUR

York

The streets of York were more crowded than the small local woman in her late thirties had ever known.

She found herself having to push her way through hundreds of men, women and children as they flowed past her like waves around a solitary rock, all rushing to secure the best place to see the Queen. She smiled to herself; they did not have what she had – a top-floor window that overlooked the Queen's procession route. The ramshackle timber-framed house she shared with her husband was only a couple of hundred yards further along the street, although with these crowds, it could have been ten times more for all the progress she was making. Clutching her recent purchases under each arm – a loaf of bread and a keg of ale – she battled her way up the cobbles, breathing a sigh of relief when she finally made it to her small wooden front door. The keg was becoming heavier with every step.

As she lifted the latch, she felt a hand on her arm, and turned.

A thin man in a leather jerkin was standing beside her. He lifted his cap to reveal hair that stood up in spikes, then smiled.

"Good day, mistress," he said, replacing his cap. "Do you live in this house?"

"Aye," she said cautiously.

"I am sure you are most keen to see Her Majesty," he continued, "when she makes her triumphant progress through York."

"Indeed," she replied. "It is a rare honour to see the Queen, but pray tell, what is your purpose?"

The man smiled again. "I have a request which maybe you can help me with."

She shifted the keg under her arm to try and get a little more comfortable. "Well, be quick with it – afore I drop this thing."

"Here," he said, taking it from her, "allow me."

She flexed her arm and shook it to try and clear the stiffness. "Most kind, sir, but I know not what you want."

"I want very much to see the Queen," the man replied, "but I have an uncommon fear of crowds. And as you see…" he waved cautiously at the stream of people still rushing past and starting to line up under the houses on either side, "there are too many people for my comfort down here on the street. So…" he finished with a hopeful raise of the eyebrow.

"So you would come up to the top of our house and watch from there?" the woman finished for him.

He nodded.

"Then yes," she said after a pause while she studied him carefully. "You can come and observe from our window, and you can stay until Her Majesty has passed."

He bowed slightly. "I am in your debt, mistress..?"

"Carter. Beth Carter. Wife of Amos, who waits above for his bread and ale."

"Richard Hornby, at your service."

"Well, Master Hornby," she replied, "Amos and I had planned to watch quietly, without a crowd at our window." She took a small breath, almost as if to reassure herself, and added, "And I have no doubt Amos will protest, but you have shown me kindness and one man is not a crowd, so I will let you up to see the Queen's progress from our window."

Picking up his sacking bag with his free hand, the Alchemist followed Beth up the narrow stairs to the top floor of her house.

---0---

It was half an hour later and the noise of the crowd below the Carters' open window was becoming deafening. The Alchemist shifted his position slightly. The slim gun was beside him on the table, which he had pushed under the window. His last three cartridges, not counting the one already in the breech, were standing in a row alongside the gun.

He took a sip of his ale and glanced round. Beth and Amos Carter were sitting with their backs to the wall. They had their arms tied behind them and linen rags were stuffed in their mouths, then secured round their heads with more rope. As he looked back, Beth struggled against her bonds and glared fiercely at him. Beside her Amos sat quietly, and the Alchemist saw him glance frequently over to a heavy metal poker leaning by the fire.

"I have tied you well, old man," he observed. "So give up all thought of reaching that poker."

Amos glared round at Beth, with eyes that said plainly that it was all her fault for letting this man in. Beth looked down and shook her head, as if to say how sorry she was. The Alchemist gave a small chuckle.

"You will live, fear not," he said. He took a bite out of the loaf of bread. Beth struggled again, her impotent rage clear in her burning stare. "Sit still," he ordered. "If I meant you harm, you would be dead by now, both of you." He turned back to look down the street at the crowds below, before adding over his shoulder, "You are more use to me alive, as I need you to bear witness to what I will do today. So calm down and this will soon be over."

He moved the gun further back on the table, before peering out to scan the crowds. "Best to keep this thing out of sight till the last minute," he said conversationally. "I would not want anyone spotting it before Her Majesty appears, now would I?" He took another gulp of ale and lovingly caressed the stock of the gun. "Everything I have worked for – everything – is for this moment."

---0---

Mary glanced behind as she pushed her way through the excited crowds that lined the street, checking that Wychwoode's two men were still with her. They were a few yards behind as planned, keeping close in case she spotted the Alchemist, but not too close that he would become suspicious. Mary glanced up from under her cap and scanned the windows of the houses above. As expected, they were all open, each with as many people crammed into them as possible, all waving and cheering at the distant royal procession as it made its way up the street behind her.

Mary's breathing was in short, ragged gasps – not only because she was feeling almost sick with fear, but also because the stench of the people she was pushing through was indescribable. At least the street itself had been swept clean of its usual human waste and laid with fresh straw for the Queen.

She came to a place where the pavement narrowed to a few feet, and the space was occupied by a couple of burly yeomen. One was the largest men she had ever seen; he must have been close to six and a half feet tall and had the build to match. She tried to push past but the two men refused to get out of her way.

"Please excuse me," she muttered.

"Hold your peace, boy," answered the giant man. "Wait here and you will see the Queen pass."

Mary took a breath to steady herself, and immediately wished she hadn't. Fighting the urge to retch at the man's smell, she said, "Forgive me sir, but I must get to my master's house up yonder before Her Majesty passes."

"Well wait, boy, and see Her Majesty first." The man chuckled. "What in the name of the Lord is the rush?"

"Belike he wants to find a better spot?" suggested the other man.

"Aye, in truth," said the first, and just as Mary tried to dodge into the open street to get past them, she found herself being grabbed around the waist by two massive arms, and hoisted up onto the man's shoulders as if she weighed no more than a fly.

"Let me down!" she yelled, and kicked at his chest.

The man laughed. "The lad has spirit, I say that!" He grabbed at Mary's legs so she could no longer kick. "Peace boy, you now have the best spot to see the Queen. See – she comes presently."

Mary looked back down the street. From this height she could see the procession clearly. Elizabeth was on her horse at the front, with Tom in a magnificent white doublet riding beside her and the Earl of Leicester on her other side. The Queen was waving at the cheering crowds and smiling, seeming to delight in the adoration of her subjects.

The procession was not more than three hundred yards away.

"Let me down, I say!" she yelled again, but the noise of the crowd meant her words were all but lost.

The procession was getting closer.

She glanced to her right, along the route.

There was a fork in the street ahead, with a small lane branching away up a hill. The lane was empty and had no straw laid down, so it was clearly not part of the royal route. A row of houses ran along the main part of the street backing onto the lane, with a ramshackle house sitting directly in the fork at the junction. She glanced briefly up at the top floor.

The window was wide open, and it was empty.

Every other window was crammed full of people. This window, with a prime view directly along the route below, had no one.

She glanced quickly up again, just in time to see a dark spiky head appear briefly then withdraw into the room.

She looked back at the Queen, sitting high on her horse, now only a couple of hundred yards away, a clear target with full line of sight from the window.

"Let me go!" she shrieked at the man, trying to kick against his arms and chest.

But it was too late.

In sick horror she saw the barrel of the gun glinting in the sunlight as it slid out of the window, and hold steady as it pointed directly at the Queen.

Drawing in her deepest breath she turned towards Tom and yelled as loud as she possibly could, "Tom!"

The yell, coming as it did from above the heads of the crowd, carried across to Tom, just as her yell had done once before in the forest. She saw him look across at her, and she pointed up at the window. She must have been a distant figure but she was high above the crowd so he could not miss her. She saw him lift his head and follow her finger up towards the window. Immediately she saw him grab the Queen's bridle, then he turned Her Majesty away.

At the same moment Mary heard a sound like a breaking branch and saw a puff of smoke come from the window.

She looked back at Tom and the Queen.

The scene appeared frozen still; Tom with his back to her and the Queen out of sight behind him.

Then a small red mark appeared between Tom's broad white shoulders.

It started to get bigger, just as a rosebud opens and grows, until his whole back was bright red.

Then he slowly slid off his horse and disappeared from view.

"Tom!" Mary screamed again, and this time the Queen looked up. Even across the distance between them, Mary could see the fear in the woman's eyes. She was hemmed in by all the courtiers around her, unable to turn and ride away, again exposed to the unseen assassin. If she were hit, then not only would history change forever, but Tom, presumably mortally wounded, would have died in vain.

Mary looked back at the window. The gun barrel had disappeared – presumably the Alchemist was reloading.

Just then one of Wychwoode's men appeared below her, his sword unsheathed. He pushed it up at the yeoman's chest.

"Let her down," he commanded, taking a stance which showed he was prepared to back up his words by thrusting the sword.

The yeoman reached up and lifted Mary off his shoulders. "Her? I thought it was a boy?"

Immediately Mary was back on the ground she called to Wychwoode's man, "That window there!" She pointed up. "Come!"

Together they ran to the door of the end house. The man kicked it in easily, and Mary followed him up the dark stairs. At the top there was another door. The man kicked this one in as well and ran into the room.

Mary saw the Alchemist at the window, leaning along the table, his sleeves rolled up and the tattoos of guns clearly visible on both arms.

The sniper rifle was pointed towards the Queen, and the Alchemist was looking as if he was preparing to take the second shot. At the sound of the door bursting open he swung round and fired at Wychwoode's man. The sound of the gun was unnaturally loud in the small space.

Blood exploded from the man's back and he went down like a felled tree.

Mary froze.

Despite all the preparation for this moment – both mental and physical – she froze.

Now that she was in front of Rick, with the gun in his hand, all her planned responses went out of her head. The only thing in her mind as she watched him pick up one of the two cartridges from the table was the phrase 'rabbit in the headlights'. He opened the breech of the gun, then quickly shook it to release the spent cartridge. It fell out with a puff of smoke. He smoothly slotted the new cartridge in and closed the gun. Then he raised it so it pointed directly at Mary's chest.

"I had thought you had both died in the fire," he said, "till I saw lover boy there leap out in front of the Queen and get his back blown open."

She shook her head. Tom was dead. The thought of it was like a block of ice in place of her heart.

"Yeah," the Alchemist continued, "so it is no surprise that you've showed up like a fucking bad penny."

In the distance, the Queen could be seen starting to wheel her horse round and shouting for the courtiers to let her through. "It looks like I have to make a choice," the Alchemist said. "Do I kill the Queen before she gets away, or you?" He turned back to the window and lined up the shot. "The Queen first, then we'll see about you."

In that moment, Mary's head suddenly cleared and she knew exactly what she had to do.

Leaping swiftly over the body of Wychwoode's man, she grabbed the heavy poker propped up by the fireplace. As the Alchemist started to glance back over his shoulder, she brought it down with all her might on his right arm, directly on the tattoo of the crossed rifles.

It landed with a sickening thud that she felt sure had broken the bone.

The Alchemist gave a thin, agonised shriek and stood up, keeping hold of the stock of the gun in his left hand; his right arm now hanging uselessly at his side.

"You bitch!" he yelled. "You fucking bitch!" He started hefting the gun to get his left hand down towards the trigger, while at the same time raising the barrel towards her chest. Mary lifted the poker again and this time brought it down as hard as she could on his left arm, directly on the tattoo of the single pistol.

The Alchemist let out a bellow of pain and rage and dropped the gun. As it fell, the trigger must have hit the leg of the table, and it fired. Mary saw the shot slam into a wooden chest and the gun recoil across the room into a far corner.

"Damn you Justine, you meddling little bitch!" yelled the Alchemist, standing with both arms hanging by his side. "What the fuck do you think you're trying to achieve?"

"I'm saving history. The history we know." Over his shoulder, she could see the Queen riding away, and men carrying Tom's body back down the street.

"Saving history? What fucking history? It hasn't happened yet," the Alchemist sneered at her. "And now you're here, it probably never will, anyway." He looked her up and down, his mouth twisted in pain. "You had kids?" She nodded. "Then it's never going to be the same, is it? Who knows what changes they'll make? So me killing Gloriana there, that might not be as big a change as you've made already."

"What about you changing things so I'm never born at all?"

"Is that what this is really all about?"

Mary saw the Alchemist's eyes flicker across to where the gun lay, seeming to measure the distance. She wasn't sure what he could achieve with two broken arms, but she gripped the poker and raised it higher just in case. She glanced at his arms; the tattoos of the guns and the pistol had almost disappeared under the rapidly blackening wheals.

"Listen," he said through gritted teeth, "you and me, we were born in the 1980s. At the time we were born, history had not changed. So whatever difference you make now, nothing can alter the fact you were born when you were – and any changes you or I make, it's to a parallel future, not the one we came from." He stopped and his face twisted once again with the pain. "And you're still fucking here aren't you? You haven't suddenly disappeared because of some change to the future, have you?" He shook his head. "More's the fucking pity. So you know what, Justine, you little bitch," he winced in pain, "nothing you or I have done has stopped us being here, but whatever the future will be now, it's never going to be what we knew. That's gone." He nodded across to the open window. "A bit like Gloriana there. Looks like she got away today – but who knows what might happen the next time?" He glanced for a fraction of a second across to the gun. "At least lover boy there took one for the team."

If that was meant to distract Mary so he could get to the gun, it failed.

Keeping hold of the poker tightly in both hands, she flexed her wrists, lifting the tip higher.

Then she waited for her moment.

He stared at the poker, then back at her, with ill-concealed loathing.

She watched his eyes, as intently as a hawk watches a mouse.

No doubt he knew that to look away was a disastrous move, but eventually he stole the briefest glance across at the gun.

It was all she needed.

As his eyes slid off the poker, she hefted it back and in one clean move, swung it down and round as hard as she could on his left shin.

It connected with the noise of an axe hitting a tree trunk, and this time she was sure there was an additional crack as the bone snapped.

Rick went down with a thin scream, hitting his head with a sickening thump on the side of the table as he went. He collapsed on the floor and was immediately still.

She waited what seemed like an age, but he remained motionless.

Was he bluffing?

She crouched down, the poker raised in case he made any move. Slowly, carefully, she touched his eyelid. There was no response. She eased it open, to reveal that his eye had rolled up into his head.

He was out cold.

She looked at his impassive face. Rick, the catering manager at Grangedean Manor who had been nothing more than an annoying colleague in the 21st century, had become a time-traveller like her – and so had become the only person in this strange Elizabethan world who could really understand her. But he had turned out to be a monster, attacking women and trying to assassinate the Queen.

Yet it was he who had worked out the time-travel conundrum – that the time-traveller can never actually endanger their own existence, because their birth took place in a parallel version of the future, one that could never be altered. No changes made to the future by her and her family could possibly prevent her birth in the 1980s.

But was he right? If so, then maybe one good thing would have come from this encounter; she could finally put her concerns about her existence to rest.

She was never going to just 'disappear'…

Mary sighed. All those years of hiding at Grangedean Manor! All those years of fearing to set foot outside in case she changed something pivotal – had that all been a mistake?

What excitement and adventures could she have enjoyed in Elizabethan England, if she had just been a bit braver and a bit bolder?

She glanced down at Rick.

Maybe this adventure had more than made up for it – except that too many good people had got hurt, or worse, along the way. She leaned down over the still body of the Alchemist.

"Rick Hornby," whispered, "I once promised Thomas Melrose I would beat you for what you did to Olivia." She looked at the poker in her hand. "That was for her – and for Agnes and for Ursula," she paused a moment, "and for my dear friend, Juno." She prodded him with the tip of the poker and he groaned slightly. "And, more than anything, that was for Tom."

There was the sound of a different, higher-pitched groan behind her.

She turned and noticed a man and a woman sitting up against the wall, bound and gagged.

Their pleading eyes met hers.

Quickly she untied them, and while they were carefully standing and easing the blood back into their arms and legs, she checked the Alchemist's pulse. It was faint, but still there, so she used the ropes that had so recently bound the two of them to bind his blackened arms tightly behind his back.

"By Heaven, mistress," the man said slowly, "I have ne'er seen such skill with a weapon – and ne'er by a woman – as you showed with that poker." He shook his head and turned to the woman as if for affirmation. "Such targeted strikes to stop the man in his treasonous endeavour! One on each arm and one on the legs, eh Beth?"

"Aye, t'was well done, Amos," replied Beth. "The man got his just rewards."

Just then there was the sound of feet pounding up the stairs, and Wychwoode burst in. He took in the Alchemist lying bloody and bound at Mary's feet and the open window with its view down the street.

"By Heaven, my lady, you have succeeded! The man is stopped while the Queen is safe and unharmed!" A deep frown crossed his face. "But Mary, I have to tell you that Thomas Cobham is hit."

"I know. I saw him killed."

"But no! He lives still. He asks for you."

A sudden hope rose, like a flame coming back to life in a dying fire. "He still lives?" Mary asked, her voice rising unnaturally high. "Where is he? I must see him!"

"There was a barber-surgeon living close to the place where he was hit – it is the house with a green door. He was taken there and the man is doing all he can for Cobham's comfort. Go now, go! I will see to this filthy monster who you have bound so well for me." He crouched down and put a finger to the Alchemist's neck. "By Heaven, he has been beaten most soundly. It is a wonder that he still lives!"

---0---

Mary ran up to the green door. A soldier with a halberd and silver breastplate was standing guard.

"Let me in!" Mary shouted. "I must see Tom Cobham!"

"Art Lady Mary de Beauvais?" asked the man, staring curiously at her clothing.

"Yes!"

He stood aside. "I have been ordered to let you in if you arrived, disguised in the garb of a boy," he said.

Mary ran past him and into the front room, taking off her cap and shaking out her hair as she ran.

It was dark, with only a couple of candles casting a meagre glow in the room. As Mary's eyes became accustomed to the dim light, she could see a man lying on a table, with a woman leaning over him, sponging his forehead gently with a damp cloth. A man in a red velvet cap stood at the end of the table mixing some powders with a pestle and mortar, and a dark-haired nobleman stood beside him. Mary realised that the man on the table who was breathing quick, shallow, ragged breaths was Tom.

Then she gave a small gasp. The woman gently tending to him was Queen Elizabeth.

She went up to the table. She could see that Tom was conscious, as his eyes followed her as she approached.

Mary bowed to Elizabeth. "How is he, Your Majesty?"

Elizabeth looked up. "As well as can be expected, given that he shielded me with his body and took the shot aimed at me." She stared at Mary. "A woman dressed in boy's garb? Then you must be the Lady Mary he has been asking for." Mary nodded. "Then do you wish to tend to Sir Thomas yourself?"

The Queen stood back and handed over the cloth. Mary knelt by the table and stroked Tom's cheek. "Sir Thomas, eh?" she said softly. "That was nice." She wiped his forehead. "What did you have to get yourself shot for?"

"I heard your call," he whispered. "Your loud fishwife shriek was just what we needed."

"But you were supposed to pull Her Majesty out of the way. Not shield her and take the shot yourself."

"Aye." He coughed, his eyes never leaving hers. "But it seemed the right thing to do."

"And it got you wounded."

"It got me killed."

"No!" she whispered.

"Aye. It has to be said. And anyway," he said softly, "it saved the life of the Queen, did it not? See how she lives now, and has seen fit to make me Sir Tom."

"Yes, but…"

He frowned. "Was that not what we intended?"

"Well, yes, but…."

"So, that is settled." He coughed again and some blood appeared at the side of his mouth. Mary wiped it away. "It is a story to tell, is it not? We had some good times together." He coughed another time, and his breathing became more ragged.

The man in the red velvet cap came over with a glass. "Some tonic, Sir Thomas, to restore your health?" The man held the glass below Tom's mouth. Tom took a sip, then the man stepped back. "This fellow is a surgeon, who thinks a tonic will mend the hole in my back," Tom whispered to Mary. "He is either a fool, or he thinks I am one."

"For sure, we will have you restored to health again, Tom," blurted Mary. "For I will die as well if you are not with me."

"Please, my love, do not say such a thing," breathed Tom. "You have a husband who loves you well, and who needs you more than I." He reached out a hand and gently stroked her cheek. "Ask Wychwoode," he breathed. "He will tell you all about Sir William."

"Ask him what?"

"Do but ask him."

"I will."

"Good." He took a couple of laboured breaths. "But I do have one question for you."

"What is that, my love?"

"Back in the forest," he whispered, so faintly that she now had to put her ear right up to his mouth, "the Alchemist called you by some other name, and talked of the future." He coughed again quietly. "At the time I thought it strange, and I must confess I wondered if you were somehow in league with him."

"Nay, my love. I wanted to stop him. I had to stop him," she answered.

"So you were never in league with him." She felt his breath on her cheek as he sighed. "That is good. I needed to be sure of that."

"I swore so at the time," she whispered.

"I know, and I needed to confess to you how I did not fully believe you. I am so sorry, dearest Mary. Will you forgive me? I must know."

She turned and looked into his eyes. "Of course I forgive you, my love."

"Good," he breathed. "Then I go in peace." He paused again as he tried to draw in a ragged breath. Then he said in a louder voice, "Farewell Mary. Fare thee well, my dearest love."

He took two more rasping breaths, then was still.

Mary threw herself onto his neck, as great sobs racked her body. Tom had gone… Tom, who had saved her from that foul man in the Blue Maid; who had been her constant companion and friend; who had always been the perfect gentleman; who had made the ultimate sacrifice to save the Queen's life. Tom, who had said his heart was hers…

She felt a hand on her shoulder. After a moment she looked up. It was the dark-haired nobleman – whom she now recognised as the Earl of Leicester. "Come, Lady Mary," he said gently, "he is gone. We will have him removed for burial."

Mary stood, and Leicester steered her gently out of the room, along the corridor and out into a small courtyard. The Queen followed.

As Mary blinked to re-accustom her eyes to the bright sunlight, there was the sound of boots coming through the house, and once again Wychwoode appeared. He bowed to the Queen, and Mary saw he was carrying the gun.

"This is the weapon, Your Majesty," he said, holding it up. "The man had fashioned it himself." He held up the one remaining cartridge. "He combined both powder and ball into one capsule, so he was able to prime and load the weapon in but a few seconds."

Leicester reached for the gun and turned it over in his hands, then peered through the telescopic sight. "This is a most remarkable piece," he said slowly. "We must study and learn from it, so we can use its superior fire power and accuracy ourselves. It will give us great advantage over our enemies – we will win many more battles with this."

"I agree, but let us address this in good time, Robin," said the Queen. She turned back to Wychwoode. "For now, what of the murderer himself?"

"He is bound and secured, madam," Wychwoode answered, taking the gun back from Leicester.

"He must be dealt with appropriately," the Queen said.

"Of course, madam," answered Wychwoode, then he added, "though he has already taken grievous wounds to both arms and to one of his legs."

The Queen raised an eyebrow. "Why? How did he come by such injuries?"

Wychwoode looked at Mary. "It seems Lady de Beauvais set about him most grievously with a sturdy poker."

"Did she indeed?" Elizabeth turned to Mary. "I must respect your strength."

"I used the poker on the first arm to stop him firing on you after he had shot Tom… Sir Thomas, Your Majesty," Mary answered. "Then he tried to fire the weapon at me, so I hit the other arm. Then…" she stopped, and shook her head. "I wanted to stop him for good, so I hit his leg to bring him down."

"With the force to give it a clean break, madam," added Wychwoode. "The man will surely not walk to the gallows."

"Well, it sounds as if you were successful, my dear Lady Mary." The Queen turned to Leicester. "You see, Robin, a woman can be as strong as a man, if she is driven to it." She thought for a moment, her piercing dark eyes fixed on Mary. "And I saw you in the crowd, did I not? It was your cry that Sir Thomas heard... so, Lady Mary, it was your actions that saved my life – not once, it seems, but twice." Without taking her eyes off Mary, she said, "You know, Robin, I have long been saying that we should look at how much we subjugate women by law. Lady Mary here is perhaps real proof that those laws are in serious need of review."

Leicester nodded. "As you wish, madam."

The Queen turned to Wychwoode. "And what of the man's motive? Is he backed by a Catholic plot or was this a lone action?"

"We believe he has Catholic backers, madam," replied Wychwoode, "and we are in the process of arresting them shortly." He paused. "But we also have some insight into the man's own motives, as he confided in the owner of the house and his wife, who were his unwilling captives. It seems he was not himself a Catholic, nor was he motivated by religious zeal – for all it seems…" he paused, seeming to struggle to contain his emotion, "…it seems, that he worshipped Satan instead." He fished for something in his pocket, then opened his hand to reveal Rick's lighter. The skull looked up at them, glinting wickedly in the sunlight. The Queen drew back with a gasp. "This is a miniature tinder box," explained Wychwoode, "and it is clearly a talisman to Satanic worship. It was found in his bag."

The Queen appeared to go whiter than Mary thought possible. "We shall not have such devilry in our presence," she commanded in a strangled whisper. "Take it away now." She paused a moment, then added, "It shows us how this man is beyond any form of understanding."

Leicester took it and examined it dispassionately, as Wychwoode continued, "It appears his motivation was also self-advancement – he expected ennoblement from the Queen of Scots, were she to have usurped your throne."

"Thanks to the quick actions of Lady Mary and Sir Thomas Cobham, we are spared that disaster, are we not?" said Leicester, handing the lighter back to Wychwoode. "And what of his Catholic backers?"

"We believe we know their ringleader, my lord," answered Wychwoode, wrapping the lighter gingerly in a cloth and putting it back in his pocket.

"I want him found and caught," said the Queen firmly, seeming to have recovered her composure now the lighter was out of sight. "I do not want him to escape justice, nor be free to start another plot."

Wychwoode nodded. "We will be making every effort to apprehend him."

The Queen stared at him a moment. "Well, see that you do. Or I will ask Lady Mary here to do it for you. She seems to have a way of stopping my enemies in their tracks."

Wychwoode bowed but said nothing.

The Queen drew Mary to one side. "I have never seen such devilry as that tinder box," she said, shaking her head. "This man must pay dearly for all he is, and all he has done."

Mary nodded, and said nothing.

"In faith, we are forever in your debt, my dear Lady Mary," the Queen continued quietly. "Your husband is Sir William?" Mary nodded again. "I have heard of him, of course, but never had him presented. You are both most welcome at Court. We would see more of you and greatly enjoy your council in future."

Mary curtseyed. "As you wish, Your Majesty."

Elizabeth studied Mary again with her dark eyes. "You know…" she began, then paused and took a breath, "…when Sir Thomas took the shot in his back, his face was before mine. As close as you are now… I saw the moment he was hit." Mary said nothing; Elizabeth was clearly finding this difficult, but wanted to get out what was on her mind. "When the ball struck… I saw the shock and pain in his eyes – and… he knew it was mortal, but…" she shook her head, "he seemed almost *pleased*… as if he knew he *deserved* it…" Elizabeth nodded. "I wanted you to know, my dear. In case that meant something to you."

"Thank you, madam. Yes, it does."

There was a moment of pure understanding that passed between the two women. It was only brief, but just for a second, Mary felt closer to Elizabeth than she had ever felt to any other adult.

Then the moment passed, and once more the Queen became the decisive monarch. She turned to Leicester. "Come Robin," she said, "we must return to Wyvern Castle. Tomorrow we prepare for our journey back down south. Good-bye, my dear Lady Mary. We shall see you back at Wyvern, no doubt." With that, she swept out, followed by Leicester.

Mary turned to Wychwoode. "Tom said a strange thing before he died. He said there was something I was to ask you about William. What did he mean?"

Wychwoode drew a long, careful breath. "There is indeed some news I have to give you, Lady Mary, concerning your husband Sir William, and your son Ambrose, and the dangerous situation they now find themselves in…"

CHAPTER TWENTY-FIVE

Mary gripped her knees tighter on the saddle and lowered her head, coming down so close to the horse's mane that it whipped across her face with every galloping stride.

Beside her, Olivia Melrose was also crouched low over her own horse's mane, as the two of them thundered along the path from York to Hetherington Hall, their hair flying loose behind them.

It was not more than half an hour since Wychwoode had given her the news that not only had William remained at Hetherington Hall for all this time, but that now he and Ambrose were being held hostage by the lead plotter – and that was Lambert Moreton.

But worst of all, Wychwoode had reason to believe that the lives of her son and husband were dependent on Moreton hearing of the death of Elizabeth. And since she had just prevented that from happening, their lives were now hanging by the slimmest of threads. Which was why it was imperative that she get to Hetherington Hall as fast as possible, before any message reached Moreton from York.

Wychwoode had also muttered something about a promise to Tom to send men to Hetherington, but Mary had neither the time nor inclination to wait while he arranged this – no, this was her mission, her responsibility. With a parting yell to send them as soon as possible if he cared to do so, she had raced out of the surgeon's house and found a mounted soldier. Shouting that she was on the Queen's business, she demanded that he take her to Wyvern Castle with all speed. Fortunately the man had not asked questions, but helped her mount up behind him and had ridden like the wind.

It had been but a few minutes' work to secure a horse from the Wyvern stables, just as Olivia had arrived back in her carriage from York. Seeing Mary so desperate to ride out, Olivia had insisted on coming as well. Despite Mary's protests, the girl had leapt onto the next available horse and galloped out after her.

As she rode, Mary tried to think what she would do to rescue her husband and son when she arrived at the Hall. What she really needed was a plan.

Although what she did have, was the gun.

She had grabbed it and the last remaining cartridge from Wychwoode as she ran out – with something about her need being greater than his – and it was now strapped to her back as she rode.

As if reading her mind, Olivia shouted across, "What is your plan, my lady?"

"My only thought is to take up position to watch from a distance. Then we can decide what is best to do."

A few minutes later a high stone wall appeared through the woods, and the path turned to follow it. Mary slowed her horse and trotted alongside it for a few minutes. "I think this is the wall of the Hetherington Hall grounds," she said. "We need to get over."

She pulled her horse up and it skittered to a stop, breathing hard and steam rising from its flanks. Mary stood in her stirrups and slowly raised her head over the top of the wall. There was Hetherington Hall. Even from the side it was easy to identify the magnificent wings and the main steps beyond with their guardian stone lions. "Aye, it is," she said.

She sat back in her saddle. "We should tie the horses here, and drop over the wall."

Olivia nodded, and tied her horse to a nearby tree. Mary did the same, then together they stood in their stirrups, stepped up onto their saddles and lifted themselves onto the wall.

Dropping lightly down onto soft earth on the other side, Mary crouched and started studying the land ahead of them. There was a soft thud behind her, then Olivia appeared alongside.

The woodland trees extended a few yards in front of them, before opening out into separate cultivated gardens, each bordered by box hedges at around five or six feet high. Beyond these was an incline up to the side of the house, which rose majestically into the blue sky; its red brick walls set with diamond-paned windows and topped with twisted brick chimneys.

Mary reached behind her and took the gun from its strap, then dropped to her belly, sinking down into the soft leafy earth. She settled herself with the gun pointing up at the house and squinted through the sight. Immediately the building leapt into sharp focus. The Alchemist had certainly known what he was doing – the magnification and clarity were excellent. He had even added cross-hairs for better aiming. Mary shivered as she imagined him centring these on Elizabeth and squeezing the trigger, at precisely the moment that Tom's back had appeared instead.

"Pray tell, my lady, what exactly is that silver stick in your hands?" asked Olivia, lying down beside her.

Mary swept the scope across the side of the house, but saw no movement. "You recall I told you when all this started, that I was going to London seeking out a man? A man that I would ask questions that only he could answer?"

"I do," said Olivia.

"And I also told you when we met at the gates, that there was a plot on the life of the Queen?"

"Of course."

"Well, I found the man. And it turns out I was wrong to seek him. It was he who would kill the Queen – and he made this weapon to carry out the killing."

"By Heaven, my lady!" Olivia squeaked. She paused a moment. "So that was why we at the rear of the progress were sent back to Wyvern early. This man made his attempt on the Queen's life!"

Mary caught some movement out of the corner of her eye and trained the scope on the place she thought she had seen it, but there was nothing more than the branches of a willow tree swaying in the gentle breeze. She moved on to study the side of the house but there was no sign of life. She let her breath out gently; she had not even been aware that she had been holding it. "Yes," she said. "The Queen was saved by Tom, throwing himself in the path of the shot."

"Master Cobham did that?" asked Olivia. "Does he survive?"

Mary looked up and shook her head. After a moment, Olivia put her hand on Mary's and said, "I am so sorry, my lady. I know you were close to Master Cobham."

"Sir Thomas." Mary squinted back down the scope again. "Her Majesty saw fit to knight him before he died."

"Oh. That was kind of her."

There was another flash of movement and Mary swung the gun round.

Then her heart skipped a beat.

Moreton and three men were walking down the main steps and out of the house.

"She is most..." Olivia began, in the same loud conversational tone.

"Shh!" Mary hissed.

Olivia was immediately silent, but perhaps it was already too late. As Mary watched through the scope, Moreton stopped abruptly, signalling to the men behind him to stop also. He stared slowly around, as if searching for the source of the distant sound he had just heard. Mary tried to sink further into the soft earth, but she knew that if she could see Moreton above the box hedges, then he could potentially see her.

She lay as still as she could, scarcely breathing, as Moreton stared across the park. Had he heard Olivia? Something had made him stop – did he know it was a voice, or would he perhaps think it was something else? Beside her, Olivia lay still as well. Both were wearing dull-coloured clothing – with luck they would merge into the leafy floor of the woodland. The stock of the gun felt clammy in her hands. It was still raised, but she dared not move it down, for fear that the movement itself would catch the sunlight and be spotted.

As Mary watched through the scope, Moreton continued to sweep his gaze across the grounds. Her finger hovered over the trigger, as she eased the cross-hairs into position, placing his head dead centre. How easy would it be to squeeze the trigger and rid herself – and Elizabeth – of this vile plotter?

But right now, the gun was not loaded.

Moreton gestured to one of his men, but the man was beyond Mary's view. She remained still, not daring to move the gun a millimetre. The man came into view. She saw Moreton gesture to him again, pointing towards the trees where Mary and Olivia lay. The man nodded, and started walking directly towards them.

Almost as if in slow motion, the man made his way down from the path onto their level. Now Mary could only see the top of his head above the box hedges, heading in their direction. Soon he would emerge onto flat ground and have a clear view of them.

Mary felt in the pocket of her jerkin for the last remaining cartridge. There it was, solid and reassuring. Slowly she grasped it between thumb and forefinger, and eased it out. It may be her only shot, but she couldn't think of any other option than to use the weapon on this man and prevent him finding her and Olivia. Shooting him would give them time to escape back over the wall to their horses, then ride for help in finding William and Ambrose.

She shifted the cartridge into the palm of her hand, so she could release the catch and open the breech with her fingers, just wide enough to insert the cartridge.

The man was now only one hedge away from the open.

Mary winkled the cartridge back towards her thumb and forefinger, ready to slide it into the breech, snap it shut, and shoot.

But her hand was too sweaty.

As she felt the metal case on her fingertip, it slipped out and dropped onto the rough earth at her side.

Desperately she patted the earth around where it fell, trying to find it.

She saw the man turn his head to one side – he was looking for a way round the last hedge. He started walking along it.

As he did so, Mary knew she only had seconds while his attention was diverted, to find the cartridge, load and fire. She looked down at her side, but there were leaves all around, and she could not see it.

But she did see Olivia's arm make a sudden sharp movement and something dark fly out of her hand.

The man came to the break in the hedge and started to turn.

Then there was a sudden loud cawing from a tree further along, as a number of birds shot up into the air. The man looked startled, then craned his head up to watch the birds as they circled noisily overhead.

By the time he looked down again and stepped round the hedge, Mary and Olivia had run back and were now hiding behind nearby trees.

Mary held her breath and waited.

She heard the man shout, "T'was naught but rooks!"

She waited another few minutes, then peered cautiously round the tree. All four men were now walking along the path away from the house, and were nearly out of sight.

Signalling to Olivia to stay where she was, Mary dropped into a crouch and ran back to where they had lain. There was the cartridge, poking out from under a leaf. Picking it up, she ran back to Olivia.

"That was close," she said. "You threw a stone at the tree?"

Olivia nodded. "I saw the rooks up there and took the chance while he looked away."

"Good. Well done. It diverted them all." Mary looked back at where Moreton and his men had gone. "We must follow them. Come."

---0---

Mary squinted through the scope and swung the gun back and forward, but could see nothing but trees, sky and grass. She lowered it slightly, then tried again.

This time Moreton and his men flashed past. She swung it gently back a fraction, and the four men came into view, walking together along the path. She followed them for a moment, then swung the gun past them, looking to see where they were heading. After a moment the magnificent main gates came into view, looking solid and impenetrable in the early afternoon sun. She panned slowly back, once more picking up the four men, but at this distance and with the foreshortening effect of the scope, it was impossible to tell how far they were from the gates. She followed them further, her cross-hairs trained on Moreton's thin, sandy head.

The men reached the heavy wooden gates and stopped.

Then they seemed to wait, standing silently in a small group.

Why did they not go through? What were they waiting for?

"What passes, my lady?" whispered Olivia, her voice no more than a breath in the still air.

"They wait, standing about as if with naught to do." Mary's voice was equally quiet.

"By the gates?" asked Olivia.

"Aye." Mary shifted her position slightly; her arm holding the stock was starting to protest at being kept so long in the same position. "I know not why."

"Belike they await news from York?"

Mary cursed under her breath. Of course! They were waiting for a messenger to tell them news of the Queen. News that would be catastrophic for her husband and son.

Once again, she trained the sight on Moreton.

Should she kill him now, to stop him hearing the news?

She lined up the cross-hairs so that Moreton's head was dead centre. Her finger found the trigger, and started to curl round it. She slowed her breath… and started to pull.

"Oh by the Lord!" Olivia breathed suddenly.

Mary's finger came off the trigger and she looked up at Olivia. "What passes?" she asked, her voice shaking and her breath now rasping in her throat. "I would have killed him in that instant."

"See!" Olivia pointed. "The gate is opening. It must be a messenger who comes!"

Mary looked back through the scope. Sure enough, two of Moreton's men were pulling the heavy wooden gate open, and Moreton was walking towards it with a look of anticipation.

Mary shifted the gun slightly, moving the cross-hairs to head height at the side of the gate, waiting to see a man's head appear.

If this man was a messenger, maybe the better option would be to silence him instead, before he could announce the news that the Queen was not dead.

She brought her finger back to the trigger, and slowed her breath.

The gate continued to swing, until it was fully ninety degrees open. But whoever the man was, he remained hidden, apparently talking to Moreton from behind its solid cover.

"Blast!" muttered Mary, "Why does he not show himself so I can get a shot?"

But suddenly it was too late.

Moreton staggered and clutched at the side of the gate for support. His mouth made a small 'O' shape and he shook his head vigorously. He looked back at the hidden man and asked a question. The man must have answered, most likely confirming the unwelcome news, for Moreton then turned away and let out an anguished howl that could clearly be heard by the watching women. Then he snapped back, and suddenly an evil looking rapier was in his hand, glinting in the sunlight. With another howl, Moreton thrust the rapier out of sight behind the gate, then withdrew it almost as fast.

As Mary watched in horror, a man in a black cape and hat toppled like a felled tree from behind the gate and lay prostrate on the path.

Without a backward glance, Moreton shouted an order to his men, then stepped over the body and walked out of the gate. The other three followed behind. The last man tried to pull the gate shut behind him, but the messenger was in the way. After a brief and half-hearted attempt to kick the man's body aside, he left the gate open and scurried through.

Mary pushed the gun into the makeshift sling on her back and jumped up.

"Come on," she said to Olivia. "We must follow!"

Together they ran across the lawn and soon arrived at the gate.

Mary took in the sight of the man lying on the path, the stones all around him running bright red with his blood. As she reached him, she dropped to her knees and put a finger to his neck. As she suspected, there was no pulse. "We can do nothing for this unfortunate fellow," she muttered, "though I would have killed him sooner myself if I could." Then she ran around him and out of the gate.

They quickly reached a fork in the path.

Mary gave barely a glance to the left fork, and immediately turned right.

"This way!" she hissed. "I think I know exactly where they have gone!"

Without waiting for Olivia, Mary ran along the stony path until it reached the edge of the ravine. She skittered to a stop on the loose pebbles and turned to find Olivia right behind her.

"Wait a moment," she whispered.

Together they peered cautiously over the edge of the path. It dropped away from them down the side of the ravine, then zigzagged its way to the floor below. Some way down, they could see the heads of the four men walking along.

Mary pulled back.

"Art well, my lady?" asked Olivia. "You are as white as the snow."

Mary shook her head. "Nay," she muttered. "They go to a watchman's hut at the bottom, I am sure of it. That is where they hold my husband and my son." She looked up at Olivia. "And unless we can stop them, they go to kill both my men."

"We must do something to stop them, my lady!"

"Yes," said Mary, then turned to Olivia. "And I think I have a plan for that – in which you must play a major part."

Olivia smiled. "Whatever I can do, Lady Mary, that I will."

---0---

Mary took aim through the scope, lining up Moreton's thin head once again in the cross-hairs.

"Moreton!" she called out as loud as she could. Her voice echoed around the still air, crashing off the stone walls and whipping around the trees that lined the base of the ravine where he stood.

Moreton turned around and around, spinning on his heel as he tried to locate the source of the call.

"Who's there?" he shouted back. "Reveal yourself!"

"Up here!" called Mary.

He looked up, continuing to spin round. Then he must have spotted her as a distant figure standing on the path high above him and he stopped, staring directly at her; his face in the centre of the scope. Mary moved the cross-hairs up from his sharp, thin nose to the wispy hair falling over his forehead.

"Who's there?" he repeated.

"I am Lady Mary de Beauvais, who you would have dismissed as a vagrant serving woman."

There was a silence, as Moreton continued to stare directly at Mary.

"Then you know I hold your husband and your son," he shouted back. "Do you give me cause that I should not kill them now?"

"I do." Mary called. "For I hold the very weapon that the Alchemist would have used to kill Queen Elizabeth on your orders." She paused. "And I am pointing it directly at your head."

"The very weapon?" He gave a sly smile. "Then I must assume you took it from the Alchemist by force, for I do not think he would have given it up willingly."

"I took it after I stopped him from using it on Queen Elizabeth."

He nodded slowly. "I am impressed. You have shown yourself a match for a man." He whispered something out of the side of his mouth that Mary could not catch – presumably an order to one of his men. "Too bad that your companion, Tom Cobham, was not so fortunate. I never met him, but I was told he cleaved to our cause, and even helped us secure the Alchemist. Now I see he was working against me. Or you turned him – I know not which." He looked away again and nodded to one of his men. "I understand he performed a sterling service for the heretic bastard that styles herself 'queen' – by choosing to die in her place."

Mary's finger tightened on the trigger.

"Aye!" she called back. "A noble gesture, Moreton, if that means anything to you."

"Oh indeed, it means something to me. It means that you and Cobham together have stopped my plan to rid us of this bastard heretic and place the true Queen Mary of Scotland on her throne. Cobham is dealt with, but you are not."

"You forget I am pointing a weapon at your head. I can split it open like a sack of flour."

Moreton did not reply. Instead he smiled broadly at her, then he nodded again to one of the men standing beside him.

Taking her finger off the trigger, Mary looked around the scope to get a full picture of the scene below.

Although the figures were distant, she could see that Moreton was standing a few yards in front of the watchman's hut. Two of his men were standing close to him, and the third was holding a small boy that struggled and wriggled in his arms.

Ambrose!

As Mary watched, Moreton crossed over and took Ambrose from the man. Then he crossed back to where he had been standing.

Mary put her eye back to the scope.

With surprising strength in his thin frame, Moreton was holding the boy up so that Ambrose's body acted as a perfect shield.

"Go ahead, Lady Mary!" Moreton called out from behind Ambrose. "Please discharge the weapon. Marry, you just might cause me a fatal wound, but I fear it is much more likely you will hit this fine boy here."

"Damn you, Moreton! Let my son go!"

"Ma!" called out Ambrose. "Ma! Is that you, Ma? Make him put me down!" He started kicking at Moreton's thighs.

"The boy has spirit, does he not?" called Moreton. "Truly his mother's son! But I warrant that if he does not cease to kick me, I will have his throat cut."

"Stay still, Bambi!" Mary shouted. She studied her son's face in the scope, his little features set into a scowl as he stopped kicking at Moreton.

Then suddenly a knife appeared by his throat.

She swung the gun round, and saw one of Moreton's men was now standing next to Ambrose, holding the knife. The man gave a broad grin in her direction, revealing a mouth containing only a few blackened teeth, then settled his stance.

Mary swung the gun the other way, until she could see the other two men, each standing watching Moreton, her son and their knife-wielding comrade.

She also noted what was happening behind these two men.

It was time to end this.

She shot the man with the knife.

A dark, angry red spot suddenly appeared in the centre of his forehead, and he fell back like an axed tree.

As Moreton turned to see what had happened, his grip on Ambrose loosened and the boy slipped down, until his head was close to Moreton's hand.

"Ambrose!" Mary shouted. "What would Kat do?"

Ambrose bit down hard on Moreton's hand; so hard that Mary saw blood appear.

Moreton screamed and let the boy drop to the ground.

Ambrose immediately scurried off towards the hut, as Olivia appeared behind one of the other men and in one swift movement, pulled the man's own knife from its scabbard and thrust it up to the hilt into his chest. The man gave a grunt, and went down.

His other comrade saw what happened and started to run over, just as William appeared behind him.

William put his foot out and the man stumbled, then went flying forward and landed in a sprawling heap at Olivia's feet.

Olivia wrenched the knife out of the first man's chest, leant forward and thrust it into the second one's back. With a gurgling, rattling yell, the man arched upwards, then flopped forward and was still.

The whole thing had taken no more than twenty seconds.

Moreton looked from one body to the next, then up at Mary. It was clear that he was considering his options – perhaps working out if Mary was able to fire the gun again and he should run, or whether he should stay and keep talking. Then it seemed that he had made his decision – and that was to get away as fast as possible. He turned and started running towards the far side of the ravine. Almost immediately he was out of sight among the trees.

Mary quickly put the gun back in its strap, then set off down the path as fast as she could.

She arrived to find William sitting on a log nursing his foot, while Olivia was cutting away the hose at his ankle. As Mary came up to them, Olivia pulled it up to reveal a blackening bruise darkening the side of his shin.

"I stopped that ruffian, Mary," he said with a wince of pain, "but I think the fellow has broken my leg as he came down. I cannot put weight on it nor walk a step."

There was a moment's silence, as he looked up at her. Then they both spoke at once.

"I thought you were at Grangedean!" Mary said, while he asked, "How are you here and not with the girls at home?"

There was a pause, then Mary said, "Why are you still here, William? You should have set off weeks ago!"

"I was concerned for Ambrose's safety, my love," he answered. "Which I was right to be."

Ambrose! In the heat of the moment, Mary had forgotten how desperate she had been to see her son again. She turned to the small boy who was standing quietly a couple of feet away. She knelt down, then pulled him into her arms and hugged him tight, savouring the smell of him again after all these months. After a moment, she broke off the embrace and looked deep into his eyes. "I am so sorry, Bambi," she said. "I failed you." She stroked his hair. "You said the Grenvilles were Catholic and I made light of it. Will you ever forgive me?"

"Of course, Ma," he answered. "And anyhow, Pa looked after me well."

She walked over to William.

Then suddenly they were in each other's arms, and their mouths came together and Mary kissed her husband with an intensity she never knew she could ever have had.

She pulled back and looked into his blue eyes, as if seeing them for the first time. "Oh William, I have missed you so!"

"And I you, Mary, my love." He smiled. "I thought of you each day, back at Grangedean, worried for my safety."

"And I thought you would be out searching for me!"

"That I would have done, had I arrived home and found you not." He became serious. "But what of Kat and Jane?"

"Oh, William, I know! They will be worried sick, I am sure." She paused. "Or at least Kat will be. She was fearful of a bad man attacking me."

He searched her eyes. "And did any?"

Mary nodded. "One or two did, yes. But I came to no harm. How about you?" she asked quickly, to head off any further discussion about how she had managed to stay safe.

Tom was dead – that was an end to it.

William said, "I thought Ambrose and I were to be slaughtered like a pair of sheep when we were led to that hut and manacled up these two days past. So when that ruffian came in just now and took Ambrose, I thought the worst." He turned to Olivia. "Never did I think that an unknown young girl would then come in and break open my manacles with a bar so I could help slaughter our captors instead. I must thank you for your plan, and your companion – Olivia, is it…?" The girl nodded. "…Olivia here, for carrying it though."

"And it worked," Olivia observed, looking as if she was trying to stay calm despite having just killed a man.

"But I fear I have broken my leg," continued William, "and Moreton has escaped." He winced with pain. "I would follow the rogue and beat him to death for all he has tried to do."

"You are not going anywhere on that leg, William de Beauvais," said Mary. "But I will follow him. It is a steep path up the other side of the ravine, and with luck he will not have got far," she smiled grimly.

She put the gun in its sling.

"All of you, wait for me here."

---0---

Once again, Mary found the scope of the gun invaluable as a telescope.

She aimed it at the path leading up and out of the ravine on the other side, sweeping it across each straight section and around the hairpin turns.

It wasn't long before she picked up the figure of Moreton, walking slowly upwards, some distance above. As she watched, he turned at a hairpin, making the rapier at his waist flash in the sunlight, then he set off up the next section of path, his pace slowing further.

He stopped completely, leaning back against the rock wall, his thin chest heaving for breath.

She put the gun back in its sling and set off in pursuit.

The path was steep and very stony, with loose rocks of many shapes and sizes. Even though she took it slowly in the still, hot sunshine, it was not long before her legs were burning and the air was rasping in her throat.

She rested for a few seconds, then took a deep breath, squared her shoulders and continued after Moreton.

She was making good progress, when suddenly a hail of large stones crashed onto the path in front of her, creating a dust cloud and sending a few smaller stones flying up. She stopped and looked up, but saw nothing.

A minute or so later she had just rounded a hairpin bend and was starting up the next straight, when a single rock the size of a large melon hurtled down with a whooshing sound, followed by an almighty *whump!* as it landed a couple of feet behind her.

Mary gave out a strangled yelp; it was large enough and falling fast enough to have killed her outright.

She looked up again, just in time to see the toe of a man's shoe withdraw from the edge of the path above her.

Mary leapt for the rocky wall beside her, flattening herself against it.

As she did so, another large rock crashed down – this time landing exactly where she had just been standing.

She looked up. Above her the wall sloped forward, giving her natural protection from the overhanging ledge above. She looked down the slope behind her. A few yards back, the wall changed angle and sloped away from the path – so if she went back, she would be exposed.

Ahead, the overhang got steeper – so if she went forward, she would have protection nearly all the way to the next hairpin.

Mary took the gun out of its sling and went forward, gripping the stock tightly.

Staying as close as she could to the wall, she eased her way along inch by inch, trying hard to be silent so that Moreton would not be able to pinpoint her.

Soon she reached the next turn and stopped just before it, while still protected by the overhang.

Leaving its safety to step out onto path and around the hairpin would mean being completely exposed.

She pressed close to the rocky wall, listening hard for any sound, but there was nothing.

Was he standing just above her, holding another rock, waiting to throw it down?

Or was he hidden in a shadow with his rapier drawn, ready to leap out and run her through?

She looked down, and spotted a stone the size of her fist just by her foot. Cautiously she bent and picked it up, then threw it gently down the path she had just climbed.

It made a loud clattering noise in the still air as it landed, and almost immediately there was the sound of footsteps moving away on the path above her.

Quickly she dashed out onto the hairpin, then skidded round the corner.

Moreton was just ahead, standing on a part of the path where it narrowed to just a couple of feet wide. He was hanging on to a branch growing from a fissure in the rocks, and was leaning over the ledge and staring down.

She slithered to a stop. At the noise he pulled himself upright, then turned and drew his rapier.

In response, Mary raised the gun to her shoulder. She pointed it directly at his head.

"See, Moreton," she said, advancing up the slope towards him, "this is the Alchemist's weapon. It is the weapon that killed Tom Cobham, and you saw how it killed the man that held a knife to my son's throat." She steadied herself. "And now it is aimed at your head."

Moreton gave a sneering smile and walked down until he was only a few yards from her, his thin face filling the scope. "So what would you have me do, Lady Mary?" he asked.

"Lay down your rapier."

"And if I do?"

"Then I will take you to Master Wychwoode, who will arrest you.

"And if I do not?"

"Then I will kill you."

Moreton smiled again. "Then you had better kill me," he said. He stepped back a few paces and Mary followed.

"You want me to?"

"Oh yes, Lady Mary." Moreton answered. "For you will be doing me the greatest service. Your killing will perhaps be swift and free of pain – whereas that heretic bastard will have me hung, drawn and quartered."

Mary said nothing, continuing to point the gun at his head.

"I could wound you only."

But I'm bluffing. The gun is not loaded – the last cartridge was used on the man with the knife.

Moreton stared back at her, then sneered again.

"But you do not kill me, nor do you aim elsewhere on my body to wound." He stepped back and again she followed. "Which means that either you have not the will to kill or wound me, or you do not have the means." He raised his rapier. "And since you had no hesitation in killing Charlie down there to free your son, before he wounded me so grievously, I do not think you lack the will." He studied the bite mark on his hand dispassionately, then made another step back. Again, Mary stepped towards him.

"So," Moreton continued, "I surmise you do not have the means. That although the weapon is in your hand, perhaps it is not primed and loaded with shot. In which case," he added, "I would prefer to kill you instead, and make good my escape."

Mary braced herself.

Almost as if in slow motion, she saw the tip of the rapier start to drive towards her. She shifted the grip of her left hand on the barrel of her gun, and in one smooth movement swung the whole gun round, while at the same time turning sideways. The rapier blade sliced harmlessly through the air a couple of inches away, as she brought the stock of the gun swinging round in her left hand with as much force as she could. It made contact with Moreton's arm, sending the rapier clattering down against the rock beside them as he yelled with pain.

Or was it triumph?

Mary suddenly realised why Moreton had been stepping back and she had been so blindly coming up after him – he had been deliberately leading her onto the narrowest section of path.

And now her momentum was taking her over the edge.

She scrabbled to get a grip on the loose stones, but it was too late. She felt her feet slipping.

As she went down, she let go of the gun and reached for the only thing she could.

Moreton's ankles.

The force of her falling pulled both his legs over the edge and he started to fall with her – until he stopped with a sudden arm-wrenching jerk that nearly sent her sliding off.

She looked up.

The only thing stopping them both from plunging down the long drop to the next path below, and possibly on down to the rocks at the bottom of the ravine, was the branch that Moreton was now gripping with both hands.

"Let go of me, you infernal bitch!" he yelled. "For the sake of Sweet Jesus Christ, let go!"

Mary did not answer. Instead she looked across to her right. There was a small outcrop of rock less than a yard away.

It could give her a foothold – if only she could get to it.

She looked up at the rock face above it. There was a small fissure above and to the left.

A hand-hold.

An idea began to form.

She started to swing her legs – first to the left, then to the right.

"Christ's holy cross, what are you doing?" came the cry from above.

Again, Mary did not answer – she was concentrating on reaching the outcrop.

Two more swings, accompanied by increasingly belligerent shouts from above, and she managed to get a toe onto the rock – but it did not hold, and she swung back once more.

"By Heaven, stop this now or I will let go and we both will perish!" shouted Moreton.

The next swing had more momentum and she got her toe on the rock. It held, leaving her suspended at an angle – one foot on the rocky outcrop and both hands hanging onto Moreton's legs.

Mary gripped even more tightly to his left ankle with her left hand, then slowly released her right hand.

"God's wounds!" shrieked Moreton as all her weight went through his left leg. "You vile harridan! You will kill us both!"

"I thought that was what you wanted," Mary muttered.

She eased her right arm towards the fissure, stretching as far over as she could. She nearly got her fingers inside, when suddenly he pulled his leg back and instead of gripping the fissure, her fingers scraped back across the rock and leaving a bright red trail behind them.

Wincing, she looked up.

"I see what you do, you vile jezebel!" Moreton snarled down at her. "But it will not succeed." He pulled again on his leg, scraping her fingers even further away from the fissure, until she felt them hit a small outcrop.

With a gasp of pain as her shoulder nearly dislocated, she clutched at it.

For a moment they were both still; Mary with Moreton's left ankle in the vice-like grip of her left hand, and her right at full stretch with her bloody fingers locked around the small outcrop.

Then she started to pull back.

With her heart thumping and the blood pounding in her ears, she slowly brought Moreton's leg back towards her hand.

"By Christ!" he yelped. "You have Satan's strength!"

Ignoring his shouts, she gathered herself and gave one last pull, then lunged across to grab the edge of the fissure, screaming in pain as her fingers curled into the little gap.

They held firm.

She looked up at him.

"Fare thee well, Lambert Moreton," she said, and gave a sharp pull on his ankle.

Possibly his arms had lost all strength, but it was enough.

Moreton's hands slipped off the branch and he fell past her with a blood-curdling shriek.

The sound cut off abruptly as he hit the path below a sickening thud.

Mary looked down. He was lying on his back with his arms spread out.

She looked back up.

Trying to ignore the pain in her fingers, and the bright red trail of blood dripping down the rock, she searched for a ledge to take her left leg.

There was an outcrop in roughly the right place, but it looked very small.

With little mewling noises coming from the back of her throat, she eased her foot over, pushed the side of her shoe hard into the rock, then let it come down to rest on the tiny ledge.

She clenched her jaw, then raised her right leg and found a small ledge

Reaching up with her left hand, she scrabbled for a little outcrop, but it was half a hand higher than her full stretch.

Damn!

She took a breath, then reached again.

Again she could not get her fingers onto it.

With a scream of rage and frustration, Mary threw herself upward, using her right hand to pull herself higher, and feeling her left leg come clean off its little outcrop.

It was an all-or-nothing move.

Her hand rose up just beyond the top of the piece of rock, and she crooked her fingers onto it.

Her grip held.

With a further yell to herself, she got her left leg up to another small ledge, then her left hand up to another fissure, and was soon able to get both hands to some rocks at the edge of the path above her.

She pulled herself up over the edge, wriggling like a wet fish on the edge of a boat to get her weight up and over – but she was soon lying safe on the path itself, her breath rasping in her throat as she shook with relief.

Slowly she stood up, then retrieved both the rapier and the gun. As soon as she picked up the gun, she could see that the barrel was badly bent. The Alchemist's work was destroyed – the gun would surely never fire again. She tucked it into the sling on her back and pushed the rapier through her belt, then set off down the path.

Moreton was lying on the path where he had fallen, laid out on his back with his arms outstretched and his legs rocked over to one side.

She approached him carefully, holding out the rapier in case he was bluffing. But when she got to him, she could see his eyes were fluttering and the top half of his body was shaking. She crouched down beside him.

"Moreton?"

His eyes opened and his head turned towards her.

"You servant of Satan," he muttered. "I cannot feel my legs."

Mary looked down at them, then at his lower back, which she could now see was slightly arched. She put her hand under and felt something cold and smooth. She pushed him slightly to his side, and revealed the object.

Moreton had fallen directly onto one of the large rocks that he himself had thrown down at her – and it had severed his spine.

---0---

It was half an hour later and Moreton was laid out on some soft earth at the base of the ravine. He had been roughly carried down the rock face by a couple of Wychwoode's men, screaming and cursing as they went, after the lawyer and his soldiers had arrived at the bottom of the ravine and had been urgently sent up the other side by Olivia and William.

Mary was standing a few yards away from the hut with Wychwoode, William, Ambrose and Olivia.

She turned to Wychwoode. "What will happen to Moreton?" she asked.

"He will be interrogated about possible co-conspirators, then he will be hung, drawn and quartered," the old man answered. "That is the punishment for a treasonous plot on the life of the Queen."

William nodded. "I cannot say in truth that I am sorry. He thought to play me as a cat plays with a mouse. I am well pleased that his plot is ended."

"Please, Master Wychwoode, what of Sir Nicholas and Lady Grenville?" Ambrose asked. He had been standing to one side, holding Olivia's hand.

"I understand they have observed mass in secret and hid a priest," Wychwoode looked at William, "which is an offence in itself." He gestured back to Moreton's prostrate body. "But I also understand they were under the influence of this firebrand here, and have sworn to uphold the law in future and embrace the true religion. They will lose their lands and their position, but not, on this occasion, their lives." He looked at Mary. "Doth please my lady – this outcome?"

"I suppose so," Mary answered. "I have no anger for them." She glanced over at William. He was shaking his head slightly. "What of you, my love?" she asked.

"I have concerns about Sir Nicholas," he answered. "I heard him call Her Majesty a bastard." He paused. "Although I will warrant he knew naught of the plot."

"Then what will be done is for the best," said Wychwoode. "Now," he said, becoming very business-like, "I must take this Moreton into custody. And you, madam," he pointed a bony finger at Mary, "must make haste to Wyvern Castle and once more dress yourself as befits a lady, and one much beloved of our Queen. She has now decided to hold a banquet in your honour this night, and I would not have you be late, or not look as good as I know you can, for this great occasion."

"Me?" squeaked Mary. "Why?"

"If you have to ask, then you are more deserving of the honour than even I thought," said Wychwoode, and he marched off towards the hut.

"Ma!" said Ambrose, his eyes as wide as saucers. "You are to be honoured by the Queen!"

Mary crouched down and scooped Ambrose up in one arm, stood up and pulled William close to her with the other, then nodded at Olivia to come over as well. "Do you know," she said, "that when I was up on that rock face, with nothing more than the tiniest of ledges to stop me falling, the only thing that kept me moving upwards was the thought of seeing you all again." She looked from one to the other. "The only honour I seek," she said, "is to have you men both close to me, and to be home in my beloved Grangedean Manor, with nothing more pressing to concern me than the state of the rushes in the Great Hall, and to have my dearest friend Olivia come and visit me as often as she wishes."

CHAPTER TWENTY-SIX

Mary turned to William and muttered, "Hanging above a hundred foot drop, I was not so fearful as I am now."

"Courage, my love," he muttered back, squeezing her hand, then apologising when she winced with pain. "All will be well, I promise."

They were standing in the dimly-lit antechamber outside the doors to the Great Hall at Wyvern Castle, with William leaning on a stick to support his leg. Beyond the doors, they could hear the noise of more than two hundred people laughing and shouting together, waiting for the banquet to begin.

But that could not happen without the guest of honour.

"What a pair we are," she observed, "you with your leg nearly broken…"

"But thankfully, it turns out, only bruised most sorely," he said.

"…and me with my hands torn to shreds on those rocks." She smiled at him. "We have both had our adventures, have we not?"

"Aye, my love," he agreed, "we have." He paused. "But you have not told me why you set off from Grangedean in the first instance?" He peered at her in the gloom. "And what of this man I am told of – Sir Tom Cobham, was it? What of him?"

The question hung in the air.

Mary took a breath and was about to answer, when there was a heavy knocking from inside the hall, sounding like someone was banging a wooden staff on a table. Then some indistinct voice made an announcement, and slowly the doors swung open. Mary and William were almost blinded by the light that flooded over them, as they stepped forward.

"…And I present to you the Queen's Guest of Honour, and beloved friend, Lady Mary de Beauvais and her husband Sir William de Beauvais!"

It was Leicester who was the Master of Ceremonies, and as William hobbled slowly into the room with Mary beside him, Leicester raised his hands to encourage the cheers from the assembled crowd. Mary smiled nervously at a few people close to her, then looked up to see Queen Elizabeth sitting at the centre of the top table, resplendent in a white and gold gown with an enormous winged headpiece of pale cream silk rising from her shoulders and framing her red hair.

Mary approached the table, then stopped and sank into a low curtsey, while William bowed his head.

The Queen rose slowly to her feet. As if this was the cue everyone had been waiting for, they all stood as well, and the cheering and clapping that was already louder than could be thought possible, increased in volume even further.

Elizabeth gave a small, almost imperceptible nod as a sign of her approval, then indicated the two empty seats, one on either side of her. Mary and William then went round each side of the table to their places.

As Mary sat, the Queen turned to her and said, "You are well met, my dear Lady Mary."

"Thank you, Your Majesty. This is most kind, but…" she almost said 'unnecessary'… "but I was only doing my duty."

"Your duty? Aye," the Queen observed with a half-smile. "But I think you went a little further than that. Let me count the ways." Elizabeth held up her hand and counted off on her slim fingers. "The first, you pursued this Alchemist across many counties and made plans to thwart him. The second, you warned Sir Thomas so that he performed the ultimate sacrifice and saved my life. The third, you stopped the Alchemist from making a further attempt to kill me by the judicious use of a poker on his painted arms. The fourth, you used the said poker to give the Alchemist a beating on his leg that prevented him either escaping or causing any further harm. And the fifth," she made a deliberate show of counting off her little finger, "the fifth, you pursued my Catholic enemy, this Lambert Moreton, to bring him to justice, at considerable risk to your own life." She raised a quizzical eyebrow, "Or have I missed anything?"

Mary shook her head. "Nay, madam, I think you have summed up excellently."

"There, then no more shall be said on the matter." She turned to William and observed, "Your wife is quite the woman of action, Sir William. You must be immensely proud of her."

"Oh, I am, your Majesty…" he answered, and the two of them fell into conversation that Mary could not catch.

She glanced to her left, and caught sight of Wychwoode, seated between Olivia and Ambrose. Wychwoode was clearly regaling them with some story of daring-do – and to judge by the way he was waving his arms about, and the rapt expressions on their faces, he had their complete attention.

Ambrose looked up and caught her eye, giving her a look that said plainly that the stories he was hearing were about her – and that her exploits were causing him to see his mother in a whole new light.

The voice of Jesus, Ma? he mouthed in amazement. No doubt he was referring to the moment ten years before, when a crowd, who had been whipped into a frenzy by the witchfinder Hopkirk and wanted her drowned in a well for sorcery, had heard a divine message telling them that she was not a witch, and should be saved.

She smiled and shrugged. *I am still your Ma, whatever Jesus might say…*

The Queen turned back to her. "I have just set out a course of action to your husband that I wish to be followed," she said.

"Indeed, madam?" answered Mary. She saw William lean slightly forward and smile reassuringly at her.

"Yes. But before I share it, I understand that you, Sir William and your charming son will shortly be setting off to journey back to your home of Grangedean Manor?"

"Yes, madam," Mary answered. "I have two other children, two daughters, and I would see them again as soon as I can."

"I wish you God speed and a safe journey." The queen regarded her thoughtfully. "But I would ensure that this is done as far as possible without troubling the Lord God too greatly, so I shall make available a detachment of my finest guards, as well as a warm and secure carriage, so that your journey is swift, comfortable and untroubled by any brigands."

"Thank you, madam," Mary answered cautiously, "that is most kind."

"Although perhaps I should simply arm you with a poker and let any brigands take their chances?"

Mary smiled. "I am content to travel quietly, and leave my days of action behind me."

Elizabeth smiled back. "I respect that, and would have you attend me at Court, so I may benefit instead from your wisdom and calm council."

"I will be honoured, Your Majesty," answered Mary, still wondering what course of action the Queen had put to William.

"Which brings me to my main point," said the Queen. "This whole episode has been most unfortunate, and I do not want any other would-be armourers thinking to create such a weapon, nor to copy this Alchemist and plot against my life or my crown. I wish for the events of these last few days to be struck from the historical record, as if they never happened. So I shall make my progress down to the Earl of Leicester's castle of Kenilworth in Warwickshire, and we shall record in all documents that there was no progress beyond Kenilworth this summer. York simply did not happen." Mary must have looked surprised, for the Queen said quickly, "That is not to take anything from your bravery here and your actions, my dear – which you and I will always know and cherish – but the records will only talk of Kenilworth." The Queen regarded her a moment, then added, "Your husband knows that you do not seek any glory for yourself, and he is concerned that if your deeds here became too well known, then you would forever be the subject of conversation – from great halls down to lowly ale-houses. He is anxious for your well-being, and agrees that this as the perfect way to safeguard it."

She leaned forward and again saw her husband smiling at her from the other side of the Queen.

"It is an excellent plan, Your Majesty."

"Indeed." Then the Queen leaned in close and dropped her voice. Once again, they were in the surgeon's house in York; once again two women with a shared bond. "Mary, I understand so well that you have loved and lost." Elizabeth paused. "And that in death the man you loved has given us both the chance to renew our lives. I will use well the opportunity he gave me…" the Queen's dark eyes held Mary's, "and I would you do the same. You have a man right here who loves you most deeply. You have a wonderful future with him, and with your charming son, and your daughters back at Grangedean Manor." The Queen put her hand on Mary's arm. "They are your future, Lady de Beauvais. I would you mark it well."

"I will, madam. Yes – yes I will."

"Good." The Queen leaned back and took her hand off Mary's arm.

Mary also sat back.

Then it seemed that the noise of the room receded into the distance, and for the first time in many months, a warm glow of contentment spread over her.

The Queen was right! Finally, Mary had been given back her future. As the Alchemist had made clear, nothing she had done by saving William or having her children would endanger that. The Alchemist, Moreton and their awful plot were gone, and now she could relax, enjoy her life at Grangedean with her family and, it seemed, her new life at Court as well.

How fortunate she was to be a valued part of Tudor history.

There was a life outside Grangedean, and now she was going to enjoy it!

Mary felt a touch on her other arm and suddenly the sounds of the room came rushing back. She looked round. It was Leicester. She realised with a start that such was the dominant presence of the Queen, and her new-found contentment, she had not even registered that the Earl was next to her as well.

"I must ask you, Lady Mary, what of the Alchemist's incredible musket?"

"Oh." Mary cast her mind back to the path above the ravine. "I dropped it when I fell from the ledge, my lord. It was damaged beyond repair."

His mouth fell. "That is indeed a shame. I would see how it was made so it can be copied." He narrowed his eyes. "Belike its function can still be understood, for all it is damaged?"

Elizabeth leaned across. "Nay, Robin, it is an evil thing; the work of the devil and of a man who worshiped the darkness. We will have naught to do with it." She turned to Mary. "I command you take it to a blacksmith's forge and have it committed to the fire. I want no trace of it to remain."

"But madam…" Leicester started to rise out of his seat. Elizabeth held up her thin, white hand.

"I am resolute, Robin."

He subsided back again. "As you wish, madam."

"I do wish, Robin." She gave a small conspiratorial smile at Mary, then looked at Leicester with wide, innocent eyes. "So Robin, how are you going to impress me at Kenilworth?"

CHAPTER TWENTY-SEVEN

The Tower of London, early June 1575

The thick stone walls glistened in the flickering candlelight, as Wychwoode walked slowly up to the near-naked figure spread-eagled on the platform in the middle of the room; his groin covered with just a dirty cloth.

The platform was made of rough, dark wood, its open grain scuffed from the repeated impact of writhing limbs, and stained almost black by years of being soaked in blood, sweat and urine.

The figure lying on it was tied by ropes around each ankle and wrist. His feet were secured to strong metal rings, while the ropes to his outstretched hands passed round a large wooden drum beyond his head. A muscular man in a leather jerkin stood next to the drum, ready to turn it by means of a cross-bar on the side.

Wychwoode came up to the spread-eagled man's head, and looked down at the short, spikes of hair plastered to the man's sweating skull.

"You will know what this contraption is, I am sure," he said in a dry, flat voice. "We need to know all the details of this plot and your part – and you can either tell me now, or tell me after my associate here has pulled your arms and legs out of their sockets. That is," he added, "if they do not first come apart where Lady Mary has hit them. The choice is yours."

The Alchemist stared at him with hate-filled eyes. "There's nothing to tell," he muttered. "I worked alone."

"But you were in league with Alleyne and Tyler, and were led by Moreton," said Wychwoode. "I do not call that working alone."

"As Cobham must surely have told you, since he was your agent all along," the Alchemist growled, "once Alleyne died and you had Tyler, I contacted no-one. Not even Moreton. There was no others involved."

"What of Grenville?"

"Who?" The Alchemist turned his head away. "I never heard of him."

Wychwoode nodded. "I though as much." He paused, considering the Alchemist's prone figure, with his blackened and bruised arms and leg. "So then tell me, what of this?"

He held up a small metal object with a white skull motif. The Alchemist turned his head back and stared at it in the flickering candlelight. "Is this a sign of devil worship?" Wychwoode asked. "Are you a disciple of Satan? For if so, then you will be burned alive to cast out the devil."

"Where the fuck did you get that?" asked the Alchemist, his eyes wide. "I haven't seen that since…" he stopped himself.

"Since when?"

"Since… fuck. I can't say."

Wychwoode nodded to the man in the leather jerkin, and the man put his weight against the cross-bar to turn the drum.

A few minutes later, once the Alchemist's screams had died down to a soft whimper, Wychwoode asked again.

"Since what?"

"Since… since… oh, fuck it. Since I arrived in this shit-hole time."

"I do not understand. Tell me what you mean." He turned towards the torturer and nodded again. The man started to push on the cross-bar.

"No!" screamed the Alchemist. "Wait! You have to let me explain!"

Wychwoode held his hand up and the man paused.

"Listen," panted the Alchemist, "in life, one day follows the next, right?"

"Yes," said Wychwoode slowly, "but I do not see…"

"So you travel forward through time, always you go forward, right?"

"Yes..."

"But I went the other way. I went backwards."

There was a long silence, then Wychwoode said, "You speak nonsense."

"No, you have got to listen." The Alchemist paused, as if gathering his thoughts. "This year, it is 1575, right?"

"Yes it is."

"What if I said to you, you could wake up tomorrow, and still be the same person, but instead of it being 1575, it was now 1135?"

"Then I would say it was impossible, and against the God's laws."

"Well, it is not impossible, because I have done it."

Wychwoode stared at the Alchemist a while, trying to process what he had just heard. "You mean," he said slowly, "you have travelled *backwards* in time – through four hundred and forty years?"

The Alchemist nodded. "Exactly."

"From the year of our Lord…" Wychwoode paused while he did the calculation, "…2015?"

"Exactly."

"This is arrant nonsense," Wychwoode began, and turned again to the torturer.

"No!" the Alchemist shouted. "You have to believe me! How do you think I made the gun? With future knowledge! How do you think I made the shells – the powder and ball in one capsule? How do you think I made the scope to see the target close up?" He looked down at his arms. "These tatts, pictures, on my arms – they are of weapons from my time! If that fucking bitch hadn't hit them, you'd see more clearly – they're like nothing you would ever find today." He glanced at the object in Wychwoode's hand. "And that lighter you're holding; it's nothing to do with devil worship – total nonsense! It's just a fucking lighter that I must have dropped when I first arrived, that's all."

Wychwoode observed the Alchemist dispassionately. "So you say you travelled here from the year 2015?"

"Yes. Yes, I did."

Wychwoode pursed his lips, then said, "How, exactly? By sorcery?"

"No!" The Alchemist shook his head violently from side to side. "I got caught in a storm. There was lightning – lots of lightning. Then I found myself here."

"I see."

"You believe me?"

Wychwoode was silent a moment, then said, "At this time, no. I am a lawyer by profession. I need to see clear evidence." He paced away from the rack a moment, then turned back. "I assume when this lightning storm sent you to our time, you would have appeared as if by sorcery from thin air. Did any person witness this?"

The Alchemist stared at him with desperate eyes. "No," he said. "But I went to the Grangedean tavern and sought food from Agnes. She will vouch that I was dressed in my future clothes and offered her coin with the head of our Queen on it – the Queen from my time. Ask her. She will confirm it!"

Again, Wychwoode paced away. Was this nonsense? An attempt by a condemned man to create a diversion? He looked at the bruised and battered body on the rack. If it was a diversion, it was remarkable in its invention. What a notion – to come from the distant future… Yet this Alchemist had fashioned a weapon that no man had ever seen before… Such knowledge could be explained by rational means – but equally, it *could* be true… And those pictures on his arms – now more visible since the bruising had started to fade – they also depicted strange types of musket, ones that had no known equivalent… What if this *were* real? But even if so, the talk of lightning was nonsense. What other explanation could there be than this was the devil's sorcery?

Wychwoode again observed the bruised man on the platform. "I am minded to accept that you may be a traveller through time, for there is some proof in the weapon you fashioned and the images on your arms." He paused, considering his words carefully. "But I cannot accept there is any other explanation than sorcery – and the devilry on this object you call a 'lighter' convinces me. So unless you recant this claim, I will have no choice but to have you burned at the stake."

The Alchemist let out a low groan. "And if I do recant?"

"Then you will suffer the fate of a traitor – the same fate as Moreton did these two days past – you will be hung but not killed, then cut down and disembowelled, before your head and limbs are removed."

The Alchemist stared at him for what seemed an age, his eyes glowering in the flickering light. Eventually he said, "So if I recant, I will die as Moreton died. If I do not recant, I will burn as a sorcerer?"

Wychwoode nodded.

"But you know what? You know fucking what?" the Alchemist said slowly. "If I am to burn, then another must burn as well. I am not the only one from the future."

"You would have me believe there are others from the year 2015?" Wychwoode asked sharply.

"Yes, there is – one other. And do you know what? I can prove it!" The Alchemist's voice suddenly rose to a triumphant shout. "Fuck, yes, I can actually prove it!"

"How?"

Despite the pain he must have been in, the Alchemist smiled. "Because I had a conversation with this other time-traveller, and it was in front of witnesses. Honest townspeople of York who will vouch that we spoke of future times and everything the other person said showed that they were as familiar with the future as me."

Wychwoode stared at the man. "If I find your witnesses do support your claim, then I must question this other person also."

"Yes, you must!"

"And if I am satisfied that he is also a sorcerer, then he will burn as well."

"Yes," the Alchemist said, "only it is not a 'he'. It's a 'she'..."

Then he smiled; a broad smile of triumph.

A smile of revenge.

"It's Lady Mary," he said. "It's Lady fucking Mary de Beauvais."

He laughed.

"That bitch is from the future like me, and you're going to burn her to death…"

END OF PART 2

PART 3

THE SOVEREIGN'S SECRET

CHAPTER ONE

The Tower of London, July 1575

The gaoler rose from his stool and pointed at the dark stone archway. "The cells you want are that way, sir," he muttered.

He put his tankard of ale down on the table and looked closely at the man who had just walked in unbidden, showing a warrant to see his most high-risk prisoner. The man seemed tall, although it was hard to gauge his actual height as his doublet, hose and cloak were such deep black that he seemed to be an integral part of the heavy shadows. Only his pale, deeply lined face could be seen clearly in the candlelight, set under the shock of grey-flecked white hair that flowed out from under his black woollen cap. The man's close-set blue eyes made the gaoler catch his breath. They reminded him of the hard-edged captains who used to make him squirm as a conscripted fighting man; the ones whose authority could never be questioned.

"This prisoner – he lives still?" the visitor asked, making no move towards the archway. His voice matched his face; deep, gravelly and heavy with long-held authority.

"Indeed, sir, yes, sir," the gaoler answered, shifting his weight from one foot to the other. He paused. "Although I warrant it is by the narrowest of threads."

"How so?"

"He eats very little, by his own choice, and is oft seen letting the rats take the bread and small beer I allow." The gaoler paused awkwardly, but the white-haired man nodded at him to continue, so the gaoler stood a little more easily. "He is clearly in the greatest of pain," he said, "with heavy bruising on both arms and a leg that is broken. He needs must keep the leg still, so he has bound rags around a stick on each side of his shin, which will allow it to set straight." The gaoler paused again, then permitted himself a small smile. "I have told him his fate is to die a traitor's death, and that the same leg, along with his manhood, his guts and finally his head, will all be removed." The visitor nodded again, so the gaoler finished with a little black humour. "If he wants to walk to the gallows then God speed his bones to mend, but I warrant it will be a short-lived victory!" He gave a small laugh at his own joke, then asked, "Master...?" while raising an enquiring eyebrow.

"Wychwoode," the other man answered. "Master Wychwoode. And yes, indeed it will indeed be a short-lived victory."

"I have heard..." the gaoler began, then stopped. Wychwoode said nothing, so the gaoler took a small breath and continued. "…I have heard him say that his wounds were inflicted by a noblewoman… the one he calls the 'fucking bitch', begging your pardon, sir."

There was a silence, and the gaoler began to think he had gone too far.

"That is indeed God's truth," Wychwoode answered.

"By Heavens, sir…'tis indeed so? A noblewoman?" The gaoler shook his head slowly, "Who broke his leg clean in two, and hit both his arms with such force that the bruising still remains, even to this day? I would credit a lowly woman or one from the stews might do that… but a noblewoman?"

"That is correct."

"Then I see clear why he talks of her with such venom."

The old man narrowed his eyes. "She stopped him in the act of attempting the treason that brought him to this place."

"Then I would surely bow before her, should we ever meet," muttered the gaoler, "while I would have my dagger to hand, for she sounds most dangerous."

"She is a fine and brave woman, fellow," Wychwoode said. "Resourceful, loyal and an upholder of the law. Qualities to be valued. She did what she needed to do."

---0---

Wychwoode fell silent, lost in his thoughts.

This cold stone place seemed to fade away, and with it the swarthy gaoler in the leather jerkin with tendrils of matted black hair sticking to his grimy forehead. Instead he was seeing scenes from a few weeks before, and in particular, the glorious exploits of the very noblewoman he had alluded to; Lady Mary de Beauvais.

Lady Mary standing over the bound and bloody body of the Alchemist, the man she had stopped as he attempted to use the powerful musket he had fashioned himself to assassinate Queen Elizabeth. She had achieved this by beating his arms with an iron poker, then using it to break his leg…

A forest clearing. Lady Mary casually holding the same musket, close by the body of a man she had killed by its power; a neat hole punched in the centre of his forehead, as if placed there with a driven nail…

Lady Mary presenting the supine form of one Lambert Moreton, his spine severed so he would never walk again… Lambert Moreton who had conceived and planned the whole plot; injured from a fall onto his back that she had caused…

He became aware that the gaoler was again talking, and with an effort dragged himself back to the present, and the cold stone jail.

"And the prisoner, sir, the one they call the Alchemist? Are you here to take him to meet the executioner?"

"Nay, fellow," he growled, "for now I must only talk with him."

The gaoler nodded and pointed again at the dark archway, set deep into the stone wall behind him. "Then that is the way we will go, sir."

Wychwoode looked into the darkness. "You will lead," he ordered, "with a brazier to light the way."

Their steps echoed loudly as they passed along the stone passageway, with the glow from the gaoler's brazier making the walls turn a fiery flickering red.

Wychwoode had to stoop to avoid hitting his head on the stone ceiling, and was relieved to make it to a heavy oak door. They passed into another long stone corridor with further archways set into the walls at regular intervals.

Each arch was the opening to a cell; each secured with a barred gate. The bars were covered in a mixture of black pitch and occasional brown streaks – rust or dried blood, Wychwoode was not sure. He permitted himself a curious glance through the bars at the unfortunate prisoners inside. None looked up or even acknowledged his passing; they were all pathetic bundles of rags, sitting slumped in the corner, or, in one case, hanging by the arms from a set of manacles attached to a high wooden post. Then, towards the end of the passageway, they came to a cell with a single prisoner, sitting back on a wooden bench with his head resting on the wall behind him.

As they passed the front of the cell, the man looked up, and for a brief moment, their eyes met. The prisoner scrambled up and staggered quickly to the gate, putting his hands through the bars.

"Master Wychwoode?" His voice was cracked and hoarse, as if this was the first time he had spoken in days. "Is that Master Robert Wychwoode?"

Wychwoode stopped and turned slowly with a look of indifferent enquiry.

"Aye," he said. "I am he."

"By Heavens, sir, you are well met!"

Wychwoode stood in front of the cell, just far enough back from the bars to be out of reach. There was a moment of silence as they observed each other. The prisoner was a tall, heavily built man in his mid-thirties, with a beard that looked as if it had been trimmed not too long ago, but was now somewhat unkempt. He was reasonably well-dressed in the garb of a merchant, although his clothes had clearly suffered from his stay in this filthy cell.

"Have we met before?" Wychwoode asked, with an edge of chill to his voice.

"Yes, yes…" The man nodded briefly. "I came to see you at the Inns of Court a few months ago." He gave a small bow of his head. "Roger Rolleston."

Wychwoode did not answer immediately; he was comparing the dirty man in front of him with the memory raised by the name – the memory coming back of a man whose manner was over-confident to the point of arrogance, and who was there to petition for… what was it? Ah yes – it was for the bond-release of goods from a merchant ship that he had invested in.

"I recall well," he said. "So, what brings you to this unfortunate position?"

Rolleston shook his head. "I was in the wrong place at the wrong time."

"As do most prisoners observe."

Rolleston grimaced. "No, no! This is God's truth, I swear! I was visiting some acquaintances with a view to dealing on a consignment of spices, when the local Pursuivants came to arrest my hosts for Catholic sedition." He shook his head again. "I was accused of being a Catholic simply by being in the company of such recusants, and all my protestations of innocence since have fallen on deaf ears."

"Then you will be brought to trial? That is the proper forum for you to put your case."

"I trust it will be soon, so I can show clearly that I am innocent of all charges."

"Well Master Rolleston, if your case is strong, you will have naught to fear." Wychwoode considered the man before him, clutching at the bars and looking at him with an expression of hope.

"Master Wychwoode, will you intercede on my part?" Rolleston asked.

The older man sighed. If every fellow who had brief acquaintance could call upon his services, he would never have the hours in a day to conduct his business in the law, let alone serve his true master, Francis Walsingham, and above him, Her Majesty Queen Elizabeth. "Nay," he answered with a shake of his head, "I have many more pressing matters. I am engaged on affairs of state as well as with the law."

Rolleston stood back, then suddenly he punched the bar with such force that Wychwoode thought his knuckles must surely be broken. "By Heavens, Master Wychwoode," he growled, "fate has brought you to me, and you are my only hope! I am wholly innocent – I have attended Protestant services with faith and with diligence ever since Queen Elizabeth ascended the throne! I have never missed a service, nor would wish to – go ask!" He shook his hand as if that was all that was needed to clear such pain as the hit would have caused. "Go ask in the parish of Egham, and particularly the church of St. John. The priest there will tell you that what I say is God's truth!"

Wychwoode nodded. "You speak with passion." He considered Rolleston again for a few moments. Maybe he had been too quick to condemn the fellow. What if he did as asked, and used his influence to gain the man's freedom? Then this Rolleston would be in his debt – which might make him useful in future.

It is always good to have resources at one's disposal…

"Very well then, I will ask," Wychwoode said slowly. "If your claim is corroborated, I will see what I can do."

Rolleston gripped the bars again and stared up at him. "I will forever be beholden to you, sir!"

Wychwoode glanced at the man's knuckles, that now had a line of blood running across them. "Indeed you will," he said. "But I make no promises."

As he turned back to the gaoler, who was waiting by another heavy oak door, Wychwoode shook his head to clear thoughts of Rolleston and his troubles. He needed to focus on the man he had come to see, the man known as the Alchemist.

The gaoler silently unlocked the door, then stood back to let Wychwoode through.

On the other side there was only one cell. It was dark, lit by just a thin beam of light coming from a small, barred window high up one wall.

In the corner sat a painfully thin prisoner with spiked hair and a rough beard, wearing only a torn shirt and breeches which appeared to be soiled with his own waste. A chain secured him to the wall, ending in a tight black collar round his neck. Both arms were covered in old yellow and purple bruises, under which faded images could just be seen; images that appeared to be crossed pistols on one arm and crossed muskets on the other. His left leg, blackened and swollen below the knee, was bound by rags and wooden sticks as the gaoler had described.

The two men walked up to the barred gate. The prisoner looked up slowly, his eyes seeming to change their focus from an inner world of pain to the new arrivals.

"Wychwoode," he said tonelessly. "Are you here to stretch me on the rack again?" He pointed down. "I have put my leg in splints and I feel the bones are starting to knit back together. Do you plan to undo all that good work?"

"Nay, Alchemist," answered Wychwoode. "I am not here to put you to the rack again. For as you know, the law has a different – and more permanent – fate for you."

"Ahh, yes. The gaoler here has delighted in confirming to me in great detail what that fate will be. But," the Alchemist looked up, "it has been over three weeks now," he pointed to a regular series of marks scratched into the wall, "and I am still alive."

Wychwoode studied the man. That he had lost weight and was now no more than a set of bones covered by skin was to be expected, for no man would grow fat in this place, and especially not if he used his meagre rations to feed the rats. That he had splinted his leg – this too was to be expected, for why would he not want to give himself some purpose and small comfort, even with the certainty of execution to come? But these were not the topics he had come to discuss. He whispered his instruction to the gaoler, who nodded, and unlocked the gate.

As Wychwoode walked into the cell, the gaoler muttered, "He is on a short chain, sir, but I would keep my distance if I were you."

"I thank you, good man, for your information and advice," Wychwoode snapped, "but I am confident I can take it from here."

The gaoler nodded. "Yes, sir, yes," he stammered. Then he backed out, closing and locking the gate behind him.

Wychwoode waited until the heavy door could be heard closing further up the corridor, then he walked up to the Alchemist. "Aye," he said, "you are still alive. For now."

The Alchemist said nothing but watched the older man, as wary as an exhausted deer regards the huntsman. Wychwoode moved back to the wall opposite, then leaned against it and folded his arms.

"I came to see your state of health," he said eventually.

"As shit as can be expected," replied the Alchemist, "after what that bitch did to me with her poker; you with your torture on the rack, and what I get to eat in here." He indicated a mouldy hunk of bread beside him, that seemed to move of its own accord. "Full of weevils," he observed. "And the beer stinks of piss. Even the rats have to be persuaded to take it." He shook his head. "No, my health is not good right now – as if that mattered." He shrugged. "But then I'm sure you knew that. Why are you really here?"

Wychwoode went back to the gate and peered through the bars. The gaoler had definitely gone. Even so, he lowered his voice as he came back to the Alchemist. "I wanted to know if you still maintain your extraordinary claim to have travelled here through time, from the year twenty fifteen."

The Alchemist shrugged again. "I still die an agonising death if I do admit it – you'll burn me as a witch. But if I deny it…" He started to cough; a thin wheezy sound. Once he regained his breath he repeated, "If I deny it… then I get to see what my insides look like." He paused, as if to let the true horror of that sink in, "and your precious Queen gets to see my head on a spike. Either way, I am dead."

There was a silence, then a narrow, calculating look came into the Alchemist's eyes. "Oh, but wait a minute! Wait one minute! It does matter, doesn't it? To you! Oh yes, to you and that bitch Lady Mary de Beauvais... Because I have accused her of being a time traveller as well, and now…" the Alchemist's voice suddenly rose, "*You know it!* Now you *know* she's actually from twenty fifteen!"

Wychwoode remained impassive.

"You have spoken to that couple in York, haven't you?" the Alchemist said. Then a thin smile played around his mouth. "The ones I tied up when I used their room to take a pot at the Queen. They must have heard me and the bitch talking about the future together! So, you *know* it's the truth!" He started to shuffle forward, until stopped by the short chain to his collar. "If I deny it," he said, his voice dropping to a whisper as his eyes burned into Wychwoode's, "then there's no sorcery. I still get ripped apart for treason, but she gets off free as a bird." He shuffled back to release the tension on his chain. "*That's* why you're really here, isn't it? You want me to deny what I told you on that infernal rack, to help make sure your precious Lady Mary is in the clear."

Wychwoode gave a small nod. "I have spoken to Beth and Amos Carter, and they have – reluctantly, I may say, for they hold you in the lowest esteem – agreed with your story. They confirm that you and Lady Mary talked of the future in a way that showed you both had knowledge of it, and in such a manner that could not be explained by aught except by sorcery."

The Alchemist pointed at his scratches on the stone wall. "So that's why it has been over three weeks! You've been up in York checking out my story." He gave a triumphant grin. "Well, then, let's make this official!"

He struggled to his feet and stood stiffly on his good leg. Wychwoode could now make out the red chafing sores on his neck around the collar. "I am not going to do what you want!" the Alchemist snarled. "I will confirm to everyone that I am a time traveller from twenty fifteen, and therefore, in your eyes, a sorcerer!"

He hopped forward and glared up at Wychwoode from under his brows. "I will shout it from the gallows if necessary, in front of whatever crowd of ghouls turn up to see me die! So, it will be public knowledge! You will have to bring her in!"

He slid back down the wall and once again was consumed by a fit of coughing. "You and your Queen can do what you want with me," he muttered eventually, "but you will have to do the same to that bitch! I said it on that blasted rack, and I'll say it again now. If I burn, then she does too."

Wychwoode shook his head slowly. "I thought as much," he said. "Given the choice of two equally painful deaths, you have chosen the one that means I am bound by my duty to the law, and to my mistress the Queen, to level an accusation of witchcraft against the very woman who twice saved her life. A woman who is even now, to be honoured with a summons to Court."

"Yes, well, all I know is that she stopped me assassinating your beloved Elizabeth and getting money and a title from a grateful Queen of Scots instead. So forgive me if my heart does not exactly bleed for Lady fucking Mary too much."

"She was accused once before of witchcraft, and nearly drowned in a trial by ducking in a well," observed Wychwoode thoughtfully. "Which means this will be the second time she has faced such an accusation."

The Alchemist groaned. "You mean she very nearly died?" He gave a snort of derision that turned into another bout of coughing. Once he had his breath back he said, "That would have saved me so much trouble, believe me." Then he added, "But if she didn't die, didn't that prove the witchcraft?"

"Not at all," said Wychwoode. "For the truth is, God himself took her part." He paused, choosing his words for maximum effect. "As she went down the well, the voice of Our Lord and Saviour Jesus Christ was heard, saying she was his loyal handmaid, and that the witchfinder who accused her was a servant of Satan."

There was a long silence as the Alchemist considered this. Then he gave a slow, knowing smile. "The voice of Jesus?" he said. "Seriously?" He made a short, hollow-sounding laugh. "The voice of Jesus?" He shook his head as he stared at the older man, his breath wheezing at the back of his throat. "And you actually fucking believed it? You have got to be kidding me! She probably had her phone set to play a voice track or something. Easy trick! And she had all you superstitious yokels fooled!" He slumped further down the wall. "The voice of Jesus?" he muttered again. "Give me strength."

"Her 'phone'? What is that?"

The Alchemist gave a long sigh, his eyes burning into Wychwoode's. "It's a twenty fifteen thing. She must have brought it with her. All she had to do was prepare the phone, hide it somewhere and make sure it played the 'voice of Jesus' at the right moment." A smile cracked his thin face. "You check out that phone, Master Wychwoode, and you've got her for blasphemy as well as sorcery!" He laughed. "Oh, it just gets better and better!" This seemed too much for him. Running his fingers under the collar, he once again broke into an uncontrolled fit of coughing.

Once he was able to speak, he said, "You make damn sure you put us side by side when we are staked on that pyre, Master Wychwoode. I want to watch her burn and I really, really, *really* want to hear her scream for mercy as she dies."

CHAPTER TWO

Lady Mary de Beauvais pulled the little girl's head close into her stomacher, so the child's nose was pressed up against the stiff material.

"Mother! I can scarcely breathe!"

Lady Mary smiled as she unpeeled her daughter and held her at arm's length. "My dear, sweet Kat," she said, "I have missed you so much while I was away these many months, that I must hold you to me at every possible moment!"

"Yes, but you must not press my nose like it is a wildflower."

Lady Mary sank to the ground, her skirts billowing out around her, until she was level with her daughter's big brown eyes. "No, I must not, but you *are* like a flower, my precious one!" She placed a stray lock of the girl's hair behind her ear. "You have such beauty! And I cannot credit how much you have grown while I was away!"

"Well, you should not have been away so long, for then I would not have grown so much."

Lady Mary laughed. "Nay, my pretty…" she began, then stopped, as she noticed there were tears now welling up in the little girl's eyes. With a feeling as if a spear had been thrust through her heart, she pulled her handkerchief from her sleeve and gently wiped the tears away. "I am so sorry, Kat," she whispered. "I am so, so, so sorry. I know I said I would only be away a few days…"

"You were gone for such a very long time, Mother," Kat whispered, "I thought for sure that a bad man had crept up on you and you were… you were…" She sniffed hard, and more tears started to flow.

"I know, baby, I know," Mary replied. "But I am here now, and I am safe. I am back to look after you, and to love you." She paused. "Do you know," she said slowly, "some bad men did try to creep up on me, but..." As she said these words, she knew it was too much. The little girl's eyes widened further, and she took a small step back.

"You mean you did face danger, Mother?" she whispered. "Truly?"

"Yes… but…"

Mary stopped again. How on earth could she tell Kat what had actually happened on her journey to York this past spring? How does one tell a seven-year-old that her mother had killed and maimed men, however bad? Yet did she not owe the girl some form of explanation? After all, she *had* been gone for many months.

Or maybe she could make something up?

Mary smiled inwardly. What story could she tell that would satisfy a seven-year-old's curiosity? Maybe some tale of a cartoon-style baddie would be enough? Then the smile died, and she groaned to herself. Her fib would inevitably be found out. Her son Ambrose had been right there for some of the grisly events, and he would be bound to tell his little sister his own version. Indeed, it was lucky he'd had no chance to do so since they had returned the night before. It would be much better to get a more truthful version in first.

"Yes, there were some bad men," she said. "And do you know what I did?"

Kat shook her head, her big eyes fixed on Mary's.

"Well, there was a bad man who wanted to hurt the Queen. So I struck him with a poker, and he was not able to hurt the Queen anymore."

"You struck him?" Kat whispered. "Did that please the Queen?"

"It did. She said she wants me to join her at Court in London soon, and she wants to ask my opinion on things."

"The Queen said that?"

"Yes."

"The actual Queen?"

"Yes. The actual Queen."

"Oh." Mary waited as Kat digested this information. "And the other men?" she asked eventually.

"There was one who wanted to hurt Ambrose."

Kat's eyes widened. "Did you beat him with the poker too?"

"No, I had a very powerful musket, so I shot it at him, and he let Ambrose go."

"Oh." There was another long silence, while Mary tried to return her daughter's steady gaze. "Was there another man?"

"Well, there was a man who wanted to hurt me. So I threw him off a cliff and he fell onto his back and it broke, which meant he could not walk anymore."

"Oh."

There was a silence as Kat digested this information as well, while Mary dried her eyes again.

"So, my little kitten," she said, tucking her handkerchief back in her sleeve, "your mother had some adventures, and did in truth see off some bad men, but got back safely to you in the end."

"And you will not be having any more adventures, will you?" asked the girl. "You are staying here now?"

Before Mary could answer, a dark-haired girl of around eighteen walked up to them, followed by a tall aristocratic blond man holding the hand of a boy of around nine.

"I thought we would find you both in the gardens…" began the girl, but did not get any further as Kat ran over with a scream of "Livia! You are here too!" then jumped into her arms, sending her staggering back.

"Olivia also returned with us from York last eve," Mary said, standing up and smoothing down her skirts.

Olivia regained her balance and started to swing the child round in a circle.

"Livia! Livia!" Kat shouted into her face as they spun round. "Ma said some bad men did creep up on her, but she beat them with a poker and she shot them with a musket and she threw them off a cliff!"

"So she did!"

"And what of you, Livia?" Kat asked, as Olivia stopped spinning and lowered her unsteadily to the ground. "Did a bad man creep up on you as well?"

There was the briefest pause, then Olivia smiled sweetly, and said, "No, no. Not at all. I left all the adventures to your mother."

Mary looked away, to make sure she didn't catch Olivia's eye. For a bad man called Lionel Shelton most definitely had crept up on her, and had forced himself on her in the most brutal way. But this was their secret, and would never, ever be shared. She glanced over at the man and boy, who were standing in the shade of a nearby tree. They seemed oblivious to what had just passed between her and Olivia.

She walked over to them. "Art well rested from your first night back in your own bed, after three weeks on the road, Ambrose?" she asked the boy.

He nodded. "Yes, Ma, it was lovely." He looked up at the man. "I told Pa when we first rode up north in the snows that I missed my own bed, and I missed you telling me stories. So it is nice to be home, Ma, truly it is."

"You have stories of your own now, son," his father said, ruffling his son's hair with a grin. "Real boys' adventures that actually happened, not like the mawkish nonsense your mother tells you of the tragic Princess Diana and other made-up tales."

"Really William, let the boy alone," Mary said. "It must have been so frightening for him." Then she added, "It certainly was for me,".

"But Ma," Ambrose exclaimed, "Master Wychwoode told me all! He told of your adventures with Pa before I was born, and he was most insistent that our Lord Jesus himself said you were blessed!"

"Yes, well, we do not like to talk of that, Ambrose," Mary muttered, with a glance at her husband for him to support her.

Sir William nodded, his expression now serious. "Indeed, son, your mother is right. Such matters are not for discussion outside the family."

Ambrose nodded slowly. "As you wish, Father."

"I do mean it, Ambrose, most firmly." William put his hand on the boy's shoulder. "Now, you and Kat may amuse yourselves a while, as I need to talk with your mother."

---0---

"We need to decide on Ambrose's education," William said, when they had walked away from Olivia and the children. "The Grenvilles would have had him for a year or two, and schooled him in Latin, Greek and religion, not to mention how well he was doing at the butts with his archery."

Mary gave her husband a stern look. "Given that the Grenvilles turned out to be seditious Catholics, as well you knew they might be," she left a significant pause so that could sink in, "I am well pleased he was only there a few weeks and is no longer learning religion with them."

William had the grace to look sheepish. "Mary, my love, I have admitted my error, and we have all been through much pain and suffering as a result. I pray you do not keep the subject alive anymore."

Mary nodded. "As you wish," she said, making a mental note to leave the matter very much alive and open to being re-visited as and when it might suit her purpose. "I would that we make arrangements for Ambrose to be tutored here in his scriptures, as well as in Latin and Greek," she said. "I would not have him leave us again."

"I agree," said William. "I too, have no wish to send him away to another house. It was too painful for us all."

"Good. Then that is settled. We will find him a tutor here." She stopped. "And another thing," she said suddenly. "Kat can be tutored with him. In all his lessons."

William turned back to her, "Now you are being absurd," he said. "Whoever heard of a girl being tutored in such subjects?"

Even though the thought had only just occurred, Mary knew it would be the right thing. After all, why should girls not be as well educated as men? One day in the future they would have equal learning opportunities – why not start it now? And especially with Kat, whose sharp little mind was just crying out to be broadened. Yes, this did need to happen.

But Mary did not answer immediately. Instead, she raised one eyebrow and gave her husband an intense, challenging stare. After a few moments, he coughed and said, "I mean, my love, it is not natural…" Maintaining the stare, she raised the eyebrow slightly higher. He coughed again. "Well, perhaps we could consider it when she is a little older..."

"She will be tutored with Ambrose, now," Mary said finally. "She may have opportunities in life, such as a position at Court. The better educated she is, the better she will be able to secure such a position. And with it a good marriage."

William looked as if he were struggling to assert himself, then his shoulders dropped. "Yes, of course," he said. "I shall see to it."

Mary nodded. "Good." She walked on. "Then that is also settled."

As they proceeded to the house, Mary's satisfaction was tinged with a small, but niggling sense of unease. Educating Kat fully was the right thing to do – that was unarguable – but it opened up the possibility that her feisty daughter would grow up to have expectations; ones that society was not yet ready to deliver. Not only could that cause her dissatisfaction in later life, but it could also turn her into something of a rebel.

And rebels are people who cause history to change.

This had been Mary's greatest fear ever since she had fallen through a time wormhole into Tudor England ten years earlier, arriving as a confused time-traveller called Justine Parker. Would she cause history to change so much that her own birth in 1988 would be endangered? If so, would she suddenly just 'disappear'? After all, within two weeks she had saved William's life, when history had fated him to die.

This thought had eaten her up inside, and had kept her a virtual prisoner at Grangedean Manor for all that time. That was until she found out there was another traveller from her own time and place who seemed to have fallen through a similar wormhole. So now she had the means of validating her future existence – for if this other time-traveller knew her, and knew her name, then it would mean she had still existed in his time, and had not suddenly 'disappeared'.

So she had ventured out of her safe home environment in search of him, and eventually she had found him.

His name was Rick, but he called himself the Alchemist. Not only had he known her, but he had also presented her with the unassailable logic that nothing could endanger her birth. His explanation of parallel histories made perfect sense, and had finally set her mind at rest about the future. As he put it, her birth was a fact, and nothing she did now could alter it.

However, the future itself – the 21st century one that she knew of cars and phones and computers – that future now existed only in their memories. The potential changes that she had caused by saving William, then by having three children who were never meant to exist, and leaving Grangedean – those meant that a whole new long-term future would now be written.

So even though she no longer feared for her own existence, she could not help but feel concerned when her actions could so clearly have an effect on the future. Who knew what Kathryn de Beauvais could achieve as an educated adult, and her potential to send events in new and unexpected directions?

So even though she knew it was the right thing to do, Mary could not help a small shiver of fear that it was one more nail in the coffin of the 21st century world that only she and the Alchemist had known.

"...Mary, my love, did you hear what I said?"

William had stopped and was staring at her, his hands on his hips and his shoulders back.

"For sure," she replied, then added, "what was it again?"

William rolled his eyes. "By Heavens, woman. I asked if you wanted Jane tutored as well as her brother and sister?"

"In good time, yes. But now she is only five."

Mary walked purposefully back to the house, where they found Olivia waiting for them in the Great Hall.

"Sir William. Lady Mary," Olivia said as they entered, "I thank you for your hospitality, but I must take my leave. I would return to London as soon as I can, to resume my duties as lady-in-waiting to Lady Burnham."

"Indeed you must," answered Mary. "Her Ladyship was most generous in allowing you to journey back with us from York, so we could enjoy your company a little longer."

"But you must stay tonight and dine with us," said William, "for I have invited your father to attend, and half the nobility of the county, to welcome us all back to Grangedean!"

Olivia smiled. "Oh! My father? Of course!" She looked at Mary. "I had not thought I would have the time and opportunity to see him, but if it is such a banquet I am sure Lady Burnham will forgive me one more night!"

Mary put her hand on Olivia's arm. "I am sure she will. So come, let us choose our gowns and have my own lady-in-waiting, Sarah, fix our hair."

---0---

Some hours later, Olivia and Mary made their triumphant entrance into the Great Hall, where all the local nobility and dignitaries were already seated for the banquet, and were starting to get merry on Sir William's finest wines.

A servant opened the doors and announced them, but his voice was lost in the shouting and laughter of the guests. Then William broke off his conversation with the thin, grey-haired man beside him. He stood, and banged his knife handle hard on the wooden table. When eventually he had everyone's attention, he announced, "My Lords, Ladies and Gentlemen! I pray you, make welcome my wife, Lady Mary de Beauvais, and Olivia, the esteemed daughter of my dear friend here, Thomas Melrose." He waved a hand at the grey-haired man. "Please," he raised his goblet, "be upstanding and raise your glasses to these two brave and worthy ladies!"

Everyone got to their feet, stamping and cheering, as the two women progressed up the hall. Olivia glanced at Mary and got a reassuring smile that seemed to say, 'be confident in your yourself, and in your beauty!'

And indeed, they both had good reason for such confidence. Their elegant gowns were made fashionably wide by the latest farthingales, and their waists were pinched in by the tightest lacing. Their hair was pulled back from their foreheads – in the style made popular by the Queen – and formed into the heart-shape that her Majesty so favoured. Their pale faces were softly accentuated by rouged lips and cheeks, and Mary had insisted on applying additional kohl around Olivia's eyes, "to enhance their natural beauty."

Even so, Olivia was relieved once she had taken her seat at the top table and the normal hubbub of conversation had returned. What had all these men been thinking as they stared at her just now? To bed her? To take her by force? She shook her head as she sat and arranged her skirts, then washed her hands in the silver bowl proffered by a servant. No, they could not all be as bad as that despicable Lionel Shelton who had attacked her a few months before. But she could not shake the wariness she now felt around men. If Shelton's assault had taught her one thing, it was now to trust her instincts in regard to them.

"By Heavens," said Thomas Melrose as she pulled a piece of guinea fowl onto her plate, "it gladdens a father's heart to see you again!" He shook his head slowly. "But in truth, it is hard to recognise you! You are such an elegant woman now, not at all the young girl I waved off last winter!" He regarded her a few moments, then he frowned: concern written in every deep line of his thin face. "My dear, I had thought you were in London or Essex with my Lady Burnham, but I understand from Sir William you were on Progress with the Court, and that you were involved in some dangerous actions and adventures… He has said that you showed great daring and bravery. Is this true?"

She inclined her head. "I did only what was necessary, Father."

"Whatever it was, it has made a fine woman of you."

"Perhaps," she answered, as she held up her goblet for wine to be poured by a servant. "But better to thank the good Lady Mary. Without her support and guidance, I am not sure I would have had the strength to prevail."

"Ah, Lady Mary." He nodded. "She is indeed a special person; blessed by the Lord Jesus himself. There was no other woman in this realm I would have entrusted with your safety." He put his hand on hers. "And in truth, it seems my faith in her was well-placed."

Olivia was about to answer, when the doors to the Great Hall were again thrown open, and a tall, white-haired man dressed in black strode in, followed by four men-at-arms.

Immediately the hall was silent.

"Master Wychwoode!" exclaimed William. "You are well met, sir, and most welcome in my house." Wychwoode did not respond, but stared hard at Lady Mary instead. "May I ask the purpose of this visit?" asked William, an edge of concern now creeping into his voice.

"Sir William," Wychwoode growled, his voice low but carrying to all in the room. "It gives me no pleasure, and indeed much sorrow, but I have come on Her Majesty's business." He walked up to the top table. "I have come to arrest Lady Mary de Beauvais."

Mary stood. "Arrest me, sir?" she demanded; her voice surprisingly calm. "On what charges, may I ask?"

Wychwoode gestured to the men-at-arms to come up behind him, until all five were standing before the high table.

"Lady Mary de Beauvais," he said. "I have come to arrest you on charges of sorcery and blasphemy."

CHAPTER THREE

Lady Mary de Beauvais said nothing as Wychwoode studied the little jewelled box she kept beside her bed. He tried the lid.

"It is locked. Open it, please."

"If I refuse? It is my private property."

"I have a warrant to search the house for evidence of sorcery and blasphemy. So, I have the right to have it opened – by a key, or if that is not forthcoming, on the point of a blade." He put the box down and studied her a moment. "Mary," he said, his voice soft and tinged with sorrow, "as I said in the hall earlier, I take no pleasure in this."

"Yet you come into my home to arrest me in front of my family and friends, and your men go through my possessions like I am a common criminal?"

"It is the law." He shook his head. "I have no choice."

They were alone in her bedroom, after Wychwoode had insisted that the search of her most private spaces was conducted by him on his own, while his men searched the rest of the house. William had initially demanded that he accompany them for the sake of propriety, but Wychwoode had been very clear that his interest was purely to gather evidence, and William need have no fears for his wife's modesty. Even Mary had spoken up to assure William she was perfectly capable of looking after herself. Eventually William had accepted this with very poor grace and had marched off after Wychwoode's men instead.

"But you have not yet told me by whom I am accused," Mary began. "Three weeks ago, I prevented the Alchemist from killing the Queen, and now…" she stopped as a dreadful realisation came to her, staring wide-eyed at him. "It was the Alchemist, was it not? It was he who accused me?"

She could see in his eyes it was true. She reached over and put her hand to his sleeve. "Robert," she said softly. "It is good we are alone to discuss this." She paused. "A man who is facing certain death will no doubt say anything to try and save his skin."

He looked down at her. "He might." His gave a slow shake of the head. "I am most sorry Lady Mary, truly I am, but the man has made allegations of you that in all conscience I simply cannot ignore."

Mary removed her hand. "You could try," she said quietly, feeling a bead of sweat start to run down her back. "Do I not deserve that?"

He looked away, as if there were nothing he could say.

"You would believe the word of a traitor over me?"

Wychwoode took a deep breath. "My dear Lady Mary, he has inferred sorcery, evidenced by talk of future times in front of witnesses… I cannot ignore such things."

"Witnesses?" Then she shook her head in realisation. "Of course! That couple in York, the ones he tied up – they must have heard us talking about the future…" He inclined his head. So it was true. Then another thought came to her. "But you said I was also accused of blasphemy. Talk of the future may be construed as sorcery, but there is no blasphemy in such a thing."

Wychwoode sighed. "Lady Mary, you know I hold you in the highest regard?"

She said nothing, as her stomach started to knot up. Where this would lead?

"I have witnessed your brave deeds and leadership with my own eyes," he continued. "I know such forcefulness in a woman would be seen by many as a form of sorcery in itself, but I also see daily how the Queen shows the same, so I know it has precedence. But…" he paused. "I also have knowledge that you could not be a sorcerer, for you are favoured by the Lord Jesus – as all who were at the nearby well these ten years past heard Him say so clearly. His 'loyal handmaid' I believe he called you."

She stayed silent, letting him continue.

"Yet, the Alchemist has led me to believe the voice came not from our Lord, but from some blasphemous means instead."

So that was it.

The Alchemist must have worked out how the 'voice of Jesus' trick had been achieved. He would have known she would have most likely had her phone on her when she fell back through time, so she had set it up to play the 'voice'. Which meant Wychwoode was looking for her phone to prove blasphemy; the phone she kept locked in the little jewelled box he had just been trying to open.

"When you told the Alchemist of the voice of Jesus…" she began, then faltered to a stop. Maybe she had imagined it. Maybe this was not about her using her phone, but this was all about something else; something she could more easily dismiss.

But Wychwoode confirmed her fears. "He talked of a thing called a 'phone' – which would have produced the voice by sorcery, or by some functional trick, or some such."

Mary looked down, as if to reassure herself the floor of her bedroom was still solid, and not starting to swell like a murderous sea. Then she took a deep breath to try and steady her nerve.

"He challenged you to find it, before he was put to death?" she asked.

"Yes." Wychwoode paused. "But he told me this only two days ago."

"You mean he still lives?" She stared at him with wide eyes. "He has not been executed like Moreton?"

"Nay," he answered. "He remains a prisoner in the Tower of London. He will be put to death very soon, rest assured. But in the meantime, I need to address the allegations he has made, as the law demands. Allegations which have been independently validated."

"Master Wychwoode," she said, trying to keep her balance, "I have once before been accused of sorcery – an accusation which was not carried through at the time. Must I be so accused again?"

He sighed. "Mary, as the Lord is my witness I must say again this gives me no pleasure, but I must carry it through." He paused. "And you do not question this talk of 'phones' – which leads to me to believe you know what such a thing may be." He looked her hard in the eye, then said the words that turned her stomach to ice. "Mary, do you have such a phone, and did you use it to conjure up the voice of Jesus?"

There was a long silence, as his words reverberated over and again through her head.

'Do you have such a phone, and did you use it to conjure up the voice of Jesus?'

The words seemed to grow louder and louder each time, until she wanted to scream at them to stop, to leave her alone…

'Do you have such a phone, and did you use it to conjure up the voice of Jesus?'

There was nothing for it. To be seen to co-operate might just help, even if only a tiny bit.

She reached into a recess on the carved bed post and took out the key. Like an automaton, she opened the box and handed over her most precious and secret possession.

Even though she had known him for many years and trusted him, he was still at heart a medieval man. So it felt as if part of her soul had been laid bare when he turned her phone over and over in his hand, studying it from every angle and tapping it curiously.

"This is the thing they call a phone?" he asked quietly. She nodded. "And it can conjure up the voice of Our Lord by its sorcery?"

"It is made by the hands of men. It does not work by sorcery."

"Then show me how it so conjures His voice."

Mary shook her head. "I cannot," she answered, "it has no power."

His hands stilled, and he looked back at her. "I know not what you mean," he muttered. "Can you not simply say the necessary incantations?"

"That is not how it works." She paused. The phone had been in the box for months while she had been away. How do you explain a flat battery to someone who has no concept of what a battery is?

"Imagine a water wheel turning a mill stone..." she suggested.

He nodded curiously, so she continued. "If the water does not flow, what happens?"

He shrugged. "The wheel must stop."

"Exactly. It has no energy to turn it. No power."

He nodded again slowly, as if the comparison now made sense. "So this phone – it needs energy to make it function?"

"It does."

"Should it then be held in a mill stream?"

"No." She took out the solar charger and plugged it in. "It takes its energy from the light of the sun."

There was a silence as they both stared at the black screen. Nothing happened.

Mary willed the phone to start up. Maybe he would see that there was no sorcery in it. Although she had to admit that was hardly likely.

"It does not function," Wychwoode said after a while.

"Wait!" she snapped, then added quietly, "please!"

Eventually the start-up screen opened. He was silent as the logo appeared, and when she put in her pin code. Then, when the home screen lit up, he looked at her and observed, "You say this is not sorcery, which would make a smooth black surface come alive with pictures?"

"It is the work of men," she repeated, staring at the screen.

"And it is the work of men that enables this thing to conjure up the voice of Our Lord?"

"Yes," she said in a small voice.

"Show me."

Mary looked up and swallowed hard to try and control her racing heartbeat. "Robert, please do not make me..."

His face was set sterner than she had ever seen it. "Show me, I say."

With a nervous sigh, she opened the voice app, then she paused, her finger hovering over the play button. "If I had not used this," she said, "I would have died down that well."

He shook his head. "Blasphemy is blasphemy, Mary. Better to have died with your immortal soul in a state of grace."

She shook her head. "That is not how I saw it at the time."

She tapped on the play button.

Once again the voice issued the order to the witchfinder Hopkirk to spare Mary Fox, as she had been called then. "Matthew Hopkirk – I am the Lord Jesus Christ and I say before these people that you do not act in my name. Mary Fox is my loyal handmaiden – she is not now, nor has she ever been, a witch. Matthew Hopkirk, you are a servant of Satan, and I call on you in the name of God my Father, to end this trial now." Hearing it again after all these years, and with the accusation of blasphemy riding on it, made it too painful to bear; and when the voice had claimed to be Jesus himself, Mary could not help but wince.

"There was no intent to blaspheme," she said, breaking the long silence after she closed the app.

"Such is for a court to decide," he muttered. Then in a stronger voice, he asked, "And the men who made such things – in what year do they make them?"

So, with the blasphemy clearly proven, there only remained the matter of sorcery...

"In twenty fifteen," she breathed.

"Speak more clearly, please."

"Twenty fifteen," she repeated. "They are made in twenty fifteen."

He put both hands on her shoulders. "Then Lady Mary de Beauvais, I must ask this question, and I need you to answer me most honestly, as God is your witness, and if there is any hope your immortal soul can be saved."

He took a careful breath, and said, "Are you a traveller through time, come here from twenty fifteen?"

CHAPTER FOUR

Wychwoode led Mary back into the Great Hall. His hand was an iron grip on her arm, as if to stop her trying to escape. But he must have known she could hardly put one foot in front of the other without her legs buckling under her. Running would be the last thing she could manage.

His men were there, and at a nod from Wychwoode, they came up to her. Two of them took an arm each, while the other two stationed themselves in front and behind her as close guards.

Apart from the guards, William, Melrose and Olivia were alone. They stood, their faces showing confusion and concern.

"I must inform you," said Wychwoode in a flat voice, "Lady Mary de Beauvais is under arrest, on suspicion of using sorcery and dark arts to perform the most unnatural act of travelling through time itself, from the year twenty fifteen. She is also charged with blaspheming the Lord by causing His voice to be conjured up using an ungodly tool from the future. She will therefore be taken from here to the Tower, to await her trial for such sorcery and blasphemy."

Olivia went white then collapsed onto her chair, her head flopping to one side in a faint. As Melrose bent over and clasped her hands, William stormed round the table.

"This is an outrage! Robert, what manner of nonsense is this? Mary is innocent of these charges, as well you know! Withdraw this accusation this instant!" His hand went to his belt as if to draw his sword, before realising he was not armed in his own house. Instead he marched over to Mary and pushed Wychwoode's man aside. "Mary, my love," he ordered, "tell them this is untrue!"

She said nothing, but could feel a tear emerge and start roll down her cheek. William stepped back; his face drained of all colour. "You do not deny it?" he whispered. "Blasphemy and sorcery?"

Mary gave him the smallest shake of her head, as another tear emerged.

"Well I do not give it credence!" William shouted. "It is but a misunderstanding – that is all! We will fight against it! We will not let this go its full course." He turned to the older man. "I demand you retract this, this, this – nonsense – immediately!"

"I cannot."

"But we are summoned to Court!" William actually stamped his foot. "Her Majesty will be most angered if we do not attend!"

"I am sorry, Sir William, but that summons is withdrawn."

William scowled at Wychwoode, then looked back at Mary. "I repeat, this is but a misunderstanding, and we will fight it to our last breath!" He put his hand up to Mary's cheek. "My love, fear not," he whispered. "I will do all I can to end this nonsense. The de Beauvais name will be not tainted by such falsehoods."

She gave him a weak, watery smile, and he moved back, shaking his head.

Thomas Melrose stepped forward. "Come now, Master Wychwoode," he said. He drew himself to his full height and looked the lawyer in the eye. "You know, as we all do, that Lady Mary is a person of the soundest character, who has proven time and again how worthy she is, and who deserves not to be treated this way. My daughter tells me that were it not for Lady Mary, then the life of our dear Queen may well have been lost." He took a step forward. "Yet you put her under arrest for actions of ten years past?"

"Aye, Master Melrose, I do. I am bound by the law."

"For all that every man who knows her can vouchsafe her good character?"

"Which you, and any other man, can do when the matter comes to trial."

Melrose stepped back, his shoulders dropping. "Then in truth, you are resolved to see this through?"

"I am, so we leave immediately," Wychwoode answered. "Lady Mary can take one female companion with her to the Tower." He gestured at Olivia who was now sitting up, her face still pale. "I assume it is to be Mistress Melrose."

He turned back to his men. "Escort these women to the carriage and ensure they are held securely within. We will then take them both to confinement in the Tower of London."

---0---

William accepted some wine from Melrose in one of his finest glass goblets, as he sank into his chair by the fire in the solar. It was an hour or so later, and Grangedean Manor was very quiet – all the guests having been sent home immediately after Wychwoode had started his search of the house, and thankfully before Wychwoode had taken Mary and Olivia away. William had pressed upon the guests the need to keep this matter silent until he had cleared his wife's name. There had been much drunken nodding and muttering, but he knew it was extremely unlikely that this matter would be contained. No doubt it would become the hottest topic in the county, with much speculation on his wife's guilt or otherwise.

Her guilt…

"By Heavens, Thomas," he muttered, staring into the fire, "did you not observe Mary when Wychwoode accused her of travelling through time itself?" He drained the goblet in one go and held it out for more. "She did not deny it, withal. By the Lord's dying breath, she said naught in her defence."

"Nay," observed Melrose as he refilled the goblet, "she seemed accepting of it."

"At least we were alone when that was said," William observed. "All those drunken fellows and their wives did not hear how Mary as good as admitted… that she is a sorcerer." He faltered to a stop and stared silently into his goblet. "Why did she not fight?" he said eventually. "Why did she not call it out for arrant nonsense? For all that in truth, such talk of sorcery itself is nonsense."

"It is believed by many."

"Yet why did she not deny it?"

Melrose gave a small shrug. "For the only reason, Will." He paused and shook his head slowly. "For the reason we both know in our hearts. She believes it to be true."

"That she travelled through time from the distant future?"

"Indeed so."

"But it is not to be believed!" William shouted, slamming his goblet down hard on the table beside his chair, causing most of the wine to slop out. "By Christ alive," he continued, ignoring the red puddle spreading out, "how can any man of a sound mind accept such a thing?"

"She does."

William stared hard at his friend.

"As I see it," Melrose continued, "there are two choices here." He paused, appearing to consider his words with care. "On the one hand, we can accept that your wife has lost her mind, and in her madness, has convinced others that she is a time traveller."

"But why would she do that? Bringing others in on her mad conceit harms no person but herself. And anyway," William bit his lip as he thought, "we both know there is no madness in her. She is more settled in her wits than even you and I."

"Precisely." Melrose nodded. "So then we have the only other choice. That Lady Mary de Beauvais is indeed come here from the year – what was it? Twenty fifteen."

There was a silence as William tried to process this thought.

Of course it was nonsense. For if she was such a traveller, then she would have appeared suddenly, as if from nowhere; when in truth she had told a plausible tale of falling from her horse when riding past. But… Mary was a consummate horsewoman, who could ride any beast and tame even the feistiest of mares, so how would she have fallen? And where was the horse she had been riding? Would she not have insisted on sending a servant out to retrieve it?

No, no… she was not to be doubted. if she said she had fallen, then that was what occurred.

Although for sure, she had not been dressed for riding – at least not in women's clothing. She had been wearing a semblance of male attire, if William recalled correctly. She had been clothed in an unfinished woollen doublet and tunic down to her knees, hose so thin she was all but bare-legged, and boots. And she said she came from Hammersmith, but remarked on this as if such a place was part of London, when as any well-travelled man knows, it is but a village many miles from the city.

William caught his breath. Maybe in 2015 London will have grown so far beyond its walls that Hammersmith will have been swallowed up, as a pike swallows a minnow?

Then he frowned. Was he now starting to believe she could in truth be such a time traveller? That she had not fallen from her horse, but had appeared as if from the air itself? That she was dressed in clothing appropriate to a girl of 2015, not 1565? That she did come from both Hammersmith and London?

To think on it now, her behaviour was always most strange, even to the point of pretending to be a deer when they were alone in his chamber, and dressing as a boy to save his life in the tavern.

In which case, maybe the truth was indeed that she *had* travelled through time…

He looked sharply across at Melrose, and it was clear from the expression on his friend's face that had come to the same conclusion.

"By Heavens, Tom," he whispered, "Can it really be true?"

"I fear so, Will." Melrose answered. "I see you have reached the same understanding as I have. It is the only explanation that covers all the facts of the matter."

William felt his face suddenly flush red, and he stood so quickly that his chair pushed back with a loud scraping noise. "So in truth I am married to a sorcerer come from more than four hundred hence!" he shouted. Then he flung his goblet into the fire, so it flew onto a burning log and shattered into a thousand hissing and steaming pieces. "By Christ's Wounds, Tom, if this is true…" He took a couple of sharp breaths, "If she is indeed such a sorcerer, then she has lied to me all these years! Everything we had together has been false!" He thumped the table hard with his fist. "Why did she trust me not, Tom? Why did she not tell me herself – that I must discover the truth in this dreadful manner? By her arrest in public?"

"Because you would have reacted just as you have this moment, perhaps?" Melrose said quietly, taking another goblet off the shelf and refilling it for William. "And she preferred to keep you in happy ignorance rather than risking your anger?"

"But she has played me for a fool!"

"Belike she has. Although not through malice, I warrant, but through love."

William took a deep drink. For all his anger just now, maybe Tom was right? Could he really blame Mary for her deceit? Maybe it was as his friend had said – that it was for love that she had planned to take her secret to the grave and keep him in happy ignorance? Could she be blamed for that? The Mary he had always loved? The Mary who had always been a good wife and mother to his children?

It was almost as if Melrose had once again read his thoughts. "And do not forget, Will," he observed. "She did save your life in that tavern. It was as if she knew what was to come to pass and was there to stop it."

William sat down and nodded slowly as he stared at the pieces of glass glowing in the fire, the heat now gone out of him.

"She was most insistent I stayed in a cottage in the woods that very night," he observed.

"For sure," Melrose answered. "So she must have known, and was trying to keep you from your fate."

"But she did deceive me, Tom," William said, looking at his friend with wide eyes. "I say again, she never said aught that she was a woman come from the future."

"Yes, but we both know the truth of this. She is a brave, strong and caring woman, wherever she may be from."

"Caring indeed," William said. "You are right, Tom."

"Indeed so." Melrose paused. "And she has ever been a worthy mother, that none can fault in her love for her children."

William turned back to the fire. "The children! The truth of this would destroy them! So we must let them think only that she has been arrested on false charges – no more." William refilled their goblets. "And I must do all in my power to get her home and have such charges dropped, before Wychwoode and his officers…" he stopped and took a deep breath. "Before they put her to trial and…"

They looked at each other, but neither could bring themselves to utter the awful words.

'…and to death'.

CHAPTER FIVE

The rooms in the Tower were unexpectedly well-appointed.

Mary and Olivia peered into a bedchamber with just enough space for the four-poster within, its frame hung with heavy woollen drapes. Then there was a formal sitting room with a blazing fire already burning in a stone-arched fireplace. This room also contained a couple of high-backed chairs before the hearth, a small writing table, and a *prie dieu* – an oak prayer desk with a sloping top and a kneeling platform at the front.

"I had assumed we would be cast into some sort of dungeon," Mary observed as they were ushered into the room by a yeoman warder, then heard the door locked behind them.

Olivia sat before the fire and kicked off her shoes.

"It is not like you to be so quiet," observed Mary, sitting beside her. "You have hardly said a word since we were taken from Grangedean in the carriage. Do you not have questions for me?"

There was a long silence, as Olivia stared into the fire. Eventually she said, "I have but one question."

"Go on."

Again, a long silence. Then Olivia turned and looked searchingly at Mary.

"Is it true?"

She said the words so softly that Mary almost didn't catch them above the crackle of the fire. The flames danced merrily away in the grate, as if unaware of the significance of the question now hanging between them.

Mary sighed. "Yes," she said. "It is."

Olivia considered this a while, then must have decided that further questions were now needed. "You have travelled through time itself, from the distant future?" she asked.

"Yes. I have."

"Aye, now I think on it, you always had a strange way about you." Olivia said with a frown. "You were so certain that women would one day be the equal of men. That was from your knowledge, not just from hope?"

"It was truer of the world I lived in." Mary paused. "And although there is still much to be done to achieve full equality, essentially yes."

"So all the advice you gave me, that I should be strong and that it is not my fault if a man forces himself on me – that was from your actual experience of things yet to come?"

"Again, yes." Mary put a hand on the girl's arm. "Olivia, I had a different view on this world – a view no person born in these times could possibly have. I wanted to challenge your beliefs; to make you see there are always alternatives." Mary sat back. "And I think I might have helped, just a little bit?"

"Perhaps." Olivia stared into the flames for several long minutes. Then she turned to Mary and said, "The voice of Jesus, that Wychwoode himself told to me and Ambrose up in York – was that not real?"

Mary sighed again. It had been all very well telling the truth about being a time traveller, but to come clean about her deception with the phone? That might place a heavy burden on Olivia if she were called as a witness at the trial. But wouldn't a lie be even worse? After all they had been through together, she owed the girl that, at least.

"No," she said. "I caused the voice to come forth by using the phone. It was as Wychwoode said."

"But causing the voice of Jesus to be heard – that is blasphemy indeed." Olivia shifted in her chair, as if the fire had suddenly become too hot.

"It troubles you?"

Olivia turned to her with a look of sadness. "That it does, Lady Mary. It troubles me for the sake of your soul," she shook her head slowly. "And indeed, for mine as well."

"So what would you have me do?"

"I would have you pray with me for forgiveness," She gestured at the prie dieu. "For then I will know that you are penitent, and can still receive God's grace."

Mary sighed inwardly. As a 21st century English girl, she had never been particularly religious, ever since the occasion when she had been sitting in a school chapel service and the chaplain had been talking of God's love for innocent children. Something in his tone, or maybe it was the way he held himself, made her think that he was simply saying words he'd said a thousand times before and not even thinking about what he was saying. Which meant that she started questioning the words for herself – and finding she had more questions than answers. If God is willing to prevent such things as the suffering of innocent children, but not able to do so, then he is not omnipotent. And if he is able to prevent it, but chooses not to, then he is not good. And if he is neither omnipotent nor good, why should she have to worship him? This sceptical mind-set had set her up for an adult life where religion had no necessary place, and this had served her well in 21st century England. But England in the 16th century was an altogether different place, and she had been quickly accused of witchcraft on the basis of a casual expletive that would not have even raised a modern eyebrow. So she had been forced to adjust her outlook, and accept that an outward show of religious belief was necessary to survive in the Tudor world. She attended church as often as she had to, and had been strict about bringing the children up in the Protestant faith. But her secret scepticism had remained intact, and had made her deeply suspicious of those whose religion was so fanatical that they were prepared to kill for it.

Both Protestants and Catholics.

But for the Catholics she reserved her strongest hatred. Not only had the recent plot to kill Queen Elizabeth been driven by Catholic fanaticism, but one could not ignore the Pope's recent Papal Bull which specifically instructed all Catholics that it was their duty under threat of excommunication not only to disobey the Queen, but actively to seek her death.

Mary knew she was privileged to have seen a different side of Elizabeth to the stern monarch that everyone else knew. A bond had been forged between them over the dead body of Tom Cobham in a little house in York; a special moment of understanding between the two women. So for the Pope to seek the death of such a woman – a friend as much as a queen – meant Mary would do all in her power to stop that happening.

"Will you come and pray with me?" Olivia asked, dragging Mary back into the present.

Mary stayed still. How could she be honest about such a personal matter? But then again, if a prayer would help set Olivia's mind at rest, however insincerely it was said, then surely the end justified the means?

Mary stood and went over to the prie dieu. "Come, then" she said, "I will pray with you."

They both knelt, squeezing tightly beside each other on the narrow platform. Mary put her hands together.

"I pray to Lord Jesus,…" she began, then stopped.

What should she pray to Lord Jesus? To end this nightmare? It would take one heck of a miracle to get her out of this mess – and anyway that was not what Olivia wanted to hear.

"I pray to Lord Jesus…" she repeated, "to grant me pardon for my sins. For the sin of…" she stopped again.

This felt so wrong.

What was it the religious used to say back in the 21st century? That there are no atheists in foxholes? Well, this was a definitely a 'foxhole', so was she suddenly going to find religion? Judging by the tense knot in her stomach, the answer was 'definitely not'. Mary glanced across at Olivia, who now had her eyes shut and was moving her lips silently. How nice would it be to have that 16th century certainty, the total assurance that there was a god and he loved her…

Love…

In that moment, Mary knew exactly what she should pray for.

"I pray to you Lord Jesus…" she said again, "to grant me pardon for my sins. For the sin of blaspheming you by pretending to conjure your voice…"

she glanced across at Olivia, who had stopped her own prayers and was now listening, "and for the sin of sorcery, in that I was sent unwillingly across time itself to Grangedean Manor. But more than both of these, I thank you Jesus from the bottom of my heart that when I arrived there, I was able to do your good work. I was able to save the life of Sir William de Beauvais, then marry him and love him, and by him to bear three beautiful children, whom I love more than life itself. So while I accept that this life may soon be over, I pray to you, Lord Jesus, to watch over my husband and children and make sure they know that I am not a true sinner. To have them remember me as a warm and loving wife and mother, not a person worthy of incarceration and death. To know that I have always loved them and will continue to love them for all time."

Mary felt Olivia shift beside her, pushing herself slightly closer.

"And I pray for Olivia Melrose, whom I have come to love as much as if she were my own daughter. I pray you also keep a watch over her, for she is your good and faithful servant. She is so honest and so true that I am not worthy to touch the hem of her robe, and if I could have but one tenth of her courage and integrity, then I would be content to face my death knowing I am worthy of your love."

There was a long silence, then Olivia whispered "Amen."

"Amen." Mary repeated.

Olivia twisted her body and opened her arms. Mary did the same, and as they knelt on the prie dieu, they embraced with such intensity and warmth that it was as if nothing, not distance, or even death, could ever split them apart.

CHAPTER SIX

It was a few hours later and Mary and Olivia were seated by the fire when they heard the key turn in the door. A swarthy man in a leather jerkin with filthy matted hair came in, carrying a wooden tray of meats and wine.

"Mistress de Beauvais?" he said, as he put it on the table.

"Yes?" Mary stood up.

The man bowed low, then stood back and looked her up and down. "I swore I would bow before you. Aye," he continued, "I had thought you would be tall. I can see you might be one to break a man's leg with a poker."

"I see my reputation precedes me," Mary observed. "And how does it concern you?"

"Indeed, not at all," the man replied. "But I wanted to meet the noblewoman who had behaved as a common crone and inflicted such wounding on a man."

"Know your place, churl!" snapped Olivia as she also stood up. "Lady Mary should not be spoken to with such familiarity by the likes of you!" She paused. "Where is the Constable of the Tower? Why do we not have him to welcome us to this place?"

The man gave Olivia the same inspection as he had given Mary. "And you might be?" he asked.

Olivia drew herself to her full height. "My name is Olivia Melrose."

"Well, Mistress Melrose, we do not currently have a Constable, since Sir Peter Carew left the post some three years since. So I suggest you learn that here in the Tower, I am the gaoler, which means I say as I wish, to any prisoner." He waved his hand at the tray of food. "I am minded to take this away, and bring instead the mouldy bread and small beer we serve the prisoners in the dungeons below. Would that be more to your liking, Mistress Melrose?"

Olivia said nothing, but crossed her arms and sat back by the fire.

Mary said to the gaoler, "You must have spoken with the Alchemist. Is he still here? Has he not yet been taken to his execution for treason?"

The man gave a snide smile in the direction of the back of Olivia's head, then answered, "Nay, mistress. He lives for a few days more, and is yet chained by the neck in my most secure cell below." He paused a moment and smiled again. "Would you like me to take you to him?"

"Oh no!" Mary exclaimed. "I am the reason he is in jail awaiting execution! For sure I am the last person he would see."

"Indeed," answered the gaoler. "He has said things of you I ought not repeat, for fear of upsetting Mistress Melrose here, and her fine sensibilities." He chuckled. "I just thought it would please you, to see him, is all. Like a dog sees the bear chained to his post, eh?" He nodded at Mary and opened the door. "I will return for the tray in good time," he said, then left.

"Thank you, Olivia," Mary said, after they heard the key turning in the lock. "For taking my part with that man."

"He called you a dog! He is naught but a ruffian, my lady," exclaimed Olivia, her eyes wide. "A cur himself, who should know his place."

"Unfortunately, his place is to keep us locked in these rooms and to decide what we are to eat," answered Mary. "So, although you are right, I fear we must allow him to treat us as he will."

"Indeed, but we do not have to like it."

"No." Mary thought a moment. "But what I do not like, is the fact that the Alchemist is even in the same building as us." She shivered, despite the heat of the fire. "I had never thought I would see him again, and it upsets me to know he is near." She paced away from the hearth then turned back. "I have enough to worry me, with accusations of sorcery and blasphemy hanging over my head, to worry about the Alchemist as well."

"Too true," answered Olivia. "Have you thoughts on how we should respond to these accusations?"

Mary sighed deeply. "I know not," she said. "I had hoped Master Wychwoode would take my side, but it seems not to be."

"He serves the law before his friends."

"That he does."

"But I will speak for you, my lady," said Olivia, coming over and taking Mary's hands in hers. "I will tell how heartfelt your prayers were earlier, and how you have always been so steadfast and true. I will tell all that you are an honest woman now, whatever you may have done before, or wherever you have come from."

Mary smiled. "Then let us hope they believe you."

---0---

It was early afternoon three days later. Mary and Olivia were chatting by the fire as usual, sipping red wine from the gaoler's daily tray, when they heard the key turn in the lock.

"'Tis not time for the tray to be collected," Olivia observed casually. "I wonder who is here?"

Mary put her goblet down carefully and stood up, smoothing down her skirts as she turned to face the door. "Maybe they have come for me," she said softly. "Maybe it is time."

"By Heavens, no!" Olivia exclaimed, standing also.

The door opened, and Mary's heart sank as the tall familiar figure of Wychwoode strode in, followed by the gaoler.

Wychwoode turned to the man and growled, "Begone, sirrah. This matter is private."

When the gaoler had shuffled out, the lawyer gestured for Mary and Olivia to sit. Then he placed himself by the fire, his hands hooked behind his back.

An uneasy silence developed.

Mary shifted uncomfortably in her seat. Had the time really come for Wychwoode to escort her out of these rooms? These rooms that had become something of a home from home with Olivia's friendship and company these past few days, so that occasionally, just occasionally, Mary had almost forgotten about the reality of the fate awaiting her.

But had it now suddenly become all too real?

She took a sip of wine to try and moisten her mouth, which had now become so dry her tongue felt like a large, gagging ball of cloth. She tried to keep her hand steady, but she could not stop the pewter goblet rattling against her teeth.

Was she about to be taken to her trial?

She gave a small gasp. Or maybe there would be no trial! Maybe they had already decided on her guilt and she would be taken straight to her death! Was Wychwoode here, not to take her to some dusty courtroom, but directly instead to a rough tumbril cart? And from there to some field where there would be a stake set into the ground surrounded by dry wood at its base. And would she then be forced up to the stake and have her hands tied behind it, before some man advanced with a burning torch to… to…

Mary took another sip of wine, and thought she was going be sick.

The old man's gravelly voice forced her back to the present.

"Are you being treated well in this place?" he was asking.

Mary nodded as she tried to swallow the wine.

"As well as can be expected," Olivia said.

"And you are well fed?"

"It is not what we are accustomed to having," answered Olivia, gesturing at the remains of ham and bread on the tray. "But it will suffice."

"Good." Wychwoode paused, observing them in turn from under his brows. "Now, to business. I am come here this day to take you…" A strangled gasp from Mary interrupted him. She fell back in her chair and her goblet slipped from her nerveless fingers, landing with a clatter on the stone floor by Olivia's feet.

Ignoring the splashes of red wine now staining the side of her skirts, Olivia grabbed Mary's hand and squeezed it for reassurance. She looked up at Wychwoode. "Art come to take Lady Mary for trial, Master Wychwoode?" she asked.

Mary found her voice, and croaked, "Or has that formality been dispensed, and we are to proceed directly to the execution?"

"I am come here this day," the old man repeated, wagging his forefinger on each word, "to take you to neither trial nor execution, although those events sadly remain an inevitable part of your future. I am taking you both by boat to meet someone in his house in the country. Someone who has expressed a wish to meet you before…" he cleared his throat. "Before it is too late."

"I see." Mary took a few deep breaths to try and restore some sort of calm. "And this person – he knows that I am from future times?"

"He does, and he is most curious about you. He wishes to understand you better."

"I see," she repeated. So it was not to be a trial or burning today – that was at least something. She picked up her goblet and poured herself some more wine. Then another thought struck her. "And is he the only one, Master Wychwoode," she asked coldly, "or are my last days to be filled with many such meetings, so that the great and good of the land can all say they met the sorceress from twenty fifteen before she was burned to death?"

Mary felt Olivia squeeze her hand again.

"I cannot answer for others," he answered, "but I am sent to bring you both to meet this man now, so I would you get yourselves prepared and we will depart."

Mary glanced down at Olivia's stained skirts. "Then we will need a little time, to ensure we are both made presentable," she observed.

"I would you both make haste," Wychwoode said. "We need to catch the ebb tide if we are to get under the bridge."

CHAPTER SEVEN

The boat proceeded swiftly away from the Tower, heading west towards London Bridge. Mary and Olivia were seated in the stern, facing the eight uniformed oarsmen who were keeping good time from the regular shouts of a coxswain calling the strokes. Wychwoode was seated a little further forward.

Mary looked up as they came towards the bridge. Although she had previously seen it from the bank side, this was the first time she had been able to appreciate its scale and magnificence from the water. It was supported on many thick stone pillars, each with a large foot shaped like the bow of a boat, so the water could flow around. Above the stonework the bridge itself was like a busy street, with buildings along most of its length and only the occasional gap. At the centre was a church, then an arched building, then a drawbridge covering the largest central arch. The top of this building seemed to be decorated with what looked like a number of gargoyle heads, and Mary was just trying to work out what these were, when Olivia put a hand on her arm and said, "The heads of traitors, put on spikes for all to see."

Mary could not help but shudder. It was small comfort that she was fated to be burned at the stake and her own head would not be joining them, but it was still a deeply sickening sight. She looked more closely as they approached the bridge, trying to see if by any chance the Alchemist had now joined them, but could not make out one that looked anything like him.

She looked down to see Wychwoode had made his way back to them.

"I strongly suggest you both take a firm hold," he said. "We will shortly pass below the bridge and be subject to the strong currents and eddies that swirl between the supporting starlings. Many a boat has foundered on the stonework, and lives have been lost."

Mary glanced at the water between the nearest pillars, and she could now see that it was churning and foaming, creating white-capped waves that crashed from one pillar to the other. She must have had a look of concern, as Wychwoode added, "By good fortune, the coxswain has steered this course many times, and has never yet lost a passenger."

As Wychwoode went back to his seat, Mary grabbed onto the rail beside her with one hand, while her other sought out Oliva's and grasped it tightly. She glanced across at her friend and got a nervous grin in return.

"Hold on, then," she muttered, as the boat suddenly pitched forward into the semi-darkness below the bridge, then flung them violently to one side as the bow was pushed towards a pillar. Mary thought her hand clutching the rail was going to be ripped off by the force of it. Then the bow came round so sharply that she was sure they were about to crash, but the coxswain called, "Hold a' starboard! Pull hard a' port!" and at the last second the bow flipped round and headed now towards the opposite pillar. Mary had to push so hard against the rail to stop herself being flung out that she thought her elbow would snap, then the coxswain shouted once more and the bow flipped the other way, and she had to hang on to stop herself crashing into Olivia… and then the welcome daylight came back, the boat suddenly settled, and they emerged safely into the calm waters beyond.

"Art well?" Mary asked, keeping a firm grip on Olivia's hand, but aware that her voice had a catch in it.

"I was so certain we would be pitched out and drowned," Olivia said.

The boat now glided serenely on its way like a contented swan, so it was almost hard to believe what had just happened.

Mary nodded. "As was I," she said, then glanced back at the bridge receding behind them. "In the future people ride through rapid waters such as those purely for excitement, or go on large machines at something called a fun fair, that throw them one way then the next, just as we were."

"Why in Christ's name would they do that?"

"It is so they can be thrilled by the semblance of danger, although there is almost no chance that they will come to any harm."

Olivia considered this a moment. "Is this the women as well?"

"For sure. Girls participate in all these things just as much as boys."

"That is indeed remarkable," Olivia said. "And belike it is a little… unwomanly?"

"By our standards now, yes," Mary answered. "But not by the standards of the future I know."

The oarsmen continued to row in perfect time, carrying them ever closer to this mystery meeting.

Olivia observed thoughtfully, "For sure, it must have been so difficult for you to find your standing when you first arrived here, where a woman is beholden to a man all her life – her father, then her husband."

"It was," Mary said. "And if I had known then what I know now, I might not be in this dreadful position."

"Why, what would you have done differently?"

Mary thought back to her first day in 1565, when she had blundered around like a drunk at a party, casually swearing in front of a superstitious serving girl called Margaret. Looking back, all her woes had stemmed from that one stupid moment; from that one blunder that had ultimately set her on this path to the stake. "I would I had guarded my tongue," she answered. "For there were things that I said and things that I did that marked me out as different, and thus a possible witch. I would I had instead learned quietly how to live in these times before setting forth." Then she added, "But then belike we would not have met."

"For all our adventures together have been hard." Olivia said, giving Mary a troubled look. "We have both slain men, and I have had my maidenhood so cruelly taken. God sees these things, and it will count against me at the final reckoning."

Mary shook her head. "Nay," she answered. "I meant what I said at prayer. God sees that you are a good woman, Olivia Melrose, and that you carry no blame for either of those things." She gave Olivia a weak smile. "I have no doubt I will see Him very soon, so believe me – I will put in a good word for you."

---0---

As they progressed through the calm water towards whatever was their final destination, Mary and Olivia became silent, each lost in their own thoughts.

For all she had joked with Olivia that she would put in a good word with God, Mary felt she should not give up on life just yet. For the sake of her sanity, she was going to have to take each day as it came. And this day she was not to be drowned or tried or burned to death – but simply to meet some curious person who apparently wanted to know more about her.

So be it. Whoever this person was, meeting him could not be worse than a trial – so it would be best to calm herself down, see what this person's interests were, and if she could turn any part of this meeting to her advantage.

Mary lifted her face to the fresh breeze whipping up off the river.

While there is life, there is hope.

She glanced over at the north bank with its shingle beaches, rickety warehouses and wooden wharfs. It was impossible not to compare this with the 21st century London she remembered; the shining steel and concrete buildings mixing with older classic architecture; St. Paul's Cathedral peeking out above the Millennium Bridge, or the magnificent Somerset House next to modern blocks. But these were all in the future, and now her view was of wharfs giving way to houses, which then grew progressively grander as they came level with the Strand.

"My Lady Burnham's house," Olivia remarked, as they passed a particularly fine half-timbered building with a colourful painted boat tethered to its private jetty.

"Have you got word to her?" asked Mary. "She will be concerned you have not returned after the journey back from York."

"Nay." Olivia paused a moment. "Although I warrant I will be dismissed on return, whether I get word or not." She turned back to stare at the receding house. "She lacks tolerance for tardiness or dereliction of duty, whatever the cause."

Gradually the houses and buildings thinned out, until there was only trees and shrubbery lining the bank. The oarsmen kept time for another half hour or so, and then turned towards a small landing stage on the south bank, close to where Mary thought Putney Bridge might be one day.

With a shouted command from the coxswain, the oarsmen shipped their oars, allowing the boat to bump gently against the stage. Mary and Olivia were helped ashore, then followed Wychwoode up a track towards a large manor house surrounded by majestic elms.

"You are to meet Francis Walsingham," he said over his shoulder, as they passed a magnificent yard that must have held over fifty stables. "You are to address him as Master Secretary, understood?" The women nodded, as they walked up the steps to the front door, which was opened by a man in black.

Walsingham! The legendary spymaster, who singlehandedly created a network of 16th century spies and 'intelligencers' that would make even the modern-day MI6 envious. So this was the curious person who wanted to meet her?

As she lifted her skirts and hurried after Wychwoode, Mary had a sudden thought. If anyone in this land, save the Queen herself, could get her off these charges, it had to be Walsingham! If only she could think of a way to make it worth his while to do so.

Resolving to find a way, and with a small flutter of hope rising, she followed Wychwoode and Olivia down a wood-panelled corridor and was shown into a dark room.

It was lit only by a few candles and the light from a small window. There was a large desk in the middle and a table with four chairs in the corner, with several bookcases around the stone walls, each filled with neatly arranged books and wooden trays of documents. The desk had several piles of papers on each side, stacked neatly in ascending order of height.

A man was seated behind the desk, staring hard at them with pebble-black eyes as they came in. He was dressed in black apart from a white ruff; his thin dark face under a black skull-cap ending in a sharply-pointed beard, and his hands arched together under his chin.

Mary glanced at the table, and was horrified to see her phone sitting like an incongruous paperweight on top of a piece of paper.

The dark man gave a small cough. "Master Wychwoode," he said as he rose and came round the desk. "You are well met." His voice was soft, but with a strong undertone of authority.

"Master Secretary," responded Wychwoode, sweeping off his cap and bowing. "May I present Lady Mary de Beauvais and Mistress Olivia Melrose?"

Walsingham waved at the chairs. "Welcome to Barn Elms. Please be seated. Some wine?" Without waiting for an answer, he rang a small bell. As they were sitting down, a woman's head appeared round the door.

"Some wine for our guests, please Ursula."

While they waited for the wine, Walsingham said, "I am honoured to meet you, Lady Mary, and you too, Mistress Melrose. I have heard tell of your exploits in York recently, and I am deeply grateful for all you have both done to safeguard the person of Her Majesty, and to bring her enemies to justice."

"Thank you, Master Secretary," Mary replied carefully. "We only did what was necessary for the protection of the Queen."

"Indeed, indeed." Walsingham replied, then he leaned forward and began to study Mary intently. She shifted in her chair under his unblinking gaze, returning it as confidently as she could, while her stomach turned to ice. Being on the receiving end of this man's penetrating scrutiny felt like her very soul was being exposed for his inspection.

Just then the door opened, and the woman reappeared with the wine. While it was being poured, Walsingham sat back, and the moment passed. He brought his fingers together again under his chin.

"Thank you, Ursula," he said, as the woman withdrew. "Now, to the matter in hand." His tone became more business-like. "We have here a very interesting situation." He looked from Mary to Olivia. "On the one hand, we have your exploits in York, in which you and Mistress Melrose have demonstrated your capabilities as dedicated agents to the cause we all hold so dear – as you say, to the safety and sanctity of God's anointed Queen. Then we have, let us say, a counter-situation." He gave a small cough, as if to punctuate the change in topic. "Under the law, you are charged with two counts that both carry the death penalty; in that you are charged with sorcery, on the basis that you are a person born in the distant future, and have travelled here by witchcraft or other black arts."

Mary took a breath, preparing to refute this with her original tale of her time travel being the result of her being a victim of witchcraft, rather than the perpetrator. But Walsingham raised a hand.

"Nay Lady Mary, this is not a trial. I do not expect to hear your defence, for the facts are established and not denied, that you travelled here from…" he glanced down at the paper on the table, moving the phone to one side, "…from the year of our lord twenty fifteen. The means of travel are not relevant, for they are evidence of sorcery however they occurred." He cleared his throat. "And then we have the count of blasphemy, in that you used this thing called a…" again he glanced at the paper, "…a 'phone', to conjure up a voice and words purporting to be those of our Lord Jesus Christ himself, which is irrefutable evidence of the sin of blasphemy." Mary stayed silent as he picked up the phone and studied it, turning it over in his hand and tapping it thoughtfully. "Master Wychwoode tells me it only works when it is shown to the sun, so this has been done." He passed the phone over. "Please demonstrate how it functions, Lady Mary."

Mary pressed the button, and as with Wychwoode there was a pause as nothing happened, then the white logo lit up the screen, casting a strange glow across the four faces at the table. When the start-up was complete and the colourful app icons had appeared, Olivia gave a small gasp.

"Tis like magic!" she muttered.

"Nay," Mary said quickly, resisting the temptation to kick the girl under the table, "it is the work of men. In my time there are thousands upon thousands of such devices. Everybody has one, and they all work in exactly the same way."

"So they can all conjure up the voice of our lord?" asked Walsingham, incredulity in his voice. "Is your society so godless?"

"No." Mary answered, desperately trying to retain a sense of proportion while explaining a 2015 mobile phone to a candle-lit meeting of Elizabethans. "It is mainly so they can talk to each other."

"But can they not simply talk?" Walsingham asked.

"They can talk over long distances, without being in the same place," Mary explained. She opened the contact app. "See here," she said, showing her list of family and friends. "Here is my mother. I can tap on her name, and her own phone will make a noise to alert her. Then she can talk into it, and her voice will come out here," she pointed to the speaker. "I can answer by talking into this hole here, and she will hear me. That way we can have a conversation, however far apart we may be."

"And this is not sorcery – that you may converse with your mother despite not being in the same room?" asked Wychwoode.

"Nay – as I have said, it is the work of men."

"And if your mother is not willing to have a conversation?" the lawyer asked. "You have no idea what she may be doing if you are not close to her."

"I can leave her a message," answered Mary. She opened the messaging app. "I can write my message by touching the letters on this keyboard, and it will come up on her phone. She can then reply at a time that is convenient to her." She brought up the last text conversation with her mother and passed it over to Walsingham. "It records all the messages between us. The green ones on the right are my messages and the grey ones on the left are hers."

Walsingham and Wychwoode studied the texts together, their faces lit by the glow from the screen. Walsingham looked up. "This is truly a wondrous tool for passing messages." He pointed at the screen. "What time does it take for these to pass? This one for example – where your mother is concerned you have something called 'clean knickers'? Your response – which does seem to be somewhat less than respectful – how long did this take to appear on her phone?"

Feeling herself blushing deeply, and wishing she had opened a business contact's texts instead, Mary answered, "It is immediate."

"Truly remarkable. Yes, truly remarkable." Walsingham handed the phone back. "Please return it to its original blackness. We have much to discuss."

While Mary switched it off, Walsingham said to Wychwoode, "If I could have each one of my intelligencers equipped with a phone such as this, I would be able to pass messages and orders, and receive their reports, in the blink of an eye. We would have an inestimable advantage over the Catholics and that devilish woman who still styles herself Queen of the Scots, for all she has abdicated her throne." He looked up at Mary. "Do you have the ability to create more of these?"

Mary shook her head. "I wish I could, Master Secretary, but I have no knowledge of how they are made. And anyway," she added, "there needs to be infrastructure… er… other devices that carry the messages between phones. Without those, you would simply have two phones that have no means of communicating with each other."

Walsingham gave her a blank stare. "Tis a pity." He paused, his long fingers tapping together in sequence under his chin. Mary couldn't help being reminded of a flower opening and closing. She forced herself to look away.

Then he said, "This 'phone' device is indeed a wondrous piece. Belike it is not the only such thing that is the work of men in twenty fifteen? Perhaps you can enlighten us on what other devices are commonplace in these times?"

Mary drew a slow breath. Where should she start?

"We have many devices that save us time and effort," she said. "We call them machines."

"A machine?" asked Wychwoode. "I understand this to be a functional object, usually used in war." He looked at the two women in turn. "The ancient Romans, I believe, had machines that used tension on a lever arm to propel a rock against fortifications."

"Yes." Mary smiled. Maybe this wasn't going to be as hard as she had thought. "A device that performs a function over and over again, and can be produced in very high numbers, becomes affordable for every household." She glanced at the faces in the candlelight, staring at her in rapt attention. "So, for example, after a meal, the dishes need to be cleaned?"

Olivia nodded. "For sure. The servants fetch a bucket of water and use fine sand and horsetail plants to scour them. It is hard work, but rewarding to have clean platters."

"Well, in twenty fifteen, I would have simply put them inside a machine that looks a bit like a white chest, and the machine cleans them for me, so I can do something else."

"By Heavens," exclaimed Walsingham. "Again, how remarkable!" He was silent a moment. "Does this give your servants more time to do other, more laborious tasks, like washing your clothing?"

"No – I have no servants."

"None to run a household?" Walsingham's eyebrows nearly disappeared under his cap.

"Very few households have servants." Mary paused. "They are not needed. We have a machine to do most things, such as one to wash clothes, another to remove dirt from the floor, or one to keep food cool and fresh."

Wychwoode observed, "I warrant that these machines do every task, in place of servants."

"Indeed, indeed," said Walsingham, with a vagueness that suggested he had lost interest in 2015 white goods. Once again, he silently stared at Mary.

"Now, Lady Mary," he said after a moment, "let us consider something else that fascinates me – to wit, this curious musket fashioned by the Alchemist. It is of course the one that you used to such effect in the Yorkshire forest."

"That I later destroyed in a forge, on Her Majesty's express orders?"

"Yes, that one. You could not have anything more precise than a musket that can punch a hole in the centre of a man's forehead from many hundreds of yards away." He paused a moment, and once again Mary was in the forest, staring through the scope at the man who was holding a knife to her son's throat, holding her breath as she centred the cross hairs on his head, then squeezing the trigger and feeling the gun recoil into her shoulder as the man went down like a ninepin.

"Yet you must have had great faith in the accuracy of the weapon, must you not?" Walsingham asked, bringing her back to the candle-lit present. "Your son was but a few inches away." Then his voice dropped to a low whisper, as he stared down his long nose at her. "Yet you thought not for his safety?"

Mary felt herself flushing; despite herself, her anger was starting to rise. Was he testing her; deliberately trying to provoke her to see her reaction? She took a careful, steadying breath. "I had seen the accuracy of the weapon when the Alchemist fired on Her Majesty and hit Sir Tom Cobham in the back." She held Walsingham's gaze. "I saw it hit my horse Juno in the neck as we took a fast jump over a log." She paused again. "And I heard tell of the Alchemist hitting a coney from a long distance with deadly accuracy. So no, I thought not of my son's safety, for I knew he was in no danger."

Walsingham nodded slightly, and was silent again for a moment. Then he leaned forward, and said, "And your own faith in your proficiency to fire this weapon, that you, a mere woman, had ne'er before discharged?"

"Indeed, Master Secretary," she answered, finding it becoming harder to hold in the anger that was now starting to rise like hot lava from a volcano, "when you are in a situation where there is pressure on you to act, even as a…" she paused, "as a mere woman… you do what needs to be done."

"That may be so," said Walsingham. "Yet the first time you fire this weapon – that you know to be accurate, but which you have never before fired, you are prepared to take the risk to discharge it at the man standing directly beside your child?"

"Yes, I did." And if she had it in her hands now, she would show him just how dangerous she could be...

Walsingham pulled on his earlobe a moment. "I understand why you acted as you did, Lady Mary," he said, seemingly oblivious to the temper she was only just about managing to control. "But I am sad to say it will all come to naught. The law must take its course. You will be returned to the Tower shortly, then arraigned on the charges against you, and once found guilty you will be executed by being burned to death."

That was the last straw. Mary had had enough.

Use the anger. Work it.

Suddenly she pushed her chair back and stood, causing Walsingham to look up in surprise. "For all I have demonstrated my loyalty and value to the Queen, Master Secretary?" she demanded in a voice that echoed off the bookcases and stone walls. "Loyalty that seems to mean naught to you, who professes to be her servant?" He did not answer, but his eyes narrowed in the flickering candlelight. "As Her Majesty herself said to me, I did her great service not once, not twice, but on five occasions this summer past. Yet you choose to ignore it, because I am a 'mere woman'?" Mary stared down at the dark man. "Master Secretary," she snarled, "you, who questions my motives in protecting my son, and who seems to take delight in my impending execution – you forget I have saved the life of the Queen, and by Heavens, that has got to count for something!"

She breathed hard, then forced herself to lower her voice. "You say the law must take its course, but the Queen you and I both serve – she *is* the law. If she is prepared to pardon me, then I would give my all to protect her, as I did in York." Then she leaned forward with her hands on the table and brought her face down so close to Walsingham that every individual hair of his beard could clearly be seen in the candlelight. "Let me talk to the Queen, Master Secretary. Let me see her, so I can swear my loyalty to her myself." She stood back. "And do you know what I would tell her?" She paused to let him answer, but he shook his head slightly, his eyes wide like a rabbit watching a snake, "I would tell her that letting me go to my death would be a terrible loss to her directly. Do you know why?" Again he shook his head. "I am surprised that I, a mere woman, must point it out, but as we both know, I am from the future." She tapped the side of her head. "Which means I hold great intelligence in here about the things yet to come. I made a study of the history of these times, and I can tell you of plots to put the Queen of Scots on the throne in place of Her Majesty; of the badly-executed beheading of the Queen of Scots against the Queen's wishes, leading to a sea-borne invasion attempt by Philip of Spain that nearly causes the end of the English throne – and I can tell you of more besides. Can you even begin to imagine how far ahead of the Catholics this will put you? But no – I am a 'mere woman,' and worthless in your eyes, so you ignore this, and choose instead to let the law take its course! Well shame on you, Master Secretary!" She shook a forefinger in his face. "Shame on you for a short-sighted fool!"

Then she dropped back onto her seat, as she continued to hold his eyes, letting this sink in.

"Make me go to my death, Master Secretary, if you must. If the law is so important to you. But will you wonder for the rest of your days what valuable intelligence you will have allowed to die with me?"

CHAPTER EIGHT

Wychwoode seemed to be unable to sit down as the boat was rowed back up the river, while a blood-red sun sank slowly in the western sky.

He continually strode up and down the lowered gangway between the oarsmen, before coming back towards the two women seated in the stern, shaking his head in disbelief, then striding away again.

Eventually he stopped in front of them. "I have never, ever, *ever*, in all my years, heard a woman address the Master Secretary in such a manner!" he barked. "I am surprised he did not run you though on the very spot, for being a brazen, wanton, shameless..." Wychwoode shook his head again and stalked away along the boat, before striding back and shaking an angry forefinger at Mary. "What in the name of all that is holy were you thinking?"

Mary looked up at him as steadily as she could. "He was most disrespectful," she said clearly. "He called me a 'mere woman' – after all I had done to protect the Queen. He made me angry."

"He made... He made...?" Wychwoode spluttered. "Francis Walsingham made *you* angry...? By Heavens!" His mouth opened and closed wordlessly.

Mary sat back on the bench seat, observing the usually calm and lucid lawyer struggling to find words. She had sometimes wondered what it might take to make him lose his customary composure. And now she had found out. Heaven only knew what Walsingham had said to him in private after she had finished her tirade. The two men had stalked off to another room, leaving her and Olivia sitting in an uneasy silence.

Wychwoode glared at her.

"I did not like his tone," Mary said.

"That is not for you to like or dislike!" He leaned forward, so his lined face was uncomfortably close to hers. "You do realise, that your attempt to influence him can only rebound most dreadfully? That he will never allow you to see the Queen, or gain you a pardon?"

"Then I am in no worse a position than I was before," she observed. "But at least I tried."

"No worse? No worse? Oh, yes, your last days will be markedly worse, Lady Mary!" He pointed at Olivia. "I am now ordered to disembark Mistress Melrose at Lady Burnham's house this very evening, so you will be in solitary confinement in the Tower from here on." He stood up. "At least you will remain in your rooms, and not be cast into a dungeon like the Alchemist. Be thankful at least for that." Then he strode back towards the bow.

So now she was to be alone...

Mary took Olivia's hand in her hers. "I am so sorry," she said, "I did not mean for us to be parted. I have very much valued your company these past months."

"And I yours," said Olivia. She gave a small smile. "I admire you for trying, Lady Mary, and for standing up to that man. 'Tis only a shame he would not listen to reason, for it makes perfect sense to make use of your future knowledge."

"Aye," Mary nodded slowly. "But he would not hear it from a hot-headed woman."

"True."

There was a long thoughtful silence between them, punctuated only by the regular splash of the oars and the call of the coxswain. Mary stared across at the river bank, as houses started to appear and the countryside came to an end. Should she have let her anger take hold with Walsingham? Should she have given the dry spymaster both barrels in the way she had? True, she had said what she planned to say – for it had quickly occurred to her that her future knowledge should make her valuable – but should she have let it come out on a wave of anger, or been more measured; more considered? Mary sighed. What was done was done, and as she had said to Wychwoode, she was no worse off than before.

Apart from losing Olivia… In the deep red glow of the setting sun, Mary could see the girl was now struggling to put something into words – something that seemed troubling her greatly. It was not hard to guess what that might be.

"Yes, my dear girl," Mary said softly, "this will most likely be the last time we shall see each other."

At this, Olivia leaned across and threw her arms about Mary's neck and said with a sob, "I shall miss you so!" She buried her head into Mary's shoulder, and hot tears started to flow. "You truly have been as a mother to me! I have learned so much from you, and all to make me stronger and much more of an adult! And now I know why you have had such confidence to give me, because you have seen things I will never see, and lived in a time where women are the equal of men, and… and… and I cannot bear that I will never see you again!"

Olivia sat back. Mary took the girl's tearful face in both her hands. "Then you must honour me by living your life as I would have lived mine, Olivia Melrose," she said. "By remembering what I have taught you, and by blazing a trail for women in this society."

"I will, I will." Olivia sniffed loudly, prompting Mary to take her handkerchief from her sleeve. "Is there aught I can do for you?" Olivia asked as Mary gently dabbed her eyes. "Any service I can perform?"

Mary thought a moment. "Yes, there are two things I would have you do for me."

"Name them."

"Firstly, I ask you not to attend my execution. I cannot bear to have you see me die in such an awful way."

Olivia sniffed again. "For sure," she said with another sob. "I would not wish to see it either." She took the handkerchief and blew her nose. "And the second?"

"I would have you give my last messages to my family."

"Of course. What shall I tell them?"

Mary thought a moment. "Tell my daughter Kat that I never meant to go away and leave her again. Tell her that I will always love her, that she will be in my thoughts until the very end. Tell Ambrose that I could not be more proud of him, and to keep the stories I told him close to his heart as he grows into the strong and confident man I know he will be. And little Jane…" Mary's voice caught as her throat closed, so she had to stop and swallow hard. "Little Jane," she continued, "please tell her that her mother will always be watching over her, making sure she eats her food…" she gave Olivia a little smile. "And washes behind her ears."

"And Sir William?" Olivia sniffed.

"Please tell William I have loved him ever since I first saw his picture in the 21st century. And tell him I am so, so sorry if I have brought shame on the de Beauvais name. I never meant for this to happen, and all I ever wanted was to be a good wife and mother. I want him to know that he should find a good woman and marry again, so he can have the wife, and the life, he deserves." She swallowed again. "And maybe one day restore the good name of de Beauvais."

The two women hugged each other tightly all the way to the Strand.

CHAPTER NINE

Wychwoode was silent as the boat passed under forbidding portcullis of Traitor's Gate, then bumped up against the stone landing jetty. The gaoler was waiting on the steps with a couple of burly yeoman warders.

"Take her to her rooms," Wychwoode ordered.

"And Mistress Melrose?" the gaoler asked.

"She has been disembarked and will not be returning," Wychwoode growled. "Lady Mary is to be kept completely alone and isolated." He waved a dismissive hand. "Now take her, and make sure she is held secure, and does not converse with any person, even yourself. She is a prisoner to be punished rather than to be cared for."

The gaoler gave a sickly grin. "Why, what has the woman done, master, that she is to be so treated?"

"Hold your tongue, man," Wychwoode barked. "That is no concern of yours. If I hear you have disobeyed me, you will lose your position here. Do you understand?"

The gaoler's gaze slid over to Mary, and he gave an even more sickly smile. "It will be a pleasure, master."

As Wychwoode sat down in the stern, the gaoler indicated to the two warders to take Mary off the boat. They reached across and pulled her none too gently onto the steps. Securing their hold under each arm, they then marched her between them through a stone archway, with her feet barely touching the ground. It all happened so quickly that she did not have the chance to bid any form of farewell to Wychwoode. For all his rage against her this evening, he had been a firm friend for almost all the time they had known each other, and she would have preferred to have said at least one word before parting.

"You are hurting my arms," was all she could say as the warders gripped her tightly. Neither one replied, and if anything, they increased their grip and lifted her slightly higher. This left her hardly able to walk for herself, while it felt like her shoulders would soon dislocate.

"I would you hold your tongue," came the voice of the gaoler behind her. "You do not have your iron poker now, eh?" He was silent a moment. "You will have more to concern yourself than bruised arms in time, I warrant." She could imagine a salacious grin spreading across his coarse features. "And, mistress, it is fitting that your arms are so affected, given what you did to the Alchemist."

"It is 'Lady Mary' to you, churl," she muttered, as they started up a stone stair.

He must have heard this. "Nay," he said. "Your title counts for naught in here. If I say 'mistress,' then 'mistress' it is." Then he added, "Or maybe just 'woman' will suffice." They emerged onto a cold grey stone passage lit by occasional braziers, with Mary frog-marched by the guards. "And I told you to hold your tongue, woman." He paused. "Or I will have it cut out, so your final days are truly silent."

This had the effect he must have wanted; Mary resolved never to talk to this vile man again for as long as she might live – however long that would be.

They came to the end of the corridor and went through a heavy-looking wooden door into the open air, then proceeded along a moonlit path between two tall buildings. The gaoler came into view in front of her, scuttling sideways like a crab as the warders kept up their pace. "I know not if you have hours, days or even weeks more in my keeping," he said, "but I do know this. I am charged by Master Wychwoode to make sure you are kept silent and alone. So you do as I order without question, and without complaint. Or I will make your last days in this world the most unpleasant you can imagine."

Mary said nothing, staring at the man with burning hatred.

"I will make it so hard for you, that you will beg them to take you to the pyre as a blessed release – do you understand?" Again she said nothing. "You understand?" he repeated. She nodded as best she could, while the guards marched her briskly between moonlight and deep shadows. "Good. Then we are of one mind on this."

They went through another door, up some steps and along an oak panelled passage, with occasional pictures of stern-faced nobles hanging between candle-bearing sconces. Mary recognised the fine plasterwork ceiling studded with embossed Tudor roses; they were coming to her rooms. She waited while the gaoler selected a key from the ring on his belt and unlocked the door. The warders threw her in so roughly that she staggered and almost fell. Managing to steady herself by grabbing hold of the prie dieu, she scowled at the gaoler as he followed her in.

"I also know not what you have done to upset Master Wychwoode, that he has removed your companion and demanded you be kept in silence," he said. "But what e'er it might be, it is enough for me. I hold no care for your well-being, for all that you beat the Alchemist senseless and broke his leg." He walked to the door, then stopped and looked back. "This the last conversation you will have with me, and belike it is the last conversation you will have before you are brought to trial. I will deliver one tray each morn, and we will not converse." With that, he left, locking the door behind him.

Mary stoked the fire back into life, then sank into a chair and muttered, "Good. It is not like you had anything to say anyway."

She stared at the flickering flames, rubbing her upper arms thoughtfully.

So it had finally come to this. Ten years after time-travelling to Tudor England and being accused of witchcraft, was she finally going to be put to death as a sorceress?

She watched the flames starting to lick around one of the logs on the fire. And it would be flames such as these that would curl around her body, devouring it and turning it cracked and black, just as they were doing to this log...

Despite the heat from the hearth, she shivered.

How does it actually feel to be burned to death? To imagine it would be to die a thousand times before the event – yet to ignore it was impossible.

A piece of the log flared briefly, then broke away and fell into the glowing embers below. Suddenly she could not bear to look at the flames a moment longer.

Getting up, she glanced around the room. The prie dieu caught her eye, standing tall and forbidding, with the kneeling platform at the front. Should she pray for deliverance? She had prayed with Olivia; maybe she should try it again. She knelt on the platform and put her hands together. "Dear Lord…" she muttered. "Dear Lord… Dear Lord…"

Nothing.

She shook her head sharply and stood up. "Oh, for goodness' sake!" she said to the room. "As if that is going to make a difference!"

She went into the little bed chamber, pulled the drapes apart and climbed in, lying fully clothed on the bed. She stared blankly at her feet in their pantofle shoes, peeping out from under the hem of her skirts.

Her feet…

They had been too big for the slippers she had been given when she had first come into Tudor England – making her feel like an ungainly giant, forced to wear her modern-day boots under her first Tudor gown.

Despite herself, she gave a small chuckle. Now her shoes were made to fit her perfectly by the finest shoemakers. She kicked off the pantofles and waggled her toes.

It would be such a waste for fine shoes like these to be burned…

Or would they?

Would she be forced to walk barefoot to the pyre?

Then her feet would be the first part of her to burn – turning black as she screamed in pain…

Mary got up, put her shoes back on, and wandered into the main room.

She turned one of the chairs away from the fire, then dragged the prie dieu over. Resting her heels up on the platform, she sat with her back to the flames.

What would she be doing now, if she had never fallen into 1565 through the wormhole in time? Married with kids? Most probably. No doubt living in some suburban semi, with a husband away on business most of the time. Or was it really business? Maybe he was actually having an affair with some emaciated blonde called Helen from Accounts? What else would he do, now that his wife Justine was fast approaching forty and had lost her figure to childbirth, processed snacks and boredom?

Her mother would drop in occasionally of course, bringing bags of jellied sweets for the kids, staying just long enough to have a cup of tea, complain about her bunions, then be out the door before the sugar high sent the kids into hyperdrive, destroying all in their path around the house.

Her father would sometimes amble in with her mother, make himself a cup of tea and settle in front of the cricket, then get halfway through explaining the rules of the game to her youngest, before being unceremoniously dragged out again to drive his wife home.

It was so sad to think she'd never see them again. Never introduce them to William, or see them burst with pride when they first met their actual grandchildren. Never have her mother tell her to stand up straight ('stomach in, boobs out, Justine!') or have her father tell her to pull herself together, as 'there are plenty more pebbles on the beach, young lady...' when some boy or other had dumped her. 'He was clearly not good enough for you, anyway,' he would add.

They would never see her 'standing up straight' in her finest Tudor gown, her slim stomach most definitely 'in' behind the tightest lacing and firmest stomacher, her hair swept back in the latest style, being applauded by the assembled nobility at a royal banquet, and being welcomed as guest of honour by Her Majesty Queen Elizabeth herself.

They would never see how their little Justine had become the fine Lady Mary de Beauvais, mistress of Grangedean Manor, mother to three fine children, celebrated Tudor adventuress and most recently, saviour of the Queen's life...

And nor would they see the same celebrated Lady Mary in a plain shift dress, being led barefoot from a dirty wooden tumbril up to a stake surrounded by kindling, before having her hands bound behind it and some rough peasant executioner applying a flame, nor hear her scream as the flames licked around her and turned her still-slim body into twisted black charcoal...

CHAPTER TEN

A loud snapping sound from a burning log in the dying fire jerked Mary awake.

Slowly she lowered her stiff legs from the prie dieu and bent her knees with a small gasp of pain as they popped in protest, making the sound of a dozen firecrackers.

How long had she been asleep? The dawn light was streaming in through the window – so it must have been all night. No wonder she was stiff.

Slowly she got up from the chair and crept across the room to try and get some feeling into her legs.

She froze at the sound of the key turning in the lock, then breathed a small sigh of relief as the gaoler came in with his customary tray.

He put it on the table, then left without a word.

Mary surveyed the contents of the tray with little enthusiasm. A mouldy-looking hunk of bread sat on a wooden trencher plate, alongside a dirty tankard. She sniffed the contents and decided it was some cheap ale with some unidentifiable grey solids floating in it. She sniffed again, now catching a slight whiff of stale biscuits.

She almost gagged – that smell took her back to the portable loos at a festival she'd once been at. Which meant the most unimaginable thing; the gaoler had most probably peed in her ale. With a grimace she put the tankard down, and decided not to eat or drink. If the gaoler meant her to starve to death, he'd just be doing her a favour.

---0---

By the next day, Mary was too hungry and thirsty to care, and when the gaoler left a new tray of bread and ale, she was devouring the bread before he was barely out of the room.

It left her mouth as dry as an old dustbin. She stared at the tankard. She desperately had to drink, but how could she bring herself to put this foul liquid to her lips?

An idea came to her. She went into the bedchamber and rummaged in her bag. Triumphantly she produced an old wooden bowl that she had brought from Grangedean in case it might be useful, then rummaged again and drew out a spare silk stocking.

Pushing the bowl inside the stocking, she took it into the sitting room, then stretched the fine material tightly across the top. She carefully poured the ale into through the filter into the bowl, trying not to gag again at the sight of the grey, scummy residue it left behind.

Sliding the stocking off the bowl, she surveyed the pale liquid, then sniffed it cautiously. It did not smell so bad, so she concluded the gaoler had not bothered to foul it this time.

She took a tentative sip. It tasted rank, but the feel of liquid in her mouth was too tempting, and with a small groan she knocked it all back. She felt it gurgle in her stomach and for a brief and worrying moment she thought she was going to throw it straight back up, but thankfully all she did was belch loudly and the feeling passed.

She shook out the stocking and was about to put it back in her bag with the bowl, ready for tomorrow's filtering, when she paused, and studied it. It was a particularly fine silk stocking, and a shame to soil it so badly. Then she shrugged. What use would she have for it now, other than as a filter?

---0---

It was three days later, and Mary had just finished drinking her filtered ale, and belching as before. She had been idly amusing herself by seeing how loudly she could burp after each drink. By now she had perfected her art and was achieving a deep, rolling belch each time.

As she came into the sitting room after returning the stocking to her bag, she heard the door open and close behind her. Assuming it was the gaoler again, she did not bother to turn round.

"Do you put your back to me, madam?" came the voice of a woman. There was something vaguely familiar about it, and she spun round.

In front of her was a slight figure in a hooded cape. As Mary watched, the woman pushed back the hood to reveal a pale white face under flaming red hair.

Mary dropped to her knees. "Your Majesty," she whispered.

The woman came forward and held out her a slim hand. Mary pressed her lips to it.

"Pray be upstanding, Lady Mary," the Queen said softly. "I am not here officially – indeed only one other knows I am here at all."

"Madam, I am deeply honoured," Mary began. "But…"

"Why am I here?" the Queen said. "And come in the manner of a furtive outlaw?"

"Well – yes."

Instead of answering, the Queen went over to the table and picked up the empty tankard. She sniffed it cautiously, her dark eyes fixed on Mary's, then put it down hurriedly. "You have supped from this?" she asked, her thin eyebrows raised.

"I did, madam."

"You must have had a thirst."

"Yes, madam" Mary said, hoping the Queen had not heard her belching from outside the room. It had certainly been loud enough. "I resisted drinking the foul ale to start, but I had such a thirst I could resist no longer."

"Quite so," the Queen observed. "I was held prisoner here myself you know, as a young girl. I recall well that one is at the mercy of the gaoler for food and drink." She sniffed the tankard again. "Although I fear your treatment is far worse than ever I experienced. This smells most unpleasant. I am surprised you were able to keep it in your stomach," then she added with a smile, "if not the wind it might produce."

Oh God! The Queen of England had heard her burping like an old navvy!

"I...er... filtered it through a silk stocking first," Mary said, feeling her face flush redder than the Queen's hair. "It removed the worst of the... er... solids."

The Queen grimaced, then smiled. "Indeed, you are ever resourceful, Mary. I would expect no less of you." She indicated the chair, still turned away from the softly glowing embers of the fire. "I see you would not look to the flames. Most understandable." She gestured at the other chair. "Please sit with me. We have much to discuss."

Glad to have got off the subject of her noisy stomach, Mary turned the other chair round and waited until the Queen was seated, before sitting beside her.

"I am told you are to be tried as a sorceress and blasphemer," the Queen began.

"So I understand, madam," Mary answered, shocked to hear the accusation that had lived in her imagination these last few days being made painfully real by coming from the mouth of the Queen.

The Queen glanced across at her. "I am not here to interrogate you," she said. "You need have no fear of that."

A small flutter of hope rose in Mary's chest. Maybe, just maybe, the Queen was here to give her the pardon she'd demanded from Walsingham?

"Time enough for that at the trial itself," the Queen continued.

The flutter of hope curled up and died.

It seemed more likely that the Queen was just another thrill seeker like Walsingham, looking to satisfy her ghoulish curiosity and meet the sorceress before it was too late.

The Queen tapped her slim fingers on the arm of the chair. "But I must confess I am fascinated with this accusation of sorcery," she said. "I am told you travelled here across time itself?"

Mary nodded. "Yes, madam," she said with a small, resigned sigh. "That is true."

"From a year so far ahead, it is hard to comprehend it can even exist." The Queen paused. "Tell me, Lady Mary, by what name were you known in... the year of Our Lord two thousand and fifteen, I believe?"

"Justine Parker, madam."

The Queen raised an eyebrow. "Justine? Is that a French name?" Mary shook her head. "I see. I feel Lady Mary is altogether a better name, and we shall continue to call you as such, for now." Then she asked, "And in what year were you... will you be... born?"

"In nineteen eighty-eight," Mary answered, staring at her feet.

"So you were twenty-seven when you travelled to our time?"

"Yes." Mary looked up. "But it was not by my will."

"I see," the Queen said. "I have no doubt."

Mary took a careful breath. Maybe she could get the Queen on her side after all?

"I wanted to say as much to Master Secretary Walsingham, madam" she said. "But he would not hear my side of the story."

The Queen gave a wry smile. "Indeed," she observed. "And I hear you called him a fool?"

"I did, madam. And I apologise most deeply. It was my anger talking, not me."

"Oh, there is no need to apologise." Elizabeth smiled again. "Least of all to me." She lowered her voice conspiratorially. "I have thought the same on many an occasion. I wish I had been there to hear it for myself." She gave a small chuckle. "How did he take it?"

"Not well." Mary answered. She bit her lip. "He sent my companion Olivia Melrose away and I am ordered to end my days in silence."

"In truth I was aware of this." Elizabeth said, turning serious. "I have spoken with Mistress Melrose, and she was deeply upset to be parted."

"You have spoken with her?" Mary leaned in and put her hand over Elizabeth's, all protocol forgotten. "Is she well?"

Elizabeth looked down but made no move to withdraw her hand. Mary suddenly realised what she had done. She pulled her hand back to the arm of her own chair as if it were on fire. "Your Majesty," she said with rising panic in her voice, "I must apologise..."

Then Elizabeth did something totally unexpected. She put her own hand over Mary's.

"No," she said, her voice low and intense. "There is no need for you to apologise." She leaned in, her dark eyes never leaving Mary's. "You and I have been through so much together." She shook her head slowly. "Have you forgot how we both grieved over the body of Sir Thomas Cobham in that little room in York? Or how we talked of the life opportunities he had given us both, at the banquet afterwards?" She leaned in further. "I now understand how we formed such a connection, for you are not of this world. You are not like those fawning creatures who surround me at Court."

She sat back, but her hand stayed where it was.

"Mary," she said in a stronger, more urgent voice. "You carry knowledge of times yet to come. I too have secrets I can never share with others around me. Which is why I need someone I *can* share them with; someone such as you. I need your understanding and your counsel."

Then it was if she was no longer a queen, but just another woman; a friend in need, her pale face lined with worry. "I need your strength and your love; by that I mean I need you as someone with whom I can confide, and who will answer with honesty and without seeking favour." She looked down at their hands. "I need someone who will do as you did just this moment, who will put her hand upon mine and not be concerned about protocol – but do this because we are friends who understand and will help each other."

As Elizabeth's words hung in the air, it was clear that there was one massive elephant in the room that had to be addressed first.

"But I am to be tried and executed as a sorceress and a blasphemer," Mary said softly. "What then?"

Elizabeth stood up and paced across the room. "I know, I know," she said, then turned back, her face under the pale make-up still lined with deep concern. "And please believe I cannot simply pardon you, much as I wish to. For the crimes of which you are accused – and will inevitably be found guilty – are ones that raise terror in all God-fearing people. If I pardon you, it will raise questions of my own nature."

Mary gave a small despairing cry. To be so close to a real chance of a pardon – and now it was being snatched away.

Elizabeth crossed quickly back to her. "Nay, sweet Mary, for why would the Queen suddenly pardon a proven sorcerer and blasphemer unless she was enchanted in some way, or shared some of the sorcerer's beliefs?" She shook her head. "I am sorry, but I cannot do it."

Then she paused, before dropping one little word into the space between them.

One simple, hopeful little word.

"Unless…"

Mary's head snapped up. "Unless?" she demanded, hardly daring to believe what she had just heard.

"Unless you perform a singular service for Secretary Walsingham, and through him, for me."

Mary suddenly came to the sickening realisation that all that had just passed was simply a means to reel her in like a fish on a hook.

"Oh, right," she said coldly. "Do I have a choice?"

"For sure. You could refuse and would die at the stake as planned."

Mary stood up, and drew herself to her full height, looking down on the Queen. "Then in truth I do not have a choice, do I?"

Elizabeth looked up at her. "I know what you think, Lady Mary, that my words just now were to bend you to my will, and to have you perform such a task, but I would have you know two things." She gestured back to the chairs. "Let us sit again and I will explain withal."

When they had sat, the Queen said, "The first is that I meant every word I said just now. I value you and I need your counsel as a friend, but I cannot simply pardon you. Yet if you perform this service successfully, then time will have passed, so Walsingham and I can find a way for you to live a long and fulfilling life thereafter, and see out your days in comfort with your family, if that is what you most desire."

"And the second thing?" Mary asked, reserving judgment until she had heard both parts of this plan.

"The second may give you cause for surprise."

Mary raised an inquiring eyebrow.

"Indeed," the Queen continued. "You may have been left with the impression that Secretary Walsingham was much angered by your outburst at his house. But in truth, what you said impressed him greatly. To have knowledge of future events would be most useful, and, for all you called him a fool, he would have you pass on this knowledge in full." She paused. "Yet he also knew that you would not simply give him this intelligence while under threat of death by fire, so he needed to take this threat away and by doing so, bring you into his network of intelligencers."

Mary drew a sharp breath. "You want me to become a spy for Walsingham?"

Elizabeth smiled. "If that is how you see it, yes."

Mary thought a moment. There was one part of all this that still seemed to be shrouded in mystery. "But I know not what is this task you would have me do."

Elizabeth took a deep breath. "You will recall when I first came in, that I said there is only one other who knows I am here?" Mary nodded. She had meant to ask about it at the time, but the conversation had moved on – then it had slipped her mind. "Well, it will not surprise you to know that this other is here now, and will tell you of the task he has in mind. And being privy to the plan will admit you to a very exclusive circle; who are currently only myself, Secretary Walsingham and his man Master Wychwoode." Elizabeth leaned forward. "Secretary Walsingham is in the corridor without, and I will call him in here presently to explain in detail what you must do." She paused. "But I must impress on you that this is most important to me as your sovereign, and it must remain at the highest level of secrecy." She stabbed at the air with her forefinger. "If it becomes more widely known withal, I will deny it absolutely."

Before Mary could answer, Elizabeth stood and opened the door. A dark man in black came in and crossed to where Mary sat.

"My Lady," he said, sweeping off his cap and bowing.

"Master Secretary." Mary stood. There was a brief but somewhat awkward silence. "I must apologise for my outburst at your house," she said.

"Nay, 'tis no matter," Walsingham replied with a thin smile. "Even in the one speech you mentioned several events yet to come that gave us much useful intelligence." He paused. "And cause for concern." He glanced at the Queen, who nodded. "All because I was prodding at your anger to see where it may lead."

"Oh." Mary thought a moment. "Then Master Wychwoode on the boat after – was his anger not genuine?"

"It was not. He was instructed to play the role of a virtuous man enraged, as if a mummer performing upon a stage." He looked at her enquiringly. "I take it he played the part well?"

Mary shook her head in wonder. "Yes he did," she said. "He was most convincing."

"Good." He paused. "Now, your sovereign and I – we would discuss with you the task that needs to be performed, and as I am sure you have been told, in the utmost of secrecy."

---0---

Half an hour later, Mary sat back and looked at Elizabeth and Walsingham in turn.

"You cannot be serious!" she gasped. "You really want me to do that?"

Walsingham nodded. "From what you have told us of the future, it seems the ideal way to avoid such dreadful events coming to pass."

"But it is outrageous!" Mary said. "It will never work!"

Walsingham smiled slowly. "Oh, it will work, Lady Mary," he said. "You will make sure it works."

Then his smile disappeared.

"Or we will commit you once again to trial and certain execution."

CHAPTER ELEVEN

Wychwoode had the grace to give Mary a sheepish smile when he entered her rooms a couple of days later.

"Master Wychwoode," she said, in a voice that would have frozen a blacksmith's forge. "Do you come now to apologise for your behaviour after we visited Master Secretary Walsingham?"

He swept off his cap and bowed low. "I do humbly beseech your pardon, Lady Mary, but I was under instruction from my master to make such an act." Then he added, "I took no pleasure in it."

"I would certainly hope not," she said. "For sure I took none myself."

"It was a means to the end," he said. "It needed to seem genuine, so you understood the seriousness of your situation."

"I do understand that now, for all it was most unpleasant at the time." She went over to the table and poured some of the wine that she was now allowed. "Anyway," she said in her most conciliatory tone, "something to drink, Master Wychwoode?" As he took the proffered goblet, she added, "I am fairly sure that, unlike the ale served to me after your instructions to the gaoler, this has not been pissed in."

He took a sharp breath. "The fellow did that?" He sniffed cautiously at the wine, then put it carefully down on the table.

"I warrant he did." Seeing his obvious discomfort, she decided to soften a little more. After all, they were going to have to work together on this madcap scheme. As he sat down by the fire, she said, "Although I will admit you played the part well. Master Shakespeare himself could not have done better."

"Master who?"

Mary cursed herself inwardly – why did she not think? Shakespeare was still a small boy in Stratford. "Oh 'tis no matter." Quickly she poured herself some wine. "Anyway, I believed you, as did Olivia and the gaoler."

He watched her carefully as she took a drink from her goblet, then picked up his own, sniffed it again and took a small sip.

She settled herself in the other chair. Together they stared at the flames flickering around the logs. "If this plan is a success," he observed after a while, "you will no longer need to be in fear of flames such as these."

There was another silence. "If it succeeds, and I no longer face death by burning," she said eventually, "I will in truth want only to live at peace with my family at Grangedean Manor." She looked deep into the fire. "I would have nothing more to do with such madcap schemes."

"Nonsense," he growled.

"I beg your pardon?" She shot a look of surprise at him.

"You fool yourself, Lady Mary." He took another cautious sip of his wine. "You are one who thrives on danger." He gave a dry chuckle. "You would retire to be a plain wife and mother again? Nay, I warrant you would be dead within six months, but of boredom."

Mary frowned as she thought over his words. Was she really addicted to action and adventure? An adrenaline junkie? No, no, not at all. She shook her head. Her idea of an idyllic existence was to be living in peace and quiet, with nothing more challenging than balancing the household accounts and making sure Kat had a new kirtle. That was it.

So why did the thought make her feel slightly nauseous?

"Do you seriously think that it can succeed?" she asked, bringing the conversation back on track.

He glanced across at her, a deep frown on his face. "Do you not?"

"There is much to go wrong."

"Then we must plan most carefully," he answered. "Starting with your name."

"My name?" she asked. "What of it?"

"Oh, come now," he said. "If you will act as a spy, you cannot be roaming abroad in the country as Lady Mary de Beauvais. Not if you want the chance of a quiet life thereafter." He paused. "Who knows what trouble you might cause for others, let alone as part of the plan itself. Would you have those you have harmed turn up at Grangedean Manor, seeking the Lady Mary de Beauvais that has done them wrong?"

She nodded. "So be it," she said thoughtfully. "Perhaps it is best to be unknown." She looked up. "What name shall I take?"

"Make your choice."

Fighting back an initial suggestion of 'Jemima Bond', she gave it some consideration. Then she brightened, and said, "Something simple and forgettable. How about Anne Carter?"

"Very well," he replied, "Anne Carter it is." He sat back. "Now, Mistress Carter, we come to the other key element of this enterprise. The remarkable musket fashioned by the Alchemist."

She shot him a look of surprise. "The one that was damaged beyond repair at the gorge by Hetherington Hall," she asked, "before being consigned to a forge and destroyed completely, on the orders of Her Majesty?" She paused. "That remarkable musket?"

"Aye. That one." He took another small sip of wine. "I have kept the Alchemist alive against just such a need." He took a deep breath and looked over at her. "We will have him make another one."

"And if he refuses?"

"Then he is to be hung, drawn and quartered, as a traitor."

"And you do not have your musket."

"True."

"So how do you propose to have him comply?"

"We will offer him the chance to be released from imprisonment for the time it takes to construct the new firearm. After the weeks he has spent with only the gaoler and the rats for company, he will welcome the respite."

Mary stared at the old man. "I fear that will not be enough to persuade him," she said. "He will want more."

"Perhaps."

"Especially if you want him to take as much time as he can in the construction," she observed dryly, "then that is a good way of ensuring it."

"We are aware of that," he answered. "So we will need someone to help him in the task, keep him under daily observation, and report on his progress."

There was something in the way he said this, or maybe in the way he glanced over at her, that made her realise just who he meant for the job.

"Oh no!" she exclaimed. "No! No! No!" She turned back to the fire. "I am the last person on earth he would allow to observe him even scratch his nose, let alone help him make a new musket."

"Yet as a fellow traveller from distant times yet to come, who else would be better suited?" He smiled. "I warrant the legendary charm of Lady Mary de Beauvais will work its magic ere long."

"An unfortunate turn of phrase," she muttered, trying to ignore the vision it conjured up of once again being led to her execution.

"I apologise most deeply," he said. "But it cannot be ignored that someone must ensure that not only does he work to our schedule, but that he is also able to function effectively. The man has suffered grievous wounds that must impair his abilities – so he will need assistance. Who better than someone who understands his language and his background?"

Mary pushed her chair back in a rush of anger, and snapped, "And who worse than the person who gave him those grievous wounds?" She glared at Wychwoode. "It is utter madness! He will refuse to be in the same room as me, let alone have me assist him!"

Wychwoode looked up, his face a blank mask. "May I remind you, Mistress Anne Carter, that Lady Mary de Beauvais is equally under sentence of death? I would advise you to accept this as part of the plan devised by Walsingham and your queen, and concede with good grace." As she slumped back in her chair with crossed arms, he added, "You must find a way to work with the man. That is your challenge, and I would most strongly suggest you accept it."

CHAPTER TWELVE

Mary hung back outside the cell gate, drawing warmth from a brightly burning brazier as Wychwoode was let into the dark room at the end of the passageway. The longer she could delay meeting the Alchemist, the better.

She heard the old man greeting the prisoner inside.

"Master Wychwoode," she heard the Alchemist reply, his voice sounding hoarse and thin, although still recognisable. Mary shuddered as the hated sound took her immediately back to the forest after he had shot her beloved horse, Juno. "Once again, are you come to take me to my death?"

"Nay. I have better news, sirrah."

"Better news?" She could imagine the Alchemist's look of sarcastic surprise. "What could possibly be better than being put out of the misery of this place?"

"I am come to take you back to your dwelling in Southwark."

There was a long silence. Then the Alchemist simply said, "Why?"

"We would have you make another of your special muskets."

There was another long silence. "Why?"

"We have need of it."

"And the first one? Can it not be used?"

"Nay. It was damaged by Moreton, then destroyed on the orders of the Queen."

"A pity..." The Alchemist's voice was cut off by a fit of dry coughing, with each racking cough accompanied by the sound of a chain rattling. "A pity that you no longer have it. It would be easier to mend that one than create a new one."

"Indeed," Wychwoode agreed. "But this is the truth of our situation."

"Whatever." There was another long silence. "I do not move very easily, since that de Beauvais bitch hit me with the poker, and you stretched me on the rack. It will not be a quick job to make a new piece."

"You will have assistance."

"Oh." The chain clinked. "I trust it will not be her, eh?" There was the sound of a bitter laugh, ending in another bout of coughing. Eventually the Alchemist's voice rasped out again, "I trust she has already met a most painful end as a sorceress and blasphemer?" He gave a wheezy chuckle. "I trust she screamed very, very loudly as the flames took hold?"

Mary stepped into the cell.

"No," she said softly. "She lives still."

There was a heavy silence. As her eyes adjusted to the dimness, Mary could make out what looked like a thin scarecrow slumped in the corner, a dull beam of light shining down on him from the window like a grotesque stage spotlight. A black chain was secured to the wall behind his shoulder, ending in iron collar disappearing under his long beard.

"Hi, Rick," she said. "Long time, no see."

The scarecrow's eyes glinted as he turned to look up at Wychwoode.

"Are you fucking serious?" he whispered, his voice made all the more menacing by its quietness. "Are you telling me that I have to work with this bitch?" The old lawyer looked down at him with crossed arms and said nothing. "Are you telling me that this evil witch, who should have been burned to a crisp, is not only still alive, but is going to be assisting me in my work?"

"Nice to see you, too, Rick," Mary observed, making her voice drip with irony. "Working together again will be such fun."

"Not in a million *fucking* years!" the Alchemist spat out, crossing his arms and staring pointedly at the opposite corner of the cell.

Wychwoode cleared his throat. "So be it. Then let me tell you what will take place," he said, his voice low and gravelly, as if clearing his throat had made it worse. "At dawn on the morrow I will have you removed from this place and taken to Tyburn. And in case you have forgot, let me remind you again what will happen there." He dropped into a squat, his face nearly level with the Alchemist's. "Firstly, you will be hung by the neck. Then, while you are barely able to draw breath, yet you still live, you will be taken down. After that, your genitals will be removed and displayed before you, although you may not be able to see them clearly, for your eyes will be screwed with pain. But that, sadly, will be nothing to the pain of what comes next." He paused a moment, then cleared his throat again. "You will have your belly opened, your guts severed and removed, then your heart, still beating, will be cut out of your chest, before being burned."

He stood up.

"That, my friend, will be the last thing you see, before finally, merciful death takes you into his arms." He looked up at the window a moment, then turned back to the prisoner.

"But even death will not be the last horror to be borne by your body. For then your head will be removed and placed on a spike for all to see as they step upon London Bridge, and your remains will be quartered and disposed of in pieces."

There was a long silence, and Mary wished she could sit down. But the floor of the cell looked filthy; covered in rat droppings and something that looked suspiciously like a dried human dropping as well. She remained standing.

Wychwoode stared down at the Alchemist. "Or, let me put a different scenario to you," he said quietly. "As before, on the morrow, I will have you taken from this place, but not to Tyburn." He shook his head. "Nay, instead I will have you taken to your own house in Southwark, where you will have the finest bread and ale for a few days in order for your strength to return." He paused, "Or meat pies? I believe you are partial to the pies sold by one Mistress Somerville in the shop close to your house?" The Alchemist gave a tiny nod, despite looking as if he was trying to avoid giving anything away.

"Then you will be provided with all the metal, glass, gunpowder and shot you need to ensure another of your remarkable muskets can be made in the workshop you previously constructed in the outbuilding behind your house, and which has been preserved as you left it." He paused, "Although now it occurs to me that it should not be you who does this work, as not only are you somewhat incapacitated, but you will also need to be secured by a strong chain to the inside of the house." He gave a dry chuckle. "We would not want you trying to disappear into the night, now would we?"

"I can hardly walk, after what you did to me on that fucking rack," the Alchemist muttered.

Wychwoode shook his head. "Nay. You experienced but a single turn of the wheel. Had there been further turns then your bones would have been parted from eachother, and for sure you would never walk again. But I warrant that in a few weeks, your joints will knit together, just like the bones in your leg." He gave a thin smile. "Then you will once again be able to stand and move yourself." He gestured at Mary. "But while you are so... inconvenienced, my thought is that it should be Lady de Beauvais here who will be your hands for this task." He nodded to himself. "She will be quartered in a house close by and will attend on you each day. You will be able to instruct her on each part of the work, which, as you both come from the same future time, she will readily understand. That way the tasks necessary to construct the weapon will be carried out."

The Alchemist drew a sneering breath as if about to respond, but Wychwoode cut him off with a raised hand. "One more thing," he said. "Lady Mary will report each day on your progress to one of my men, who will also be quartered nearby. And if..." here he gave a piercing glare at the prisoner, "...if she does not report one day – let us say, for example, she has met with some unfortunate accident in your dwelling, then you will be taken immediately to Tyburn, and the first scenario enacted in full."

There was a long silence, during which the Alchemist seemed to be considering his options, giving little snorts through his nose as if to punctuate each thought.

"Seriously? You think this cow here can make a gun?"

"Under your instruction, yes. Now I think on it, it is our best option."

"And if I choose Tyburn over working with...her?" he said, without looking at Mary.

"That is your choice, of course," Wychwoode replied. "Although it does seem a perverse one to me."

The Alchemist's head snapped up, making his chain clink. "Why?" he demanded. "Why perverse? I would only be delaying the time I go to Tyburn anyway."

Wychwoode shook his head. "Nay," he said. "If you successfully perform the service I have set out, then you will be taken to France, Germany, the Low Countries or such continental realm of your choice, given a large enough purse of coin as will set you up in one of their cities, and left there to build a new life for yourself."

The Alchemist's eyes widened in surprise. "You would have me banished with a pardon?"

"Aye, although, I would caution you clearly, that if you ever try to return to England, you will be taken to Tyburn for the full sentence of death as I have described."

The Alchemist rubbed his hands across his eyes a moment, then he looked up and said, "Fine. I will do it. I will not like it – working with her – but I will do it."

Wychwoode breathed out a deep sigh. "Good. Then that is settled. It will be as I said, you will be taken back to Southwark on the morrow." He turned to Mary. "And you are ready to play your part in this, Lady Mary? Or should I say 'Anne Carter'?" He looked back at the Alchemist. "For this will be her identity for the length of this enterprise, and I would thank you, Alchemist, to forget all talk of 'Lady Mary' or even 'Justine', as I believe you first knew her, and use only her new identity, even when alone."

Mary said, "If I must work with him I will. Although I will not like it any more than he does." She looked down at the prisoner. "You had better keep to your side of this, Rick."

He gave her a sickly smile, that was more a sneer. "I will, Mistress Anne Carter," he said. Then he added, "Although you know something?"

She shook her head.

He gestured for her to come closer. Cautiously she bent down until his mouth was by her ear.

"I was always going to agree," he whispered. He gave a small, throaty chuckle. "He had me at Mistress Somerville's meat pies."

CHAPTER THIRTEEN

If Mary had expected her working relationship with the Alchemist to be strained, she was not mistaken. The next day they were thrown together in his dingy little Southwark house, and he was as vile as she would have expected.

"Listen, you evil bitch," he began, once Wychwoode's man had secured him to the bed by a chain long enough for him to reach a chamber pot on one side of the room and a small writing table on the other, "we have to make this new gun..." He paused, glaring up at her from under his brow, "...which we wouldn't if you hadn't fucking destroyed the first one, but anyway..." He broke off as a fit of coughing overtook him; each wheezing cough forcing the air out of his thin body, leaving him red-faced and struggling to breathe. "But," he continued, once his ribs had stopped heaving, "we have to make it together. Which means I give you instructions, and somehow, fuck knows how, you are going to make it." He shook his head. "Have you ever, in your pampered, spoiled little life, actually made anything? And by that I mean something in metal or wood, not a dress or a beef fucking casserole?"

Mary felt her lip curl in response. "Listen Rick," she said, trying hard to keep her voice steady, "I do not want to do this any more than you do, but if we do it, and if we get it right, then there is a chance," she paused, "a slim chance, that we can both get to stay alive. And what is more," she added, "we get our freedom back as well." She took a deep breath. "So I suggest you trust me, give me clear instructions and drawings, the tools to do the job, and let me get on with it."

Which he did. Initially it was with barely concealed bad grace, but as she got more practiced at using the tools in his little workshop in the back courtyard, the Alchemist started to give her his grudging approval. Gradually the number of times he made her go back and remake a part reduced, until one day he actually remarked on how well she was casting and working the metal, as well as shaping the wood.

After a few further days they were able to converse a little more easily, even to the point that he no longer referred to her as 'you fucking bitch' and started addressing her by the name of Anne Carter. After another week he even teased her for having smudges of soot on her nose when she presented a particularly fine casting. It was almost as if the casual working relationship they had once enjoyed in 2015 Grangedean Manor was back, and she found herself almost welcoming his comments on her work – taking pride in his approval.

But more than anything, the fragile bond forming between these two bitter enemies was forged through their shared antagonism towards Wychwoode's man. A man whose combination of arrogance and ignorance meant he was constantly upsetting one or other, or even on some occasions, both of them.

A man called Roger Rolleston.

---0---

At first it had been easy. Wychwoode had introduced Rolleston as his new man, and instructed her to report to him each day at a nearby inn. "It is for your own safety," Wychwoode had explained. "The Alchemist needs to be aware that if he causes some accident to befall you, we will know swiftly, and he will suffer the death of a traitor. That way he will be minded to ensure you are kept in good health, for all you will be dealing with sharp tools and hot fires."

But it soon became clear that Rolleston thought he was working to a wider brief. He had started to appear at the Alchemist's house each day and asking – no, demanding – to see the progress of the gun itself.

The Alchemist, issuing his instructions and providing drawings from chained imprisonment in his bed chamber, had initially ignored this additional imposition. Eventually it had become obvious that Rolleston was starting to see himself as the de facto director of the project. Perhaps it was because the Alchemist was chained and unable to walk, and Mary was simply a woman, but whatever it was, the man had started throwing his weight about and issuing orders, for all they had no benefit to the outcome of the process.

It took a couple of weeks before the Alchemist finally snapped.

"By Heavens, Rolleston, you are an ignorant fucker!" he had yelled one day, after a particularly arrogant comment from the merchant. "You know sod all about this, so keep your long Tudor nose out of it!"

"I know this, you traitorous cur!" Rolleston yelled back, putting his hands on his hips and standing at the end of the bed with his shoulders back and his feet apart, like a Roman gladiator squaring up to his opponent. "I know that you are a filthy little peasant but a step from the gallows for your crimes!"

"And how do you know that, pray?"

Rolleston gave a slow smile. "I was briefed by Master Wychwoode, with enough information to do this work. So I know you are some sort of sorcerer, who was racked for trying to kill the Queen with your self-made musket."

"So you know why we are making another such musket?" Mary interjected with a note of caution. It would not do for this Rolleston to know too much about the mission.

"Nay, that I do not." He transferred his glare from the Alchemist to her. "But I warrant it is for some clandestine purpose of Wychwoode's." He turned back to the Alchemist. "And I doubt very much that Wychwoode has shared such a plan with a traitor such as you."

"Fuck you!" the Alchemist snapped.

"Listen, you Alchemist," Rolleston replied, "if you do not defer to your betters, then you will soon find yourself sprawled at the base of the gibbet, propelled there by the toe of my boot!"

"You are no better than me!" the Alchemist responded, grabbing his chain as if he would use it as a weapon. "I know full well you were in the Tower as a Catholic traitor yourself!"

"Nay churl," the merchant snarled. "I was falsely accused, while you are a proven traitor and witch, caught in the act of firing your unnatural musket at the Queen." He wiped spittle off his mouth with his sleeve. "You are in no position to pass judgment on your superiors!"

"Not a witch, you fucker," snapped the Alchemist.

"Nay?" answered Rolleston with a twisted smile. "Then where, pray, did you get the knowledge, and indeed the funds, to make your evil musket in the first place?"

"My knowledge is none of your business," answered the Alchemist, "and as for funds, it is amazing how you can earn good money by making household items that no-one has ever seen before and never knew they needed, but now cannot live without."

The Alchemist looked at Mary with an eyebrow raised, as if asking her to step in and take his part.

For a moment she hesitated, captivated by the image of Rick turning out modern-day items for the good wives of Southwark. What had he been making, that had allowed him to build up the money to live on, as well as ultimately to make the gun? Something as prosaic as maybe table forks, previously unknown in Tudor times? Or something more exotic, like a frying pan or a wok? She shook her head to clear the thought, and to concentrate on his request for help.

"I would not have you take such an attitude with the Alchemist, Master Rolleston," she said in a level tone. "He has been offered a full pardon if he helps with this work on the new gun, and that he is doing."

Rolleston stared at her open mouthed. "You would not have me take such an attitude…? You, who he calls a… a fucking bitch?" he asked in a strangled whisper.

"Aye," she replied, with what she hoped was a suitably passive-aggressive smile, "but he is central to this endeavour. So I suggest you learn how to control your temper and leave the Alchemist and me to finish this task without poking your 'long Tudor nose' in." He started to draw breath, but before he could say anything more, she added, "and lest you dismiss me as a 'mere woman', I would remind you that I have the strength and guile of a man –

and," she added, pointing her finger closer to his red face, "a much better one than you."

---0---

After a couple more weeks, the gun was nearly finished.

Mary stood in the courtyard and peered through the barrel section, lining it up against a patch of bright sky between the autumn clouds, enjoying the way the light bounced down the smooth metal inside and created swirling kaleidoscopes of silvers and blues. No kinks or burrs. That was good.

She glanced over as Rolleston stepped out of the rickety back door of the Southwark house and came up to her.

She took another long look through the barrel, then lowered it slowly.

"This is completed," she observed. "I am satisfied it will shoot straight and true."

"Good," he answered. "So now you will show me how the whole weapon comes together."

"In good time, Master Rolleston," she demurred. "I must show it to the Alchemist first and have him check all the parts. He is most particular."

"But you have made it to his precise instructions these few weeks," he said, sounding like a small child denied a treat. "Each day you have shown him your efforts – and if he has not been satisfied he has had you rework or remake each part, on occasions many times. So for sure, the final whole will be fit to function to his standards."

Mary took another slow look through the barrel, enjoying the increasingly impatient snorts of the man beside her. It was his own fault; if he had behaved in a more civilised manner then perhaps she would be more accommodating towards him. She lowered the piece again with a small sigh.

"Marry, sir," she said quietly, "for sure it is made to his design, but until he has approved it, then it is not complete."

"So go to it," he snapped. "I am required by Master Wychwoode to arrange for a demonstration of the power of the weapon. He would see it fire and prove itself for range and accuracy."

"Then he must wait until I have tested it first," she said firmly. "I will not demonstrate it to anyone until I am satisfied for myself it works as it should."

She watched as a red flush crept up from under his lace collar and dark beard, filling his cheeks until they were the colour of beetroot. "By thunder," he snarled, "I have had my fill of your insolence since we have been forced to work together."

Mary took a deep breath to calm herself, becoming aware that she had shifted her grip on the barrel as if she would use it to beat this boorish oaf about the head, but managed to restrain herself as she strode past him and into the house.

She stooped as she entered the bedroom, then paused to let her eyes adjust to the gloom. The Alchemist was sitting on the bed as always, finishing a meat pie. He took a swig of ale from a tankard and looked up.

"The barrel is complete," she said, trying to ignore Rolleston as he pushed in behind her. "I have held it to the light as you have said, and there are no kinks or burrs within." She handed it over and watched as the Alchemist studied it carefully close to the candle, turning it each way against the light. Then he put it to his eye and peered through, holding the end directly against the bright flame. Eventually he nodded.

"It is good," he said slowly. "I am impressed. Have you checked how it locates to the chamber?"

"Yes," she replied. "It is a little tight; I need to work it a bit more, but it will fit."

He breathed in deeply, which he could now do without coughing, and said, "Excellent." He passed the barrel back up to her. "I suggest you now assemble the whole piece and bring it to me. We can decide if it is ready to be tested."

Mary pushed past Rolleston, then made her way down the narrow corridor to the courtyard, with its little workshop on the far side. She was aware that the merchant was following close behind her, and as she got to the workshop door, she turned and said firmly, "I would you leave me to go in alone. I need to concentrate on the work, which I cannot do with you breathing down my neck."

"I am charged by Wychwoode to ensure the work is done well," he answered.

"No, you are not," she said, tapping the end of the barrel on her open palm to emphasise her point. "You were originally charged with remaining in the tavern and reporting back to Wychwoode that I am safe each day. The fact you choose to spend all your time here is your own decision." She waved the barrel towards his face, and was pleased to see him pale slightly as he stepped back a few paces from the door. "But it is not by Master Wychwoode's instruction. And anyway," she added, "the best way you can ensure the work is done well, is to keep your interfering nose out of it." With that, she marched into the workshop, closing the door firmly behind her and throwing the bolt to secure it.

Once inside, she breathed out a deep sigh that ended in a whispered "and – relax…" before surveying the room that had been her place of work these past few weeks.

Immediately in front of her was the forge – an open grate full of glowing coals that she kept alight at all times. A pair of bellows was secured at its base with the tip just below the grate, so she could work it with her foot to blow in air and raise the temperature sufficiently to melt the metal before pouring it into the sand moulds. Above the grate was a brick chimney, allowing the hot air to escape and preventing smoke build-up inside the workshop.

To the left was the lathe, which the Alchemist had made by adapting the pedal mechanism of a spinning wheel, and which he had geared up substantially with a belt-driven flywheel turning a much larger wheel on the side of the lathe itself. This meant that although it took quite some effort to start it off by working the pedals with her feet, Mary could then make the lathe spin extremely fast, and could therefore run her sharpened chisel and polishing cloths along the rest in order to create the smooth barrel and metal stock, as well as the bullets.

On the other side of the grate there was a shelf, on which stood the wooden forms the Alchemist had originally made for each part of the gun. There was the half-barrel form, two castings of which could be welded together and finished on the lathe. Then there were the two half-forms for the firing chamber, a form for the trigger, one for the bolt and one for the bullets. Mary had learned how to embed each form in fine sand to make the mould, with a rod to make a pouring tunnel for the steel. Then she would melt the metal in an earthenware crucible, adding small pieces from offcuts she had been supplied by Wychwoode using his contacts with armourers. She would watch with fascination as the metal started to twist and settle into the crucible, turning from a dirty grey to shining mercury-like silver, and finally into a glowing liquid. Then, once she had scraped off the dirty surface slag to get pure metal only, she had learned how to pour the liquid steel into the mould, break out the piece once cooled, before shaping and finishing it with the rudimentary tools made by the Alchemist or purchased from a blacksmith.

On the other side of the room was the woodwork bench, where she had made the butt and the fore-stock, learning through trial and error how to cut and shape the wood, then polish it with rough sanding cloths and oil it to a fine finish.

Mary unwrapped the completed firing chamber from its protective waxed cloth and gently applied the barrel to the aperture. As she had said to the Alchemist, it was a little too tight – but that was not a bad thing, as it would give a firm fit. But she would need it to be assembled and disassembled easily, so it had to be just right. A shame she didn't have the tools to cut a screw thread – but unfortunately the Alchemist had explained that this was beyond his capabilities, so a push-fit would have to do.

She roughened the inside of the aperture with a sanding cloth for a few minutes, then tried again. Still too tight. After more sanding and a few more tries, it finally slotted into place. Then she clipped on the two steel retaining strips she had made to hold the barrel in place against the force of the gun being fired, added the trigger, the metal stock and finally the wooden butt. She clipped the sight into place, made from a piece of tubing fitted with two ground glass magnifying lenses obtained by Wychwoode from a maker of spectacles.

She held the gun at its central point in front of the trigger and gazed proudly at the result of her work; a well-balanced, light and simple piece, with smooth, polished metal and a shining, shaped wooden fore-stock and butt. Lifting the gun up to her cheek, she pointed it at the little window and took aim through the sight. Her finger curled round the trigger, as she centred the crosshairs on the beams of an old wooden house across the street. She took a breath and gently squeezed the trigger, then allowed herself a small smile as the bolt slammed against the firing pin with a satisfying *clunk*.

She lowered the gun and glanced across at a shelf on which stood fifty cartridges, lined up in five rows of ten like gleaming little soldiers. Gathering two and putting them in the pocket of her gown, she left the workshop and walked back into the house.

CHAPTER FOURTEEN

The Alchemist turned the finished gun over and looked up, shaking his head slowly. "I would never have thought that you could have done this," he said. "I'd have put money on you doing a cack-handed job that wouldn't work at all, but fuck me, you go and produce this!" He lifted the gun to his cheek and took aim at Rolleston standing against the wall, then pulled the trigger. The bolt clicked and the Alchemist chuckled as the merchant flinched. "Not loaded, mate. More's the pity." He put the gun down on the bed and said to Mary, "Show me a bullet."

She fished one of the cartridges from her pocket and handed it over. He studied it carefully, then, seeming satisfied, he pulled back the bolt to open the chamber and slotted it into place. He casually pointed the gun at the wall between Rolleston's legs and pulled the trigger again.

The report of the gun echoed around the little room like a thunder-crack, leaving Mary momentarily deafened. There was also an overpowering acrid stench of gunpowder. Rolleston leapt like a scalded cat, as the plaster between his knees exploded in a big puff of smoke and dust. "By Heavens!" he yelled. "Have you taken leave of your senses?"

The Alchemist gave the gun back to Mary, observing levelly, "It seems to work. Now I suggest you test it in the woods to make sure the sight is lined up." He studied the mounting of the tube containing the two lenses. "See how I said to make the mount move?" She nodded. "Fire some shots and move the sight to get it lined up, then pack some soft clay in here," he pointed at the base, "so when the clay sets, you'll have it right." He fixed her with a firm stare. "*Day of the Jackal* – know what I mean?" Mary nodded again, understanding the reference to the film, where the Jackal takes his sniper rifle into the woods and tests the sight by shooting at a melon.

She glanced over at Rolleston, who had turned as white as a sheet. "I know not what is this jackal he talks of," he said in a strangled whisper, "but I know that the madman has fired his weapon at my legs in the most reckless and dangerous manner, and this shall be reported to Master Wychwoode."

Mary shrugged. "I have no idea what it is you are complaining of, Master Rolleston," she said with her most innocent expression. "Surely you were in fact on the other side of the room when the weapon was test-fired into the wall?"

"You would tell an untruth to protect this man?"

"It would be my word against yours, sir," she answered, smiling sweetly. "And as I have earned the trust of Master Wychwoode over these past years, I am sure it will be my word that will be believed."

"Then I would take it to Master Secretary Walsingham."

Mary chuckled. "Big mistake," she said. "Big. Huge."

"Your comment is pretty, woman," observed the Alchemist, appearing to be struggling to keep a straight face.

Rolleston's mouth opened and closed silently several times, then, without any warning, he suddenly turned and punched his fist hard into the wall beside him, with such force that it caused a crack in the plaster, running all the way down to the hole left by the Alchemist's shot. Seeming to ignore such pain as must have been caused, he snarled, "By the Lord's Wounds, madam, I shall not take this lightly. You will regret this, I assure you!" Then he marched out of the room, leaving Mary and the Alchemist staring wordlessly at the crack in the wall.

The Alchemist waited until the front door was heard to slam, before observing, "Fucking nutcase." Mary dragged her gaze away from the wall and back to the man on the bed. "Right," he continued, "back to business. How many bullets do you have?"

CHAPTER FIFTEEN

Mary moved her leg wider and settled her position. She was lying on the forest floor, the gun pushed into her shoulder, with her right finger on the trigger and her left hand supporting the fore-stock.

A foot in a black shoe came into her peripheral vision. "I would you take a step backwards, please, Master Secretary," she said, "and stay behind me for safety, as I demonstrate the power of the weapon."

The foot disappeared as Francis Walsingham moved further away behind her.

"You would hit that red apple over yonder, from this distance?" came the voice of the only other person in this quiet forest clearing; a woman with her pale face hidden under a cowled cloak.

"Yes, Your Majesty," Mary answered softly, keeping her breath even as she brought the sight onto the distant apple hanging from the branch. "Do I have your permission to fire?" she breathed.

The Queen was silent a moment, then she said, "Go to it, Mary, I prithee."

Mary stilled her breathing to the slowest she could, feeling her heart rate drop to what felt like no more than a beat a minute, as she moved the crosshairs to the centre of the apple and started to squeeze her finger on the trigger.

As her finger tightened, she couldn't help but think how she had got to this point; the promise to the Queen to go along with this madcap plan; the weeks spent following the Alchemist's instructions to cast and make the gun; the hours in the forest firing the weapon and adjusting the sight before fixing it with clay packing, and now, demonstrating it in front of Walsingham and the Queen.

She forced herself to concentrate on the apple in the sight. Nothing else could matter; nothing other than the round red image in the crosshairs.

She held her breath and squeezed a little bit more.

The bolt slammed the firing pin into the base of the shell and, with the familiar cracking sound, the gunpowder inside exploded, sending the bullet down the barrel at close to the speed of sound. Mary exhaled slowly as she saw the apple in her sight evaporate in a puff of smoke. For a moment she remained still, then she lowered the barrel and rolled to her side, so she could look up at the two observers behind her.

"Your Majesty. Master Secretary." she announced. "You will see that this weapon is accurate at this distance. It is, I believe, fit for the purpose you have in mind."

"Indeed it is," said the Queen. "I cannot be ought but impressed that it does what we have asked." Mary got to her feet. "And you have manufactured it yourself?" the Queen continued, her thin eyebrow raised as Mary stood before her, "by your own hand at every stage?"

"Yes, madam," Mary said. "I did, from instructions and tools given to me by the Alchemist."

"Remarkable. Quite remarkable." The Queen paused. "You are a talented woman, Mary, and I am most pleased we have had you released from the Tower for this purpose. Let me see the weapon." She held out her hand and Mary passed the gun across. "This is an amazing piece," the Queen said, as she turned it over and studied it closely. "So simple in essence, yet it fires with such ferocity." She gave a small shudder as she handed it back. "I cannot but think of how just such a weapon was aimed at me, and what would have happened if our noble protector Sir Thomas Cobham had not put himself in the way of that ball."

She turned to her spymaster. "Master Secretary, once again we have such a piece in existence, and it becomes a threat to our person if it is ever to fall in the wrong hands." He nodded, as she continued, "so again, once Lady Mary has completed the mission we have charged her to carry out, this must be destroyed, and with it all the tools made by this Alchemist for the express purpose of constructing such a piece."

"It shall be done, your Majesty," he answered with a small bow.

"And the Alchemist himself?" she asked. "Will the full sentence of death for a traitor now be carried out?"

There was an uneasy pause. "He was made a bargain, madam," Walsingham said carefully. "In return for his co-operation and for his instructions to Lady Mary, he was made an offer – for his life to be spared and for him to be sent into exile with enough of a purse to start a new existence." He paused. "But with a stricture to face certain death if he is ever to return to your realm."

The Queen was silent a moment. "It sits most ill with me, Master Secretary, to think that a man who set out to cause my death and to put that Scottish woman on my throne is spared his life."

"It was expedient, madam. He would not have co-operated otherwise."

"And you gave him your word?"

"Through my man, Wychwoode, yes."

"But not with my knowledge or consent?"

There was another uncomfortable silence. Mary could see the Queen was on the verge of issuing a command for the Alchemist to be executed anyway. She carefully placed the gun on the forest floor and bowed to the Queen.

"Your Majesty," she said, "you once told me you valued my honest counsel, and by your leave, I would offer it now."

"Indeed, Lady Mary," the Queen replied, with a look on her pale face that was almost of relief. "What say you on this matter?"

Mary took a breath while she ordered her thoughts. This had to be right. "It is true that the Alchemist set out to cause your death and put Mary, Queen of Scots on your throne," she began. "But it was not done out of Catholic conviction, rather it was done for greed; he thought he would be elevated to a high position and given much wealth by a new regime. So by pardoning him, and giving him money, he is no longer any threat to your person or your throne. Rather, it is to your credit as a wise sovereign that his contribution to this secret plan is recognised – and it is better that the promise made to him in good faith is honoured, than he is torn apart at the gallows."

The Queen observed Mary steadily from under her hood. "You take his part now?" she asked quietly. "Even after you beat him senseless in my defence?"

"Yes madam." Mary said. "I hold no love for the man, as you say, but I recognise that he has done what was asked of him, and he has done it in good conscience. To keep the bargain made with him now would be the honourable and merciful thing."

Elizabeth pursed her lips, her dark, unblinking eyes not leaving Mary's. Eventually she gave a small nod. "Very well. Have the man sent into exile as promised, with sufficient purse to establish his new life. But," she added, "I want him to have a new name, so that no connection can be made with this traitor, and Master Secretary, I want your intelligencers to keep watch on him without his knowledge, so we may know if he ever does aught of concern."

Walsingham bowed, and said, "As Your Majesty wishes."

"And one further thing, Master Secretary," the Queen added. "I would you find some condemned man; one who is already destined for the noose for his crimes, and make the artifice that this is the Alchemist, being executed for the traitorous attempt on my life, and for the murder of Sir Thomas Cobham. For all we have made to keep the events in York this summer out of the records, there will be those who know of this Alchemist and his treasonous crimes. I want it to be clear to them, and to any others who think to commit such a crime that the price of treason is always death, without exception." She paused. "Do I make myself clear?"

"Very clear, Your Majesty."

"Good." The Queen smiled. "Now, pick up your weapon, Lady Mary, and let us now execute this covert plan. There is no time to lose if we are to change the future and avoid all the troubling events of which you have so clearly warned us."

CHAPTER SIXTEEN

Sir William de Beauvais marched confidently into the room and bowed low to Walsingham and Wychwoode, sweeping off his cap.

"Pray be upstanding, Sir William," said Walsingham. "Welcome to Barn Elms." He waved his hand towards the table in the corner, where some goblets and a bottle of wine were standing by a single candle.

William replaced his cap and took a seat. Once all three were settled and the wine was poured, Walsingham said quietly, "You have requested this meeting and we have agreed. How may we be of assistance?"

William cleared his throat. If Walsingham didn't know what this was about, then he was either a fool or a liar. Judging by the man's reputation, it was the latter.

"As you know most well, Master Secretary," William began, with a cold smile, "my wife has been arrested on charges of sorcery and blasphemy – yet I know of no trial that has taken place, nor…" he cleared his throat again. "Nor any execution." He took a long breath, then let it out slowly, glancing at Wychwoode as he did so. The old man's furrowed face remained impassive, deeply shadowed in the flickering candlelight. "Sirs, I would know her fate this day."

"Your wife was held in the Tower, pending the trial," said Walsingham. "This you know, and there is no more to tell."

"Master Secretary, I pray you be more understanding!" William blurted out. "She is my wife and mother to my children. We are consumed with anxiety about her! My children do not sleep and cry out for her in the night! I say again, we would know her fate!" A sudden thought occurred. "Was?" he queried. "You said she 'was' held in the Tower. Is she no longer there?"

"My dear Sir William," said Walsingham, his voice so honey-smooth that it set William's teeth on edge. "Your wife is under arrest with the gravest of charges set against her. She will be tried as the law demands, and if found guilty, she will face the appropriate sanction." The corners of his mouth turned up in an approximation of a smile. "I understand this is not what you wanted to hear, but I am afraid it is the truth of the matter."

"And if this trial takes place, although it seems to have been delayed by many weeks, will I be allowed to attend?"

Wychwoode said, "I am not sure that would be wise, Sir William."

"Why? Good God, man, she is my wife! I have a right to hear her defend herself!" He shook his head. "And she has the right to see me there to support her. I must be there!"

"As I say, I am not sure that would be wise."

William clenched and unclenched his fists under the table a few times, trying to release the tension that was now crackling like lightning bolts in every part of his body. He had only been at this table a few minutes, yet already he was being blocked by these men. How satisfying it would be to leap across the table and smash their two thick heads together, then swing punches at each of them in turn, until they begged for his mercy, which he would only give if they agreed to bring Mary to him so he could take her home to her family…

But instead he took a deep breath and said levelly, "Come now, Robert, we have known each other these ten or more years, and have shared many a glass of wine in friendship. How can you be so unfeeling in this matter?" Wychwoode remained impassive, so William continued. "You have said on countless occasions that you value Mary's wisdom and bravery. How do you abandon her now?"

Wychwoode was about to answer, when Walsingham stood up.

"This meeting is finished, Sir William. All that can be said on this matter has been said. I bid you good day, and I wish you a pleasant journey back to Grangedean Manor."

William also stood, but instead of leaving the table, he leaned across and put his face close to Walsingham's.

"Master Secretary, I…" he began, then he stopped. What could he possibly say that would prise open the iron bars that closed off this man's mind? "Master Secretary, I…" he tried again. But no, it was hopeless. "Master Secretary, I wish you good day," he snarled, then turned and left without another word.

It was only as he was striding down the corridor that he realised what he should have said.

"Listen Master Secretary, I wish you never find yourself in my position – find yourself with one you love in mortal danger and beyond your help. For if you do, you will know what it is to feel powerless when your loved one needs you to come to their aid. It is that powerlessness, Master Secretary, that destroys you inside. You, who has power over so many people, I hope you never know what it feels like to have that taken from you. Good day to you too."

---0---

There was a long silence after Sir William had left.

Eventually Wychwoode observed, "As the man says, I have known him these many years. I do wish I could help him, but…"

"But this mission is more important than your friendship," finished Walsingham. Then his voice softened. "I do know that, Robert, God knows I do. But we cannot put this enterprise in jeopardy."

"Indeed no."

Walsingham sat back and put his fingertips together under his chin. "Curious, is it not," he observed, "that we have managed to have both a wife and husband lean across this very table, and seek to lecture me on how best to do my work.?" He gave a little snort of mirth. "Although the wife was considerably more lucid than the husband. When it came to it, the man was unable to give expression to his feelings." He looked up at Wychwoode. "Curious, I say."

Wychwoode nodded. "I felt sorry for him. His anger stopped his mind from working, whereas her anger had the opposite effect."

"True enough." Walsingham parted his fingers and leaned forward. "But enough of that. To more pressing matters. The secret mission."

Wychwoode swirled his wine around his glass, then took a sip and nodded. "For sure. Is the weapon ready?"

"Aye. I saw it demonstrated yesterday in the forest near the village of Clapham. Do you know, it puts our crude and cumbersome weaponry to shame." Walsingham shook his head slowly. "Lady Mary hit a small apple from more than a furlong distant. A furlong and a half, even. It shows the reality of her claims of the accuracy of the weapon." He nodded. "And Lady Mary – she is truly remarkable. If she is indeed from future times, then women are changed, Robert. They are not the same as our women. We are fortunate to have her working for us."

"Indeed," Wychwoode agreed. "It is as I have said before, she has the bravery and resourcefulness we need for this mission."

"And future missions as well, if she wins though this one," Walsingham observed.

"Nay. She says she seeks only to stay home and run her household," said Wychwoode. "Indeed, I am sure if we allow her, she will run home to see her family, even before undertaking the mission."

"If what Sir William said is true, I have no doubt you are correct."

"But this we cannot allow, Master Secretary," said Wychwoode. "It would put the mission in jeopardy. Who knows what secrets she may reveal?"

"As you say, Robert," said Walsingham. "So we will bring her to my London house at Seething Lane and keep a close watch on her."

"It is for the best, I agree." Wychwoode took a sip of wine. "But let us return to the plan. We are agreed, are we not, that this mission depends on Lady Mary taking a shot at our chosen target from a great distance, using the accuracy of the weapon to ensure success?"

"Aye. That we do."

"And we are fully agreed that a shot is the best way to achieve the desired outcome?" asked Walsingham. "Not a clandestine smothering in the night, or a quiet dose of poison in the food?"

"Yes, the conceit relies on the shot being taken in full public view, so the second part can then be put into motion."

"And if Lady Mary is captured and revealed as the killer?"

Wychwoode shook his head. "It will be regrettable, of course, but we will deny all knowledge. She will be a lone assassin, motivated by religious zeal, nothing more."

"Agreed. And your plan to ensure she gets to the place itself? I warrant she is brave and resourceful, but will be no match for a pack of determined thieves if they come across her on the way. Do you have some four or five men to accompany her?"

"Nay," answered Wychwoode. "This is to be a clandestine journey. To have that many men around her will surely attract attention. I propose one man only – so she will travel easier and faster, and can stay out of trouble more easily."

"If you say," answered Walsingham. "I trust you have a good man for this task?"

"I do," said Wychwoode. "He is perfect."

CHAPTER SEVENTEEN

Mary almost dropped her glass of wine as she stared open-mouthed at Francis Walsingham and Robert Wychwoode.

"You are sending *who* with me on this mission?" she asked in a strangled whisper.

"Roger Rolleston," confirmed Wychwoode. "We need someone we can trust to look to your safety."

"My safety?" Mary knocked back her wine and put the glass down, aware that her shaking hand made it quite clearly clatter against the wooden tabletop. "My safety?" she repeated. "The man is an interfering oaf who could not keep a mad dog safe. Why on earth must he come?"

"He is strong and resourceful," Wychwoode answered, his lined face frowning. "He has been briefed, but only on the destination and the need to ensure you are kept secure, not the purpose of the mission."

"And you say you can trust him?" she asked.

"Aye," Wychwoode answered. "I had him released from the Tower after his wrongful arrest for Catholic sedition."

"Yes, he said he was falsely accused," observed Mary. "How do you know he tells the truth?"

"I checked most thoroughly that he has worshipped at Protestant services ever since Her Majesty ascended the throne." He paused. "He was conducting merchant business with a gentleman at a house in Nottinghamshire, when it was raided by some Pursuivants. Rolleston was arrested also, but I am satisfied he was not of their faith, nor in league with them."

It was a week later, and they were in Walsingham's study at his house in Seething Lane, London, where Mary had been staying while the final elements of the plan were being put in place. Her initial demand to visit Grangedean Manor and see William and the children had been firmly blocked. Walsingham had been adamant that she should remain under cover until the mission was complete and had even muttered darkly that it was better for their safety that they knew nothing of her actions. This, and the fact that she was locked in her room every night, had made her extremely anxious. It had taken much reassurance from Wychwoode to convince her not to worry – which naturally had the opposite effect, making her worry all the more. It had also not helped that Seething Lane was only a couple of streets from her recent prison, and she could clearly see the turrets of the White Tower from the tiny window of the small bedroom they gave her on the top floor, making it painfully obvious that her position was still very precarious.

"I have worked with Rolleston these past few weeks," she tried, "and in my opinion, he is most ill-suited to this task." Not to mention how they had parted on the worst of terms after the Alchemist had fired between the man's legs.

Walsingham poured her some more wine. "I accept your reservations, Lady Mary – I mean Mistress Carter," he said as he wiped the neck of the bottle, "but Rolleston meets our needs well; he is a new intelligencer and therefore unknown to the Catholics…"

"Apart from some in Nottinghamshire," she pointed out.

Walsingham inclined his head. "…Apart from those Catholics, I grant you, but in the main, he is unknown. And he has worked with you, so he knows how you operate." He glanced across at Wychwoode, as if seeking reassurance from an earlier conversation. He added, "And marry, my lady, we need you to trust that we have the success of the mission, and your well-being, at the front of our minds."

Mary tried another angle. "Why do I need a man to accompany me at all?" she asked. "Can I not take Olivia Melrose? We have proven ourselves together previously."

"Two women on such a dangerous mission? It is a risk we cannot take," answered Walsingham. "We cannot allow the success of the venture to be dependent on there being no cut-purses or brigands between here and Sheffield." He smiled in what she felt was a distinctly patronising manner. "No. Rolleston's brief will be to ensure your protection on the road, my lady, and to see you safely to the place where you will use the weapon." He paused, still with the sickly smile, "So we would ask you to trust us in this matter."

Mary knew when she was beaten, and gave back an equally sickly smile. "So be it," she murmured. "But I say now, I do not trust the man an inch."

"For sure," agreed Wychwoode. "But he has made a solemn oath to ensure the success of the mission – and that means looking to your welfare."

"He had better," muttered Mary. '*Or I'll have his nuts for earrings*,' she added to herself.

Wychwoode, oblivious to her unspoken threat, turned to Walsingham.

"Now, Master Secretary," he said, "I would we run through the plan one more time to have all parts in good order."

"Indeed, that is most expedient." The spymaster turned to Mary. "Now, my lady, you have told us with your foresight of future events, that Mary, Queen of Scots becomes an increasing thorn in our side over the next few years, and that she becomes an ever more present magnet for seditious Catholic factions, with plots by men such as Babington to release her so she can usurp our rightful queen's throne. You have told us that eventually a warrant is issued for her execution, despite Her Majesty's reluctance to execute another prince anointed by God, and that in the year of Our Lord fifteen eighty-seven the beheading is carried out. However, it is most casually executed," he gave a dry chuckle, "if you will forgive the expression." He became serious again. "And the Queen of Scots dies an unimaginably painful death." He cleared his throat and continued. "This event is then used in part in the following year by King Philip of Spain to validate an attempt to invade this realm with a sea-borne army – and that although this armada ultimately fails, there is much loss of fine English men." He paused, allowing Wychwoode to take over.

"So we have determined that it is best to cut out this canker of sedition now," the lawyer continued. "Thereby saving not only the need to fight the Spanish with their invasion force, but also the plots from taking place around the Scottish Queen. We will take away the focal point of all these events. Your weapon, and your skill in its deployment, affords us the ideal opportunity to cause the swift and painless death of the Scottish Queen, while she is out taking the daily walk she uses to soften the pain of arthritis in her joints. She is currently held by the Earl of Shrewsbury at Sheffield Castle, and you will secure a suitable position to use your remarkable weapon to kill her, and with sufficient accuracy for our purpose."

"May I just point out," Mary interrupted, "that I am not at heart a cold-blooded assassin, and the thought that you see me as one fills me with horror?"

"I do understand," answered Walsingham, "but you must agree that you have previously shown that you are capable of killing in such a fashion, Lady Mary. We are merely harnessing your proven skills."

Mary opened her mouth to reply, then shut it. He did have a point, however uncomfortable that made her feel.

"The Earl has agreed to the plan in the barest outline, although he has none of the detail," continued Walsingham. "Sufficient for now that he has committed to making sure the Scottish Queen walks alone on the appointed day." He nodded in satisfaction. "We will reveal the remainder of the plan to him in due course. This being, that as soon as she falls, and amid the general consternation and reaction to an assassination in plain view, we will substitute the dead woman with a live one who has been trained these many weeks to take on her person and manner, and whose likeness to the Scottish Queen is so far beyond remarkable to be as if God himself has sent her to us. She will be wearing the same clothing as the Scottish Queen, and will have a wound that matches hers closely enough that none will question it – yet the substitute queen's wound will be produced from bursting a bladder of pig's blood, and will be declared not to be fatal. Which is why we need the accuracy of your weapon. Your shot will pierce the Scottish Queen's heart, while the new queen will appear to have taken a hit but a few inches across, to the shoulder. This will, of course, allow her to appear to make a remarkable recovery. This she will put down to God's grace, thereby opening up the second part of the plan.

"What will happen to the body of the real queen?" interrupted Mary. "Once I have..." she paused to steady herself. "Once I have killed her?"

"The body will be taken to a small room near," Walsingham said, "and held securely until it can be given a quiet burial."

Wychwoode then picked up the tale, "Meantimes the replacement, one Frances Barwell, will then become to all intents and purposes, Mary, Queen of Scots. She has been receiving secret daily intelligence from one of our men inside the Earl's household, so she has all the knowledge she needs to maintain the deception. She is a fluent speaker of both the French and the Scots tongue, so she can easily mimic the Scottish Queen's language and manner of speech, and can converse in either as required. Any lapse in memory or any misunderstanding can be put down to the traumatic effects of surviving such an assassination attempt."

"As soon as we have Mistress Barwell in place," Walsingham continued, "she will be taken to a new location to recover, most likely Tutbury Castle, which recovery will be speedy enough that she can very soon travel. Then," and here he gave an uncharacteristic smile, "she will perform the perfect endgame to our plan; she will make it known that that the attempt on her life has made her re-think her faith, and given her cause to convert away from Catholicism to become a true Protestant." He nodded briefly. "And we will also let it be known that the assassin is believed to be a disaffected Catholic – thus giving credibility to her desire to move away from that faith. She will then be brought to London, pale and wounded so she gains the most sympathy, and renounce all claim to the throne of England. A binding legal article will be drawn up to give effect to her decision, and she will sign it. The conversion and renunciation will then be proclaimed throughout the land."

Wychwoode added, "The Catholics will no longer have a person they can champion for the throne, as her son, the nine-year-old boy James, has been raised in the true faith of the Church of Scotland. So they will be forced to live more loyal and holy lives, and we will, with God's good grace, have peace in the realm and less of a threat to the person and throne of our true Queen Elizabeth."

"So we are all of one mind on this?" Walsingham asked.

Mary nodded. Yes, she was of one mind with these men, as she had little choice other than to go along with this incredible plan. But naturally she had her reservations – there was much that could go wrong, and not to mention the sickening and questionable logic of killing the Queen of Scots now, thereby saving her from a painful death in eleven years' time. Given the choice of eleven more years of life and a painful death, Mary wasn't sure she would choose that option for herself.

Not to mention that this plan would make her into a cold-blooded assassin.

To be a spy was one thing – but an assassin...?

Good," said Walsingham. Then he opened a drawer in his desk and produced an unsealed, folded letter. "Take this," he said, handing it over. "'Tis the final instruction to the Earl of Shrewsbury, appraising him of the plan, or as much as he needs to know, and his part therein."

Mary took the letter and opened it cautiously, then frowned as her eyes skimmed across the page. None of the writing made any sense; it was all in blocks of five characters and none was a recognisable word. She glanced up, to see the two men staring at her intently.

"Aye, it is in code," said Walsingham. "In case it falls into the hands of our enemies."

"And Shrewsbury can decipher this?" she asked, as she folded it again.

"For sure – it is our usual code with him." He paused, and Mary thought he had further information, but was unsure of revealing it. She raised an enquiring eyebrow, and after a moment, he continued. "It has a secret mark that sets it apart from any copies or forgery." He cleared his throat cautiously. "If ever you need to have proof it is genuine, then hold the top left corner to the flame of a candle. If the heat shows forth a secret mark, then you know the paper is genuine."

"And the secret mark is…?" she enquired, then waited as the two men remained silent. "Should I not know this?"

Walsingham paused, then nodded to himself, as if he had decided he could trust her. "The mark of this paper is to have 'GX' – the two letters that each follow my own initials – then a code number. That number will be a high prime number, to wit, one that can only be divided by one or by itself. That way you will know it is not a copy."

"How can I determine if it is a prime number?" Mary asked.

Walsingham smiled. "You must do some thinking," he said. "Can it be divided by two? Then it is not prime."

"For sure," she answered. "That much I do know."

"Then you try three, four, five and seven. If none of those result in a complete number, then it is prime."

She nodded, "Thank you for the lesson in mathematics."

"But you must keep it safe," said Wychwoode, with a small grin at her irony. "I need hardly add that we would not have it fall in their hands, for all it is so encoded."

"And if it did fall into the enemies' hands, and they were able to understand it?"

Walsingham shrugged, "Then naturally we would deny all knowledge of any part of this conceit."

Despite the warmth of the fire beside her, Mary shivered. "And leave me to carry the blame?" she demanded. "Is my name in this, as the person to execute the plan – even as Anne Carter?"

"Not by name, I assure you," said Walsingham. "Neither that one nor your true name, naturally. Your identity is not compromised by this, even if it is decoded."

Wychwoode put his hand on her sleeve. "Lady Mary," he said softly. "We would bring you in safe – you have my word." He gave her a half-smile that seemed to offer reassurance.

But Mary was not convinced, and it felt as if the temperature in the room had fallen even further. "I have now seen your play-acting Robert," she answered. "How can I trust you in this matter?"

"By my word, honestly given," he said. "We have known each other these many years and been through much together." He nodded, as if to convince himself as much as her. "So this is my heart to yours. Trust me in this; if the plan fails, I will shield you from blame."

"You had better," she answered. '*Or believe me*,' she thought, '*I'll have your nuts as well.*'

CHAPTER EIGHTEEN

Mary settled into her seat as the carriage started to roll forward on the journey north.

As Rolleston sat opposite, she gave him her hardest stare, intended to show just how much she disliked being forced to endure his company.

A few minutes before, they had been taken to the carriage as it stood at the end of Seething Lane, with two horses in the traces and a grizzled-looking man sitting on the open seat at the front holding on to the reins.

The carriage itself seemed well-made; essentially a sturdy wooden box that reminded Mary of a section of a London Tube train with an over-sized curved roof. There was a small door in the middle of each side, with glassless windows all round and thick velvet curtains to provide warmth and shelter from the wind. Inside, there were two bench seats covered with stuffed leather – one facing forward and the other backward, with leather straps beside each one to hang on to when things got bumpy.

Rolleston gave Mary back an expression that was somewhere between a frown and a sneer. "What ails, Mistress Carter? Art sickening for something?"

"In a manner," she answered, grabbing at one of the leather straps as the carriage bumped across the cobbles. "At the thought of sharing this journey with you."

He shrugged. "It pleases me neither, I can assure you." He looked away from her and appeared to study intently the London houses passing by the window.

Mary glanced down at his right hand as it rested on his knee. There was still heavy bruising and scabbed skin on his knuckles. She watched in fascination as he flexed his fingers a few times, which suggested that nothing was broken, despite the force of the punch on the wall of the Alchemist's room.

"By Heavens, what were you thinking?" she asked, pointing at his hand.

He glanced down at it, then resumed his study of the passing houses. "I was much angered," he said, in a tone which suggested the matter was closed.

But Mary was not about to let it drop. If they were going to spend many days in each other's company, then she supposed she ought to know more about this man; about what made him tick.

"Strange to turn the anger on yourself," she observed.

There was such a long silence that she thought he had not heard. She was about to repeat herself, when he said, "That Alchemist nearly unmanned me."

Mary raised an eyebrow. "You flatter yourself, sir," she said drily. "The shot was at the level of your knees."

"Belike," he answered, "but as I say, I was much angered."

"But strange as a result," she persisted, "to cause pain to your own hand."

"Nay," he said, turning back to her, "I felt no pain."

"No pain?" she asked. "How so?"

He shrugged. "I do not experience it at all, as others do."

"Seriously?" Mary gasped. "How so?" she repeated.

"I know not. It is some affliction chosen for me by God, that I do not have this feeling."

"Affliction?" Mary asked, conscious her voice had risen to a squeak. "Surely it is a blessing? I would love not to feel pain."

To be spared the agony of Tudor childbirth not once or twice, but three times – now that would have been a blessing...

"Nay, mistress," he said, the corner of his mouth turned up in a sneer, "I assure you it is an affliction. I can tell tales of grievous wounds received in daily life, that would, in normally disposed people, not have occurred." He paused. "Such as severe burns, known only by a smell of cooked meat… or of cuts received in play combat with swords, known only when my blood splashed across my opponent's arm…"

"I see," she said. "But there must be some benefits?"

"I can see very few." He paused, "Except, perhaps, when I was under threat of torture in that infernal Tower."

"True." Mary thought a moment. "But then, you were not tortured," she observed. "Wychwoode had you released to work as an intelligencer before such a thing occurred. To accompany me on this journey."

"Aye." He turned back to the window, then added out of the side of his mouth, "Which I can assure you is pain enough."

There was a long silence after that. The carriage trundled through the cobbled streets with Mary and Rolleston each staring out of opposite windows at the passing houses and yards.

A blacksmith's forge shone briefly in a gap between two buildings, and Mary saw the smith working a piece of glowing metal with his hammer. She craned her neck round to see more, before the second building closed off her view. How remarkable it was, that just a few weeks ago such a sight would have been of passing interest only – no more than a historical curiosity – yet now she regarded the blacksmith's work with an almost professional eye. How had he cast and cooled the piece? What tools would he be using to finish and polish it? What pride would he take in the final object?

"If this mission fails, and you still live, then you could earn a few pennies as a smith," Rolleston said, giving her an amused look as she sat back in her seat. "Or maybe an armourer's assistant." He gave a dry chuckle. "For if it does fail, then for sure you will no longer have any manner of life – if you even have one at all."

"I have assurances that I will not be blamed if it fails," Mary answered.

"Then you are more of a naive fool than I took you for," he observed. "If you are caught before you have successfully used the weapon you have fashioned – whatever that purpose may be – or discovered after, then you will be blamed for the failure of the operation, and Walsingham for its conception."

"And you also, if you fail in your duties."

He shrugged. "Perhaps. My duty is to get you safely to your destination and back, and I have given my oath upon it. After that, you are on your own. So the failure will be yours and yours alone."

Mary leaned forward and looked him hard in the eye. "Then I suggest we stop this talk of failure and talk instead of success." She paused a moment. "And as you are here, charged with ensuring my safety, I would have you assure me that you have plans for the success of this journey." She glanced away, then back at him. "What if we are attacked by brigands or cut-purses?"

He patted the sword at his belt. "Then I will fight to protect you, Anne Carter," he said, making it sound more like a threat than a promise. "And if I take a cut or two in your defence, then be assured I will feel no pain, and will fight on withal, to win your approval."

"I will take what comfort I can from that," she replied. "Though you will understand I shall keep the gun to hand as well, in case it is needed."

"As you wish."

And not just the gun, she thought. There was another form of self-defence that the Alchemist had patiently taught her, in preparation for her mission.

"What if you're tied up, and your attacker is advancing on you with, say, a knife?" the Alchemist had asked casually, when she had visited him briefly a couple of days before to say farewell, and they were sharing an ale alone in his room. "How will you turn the tables on your attacker?"

"Kick him in the crotch?" she had suggested.

"Maybe, but as I said, you're tied up. Say he comes in close, what then?"

"Not sure," she said. "What are you suggesting?"

He smiled slowly. "Come now, Justine, what do you have that is thick and hard and can cause real damage?"

She raised an eyebrow. "As a woman, I'm not sure what you mean…"

"Don't be daft." His smile broadened. "Your head. Have you never heard of a head-butt; the good old 'Gorbals Kiss'?"

"For goodness' sake," she answered, "I'm not going around head-butting…"

"But you're happy to use a sniper gun?" He paused. "You're being sent on what sounds like a very dangerous mission, Justine, from the few snippets I have picked up. You need to have more than one way of protecting yourself. Especially if you don't have a poker to hand."

"That's not fair, Rick."

"I'm serious." He paused again. "I know we were sworn enemies before, but since we've been working on the same side, and you've been doing what I have told you…" He nodded, as if reassuring himself that his instincts were correct, then he continued, "I've sort of understood you better."

"I'm not sure whether I should be surprised or pleased."

"Yeah, well, whatever…" he muttered. "Look," he shuffled forward clutching his tankard of ale, his chain clinking behind him. "If you're attacked, and you're tied up, then you need to know what to do."

"I will have Rolleston with me when we travel north," she said. "He is supposed to be protecting me."

"Rolleston is going with you?" The Alchemist made a violently dismissive gesture, causing ale to slop across his blanket, although he seemed not to notice. "Fuck me, you'll need protection from him, not by him! Did you not protest?"

"Of course," she answered. "But Wychwoode did not give me the choice. It's a long journey and they wanted to ensure I had a companion."

"Keep a close eye on that one, Justine," he muttered. Then he added, "North, eh? Any idea where?"

"I cannot say, Rick," she replied. "Sorry."

He nodded, as if he had expected her to say that. "Well, as I say, keep your eyes open with that prick Rolleston."

"I will," she answered. "Although I asked to have my true friend Olivia, who fought with me against your co-conspirator, Lambert Moreton. I would trust her a lot further than Rolleston."

"Yeah. Sounds like that Moreton was a right tosser." He considered her a moment. "Anyhow, let's put that all behind us." He smiled. "But this Olivia – she sounds fun."

"She's very brave, and very loyal. And fearless, too."

"Everything Rolleston is not," he said. "In which case you really do need to know how to give a good old head-butt.

Mary nodded slowly. It did make sense to be prepared, although she hoped she would never need to put this into action. "Okay, go on, then. Show me."

He nodded, tapping his forehead just above his eye "Solid bone, here." Then he went to his jaw. "But thin and delicate here. So what happens if a solid and heavy object meets a thinner, more delicate one?"

"The delicate one breaks?"

"Precisely. So if someone comes in close, bring your forehead hard onto his jaw. It doesn't take much force if you hit it right; just make sure you carry it through."

"How do you mean?" Mary could not believe she was having this totally surreal conversation, but she asked anyway.

"Listen, if you hit a nail with a hammer, it's easy to 'bounce' it, like so." He mimed hitting a blow that flicked back up at the moment of impact. "All the force is gone because you're not committed to the blow. But if you push through instead, the full force is transferred." He mimed again, but this time carried the blow through without the flick. "So don't go in half-hearted, but full-on. Committed."

"Will it hurt?" She asked the obvious question.

He shrugged. "For sure, you'll have a sore forehead for an hour or two. He, on the other hand, will have a broken jaw." He smiled. "Go figure."

"Well, let's hope I don't need to do a 'Gorbals Kiss' as you call it.

"Yeah." He stared hard at her; his eyes narrowed. "But if you do, be committed."

Rolleston's voice cut across her recollection, dragging her back to the present. "You nod to yourself repeatedly, Mistress Carter." She looked up. "Are you suffering an ague?"

"No." She didn't feel any further explanation was either necessary or justified.

"Yet that was the look of it." Rolleston sat back with his arms folded, as if that was the truth of the matter.

She observed him across the carriage. This was the second time she was travelling north alone with a man in less than a year. How different this Rolleston was from Tom Cobham, her companion from last time. Tom, who had been as honourable and as upright as Rolleston was devious and underhand, had actually saved her in her moment of need and never asked for her approval, or anything in return.

"If a fight is necessary, and God willing it shall not be, then I would you fight for my honour alone," she observed, drumming her fingers lightly on the seat beside her. "A few months ago, a man fought for my honour when I was attacked in a tavern," she said. "He asked for naught as a reward," she paused and held his cold blue eye. "And for that I valued him all the more greatly."

"So if I want your approval, I must not ask for it?"

"Something like that."

He sat back and looked out of his window. "Never can I understand the mind of a woman," he muttered.

Mary let this pass. Instead she said, "And when we arrive, I would you leave me to carry my part of the plan through." Then she also sat back and looked out of the window at the green fields and spinneys that were now rolling past. "I suggest you remain in whatever lodging we have while I undertake the mission, then you can escort me safely back to London."

"As you wish," he said. Then he asked, "And what is our destination? I feel I should know this if I am to protect you on the journey."

Mary thought a moment, then decided to give him one small nugget of information – one that he would be finding out soon enough anyway. "I will tell you this, sir, and no more. We are proceeding to Sheffield, in the county of Yorkshire.

"And what exactly is this mission in Sheffield? You are most secretive."

"And will remain so, Master Rolleston, I can assure you." Mary shook her head. "Believe me, I will not be sharing any further secrets with you."

CHAPTER NINETEEN

The evening moon was casting long shadows through the skeletal winter trees as the driver pulled the horses to a stop in the courtyard of a roadside inn. Mary felt the carriage rock as he jumped down from his seat.

The driver's grizzled face appeared at the window. "We stop here for the night," he said in a gravelly voice that sounded like pebbles being shaken in a bag.

"Thank Heaven," muttered Rolleston, "It has been a long journey thus far. I must make haste for the jakes." He leapt out of the carriage and started to run over to the inn.

Mary stepped down more sedately, then retrieved her bag from under her seat and made her way into the building.

As she entered, a large woman with a red face under a stained coif approached her.

"A room for the night, mistress?" the woman asked.

Mary nodded as she put her bag down and stared around the inn.

Like most of those she had stopped in since she had first left the comfort of Grangedean Manor all those months ago, it was a simple, open room with many oak tables and benches, each with a yellow tallow candle. Stairs led off one side of the room, presumably up to the bedrooms. She had stayed in so many such establishments that it was hard to distinguish one from another, but there was something vaguely familiar about this one, and its landlady. Perhaps she had stayed here before? Most probably, when she had previously travelled up to York with Tom Cobham on their mission to prevent the Alchemist in his attempt to assassinate Queen Elizabeth.

Mary gave an involuntary shiver. How different to be staying here again, but this time with a boorish oaf like Rolleston and not with a true gentleman like Tom Cobham.

Then she chuckled under her breath. Tom was indeed such a gentleman, that he had even managed to maintain control when they had inadvertently found themselves naked together after washing in a stream. So when she had ordered him to step away, he had done so – for all it was perfectly clear that it was not what his heart – or indeed his body – had desired.

How different would her life have been if she had submitted to the passion that she had also felt, and had allowed nature to take its course that spring day? Maybe their mission would have taken second place to their feelings for each other, and their purpose for travelling to York would have been lost? And then what? Poor Tom would still be alive today, and her marriage would have been put in desperate jeopardy – and in truth, she could never have done anything to hurt William. Not to mention that the Alchemist would most likely have succeeded in assassinating the Queen, so that English history would have changed forever under the Catholic rule of Mary, Queen of Scots.

But was she, Lady Mary de Beauvais, now deliberately setting out to change history?

It may be that ultimately her mission was to prevent Catholic plots and the Armada by assassinating the Queen of Scots, but either way the future would still be very different. The comforting world of 2015 that only she and the Alchemist remembered would surely disappear into the mist. It would be replaced by some unknown future that was yet to be written; yet to be reshaped by a million new events.

Mary gave a small sigh.

Had she not already started the process by saving William when he was destined to die, then by having three children who were never meant to exist? So what would it matter now if she caused even more changes?

And what of her original fear that if she changed history too much, she would cause her own birth not to happen and she would suddenly disappear? But the Alchemist had convinced her that nothing she could do on this timeline would endanger her birth in a previous one. She had been born in the old 1988, and that was a fact that could not be altered, whatever the new 1988 looked like.

"I have but one room remaining," the landlady was saying, dragging Mary's attention back to the present, as Rolleston joined them, adjusting his trunk-hose. The landlady continued, "It is my best room, well suited to quality travellers such as you and your fine husband here."

"Oh no, we…" Mary began, but Rolleston interrupted her.

"My wife and I appreciate your kindness. I am sure it will be ideal." Mary shot him a look of pure venom, but he continued, "We will have a brief rest before we take our supper, as it has been such a long journey." He smiled at the landlady. "I am sure my dear wife is in need of some stillness after the rigours of the road. Are you not, Anne, my love?"

Mary returned a sickly smile, keeping her anger inside, saving it for later.

---0---

"How dare you!" she snarled when they were alone in the room. "How dare you presume to call us husband and wife?"

"And have questions asked as to why we are not married, yet travel together?" he demanded.

"I do not give a fig for any questions being asked!" she shot back, "I would rather answer questions than have folk think I am married to one such as you!"

"Which would naturally lead to further questions, covering perhaps the nature of our journey, and thence to your secret mission itself." He stood before her with his hands on his hips and his shoulders back. "I would have thought, Mistress Anne Carter," he snapped, "that you of all people would understand the risks involved and the need to avoid suspicion." He paused a moment, then added, "or to prompt folk to recall us later, if asked."

"Whatever!" she muttered, annoyed at the thought he might actually be right. "Anyway," she said, pointing at the floor, "that is where you sleep, as you certainly will not be sharing the bed with me."

He shrugged. "For sure, that is no problem." He gave her a sickly smile. "To sleep on the floor is not a hardship to one who feels no pain."

Mary flounced over to the bed and flopped down on her back. "I do need some rest after the journey," she said, before turning to her side and trying to plump the thin pillow, then giving up and resuming her previous position. "So you can close the door on your way out."

CHAPTER TWENTY

A pale beam of autumn sunlight shone down through the thin curtains, warming Mary's cheek and jolting her awake. She gave a small groan and opened her eyes, staring at the rough plaster wall opposite. For a moment she had no idea where she was – searching for the familiar table and chair that usually greeted her each morning while she had been staying at Francis Walsingham's house in Seething Lane. Then she remembered the previous day's travelling with Rolleston; their arrival at the inn and his dreadful assertion that they were married.

She sat up with another groan, and was surprised to note that she was still fully clothed. She recalled she had lain down to rest before supper and had dismissed her would-be husband; she must have slept the whole night in her clothes and missed supper completely. A loud rumble from the region under her stomacher confirmed this. She glanced out of the window. From the height of the sun, she reckoned it was probably around 9am.

She got up, expecting to see Rolleston asleep on the floor as instructed, but there was no sign of him. Thinking that he had already gone down for breakfast, Mary fished in her bag for her hand mirror, pins and comb, then spent a few minutes trying to get her hair into some semblance of order. Her stomach gave another loud gurgle as she glanced in her bag at her travelling pots of make-up. She paused, before closing the bag. Breakfast was the priority, and if Rolleston and her fellow travellers found her natural look too scary, that was their problem not hers.

She took herself down to the tavern and sat at an empty table, looking around the room for Rolleston. There was no sign of him, so when a pretty young girl appeared with plates for another table, Mary beckoned her over.

"My husband…" she began, then forced a smile to cover her distaste at saying those words, "said he would, er... step out a while. Has he returned?"

"Your husband, mistress?"

"A tall man with a dark beard, wearing the garb of a merchant."

The girl's eyes widened briefly, then she said quickly, "Nay mistress, I have not seen such a man." She looked down and muttered, "Meantimes, will you have some bread and cheese to break your fast?"

Mary nodded, and the girl hurried away to serve other guests. Mary again glanced round the room, in case anyone was in some way suspicious and should be noted.

Had Walsingham sent any of his intelligencers to keep an eye on her and Rolleston?

How about the elderly couple in the corner? The old man was squinting in a short-sighted way and the woman had a lazy eye. They didn't look capable of observing anyone.

Then there were the two yeomen whose table the girl was now clearing. They were so absorbed in their own conversation that it was hard to think they were spying on anyone.

Mary felt a hand on her shoulder and looked up, to see Rolleston standing beside her.

"Good morrow, wife," he said, with a cold smile. "I trust you have slept well this night?"

"Do not use that word unless we are in company," she snapped.

He raised an eyebrow and glanced at the room. "I see others around."

"You know what I mean."

"Belike." He paused. "So, wife, I asked a question, and I would have an answer."

"Oh, you would, would you?" she said. "Well, as we are in company…" she paused to give him her coldest stare, "I did, as it happens," she replied, "I must have been very tired, as I slept through supper."

"So I noticed," he said as he sat down opposite. "I thought best not to waken you, so I dined alone."

"I am not sure to be pleased you let me sleep, or annoyed to have missed supper," she said.

"Please yourself," he said with a small smile, as if amused at his little play on her words.

"And where were you last night?" Mary asked, annoyed for wanting to know but curious, nonetheless.

"Were you my wife in truth, Anne," he said with a shrug, "then I would vouchsafe an answer to that question. But, as you so readily point out, you are not." He paused, "So my answer is that it is no business of yours."

Before Mary could think of a suitable retort, the serving girl came over with a plate of bread and cheese, and a tankard of ale. As she glanced at Rolleston, a brief, but deeply guilty look flashed across her face, then she quickly looked away.

"So, mistress, you have found your…" she bit her lip, "your husband?"

"Yes," answered Mary, forcing a cold smile. "I have."

The girl put the food and drink down and muttered, "Something for you, master?"

"Aye, some bread and cheese also, and ale," he replied with an easy smile.

Mary watched as the girl scurried away. Once she was out of earshot, Mary said, "So I think my question is answered, is it not? Now I think I know where you spent the night."

He reached across and broke off some bread from her plate. "Aye," he said as he put it in his mouth, "she is most comely." Then he added, "And most willing in bed."

Mary pulled her plate closer, and said drily, "She would need to be."

CHAPTER TWENTY-ONE

Olivia Melrose stood outside the doors to the Great Hall at Grangedean Manor, fingering her gold necklace as she waited to be admitted.

The servant beside her gave her a curt nod, then pushed them open and strode through. She saw him stop, cough loudly and wait for silence. Once the chatter had died down, he announced, "Mistress Olivia Melrose, Sir William." He stood back and gestured Olivia forward.

She took a deep breath and walked in, conscious that the family at the high table was watching her closely. She had dressed to befit her new status; deciding on a cream silk gown edged with gold thread to set off her pale face and rouged lips, while her dark hair was combed back to give her a fashionably high forehead. She had finished it off with a delicate gold tiara and matching pendant earrings. Hopefully she had judged the look right – grand, but not too grand. Not overwhelming. A look that would have made Lady Mary proud.

As she walked up to the high table, she could not help but notice how different the hall looked in comparison to the home-coming celebration of two months earlier, when she and Lady Mary had made just such an entrance. Then there had been hundreds of bright candles making the room sparkle like a magnificent diamond; now there were only a few flickering stubs in sconces on the walls and a couple on the high table. It made the room seem so much darker, and so much smaller. Maybe God wanted her to realise the difference with last time she had been here, as that was the day that Lady Mary had been arrested and they had both been taken to the Tower.

She looked at the high table, which was the only one occupied – another change from the last time, when there had been long tables filling both sides of the room, crammed with noisy nobility and joyfully drunken friends. Sir William was seated in the centre with Ambrose on his right, then an older lady in a simple brown dress. Kat was on his left, with an elegant woman in her thirties beside her. Beyond her was little Jane, Mary's third child, who was the only one more concerned with her food than with Olivia's approach. Olivia recognised the older lady as the housekeeper Ruth, and the elegant woman as her daughter, Sarah – Lady Mary's lady in waiting.

There was an uncomfortable silence as she walked up to the table, then dropped into a deep curtsey before Sir William.

"Pray be upstanding, Mistress Melrose," he said, "You are most welcome here." As she stood, she could see how badly he had aged. His bright, twinkling eyes had sunk into his face like pebbles into the bed of a dried-out stream, and his once smooth, clear skin now looked paper thin and lined. Even his beard, previously sandy throughout, was now peppered with grey.

She glanced at Ambrose. She thought he looked older than his nine years, as if the worry caused by his mother's arrest had forced him to miss out on so many precious years of his childhood. It was easy to see how like his father he was becoming; the same eyes, mouth and chin. In a few years he would be the very image of Sir William.

"I came as soon as I could," she said, "Once the Queen gave me leave from her service to attend on you here at Grangedean."

"Aye," he said, giving her a wintery smile, "I had heard from your father that you had been elevated to Her Majesty's service." He glanced down at Kat, who was hanging on to his arm, and added, "We are honoured that one of the Queen's maids of honour has graced us."

Kat gave her a weak smile. Like Ambrose, she looked older than her years. There were frown lines on her pretty little face that had no right to be there.

"Livia, I pray you come and sit beside me," she said, her little girl's voice sounding strangely at odds with the adult tone of her words. "I would you tell me all." How different from last time, when she had thrown herself into Olivia's arms, shrieking like a mischievous little imp, to be flung round in a circle.

Sir William nodded his approval, so Olivia made her way round the table. A manservant pushed a chair between Kat and Sarah. Once she was seated, the man placed a pewter plate, a napkin and goblet before her, and filled it with wine. Olivia took a sip, then said, "What shall I tell, little Kat?" Although it was clear to her what they would all want to discuss.

"I would know about my mother," Kat replied, staring up with big eyes and biting her lip.

"We are sickened with worry," added Sarah.

"Is Ma still held in the Tower on false charges?" Ambrose asked from the other side of Sir William. "We would visit her there if we could, but Pa says they will not let us."

"We know not as to whether she has been tried, or if she is condemned and executed already," explained Sir William. "They will not tell us anything." He shook his head. "It is wholly unnatural that her family are left knowing naught on such a matter. Every petition I make for information is met with silence and obfuscation. I cannot get a straight answer from any man; not Walsingham or Wychwoode, nor any other I have asked since I spoke with those two directly. I am continually turned away and left powerless in this matter."

"Please, Livia," said Kat, looking up at her hopefully, "what has become of her?"

Olivia put her hand over Kat's and gazed into the little girl's troubled eyes. "I am so sorry, but it is God's truth that I know no more than you. My own questions on Lady Mary's fate have been met with the same wall of silence as have yours."

No one said anything for a moment. Kat gave a small sob, and Sir William shook his head slowly.

"Please forgive us, Mistress Melrose," Sarah said, leaning across and dabbing away the tears that had welled up in Kat's eyes, "but when you sent word you were coming here, we took it that you would be bringing some news of Lady Mary."

"Even bad news would at least let us know what has become of her," added Ruth.

Olivia looked at each of them in turn. "As Christ is my witness, I wish beyond all measure that I could tell you something of value," she said, "but the dreadful truth is that I hoped maybe *you* had news for *me* – that is why I came here."

It was not only that; she had also originally planned to pass on to each member of the family the personal messages that Lady Mary had given her that night on the boat. But now she was sitting beside them and seeing their distress – and with the smallest possibility that Lady Mary was still alive – she knew it was not the time. Those messages would have to wait.

She became aware of a distressed sniff from beside her. Kat said, "Each day you see the Queen – can you not ask her to tell us about Ma?"

"I am so sorry, my little puss, but that is not the thing you ask of Her Majesty." Olivia thought a moment. "I have so recently been elevated to this royal position; I cannot have the Queen think poorly of me for asking too many questions…"

"But Livia…" Kat began, when Sir William raised a hand for silence.

"Mistress Melrose has most clearly set out her situation," he stated. "We cannot demand more of her than she is able to give. The truth of this matter is…" he looked at each of them in turn, "…the truth of this matter, is that none of us here knows what has become of Mary, my wife and your dear lady mother. So we must wait until such times as we are told, and cleave to the thought that no news of her trial or execution means that we can live with the hope that neither has yet happened." He nodded, as if to reassure himself as much as them. "Yes, we will have to wait. Now," he said with a weak smile, "Mistress Melrose is here as our valued guest, and we must give her our warmest welcome and finest hospitality." He pulled himself to his feet and raised his goblet. "I would we raise our glasses to the health of Mistress Melrose, and to the hope that God sends us back our beloved Mary soon."

Everyone stood and raised their glasses except little Jane, until Sarah leaned down and pulled the child to her feet.

"To Mistress Melrose for her welcome presence here this eve," said Sir William, "and to Lady Mary – may God end these false charges against her, and send her safely home to her family."

"Amen," they replied in unison.

---0---

After the meal had finished and Sarah had taken the children up to bed, Sir William and Olivia retired to the solar, settling themselves before the fire.

"Will you stay with us at least a day or two?" he asked, swirling the wine around in his glass.

"That is most kind, Sir William," she replied. "Her Majesty has instructed me to return to the Palace of Whitehall in two days, so I would be delighted."

"Good. Then that is settled." He regarded her thoughtfully. "I must tell you, it gladdens my heart that you attend us here, as it makes me feel just a little closer to Mary."

She inclined her head with a smile. "As do I also, with you."

"Then we are well matched in this," he observed. "Now pray tell, I must know how it was that you were elevated to Her Majesty's service?"

Olivia took a sip of wine. "It was the strangest occurrence," she began. "I was but a few days after I was fortunately taken back into the service of my lady Burnham, when I was summoned to Court at Whitehall. I was concerned that I was about to be thrown into the Tower myself – belike for my association with Lady Mary – so I said a fond and tearful farewell to my dearest companion Maggie Tyndall, before I boarded the barge. When I got there, I was taken to a chamber where the Queen herself was seated, with no others but Master Secretary Walsingham and Master Wychwoode. Then I was truly afraid, as the last time I had been in the presence of these men, it was when Lady Mary had called Master Walsingham a fool…"

"She did *what*?" Sir William nearly choked on his wine.

Olivia smiled. "She had observed that as a person coming from future times, she had knowledge that would benefit the Queen, and that Master Walsingham should heed this remarkable intelligence before wantonly casting her into the flames."

He nodded briefly. "That is indeed good logic, and just as I would expect from Mary." He paused and frowned as he stared into the fire. "You know, Olivia," he said, "as I said to your father at the time, it troubled me greatly when I learned about her history. I felt most uneasy when I heard that she was born in another time, and angered that she had not trusted me to tell me herself. But," he continued, "I gave it much thought, and I came to see that it did not change the Mary I knew and loved. It did not make her a different person to the girl I married. And indeed, it did make sense of her strange and sudden appearance and her most awkward behaviour when we first met." His intense look as he said this sent a shiver up Olivia's spine. "It made me realise what a truly remarkable woman she is, and how lucky I am to be the man she loves."

"And I too," Olivia replied, finding herself strangely compelled to match his feelings with her own. "She helped me to see how a woman is the equal of a man in many things, and once I knew that she had sight of a future where that becomes so, then it was real for me too." She gave a small chuckle. "Which was in truth, the reason I was commanded to enter the Queen's service."

He raised an eyebrow. "How so?"

"Well, when I was in the Queen's presence, she asked me to tell her how I found Lady Mary's character, and particularly how I believed Lady Mary would act when put under pressure."

"Under pressure?" he asked.

"Indeed, that was Her Majesty's question," Olivia replied. "So I told her God's truth, which is that my lady would always do what is right, however hard it might be, and however much danger it might put her into. Then Master Secretary Walsingham observed that as a woman, she could not be so relied upon. I recalled how my lady would have reacted to such a statement, so I told him to his face that he was mistaken and that my lady had the courage of twenty men. I told him that if I was in peril, there is not another person on God's earth that I would rather have come to my aid." She chuckled again. "I was most forceful, and I swear he physically stepped backwards when I spoke my piece."

"I see. And how did the Queen act on this revelation?"

"For sure, I warrant that she looked on it most favourably. She smiled at me and asked if I missed my lady. I said I was greatly upset when we were parted, and I miss her most dreadfully."

"As do I," he muttered.

"Then the Queen said something I did not quite understand." Olivia twisted her glass as she stared into the fire. "She said that I spoke with the honesty of Lady Mary – and that while my lady was otherwise disposed, she would keep me close by her from this moment on, as my lady's proxy. As one who could give her the same council." She turned to Sir William. "What might she have meant by that?"

He was silent, as he appeared to think this through. Then he said, "Otherwise disposed? That is most singular." He shook his head slowly "Might it mean simply that she is in the Tower?"

"I thought maybe so. But if the Queen wants her council, she has only to have her brought to court and to ask it. Whether a prisoner or no."

"I agree," he said slowly. "And it would not have been said if she was tried and executed." He gave a small shudder. "So belike she is no longer in the Tower, is still living, but is now elsewhere – somewhere that is secret, as no man will tell either of us where she is or what she is doing."

"I had not thought it," Olivia answered slowly. "But as you put it so, I can see that this could be the case."

He was silent a long while after; the flickering flames reflecting in the sides of his eyes as he stared ahead. Eventually he gave a deep sigh and turned to Olivia.

"I warrant that Mary is out of the Tower, alive – God be praised – and is even now undertaking some clandestine enterprise for the Queen. Her Majesty wanted to know if Mary has the courage to act under pressure – and that suggests a dangerous mission, no doubt dreamed up by that arch-schemer Walsingham."

He got out of his chair and did something Olivia would never have expected. He knelt down in front of her and clasped her hands in his. "My dearest Olivia," he said quietly. "I beg you; I plead with you on my bended knee, to use your new-found position at court to find out what my wife is up to. I warrant that if she is in the gravest danger, then we must do all we can to get her back safely."

CHAPTER TWENTY-TWO

If the atmosphere in the carriage had been cold on the journey so far, it was positively frigid after Rolleston's behaviour with the serving girl at the inn. Very little conversation now passed between them, other than was necessary regarding stops for food and sleep, and most of the journey over the next few days was spent staring out of opposite carriage windows at the passing forests and hamlets. Meals at each tavern were taken in an uncomfortable silence; nights were most definitely spent in separate rooms – for Mary had insisted she had no stomach for the conceit that they were married, whether or not others had concerns.

And if Mary had her suspicions about Rolleston continuing his nocturnal activities, she kept them to herself.

So when the carriage rolled slowly to a standstill in the middle of a forest clearing late one afternoon, it was a few moments before Mary felt the need to break the silence.

"Why have we stopped, I wonder?"

"Belike one of the horses is lame, or cast a shoe," muttered Rolleston, pulling back the curtain and peering out of the window. "Or a stag has blocked our path." He sat back. "I have no doubt we will be on our way again in short order."

Just then there was a whooshing sound, that ended in a sickening thud and a grunt from the front of the carriage. Mary immediately looked out of her window, just in time to see the driver topple slowly from his seat and fall to the ground, an arrow shaft standing proud from his chest.

"By Heavens!" she exclaimed. Her hand went to the door handle.

Rolleston jumped up and pulled hard on her sleeve. "You will stay here," he ordered.

"But the driver is wounded. I must go to him."

"Do not be a fool," he said, glancing out of the window at the body of the driver. "There is naught you can do for him." He drew his sword and opened the door. "You will leave this to me. If there is an archer out there shooting at us, it is best you remain in the carriage."

"Then you have a care," Mary snapped. "Your safety is mine as well,"

He glanced back briefly. "I gave my vow to protect you," he said as he jumped down, then looked back through the window, "and that I will."

His face disappeared, just as an arrow smacked into the side of the carriage, close to where his head had been.

Mary gave a small cry.

There could only be one reason for this ambush – they were going to be robbed!

Another arrow appeared with a whoosh and embedded itself close to the first. She slid down onto her knees.

And then, once the brigands had helped themselves to her possessions and money…

She curled into a small ball on the floor of the carriage.

…No doubt they would have her as well...

She heard Rolleston's sword swishing through the air. "Come out, devil take you!" he yelled. "Show yourself!"

As if that was going to help! The man was going to be shot out there...

Mary turned her head and caught sight of her bag under the seat. "Oh, sod this," she muttered to herself, "I can't just stay here – I have to do something." She pulled the bag out and quickly assembled the gun while staying low on the floor. Fitting a cartridge into the breech, she lifted her hand carefully to the door handle on the side of the carriage away from the arrows and slowly pulled it down.

She emerged at speed, crouching as she ran into the forest, her breath rasping in her throat as she reached the shelter of a large oak.

Trying to ignore the pounding in her chest, she peered back towards the path. Rolleston was standing out in the open with his feet planted squarely and his sword tip raised, looking left and right for the hidden archer.

"Take cover, you fool!" Mary hissed. "You will be shot any second!"

As if to make her point, another arrow swooshed past Rolleston's head and embedded itself in a tree a few yards further back. He turned in the direction it had come, but Mary had already spotted the archer's movement by an oak some twenty yards further up the path. She raised the gun to her shoulder and focused the scope. For a moment she saw nothing but the deeply pitted silver green bark, but as she swung the gun slightly to the right, a shoulder came into view. She followed it down to a hand holding a bow.

"By Heavens, woman, get back in the carriage this moment!"

Ignoring Rolleston's shout, she forced a few more deep, steadying breaths, then raised the gun until it was again pointing at the shoulder. Almost immediately, a sandy-haired man with a face reddened by broken veins stepped round the tree, fitting an arrow to the bow. He started to draw it back.

Mary's finger tightened on the trigger.

Shoot to kill?

Or shoot to wound?

The man had almost drawn the bow string to its full length. She could see the wicked-looking barbed arrow-head quivering under his forefinger.

Mary raised the gun until the man's head was in view, his frowning brow lined up in the crosshairs and one eye closed as he sighted the arrow.

Her finger tightened further.

Then she swung the gun fractionally down and to the right. She shot him in the hand.

The crack of the shot echoed out across the forest, followed by an agonised yell from the archer. The arrow flew high, landing harmlessly behind Rolleston.

Mary lowered the gun. She was about to walk over and check the archer, when her wrists were suddenly grabbed hard from behind and forced up her back. The gun clattered to the forest floor beside her.

"God's blood, woman!" a strange man's voice hissed in her ear, "you will regret that shot."

"Let me go!" Mary pulled against the unknown assailant's grip, but he was too strong. "Do you know who I am?"

There was a slight pause, then the voice said, "Nay, and by the Lord, I care not."

"What do you want with me?" she said, trying to sound strong.

"I will take from you what I will. What I can carry…" there was another short pause, then the voice added in a whisper, "and what I cannot."

"There is a man with me," Mary said. "He will stop you."

"Aye, there *was* a man," the voice said with the sound of a smile, "but he has disappeared." The rough scratching of a beard rasped across her ear, and she thought she would retch. "I warrant he has seen sense and left you to our mercies." Mary flicked her eyes across to where Rolleston had been standing.

The clearing was empty.

"He would not do that," she asserted.

'I gave my vow to protect you!' he had said. Was that an empty promise?

Of course it was.

The man pushed Mary towards a small tree, then spun her round and pulled her back against the rough bark. She felt some rope being passed around her wrists, and tried not to flinch or make a sound as it was tightened to the point of cutting into her skin. After a moment the man stepped out in front of her.

Her attacker was dark haired, with some grey at his temples and much more in his beard. He was of medium height; dressed in a dirty old wool jerkin and brown breeches.

He drew a sword and placed the tip on her breastbone. "You will stay here while I see what you have done to my companion," he said. Then, with his cold blue eyes holding hers, he traced the sword down her chest to the top of her bodice, so lightly that it did not cut into her skin, before moving it down her stomacher until it was resting on the top of her skirts, pointing at her lower belly. "Then I will return to deal with you." His eyes held hers a moment more, then he pushed the sword tip a couple of inches into the soft material, "Do you understand me well, woman?"

All Mary could do was nod slightly.

"Good." The man sheathed his sword. "Good." He strode away across the clearing, to where the archer was kneeling beside the tree, his bloodied left hand held close to his body.

Mary let out her breath and looked down. The gun was still there in the undergrowth. It was amazing that the man hadn't picked it up. It didn't bear thinking as to what he might do if he decided to examine it more closely.

She tried to hook her toe under the barrel, but her foot would not quite get that far, and all she ended up doing was waggling it uselessly in the air above the gun. Ignoring the pain in her wrists, she inched herself round the tree so she could extend a bit further, but it was not enough.

Muttering curses under her breath, she leant forward to ease the pressure on her hands, then slid down the tree so she could extend her leg out further, like a crouched Russian dancer. With a small triumphant 'yes!' under her breath, she managed to hook her heel over the gun's breech.

She quickly glanced over at the archer. He was still by the tree, while his companion had his back to her and appeared to be winding some cloth around the man's bloodied hand.

With a small smile of satisfaction that the man's sniping days were probably now over, Mary slowly stood up, inching her hands up the tree to give herself leverage. Once she was fully upright, she pulled the gun again with her heel, until she had it fully hidden under her skirts.

It was not a moment too soon, as the attacker reappeared in front of her, his sword out once again.

"By Heavens, woman, you have done great damage to Nathan's hand." He shook his head. "The ball has passed clean through from one side to the other."

"Good," Mary answered, lifting her head and looking down her nose. "It was his own fault for loosing arrows at us. I warrant he has killed our driver, and would have killed my companion and myself as well, if I had not stopped him."

"You are in no position to argue this matter," the man answered. "Meantime, I will help myself to the contents of your carriage." He gave a cold smile. "A fine lady such as you will have jewels and gowns that will fetch a fair price to compensate for my companion's wound." He glanced back at where the carriage stood, with the driver's boots still visible on the forest floor beyond. "Or I warrant we will simply take the carriage for ourselves, with all contents included."

Mary stared at the man in silent disgust.

"Nay churl, you will do no such thing!" came a loud voice, as Rolleston stepped out from behind a tree with his own sword raised. "Begone, sirrah," he barked, "or I will do to your chest what my lady here has done to that fellow's hand!"

"Fie!" the attacker snarled, turning to face the merchant, "I will deal with you first if I must." He glanced back at Mary. "Then I will continue to attend to your lady."

Rolleston did not answer, but instead took guard, his sword raised and ready.

The man responded with his own guard, and they circled warily for a few moments, as if neither wanted to commit to the first move. The man had a look of fierce concentration, while Rolleston now had a small smile, as if this had all become a bit of a game.

"Come, Greybeard," he called eventually, "make your play, or shall I win by just tiring you out?"

"Nay, fellow," the man replied, "I shall not make it so easy." Then he made a sudden lunge at Rolleston's head that caused Mary to gasp.

Fortunately Rolleston only had to lean away slightly, so that the other's blade passed harmlessly by, then Rolleston made a sudden lunge of his own. Greybeard parried with ease, knocking Rolleston's slimmer blade away. With that, the fight began in earnest.

Mary found herself biting her lip as the two swords clashed at lighting speed; each man turning the other's blade, not only to avoid a thrust that looked potentially mortal, but also to force his opponent to leave his side or his chest exposed. Each time Rolleston looked in danger her jaw tensed, and at one particularly late parry, she bit her lip hard enough to taste blood.

As the fight moved around the clearing, Mary could see that it was too evenly matched for a quick victory by either man. Maybe it would be as Rolleston had joked initially – the winner would be the one who could simply tire the other out.

But both men seemed to have enough energy for now, keeping the fight going with successive thrusts, parries, blocks and cuts, so that Mary could only watch and hope that Rolleston would prevail.

Eventually she sensed that both were beginning to lose energy. Their swords no longer flashed at high speed and their shoulders were starting to drop.

"Have a care, Rolleston!" she called, as he made a small stumble, but thankfully recovered, before finding some new vitality and driving Greybeard backwards towards a tree. As Greybeard came up against it, she could see an angry frown forming in place of his look of concentration, and he made a sudden lunge that caught Rolleston on the thigh, just below his trunk hose.

Mary gasped and called out "Rolleston! Your leg!"

Rolleston looked down, then gave a surprised grunt and clasped his free hand to his thigh. The grey material of his hose began to turn red under his fingers.

Greybeard seemed to see his opportunity and lunged forward, flicking his wrist so the blade flew from Rolleston's hand and dropped to the ground. With a snarl of triumph, Greybeard took a further step, his own blade now pointing at Rolleston's chest.

"On your knees, fellow!" he commanded. "Let us finish this."

Mary stared in horror as Rolleston dropped down and Greybeard held up his sword to strike.

Rolleston was going to die – and she was next!

"No!" she screamed; a guttural, primeval drawn-out cry that distracted Greybeard as he moved to strike. This gave Rolleston his opportunity. He grabbed Greybeard's ankle and pulled the man off balance. Greybeard stumbled back a few steps until he hit the tree. As he did so, Rolleston quickly stood, retrieved his sword, then stepped forward and used it to flick the blade from Greybeard's hand.

Unarmed and with his back to the tree, Greybeard was at Rolleston's mercy. He stared down at the blade that was now pressing into the coarse wool of his jerkin, the whites of his eyes showing.

"Do you go to it, fellow?" he said, his voice high and hoarse. "Are you going to finish me now? For naught but an attempted robbery?"

"Yes," answered Rolleston, "I am. Like I would any brigand attempting to rob lawful folk."

Mary screwed her eyes shut, not wanting to witness the sword being driven into the man's chest, wishing she could also bring her hands to her ears to block out the gruesome sound of his death groan.

In the event there was only a gasp, a cough, then the sound of a body sliding down the tree and a thump as it hit the ground.

She cautiously opened her eyes.

Rolleston was standing over the body, his sword covered in blood. Greybeard was lying face down, with a small red stain growing on his back like an opening flower.

Rolleston wiped his sword on the body's jerkin, then looked over at Mary.

"The archer has run off," he said. "And I suggest we do the same. If the bodies of this man and our driver are discovered, we do not want the hue and cry after us."

"Indeed," she said. "But you had better untie me first."

---0---

It was a while later and they were in a room at a traveller's inn at Stanford, some miles from the scene of the ambush.

Rolleston bent down and peeled back the edges of his hose around the wound. With a look of curiosity, he pressed his fingers either side.

"Let me see it," Mary said quietly. "I may be able to help."

"'Tis not deep, and will soon heal, methinks."

"It needs binding. You do not want it to fester." She paused. "You will not be alerted by the pain if it does."

"Aye. Belike."

"Give me your knife."

He raised an eyebrow. "You would make more cuts to my leg?"

"No, give it to me."

He handed it over, hilt first. She lifted the hem of her gown to reveal the kirtle below, and used the knife to cut away a strip of cloth all round. Then she knelt by his leg and pulled his hose away from the wound, before winding the material round and securing it in a tight knot. "There. It is not perfect, but it will hopefully stop any festering."

"Thank you."

She stood up. "And thank you, too, for fighting for me back there. I do not know what I would have done if you had not prevailed, Master Rolleston."

He shrugged. "No doubt you would have been slain also, Mistress Carter."

"I was so sure you were to be killed when he had you on your knees."

"But it was your yelling that distracted the man," he observed. "So I could turn the fight to my advantage."

She gave a small chuckle. "I have been told before that my voice is loud."

"That it is," he said. "I thought perhaps a cat was being disembowelled."

CHAPTER TWENTY-THREE

Rolleston slowed the carriage and came to a stop, calling out to the horses, "Whoa there! Whoa!"

The alarm in his voice made Mary give out a small fearful cry. She held on to the seat and looked around the dim interior, lit by just a trickle of light coming in around the thick curtains. It was the day after the ambush, and they had only been going for two or three hours since finishing breakfast, so there was no reason to stop.

Her hearing was suddenly heightened, expecting at any moment for there to be the whoosh of an arrow or maybe the thud of a crossbow as another set of brigands tried to rob them.

Quickly she reached down to the bag under her seat and drew out the gun, which she now kept fully assembled at all times. She fumbled for a cartridge and managed to slot it into the breech with trembling hands.

There was silence, so she waited a moment to steady her heart, then pulled the curtain back a few inches with the tip of the barrel and squinted out against the sunshine. "Is all well?" she called out, trying to keep her voice steady. "Why have we stopped?"

The carriage rocked and there was a thump as Rolleston jumped down from the driver's seat, then his face appeared at the window. "No matter," he said with a small grin. "No man is trying to attack us again." He gently pushed the barrel of the gun away, so it was no longer pointing up his nose. "You can put your weapon back from where it came, Mistress Carter. We have stopped for a different reason."

She let out a careful breath. "I am pleased to hear it," she answered, resisting the temptation to chide him soundly for giving her such a scare. "And what reason might that be, pray?"

"Come out and I will show you," he answered.

She put the gun back in the bag, and stepped carefully out into the late-Autumn sun. They had pulled slightly off the track, and were stopped alongside a signpost at a crossroads. One route led to Newark, one to Nottingham, and one to a place called Bridgeford. "Well?" she asked.

"I would show you where I was taken and accused of popery and treason," he said. "It is but a short ride from these crossroads." He paused a moment, as if unsure what to say next. "As I said to you and that Alchemist fellow, I was guilty only by association, as I was there to conduct the business of trade. Belike if you saw the place, you would see that a great injustice was done."

Mary couldn't see anything of the sort; surely a house was just a house, whatever may have happened within its walls? But the look of hope on his face was too hard to ignore, so she said, "I will see the house if you wish, so long as it does not add too much time to our journey."

"Very little," he said with another grin, then pulled himself up into the driver's seat. Mary settled back in the carriage, as he turned the horses and headed in the direction marked 'Bridgeford'.

This path was more rutted and less finished than the main road they had left, so she had to hang on to the leather straps either side of the seat as the carriage swayed and rocked along. "Is it far?" she called out. "This path is most uncomfortable."

"Not too far, Mistress," he called back.

Sure enough, it was only a few minutes later that he pulled the horses to a stop once more, and jumped down again to hold open the carriage door for Mary to step out. They were by some black iron gates set into a red brick wall, which were quite plain; nothing on the size and scale of Grangedean Manor. Beyond them was a medium-sized brick and timber house sitting squat and assured around twenty yards beyond the gate. The path from the gate wound up to the house, then swept past the dark wooden front door, round a small lawn and back to the gate again. Mary thought it looked like it had four or maybe five bedrooms; comfortable, but not particularly special. It had several square-paned windows adorned with thick swirling 'crown' glass, plus two tall brick chimneys rising above the shingle roof. There were similar houses on either side, each a few hundred yards away.

"Oak House," Rolleston said. "Home of Master Antony Brooks."

Mary gazed at the house, while trying to think of something polite to say. "A fine place."

"And as you can see well, 'tis no grand manor, nor a place for the gathering of seditious Catholics, but an ordinary house of an ordinary God-fearing and loyal man."

Mary considered it a moment. "Is Master Brooks also a merchant?"

"He invests in ships, and especially in spices from the Orient."

"So was this the business you had with him?"

"Aye. I have bought many of his consignments. I store them in bonded warehouses at the port of Harwich mainly, then find buyers for smaller parts of each consignment."

"A fine trade," she observed. There was a silence, so she asked, "And was Master Brooks arrested also?"

"Indeed he was, and Mistress Brooks as well."

One of the chimneys had smoke coming from it. "And are they back in residence now, or still held for trial?"

"They are returned here; they were quickly released by the magistrate, as they gave assurances they would observe the true faith hereafter, and were sent back with but a fine."

She turned to look at him. "So why then were you taken to the Tower? Especially as you have protested your innocence throughout?"

He gave a small rueful chuckle. "Methinks I protested my innocence too greatly. The Pursuivants, led by one Silas Taverner of Nottingham, may God strike him down, needed to justify the heavily armed raid they made on the house. The Brooks family have local standing and were well known to the magistrate, whereas I, an unknown merchant from London, was arraigned because I put up a fight."

"Which you could do without feeling the pain of any hits," she observed. "So you fought on when others would have conceded."

"Precisely."

She nodded thoughtfully. The disadvantages of being unable to feel pain were becoming more obvious. "So what happened after that?"

"The magistrate would not hear my protestations of innocence and had me sent to London, where I was arraigned and thrown into the Tower, accused of being an unrepentant Catholic, and therefore by definition, a traitor. That was where Master Wychwoode found me, and thank the Lord, he had me released in order to serve him and Master Secretary Walsingham. And you too, Anne Carter," he added.

"Yes, and I am fortunate you are practiced with the sword. We were well rid of Master Greybeard and his archer."

He nodded. "Aye."

"Tell me," she added, "where you learned to fight so well? It is unusual for one who buys and sells spices to be so accomplished with a sword."

"Ah," he replied, "but I was not always a merchant." He smiled. "As a young man I wanted to explore the continent, and spent time in Padua, in Florence and in Venice. There were many young Italians there who took exception to me and to my Protestant faith, so I needs must defend myself from their constant attack." He looked towards her, but she could see he was really seeing scenes from his past life. "I vowed I would never again be left at a disadvantage, and engaged an experienced swordsman to teach me. Through him, I learned how to defend myself well." His blue eyes snapped back onto her. "I became the master of any Italian who decided I was no longer worthy to draw breath. I would not be cowed by them, and they learned to leave me alone."

"I see," she said. "And you came back to be a merchant?"

"I met a man in Venice who shipped spices, and I learned his trade – first as an apprentice, then as his secretary. I was able to secure contracts with his suppliers for trade into England, so on my return, I set up my own merchant business." He smiled again. "So there you have it, Mistress Carter. Roger Rolleston, from young man in Italy to merchant released from the Tower by Wychwoode. My life presented to you in full."

"I see. Thank you; most interesting." She frowned as a thought occurred. "And is there a Mistress Rolleston?"

He shook his head. "Nay, I have not met a suitable woman, nor has it ever been expedient to make such a match as the nobles do, for money rather than love." He paused, considering her. "In truth, I have not had the time or inclination to seek a wife."

Not that it stopped him shagging that barmaid, and who knows else besides her…

Mary kept the thought to herself; instead she said, "Thank you again, Roger, for being more honest with me."

"We are on this mission together, Mistress Carter," he answered. "So it is good to be honest with each other."

"True." She smiled, and opened the carriage door. "Now to be honest, I would that we now resume our journey. It is a couple more days to Sheffield, and we do need to make good speed."

She climbed back in and took her seat. A moment later she felt the carriage rock as he also resumed his position in the driving seat.

Then the horses' noses were pulled round, and they headed back towards to the crossroads.

CHAPTER TWENTY-FOUR

It was a grey afternoon in the Presence Chamber at the Palace of Whitehall, with an early flurry of snow falling softly outside the windows. Inside it was comfortably warm; a roaring fire welcoming the various courtiers, dignitaries and ambassadors who came in a steady procession to discuss matters with the Queen. Her Majesty was seated close to the heat of the fire, while Olivia Melrose and the other ladies were sewing or embroidering quietly to one side. Olivia was bent over her embroidery, working on the tiny stitches that would make a colourful image of Adam and Eve in the Garden of Eden with which to decorate a small jewel-box for the Queen.

Most of the conversations between the Queen and the visitors were on mundane matters so Olivia ignored them, preferring instead to concentrate on her needlework, and on her thoughts.

Since leaving Grangedean Manor and returning to Court a few days earlier, she had been trying to work out how – or if – she could fulfil her promise to Sir William and little Kat de Beauvais to ask the Queen for information about Lady Mary. She had soon come to the conclusion that as she had said to Kat, it would be impossible for her, a newly appointed and lowly maid of honour, to approach the Queen on such a secret and contentious matter. There had, however, been a couple of occasions when she and a few other ladies had been alone with Her Majesty, and it seemed to be the ideal opportunity. The conversations had been light-hearted and inconsequential, so she was almost tempted to go up to the Queen and ask for a quiet word, but each time she had lost her courage and remained silent. This made her feel deeply disappointed in herself. Had she not overcome and stabbed two Catholic men to death in quick order, both twice her size? Yet here she was, unable to ask a simple question of her mistress.

But it was not too hard to imagine how such a conversation might go:

"Your Majesty, I would know of the fate of Lady Mary de Beauvais?"

"I am surprised at you, Mistress Melrose, to be asking questions on matters that are no concern of yours… I had high hopes of you, Mistress Melrose, for your wise counsel in place of Lady Mary… now I am disappointed in you…"

As Olivia bent over her embroidery and concentrated on the pink silk thread that formed the face of Eve, she heard the name of a particular visitor being announced. All thoughts of the Creation vanished in an instant when she looked up to see the tall figure of Robert Wychwoode bow and move forward.

Maybe he could be a potential source of information instead?

Olivia strained to catch what passed between Wychwoode and the Queen, but unfortunately he was whispering directly into the Queen's ear, so Olivia could not make anything out. She did note that the Queen seemed remarkably interested in what he was telling her; listening in total stillness, with her mouth slightly open and her eyes shining as the old man leaned over.

Olivia waited until Wychwoode had bowed once more and left the Queen's presence, before casually asking to be excused herself. On the Queen's nod, she put down her embroidery and walked quickly out.

The old lawyer was striding away down the corridor, his black cloak flapping behind him as if he were a crow about to launch into flight. "Master Wychwoode!" she called.

He stopped and turned with an enquiring look, so she lifted up her skirts and ran up to him.

"I would talk with you, sir," she said.

He regarded her a moment with a frown. "If it is about Lady Mary de Beauvais," he said slowly, "then you must know that I am not at liberty to say aught on this matter."

"For sure it is about my lady," Olivia answered, trying not to snap in irritation. How like him to have known exactly what she was going to ask, and to close down the conversation immediately!

She put a hand on his sleeve, and softened her voice. "But I must appeal to your nature, sir, and say that there are those who have the greatest love for Lady Mary, and would know of her situation."

"This much I am aware," he answered, "and indeed, I am one of those who holds the lady in the highest regard, but I repeat, I cannot say more." He turned to go. In desperation she grasped his sleeve. He stopped and looked down at her hand. "Mistress Melrose," he said, "you, I also hold in high esteem, following your brave actions in York this spring, but as I have said, this matter is not for further discussion." He pulled his arm. "So I would ask that you release my sleeve and let me go about my business."

"I have but one question, Master Wychwoode," she said. "In the name of Christ, I would you do me the courtesy of giving me just one piece of information."

He gave her a blank stare, that eventually softened into a weak smile. "If you agree to let me go, then I will consider the same."

She took a breath and looked him directly in the eye. "Sir," she said slowly, "I, and her family, would know but one thing. Does she live or is she already dead?"

He was silent, frowning as he appeared to think through his response.

Olivia felt hope rising, for the longer he was silent in thought, the more likely Lady Mary was alive – for if she was dead then he had only to say it. But if, as Sir William thought, Lady Mary was away on a secret mission, then the old lawyer would need to consider his response most carefully. Olivia said nothing herself, leaving Wychwoode the time and space to consider his response.

"Mistress Melrose, I will say only the following," he said eventually. "To the best of my knowledge, Lady Mary de Beauvais lives still."

Olivia's heart leapt at this. To know Lady Mary had not been secretly tried and executed was the greatest of news! But she needed more.

"I thank you, sir," she said. "That will be so welcome to the family to hear," Then she waited a beat, looked up at him with wide eyes and added softly, "But you tell only a part of this?"

He raised an eyebrow but said nothing.

"If this is to the best of your knowledge, sir," Olivia continued, looking away then back up at him in the kittenish fashion that worked so well on the younger courtiers, "then I take it that you know nothing of Lady Mary's current situation? Belike this means she is on… a secret mission and away from contact? Perhaps a secret mission for Her Majesty?"

Wychwoode frowned. "I have not said such a thing," he growled. "And if you say the same, it will be but supposition on your part and viewed most gravely." But he said it like he did not fully mean it.

Perhaps he was wavering…

"Yet Lady Mary herself said to Master Secretary Walsingham that she held knowledge of the future which could be of use to him in his intelligencing," Olivia purred, keeping up her pressure. "So I warrant such a mission would be a way of making use of such knowledge?"

"I say again, this is mere supposition on your part." He paused. "But I will say that you are a most persistent, and astute young woman." Then he smiled again.

So it was true!

Olivia was silent a moment as she considered how best to make use of her advantage and prise further information from the lawyer. What more could she glean that would help her piece together Lady Mary's current situation?

"I warrant Lady Mary would not be alone on such a mission," she began, then hurriedly added, "were she on one."

"Why so?" he answered. "She is supremely capable, as well you know."

"But if she possesses such valuable intelligence, would you and Master Walsingham risk her being alone? If she was not under some form of protection? Belike you have given her a large guard of armed men?"

"Nay, but one man…" he began, then stopped, with a look of shock on his face.

"One man?" Olivia was surprised. "You sent her with but one man? I am aware of her strengths, but one man? Is that all?"

"Roger Rolleston is a capable swordsman and committed to my service, and…" he began, then took a long, slow breath. "You are a most beguiling young woman, Mistress Melrose, and I applaud you for having taken advantage of an old man's good nature." He frowned. "As a consequence I have said much too much, and you will forget it all. Am I clear?"

"Most clear, Master Wychwoode," she said, letting go of his sleeve with a small triumphant smile. "I will not tell a soul."

CHAPTER TWENTY-FIVE

Olivia smiled at Sir William.

"I can tell you," she began, her eyes shining brightly in the candlelight, "that your idea was correct. They have not tried or executed my lady, but have sent her on a mission of some sort. I know naught about it, except that it is a deep secret, and for the benefit of the Queen."

They were sitting in the parlour of a small inn on the corner of Pudding Lane and Thames Street, where they had agreed to meet and share any information. Olivia had previously dreaded meeting Sir William if she had nothing to tell him, but now she had good news, she had been counting the hours until it was the agreed time and she could get away from the Palace.

"And what is more withal," she continued, "my lady has been sent on this venture with but one of Master Wychwoode's men to protect her."

"One man? That is all?" said Sir William with a look of surprise. "It is hardly seemly in a married woman," he muttered with a bitter frown.

"Aye, but I warrant she can be trusted."

"It is not her that concerns me in this matter." He sighed. "Who is this man she is with? I pray to God he will respect her honour."

Olivia nodded. "Master Wychwoode said it was a man by the name of Roger Rolleston."

Sir William sat back. "Roger Rolleston, eh? That is a name I have not heard before. I will need to find out more of him." Then he gave her a weak smile. "Meantimes, I cannot say enough how grateful I am for your help in this matter, Olivia." He regarded her thoughtfully a moment. "You have been able to get information out of Wychwoode, when to me he was like a closed document; folded, sealed and giving away nothing. How were you able to get him to reveal all?"

"Marry, Sir William," Olivia replied with a conspiratorial smile, "perhaps there are some secrets that can only be revealed by the guile of a woman, that a man will never access."

"God's Wounds!" he laughed. "You used the language of love to get that dried old stick to open up? Now that I wish I had set my eyes upon!"

For the first time since she had previously been shown into the Great Hall at Grangedean Manor, Olivia thought Sir William looked a little more at ease with himself. At least he knew that his wife still lived, for all she was sent on some dangerous mission with but one man as a protector. This was clearly uppermost in his mind as well.

"While I am most deeply relieved that she has not been tried or executed," he said, "I am naturally concerned that she is sent on some secret mission, and God only knows what and where this might be." He paused. "God, and that arch schemer Walsingham." He drummed his fingers on the table a moment. "Belike you could make even bigger eyes at Wychwoode, and get more knowledge?"

"I think not," she answered. "He realised he had told me too much already, and begged me to silence. I should not in all conscience have told you any of this."

"Nonsense!" he said. "For sure you would tell her husband. He could expect that. But indeed," he continued, "I will share this with no other, you have my word."

"As I also gave mine," she said with a grin.

"Yes, well, there it is." He paused. "But that does not prevent me investigating this man Rolleston, and seeing if we gain any useful intelligence. I would not leave Mary to whatever dangers she faces, without seeing if I can do aught to assist her."

"Would not Wychwoode help?"

"Perhaps – but as he sent her on this mission in the first place, I am not sure. I should act alone.

"I wish you much success."

Again he drummed his fingers, as if he was deciding whether or not to share something. "But I must tell you, Olivia, I have learned this day that there is another possible source of information we should also explore."

She raised an eyebrow. "Which is?"

"You know the fellow who tried to kill the Queen in York, before Mary beat him senseless with a poker?"

"The Alchemist?"

He nodded. "Well, he is finally to be executed this very day at Tyburn. I have a thought that maybe we could learn something from his last speech on the scaffold. These condemned men often give forth information which can have some meaning to those who seek it, and who know more than the general rabble."

"You would attend his execution?"

"Aye, and you as well, if you are free from the Queen's service for a while longer. You are also aware of the background facts, and something he says may have meaning to you not me."

"It does make me uneasy," she replied. "They do unspeakable things to a man, do they not?"

He nodded. "I know, Olivia, but I have also stood close by and watched as you plunged a man's own dagger deep into his body, before pulling it out and doing the same to another man. So I do not see you as any other young woman, swooning at the thought of violence. I see you as one who understands the ways of men and is able to match them, blow for blow."

CHAPTER TWENTY-SIX

Mary rode slowly behind Rolleston through the dark Sheffield streets; the sun mostly blocked out by the high, oppressive, overhanging buildings. Their horses picked their way carefully over the slimy cobbles, taking them through the constant flow of humanity that swirled about them like a fast-flowing stream breaks around a rock.

She adjusted her position on the side-saddle in an attempt to ease the constant rubbing of the stiff pommel on her thigh. It was a shame that they had left the carriage at a travelling inn outside the town's walls, but as Rolleston had said, to bring such a vehicle into these narrow streets would have been madness. She had agreed at the time, but there was no doubt it would have been so much nicer to be seated in the carriage, rather than riding on the uncomfortable saddle he had found for her.

A shout of "'Ware below!" came from above them. Rolleston immediately stopped and held up his hand for Mary to do the same. She wrinkled her nose in disgust as what was clearly human waste dropped out of an upstairs window, landing with a soft 'splat' on the street in front of them. Rolleston seemed unconcerned; merely side-stepping the stinking mess and moving on. Mary put her pomander to her nose as she passed, letting the strong scent of lavender almost, but not quite, block out the smell.

She had just passed it when a young man in a dirty jerkin backed out of a house beside her, appearing to be shouting at someone still inside. Before she could warn him, he stepped back into her path, so she had to pull her horse's head quickly round to avoid trampling him with her hooves. The man jumped out of the way, then looked up at her with a deep scowl. "Watch your step, woman!" he growled, then scurried away and was lost in the shadows below the overhanging floor of the next house.

Mary took another sniff of her pomander. Oh to be back in Grangedean Manor, walking in the parklands in the bright, crisp, clear morning air. The trees would be almost bare by now, with a light silver coating of frost to match the tiny sparkling ice crystals drifting through the air. Or strolling through the little village, being greeted by the farm workers and women with a cheery smile as 'my lady', rather than being called 'woman' by some Sheffield ruffian.

She lowered the pomander. Strange that her longing to be away from this narrow, smelly, unpleasant little street only went as far as her current life in Grangedean. She frowned. Her desire to be back in Grangedean living a life of peace and quiet with her family was deep-rooted, and she had been very clear about it with Wychwoode. But why was she not longing to be back even further; in 2015 in her previous life as Justine Parker? For sure she would rather be anywhere but here, so why not once more in her little flat in Hammersmith, drinking wine and dancing round the kitchen to her favourite music? And Grangedean – why did she long to be there as a Tudor wife and mother, not in her old life as the modern-day girl managing events for visitors?

Mary bit her lip. 2015 now seemed so distant – almost like a dream she could not quite recall. Was she was now so completely settled in Elizabethan times that her original life in the 21st century hardly entered her thoughts? That to be truly happy, she need only be a Tudor wife and mother, enjoying life in Grangedean Manor surrounded by her family, rather than being back in 2015?

Mary sighed. Yes, there was no doubting it; a life of Elizabethan peace and domestic tranquillity with her family – that was where true happiness lay.

Except there was one major obstacle in the path to this idyllic picture...

An act of cold-blooded murder.

Truly, it didn't bear thinking about.

So let's not think about it for now. One step at a time...

Rolleston turned and said, "It is not much further to the inn." He gave a small smile. "I believe it is but a couple more turns and up a hill."

"Good," Mary replied. "I am stiff, and I am most weary of these streets. It feels as if we have been in the saddle for days."

"But an hour, Lady Mary," he laughed, "since we finished our midday meal and left the last place. Naught but an hour." She didn't respond, but shifted her leg slightly to release the pressure from the lower pommel on the back of her knee.

"I am to make for a place called the Crossed Keys," Mary had said, as their food was put before them. "You can remain here."

"I know of it," said Rolleston, as he broke off some bread. "It is atop one of the many hills in the town." He paused, observing her as he chewed. "And you would go alone?"

"I would."

"For all you know not where it is, and will be unprotected?"

Mary thought this through. While she could see the benefit of having him there to guide and protect her, she would prefer him to stay back. But then again, he would be useful in ensuring she got there safely…

"Very well," she muttered. "You may accompany me to the door and see me inside safely. No further. That is all."

"So be it." He looked at her as he broke off some more bread. "And what is your business there?"

"That is not for you to know. Your role is only to get me there safely. That is all."

"Then that I will," he had said. "But first I need to take a piss."

CHAPTER TWENTY-SEVEN

Olivia followed Sir William as he pushed through the Tyburn crowds towards the rough wooden platform, on which stood a crude gibbet with a knotted rope hanging from one end. The two of them received a few curious stares as they moved through the roughly dressed throng; Olivia feeling a little self-conscious in her fine silk gown and with her fashionable hair, but they made it to the front without incident.

She looked up at the platform. A man with grey hair under a woollen cap and a grey beard over his fine ruff was standing to one side, talking with a priest. A muscular man in a black head mask and no shirt stood by a long table, holding a large knife in one hand, and a saw in the other. Olivia took it that he was the executioner.

A thin, sorry-looking man in a torn jerkin was standing on the other side, his hands bound behind his back. This man seemed to be overshadowed by the guard beside him, who was wearing a wide-brimmed blue hat with a white feather, blue breeches and a steel breastplate, and was carrying a halberd with a fearsome-looking polished blade that glowed dully in the grey light. The guard was glaring across the crowd with a deep scowl, and Olivia could not help but shrink back at one point when his eye caught hers.

"That must be the one they call the Alchemist," Sir William observed, staring at the thin man with the bound hands. "Although it looks as if he has healed well from the blows rained down on him by my wife." Olivia studied what she could see of his arms and legs through his ragged clothes, and it did seem that whatever damage Lady Mary had inflicted, there was little sign of it now.

"Aye, 'tis strange," she said, "Lady Mary was clear enough in the carriage on our return journey, when she told us the story of her attack on the man. She said she beat both his arms and broke one leg." She looked harder. "And she said he had painted arms, with images of firing weapons of the future."

"I fancy I do see those," Sir William answered, and indeed now she looked she could see there were crudely drawn images just visible on the man's forearms. "But any bruising has faded to naught," he continued, "and the leg is fully healed." He shrugged. "Forbye, we should not become concerned on the state of the man. His traitorous arms and legs will soon be parted from his body anyhow."

As Olivia nodded agreement, she heard a small snort of amusement beside her, and glanced over at a thin, well-dressed man with a trim beard standing close by. He was staring hard at the condemned prisoner, but she got the distinct impression he was actually listening to their conversation. She was about to ask him his business, when she was interrupted by a shout from the platform.

"Hear ye all!" the grey-haired man called out. He seemed to be the main official in charge, and he raised his arm. When the crowd was silent, he continued, "We are here this day to witness the execution of one Richard Hornby, also known as the Alchemist, sentenced for the act of gross treason against our sovereign queen, Her Majesty Queen Elizabeth, and for the foul murder of one Sir Thomas Cobham." He looked down at a paper he was holding. "Know ye all, that the traitor will be hung, then taken down while he still lives. His entrails in all, then his heart, will then be drawn out before him and burned. Once he is dead, his body will be quartered and dispersed. His head…" and here he glared at the prisoner, "…his head will be placed on a spike above London Bridge, for all to see and know the true price of treason."

The condemned prisoner hung the head in question in shame.

"Bring him forward!" the official barked. The guard dragged the man to the centre of the platform. "What say you, traitor, before the sentence is carried out? If you have aught to say, then do it now."

The man lifted his head and stared around the crowd, who started baying and calling out.

"Traitor!"

"Evil!"

"Die like a dog!"

"But die well for me," the man beside Olivia said quietly.

Again, she glanced at him.

The prisoner on the platform appeared to be about to say something, then he shook his head and looked down, staying silent.

"So be it," the official shouted. "The traitor has nothing to say. Let the execution begin."

The executioner pulled the prisoner over to the gibbet, led him up onto a small stool, then put the rope over his neck.

The priest came forward and muttered inaudibly up at the prisoner as he stood on the stool, then moved away and nodded at the executioner.

"By Heavens, we will learn nothing this day," Sir William said. He put his hand on Olivia's sleeve. "Come dear girl, we should be away. I care not for the rest of this spectacle."

She nodded in agreement. "I have no stomach for it either." As she turned to go, she caught the eye of the thin, well-dressed man beside them.

"Wait a moment," he said quietly. "See, they will hang him to death immediately."

"Nay," said Sir William, who was now close enough to hear this. "He will still live when they draw him."

The man shook his head. "Not this one. You will see."

Despite herself, Olivia turned and watched as the executioner kicked away the stool and the prisoner dropped to the end of the rope. Immediately he started kicking and writhing, his face turning red and his tongue emerging from his lips.

"See," said the man beside them "if they do not take him down now, then he will be dead before they have a chance to draw him."

The prisoner made a few more jerks, then the executioner lifted him by the knees and pulled off the rope, before carrying him over to the table and laying him out.

"They think he still lives," the man muttered, giving a small gesture with his hand to indicate the crowd around them. "But I say he is mercifully dead already."

And indeed, Olivia could see that the hanged prisoner was only making movement when the executioner held his arms or his head.

"He is dead. They are working him like a fucking puppet." said the man. "They offered him an easy death in return for his compliance. That is why he said nothing. They will go through the motions now, for the show – cut him open and take off his head, and all that. Probably got some stooge under the platform to scream at the right moment so these ghouls here think they are getting their money's worth."

"You are very well informed on this, sir," Sir William observed. "Although your course language rather belies the quality of your attire."

"Yes, well, things are not exactly what they seem, are they?" the man replied. "And I have an interest in all this, believe me." He turned away, then stopped and looked back. "I am guessing, you are de Beauvais, husband of Lady Mary." He looked at Olivia. "Which makes you the sidekick Olivia she talked about." He nodded to himself. "So take this from one who knows. If you are looking for the lady, then I suggest you look north."

Sir William was silent. Olivia thought he was deciding whether or not to treat this information seriously. The man clearly knew who they were, so most likely he knew of Lady Mary's whereabouts as well – howsoever that might be. In which case, his information could most probably be trusted. She glanced at Sir William and gave the smallest nod. He did the same back, then said, "Thank you sir. We do indeed seek the lady. Do you have any more for us?"

The man thought a moment. "I know she was sent on a secret mission for Wychwoode. With an utter fucking tool by the name of Rolleston."

"Rolleston, sir?" Olivia asked. "This name comes up a second time. And you disparage him greatly?"

"I would not trust that 24-carat fucker further than I could nudge him. But they went off together." He gave them a grim smile. "Seek Rolleston and you will find the lady." He paused a moment. "And seek out one called Anne Carter. That is all I will say."

"Again, thank you sir," Sir William said. "You are a good man to help us so."

"Maybe." The man nodded, ignoring the blood-curdling screams that came from the platform. "Maybe not. There was a time when I would have happily seen her burn in hell. But you know what? I was wrong – she is okay, really." He paused a moment. "Yeah, okay." He nodded again. "You make sure she gets back in one piece?"

Olivia said, "We will."

"Good. Now, I have a boat to catch which will take me abroad. Good luck." The man limped stiffly away and soon disappeared into the crowd.

There was a pause, while more screams came from the platform. Olivia said, "What was the meaning of that word he used – 'okay'?"

"I know not. I have never before heard the like," Sir William answered. "But I am guessing it meant 'worthy' or somesuch." He stared after the man, then nodded to himself. "Aye, it fits," he muttered. "It fits." Then he took her arm. "Come, we must be away."

He started to push through the crowd, who let them through without taking their gaze off the spectacle on the platform. "A strange fellow, but well-informed," he said over his shoulder. "I will find out more on this Rolleston. It seems he is the key to discovering the whereabouts of my lady. And Anne Carter." They emerged into the open field behind the crowd. "I would we meet again soon," Sir William added, "so we may decide what is best to be done."

"I have leave again in two days," she answered.

"Good. Then we will convene in the same place as before, at the same time, in two days," he said, just as a great cheer went up. "I warrant they have just lifted the fellow's heart."

"So he dies a traitor," observed Olivia.

"Thus it might appear," agreed Sir William. "For all that appearances may deceive."

CHAPTER TWENTY-EIGHT

Mary pulled her horse to a stop below the swinging sign that showed two keys in a cross-shape. "We have arrived," she said. "And I thank you for showing me the way. You may go now – I will take it from here."

But Rolleston dismounted and started tying his horse to the rail.

"What are you doing?" she asked coldly as she dismounted also. "I said you may leave."

"Oh come now," he said with a small smile. "I have come this far; I am not going to abandon you now. Who knows what ruffians there are inside this place?" He glanced at the building's chipped and tired-looking lath and plaster. "It seems most run-down. A single woman walking in alone will be easy prey for any casual fellow who fancies a piece of her." He peered through the grimy windows. "I recall well how you said a man once rescued you from an attack in just such a tavern. Will I need to stand out here and wait to hear you screaming like a wounded cat before I must run in to your aid?"

Mary tied up her horse and peered through the nearest window herself. It did seem dark, although she could just make out a few bare-headed men. "Very well," she said. "You may see me inside and sit at a far distance where you can keep a watch for my safety."

"For sure," he answered. "That makes some sense."

But when they went inside he stayed with her all the way to an empty table.

"In truth, I warrant it is better if I sit here with you," he said brightly, taking a seat.

"No, you shall not," she replied. "Go away. This is a private meeting."

"Oh, come now," he murmured, "look about you. These ruffians are just itching to scratch themselves on a fine lady such as you."

She glanced around, and it did seem he had a point. The rowdy shouting that had first greeted them as they entered had now stilled to an uneasy silence. The majority of the heavily bearded and dirty faces were turned in her direction, and were studying her with some interest.

"Belike they have never seen such nobility. You would be a new experience for them. Unless..." he paused, "unless they could see you were with your 'husband'... Under his protection..."

"Very well," she sighed, recognising when she was beaten. "Very well, you can stay. But you keep silent throughout."

"I will," he answered. "Who are we meeting? I should know, and their purpose, or I may misunderstand the conversation."

"By Heavens, Rolleston," Mary snapped. "I have said I will not share the secret with you. You have got yourself to a position where you are here, very much against my will, and that is as far as you go. Do you hear me?"

He shrugged. "In truth I am intrigued. I have come this far on the journey, and yet I know not the purpose. That has got my interest, and I would know more."

"Well, I am not telling."

"Then I know when I am defeated," he said, standing. "I will take my leave, and with it I will be breaking my oath to keep you safe." He nodded across at a couple of roughly dressed labourers who were still staring at them. "Those two fine fellows over there; I say it will be no more than a minute after I am gone that they are at your table. No doubt they will be offering to show you some fine Sheffield hospitality, if you get my meaning."

"Sit down," she ordered. "You have made your point. I will share my purpose here."

"Good," he said. "Tell me."

"I am to meet a woman named Frances Barwell, to confirm she fully understands her part in the plan."

"And her part is?"

Mary hesitated, then took a deep breath. He would find out anyway once the conversation started with Mistress Barwell.

"She is to impersonate the Queen of Scots."

"Why so?" he asked, looking away as he thought it through, before he suddenly turned to her with a face that had turned quite white. "That incredible musket of yours…" he said slowly, as he appeared to realise the full audacity of the plan. "By Heavens, you will use it to assassinate the Scottish Queen, and put this Mistress Barwell in her place?"

"I did not say that."

"Nay, it was not necessary…" He leaned back. "I see it all now. You have constructed this weapon to kill the Queen of Scots and cut off the Catholics from a credible claimant to the throne…" He nodded. "No doubt this Mistress Barwell will announce a conversion or somesuch. It is audacious indeed."

"I thank you to keep your mouth shut on this, Rolleston," Mary snapped, crossing her arms.

"Oh, you need have no fear on that score. I approve heartily! Any plan that hobbles the Catholics has my full approval!" He grinned. "Nay, 'tis quite brilliant!"

---0---

Frances Barwell was a tall, heavy-set woman with red hair, a long, aquiline nose and small, disapproving lips. Having never met the true Queen of Scots, Mary didn't feel confident to assess the likeness, but she took it on faith that Walsingham and Wychwoode had done their homework – and certainly Frances looked in her mid-thirties, the same age as the Queen.

"You plan to… er… remove the true Queen of Scots on the morrow?" Frances asked in a broad Yorkshire accent, once she had sat at their table and accepted a tankard of ale

"That is my aim, yes," Mary answered. "Will you be ready to assume her place?

"Indeed, I am ready." Her expression softened, then she added in perfect-sounding French, "Je serai comme Mary, la reine légitime des Écossais, détenue par ma cousine Elizabeth contre ma volonté et contre ma véritable prétention au trône d'Angleterre."

I will be as Mary, rightful queen of the Scots, held by my cousin Elizabeth against my will and against my true claim to the throne of England.

Mary nodded. "That's good. She spent most of her early years at the French court, so speaks mainly French."

"You can converse also in the Scots tongue?" asked Rolleston. "The Queen is from that country, so she speaks it full well. You could fail badly in your role if you cannot speak it."

Frances looked directly at Mary "This man is suspitious o me," she said. "I wad nocht hae him doutin me."

There was a silence, then Mary asked, "And the meaning?" – although it did seem fairly understandable.

"This man is suspicious of me," Frances said with a small smile. "I would not have him doubt me."

Mary inclined her head in acknowledgment. "Very well." Then she added, "Forgive my companion, he is a naturally suspicious person."

"I am but concerned for the success of this amazing plan," said Rolleston.

"As we all are," Mary responded briskly. "Now, let us talk of how it will be carried out." She looked across at Frances. "I believe you have not yet been fully briefed?"

"Only that I am to take the place of the Queen of Scots tomorrow, which role I have been schooled upon in her person and manner, and then I am to renounce her claim to the throne. I know not of the details of how the substitution is to be effected."

"So I will brief you now."

"Please do so."

Mary took a sip of ale to settle herself. "You are to be admitted to a side room in the castle by the Earl of Shrewsbury himself," she said. "It is close to where the Queen of Scots takes her daily walk, and you will be dressed in the same clothes. You are to have a bladder of pig's blood attached to your shoulder under your cloak. When the Scottish Queen goes for her walk, I will take a shot to her heart, so it will be a mortal shot. She will be removed quickly from the scene and her body brought to the room where you are concealed. You will then appear soon after with the blood all about your shoulder, and although appearing to be shocked and dazed, you will say that you are not mortally hit."

Mary glanced at Rolleston, who was listening intently, his mouth slightly open and his eyes shining in the flickering candlelight.

Mary continued, "You will then be taken to the Scottish Queen's chambers. I understand you have also been receiving intelligence on the recent events in her life?" Frances nodded. "Good. Anything you have appeared to have misremembered will be explained by the shock of the assassination attempt." She took another sip of ale. "You will then be taken to Tutbury Castle to recuperate for a day or two, before proceeding to London for the final part of the plan – the renunciation of the Scottish Queen's claim to the throne." She sat back. "All the details of that will be relayed to you by the Earl on the journey."

"A most ingenious plan," whispered Rolleston. "I am well impressed."

"Your praise should mainly go to Master Secretary Walsingham and Master Wychwoode for the plan," Mary observed. "Although I commend your willingness to play your part in this, Mistress Barwell."

"I thank you, Mistress Carter," Frances answered. "I also commend your part in this venture." She nodded again, as if confirming in her own mind the full scope of what Mary was about to do. "To conceal yourself and take a mortal shot at God's anointed Queen – that is an act of true bravery. For all she has abdicated her Scottish throne and is a Catholic, it may be that God will not accept such an act. What if your actions on the morrow condemn your soul to eternal damnation?"

Mary's eyes widened. Wow – that was direct. And a tough one to answer. If she revealed she wasn't concerned because she didn't have a faith, would she lose this woman's natural Tudor sympathy and endanger the whole plan? Or if she said she was prepared to take the risk, was she revealing herself as a reckless heretic?

She sighed inwardly. Truly, religion itself was the culprit here. Setting up one man's faith as another man's heresy created nothing but deep, intractable problems.

Mary took a deep breath. "Mary, Queen of Scots is a heretic Catholic who would have no concerns to take the life of God's rightfully anointed Queen Elizabeth, and then her throne," she said quietly but firmly. "So I, as a follower of the true Protestant faith who has sworn to protect the Queen, and who has already saved her life in the past, I have no trouble in my conscience to do this act. None at all."

She let the heavy silence after her words continue for several moments, then looked at Rolleston and added, "Is that not so?"

He frowned slightly, as if surprised to be asked, then his face cleared and he said, "Naturally, Anne. There is no doubting your intention or your conviction in this matter."

Mary turned back to Frances Barwell and asked, "My part in this venture will soon be over. Yours could continue for days or even weeks until you get to London and sign the papers renouncing the Scottish Queen's claim to the throne. Do you not have a family who will miss you?"

"Nay," Frances answered. "I have been widowed these many months, since my husband Jack Barwell died of a severe fever." She paused. A look of sadness appeared very briefly, before being replaced by her usual neutral expression. "We were not blessed by God to have children, so I live alone. My only sister lives in Nottingham, so I rarely get to see her." She shook her head. "No, God has not seen fit to allow me a loving family, but has instead given me a remarkable likeness to the Scottish Queen. So I do His will in taking her place for as long as is necessary."

"I am sorry about your husband," Mary said.

"Such is God's plan." Frances said, with a small glance upwards, as if to make sure her words were heard in Heaven. "He was a clerk with a master in the law here in Sheffield. So we had a comfortable life, not given to extravagance."

"Is that how you met Master Wychwoode?" Mary asked.

Frances nodded. "He was a visitor to my husband's employer's chambers one day, when by happenstance I was present. He kept looking at me strangely, and observed that I reminded him of someone." She gave a small chuckle and smiled at the memory. "Then it was as if a ray of sunlight had shone upon him, and suddenly his face lit up. 'I know who you look like,' he said, 'it is the Queen of Scots!' He came up and studied me closely, turning my face this way and that, before he said, 'It is as if God himself has made two copies of the same person! And you are living in Sheffield, where the Scottish Queen is held! 'Tis most uncanny!' So, when he approached me a few weeks past, and outlined to me this audacious plot, he was clear that it was God's will that I am involved, as God would not have given me the face and body of the Scottish Queen if he had no other purpose." She nodded, as if to reassure herself. "So it is with good grace I play my part – as you do also." She stood and held her hand out to Mary. "I will not see you again, I fear."

Mary stood also, and took Frances's hand. "Most probably not."

"I wish you God's grace and success on the morrow."

"And you."

"What will you do now?" Frances asked.

"I go to see the Earl of Shrewsbury, and ensure he is also ready to play his role," Mary answered.

"Then God's grace be with you for that meeting also." Frances smoothed her skirts, stood to her full, imposing height, and left the tavern without a further look back.

CHAPTER TWENTY-NINE

Sir William idly swilled his beer around the bottom of the tankard as he waited to meet Olivia Melrose in the tavern as arranged at Tyburn two days previously. He stared into the murky depths as he mulled over the results of his investigations into Roger Rolleston.

His initial enquiries had yielded little; no person he asked had ever heard of the man, which was not altogether surprising, considering that they moved in very different circles. He was beginning to despair of finding any useful intelligence, when he finally had a stroke of luck. He learned that Nicholas Grenville was in London, and could be found at his house in Blackfriars. Grenville was the northern Catholic who had been caught up in the plot for the Alchemist to kill the Queen in York that spring, masterminded by Grenville's errant nephew, Lambert Moreton, and foiled by Mary with her poker. Grenville had been spared from execution, not only because he had agreed to convert away from Rome, but also because Sir William, who had been his house guest at the time, had made it clear that Grenville had been unaware of the plot.

So here was a man with a possible source of deeper information; and who owed him a favour. He had therefore paid Grenville a visit the evening before.

"Rolleston?" Grenville had said, as he poured them both a glass of wine. "For sure I know of the fellow. Self-important merchant who puffs himself up and dresses like a peacock, as a means to satisfy his well-known and constant desire for female flesh."

Sir William flinched. And Mary was alone with this man? That confirmed his worst fears and made him sick to his stomach. Damn Wychwoode for sending his wife off alone with this fellow!

Now, more than ever, he had to go after her.

"Most interesting." he said with a thin smile. "So if I was to seek this man Rolleston, where would I most likely find him?"

Grenville shrugged. "I know not – he could be anywhere. He was held in the Tower until recently, but I heard he was then released."

"Why was he held?"

"He was found in the house of a known Catholic, one Antony Brooks."

"So then, why was he released?" asked Sir William, mentally adding the name Antony Brooks to his list of persons of interest in this matter.

"I know he maintained a story that he was an observant Protestant, regularly worshipping in some church in Surrey or some place, so I warrant the cunning fellow was able to show he was not there on seditious business." Grenville took a swig of wine. "As a merchant, he most likely had some tale of being there on the pretext of trade."

Sir William considered this. "So, he is not a Protestant in truth?"

"Heavens no!" Grenville gave a short laugh. "I will tell you, Sir William, as we have an understanding, but the truth is," he leaned forward with a conspiratorial look; "Rolleston is a confirmed Catholic, as is Brooks, in whose house he was found." Then he sat back. "There, I have said it." He frowned. "But why do you seek him?"

Sir William paused a moment. Given that the mission this Rolleston and Mary were on was secret, it would clearly not serve to tell the truth. So he picked up on something Grenville had mentioned, and he said, "I seek him on a matter of trade; I have invested in a shipment of spices from the Orient. All I know is that he has gone north."

"Ah! He has absconded with your funds, has he?" Grenville answered with an unpleasant wink. "I warrant that is why you seek the fellow." Then he said, "Antony Brooks lives at Oak House at Bridgeford, which means you go to Nottingham, then on a few miles beyond. If, as you say, Rolleston has gone north, you might consider starting your search there."

"But was Brooks not held as well?"

"Nay, I hear he wriggled off the hook like a slippery eel." Grenville laughed again. "He has good associations with the local Justices and would have leveraged those…"

Sir William looked up as Olivia arrived at the table dressed in her riding clothes. He poured her some beer, let her settle herself, then filled her in on what he learned of Rolleston, Brooks and the house in Bridgeford near Nottingham. In telling the tale, he decided to omit the piece about Rolleston being a known womaniser.

"Then we must make haste to this place, Oak House" Olivia said when he had finished.

"We?" he asked. "For sure I shall travel alone. I fear this is not a mission for a young woman."

Olivia gave him a wide-eyed look of surprise. "I warrant my love for my lady is as great as yours, Sir William," she said. "If there is a chance she is in danger, I would not shirk my duty to help..."

"But…" he began.

"…And as you stated when we were last here," Olivia continued, as if he had not spoken, "I killed two men in quick succession before your eyes. I am not just any young woman, Sir William, and I *will* be accompanying you on this mission."

"But…" he said again, then paused. When she stayed silent, he continued, "…will the Queen allow you leave of absence for such time as may be necessary?"

"The Queen understands I have need to return home to tend to my sick father. She has allowed me as long as is necessary to return him to health."

"Oh, Melrose is sick? I knew not."

Olivia shook her head with a look of bemused amazement. "Of course not; it is but a ruse to get time away from Court."

"Oh. Ah, yes, of course," Sir William muttered, as if that was what he had known all along.

"Then I suggest we set off without delay," she said, finishing her beer and standing. I have my horse without, and I am ready."

CHAPTER THIRTY

A small, elderly man in black let Mary and Rolleston into an imposing wood-panelled room inside Sheffield Castle, dominated by a roaring fire in a magnificent fireplace.

It was after they had left the Crossed Keys earlier, that Mary had tried once again to get Rolleston to leave her, but he had been adamant that he was coming to this meeting as well.

"Now I know of the plan, what benefit is there in further secrecy?" he had asked, as they walked down the hill towards the castle. "And anyhow, there are many cut-purses and ruffians in these streets. I am sworn to protect you, and that I shall."

"But you have no need to come into the castle," she had tried. "You can wait for me outside."

"Nay, Mistress Carter." He had shaken his head. "Think you that the Earl and Countess of Shrewsbury will receive a single woman? I doubt it greatly."

Mary had thought the exact opposite, but couldn't think of any way to force him, so they had entered the castle together, and been seen up to this magnificent room by the elderly servant.

Mary looked about her, taking it all in. Above the fireplace was a pair of crossed swords under a red and yellow shield bearing the image of a gold lion standing upright. On either side were imposing portraits; one of a nobleman with a long grey beard that reached beyond the edge of his ruff and was dropping over the edge like the beginning of a waterfall, while the other was of a mature woman with a long, aristocratic nose and red hair. The man looked as if he had deeply resented having his portrait done. His expression was one of pained sufferance as if he was continually telling the artist to 'get on with it'. The woman, on the other hand, looked as if the whole experience was just a bit of fun, as if her natural humour could not be repressed by standing still for such a long time.

The centre of the room was furnished with eight large high-backed chairs around a broad oak table, with further smaller chairs placed around the walls. In one corner stood a large writing desk covered with papers, while the rest of the room held a mixture of occasional tables, decorative pots and a pair of prie dieus. The ceiling was adorned with decorative plasterwork in geometric patterns radiating out from a large central boss that featured the same lion shield as the one above the fire.

The man who had let them in bowed and announced into the empty room, "Mistress Anne Carter and Master Roger Rolleston, madam." Then he reversed out of the door, leaving them standing there.

Mary was just wondering who he had been addressing, when a woman's head suddenly appeared above one of the chair backs, rising up as if pulled by an invisible string. Then the head turned, and Mary realised that she was looking at the woman in the portrait.

"I am the Countess of Shrewsbury," the woman said, as she walked towards them. Mary couldn't help glancing at her face, then flicking her eyes over to the picture to confirm the likeness. "Yes, that is indeed me," the woman said softly. Mary dropped into a small curtsey and found herself staring down at the toes of the woman's silk slippers peeping out from under her gown. "Pray be upstanding, Mistress Carter," came the woman's voice, and she felt a hand under her chin lifting her up. "You and Master Rolleston are most welcome." Mary stood to her full height, which was at least a head taller than the Countess.

"We are come of late from London, Your Excellency," Mary said, "and present our compliments to you and the Earl."

"Indeed, my husband said a woman may come, and would be bringing a message regarding our… guest… the Queen of the Scots," said the Countess. Mary nodded slightly. "Ahh, t'would be a most welcome message if it tells that she is to be moved to the care of another," the Countess continued with a look of tired resignation. "She and her retinue weigh most heavy on our purse, and we get no help from Her Majesty's Exchequer for all our troubles."

Mary gave a weak smile. "I am instructed that the message is for the Earl's eyes alone, Your Excellency."

"Of course, of course," the Countess said, and walked over to a cord hanging in the corner. "You and your companion will take some wine?" she asked, pulling it sharply. A distant sound of a bell could be heard.

"That would be most kind," Mary answered.

"For me, also," said Rolleston.

The elderly man in black reappeared, acknowledged the Countess's request for wine, then bowed and left.

"My husband has been seeing to the Scots woman's retinue," the Countess observed. "I expect him back presently."

"We are happy to wait, Your Excellency," Rolleston said.

The Countess inclined her head in acknowledgment, and said to Mary, "Is Master Carter, your husband, not here also?"

"No, madam. He has other business to attend to." Which was sort-of true enough.

"You must be pained at being parted."

"Indeed I am, my lady."

"But you have the companionship of Master Rolleston," the Countess observed, with an enquiring raised eyebrow.

"Master Rolleston here has been so good as to offer me his protection on my journey," Mary answered.

"Most kind," the Countess answered and turned to Rolleston, looking him up and down slowly, almost as if she were assessing the qualities of a horse she was purchasing. Then she nodded to show he had passed her visual inspection. "I trust you have not been called upon to draw your sword in defence of the lady's person and honour?" She gave a small smile, seeming to show that such things were never actually necessary in her privileged world, but may, of course, happen to others.

"Aye, in truth I did have to do so," Rolleston answered. "Some brigands stopped us on the road, and would have taken our valuables, as well as threatening harm to Mistress Carter. I was able to overcome them with my sword and er… see them off… before any misfortune came to this lady, or to our possessions."

The countess's mouth opened in a small 'o'. "By Heavens, is this true?" she breathed, looking at Mary. "You were attacked?"

Mary nodded. "Yes, madam, 'tis God's truth."

Just then the servant reappeared with a tray of goblets and two bottles of wine.

"I have taken the liberty of bringing a choice of wines, Your Excellency," he said.

The Countess selected one and poured them all glasses. When they all had a glass in hand and the man had withdrawn, then she said to Mary, "You are indeed fortunate that you had Master Rolleston there as your protector."

"Indeed I am, my lady," Mary answered. "And I am most grateful to him."

"Then we must drink to his health, must we not?" The Countess raised her glass. "I commend you Master Rolleston, for your bravery and your presence of mind." Rolleston gave a small bow, as they all drank. "Now, I am sorry, but I must leave you," she said, once they had put their glasses down, "as I have some household affairs that I must attend to. My husband will be here presently, as I know your business is with him." She gave them each a small nod. "Good day, Mistress Carter. Master Rolleston."

There was a silence after the Countess had left. Mary picked up her wine glass and finished off the last few drops, then poured herself another full glass and drained it in one go. "Do not ask me to feel at ease with this situation," she muttered, refilling her glass and draining it again. "To be welcomed as a guest here, knowing what I intend for the morrow – it sits ill with me. Most ill."

"I know," he said, in a tone that surprised her with its sympathy. "It must be hard, knowing what you are charged to do."

Just then the doors opened and a man of around fifty entered, dressed in a black doublet, brown trunk-hose slashed with grey, cream hose and a grey cloak. Again, Mary glanced up to the picture beside the fireplace; there was no doubt this was the same man. Except that where the picture had a look of impatience, the man before them simply looked tired, as if the weight of the world was on his shoulders.

"Mistress Carter?" he asked as he came over and made a small bow before her. "You are well met indeed." He stood to his full height, which was still half a head shorter than her, then gave a weak smile. "I trust Bess has made you welcome?" He eyed their glasses, and poured one for himself. "Those Scottish women will be the death of any man who must shepherd them from one place to another!" He gave a hollow laugh. "Shepherd! I am no such thing when it comes to them, for they are not like sheep, but like cats…" he raised his eyes to the ceiling, "Cats that spit and scratch and do aught but what they are asked…" He looked down again. "You know, all four are also named Mary? It is impossible to address them with any clarity." Then he smiled. "But enough of them. We must harry to our business." The smile faded, and he said, "You have instructions for me, I believe?"

"I do, Your Excellency." She fished in her pocket and handed over Walsingham's coded letter, which he took between thumb and forefinger as if it were white hot.

"Let us see what this says, eh?" he muttered, as he took it over to the desk and broke the seal with a knife. Then he opened it up and smoothed it with his hand, before laying the knife along its side like a paperweight, to keep it from closing again. "Let me see, let me see," he muttered, as he reached for a small leather-bound book and found the correct page. Then he selected a piece of plain paper, dipped a quill in a small ink pot, and hovered over the blank page.

"Oh yes, 'A' is equivalent to 'S'," he continued, as he looked at the book, then back at the coded letter. "Which makes 'T' into 'R'…"

Mary and Rolleston watched as he slowly deciphered the letter, scratching characters onto the blank page as he went. "By the Lord's passion…" he said to himself as the meaning of the code became apparent, "that is most singular, most singular indeed…" He looked up. "Yes, this confirms the outline of the plan that has been shared thus far; that a secret type of musket is to be used that can be accurate from a great distance. I am to secure for the assassin a suitable position overlooking the courtyard so it can be fired upon the person of the Scottish Queen when she steps out on the morrow…" He looked up. "It says not who will be the angel of death who fires this weapon, but am I to take it that it will be you, sir?" He looked enquiringly at Rolleston, who shook his head. "Nay?" He turned to Mary with a raised eyebrow. "Then is it you who will fire this weapon at the Scottish Queen?" Mary nodded. "Remarkable!" The Earl shook his head. "They have sent a woman to kill a woman! Who would have thought it could be so?"

He went back to his sheet of decoded notes. "Yes, yes; I am to bring the new substitute queen to the room beside the courtyard, then burst the bladder of blood… just so, just so… Then I must treat this new queen, who looks and speaks like the original, as if she is genuine, and convey her to Tutbury." He read further. "Oh, but there will be the conceit that the distress of the assassination attempt will account for any lapse of memory." Mary nodded again. "This is most clever – most clever indeed." He looked up at Mary. "So this counterfeit queen, she will renounce the claim to the throne and the Catholic faith? So that no further plots can centre on her in future?" Once again, Mary gave a small affirmative nod. "And I shall be relieved of the burden of keeping the Scottish Queen and her retinue of leeches who suck the blood from my family and my purse every day that God provides?"

"I believe that will be the outcome, Your Excellency," Mary said.

The Earl looked up, and it seemed that some of the weight had already lifted from his shoulders. "Then this plan has my deepest blessing," he said with a small smile, "and tomorrow, I shall play my part in it with God's good grace."

He sprinkled some sand across the sheet of decoded notes, then shook it off. "Then, once you have disposed of the Catholic Queen," he continued, "I will escort her replacement from Tutbury to London for the renouncement of both her faith and her claim to the throne." He put both papers to one side on his desk. "Come," he said, "we must view the turret where you will be stationed tomorrow, so you can be sure of your angles and distances."

Mary nodded, her head clearing of the wine in an instant.

This was getting real. All too real.

The Earl led the way out, with Mary close behind. "You really do not need to see this," she whispered over her shoulder to Rolleston as she passed through the doors. "I will meet you back at the Crossed Keys." There was no response, so she looked round, to see he was a few feet further behind. "Apologies," he said with a sheepish smile as he caught her up. "That was a particularly fine Rhenish, so I availed myself of another cup."

"For sure," she replied, then repeated her instruction.

He thought a moment, then nodded. "Yes, I concur. I will see you there presently."

Mary followed the Earl out into the afternoon sun, and as they crunched along a gravel pathway around the castle, Rolleston peeled off and headed out through a nearby gate onto the street.

"Follow me," the Earl said as he strode along the path. "I have the perfect place for the killing on the morrow."

Shit! Why did he have to put it as bluntly as that?

CHAPTER THIRTY-ONE

Sleep that night seemed quite out of the question.

It's not that Mary didn't try. After retiring to her chamber, she was determined to rest and relax so she would be sharp and alert for the awful task in the morning. So she took care to stick to her usual routine – undressing and changing into her nightshift, then cleaning her teeth with the special pig-bristle brush and peppermint paste she had made at Grangedean, before slipping under the blankets and getting 'sleep ready'. This was a procedure she had perfected in the early years of her Tudor life, starting with lying on her back and flexing, then relaxing, all her muscles in turn. She would begin at her toes; splaying them out a few times then letting them relax with a small wiggle, then pulling her feet back and letting them relax also – and so on up through her arms, hands and fingers, ending with the muscles in her neck, mouth and eyes. Not forgetting a quick 'Bewitched' nose wiggle. This usually had the effect of making sure all her muscles were totally floppy, smoothing out any hidden tensions. It also had the effect of making William laugh if he saw it, causing her to have to start the whole routine again. Then, once all the muscles were nice and relaxed, she would roll gently onto her right side, take a few deep breaths and curl into a foetal ball. She would usually be asleep in minutes.

But this night, however much she tried, all her muscles kept tensing up again; making every position she tried painfully uncomfortable.

Tomorrow she would become a sniper, an assassin, a killer. How could she possibly sleep when she was preparing to end the life of Mary, Queen of Scots in cold blood?

She tried to settle on her back.

Did Rick, the Alchemist, have such doubts before he set out to kill Queen Elizabeth? It was unlikely; the man had a free choice and, she suspected, very little conscience. Plus, he was not under threat of death by burning for sorcery if he refused to make the attempt. But did that make it all right? To kill an innocent person because if one didn't, one would be killed oneself? Better to be murdered than to become a murderer?

Mary tried her left side, thumping the pillow a few times to get a head-sized depression into the rough horsehair and straw. It didn't make her any more comfortable.

What about Lee Harvey Oswald? Or John Wilkes Booth? Did they have sleepless nights before setting out to kill Kennedy and Lincoln? Oswald and Booth... And Chapman, wasn't that the bloke who killed Lennon?

Sirhan Sirhan. Where did that name come from? Mary clicked her fingers and frowned. Oh yes, he was the one who killed Robert Kennedy. And James Earl Ray, of course, who assassinated Martin Luther King.

How did they all sleep, the night before their big days?

Jack Ruby. He shot Oswald.

Oh god! What if there's a Jack Ruby out there for me?

Mary flopped back onto her right side.

Would she be looking over her shoulder for the rest of her life, if it ever became known that the spy and assassin Anne Carter was in fact, Lady Mary de Beauvais? But Walsingham and Wychwoode had promised her security would be assured, and surely the Queen would offer her protection?

But what if it did come out – that Lady Mary de Beauvais was the assassin of Mary, Queen of Scots? Would schoolchildren of the future learn her name and her life story? How would they be taught about her first twenty-seven years – years that had never actually existed in Tudor history?

And what of history itself? The Armada? The Babington Plot? Maybe even the Gunpowder Plot? Such events that would be replaced by new ones in history; ones she couldn't even begin to imagine. All because she was going to centre the Scottish Queen's chest in her crosshairs, hold her breath, and pull the trigger…

Mary sat up with a small cry.

Now she was actually planning her shot, like a truly cold-blooded assassin!

She brought her knees up to her chest and hugged them, rocking slightly on the mattress in the dark. What a dreadful set of events had led her to this point – had led her to becoming this merciless killer…

If only the plot had been simply to kill the Scottish Queen quietly in the night. The Earl of Shrewsbury could have done it, of course; he could have crept into her chamber and dispatched her himself. After all, he disliked her intensely, as she and her ladies were eating their way through his fortune. In truth, he should have welcomed the opportunity. But that was not the plan – the public shooting had been deemed necessary by Walsingham so he could let start a rumour that the would-be assassin was a disaffected Catholic, so making the Scottish Queen's willingness to give up her claim to the throne more credible.

Mary slid back down the bed and tried once again to do her flexing routine, then took several deep breaths to 'lock in' the relaxation.

Think of something else.

Rolleston.

Imagine not feeling pain… She would have traded anything not to have had the screaming agony of childbirth…

If she'd had Ambrose, Kat and Jane in the 21st century, there would have been so many more options…

Gas and air…

Epidural…

Waterbirth…

Is Kat all right? Once again a promise not to leave her had been broken…

She'll probably never want to trust her mother again…

Is Jane eating?

Ambrose? Has William found him a tutor?

William…

William…

Mary drifted off into a dark, dreamless sleep.

---0---

Rolleston picked a piece of crustiness from the corner of his eye and examined it closely on the edge of his nail.

"Did you sleep at all last night, Mistress Carter?" he asked, flicking the tiny thing onto the rush floor.

"Eventually, I must have done," she replied. "I had much on my mind, as I am sure you will imagine."

He nodded. "I do imagine."

"And you?" she asked. "Did you sleep…" Mary paused, as she noticed his eyes were now following a pretty young maid making her way around the room. She changed what she was going to say, "…Did you sleep alone?"

He pursed his lips. "Belike I did. Or belike – I did not."

They were breaking fast in the tavern of the Crossed Keys the next morning. Mary looked at the maid as she bent over a table, her chest barely held in by her thin linen blouse. "I fear she is young enough that you could have sired her yourself, Master Rolleston."

He did not respond to this, but instead he said, "Will you be heading straight for the castle? You have note of the hour when the Scots Queen will be taking her walk?"

Mary sat back and eyed him over her tankard as she had a sip. "I do. She will be taking her walk around noon. I will ensure I am in position around one hour before, so I am ready when she comes out."

"And will she be alone?"

"Yes. Apparently she has very sore joints and does not like others to see her walk."

"Understandable."

"And you, Roger?" she asked. "What is your plan for today?"

"I will take a short stroll around the town now, then I will come back here and await your return."

"Then go to it," she answered. "I would sit here a while longer to gather myself."

"Indeed," he said, standing. "Till we meet after… the matter… has happened." Then he strode across to the front door, pausing only to slap the serving maid's bottom on the way out.

Mary sighed as the girl squeaked and mock-chided him.

Rolleston turned at the door and gave Mary a small wave across the room, then he was gone.

The maid came over. "Some more to eat or drink, madam?" she asked, her face still flushed.

"No, thank you," Mary replied, then added with a slight chill in her voice, "I see you are quite familiar with my travelling companion."

The girl blushed deeper, and stammered, "I beg your pardon, madam, but I thought..."

Mary raised an eyebrow. "What did you think, exactly?"

"That you and he are not... you are not..."

"That we are not husband and wife? Is that what he told you?"

"That he did, madam!" The girl put her hand to her mouth. "Oh, madam, I am so sorry, indeed I am! What you must think of me!" Then she added in a slightly lower tone, "And him..."

"As it happens, he is but my travelling companion, looking to my safety," Mary said, deciding to let the girl off the hook. "He has told you the truth; we are not wed."

"Oh." The girl's colour started to fade back towards normality. "But it has upset you, madam, I can see that." She poured ale into Mary's tankard. "I am so sorry, madam, if you are offended. I meant nothing by it, indeed not!" She bobbed her head and scurried off.

"Nor did he," Mary muttered after her. "Nor did he."

Mary drank her ale slowly. The distant sound of a church bell rang the hour, and she counted ten strikes. Ten o'clock! She finished her ale and stood. She must get the gun and get over to the castle now, or she might not be ready if the Scottish Queen decided to walk early.

With a muttered curse, she hurried over to the stairs and made her way up to her chamber.

CHAPTER THIRTY-TWO

Mary wiped her hand on her man's jerkin and put it back on the fore-stock of the gun. The last thing she needed now was sweaty palms. She should have brought a towel or a rag.

Her jerkin was made of leather, and she had added extra leather patches to the elbows to prevent soreness from the hard stone. She was wearing men's breeches and had her hair up under a cap. She had also blackened her face in the approximation of a beard. All this was so she could not only pass as a man – at least at a casual glance – but was also unhindered by voluminous skirts in order to make a quick getaway.

She shifted her grip and put her eye to the scope. A wall that bisected the castle courtyard sprang into view. It had a gate at its centre, topped by a fine stone arch. From this height she could see both sides of the gate – behind it as well as in front. She lined up the crosshairs on the large black door handle for a moment, then idly moved up to the stone lintel. There was the same shield with the standing lion that she had seen above the fireplace the day before. The device of the Earl of Shrewsbury. She swung the scope up to the flag flying above the castle; it featured the same shield. She chuckled softly; the Elizabethans certainly knew a thing or two about branding.

The flag flapped slightly, leading to the conclusion that the wind was blowing from right to left. Mary could see that it was a gentle, consistent breeze at rooftop level; of course, there might be some eddies swirling around the courtyard below which she should allow for. She swung the sight across to find a small tree in a decorative bed and observed the leaves a while. If the tree was any indication, the breeze at ground level was actually blowing the other way; from left to right, although it seemed very slight. Important to allow for it over this distance if she was to hit her target with absolute accuracy.

She shifted her position a little to try and stop her muscles locking up.

This could be a long wait.

She was standing in a damp-smelling circular room in one of the two turrets above the main castle gates, with the only light coming from the single arrow-slit window at the end of a very deep stone sill. She had pulled up a small table for her bullets and a costrel of water, and was using the stone sill as a rest support for the gun. It was a convenient position to fire from, as it was deep enough to support her left elbow as she held the gun. The only issue was her limited barrel movement up and down, which meant her actual field of fire was somewhat limited.

A small motion down in the courtyard caught her eye and she found it in her sights; a servant in Shrewsbury livery coming out of a door and crossing to the other side. She followed him as he walked, keeping his head in her crosshairs for practice, but with her finger well away from the trigger. The thought of accidentally shooting a servant filled her with sick horror.

As bad as shooting the Queen of Scots?

Mary took a deep breath and again wiped each palm, before settling once more in position.

Another servant came out of a door beyond the dividing wall, and she saw him walk up to the gate in the middle, then disappear behind it. She focused on the gate at head height, and was able to pick him up as he came through, getting him neatly in the crosshairs as he walked forwards. He was now coming towards the gate directly below her. She counted the seconds until her limited firing angle was too sharp and even though he was still a long distance away, she was not able to get her barrel to point that low. She reckoned that if the Queen was to walk at the same speed, then the window of opportunity for the shot would be around twenty seconds.

She wondered if the Earl had deliberately sent the fellow out there, just so she could get this information. Did the man know that his every move was being tracked by a hidden sniper? But then, the concept of a distant killer armed with a gun such as hers would be so alien to the average Elizabethan, that it was unlikely he could conceive of the threat he was under. He would be aware of arquebus guns, muskets and crossbows of course – but the accuracy of such weapons was insufficient for a sniper to be as far away as she was.

So, unless the Earl had told him (unlikely), he had been blissfully unaware that a gun was tracking his every move. A gun built to a 2015 design and aimed at him by a time-travelling woman – now *that* he would have definitely been unable to comprehend!

Indeed, if she didn't know it to be true, Mary herself could hardly believe it.

How had she got herself into this situation – and would she have done anything differently? Her original time-travel over ten years ago was unfortunate; she had simply been in the wrong place at the wrong time, and had slipped down a wormhole opened up by the electrical storm. The fact she had her phone with her, and a solar charger, meant she could use it to conjure the 'voice of Jesus' and save herself when tried for witchcraft by ducking in the well. Then saving the life of Queen Elizabeth by beating the Alchemist just as he was about to fire the fatal shot – she had no regrets about that at all. And being forced to undertake this mission under threat of execution by burning – what choice did she have?

Mary put the gun down and stood up, stretching her back until she felt the joints popping. Then she resumed her position, with the sight trained on the door that the second servant had come from.

And she waited.

The clock struck twelve.

Maybe the Queen was not coming out today? Maybe her arthritis was too painful?

The clock struck the quarter hour.

Give it another half an hour, then maybe try again tomorrow?

There was movement at the door. A tall, heavy-set woman in a clean white walking cloak came out, followed by a man in black. Mary lined them up in her sights. The man was the small elderly servant who had let her and Rolleston in the day before.

And the woman…

Mary focused on the distant figure and drew a quick breath. It was uncanny – as if she was looking at Frances Barwell, but fully made up and with her hair done.

Mary watched as the Queen said something to the servant, then he went back into the castle while she turned towards the gate and started walking stiffly. Quickly she was out of sight behind it. After a moment Mary saw the handle turning.

Then it seemed as if reality blurred, pitching her into a dreamlike state, almost as if she were sliding down a slippery slope, unable to grab hold and take control.

The wooden door opened, and the Queen walked through alone, bringing her head right into the centre of the crosshairs, and Mary's finger trembled on the trigger as the Queen started walking towards her. Twenty seconds was all the time she had available; maybe a few more as the Queen walked so slowly… the Queen kept walking… so it must be fifteen by now, fifteen seconds until she would pass the point where Mary could get a clear shot, so it had to be now, it had to be; now it was ten seconds, so it really was now or never, and then the Queen looked up and it was if she was looking directly at Mary, daring her, challenging her to take the shot; 'take it, take it' she seemed to be saying 'and put me out of my misery! Go on, girl, go on, do me the favour and give me a quick, clean death now rather than eleven more years of unjust imprisonment ending in a painful execution; go on, do it now, I dare you!'

Mary found she was holding her breath as she centred the fine, aristocratic head in the crosshairs, then dropped the sight down to the centre of the Queen's chest, right where the clasp strained to fasten the cloak, right where the heart would be, then Mary heard a small cry of pain, but it couldn't be the Queen because she hadn't fired yet, so *Christ!* it must have been her not the Queen who cried out, and the Queen was still walking; getting closer and closer to the point of no return; six seconds, five seconds…

CHAPTER THIRTY-THREE

Mary took the shot.

The cracking sound crashed round the room, reverberating off the stone walls and leaving her ears ringing. It was accompanied by the acrid firework smell of the gunpowder, and a cloud of bitter, choking smoke that burned her throat and made her eyes water.

She blinked furiously down the scope, as the scene unfolded in the courtyard below.

The Queen had been blown backwards by the shot and was lying very still on the cobbles. Her mouth was open with what almost looked like a snarl, as if instead of welcoming the shot, she had actually tried to curse Mary as she flew through the air.

A patch of bright red was growing fast and spreading out from the centre of her chest, turning the beautiful white cloak crimson.

There was a shout and a guard in the Earl's livery appeared at a run, then another, and a third. Together they surrounded the body; one cradling the Queen's head and the other struggling to undo the clasp to the cloak. Several more men appeared, and soon the body was completely surrounded. As Mary watched, it was lifted up and quickly carried to the side of the courtyard, disappearing out of sight.

Quickly she ejected the smoking cartridge case from the chamber, then broke the gun down and put it in her bag. Then she swept the spare bullets and the costrel into the bag as well, before closing and attaching it to her back with its two handles like a backpack. With a quick look round the room to make sure nothing was left, she ran out.

The Earl had shown her the way in and out of the turret room when they had scouted the location the day before. The escape was along the open walkway above the gate hidden from view by the crenelated stone walls; a structure he had called the 'allure'. Then down the steps that were within the other gate turret and out towards the street.

Crouching as she ran, Mary made her way along the allure and pulled open the wooden door at the end. Then she clattered down the stone steps to the door into the street.

Keeping her head down and walking with what she hoped was the rolling gait of a man, she pushed through the Sheffield crowds. She could sense a distinct air of alarm from those around her, and she heard snatches of conversations, with words like 'assassination!' 'a ball to the chest!' and 'blood everywhere!' as the crowds flowed past, mostly heading towards the castle.

Ignoring them, she made for the Crossed Keys where she could clean up, change into her normal women's clothes and be ready to act as if she had never left. Then she could grab her horse and Rolleston, and ride out of Sheffield to the travelling inn where they had left the coach.

And from there – back down south to a grateful Queen and Walsingham.

And an end to the threat of trial and execution?

She reached a junction between two streets, and was about to turn left up the hill to the Crossed Keys, when she caught sight of a pair of armoured halberdiers heading down the hill looking at the faces in the crowd as they passed. Without breaking stride, Mary took the right fork down the hill instead, and increased her pace to put distance between her and the halberdiers.

Were they looking for her? She bit her lip as she picked her way down the cobbles. Maybe. Maybe not. But there was no sense in taking a risk. It was clear from the reaction of the crowds that news of the assassination was spreading like wildfire – so better to assume that these men were on the lookout for anyone acting suspiciously.

Halfway down she saw a grim-looking tavern; a low, shabby building with cracked walls and broken shutters, under a faded sign that said it was called the 'Cock and Bull'. She turned and walked confidently through the door.

Inside it was very dark, with the only light coming from the fire – which suited her purpose admirably. She made her way to the back of the room, trying hard to ignore the smell of stale sweat, woodsmoke and mould. She chose a table close enough to the fireplace to be warm, but deep in shadow. Dropping her bag at her feet, she pulled her cap down and started to watch the door like a hawk.

After a few minutes no halberdiers had come in, or anyone else looking like they were searching for the assassin, so she allowed herself to relax slightly. If she had successfully evaded them, she could hope to be back on her way soon.

A red-faced woman with a dirty cap and apron came over.

"Ale, master?" the woman asked.

"Aye," Mary grunted, turning her head away from the woman's stink, which was noticeable even against the smell of the room.

"Beg pardon?"

"Aye. An ale," she repeated gruffly.

The woman nodded, as if further conversation was not worth the effort, then moved away.

Mary waited until the ale arrived, then allowed herself to sit back and take a sip, her gaze never once leaving the door.

How long to give it before she could reasonably leave? Half an hour? An hour? Would those men continue combing the town for her as long as it may take, or would they call off their search? She decided to give it an hour, then try to get back to the Crossed Keys.

An hour was a long time to wait. The first ale seemed to go down very quickly, as did the second one she ordered, then a third.

So she was no longer watching the door with quite such intensity, and was even dozing slightly with her head down when some men came in and took seats at a table in front of the fire. Indeed, it was only when one of their voices filtered into her consciousness, that she even became aware of them at all.

"A remarkable conceit, that she took only a small wound to the shoulder."

Mary's head snapped up. Right now that voice was as familiar to her as any she had ever known.

Roger Rolleston!

She pulled her cap low, then glanced up from under the brim.

Four men were now seated at the table by the fire. Rolleston was sitting to one side; his profile silhouetted against the flames. Opposite him was a man she couldn't see clearly, as his face was fully in shadow. Then she caught sight of his hand.

His heavily bandaged hand.

She stared hard as he scratched his beard with fingers emerging from the bandaging. She thought she recognised the shape of his head as he leaned forward in front of the fire – last seen… where was it?

Poking out from behind an oak tree?

Nathan, the sniping archer? The one she had shot in the forest? If so, what was Rolleston doing sitting in a dark, dingy tavern with the archer? And if that really was him, then the fellow beside him would be…

Mary gasped and pulled her cap further down.

Greybeard!

What in heaven's name was Rolleston doing drinking and chatting with the archer and how in Heaven's name could he be with a man she had seen him run through with a sword a few days before?

Only – she hadn't actually seen it, had she? She had screwed her eyes tight shut!

She pushed her cap up slightly and looked at the fourth man in the group. At first she didn't recognise him at all, but then he said something, and the low, gravelly voice took her straight back to their journey up to Sheffield. She was sitting in the carriage when he had come to the window to tell her they were stopping for the night.

The driver!

The man who she had left for dead when hit by an arrow!

Mary turned slightly away from them – both to avoid being recognised, and also to have an ear facing them directly, so she could hear their conversation better.

"Has the substitution been actioned?" asked Greybeard.

"Aye," answered Rolleston. "The Barwell woman was slotted in as neat as a ninepin, as soon as the true Queen was taken to the back room."

The 'true' Queen?

"And now?"

There was a pause, and Mary could imagine Rolleston doing his trademark shrug. "She has shown herself as planned and created the conceit that it was but a flesh wound, which she will have dressed in her chambers." Then he added, "And no doubt she claimed to be dazed and confused from the trauma of the shot."

"That was clever," came a voice Mary didn't recognise – so presumably the archer. "To ensure her ladies do not question her memory."

"And it played well into our hands," said Greybeard, "to complete our part of the plan."

"Aye." This was the driver. "The true Queen is recovering well, since we spirited her out of the room where she was left as if dead."

"She is tough, Her Majesty," observed Rolleston. "The breastplate we made protected her from the shot, but the force of the ball still sent her flying to the ground. She said she thought she had broken her head on the cobbles, but by the grace of God, she was able to walk away from the room later."

"We must be thankful for the assassin's accuracy with that musket," said Greybeard. "Not only did the shot find our bladder of blood with unerring precision, but it also hit the Queen in the middle of the breastplate, where it was strongest. Think if she had missed, and say hit the Queen in the head, then we would be in a very different position."

There was silence, then Rolleston said, "So I would we raise a toast to the woman whose blind ignorance and accurate marksmanship has made our Catholic plan so successful!" There was the sound of tankards being thumped on the table, then a pause as they drank. "To Mistress Anne Carter. Without her our plan would have been as naught!"

Mary stiffened, feeling as if a cold wave had broken over her and her whole body was made of ice; completely numbed. What more could these traitors; these vermin, say now?

She hadn't heard the half of it.

Rolleston continued, "Do you know, I thought she would never be one to carry out the attack on the true Queen. I did not think she had the strength to do it."

"Or the courage," observed Greybeard with a dirty-sounding chuckle. "I thought she was going to shit herself when I tied her up and threatened her in the forest."

"She had the wit to hide her strange musket beneath her skirt, did she not?" observed the archer.

"I agree," answered Greybeard, "but that played into my hand well, for I must let her keep it so she could use it for the assassination. I would not have wanted to question her over it, as a real brigand would."

"You are correct, Antony," said the archer. "Although I would you had taken it off her before she wounded me so grievously in the hand."

Antony? Mary almost looked round. Did that mean Greybeard was the investor Antony Brooks? Now she thought about it, he did look a bit dapper for a highwayman. His beard was too neatly trimmed for a start. How had she not seen that?

"She was like a frighted kitten before a snake," said the driver.

"Until I came to the rescue and fought for her honour," Rolleston laughed. Then his voice changed, and he muttered, "And you opened up my leg like a piece of mutton, Antony."

"Come now," answered Greybeard. "It is no different from when we were boys and you hit me in the head with your catapult."

"Yes, and as I recall, you knocked me to the ground with a wooden sword."

"So I reckon we acquitted each other equally." Greybeard paused. "Then and now."

"But that was not part of the plan for the ambush, was it?" Rolleston continued. "Make it look like show – flashing blades and every cut parried; that was what we agreed." There was a silence, then he added, "Make her think I was her saviour."

"You made as if you had killed me while her eyes were shut, did you not, good fellow?" said Greybeard. "That was enough, I venture."

"For sure. In truth, it was fortunate I had plenty of blood flowing from my leg to smear all about my blade and on your back," said Rolleston. "That was a nice touch."

"There you have it," said Greybeard. "Had I not opened your leg, we would have not been able to pull that little trick."

"Anyhow, it all worked well in the end," interjected the driver. "Did you not say that after the fight and your sad tale before Antony's house, that she bent more easily to your will? So in the end she told you all, enabling you to insert our plan into hers?"

"Almost true," answered Rolleston. "the rescue and the tale helped, but I had to lead her in a few more steps to tease out the full plan." He chuckled. "Your two ruffian friends made most convincing would-be rapists in the Crossed Keys, Nathan. That was what finally convinced her to let me stay and learn all."

"Indeed," answered the archer. "Although I had to ride hard to get to the message to them, once you told me it was to be the Crossed Keys," he gave a short laugh. "It was hard to ride one-handed." He held up his bandaged hand. "How did you get away from your lady?"

"No more than any man would say – I told her I was taking a piss," said Rolleston.

There was a silence, then the sound of an empty tankard hitting the table. "We should be going, as we have ground to cover this evening," said Greybeard. "You have the letter and the Earl's note in plain words that proves the plot, Roger?"

"I do." There was a rustle of papers, "neatly purloined from the Earl's desk last eve, when my lady thought I was taking a last glass of his Rhenish."

"I have never known you to pass up a glass of wine, Roger," said Greybeard, a smile in his voice.

"Nay, old friend," answered Rolleston with a chuckle, as there was the sound of something heavy being placed on the table. "I took the unopened bottle also."

CHAPTER THIRTY-FOUR

It was many minutes after the men had left that Mary was able to move a muscle, such was the shock of learning just how much of a fool she had been.

A stupid, blind, trusting fool!

How had she not seen that Rolleston had been playing her like a bloody harpist? Oh yes, he had known exactly which strings to pluck in order to win her round; the 'knight-in-shining-armour-battling-for-her-honour' thing – that came from her little anecdote on the first day in the carriage – when Tom Cobham had saved her from a would-be rapist. And then trotting out the 'I-was-an-unjustly-accused-innocent' sob story… so clearly designed to tug at her naturally sympathetic heartstrings.

And so clearly an evil, calculating lie! He was, and had always been, a treasonous Catholic, determined to replace Elizabeth with the Queen of Scots.

He must have planned the whole thing in league with Brooks and the others. All that business of spending the night in the beds of serving girls; he probably spent most of the night plotting with his friends. And she, Mary, had tut-tutted, dismissed him as a sexual addict and slept like a log. Meanwhile, they were downstairs, working it all out.

To start with, they had planned the fake ambush, with the driver being hit – but clearly not killed – by the arrow. Mary shook her head. No doubt he had been wearing a thick leather vest under his jerkin as protection – just like the Queen of Scots.

A cold snake of anger suddenly squeezed itself tightly around her gut as she recalled Rolleston's words that morning, dropped casually into the conversation. "I will take a short stroll around the town," he had said, "then I will come back here and await your return."

A short walk to the castle, more like – to prepare the Queen for their plan to save her life, and to fit their armoured breastplate!

The devious, scheming sod!

Mary clenched her fists so hard that her nails nearly broke the skin.

The Queen had stepped out for her walk much later than usual – no doubt as she was having her armour and bladder of pig's blood fitted.

And hadn't Mary played her part to perfection, doing exactly what the Catholics had wanted and planned for her?

Hadn't she just..?

Oh yes, their plan was even more devious than Walsingham's – especially as it used his scheme as their start-point…

Mary forced herself to unclench her fists, and to take a deep breath.

So, they have the Queen of Scots. What happens now?

The damned woman would be gloating over her freedom and travelling triumphantly towards London. And what's more, she would be able to travel openly, thanks to Frances Barwell so conveniently 'covering' for her in Sheffield.

On the way she would be presented to as many Catholics as possible; stirring them on to support her cause. There would be forces raised, as Catholic landowners, emboldened by the sight of the woman they believed to be their true queen, pledged their militias and the men in their service. No doubt the word would also be going out to the Catholics in the north, still smarting from the failure of the Northern Rebellion a few years earlier.

Walsingham's coded letter and the Earl's translation would be presented as proof of the plot, bringing not only the committed Catholics to her side, but also those so-called Protestants who still secretly believed in the old ways of worship. Damn Rolleston for sneaking back and stealing them off the table before the Earl had thought to lock them away.

Damn the unfeeling bastard to hell!

With a growing Catholic army behind her, the Queen of Scots would become an unstoppable force, sweeping towards London to claim the throne. At best she would take it unopposed, and at worst there would be a bloody battle, with many lives lost on both sides.

None of which would be happening if she, Mary de Beauvais, had not been such a stupid, trusting, bloody idiot, revealing the plot when she had been sworn to secrecy by the Queen herself…

Mary took another deep breath, forcing herself to calm down and consider how this would play out.

When the new queen was crowned as Mary II – what then?

Of course, she would restore Catholicism.

Once again every man, woman and child in the land would have to immediately and uncomplainingly change the daily practice of their religion. A wave of priests would miraculously appear, emerging from their foul-smelling hiding holes like bears from hibernation, or triumphantly stepping ashore from exile. They would replace the Protestant clergy in every place of worship, from the smallest chapel up to Canterbury itself. Anyone suspected of having an English bible would be open to an accusation of heresy; liable to be arrested and have their home searched. An open charter for petty jealousies to flourish and for society to split apart like a busting balloon.

Philip II in Spain would look on with approval, no doubt offering to help 'catholicise' England by sending over the Inquisition – and with it would come the terrible burnings and martyrdoms that had so characterised the first Mary's reign twenty years before.

And Elizabeth?

Mary put her head in her hands.

Thanks to her utter stupidity, the poor Queen was going to be faced with the one thing she had justly feared: the loss of her crown to her Scottish cousin.

And not just her crown. For how would the new Queen Mary treat her rival, who had kept her imprisoned for many years in castles that were so damp and drafty that it had given her painful arthritis, and then tried to have her killed by a secret assassin?

Mary stared blankly into the fire, and it seemed as if she was back in her rooms in the Tower, with Elizabeth putting a hand over hers.

"I need your understanding and your counsel..."

And what had that understanding and that counsel given to Elizabeth?

Imprisonment and almost certain death.

Mary felt as if she was about to throw up.

She took a further deep breath and stood, clutching the table for support.

"This is my mess," she said to herself. "My own stupid, stupid fault. So what now?"

She steadied herself and looked into the fire.

"I have to stop them. Whatever it takes, at least I have to try..."

Or die in the attempt?

Yes!

She ran out of the tavern and headed back into town.

---0---

A few enquiries later, she arrived at the market square, and found a horse dealer in one corner.

He was a tall, bald man with one lazy eye and the other constantly roving independently around the square as he talked.

"A horse for you, young master?" he asked, when Mary had stated her needs. "For sure. I have the finest beast right here."

Mary eyed the sorry-looking horse standing alone behind him. "Is that the only one you have? I need to ride at speed on the most urgent business."

"Aye, it is the only one. Trade has been brisk this day, with talk of the Queen of Scots being shot. There are those who wished to be away from the town at speed and sought a beast on the spot." He gave a small chuckle that was more of a sneer. "But, Master, the good news for you is that like all fine dealers, I have saved my best till the last." He gave her a yellow-toothed smile. "He is a worthy beast I tell you, and will take you far without complaint or tiring, at a trot, an easy canter, or even at a gallop."

"And you have a saddle, a bridle and reins?" she asked, deciding she had little choice, if she wanted to be away quickly.

She had decided against going back to the Crossed Keys for her own horse, in case any of Rolleston's men were watching it. They would no doubt be expecting her to go back there – and it was only by good fortune that she had overheard them in the Cock and Bull and avoided it.

"That I have young master," the dealer said, without either of his eyes quite meeting hers.

A few minutes later a price was agreed – which was more than Mary wanted to pay, but considerably less than he had first asked. She handed over the coins from her purse and the deal was done. Then she swung up into the saddle, gathered the reins and made her slow way out of the crowded market square, then out onto the streets of Sheffield and the road south.

CHAPTER THIRTY-FIVE

Mary urged the horse through the narrow streets out of Sheffield, surrounded by crowds who seemed to have little care for the rider in their midst with an increasingly urgent need to get past. They seemed more content to gather in shocked huddles, no doubt sharing increasingly salacious stories of the assassination attempt at the castle.

As she rode, Mary began to think the horse dealer had deliberately sold her a stinker. Far from being eager to move, it plodded along without any sense of urgency, and although it would have been difficult to proceed any quicker through the milling crowds, Mary could sense the horse was not particularly eager to speed up. It was like driving a large car with a tiny engine.

A bread seller with a barrow of loaves suddenly stopped right in the middle of the road and started to sell a loaf to a woman a grey coif, causing Mary to slow the horse even more and plod round.

"Have a care, man!" shouted the trader, looking up. "You would knock over my barrow and spoil my loaves!"

Mary did not respond aloud, but muttered "moron" under her breath as she continued past them.

Once she got moving again, Mary reviewed her plan. The first stop had to be the traveller's inn a couple of miles outside Sheffield where she and Rolleston had left the carriage. Assuming that the Scottish Queen would want to travel in some comfort after her various ordeals, it seemed reasonable to suppose that they would stop to collect the carriage. Indeed, it made sense that Rolleston had wanted to leave the carriage there, as it would be available for their journey south once they were away from Sheffield.

Mary urged the horse into a gap in the crowd and looked up. The town gate could just be seen ahead. The sooner she could get clear of all these blasted people, the sooner she could make some speed – and maybe even catch Rolleston and the Queen at the inn.

With that hopeful thought, Mary rode out of the gates and into open countryside.

Once she had a clear road ahead, she squeezed her legs to try and get the horse up to the 'easy canter' promised by the dealer.

Unfortunately the horse had other ideas, and reacted to her instructions by slowing its walking pace. "Oh come *on*!" Mary snapped, digging her heels in. But her normal empathy with horses didn't appear to work on this beast, rather it seemed to take pleasure in doing the exact opposite of what she wanted. The more she urged it, the slower it went. So in the end she stopped flapping around on its back like an angry swan, and instead tried not urging it at all. However, this seemed to be exactly what the horse had really wanted all along, and it settled itself into a leisurely walk.

So by the time they finally ambled into the yard at the traveller's inn, Mary had used every swear word she knew at it, and had even made up a few new ones as well.

She slid from the horse's back and looked it hard in the eye.

"If England falls to the Catholics, you useless, brainless donkey," she hissed in its ear, "it will be your fault. Do you hear me?"

The horse whinnied and raised its head, then bared its teeth at her, as if to say that it was all her fault and nothing to do with him. "Come on, you pathetic piece of dog-meat," she continued, dragging it into the stables.

The inside was dark. Unlike many of the inns she had stopped at, which just had a high roof supported by a single wall on one side and stout wooden pillars on the other, these stables were a secure, dry, four-walled building, giving the horses real protection from the cold winds. The only light came from the door and gaps in the wall boards that threw random beams of light around the building.

Once Mary's eyes became accustomed, she could see that there was a large hay bale at one end, and beside it a blackened wood water-trough about the size of a modern bath. The smell of sweating horses and their waste was overpowering, so she found an empty stall as fast as she could, tied the horse to the rail, then walked back out into the fresh air of the main yard.

The first thing was to see if the carriage was still there, which would mean Rolleston and the Queen would likely be there as well. If not, then she would have to think again…

Mary started looking around for the familiar shape. There was a chance she was not too late. Rolleston had probably not been too far ahead, as he would have needed time to get the Queen away from the castle, tend to any injuries she had sustained from the shooting and the fall onto the cobbles, then get her onto a horse and out of Sheffield. No doubt they would have had just as much difficulty getting through the crowds as she had. Although they would have made more speed once they had hit the clear roads.

Damn the dealer's slow, plodding horse!

There was no immediate sign of the carriage in the courtyard, so she ran round to the back of the stables, hoping to see it standing there, solid and real. But there was nothing other than some weeds, a bale of hay and a few barrels.

With a muttered curse, she went back to the yard, just as a bright-eyed old man poked his head out of the stable door.

"I be the ostler here, young master," he said. "Is that your horse put just now in yonder stall?" he pointed back into the stables. She nodded. "Shall I have some water and hay for it?"

"Thank you," Mary replied, resisting the temptation to suggest a humane killer would be more appropriate, and trying to make her voice sound as gruff as she could.

She was about to walk into the inn to ask about Rolleston, when she had an idea. She followed the old man back inside.

As her eyes adjusted again to the dim light, she could see he was putting hay in front of her horse. He then went to the water trough and scooped up a pail, which he carried back and poured into the horse's own trough.

She cleared her throat. "I am seeking some companions who may still be here," she asked. "Can you tell me if they have departed already?"

The ostler came out of her horse's stall, wiping his hands on his apron. "I will certainly try, master," he answered. "Picture them to me."

"A tall man dressed as a merchant, an older man with a grey beard, a thickset man and one with a wounded hand. They would have had a tall red-haired woman with them also."

"Oh aye, master," he said with a smile. "I recall them well. They left in a fine carriage but half an hour or so ago…"

Half an hour! If only that lazy old nag had gone at a reasonable pace, she might have caught them!

The ostler was continuing. "…The merchant – I heard one call him Rollwood or similar, and he called another Antony, I think it was – this Rollwood, he gave me a farthing for my care of his horses. The lady said not a word, and indeed she seemed quite unwell – so they had to help her into the carriage." He paused. "Most strange, I thought it, for when they helped her up, she seemed greatly dismissive of their assistance, as if she was a noblewoman, for all her lowly attire." He frowned. "Now what was her name? They called her Mistress somesuch, as they helped her into the carriage." He thought some more. "…Mistress Anne C-something, it was."

"Carter?"

The ostler smiled happily. "Aye, master, that was it. Mistress Anne Carter was her name. That was it."

Oh, really?

REALLY?

Rolleston was going to pay for that little joke!

She fished in her purse for a farthing, then took a deep breath. "But half an hour since they left?" she asked, handing it over.

"Much obliged, master." He bit the farthing, then pocketed it. "Maybe more, maybe less. If your horse is fresh, you will soon catch them."

Mary looked back at the dealer's nag, chewing on its hay. As if knowing it was being discussed, it turned and eyed her moodily. Even at its freshest, this horse would never go fast enough. She would need to find another, and quickly.

She glanced across at the other stables. There were five further stalls, with a horse's hindquarters visible in four of them. If only one of these others was her ride, rather than the obstinate mule she had come here on…

"Yes," she said. "Thank you for your help."

He nodded, and as he turned to leave, a man walked into the light of the doorway. Standing there silhouetted, all Mary could see was that he was reasonably tall and well-built, with a rakish cap and his hands on his hips.

Rolleston?

The man moved into the building, and one of the random beams of light picked out his body like a searchlight. He was wearing a fine brown doublet with gold edging, yellow trunk-hose split with brown and gold, black hose and a leather garter. Then he walked forward again, so the beam of light moved up to his face. Mary let out the breath she must have been holding. She had never seen this man before.

"You, ostler," he snapped. "Is my beast ready? I ride out in but a half hour."

"Yes, master," the ostler replied, looking towards a well-built chestnut mare in the furthest stall. "I will have her saddled and ready most presently."

"And you have brushed her well? Mane, tail and coat?"

"I have that, master."

"And her hooves, have they been oiled?"

"Indeed they have."

The man drummed his fingers on his sword hilt. "Good. I will be having my ale and pie in the parlour, and will be back before the half hour."

"She will be ready in good time, master, my word on it."

The man did not reply, but marched out of the stables and could be heard striding across the cobbles to the inn.

Mary turned back to the ostler. "I thank you, good man, for your help." She walked to the door and stopped. "My horse requires but hay and water – that is all."

Then she walked over to the inn herself.

---0---

The familiar smell of sweat and candle smoke replaced that of horses as Mary entered the parlour of the inn; a smell so strong that she could almost taste it. Taking a seat, she looked around for the horse-owning man, and spotted him a few tables away. Now she could see his face more clearly in the light of the candle on his table, she could see how he could be mistaken for Rolleston, if a little older and a little rougher around the edges. Indeed, he seemed to have the look of a yeoman about him, rather than a man of the high-status that his clothes suggested.

"Another fraud," she muttered under her breath. Then she put her hand to her mouth as a dreadful thought occurred, and she murmured, "Am I becoming an Elizabethan snob? Oh, goodness. I do hope not!"

She looked round to see if anyone had heard, as there was not much noise from the few travellers sitting at the various tables. But they were nursing their tankards of ale and plates of bread and cheese or pie, and chatting quietly. A dog was working the tables for scraps, running from one hand to the next with its tail wagging. After a moment it approached Mary.

"Sorry old chum," she said softly, "nothing for you here." The dog, which looked like some form of long-legged terrier, put its paws up on her lap and examined the table, as if it didn't quite believe her and had to check for itself. "See?" she said, "nothing there." The dog gave her a disappointed look, then jumped down and bounded across to the next table.

Mary looked back at the man, to see that a pretty young serving girl was just bringing a tankard of ale and a steaming pie to his table. As the girl leaned over to put them down, Mary saw the man put his hand up and grab at her chest. The girl froze. Then he smiled at her, as he moved his hand slowly up to her collar, before working it under her linen chemise like some dreadful burrowing insect. Then, as Mary watched in sick fascination, he slowly slid his hand down, until she could see it was clearly cupped around the poor girl's breast.

"Good firm duckies, my girl," she heard him say with a sneer. "If I was not so soon leaving, I would have a proper look at them…" He withdrew his hand and with his eyes still fixed on the girl's, he brought his palm up and sniffed at it. "…And maybe more."

The girl pulled her collar back up, as if by fixing her clothing she could undo what had just happened, then she scurried away without responding. It looked to Mary as if the girl had experienced this kind of behaviour many times before from such a man, and even if it was not unexpected, it was certainly disgustingly unwelcome.

After she had gone, the man took a deep swig from his tankard and smiled to himself as he started to eat his pie.

Mary sat back and shook her head slowly. What a total *prick*. Just like Rolleston – another heartless, misogynistic example of Elizabethan manhood.

And just like Rolleston, she was not going to let this go unpunished. It was going to be a pleasure to kill two birds with one stone; as not only was she going to steal his horse – for the sake of Queen and Country, naturally – but she fully expected this would bring the heartless sod down a peg or two when he found it gone.

Mary reckoned she only had a few minutes until the ostler had the man's horse saddled and ready. And judging by the speed the fellow was now wolfing down his pie, he would be heading out at about the same time. So she had better move quickly herself.

She got up and slipped outside, then hurried over to the stables. Peering round the doorway into the dim building, she could just make out movement by the man's horse. Then there was the sound of a hand slapping a horse's neck.

"There, girl, there. You are quite the one, are you not, my lovely?"

Mary heard a rustle of straw, then the sound of footsteps coming towards her. Quickly she moved round to the side of the building and flattened herself against the wall. She waited a few seconds, then peered round. The ostler was heading away towards the inn; no doubt to let the man inside know his horse was ready.

Mary slid into the stables and went up to where the mare was standing, fully saddled.

"Yes, you are quite the one, aren't you?" she said as she stroked its neck. "But now you are going to be mine. I shall call you Justice. Do you like that, Justice?" The mare gave a small whinny. "I will take that as a 'yes', shall I?" Mary lifted the stirrup. "Now, Justice, I need to make sure we fit each other well. Your previous master had quite long legs." She shortened the stirrup, then went round to the other side. Justice moved over slightly, giving her more room. "Thank you," Mary said as she adjusted the other stirrup, "I think we are going to understand each other brilliantly." Then she slipped her finger under the leather girth strap. "Nice and tight," she observed. She undid the halter rope and led Justice out of the stall. A mounting block was standing to one side, so she pulled it over with her foot, then used it to swing herself up and settle into the saddle. "Right, my girl, let's go."

She squeezed her heels and Justice trotted out of the stables, just as the front door of the inn opened and the mare's previous owner came out with the ostler.

"Oi!" he shouted and started to run towards her.

Mary put her head down, gave a firm kick and flicked the reins. "Come on, girl!" she urged, and there was no delay or sluggishness in Justice's response. With a neigh and a shake of her head, she was off like a Derby winner coming out of the stalls. As they passed through the gate at the end of the courtyard, Mary glanced back over her shoulder. The man was skittering to a stop on the cobbles, then snatching off his cap and flinging it down in anger.

"Forget him now," Mary said. "We've got a queen to find!"

She put her head down again, lifted her bottom like a true jockey and galloped out onto the lane heading south.

CHAPTER THIRTY-SIX

Justice was as fast and sure-footed as the dealer's horse had been slow and ponderous, but after cantering for over an hour, it was clear that she was starting to tire. So when the road went through a small village, Mary slowed her to a walk and started peering around in the growing darkness for a horse trough. She found it by a small green, and let Justice enjoy a long and necessary drink.

Eventually the mare lifted her head from the water, but left it hanging low as she fixed her dark liquid eye on Mary.

"You are tired, aren't you, old girl?" Mary said as she ran her hand down Justice's damp neck. "You've been running hard, and I am pretty sure we will have got closer to those blasted Catholics, but you do deserve a rest." Then she added, "Just a short one, mind, as we must press on. We need to get there as soon as possible, and that means tonight."

Without re-mounting, she led Justice toward some flickering lights on the other side of the green. "Look," she said, as a swinging sign became visible above the door of one of the buildings. "A tavern. I could do with a drink as well."

The tavern was a sad-looking tumbledown; a single-storied, timber-framed building, with cracks in the walls and a thatched roof with gaps that suggested it would be far from watertight in the rain. There were two windows on each side of the front door, all with dirty and crooked shutters. As she walked up through the small courtyard towards the door, she spotted a horse rail to one side, so she walked Justice over. There was a long manger by the rail, containing a few sparse bundles of hay.

"Look, Justice," she said, trying to sound bright for the horse's sake, "you get to have dinner as well!" She tied the horse with a rope long enough to let her reach the hay, then went inside and sat at a small table by one of the windows. There was a clear patch in the glass where she could see Justice across the courtyard by the light of the rising moon. The mare had her head down in the manger and seemed to be chewing contentedly.

Mary chuckled. It was good to keep an eye on Justice; heaven forbid that someone might try to steal her.

A serving girl came over, and Mary ordered a pigeon pie and ale. They arrived shortly, giving off a delicious, warm, comforting smell. She breathed it in deeply, triggering a sudden memory of being back in the Great Hall at Grangedean Manor having supper with William and the kids…

Oh to be back there in reality, in place of this shabby, dirty, run-down little tavern in the middle of nowhere, and to be with her family instead of being alone…

Mary shook her head in frustration. Now was not the time to descend into self-pity.

She cut into the pie, and this time the smell actually made her mouth water. She took a piece of meat. It was nothing like the pies that came out of the Grangedean kitchens; indeed, Ruth would never let the cook produce anything like this, but right here, right now, it was just what she needed.

Shortly after this, when the food and drink were settling comfortably in her stomach, she sat back and found herself giving a long, deep, chest-stretching yawn.

In truth, it was not surprising she was tired. It was incredible just how much had happened in the space of one day. Mary closed her eyes.

What a day it had been…

After a particularly bad night's sleep, she had tried – and it seems, failed – to assassinate the Queen of Scots; uncovered the Catholic counterplot; stolen a horse and ridden like a demon through the dusk after the Queen of Scots in order to... what? To kill her properly this time?

Mary gave a deep sigh. Somehow it didn't seem like that was a good option anymore. Somehow it seemed like the failure of the first attempt was a sign that maybe she wasn't cut out to be a cold-blooded assassin. Had it been in truth a lucky escape – when she'd pulled that trigger and not actually killed the Queen?

But then, if she didn't kill Mary, Queen of Scots, Walsingham's plot would fail, Elizabeth would probably be deposed and executed, Catholic-inspired terror would stalk the land – and if Walsingham didn't have her burned at the stake, then Mary, Queen of Scots most certainly would.

There was no doubt that bringing forward the death of one woman would save countless other lives…

She pushed with her foot at the bag she had put under the table and felt the reassuring weight of the gun inside. There was no doubt that she, Lady Mary de Beauvais, had both the means, and the motive, to make sure that finally, that death would happen.

Could she do it? Could she once again pull that trigger, knowing that fate had stepped in previously to prevent her actions having a lethal outcome?

Mary opened her eyes and let out a long, frustrated breath.

That was a decision she would have to face if she caught up with Rolleston and the Queen of Scots.

When she caught up with Rolleston and the Queen…

Because if she did not catch up with them, then her only option would be to watch Elizabeth be deposed and killed, and know, in whatever time she had left before Queen Mary had her found, arrested, tried and executed for treason, that it was all her fault. That she had a chance to put things right, and failed.

She could not – she must not fail!

Mary stood up, knocked back the last of her ale, then grabbed her bag and left the tavern.

CHAPTER THIRTY-SEVEN

The signpost at the crossroads swept past so quickly that it took a moment for Mary to realise that it was the one that pointed to Nottingham, Newark and Bridgeford. She pulled Justice up so sharply that the mare dropped her hindquarters and almost reared up, as she struggled to come to a stop. Finally Justice was standing still, her flanks heaving and her head tossing, steam rising into the moonlit sky from her neck.

Mary turned the horse round and they trotted back to the signpost.

"I am sure it was this one," she muttered, "although it looks quite different at night." She peered at the moss-edged wooden signs with their crudely carved lettering looking very black in the light of the moon. "Yes," she said, "it is definitely the right one." She wheeled Justice round to the direction of 'Bridgeford'. "Come on," she urged the mare, and they set off down the rough path.

The glow from Oak House was visible even before she got up to the gate; it was lit up like a Christmas tree with candles blazing in all the windows, giving it a cosy warmth that was quite at odds with the potential threat of its inhabitants.

Once Justice was tied securely to a tree out of sight of the house, Mary dropped to the earth by the gates and peered through. Oak House was only around twenty yards away, so she didn't need the gun's scope to see clearly who was inside.

Rolleston, Brooks, the archer and the driver were in the parlour, standing by the fire with glasses in their hands. They seemed to be very pleased with themselves; she could see them through the small panes of glass throwing back their heads with laughter, and taking great gulps of their wine. It did not need Sherlock Holmes to deduce what they were so pleased about – and no doubt Mary's ears should be burning as they re-lived their successful spiriting away of the Scottish Queen from under her unsuspecting nose.

Mary clenched her fists. It wasn't just her ears that were burning out here in the dark; once again she felt her anger flaring up after being played for a fool.

There were other men drinking and chatting with them. Mary slowly unclenched her fists and counted a further six; all dressed in the fine clothes of merchants and gentlemen, but all with the broad shoulders and heavy build of fighting men. Each man was armed, with broad swords at their sides and poignard knives at their belts.

Mary slid slightly further back, putting herself deeper into the shadow of the wall. One woman against ten men? Even if these were the only guards for the Scottish Queen and there weren't others in rooms she couldn't see, it was still scary odds.

She looked to the upstairs chamber. A pair of candles were burning in the window, their brightness making it difficult to see past them into the room. Maybe the magnification of the 'scope would help. She wriggled round to get the gun out of her bag, then decided she might as well load a cartridge into the breech, just in case. Settling herself into a comfortable position, she poked the barrel through the gate and sighted the crosshairs on the window. Now she could see into the room better, but her low angle meant that all she could see was the top of a four-poster bed.

She waited in case anyone moved inside, but nothing happened for many minutes, until suddenly the two candles were snuffed out, and heavy drapes were pulled across the window. If the Scottish Queen was in there, then she had retired for the night.

Mary turned back to the parlour, and focused on the men inside. She picked Rolleston in her sights, her finger hovering over the trigger as she kept him centred in the crosshairs. The small panes of thick, curved crown glass seemed to change the shape of his head as he moved; enlarging his chin and making his nose grow like Pinocchio.

The temptation to take the shot was strong, but Mary resisted. Not only was the thick glass likely to deflect it, but she would be giving up the element of surprise – her only chance to shorten the odds in her favour. If she took a pot at Rolleston, the others would immediately scatter, and no doubt hurry the Scottish Queen off to some place of greater safety, like the Secret Service around a US President. Then they would all spill out of the house to hunt down the lone assassin.

Better to deal with Roger bloody Rolleston later.

Mary followed him idly for a few more minutes, before spotting a woman coming into the room; well-dressed, grey-haired and looking around forty. She was carrying a large pewter jug and moved amongst the men, filling their glasses and chatting to each. She put a hand on Brooks's shoulder as she poured his wine – so presumably this was his wife. Mary moved her finger well away from the trigger as she watched Mistress Brooks finish replenishing the men's wine, before poking the fire, then leaving.

It was going to be a long night.

---0---

The dawn sun crept across Mary's face, waking her with a start.

For a moment she had no idea where she was. She stared bleary-eyed at a distant red-brick wall between the trees.

She was cold, she was stiff, and her neck was sore. Then it came back to her; she was outside Oak House, with the Scottish Queen hopefully still inside. As if a dream remembered, her situation started to become clear again. There had been the agonisingly long wait as the men laughed and drank in the parlour, seeming never likely to retire for the night. She had remained by the gate in the dark waiting for them to leave so she could do the same, until finally they had all yawned, scratched their chins and drifted off one by one until the parlour was empty.

Only then had Mary felt it was safe for her to try and get some sleep as well, so she had slunk over to the small, forested area a hundred yards back, where she had left Justice.

There she had found a small hollow filled with musty autumn leaves, and had crawled in, pulling the leaves over her to create some small warmth, and using her bag as a pillow.

And now it was morning. She stood and brushed off the leaves, then took a deep breath to steady herself. She was going to have to get moving if she was going to rescue her mission and stop the Queen of Scots from progressing south.

She gathered her bag and the gun, then glanced across to where she had tied Justice. At first there was no sign the horse, and for a dreadful moment she thought that maybe the previous owner had taken the mare back while she slept, but then there was a movement amongst the trees and Mary picked out the shape of a horse with her head down, eating some grasses. Nicely camouflaged.

She ran through the wood until she was beyond the gates to Oak House, then doubled back to a large oak. She had spotted it in the moonlight the night before, around thirty yards back from the gates. She looked at it again in the morning light. It seemed ideal – the perfect vantage point for the plan she had formed.

Putting the gun in the bag and securing it over her shoulders, she reached for the lowest branch and swung herself up. Then she climbed further until she reached a large wide branch. It was not too high, which gave her a good angle of fire, and had a number of higher branches hanging near, giving her some cover.

Settling herself onto the branch with her back to the trunk, she took out the gun and checked the chamber. The cartridge was still there, but she ejected it anyway, checked it over, then re loaded it. She jiggled her hand in the pocket of her jerkin, and felt the reassuring smooth coldness of the other cartridges. Plenty of ammo.

Then she put the gun down on her lap, and waited.

CHAPTER THIRTY-EIGHT

It was around an hour later that the driver brought the carriage round to the front of the house. He stayed in his seat, as the six men Mary had seen the night before rode up, all armed with swords. They clustered around the carriage, their horses skittering about and raising their heads as the men chatted to each other. This seemed to make the pair harnessed to the carriage also skitter nervously, until the driver called out something that seemed to calm them down.

Rolleston and Brooks came out and conferred with the driver, then Brooks went inside, while Rolleston stood to one side of the carriage, glancing around. Maybe Mary was feeling vulnerable, but it looked suspiciously like he was deliberately noting possible hiding places.

She froze as he looked directly towards her tree.

Then he started to move in her direction.

Was he looking for her, knowing she might have followed them to Oak House? Was it her imagination, or was he staring straight at her as he walked? Surely he hadn't spotted her? Mary mentally shook her head. She was reasonably high up, the tree was at least fifty yards from the house, and she was sitting far back on the branch. She glanced briefly down at her sleeve. Her jerkin and breeches were made of dark serge and were covered in dirt after she had been wearing them for a day and slept a night in the open. She had even deliberately muddied her face with a liberal smearing of dirt, in addition to the darkening she had added the morning before to look like a man. So she should be nothing more than a vague shape blended into the distant tree itself.

But he continued to walk towards her.

Now he was close to the gate, still staring directly at the tree.

There was no other option; she would have to take him out if he came through the gate – and damn the consequences. She raised the gun slowly and put her eye to the sight.

Rolleston's face jumped into focus.

She centred the crosshairs on his forehead. It seemed as if he was looking straight at her, his piercing blue eyes under the heavy brow drilling directly into hers. Then he looked down. Mary dropped her sight to see what he was looking at. His hand was on the latch. He lifted it and started to open the gate.

She raised the sights to his head again, and settled her finger on the trigger.

Just walk through that gate, Roger, just you walk through, and I swear it will be the last thing you ever do.

Rolleston stopped, almost as if he had heard her.

She held her breath, as he turned his head and looked back. She glanced up and saw that Brooks was standing a few yards in front of the carriage, his hands on his hips.

"Roger?" she heard him call out.

Rolleston stopped with his hand on the gate and glanced back over his shoulder.

"Roger?" Brooks repeated.

With a last look at the tree, Rolleston turned on his heel and strode back.

Mary let out a long, slow breath and released her grip on the gun, bringing it down to her lap.

Rolleston got back to the carriage, and spoke urgently to Brooks, who nodded and hurried back into the house.

Just then Mistress Brooks came out with a tall red-haired woman in a plain grey gown.

Right. It was time to finish this.

Mary raised the gun again and took aim. Once more the Queen's familiar head jumped into her sights.

Mary slowed her breathing, keeping the crosshairs centred on the aristocratic profile, as she settled the trigger into the crook of her finger and started to squeeze…

The Queen's head suddenly disappeared from view.

Mary released the trigger and looked up.

Brooks was helping the Queen into the carriage, forcing her to bend down as she stepped in. Once inside, the Queen was only visible through one window, and then from the waist down.

Damn! Damn, damn, damn!

So now it would have to be plan B. Wait until the carriage comes closer.

Mary lowered the gun and tried to let her thumping heart settle as she waited for the carriage to move, but it seemed an agonisingly long time. There was plenty of comings and goings from the men and horses – one riding away then back with a costrel for the driver; another dismounting and running into the house before re-emerging with a bag for the Scottish Queen – but at the centre of this maelstrom of activity the carriage itself remained frustratingly still.

Just as Mary was wondering if she should maybe climb down and sneak up to the gates for a possible shot, the driver cracked his whip over the horses' backs. With a clatter of the wooden wheels on the cobbles, the carriage started to move; the riders all following close behind.

Giving a small sigh of relief, Mary lifted the gun again to her shoulder and took aim at the moving vehicle. As it turned towards the gates she was able to pick up the window in her sights, but the angle was still too sharp, and she could not see the Scottish Queen inside.

The carriage came up to the gates and one of the riders came forward, dismounted and opened them both up fully.

"Come through, Queen of Scots," Mary muttered. "Come on through so I can see you."

Once the carriage was past the gates, it turned slowly onto the track, so Mary had the open window more clearly in her sights, with the Scottish Queen's head in plain view inside.

Now it was time to make sure she finally finished the job.

But she did not take the shot.

There was a sudden whoosh, then a loud cracking thump that was so close it almost deafened her.

With a shocked scream she looked away from the carriage, and stared in cold horror at the arrow shaft that was now quivering in the tree beside her head, only a couple of inches from her ear.

As the gun slipped from her nerveless fingers and fell to the earth below, she heard a voice, worryingly close by.

"That was to show that I can shoot an arrow as true as I please," the voice said. "Stay still mistress, or I will put the next one through your eye."

A man emerged from the woods; an arrow held loosely in his bow.

It was Nathan the archer.

Mary had no doubt that if she made a sudden movement he would bring the bow up and fire within a fraction of a second. She raised her hands, noting as she did so that he still had one of his in a bandage.

"Aye," he said as he approached the tree, "as you see I still carry my injury from your musket, although it has not prevented me making such a nice shot this moment." He paused. "I was told by Master Rolleston to observe this tree most closely, and the Lord be praised; what do I find but Mistress Carter preparing to murder the true Queen." He chuckled; a dry, empty sound. "So I needs must fire a warning arrow to stop her in the attempt, must I not?"

He came closer and she saw him clearly, as if she was observing him for the first time. He was in his mid-thirties with sandy hair and a ruddy face, dressed in a green tunic under an armoured breastplate. His arms under the tunic bulged with heavy muscles, especially his right arm. "I could have pinned your ear to the tree from a furlong distant should I have wished, you understand?"

She nodded, her mouth dry.

"Good." He stopped a few yards away, while from the corner of her eye Mary saw the carriage disappear round a bend in the lane.

"Come down," he ordered.

As she was lowering herself from the final branch, he picked up the gun and was studying it carefully. "This is the firing weapon that put a hole through my hand as if driven by a burning stick?" he asked, staring at her with wide eyes. "By the Lord, where is the matchlock? The pan for the powder?" His face went white. "Belike 'tis the work of the devil, this?"

"I fashioned it myself," she stated, raising her chin. "It has nothing of the devil in it."

"So you say, mistress," he answered. "But I will have naught to do with it." He turned and threw it into the trees. As it landed, something must have caught the trigger and it fired with a loud crack. The archer crossed himself several times. "Christ in Heaven!" he exclaimed. "And you say there is no devilry in this, that spits out a ball without a human hand?"

"Whatever you say," she muttered, taking careful note of the tree where it landed.

"Now, tis no matter," he continued, "you will walk before me to the house, and there we will find out if there are useful things you know."

Mary made her way up to the gate, which was still open after the carriage had passed through. With her jaw clenched, she carried on up to the house. As she stepped into the hallway, the archer behind her said, "Up the stairs, if you please." At the top he said, "To your left, into the bed chamber."

She had barely had time to register the room with its brightly embroidered wall hangings and four-poster bed, when there was a blinding flash of pain in the back of her head, and the rushes on the floor suddenly came up to meet her.

Then there was blackness.

CHAPTER THIRTY-NINE

Someone seemed to be beating a heavy anvil in the back of her brain as Mary slowly opened her eyes and squinted up at the archer. He was standing over her, observing her with dispassionate curiosity like a scientist studies the object of an experiment.

She groaned and tried to rub the back of her head, but was surprised to find her right hand would not move. She tried her left, but that would not move either. With her breath starting to come in fast, shallow, panicky breaths, she moved her head painfully to both sides, and saw that she was lying on the bed with her wrists tied to each of the posts, so that her arms were spread out like a perverse image of Christ on the cross.

She tried to bring her legs up to kick at the man, but neither leg would move either. She pulled at them with increasing urgency, but they stayed resolutely still. A sharp pain in each ankle made it clear that her legs were also tied up, presumably to the other two bed posts.

Mary stopped struggling and stared hard at the archer. "Let me go," she snarled.

"And why might I do that?" he asked with a thin smile.

There was no realistic answer, so she stayed silent, trying to ignore the throbbing pain in her head, now joined by the agonising tightness of the bonds on her wrists and ankles.

"Listen, woman," he said, his face becoming serious again. "I would know how much you can tell of your foul plot against the true Queen."

"And if I will not tell?" she muttered.

"Oh, in faith you will, I can assure you," he said. "The only question is how much pain you will endure first." Then he produced a short dagger, leaned over her and slowly, deliberately ran the flat of the blade down her cheek. "You will tell, mistress," he repeated, as the blade traced onto her neck and moved softly across her throat.

Mary tried to swallow the burning bile that suddenly came up. "Why ask?" she said eventually. "You seemed to have known it all anyhow."

"Belike we did," he answered, "but we would ensure there are no parts we have missed." He paused, "Parts that may prove most useful to our cause."

She shook her head, trying to ignore the dizzying pain. "Your cause has won," she said. "Your Queen is on her way to London, and I have no doubt she will gather support as she goes."

"Aye," he nodded with a real smile, pulling away the dagger. "Nottingham, Derby, Stratford, Oxford and many others besides – she will cleave each one to her side as she goes, with loyal Catholics emerging from the darkness of the bastard's heresy and embracing once again the true faith."

"Then let me go," she repeated. "I am no use to you."

He laughed; a bitter, twisted laugh with no mirth in it. "Oh, mistress, let me tell you what use you are to me." He leaned forward; his red face coming so close to hers that she could see the snot up his nose and smell the stale bread and ale on his breath. "You will tell me all, that is for sure. But before that, I would have payment for – this." He pulled back a moment, then his bandaged hand appeared in front of her eyes. Even though she tried to turn her head away there was no escaping the putrid smell of rotten flesh from the filthy cloth. He leaned back in. "Then, once you have given me all your secrets, you are right; I will have no use for you. So the only question is how I will dispatch you – mercifully and quick by a swift, deep sweep of my blade across your throat, or slowly by a small painful cut to the belly that could take days to bleed out."

"By Heavens," she said. "Your soul will face eternal damnation for this."

Unfortunately, this seemed to have little effect. "Nay," he said with a satisfied smirk, "you are a cursed heretic. Dispatching you will not only save my soul; it will ensure my everlasting place in Heaven."

She stayed silent.

"But I said first I wanted payment for your injury to my hand," he continued. He put it to his nose and grimaced. "It starts to fester, so that soon I will no longer have its use to pull my bow. And for that, woman, I would have you suffer greatly."

Mary could only look up at the man, her stomach twisting in dread as she waited to hear what particular payment he had in mind.

"I fancy I will take my payment from…" he looked down and paused a moment, then put the heel of his good hand up between her outstretched legs and rubbed slowly, "…from here."

Mary squirmed desperately as he rubbed harder – his eyes glazed and unseeing as his hand moved up and down. After what seemed like a lifetime he stopped, and his eyes focussed back onto her. Then he stood up and began to unbuckle his breastplate, before pulling down his breeches.

With a look of concentration, he turned to her own men's breeches and undid the lacing, then he pulled them roughly down as far as they would go, which, as she was spreadeagled on the bed, was not that far.

But unfortunately, it was far enough.

Mary thought she would be physically sick as she felt the air on her most private parts.

With an almost conspiratorial smile, as if this was some secret encounter that they had planned together, he climbed up onto the bed, and positioned himself over her.

"I would kiss you," he whispered in her ear, his breath making her skin crawl, "but I doubt I would find pleasure in it." Then he lifted his head up slightly as he arched his body in anticipation.

A kiss…

A Gorbals Kiss…

As the Alchemist had shown her…

The archer's jaw was right there above her…

With a force like a canon's fire, Mary brought her head up suddenly and directly into his jaw.

There was a sharp crack as she made contact; his head snapping back and his whole body jolting away as if she had hit him with a taser. Then his head hit the bed post and there was a second, even louder cracking sound, before he fell onto the floor with thump that reverberated around the house.

Mary dropped down onto the bolster, the pain in the back of her head now magnified to the level of a thousand hammers beating on a thousand anvils, and joined by an equal, if not greater, pain in her forehead.

The Alchemist had been right, and it did hurt to give a head-butt. It hurt like hell.

There was the sound of footsteps and a grey-haired woman appeared in the doorway.

"By Heavens!" she cried, "Who are you and what are you doing tied to my bed? What has passed here?" She walked over, and stopped by the archer's prone body. There was a silence as she took in Mary tied up with her breeches pulled down and her femininity on full display, with the archer beside the bed in a similar state of undress. Mary didn't suppose it would take a genius to work out what had been about to happen.

"Nathan is knocked out for sure," observed the woman, who Mary now recognised as Mistress Brooks. "For all he lives still. How came he so?"

"He was about to violate me," Mary said quietly. "So I used my forehead to hit his jaw. It was all I could do."

Mistress Brooks shook her head. "If had not seen it myself, I would scarce have believed it," she said. "And you are bleeding above your eye, which speaks further to the truth of this."

"Will you untie me and let me go?" Mary asked. "I will be most grateful."

"For sure," Mistress Brooks answered, and started on the nearest rope.

"Thank you," Mary said, with a relieved smile. As soon as the bonds were freed, she wiggled her fingers and circled her wrist to try and get some blood back into it.

But instead of moving round the bed, the other woman suddenly stopped and stood back.

"My other hand…?" Mary began, but the woman stepped further away.

"Wait! I know who you are," she said, colour draining from her face until it was as grey as her hair. "You are that Anne Carter that Antony talked of; she who would have killed our rightful Queen." She shook her head. "I would have freed you, and to do what? You would once more go about your evil heretic business."

"Please!" Mary asked, looking the woman directly in the eye. "Can you not see how I have suffered? That man would have raped me, had I not struck him first."

"That is as may be," Mistress Brooks said, her mouth now setting into a hard line. "But you are to remain tied up until my husband returns and says what is to be done."

"But that could be days or even weeks!" Mary cried. "I will be dead if you leave me here like this!" She used her free left hand to check her forehead, and found her fingers sticky with blood. "Will you abandon me here to starve or bleed to death? Have a pity, Mistress Brooks!"

"I have pity enough, but not for heretics." She grabbed at Mary's wrist and pulled it firmly back to the bed post, then re-tied the rope.

"And if that man awakes?" Mary said. "What then?"

"That is for God to decide." As Mistress Brooks stood back, Mary turned her head to look at her. As a woman she looked pleasant enough, and in different circumstances Mary felt she could have formed a friendship, but now was not the time. And indeed, time was the one thing she did not have. All she could think about was that carriage disappearing round the corner, taking all her hopes – and the future of the Elizabethan reign – with it. The longer she stayed tied to this bed, the less chance she had of catching it.

"I see you are determined on this, Mistress Brooks," she muttered. "I would you then leave me in peace to make prayers for my soul."

Mistress Brooks nodded, then went over to the door. With her hand on it, she turned back and seemed to be about to say something, then appeared to think better of it, and left without another word.

As soon as she was gone, Mary started twisting her left wrist to loosen the bonds. Mistress Brooks may have been a fervent Catholic, but, compared to Nathan the archer, she was very poor at tying knots. With a final few twists, Mary was able to slide her hand out. From there she made quick work of the rope on her other wrist; then she freed both her ankles.

Standing upright was not easy and she nearly fainted the first time she tried, but after a brief sit on the side of the bed, then using the nearest post as a support, she was able to stay on her feet. The next thing was to pull up and secure her men's breeches. "All my bits on display!" she said to herself. "I have got to get back into my women's clothes." She finished the lacing. "But first things first."

She took one of the four ropes, rolled Nathan onto his side and pulled his hands up behind his back. He started to groan as she secured his wrists, then his eyelids fluttered briefly as she ran the end of the rope down and tied it to his ankles. "There," she muttered as she pulled the last knot tight, "that will teach you."

His eyes opened and fixed on hers with a deep scowl. He tried to say something, but his jaw didn't seem to work well enough.

"Best not to try talking just now, Nathan," she instructed. "Just enjoy being tied up, eh?"

She knotted the other three ropes into one long length, which she secured to the handle of a heavy chest. Then she opened the window and threw the rope out, before clambering down and dropping lightly to the cobbles below.

Without looking back, she ran as fast as she could go to the gate, then to the tree where Nathan had thrown the gun. After a brief search among the leaves she spotted the steel barrel, grabbed it and ran to where Justice was still tied up, calmly chewing on some wild grasses.

Mary hauled herself up into the saddle, took a deep breath, then gave Justice a small kick. "Come on, old girl," she said, "I hope you're feeling fresh. We have a carriage to catch."

---0---

When Mary got to the crossroads, she was almost falling from the saddle. Despite being an experienced rider, the combination of fatigue, stress – and being hit on the head twice – had left her as weak as a newborn puppy.

"Come on, Justice," she muttered, "we have to do this. We can sleep for a week, but only if we get it done." She studied the signposts. "What was it the archer said? *Nottingham.* He said the Queen would be starting to raise her forces in Nottingham." She wheeled Justice round. "Then that is where we will go."

Mary concentrated on two things as they cantered along the track; firstly, and most importantly, staying in the saddle as Justice leapt over ruts and fallen branches; and secondly, trying to work out how far behind the carriage she might be. Assuming she had only been unconscious for a few minutes – long enough for the archer to tie her to the bed posts – and that the attempted rape itself had only been say ten minutes, then together with her escape from Mistress Brooks, she was probably no more than half an hour behind.

Assuming she was on the right road.

She squeezed her legs into Justice's flanks. "Come on, old girl, this has got to be the right way. Let's keep it going."

But after a few miles she could feel Justice starting to flag, so at the next village she stopped and found the water trough, letting the mare enjoy a long drink. Then, when Justice was done, she led her over to a nearby tavern to have some hay in a stall, while she grabbed a quick meal of pottage and ale herself. She ate as fast as she could, then re-mounted and headed back onto the lane.

Just as she was about to kick Justice back up to a gallop, she saw an old man in a brown smock standing beside a gate. A thought occurred, and she wheeled the horse back and trotted over.

"By your leave, sir," she said, "I have become separated from my companions. Have they passed this way? A carriage pulled by a pair of horses and nine or ten riders accompanying." She smiled hopefully down at him.

There was a frustratingly long pause, and she was about to repeat the question a bit louder in case he was deaf, when he coughed and said, "Well, master, the carriage I saw a while ago was a noble affair, with many fine gentlemen riding beside," he looked her up and down and Mary was conscious that she must present a gruesome sight; a wild-eyed young man in filthy breeches and jerkin, with mud and dried blood all over 'his' face. "You became separated? Or in truth, they wanted you not?" He gave her a sickly grin. "Belike they threw you in a ditch and left you to wild dogs?" He touched his own forehead as if to remind her of the cut she had there. "For I cannot be seeing you as one of their company."

"Well, I do need to catch them up," she said. Then she added with what she hoped was a suitably passive-aggressive smile, "and I thank you for telling me that they passed this way."

She wheeled round again and urged Justice into a steady canter along the lane with a renewed sense of hope. For all that the old fellow had dismissed her as some sort of lying vagabond, he had confirmed that the carriage had indeed passed this way. If she kept up a reasonable and steady pace, with any luck she should catch up with them soon.

---0---

It was not long after she had left the old man that the lane emerged out of the forest, causing Mary to shield her eyes against the bright winter sunshine.

Ahead of her the path ran straight for what seemed like many miles across an open patchwork of fields: some bare and brown after the harvest while others lay fallow.

A flock of birds appeared and started swooping in formations above, creating a series of different shapes and patterns; calling and chittering so noisily that she could hear them clearly above the thudding of Justice's hooves and the regular jingle of her bridle. Then they flew away across the fields, just as another flock appeared directly ahead, and started making new formations of their own. It almost felt like they were choreographing their displays just for her entertainment.

Mary smiled at them, glad of some small diversion from the grim task she still faced. Maybe if she could concentrate on the birds, the winter sun and the joy of riding a great (albeit stolen) horse along the open fields, she could forget why she was chasing so hard after the carriage… and what she still had to do once she caught up with it.

The birds swooped low, bringing her gaze back to the horizon.

An unexpected movement suddenly caught her eye. A loose, dark shape on the lane that did not look like part of the landscape; that seemed to shift and change.

With rising hope, she urged Justice forward to get a closer look. After a couple of minutes, the shape resolved itself into a central square that rocked from side to side, and tall, thin figures around it that moved up and down.

A coach and riders.

Got them," she said to herself.

Mary pulled Justice back and slowed to a brisk trot. Now she had the carriage in her sights, she was cautious about getting too close and being seen. Indeed, if she could make them out on the road ahead, it followed that they could just as easily spot her if they looked back. And judging by Rolleston's suspicions at Oak House that she was hiding in the tree – which he had presumably passed on to Nathan the archer – he would be ever mindful of the possibility that she was still following them.

But it was one thing to catch up with them; it was another to be able to take a further shot at the Scottish Queen and complete her mission. As she trotted along, keeping a good distance from the carriage, she explored possible plans in her mind.

It took a while, but eventually she nodded to herself.

"That's it," she said. "Got it!"

It was a plan that included not only resolving the situation with the Queen of Scots, but Mary's own escape thereafter.

And not forgetting Rolleston.

The plan included something extra special just for him.

CHAPTER FORTY

Mary kept well back while she studied the horizon for a forest that would give her cover to get past the carriage unseen, so she could then carry out the plan.

Eventually a long, low smudge of dark appeared along the horizon, and a few minutes later, she was close enough to see the crows and buzzards circling overhead and hear their calls as they swooped in and out of a deep line of trees.

The carriage ahead disappeared into the darkness of the forest, so she turned Justice off the lane and hopped her over the ditch into a field. Once they landed, Justice needed no urging to move smoothly up to a full gallop. With a shake of her mane, she put her head forward and fairly flew across the field, leaping over the ploughed ridges and dips with all the confidence of a Grand National winner.

In no time they entered the impenetrable-looking darkness, fifty yards or so across from the broad, well-worn path following the carriage.

For a moment it felt as if the lights had suddenly been switched off, so Mary eased Justice back to a steady canter. Over the next few minutes there were plenty of roots and branches to be cleared, trees to avoid and low branches to duck under, before a space opened up between the trees. She stole a quick glance to her right, expecting to be around level with the carriage by now. There was no sign of it through the thick trees. Mary only had a fraction of a second to feel reassured – if she couldn't see them, then they couldn't see her – before she had to drop her head down to Justice's neck as the mare took a flying leap over a fallen log directly under a low branch.

A few yards further on, another clearing allowed them to make even better progress through the forest. Soon after, Mary thought they must now be well past the carriage, so she decided it was time to head over to their right and pick up the lane again. Justice seemed happy with the change of direction, and they made good speed towards where Mary estimated the lane would be running through the trees.

It took a little longer than she thought, but then they jumped a root and Justice landed onto an earthy patch, before gathering herself and galloping across into the trees beyond. It was all so quick that Mary almost didn't register that they had reached the lane, but she was able to pull Justice up and trot her back to be sure.

Once she was certain it was indeed the lane, Mary cantered on in the direction of Nottingham, partly to check that she was not still behind the carriage – although at the speed they had been going, that was unlikely – but also to scout out the perfect tree for her plan.

She found it a couple of minutes later, then walked Justice a few yards further on and tied her up behind an oak.

Then she took the gun from her bag and settled herself to wait.

CHAPTER FORTY-ONE

It was quiet in the forest; the only sounds, apart from the soft thud of horses' hooves on the hard earth, were the jingle of bridles, the creak of leather on leather and the squeak of the wheels, as the nine men rode with the carriage containing the Queen of Scots.

Rolleston and Brooks were level with the driver, while the other six men formed a guard behind the carriage.

"I warrant we shall be in Nottingham within two or three hours, brother," Rolleston said. It pleased him that their mission would soon be moving to the next phase – getting the true Queen in front of her loyal subjects and ultimately, onto the throne in place of that heretic bastard, Elizabeth. It was a fitting reward for all the planning, subterfuge and dissembling needed to get them to this point – from his original pleading to that rogue Wychwoode in the Tower, to getting the Carter woman to play into his hands in Sheffield, to getting away from her at Oak House.

"Aye, brother," Brooks replied. "And we agree that we start with Francis Molineux of Haughton, who spends the winter in his town house in the city. He has stayed true to his faith and will be pleased to lead us to other noted Catholics hereabouts." He nodded. "So our movement will begin to build."

"Quite so," Rolleston agreed. "Francis is still most active for a man of… what is he… above sixty, I warrant? He carries some weight with the true believers of Nottingham." They rode on in an easy silence for a moment, then he added, "The Queen will be pleased to start meeting her subjects. Molineux will be an excellent catalyst to bring them to Her Highness's side."

"For sure," interjected the driver beside them, "And then there is Robert…"

But he never finished his sentence.

There was a sudden loud cracking sound from up ahead. Rolleston thought initially that it was a branch breaking, but then he saw that the driver had dropped the reins and brought his hands up to his chest. For a moment the man looked down in surprise at the bright red blood that started to pulse through them, then, with a small cough, he fell forward and lay still on the running board.

As Rolleston and Brooks stared in horror at the scarlet pool that began spreading out below the body and dripping down onto the path, a woman's voice rang out across the forest.

"Stop there, Roger, please."

A very familiar woman's voice.

Rolleston raised his head and snarled, "Anne Carter?"

"Hello Roger. You are indeed well met," the voice answered, sounding inappropriately conversational. There was a pause. "I said to stop the carriage, please, or should I once again use my gun?"

With a deep scowl, Rolleston put his hand to the bridle of the nearest horse and brought it to a stop. As he did so, one of the rear-guard men rode up.

"What has passed here?" he demanded. "Did I hear a musket..?" Then he saw the driver and turned to Rolleston with a white face.

"By Heavens," he said. "Are we under attack?"

Rolleston nodded. "Aye, Edmund, we are."

"I heard a woman's voice. Are we being threatened by… *that* woman?"

Rolleston nodded again.

"By the Lord's grace, I will have none of this!" Edmund drew his broadsword and started to ride forward. He had barely gone three yards when there was another loud crack from up ahead and he fell backwards out of his saddle as if struck by an axe, landing on the path with a heavy thud that reverberated around the forest. A few crows flew up from the tops of the trees, cawing loudly.

Rolleston's breath caught as he saw the neat red hole punched in the centre of Edmund's forehead.

There was a stunned silence, then Anne's voice came again. "Does anyone else want to try?" she asked. "I have more than enough ordnance here to do the same to each and every one of you. Several times over, in fact."

No-one moved.

"What is it you want, Mistress Carter?" This was Brooks.

"Oh, I think you can guess that, Master Brooks," she answered. "I set out on a mission to protect our true Queen by removing her Catholic rival, and I do not intend to fail."

"Then why do you not take the shot now?" Brooks gestured back at the carriage. "You have her at your mercy."

"Oh, I have no doubt that your heroic queen is presently lying out of my sight on the floor of the carriage. If I took a shot now, the best I could do would be to put a brand-new hole in the royal arse." There was another chuckle. "Anyway, why do you not ask Roger?"

"What you mean you by that?" Rolleston asked, feeling a small, cold chill of fear starting in his belly. Where was the she-devil going with this?

"Oh, come now, Roger, you know full well our plan. You can stop your lying now. These men will find out soon enough whose side you are truly on."

Rolleston felt the cold fear squeeze hard. "I am on the side of the true faith and the true Queen," he said

"Indeed you are, my friend," Anne Carter answered. "But do these men and the lady in the carriage know that means the reformed faith and Queen Elizabeth?"

"It does not," he snapped, feeling a cold sweat starting to run down his back. "And you know full well it does not."

"I know you are a consummate liar, Roger," she answered, her voice taking on a harder edge. Then she gave a bright, tinkly laugh. "But our plan has gone so well thus far, that in truth, I forgive you."

"Your plan?" Brooks growled, turning to Rolleston with a dark frown. "What plan was that?"

"Antony, my true friend," Rolleston said quietly, "surely you do not believe these lies? From a woman? A woman we have played all along for a fool?"

"I know not what to believe," Brooks answered. "But I do know you gained her trust on your journey north, so now I have a doubt that maybe you have conspired with her to bring us to this point? Belike she is no fool, and you have both been playing us?"

"By the Lord's grace, that is no way to address your oldest and dearest friend, Antony! Are we not as close as brothers? Have I not proved myself many times over?" Rolleston held his hands wide in a gesture of supplication. He turned round and appealed directly to the remaining men behind the carriage. "You will vouchsafe me, will you not? I have…" He paused, briefly distracted by the sight of one of them slithering into the undergrowth on his belly like a vengeful snake. "…I have been true to the cause from the start!" he finished, as the man's feet disappeared.

"As well as may be," answered Brooks, "but I fear I need better proof than just your word. This is the gravest matter, and even friends can turn their coats." He paused, chewing the inside of his cheek as he considered Rolleston. "I would you ride forward and capture the woman. Then I will believe you."

"Nay, do you take me for a fool?" Rolleston protested. "If I ride forward and am true to the cause as I say, then she will put a hole in my head just as she did with Edmund there. And if she does not slay me thus, then you will know I am false and you will want to do the deed yourself, brother or no."

Brooks was just drawing breath to answer, when the woman's voice cut across them. "A fine exchange, gentlemen!" she called out. "And I am touched by this talk of brotherly friendship. But I am running short on time. Roger, we need to move on to the next part of our plan."

"There is no plan, woman, as well you know," replied Rolleston.

"Oh, indeed there is, and…" She broke off suddenly. "Oh! Hold on a moment…" Once again the cracking sound of the gun rang out across the forest. Some further crows flew up noisily from the tops of the trees. "Sorry about that," she resumed, once the crows had re-settled. "As you were. One of your men was trying to come up on me in stealth through the undergrowth. I think I got him directly through the eye." There was a further pause, and she said, "Now. Roger. As we agreed, please fetch the Queen of Scots from the carriage and bring her forward."

"You will do no such thing!" Brooks snapped.

"I have no intent to do so," Rolleston replied.

"That is indeed a shame," came Anne Carter's voice. "As it means I will need to put a hole in the head of your oldest and dearest, friend, who you call 'brother', Master Brooks. And then every other man here, until all are felled and the lady herself is at my mercy." There was a silence, then she added, "So belike the outcome is the same in any case."

"You would kill us all?" Brooks said.

"Most certainly. After your companion Nathan hit me over the head, tied me to a bed and prepared to violate me, I find my thoughts of mercy are somewhat strained." Then she added, "And I shall not weep for Mistress Brooks becoming a widow, for she would have left me to die after I had dealt with Master Nathan."

"You dealt with him?" Rolleston asked. "How so?"

"Well, let us just say that the cut I have on my forehead will heal soon enough, but I fear his broken jaw will take much longer. Now," she continued, her tone becoming more business-like, "do I need to count to three before I make Mistress Brooks a widow?"

No-one moved.

Brooks screwed his eyes shut and appeared to hold his breath.

"So be it," she said. "One – two – thr…"

The door of the carriage swung open, and Mary, Queen of Scots stepped out.

With a brief nod to the men behind her, she turned and walked stiffly up towards where Brooks and Rolleston were seated on their horses.

The two of them bowed their heads as she walked past, and Rolleston could see her hand was trembling.

The Queen walked on a few yards further, then stopped and spread her arms out wide.

"You, woman!" she called out in her strong French accent. "*Par Dieu*, you have won! If you want me, my chest is open to you, and this time I have no breastplate to stop the ball. So make your shot and then, *bien sur*, it is done."

There was a long silence in the forest, broken only by the occasional call of a crow and the rustle of the breeze in the tops of the trees.

Rolleston felt sick, expecting at any moment to hear again the crack of the gun, and to see the Queen stagger and fall. Had it come to this, that just when he had been celebrating their success, Anne Carter had come in like an avenging demon to snatch away his victory? It would be the end of all his hopes and dreams, and those of every Catholic soul in England.

Nay, every Catholic in Christendom.

Yet the Queen stayed standing, until eventually she let her arms drop to her side.

That seemed to be the signal Anne Carter was waiting for. "Madam," she said, "it is true I have tried on two occasions to assassinate you, and both times I have failed."

Rolleston saw the Queen's head come up in a small gesture of defiance.

Then Anne said something he would not have expected.

"In truth, I find I no longer have the stomach to make the fatal blow."

The Queen turned her head slightly, as if she was looking back to Rolleston to explain this. "No," Anne continued, "I leave that to the man who you have trusted to set you on the throne, yet who has, all this time, been working against you in secret. Master Rolleston."

Now the Queen turned fully, and Rolleston felt the deep anger – and a hint of disappointment – in her piecing stare.

"Nay, madam, nay," he muttered. "It is all a lie. She is playing us…"

The Queen shook her head and turned back.

"So, madam," Anne called out, "I would ask that you kneel by yonder branch, with your chin resting upon it, and Roger, you may fulfil your destiny by being the man to make the final cut with your sword."

Rolleston looked across at the branch Anne had indicated, a short way ahead. It was sturdy-looking and maybe six inches in diameter, around three feet off the ground. There was no other branch above it, giving space for a swordsman to raise his weapon high. In place of a block, Rolleston could see it was a fair substitute.

"You win, Anne!" he called. "You win. I am sorry for all I did and all the hurt I caused you." He waited but there was no reply. "Does that not give you satisfaction, Mistress Carter?"

"A good try, Roger," she responded. "And in truth all was as we planned, so your apology is not needed. Now I know it is your deepest wish to be the final executioner, so I would you now go to it." Then she added, "I am counting the grey hairs of Master Brooks's beard in the sights of my weapon. Perhaps I will shoot them off one at a time."

Rolleston swallowed back the bile in his throat and drew his slim sword. "This rapier is too slight," he called out. "It will scarce pierce the skin."

"Then use the one from your fallen companion," Anne answered him. "It is broader and heavier."

"And if I refuse?" he asked.

"Then I will do as I promised, and end the lives of all here present, starting with Master Brooks and finishing with you, and then, if I must, the Queen of Scots."

He looked up in the direction of her voice, trying to see her among the trees, but failing to make her out. "You are a cruel and heartless woman, Anne," he said.

"No, Roger, I am not," she answered quietly, although her voice carried to them as clearly as if she had been standing in their midst. "I am an unfortunate at the mercy of powerful men and women, who forced me to act for their own ends, when I wanted nothing more than to live a peaceful life with my husband and family. It is all I have ever wanted, yet I have been wrenched away from them, jailed, threatened, nearly raped and made to become a spy and a cold-blooded killer. I have been lied to and manipulated. And do you know what Roger? I am sick and tired of being the victim in all this, and I tell you, I have really, *really* had enough. So yes, if I am being cruel and heartless, if I am barely able to control my anger, which is hard, Roger, let me tell you, and if I am killing people, it is because I am responding to those who would do the same to me." She paused. "Right now, Roger, I do not like myself. Not at all. Indeed, I do not even recognise myself anymore. But before I can become myself again and believe me there is nothing I want more than that, then we need to finish this thing." She paused again and her voice took on an authoritative tone. "So madam, I ask you please to kneel by the tree, and Roger, you are to perform the final act as we agreed."

"We agreed nothing," Rolleston muttered, but he picked up Edmund's sword in his left hand and tested its sharpness by running his right thumb down the blade, then he shook off the blood from the resulting deep cut and put both hands on the hilt.

The Scottish Queen walked slowly to the tree, then knelt by it with her hands clasped. As he went towards her, Rolleston heard her muttering "In manus tuas, Domine, commendo spiritum meum."

Into thy hands, O Lord, I commend my spirit.

Then she said some more words to him, before placing her head carefully onto the branch, turned away from him, with her neck exposed.

He took a deep breath, then in one swift movement, raised the sword up high and brought it down with all his might.

As the Scottish Queen's head fell away from her body, there was an agonised howl from Brooks. He ran forward with his own sword raised. Rolleston turned with a look of surprise, almost as if he was not expecting it, then almost by instinct he came on guard himself.

"No longer play-acting, Roger," Brooks snarled as they faced each other.

"Nay," Rolleston answered, "For all Anne Carter was an accursed liar. I am still true to our cause."

"I judge a man by his deeds, not his words," Brooks said. Then he made a sharp flick with the edge of his blade, and Rolleston's sword dropped to the ground with a thud.

Rolleston stared blankly at the weapon now lying on the forest floor, then shook his head as he peered down at his right hand.

It was also on the forest floor, still grasping the hilt.

He held the stump up before his face, staring at it as the blood pumped out.

"I have removed the hand that killed the rightful Queen," Brooks said. "And now I will dispatch the rest of her executioner to Hell." He stepped forward and raised his bloody sword. "On your knees, traitor."

"I still say it was a lie…" Rolleston began.

"On your knees!"

Rolleston dropped down and bowed his head.

Brooks came up beside him, and raised his sword over Rolleston's exposed neck.

Rolleston twisted his head and looked up. "Would you kill me without hearing my defence?"

"Aye, I would!" yelled Brooks, and brought down his sword.

Then the other four men ran up. They all crowded around Rolleston's body with their poignards out.

Such was their focus on Rolleston, that none of them saw a horse and rider emerge onto the path up ahead. The rider stopped a moment to observe the scene around the body, then turned the horse towards Nottingham, and set off at a gallop.

CHAPTER FORTY-TWO

The afternoon sun was starting to set as Mary rode into Nottingham, throwing an orange glow across the timbered houses and creating deep shadows in the streets between. There was the usual urban bustle that she had come to expect; roughly dressed men and women scurrying in and out of houses and shops; yeomen and farmers in rough woollen jerkins shepherding pigs and goats, as well as the occasional nobleman riding on a fine charger while seeming to ignore the common rabble that swirled and eddied around his feet like waves around a rock. There was even a fine carriage pulled by two horses, which reminded Mary of the one she had left back in the forest with Brooks and his men. No doubt this was now pressed into service as a makeshift hearse on the return to Oak House, taking back the body of the man Edmund whose sword had served so well as a headsman's axe, the other man who had tried to sneak up on her, and whatever was left of Rolleston.

As well, of course, as the head and body of the Queen of Scots.

This thought prompted the return once again of the horrible image of the Scottish Queen's head being severed from her neck and falling with a sickening thump onto the forest floor – an image she had been trying to block out, mostly without success, ever since it had happened. Indeed at one point she was forced to stop suddenly and run to a ditch to throw up what little she had left in her stomach, as a reaction to the horror of what she had caused to happen.

Would she ever be able to forget that sight? For all it was the objective of her mission, it was a true horror and gave her no satisfaction. Indeed, the only feeling she had as the scene played over and over in her head like a video on repeat, was of increasing disgust – with herself, with her situation, and with all the death and destruction she had caused. It made her feel as if she were a crab's shell that had been scraped clean; as if nothing remained of the living, breathing creature that once existed inside.

A sudden wave of dizziness made her sway in the saddle, and almost fall off.

She sat back and tried to regain her breath.

It must have been because she was hungry. When had she last eaten? It was hard to remember, given what had happened in the forest, but she finally recalled bolting down some pottage a while ago – that was all. So she had to get something to fill her empty stomach, before she fainted completely and fell from the saddle.

Then, once she had eaten, maybe she would be better able to think straight. And what she needed more than anything now was a clear head if she was going to plan how she was going to resolve the final, and seemingly most impossible part of this dreadful mission.

How to find and destroy Walsingham's coded letter before Brooks used it to blow the whole plan apart?

Mary gave a low groan of frustration. It seemed that ever since that fateful evening when Wychwoode had arrived at Grangedean with his men at arms, for every step forward she had taken two back, and this was just another in a long line of such setbacks to be dealt with. Added to which, she had taken two blows to the head and was finding it harder and harder to concentrate. For if she had been thinking straight, she would have found a way to get the letter off Brooks back in the forest, rather than letting the opportunity pass.

As she rode through the streets, it seemed as though the increasing blankness in her mind was like a heavy dark curtain, behind which a set of shapeless and nameless horrors were swirling about like so many demons, all fighting to get out. Whatever they were, they terrified her, so she had to keep the curtain firmly closed. Because that was the only way she could keep herself together, and keep going.

Another wave of dizziness made her grip her knees onto Justice's side in desperation, as she looked around for an inn.

"Must eat, must eat," she muttered to herself, as she stared hard at two people approaching her on horseback. "Because now I am hallucinating."

For what other explanation could there possibly be for seeing William and Olivia riding towards her in the streets of Nottingham?

---0---

Mary almost blacked out as William took her hand to help her dismount, then found herself slipping and sliding as if down a long dark tunnel that ended in his strong arms.

"Come now, my love," she heard him say as he caught her, holding her tight and stroking her head. "Oh, my love, my love, we have found you, we have found you, that is all."

She looked into his eyes and tried to say something; anything.

But no words came.

Instead his concerned face suddenly exploded into a thousand pieces as her eyes flooded with tears, then a great sob racked her body, followed by another and another, and then the heavy curtain was ripped back and all the demonic horrors flooded out; everything that had built up over the past few weeks and days, the endless procession of terrors she had suffered since being arrested; the threat of being tried and burned; the ambush in the forest by Brooks;

taking the shot and escaping through Sheffield; discovering how she had been fooled; and finally, turning the tables on Rolleston so he had been the final executioner. They all flowed out with the force of torrential waters blasting through a breached dam, until she was nothing but a helpless, howling bundle, clinging onto her husband like a rock against the torrent because she needed to know deep down that he was real, and that this was not another cruel fantasy conjured up by her stress and hunger…

Time seemed to stand still as she held on to him, sobbing uncontrollably and squeezing him tightly. He held her for as long as it took for her sobs to thin out, until eventually with a few gasping breaths, they slowed enough for her to manage a few words.

"What..? How..? Why..?" was all she could say.

A hand touched her arm and she turned to find Olivia standing beside her.

"We knew you were in danger, so we came north to find you…" the girl began, but got no further. With a cry like a wounded animal Mary unpeeled herself from William and threw her arms round her friend, once again howling and dissolving into floods of tears.

"Oh my lady, my lady," Olivia crooned softly, holding Mary's shaking head to her breast and stroking her hair, "what has happened to you? What has happened?"

"We are here now, my love," William said, once the sobs had begun to slow down again, then eventually slowed enough for Mary to pull away slightly from Olivia. "We have come to take you back home," he said. "This nightmare is over."

Mary looked up at him and sniffed loudly. "No… no… it… is not…" she managed to gasp between further sniffs and gulps. "I… have… still… got… something… got… something… to do…"

"Well, by the greatest good fortune our paths have crossed," Olivia said, "so if there is aught we can do to help, then we shall."

Mary let Olivia go and staggered back.

"This is… trouble… of my own… making," she managed to say. "My own stupid fault… So I must… must… resolve… it myself." Then she gave them a weak, watery smile. "Although… I am… very glad… to see you both."

"By Heavens, do you suppose we will abandon you now?" William exclaimed. "When we have done so much to find you, and have been blessed by God with the good fortune to come upon you here in Nottingham?"

"No… I… suppose… not."

"Then let us repair inside the nearest tavern, get some good, hot pottage inside you, then you can tell us what is done so far, and what is still to do, and we can decide how best to proceed."

"I… suppose… so," she stammered.

They found a tavern on the next lane, and Mary allowed William to half lead her, half carry her inside.

He made no demands for her story until he had ordered two large bowls of pottage and some bread, then watched as she ate her way through all of it. After that he ordered them a new candle for the table and a tankard of beer each. Then he waited until Mary had drunk half of hers, before leaning forward and saying quietly, "Tell us what you are able, Mary my love, and we shall agree what is best to be done."

Mary looked at each in turn and found that now she had some food and drink inside, her head was less painful and she was starting to think a little more clearly. William was looking at her with a mixture of love and expectation; the look of a man who still trusted her to make good decisions, just as she had for the last ten years as mistress of Grangedean Manor. Olivia was looking concerned and slightly confused, no doubt after having to comfort the woman who, the last time they were together, had comforted her.

Mary nodded slightly to herself. It was clear to her now, that her real loyalties lay with these two, not the men in London. Unlike Rolleston, she could totally trust them. She would not hold anything back. In truth, the more they knew, the more they could help.

Even if they knew the worst of what she had done.

"I was charged by Walsingham, Wychwoode and the Queen," she began, "to undertake a secret mission in return for my release from the charges against me."

"Even though Master Secretary Walsingham was deaf to your entreaties," Olivia asked.

"Nay, that was all false," Mary answered. She steadied herself with a deep breath. "It was all for show. In truth, Master Walsingham actually understood that my future knowledge would indeed be most valuable. He just play-acted."

"Then all the anger on the boat from Master Wychwoode was wholly unreal?" Olivia asked, her eyes wide.

"Indeed it was; designed to make me even more fearful of my fate as a blaspheming sorcerer, and therefore more likely to do their bidding."

"I shall never again trust that man," muttered William. "But what then?"

"I used my knowledge of the future to reveal to Walsingham all the events that are going to happen. I told him of the plots and Spanish war of invasion yet to come, that would all be centred around the life and death of Mary, Queen of Scots."

"And this mission?" William asked.

Mary took a breath. "In order to avoid such a future and to secure Elizabeth's throne," she whispered, "I was charged with assassinating the Queen of Scots,"

There was a long silence, during which Mary noticed William and Olivia exchange worried glances. Eventually, Olivia cleared her throat. "And did you?" she asked softly.

"She is dead, yes. But although I caused it, it was not my hand that struck the final blow." Mary paused, then added, "For all I tried on two occasions to kill her myself, and was unsuccessful."

"By Heavens, Mary," William said, "I would you tell us all, from the start, and with nothing omitted."

Mary nodded, took a gulp of her beer and indicated for the two of them to move in closer. They huddled either side of her, their eyes bright in the light of the new candle and their mouths open in expectation.

Keeping her voice low so as not to carry beyond the table, Mary said, "I will start with an apology to you, William, that I never told you the secret of where – or when – I am from. I am sorry that you had to find out the way you did." She gave him a small kiss on the cheek. "Were you angry with me? I will understand if you were."

He kissed her back. "I was much angered to start, for sure, but then I recalled what a constant wife and mother you are, so I forgave you." He paused, "Tom Melrose helped me see the truth of it – that where you come from does not alter the person you are."

"Well, sadly that is not how Wychwoode saw it," she said, "His arrest meant I had no choice but to undertake this mission – to use the Alchemist's special musket to kill the Scottish Queen."

"But we destroyed it in a forge on our return from York," said Olivia with a frown. "I recall it well."

"Yes, so I had to make a new one."

"You?" asked William. "In a forge? Like a common smith?"

She gave him a small smile. "Indeed, it was under the Alchemist's instruction, but yes, I made it."

"God's Blood, I would never have credited it!" His jaw dropped as he stared at her. "You are ever resourceful, Mary!"

"I had to be," she replied, "for there were times on this mission when it was most needed."

"So, tell us all," Olivia said as she and William leaned in closer.

"The start you know…" Mary began, and launched into the full tale.

---0---

The candle on the table was almost burned down to a stub as she drew her story to a close. She had not glossed over the parts that reflected poorly on herself – such as how she had been played for a fool in the ambush, how she had stolen Justice, how she had been tricked by Rolleston to give away too much information about the plot, and how she had then failed to stop him stealing the coded letter.

"…So you see," she had finished, "that letter, and its translation, are like gunpowder in the hands of this man Brooks. I could have resolved it in the forest, but failed to do so. They were so busy murdering Rolleston, that it was too late to retrieve it – but I should have had Brooks destroy it while I had him under my control. The Earl of Shrewsbury will soon be in London with Frances Barwell as the Queen of Scots, and if they try to carry through the renunciation of her Catholic faith and her claim to the throne, then Brooks has only to produce the letter to explode the whole subterfuge. The Catholics will be emboldened and will almost certainly rise up; Philip of Spain and the Pope will then get involved and most likely put forward some puppet monarch." She had paused. "And Queen Elizabeth will once again face being deposed, imprisoned and no doubt executed." She swallowed hard. "I will have failed her."

William and Olivia leaned back and stared silently at her, as if they were unsure how to process what they had now heard.

Just as Mary felt that the silence had gone on long enough, William started to nod slowly. "That you have the courage to kill," he said, "we knew already, for we have seen it with our own eyes. That you have the wherewithal to plan and execute such a conceit as had this man Rolleston acting as the Scottish Queen's headsman, then have his own companions turn murderously against him – so much I could guess, for I have seen how you can bend any man to your will," he smiled briefly, "myself included." He leaned across and put his hand over hers. "Mary, my love," he said, his eyes unwavering on hers, "I bear you no ill-will for any of this, for even though you have come to us from the distant future and you have caused deaths and stolen property, I know you act from the purest of motives, and I would be sure that God sees the same good in you as I do."

Then Olivia placed her hand over William's. "I say the same," she said, "for I have seen how you care for those you love, and I know that it is as God wills it."

Mary smiled at them. "I thank you both for your understanding," she said. "I would not have wanted to do any of this, were I not forced to do so." She shook her head. "But all of what I have done so will be as naught, if we do not destroy that letter."

"I agree," said William. "So we must construct our plan of action, and carry it through together – the three of us." He paused. "As we did near York this spring."

"Yes," Mary said. "But we need to be well prepared." She looked at them both. "Starting with the gun. You both need to know how to fire it, in case you have to."

"But Mary, my love, are you sure?" William muttered, "I warrant that is your area of expertise."

"Come now, William," Mary responded. "What if I am not able to use it? What if I am injured…" she paused, "or worse?"

Her words hung in the air.

"Then one of us may need it," Olivia said quietly, but with more steel in her voice than William had shown.

"Exactly," Mary said, giving William a small smile, to reassure him that she understood his reluctance to handle an unfamiliar weapon.

"I saw how you used it before," Olivia continued, "but I would have some more instruction, so I understand it fully."

"Then after we have finished here, I will show you both," Mary said, "so it becomes as natural to you as it is to me."

"Do we have time enough?" asked William.

"You are right, William. We will have to move quickly," Mary said. "I fired on the true Queen of Scots yesterday not long after midday. The Earl of Shrewsbury will most probably be travelling with Frances Barwell to Tutbury this day, and then on to London tomorrow or the day after, as the longer he leaves the deception, the more chance of discovery. If they ride hard they can be there in two days. Brooks will want to bury the real Queen, creating a shrine for Catholics to visit in future, but then he will want to set off to London as well, with the incriminating documents. So I think our best chance to find and take them is at Oak House tomorrow."

"But how to find these documents?" asked Olivia.

"I know not for sure," Mary answered, "but I warrant Brooks is most likely to keep them on his person. So we need to take and overpower him."

"How many men do they have?" William asked.

"There were nine originally with the Scottish Queen in the forest; Rolleston, Brooks, the driver and six others," Mary said. "I dispatched the driver initially, then one called Edmund, and another who attempted to come at me by stealth. And of course, Rolleston was killed by Brooks for treachery and beheading the Queen. So I make it that there are now five – Brooks and the four remaining men." She paused, "And at Oak House, there are Mistress Brooks and Nathan the archer, although I know not if he is in a condition to fight, after I broke his jaw. At least I think I did."

"By the Risen Christ, Mary," William said, "when this is over you will find life at Grangedean holds little excitement and adventure."

"But William," she said, leaning across and stroking his cheek, "that is my heart's truest desire – to live a quiet life of peace and order with you and the children, and not to be running through towns and forests as an assassin or spy." She paused. "Ten years ago I was just a girl living in twenty fifteen, with nothing more to concern me than pleasing my mother by finding a nice young man and settling down. Instead, I am now a cold-blooded killer, dispatching Her Majesty's enemies in return for the chance to save my own life, and live it with the nice young fellow I did eventually find." She stroked his cheek again, then dropped her hand. "Do you know, back in the forest this day I was even making jokes as I shot a man. Afterwards, I realised how much that sickened me." She sat back. "So we have one last battle to undertake – one last task to retrieve those documents. And either we succeed, and I never have to fight again, or maybe we die in the attempt." She looked at them both – her husband and her dearest friend. "So if you are with me, we do this together and risk our own deaths. If you would prefer to stay here and stay safe, I will understand, truly, and I will go alone."

She took a small breath.

"Are you with me?"

"We are," they both replied.

"Then let us make our plan."

CHAPTER FORTY-THREE

The loud tick of a crude old carriage clock welcomed Mary, William and Olivia into the back room of the tavern, its second hand staggering round the dial like an unsteady drunkard.

Mary checked to ensure they were alone, then took the gun and a cartridge out of her bag and placed them carefully on the table. In the light of the flickering candles ensconced on the walls, she pulled back on the lever to open the breech, then held up the cartridge so that William and Olivia could see it more clearly.

"The breech opens to reveal the chamber, and the cartridge goes in here, like so," she said, slotting it into place. "Then you pull the lever up and forward to close the breech." She looked at them both in turn. "Now the gun is loaded and ready to fire."

"As the Lord is my witness, Mary my love," said William, his eyes glittering in the candlelight, "I would not credit that this wonderful piece of ordnance was made by your own hand." He shook his head slowly. "It is a remarkable thing indeed."

"Yes, but it was made under instruction from the Alchemist," she replied. "He showed me all the steps to take, and approved each one before I was permitted to move to the next."

"Then he is to be congratulated," William said, "for his ingenuity."

"Not hung, drawn and quartered, for his treason?" enquired Mary, now starting to feel sufficiently rested and well-fed to give him an impish smile.

William shook his head again. "I rather think not," he said. "I fancy he is even now aboard a boat bound for foreign lands."

Mary unloaded the gun and put it carefully down on the table with the cartridge, then she looked up at her husband. "Indeed?" she asked, her voice tinged with caution. "Wychwoode did offer him a way to achieve such a fate..." She left it hanging as a question.

"Mistress Melrose and I saw a man hung, drawn and quartered at Tyburn these few days past," he said, "and all who saw it would swear it was the one known as the Alchemist who met his end."

"But you think otherwise?"

"A well-clothed man who had the appearance of the Alchemist as you described him, and had the limp in his leg that would have resulted from the beating you gave him, led us to believe that the poor unfortunate upon the scaffold was in truth another fellow, put in his place and given his name. Then he told us he was bound out of the realm on a boat."

"And it was he who gave us the information that led us here," said Olivia. "He said to look for Rolleston, and also to seek one Anne Carter – the name you said you travelled under. He said we should head north. Had we not had such information to start from, we would never have found you."

Mary shook her head. "So Rick finally did the decent thing," she said, almost to herself. "Maybe there really was some good in him after all."

For all she would once have gladly hung the man, then chopped him into bits herself, now she felt nothing but relief that he had gone free. For they had parted, if not as friends, then certainly with an understanding that as fellow time-travellers and gunsmiths, they had some sort of common bond.

But would Rick survive in exile?

Mary nodded to herself. Of course he would; he was a natural survivor. No doubt once he had established himself in Germany or France or Holland or wherever, he would set himself up again as an inventor, conjuring up items that amazed the locals and made him lots of money, just as he had in Southwark. If only he could be content with that, and find someone who made pies as good as Mistress Somerville, he would live a long, and maybe even a happy life.

Mary was about to reply when she heard the sudden 'click-clack' sound of the gun being loaded.

Spinning round, she saw Olivia had lifted the gun to her shoulder and was pointing it at the opposite wall. Before she could say anything, the girl pulled the lever back and ejected the cartridge into her palm, then reloaded it in only a few seconds, lifted it and pointed it at the wall once more.

"Again," Mary said, glad of the chance to move on from the Alchemist and back to the matter at hand. "And this time point the cartridge in towards the gun as you load, so it locates into the breech more quickly."

Olivia nodded and tried again, this time taking maybe a second off the time to reload.

"Good," Mary said. "And again."

Olivia did so several more times, until she was as fast, if not faster than Mary herself.

"Now with your eyes closed," Mary said.

Olivia picked up the gun and the cartridge, closed her eyes and reloaded. It was much slower as she fumbled to locate the breech, but after a few more tries she was almost back up to the speed she had achieved with her eyes open.

"Truly excellent," Mary said. "I am most impressed, Olivia." She handed the gun and cartridge to William. "Now your turn, my love," she said, then added with a small knowing smile at her friend. "Show us how the man can better the womenfolk."

To give him his due, William tried hard. With a determined stare at both of them, he picked up the cartridge, snapped back the breech lever, then tried to slam in the cartridge, but missed the breech completely. With a grunt of annoyance, he tried again, and although this time it went in, he wasted time making sure it was seated correctly. After a few more tries he was consistently getting it in place, but not as fast as either of the women. Then he tried with his eyes closed, and after a few fumbles and dropped cartridges, he was able to achieve at least consistent loading.

"There," he said triumphantly. "It is a simple matter, and well-proven."

"That is deserving of praise, I agree," Mary said, "but you have two very competent women here, with smaller hands, who are both able to load and fire more quickly."

"Nonsense!" he barked, and tried several more times, shaving perhaps half a second off his time. But as he put the gun down, Mary felt he could do better, and decided to make it into a competition. "Marry," she said, "I will give each of you thirty seconds by that clock there, and let us see who does the most load, aim and unloads." She put the gun on the table with the cartridge next to it. "You first," she said to Olivia.

"Eyes open?"

Mary nodded, watching the clock. As the second hand staggered wheezily up to the hour, she counted Olivia in. On the command 'go!' Olivia sprang into action. She grabbed the gun and snapped open the breech, then slotted in the cartridge, slammed it shut and brought the gun up to the firing position. Then she unloaded and repeated, managing eight further sequences before the end of the thirty seconds.

"Well done," Mary said, as Olivia replaced the gun on the table and stood the cartridge next to it. "Now your turn," she said to William. He moved to the table and stood with his feet planted and his hands hovering over the gun, his fingers flexing like the wings of a bird.

"Now to show you both how a man moves with the speed of a lightning bolt…" he said.

"This I must see," said Mary, and counted him in.

When the thirty seconds was up, he put the gun down and stood back.

"How many was that?" he asked, with an expression that expected success.

"Seven," Mary and Olivia said together. His face fell. "For sure?" They nodded. "By Heavens!" he exclaimed, then stopped, and his frown turned into a broad smile. "Well, I warrant it was a fair contest. As a gentleman I needs must recognise when I am beaten and by a woman!"

"There is no shame in that," said Mary, taking hold of his arm and giving him a kiss on the cheek. "You have speed, more than many would have in my time. It is just that we are a little faster."

"For all it galls me to say it, I can see that," he answered, "and I trust the Lord will not require me to take up this weapon when such speed is required."

"Then let us focus on our plan for the morrow," said Olivia, "And with God's good fortune, such a thing will not happen."

CHAPTER FORTY-FOUR

Brooks, his wife and the rest of the men were breaking fast in the great hall of Oak House, a large room in the centre of the building with a high vaulted roof and brightly painted wood panelling. The roof was supported by a series of strong black oak beams running across the room between the tops of the walls, and it was these beams that had given the house its name.

It was the morning of the day after their return. The previous day had been filled with activity; beginning with them bringing a Catholic priest, Father Goddard, out of his place of concealment in a secret room behind the basement of a nearby tavern, then trying to convince him that they needed to hold a funeral mass for the Queen of Scots herself. At first he had been deeply sceptical, and it had taken some passionate persuasion to convince him that this was not some trick by Pursuivants to lure him into the open and have him arrested.

Eventually he had agreed to view the body, which was laid out on the parlour table at Oak House. He stared at it silently for some time while Brooks and his wife watched, clutching each other's hand tightly. The Queen's head had been returned to its rightful place, with a small sack of flour underneath the neck to support it. If it were not for the ugly red gash running all round, she would have looked if she were merely resting serenely with her hands by her side.

Father Goddard studied the face, then moved round and turned his attention to the nearest hand. Then he raised his head upwards and moved his lips silently, while Brooks and his wife both held their breath.

Then he looked at them across the body. "Yes," he said, "God has told me this is indeed the true Queen." Then he had made the sign of the cross on the forehead, lips and chest, before placing his hands on either side of her head and leaning over it, his lips again moving silently. As he stood up, Brooks noticed that the Queen's eyes were now wet with Father Goddard's tears.

He had then gone out with them to view the burial site in the orchard behind the house, before saying the necessary words to consecrate the ground. After that the body was brought out in a shroud and lowered gently into the grave that had been dug, then covered over with soil.

It had been a moving service, with Mistress Brooks and all the men gathered around with their heads bowed as the requiem mass was said, followed by Eucharistic prayers. Then Father Goddard had given a short homily.

"My friends in Christ," he had said, "it is with the deepest pain that we bury our sovereign lady, and with her we bury our dream of a quick return to the true faith." He paused, looking around. "This is a mass said by only a small number of loyal followers, when it should have been a royal service attended by all the Queen's devoted subjects. But my friends, our cause is like a candle that has its flame put out; the light is gone, but the candle itself is still there – and it is our duty as followers of the true faith to find a way to re-light it once again. As God is my witness, the fight continues, until the heretic usurper is removed from the throne she occupies against God's will, and a true Catholic sovereign sits in her place. I charge you to do all that is in your power to bring this to pass." He gave them all a hard stare then made the sign of the cross. *"In nomine Patris et fillii et Spiritus Sancti, Amen."*

"Amen," they had all said, then returned to the house for supper and to raise a glass of wine in honour of the departed Queen.

"I can still scarce believe the true Queen is dead," Brooks muttered as he broke a piece of bread the next morning. "All our plans coming to naught, because of that she-devil Anne Carter." He stuffed the bread moodily in his mouth

"So you have said many times over," replied his wife. "Saying it again does not restore the rightful queen to life, nor fulfil our obligation to continue the fight.

"I know, I know," Brooks replied once he had finished chewing. "But it galls me nonetheless that we were thwarted by one such as her ¬– a woman.

"We could have her arraigned by the Justices for murder," one of the men suggested. "Edmund, Richard and Samuel the driver were all slaughtered by her hand.

"Nay," Brooks replied. "Have you taken leave of your senses? She will be hailed a hero for causing the deaths of the bastard queen's enemies." He shook his head. "No, we must save our efforts for destroying Walsingham's plan to have the imposter queen renounce the true faith and her claim to the throne." He took out the two pieces of paper he had tucked into the front of his doublet. "With these papers we can still dismiss the false queen as a base conceit and cause a Catholic uprising. We may not have the Queen of Scots on the throne, but perhaps another of the true faith, as Father Goddard has said. Either way," he glared at each of them in turn, "either way, we have a realm restored to the Catholic cause, and that heretic bastard removed from the throne, which will be a blessed relief."

He was interrupted by a heavy thumping on the front door. "Pray, see who that might be at this early hour, wife," he said, putting the papers back inside his doublet.

Mistress Brooks went out, and returned a few minutes later with a tall blond man wearing a rough woollen jerkin, no hose and torn breeches held in place by a length of rough rope wound several times round his waist.

"Well, fellow?" Brooks demanded, as everyone stared at the man in silence. "What is your business here?"

The man took off his cap and twisted it in his hands. "Please, sir," he muttered, "I come in haste to warn you of grave danger."

"Indeed?" Brooks asked, his voice showing only mild concern. "And what danger might this be?"

"I was in a hostelry in Nottingham…" the man began.

"And there should have stayed," one of the others muttered under his breath, but loud enough for all to hear. There was general laughter from all except for Nathan, whose jaw was heavily bandaged.

Brooks raised his own hand for silence. "Let us hear the fellow out," he said. "If he has come all the way from Nottingham on this freezing morning to warn us, he may have information of value. Come to the fire, man, you are blue with the cold."

"I thank you sir," the man replied and moved closer to the fire. "I was in the Prospect Inn last evening, and was seated near a group of fellows who, from their manner and conversation, I took to be Pursuivants. Their leader was one they addressed as Silas Taverner."

Now he had their full attention.

"I know this Taverner," Brooks said with a chill in his voice, "as it was he who arrested me once before."

"Aye, and he means to do so again, sir," came the reply. "I overheard them planning to raid your house again this very morn, so being a true Catholic myself, I awoke well before the dawn and rode up as fast as I could to warn you."

Brooks considered the man, his head on one side. "You have done well, fellow," he said. "What is your name?"

"Will, sir. Will… er… Bowyer."

"In truth, Goodman Bowyer, you are welcome this day, and your warning is well heeded." He paused. "Did this Taverner say *why* he was planning to raid this house once again, perchance?"

"He did, sir, in his conversation with the others." Bowyer twisted his hat even more in his hands. "I listened hard, for all they talked quite softly, and it was to do with your apparent conversion to Protestant heresy after your last arrest. He has heard tell you have been once again hearing Catholic Mass."

"I see." Brooks looked round at his companions, then back at Bowyer. "And you say he is coming this very morning?"

"I would expect he is but a quarter hour behind me, sir."

Brooks stood and gestured to the men at the table. "Then I suggest we make haste away to Bridgeford. We should all go to the house of my Catholic brother, Master Cornell. Then there will be no person in the house when Taverner arrives."

"If I may, sir," interrupted Bowyer, "I would suggest you stay here. Taverner will be all the more suspicious if the house is empty and it looks as if you have flown. You and Mistress Books should stay and deal with Taverner without these other men here, to give him cause to see a conspiracy. You will be no more than an innocent man and wife going about your business as normal."

Brooks considered this a moment. "The fellow has a point," he said. "You all go to Cornell's place and wait for me there."

The men stood, then made their way out of the hall, heading for the back door towards the stables.

"You, Goodman Bowyer, take some bread, and be gone as fast as you can, lest you are found here and must answer questions from that louse Taverner."

Bowyer put on his cap and bowed. "I thank you sir, and I am glad I have been able to help a fellow Catholic."

"Indeed and we thank you. Now you had best be gone."

Bowyer selected a piece of bread, took a bite, then walked over to the door through which the men had just gone. But instead of leaving as bidden, he pulled the door shut and moved the bolt across to lock it.

As Brooks and his wife watched in amazement, Bowyer then walked to the open door on the other side of the room, and gave a soft whistle. A moment later a woman came in, dressed in black breeches and a tight-fitting black jerkin. She carried a slim tubular weapon that Brooks immediately recognised from the fake ambush in the forest. Bowyer closed the door behind her and stood with his back to it.

Brooks looked at the woman's face in amazement.

Anne Carter!

She smiled, then raised the gun and pointed it directly at his chest.

"Hello, Master Brooks," she said. "You are well met indeed."

Mistress Brooks made a small movement, as if she were about to attack Anne Carter. Bowyer stepped smartly across and grabbed her hands, pulling them up behind her back so tightly that she could not move any further.

"By Heavens, Carter," her husband snarled. "I would you were out of my life."

"Oh, I will be, believe me," she answered. "Just as soon as you give me the letter and note decoding it, that were taken from the Earl of Shrewsbury's desk."

"You do know there are Pursuivants coming..." Then Brooks stopped, as Anne Carter gave him a small smile. He nodded slowly. "I see," he said. "There are no Pursuivants; just you and this Bowyer fellow concocting a conceit, to have all my men put out of the way,"

"And it has worked, has it not?" Anne replied. "They are all now gone to, where was it...?" she put her head on one side, "Aye, the house of one Cornell. I mark it well, and will perchance let Master Taverner know that this Master Cornell is worthy of further investigation."

Brooks shook his head. "By the Risen Christ, you are the spawn of Satan,

Carter." He looked at her with deep hatred. "And if I refuse to hand over the documents you seek?"

"That would be foolish, for it will be the last thing you do." She raised the gun still further, so now he was staring directly down the barrel. "This thing is close enough to blow your head clean off your shoulders. Will you risk that for a couple of pieces of paper?"

"Papers that will place a rightful Catholic king or queen on the throne of England."

"As may be," she said. "Put them on the table."

With a look that was now of pure loathing, Brooks reached inside his doublet and withdrew the two papers. Then he placed them on the table and stood back.

"Good, now you and your wife, sit in these two chairs, but put them back-to-back first." She indicated two high-backed chairs. Brooks placed them as directed, then sat in one. Bowyer pulled Mistress Brooks over to the other and pushed her down into the seat. Then he pulled the length of rope out from round his waist and tied their wrists to each other on either side, so they were immobile.

Anne Carter then picked up one of the papers – the one that was coded in blocks of letters – and held one corner over the nearest candle. Brooks could just see a small black 'GX' and the numbers 3089 appear in the corner.

Anne Carter studied the code and her lips moved silently as she appeared to be doing a calculation in her head. "Yes, prime. It is the genuine letter," she said, then picked up the other paper and scanned it. "And this is the de-coding," she added. "I trust you have not made a copy of the coded letter, as it will be dismissed as a forgery if there is not a genuine code secretly written in the corner."

Brooks shook his head.

"Good." She moved over to the fire. "Then I have great pleasure in destroying these."

She put both papers into the flames, and as Brooks watched in sickened horror, they blackened, curled up, and eventually disappeared.

"There," she said, "my mission is accomplished."

Then Anne Carter gave the man Bowyer a triumphant smile. "Now, let us be away," she said. He nodded, and said to Brooks and his wife, "Fare thee well, Master Brooks, Mistress Brooks. I trust we shall never meet again."

As they turned towards the door, it opened.

A younger woman came into the room, also dressed in the same black clothing as Anne Carter. But she was not coming in willingly; rather she was being pushed in by a tall man holding her from behind with one arm locked across her ribs and the other holding a knife to her throat.

Anne Carter took one look at the man and put her free hand to a chair as if she was about to faint.

It was Roger Rolleston.

CHAPTER FORTY-FIVE

Rolleston kicked the door shut, then stood with his back to it, still holding his knife to Olivia's throat.

"I found this young woman lurking about the house in a most suspicious manner, for all the world like a bad odour," he said. "And while she is dressed most strangely, I fancy she might be quite comely if she were scrubbed and clothed correctly." He smiled at Mary, although it was more of a sneer. "I would say you are well met, Anne Carter, but it would not be the truth. The truth is, like another bad odour, you continually turn up when not wanted."

"I could say the same of you, Roger," Mary replied, looking at his right arm clamped across Olivia's ribs. It ended in a heavily bandaged stump where his hand had been. "When I left, you were about to be executed like the cur you are. I saw the sword come down, and the others move in with their knives out…" she paused. "Yet, here you are, somehow still living."

"Aye," he said. "Is it not remarkable what a single word can do to divert a sword from its deadly path?"

"A single word?"

"I was raised in the next house to this one. Antony and I grew up together, as inseparable as if we were brothers born. I simply reminded him of this, and called him 'brother'. It was enough to send the blow into the ground rather than my neck. The other men took their lead from Antony, and they all believed me when I then calmly explained to them that the evidence of my treachery came only from you, Anne Carter. They realised that we had all been the victim of your conceit, and I had not in truth betrayed my faith."

"Yet you killed the Queen."

"Indeed, but not by my will, rather by hers. You saw how she went gladly to her death. She was wearied of the frequent changes in her fortune, so here was a quick and painless way to achieve finality and begin her new life in Heaven."

"But this is your conjecture?"

"Nay, before she put her head on the branch, she said to me these very words; 'I find I am weary of life, Master Rolleston. I welcome death with open arms and the peace it will bring me. Go to it with my blessing.' So no, it is not conjecture."

He pushed the knife closer to Olivia's throat, causing Mary to give an involuntary gasp.

"Now, what is to do?" Rolleston asked with another sneer. "We seem to have something of an impasse here. I can dispatch this girl, whom I note seems to mean much to you, Anne Carter. Indeed I have a mind to do so, unless you drop your weapon immediately." He pulled the knife closer still, causing Olivia to flinch her head back, her eyes wide like a hunted deer. He nodded at Mary. "Go to it. Place it on the floor and kick it towards me."

Mary hesitated a moment.

"I said go to it, or your young friend here will feel the bite of my knife into her pretty neck."

Mary bent down and placed the gun on the floor, then kicked it towards Rolleston.

"Good," he said. "Now you, fellow," he said to William, "untie my brother Antony and his good wife."

William took a quick look at Olivia, then went over to the chairs and untied them as ordered.

"That is well done," Rolleston continued. "Antony, do me the favour of using this convenient piece of rope now to create two nooses, and throw them across yonder high beam.

Brooks nodded, used his knife to cut the rope in two, then created noose loops in each. He tested both to ensure the loop easily slid closed, then threw each rope over the nearest oak beam a few feet apart and secured them. The nooses were now both hanging around seven feet off the ground. Then he pulled two chairs across and placed one under each rope.

"You fellow, and you, Anne Carter, although in truth I doubt that is your real name," Rolleston said, "be so good as to stand on the chairs and put your heads in the ropes."

"Have you taken leave of your senses, man," demanded William, "to think we will readily comply?"

"Then you will see this pretty young girl here disfigured by my knife being pulled across her throat," answered Rolleston. "And when you have watched her pour out her life's blood and die in pain, if you still will not do as I ask, then I will try my aim on you with the remarkable weapon you have fashioned, Mistress Carter, to persuade you even more strongly." He smiled. "Although I doubt I will be as proficient with it as you are, so I will cause only pain and suffering with the firing now, leading to a death in time that is both slow and agonising."

Mary glanced over at Olivia, and noticed the girl look down at the gun on the floor, then back at her again. She did this a couple of times in quick succession, so Mary realised it was a signal. She thought she guessed what Olivia meant, so she said, "That gun at your feet? It is not about proficiency, Roger; you would not even be able to fire it."

"Perhaps not, but as I say, I am willing to try."

Then he looked down at the gun.

This briefly distracted his attention and enabled Olivia to make her move. She twisted her head in line with his movement and slammed it sharply back into his windpipe, causing him to gag and drop the knife. Then she made a quick turn of her body and slipped out from his grasp.

As she did so, Antony Brooks started to move to Rolleston's aid. Olivia dropped to the ground and in one smooth move, picked up the gun and fired a shot into Brooks's thigh. Mary's ears rang with the thunderous crack in such an enclosed space, as the shot tore into the grey-bearded man's leg. He screamed and fell to the ground clutching at the wound. Mary flipped a cartridge out of her pocket and threw it to Olivia, who caught it and swiftly reloaded. Pivoting round, she fired the next shot upwards at Rolleston, but she did not turn fast enough, and he was already moving sideways. The shot just missed him, instead blowing one of the antlers off a stuffed stag's head on the wall behind him.

As Olivia ran over to Mary's side and thrust the gun into her hands, Mary saw William diving for the knife where it had fallen. But Rolleston saw what he was doing and made a grab for it with his good hand at the same time. Together they fell to the floor.

As they grappled, Mary reloaded and tried to get a clear shot at Rolleston, but every time she thought she had the opportunity, William had his head in the way. So she held the gun ready but did not fire.

William managed to get two hands on the knife. Rolleston had his on it as well, and they rolled over a couple more times, ending with William on top. He had the knife in both hands and was trying to bring it down, but Rolleston's strength was the equal of his, and the knife stayed a few inches above Rolleston's chest. Then Rolleston brought his stump up and crashed it into the side of William's head; a move that would have made any normal man scream in agony. With a grunt of pain, William rolled away, allowing Rolleston to get back on top. Now the knife was bearing down on William's chest. It seemed to Mary that he was pushing back with all his might, but Rolleston was a bigger man, with his added weight giving him the advantage.

Mary continued to dance round trying to get a clear shot, but even though Rolleston was now on top it was still too risky; at this range any shot could potentially pass straight through Rolleston and hit William.

Then Olivia picked up the broken-off antler, and held it high over Rolleston's head to use as a dagger. But before she could bring it down, Mistress Brooks left where she had been tending her husband on the floor and ran at Olivia, snarling like an angry cat, and leapt at her, knocking the antler to the floor. Olivia put her arms up to defend herself as the woman then attempted to scratch out her eyes.

Mary looked back at the fight between William and Rolleston. She could see that the knife point was now only an inch off William's chest, and from his red face and bared teeth, it looked like he might be tiring.

Rolleston hunched his shoulders. "Die, fellow, die!" he yelled and thrust down hard.

Mary screamed as she heard William give a short cough, then she saw his eyes open wide, staring up at Rolleston.

Then his eyes closed.

"William! No!"

As she screamed, Mistress Brooks was briefly distracted from her scratching at Olivia, giving Olivia the chance to grab the antler and get a good swing into the side of the woman's head. As the weapon connected there was a grunt from Mistress Brooks, and she went sprawling into the wall. Her eyes fluttered briefly, then she was still.

Olivia struggled to her feet and leaped across to where Mary was trying to pull Rolleston off William, but for some reason he seemed to be dead weight. She came beside Mary and together they tried to roll Rolleston away onto his back.

Mary took a deep breath to prepare herself for the sickening sight of her husband with the knife deep in his chest, as she and Olivia finally managed to get Rolleston away.

Then they both gasped.

There was plenty of blood, but William's chest was clear.

No handle was sticking out.

A groan from Rolleston made Mary look across at him instead.

The handle stood proud just below Rolleston's ribs, surrounded by a widening pool of blood spreading across his doublet like ink on blotting paper.

Now there was a groan from William, and his eyes opened.

"Mary, my love," he whispered, "that was close." He struggled up on one elbow. "I had two hands on the knife, whereas he had but one. So I managed to turn it at the very last moment as he pushed down and he drove it deep into his own body." He gave a weak grin and rubbed his ribs, "For all I will have quite a bruise as the handle dug deep into me as he came down."

"Oh, William!" Mary sobbed, as she dropped to her knees and pulled his head up to her breast, cradling him like a baby," I thought I had lost you!"

"Oh come, now, my love," he said, with his face buried in her black jerkin, "it will take more than that."

She let him go and he struggled to his feet, while she picked up the gun. Then he went over and helped Olivia up. The three of them stood together, looking at Mistress Brooks out cold on one side of the room, her husband now passed out in a large pool of blood on the other, and Rolleston on his back with the knife handle standing proud in his belly.

"I would we get away now," William suggested, "before perhaps those other men realise they were deceived, or are still close enough to hear the sound of your gun, and make a return."

"Yes, we must," agreed Mary, "and now the documents are burned, we have done what we set out to do." She looked at William, whose skin was now taking on something of a grey tinge. "Come, my love, you need rest, some wine and food, and to have your bruises tended." She turned to Olivia. "And you also, have scratches to your face."

"That woman was trying to take out my eyes." Olivia took hold of the back of a chair to steady herself.

Mary followed William out into the cool air. "I suggest we make haste for Nottingham first to get some rest and recovery, then make for Whitehall to report to Master Secretary Walsingham."

They walked to where they had left their horses.

"That woman put up a fight, did she not, Olivia?" Mary observed, as they started to untie the beasts.

There was no answer.

Mary spun round.

Olivia was not with them.

She looked at William, and together they both said the same thing.

"Rolleston!"

They ran back to the house and into the Hall.

Rolleston was standing and again had Olivia in his grasp, with the bloody blade of the knife once more held to her throat.

"Those nooses still await," he croaked. "I would you go to them, and I will not be so obliging this time."

"I am so sorry," Olivia said, her eyes wide. "He came up behind me and pulled me to him. I thought he was dead."

"That is the benefit of feeling no pain," Rolleston observed. "Far from dying, I simply pulled the blade free and am sound in body once more."

Mary raised the gun and pointed it at his head. "Let her go, Rolleston," she ordered.

He moved his head behind Olivia, so she was almost completely shielding him – with just the smallest part of his head still visible. "Do you risk killing this girl?" he asked. "Or come any closer and watch as I make her die in pain." Then he whispered in Olivia's ear, but loud enough for Mary and William to hear. "It must be such a strange sensation, pain. I would you tell me how it feels when I cut your throat, but you will scarce have time." He paused. "Or the capability of speech." He looked up, "Come, Anne Carter, who this man calls Mary, and you, Will or William, step up to the nooses, and we can end all this."

For sure it was time to end it.

Mary took the shot.

Once again the report of the gun echoed around the room. The bullet missed Olivia by no more than half an inch and entered the corner of Rolleston's eye, then exploded out of the back of his head, killing him instantly. The force of the shockwave snapped Olivia's own head to one side making the knife cut into her neck. As Rolleston fell backwards, she fell back with him, then rolled off him and lay still on her side, as if she was a sleeping infant.

Even before Mary lowered the gun, William ran over to Olivia and was examining her. Then he picked her gently up in his arms and struggled to his feet, holding her as if she were a sleeping babe.

"She still lives," he said, "but she has a deep cut to the side of her neck."

Mary examined Olivia's neck, and breathed a small sigh of relief. "It is only a flesh wound," she said. "We should bind it up, so it will heal." As she said this, Olivia's eyes fluttered open.

"You will live," Mary said with a smile.

William carried Olivia outside. "Come," he said. "Let us make haste to Nottingham before anything else occurs."

"The Lord be praised," Olivia whispered to Mary as William carried her along towards to the horses. "He has saved me."

"I rather think the Lord had less to do with it than my aim being true," Mary muttered to herself.

CHAPTER FORTY-SIX

Mary shifted from one foot to the other as she stood outside Walsingham's study at the house on Seething Lane. The door remained firmly closed, as it had been since she had first been told to wait by a servant fifteen minutes before. She adjusted her gown for the hundredth time, smoothing the thick material down with her hands. Then she patted her hair again, making sure it was still in perfect shape.

Loud footsteps coming down the corridor made her turn. Wychwoode was striding towards her, his cloak billowing out behind him.

"Master Wychwoode," she said, as he came up. Then she added through slightly gritted teeth. "You are well met."

"And you, Lady Mary," he replied with a thin smile. "I am indeed most pleased to see you back, and also in good health. I believe you are here to report on the outcome of the mission?"

"I am."

"And you are to be congratulated," he continued. "All has turned out most satisfactorily. I trust you experienced no difficulties in the course of your endeavours?" Then he raised a hand. "But no, you must save your story for Master Secretary Walsingham. I shall not steal the thunder from your tale."

Just then the door opened, and Walsingham's head poked out, his dark eyes flicking across them both. "Lady Mary?" he asked, almost as if he was surprised to see her. "And Master Wychwoode, also? Good, then we are complete." He stood back and held the door. "Please step in."

Mary made her way to the table, and noted with a wry smile that her phone was once again sitting on top of some papers. She sat down and picked it up, turning it over in her hands, surprised at how the familiar touch of the smooth plastic brought back warm feelings of security and contentment. She pressed and held the 'on' button, but the screen remained resolutely black.

"I have spent some time familiarising myself with this amazing object," Walsingham said, making her look up. He gave her a conspiratorial smile. "I became particularly enamoured of the four young men who sing the song with the oft-repeated line 'Back for Good.' The words appear to be so much doggerel, but I found the melody quite pleasant. My wife Ursula has been most insistent that I cease humming it as I go about the house." Mary put the phone down, trying hard to process the image of the dry Elizabethan spymaster watching Take That videos.

"You are free to take this 'phone' device back, Lady Mary," said Wychwoode. "But we would have your assurance it will be kept securely locked away, or else destroyed. It would not be seemly for its existence to be made public, else we would have others react negatively to its powers, as we both did when we first saw it."

Something in the tone of his voice – almost the sound of a warm smile – caught Mary's attention. "I can take it back? Does that mean I no longer face the charge of blasphemy?" she asked.

There was a quick glance between the two men, almost as if they had been expecting this very question. Walsingham put his fingers together in the same 'church roof' shape as he had at their first meeting.

"I think you can rest assured that the charge of blasphemy has been dropped, Lady Mary," he said quietly.

"I see," she replied, trying hard to keep her tone measured. "And the charge of sorcery?"

"That too," said Wychwoode. "All charges have been dropped. It has been acknowledged that such charges were in truth, quite baseless."

Mary took a couple of deep breaths, then smiled at each man in turn.

All charges dropped…

All charges dropped!

What she really wanted to do now was to jump up, lean across the table, kiss them both, then throw back her chair and shout, 'Yes! YES!' while doing repeated fist pumps.

What she actually said was, "I thank you gentlemen. That is great news. It is indeed a relief to know I am no longer under such a threat."

Walsingham smiled. "I think, Lady Mary, that it is a measure of the gratitude felt by our gracious sovereign, as well, of course by both of us here, that we must acknowledge the part you have played in her secret enterprise."

"Mistress Barwell was lately brought to London as we planned," explained Wychwoode, "and in the guise of the Queen of Scots, she signed an undertaking to renounce that queen's Catholic faith and her claim to the throne of England. It was done before Parliament, so it is fully in the public domain. I am pleased to report that no person there present questioned that it was the very Queen of Scots herself. The likeness was remarkable, and even those few that had previously met the lady in person were taken in by the deception." He inclined his head to one side and fixed her with his piercing blue eyes. "So the Catholics no longer have a focus for their seditious plotting, and we have the chance to secure a long-lasting peace in the realm."

"And we let it be known through some of our intelligencers that the assassin was believed to be a disaffected Catholic," added Walsingham. "So the change of heart by the Queen of Scots was better understood and no man thought to challenge it." He nodded. "It made good justification for the very public execution you performed, Lady Mary."

"Even though it was undermined by Rolleston and Brooks?" Mary asked.

"Perhaps," answered Wychwoode. "But the end outcome was the same, nonetheless. For which we have you to thank."

"Well, I am pleased it finally turned out so well," Mary said. "Mistress Barwell certainly impressed me when I met her in Sheffield." She paused. "What will become of her now?"

Wychwoode smiled. "She will continue in her role a few more weeks, then it will be announced that the Queen of Scots has caught a serious chill and sadly, passed away. Mistress Barwell can then resume her previous life, and the deception will remain a closely guarded secret for evermore."

"I need hardly add that you are enjoined to keep the secret also," Walsingham said, his eyes suddenly very cold.

"Of course," Mary replied. "I have no wish to share it with any person. Besides," she added, "I hardly think anyone would believe it."

"I have no doubt you are correct," said Walsingham, sitting back.

Wychwoode said, "Those events you have told us that would have occurred, such as the plot led by one Anthony Babington, the original execution of the Queen of Scots and particularly Philip of Spain's attempt at a sea-borne invasion – all these will in every likelihood, no longer happen." He nodded in satisfaction. "You have changed the course of history, Lady Mary, and it is to be hoped, much for the better. It seems that Her Majesty is now more secure on her throne, and that is a most welcome outcome."

Mary did not respond immediately. That she had changed the course of history was something she had already accepted – indeed it seemed strange now how fearful she had originally been of the idea, and how keen she had been to preserve the history she had grown up with.

Although, was wanting to preserve it in truth no more than a selfish indulgence? It now existed only in her and the Alchemist's memories, so what was she protecting? A memory? Far better to let it go, and to focus instead on the benefits she had finally managed to deliver through this mission. To focus on the lives she had saved and the plots that would now never happen. Whatever new history might now take place, there was a chance it could be a little less bloody and a little less deadly than the one she remembered. She should be grateful for that at least.

"I am pleased that the outcome was successful at the last," she said. "Although there were some difficult moments on the way, believe me."

"I am not surprised, Lady Mary," said Walsingham. "And we would very much like to have your report."

Mary leaned forward. "As you wish," she said, then paused to gather her thoughts. "Let me start by telling you that as I said originally, Roger Rolleston was not to be trusted. He was a Catholic all along, and a most dangerous one at that. He tried very hard to turn the mission against me, and he very nearly succeeded."

There was a long silence, then Walsingham whistled softly. "I had heard of this," he muttered, "but you have now confirmed it for sure." He did not look at Wychwoode as he said this.

Wychwoode appeared to be studying the table with great interest. Eventually he looked up at Mary. "I do most humbly beg your forgiveness my lady, for I genuinely believed him to be on our side in this matter." He reached across and took her hands in his own. "I would not have sent you with him if I had even had the smallest suspicion, believe me."

"What form did this treachery take?" asked Walsingham.

So Mary told them the full story, from the journey up to Sheffield, through to the final fight at Oak House, and even, with honesty, admitted to allowing Rolleston the means to work out the plot. They listened in silence throughout, apart from occasional exclamations of surprise or amazement. When she had finished, they sat still for some time. Then Walsingham got up and paced over to the fire, before turning back and asking, "This treacherous fellow Rolleston, he told you he was incapable of feeling pain?"

"Yes."

"And you saw the truth of this for yourself?"

"I did; in the forest when he and Brooks staged the counterfeit ambush, and on other occasions since. The last of these was when he pulled the knife from his belly in the Hall at Oak House."

"Ah, yes," observed Wychwoode, "Before you finished him off by the finest of shots; one that missed Mistress Olivia Melrose by a hair's width."

Mary nodded. Then Walsingham asked, "But if he had taken a knife in the belly, surely that was a mortal blow? Belike he was as good as dead already? You had only to wait a moment more, and he would have fallen?"

"I could not have taken that risk. As he felt no pain, he had no way of knowing just how badly he was struck. He genuinely believed he was recovered, and could thus have continued for enough time to have either killed Olivia or forced William and I into the nooses."

"So you took a shot that, had it been but an inch over, would have killed Mistress Melrose instead?" Walsingham's eyebrows seemed to climb halfway up his forehead. "Was that not foolhardy?"

Mary could not believe the man was asking the same question he had asked at their first meeting. "As I believe I explained before, Master Secretary," she said, trying to keep her voice calm, "I have every confidence in my ability to fire the weapon accurately. I did so when my son was close, and I repeated this with Rolleston as well. I did what was necessary."

"So it seems." He stared at her with his dark eyes, as if he was making his mind up to reveal something. Eventually he said, "It also seems from what you have said, that Olivia Melrose is equally competent to fire the weapon. How was she so able?"

"She had seen me do so, and I also gave her instruction while we were in Nottingham for just such an eventuality. She is quick to learn, and indeed, I warrant she is now faster than I at loading and firing the gun."

Walsingham put his fingertips together once more. "Good," he said, his tone measured, which made his next words sound all the more unexpected. "Which is why I have requested Her Majesty to release Mistress Melrose to my charge, so I can put her to work as an intelligencer."

"You have done *what?*" Mary asked, her voice rising.

"I have made her such an offer."

"And she has agreed?"

"She has indeed." He paused. "Olivia Melrose is a remarkable young woman; courageous, resourceful, capable with your gun and, I understand, utterly devoted to Her Majesty's cause. She is also very comely, and understands therefore how to bend a man to her will, as she did with Master Wychwoode." He paused, his eyes never leaving hers. "I already have missions in mind for her, which involve this remarkable weapon, so we will, regretfully, not be acceding to the Queen's request to have it destroyed. He paused. "I have scarce seen another intelligencer more fitted to such a role. Although," he continued, "I have in truth seen one other who is almost more suited." He was silent, clearly expecting her to respond.

"And that is…?" she asked finally.

"It is you, Lady Mary."

There was a heavy silence while Mary returned his stare, as if this had suddenly become game of high-stakes poker. "Almost?" she asked. "You said 'almost'?

"You made two errors in this mission," Walsingham replied, looking her direct in the eye. "The one; you allowed the secret of the plan to be discovered by Rolleston."

"And the second?" Mary asked, although she suspected what was coming.

"The second was that you failed in the forest to secure the destruction of the incriminating documents; the documents which were almost certainly on the person of Master Brooks, necessitating your near-fatal mission to Oak House."

"So, Master Secretary," she said. "What would you have me do?"

"Carry on in my employ, if you wish."

"Despite such errors?"

"Yes." He considered her, his dark eyes unsmiling. "For I warrant you have learned such a lesson from these errors that you will not make them again. So if you want to continue, then I would have you do so."

"I see." Mary scratched at a small itch that had started on the back of her neck. "You also know I will no longer have useful insight into events to come? As a result of this mission, the future I knew has quite gone. I now know no more than any of us."

"I understand, but it is of small consequence. I would have you more for the bravery, cunning, ingenuity and determination you have clearly shown these past days."

"I see. And if despite my bravery, cunning, ingenuity and determination, I do not want to continue in your employ?"

"Master Wychwoode here has impressed upon me your wish to live in peace with your family. I agree that you have earned that life if you want it." He regarded her thoughtfully. "I would also add that Her Majesty has expressed a wish that if you choose not to serve her as my intelligencer, then you regularly attend on her at Court instead. She says she values the calm and wise counsel that you offer, and particularly that you are honest with her, without looking for favour. Although," here he paused with a raised eyebrow, "she also asked that I pass on a singular message that means naught to me, but may have significance for you."

"Which is?" Mary asked, intrigued.

"She observed that she would only value your advice if it were based on sound thinking, and not on a sound carried by the wind." He smiled. "Does that mean anything to you?"

Mary felt her face flushing. Of all the things that Elizabeth had remembered, it was that she had been belching loudly from drinking that foul beer in the Tower.

"I have an idea, yes." Mary smiled inwardly. Perhaps this was the Queen's way of confirming just how much she wanted a totally open and honest relationship between them, with no false modesty.

Or maybe it was just her base sense of humour.

"Good," said Walsingham. "Then there are your options. Which is it to be?"

He sat back, and Mary looked from one man to the other. On one side the dark, brooding spymaster, fixing her with his hooded eyes and appearing to be calculating the odds on which way her decision would go. On the other side the old, white-haired lawyer, who had once been her friend and even something of a father-figure, and perhaps could be again if she forgave him for Rolleston and let him back in...

So, what was it to be?

Keep working for Walsingham as a spy and assassin, with all the adventure, excitement and action that would involve?

Or go home? Do nothing more dangerous than running Grangedean Manor and giving honest counsel to Elizabeth, while no doubt offering help and advice to Olivia so she could grow into an accomplished intelligencer instead?

Mary thought back to that ride through Sheffield, when the idea of a quiet life in Elizabethan England seemed so appealing. Indeed, her heart's deepest desires had been so clear as she rode through those oppressive and foul-smelling streets…

To be able to live at peace and fulfil her promise to Kat not to leave her again…

To be there to help not just Kat, but Ambrose and Jane as well – to enable them to become the fine young people they were now destined to be…

To grow old beside William, the man she had loved ever since she had first laid eyes on his magnificent portrait, before she had been thrown, a frightened girl called Justine Parker, into the confusing world of Tudor history; a world she now understood well, and indeed felt she was a valued part.

And to be there for Elizabeth – the woman not the queen – with her honest counsel…

But – and it was a very big 'but'…

How could she live without all the adventure and action, stuck in Grangedean Manor with nothing more exciting to concern her than the household accounts?

Would she end up a bitter, bored, dried-up old housewife?

What about all the obstacles she had faced and overcame on this mission? Could she live without such challenges?

Could she really just sit back and let Olivia have all the fun?

Mary picked up her phone and stood.

All things considered, there was really only one possible answer.

She stared down at both men, took a deep breath and said in firm, clear voice: "I have made my decision, sirs."

She paused as they looked up at her expectantly.

"I want to go home."

CHAPTER FORTY-SEVEN

Mary stepped carefully down from the carriage. The trees around the Grangedean Manor park were almost bare, with a light silver coating of frost to match the tiny sparkling ice crystals that drifted through the clear air of the winter sunshine. She walked across the path and looked up at the façade of the Manor.

To her, the Manor was as warm and as comfortable as an old pair of shoes; every stone a familiar friend; every beam and every window as recognisable as her own face in the mirror. She smiled as she took it all in; the only place she had ever truly called home. The only place where her soul had ever truly lived.

She proceeded alone across the frosty lawn, then dropped slowly to her knees and gripped the cold turf in both hands.

"I make you this solemn promise," she whispered, "I will always live here, and I will always be happy here. Whatever comes to pass, whatever the future may be, I will never leave."

The Manor seemed to smile back, and the breeze in the trees give a gentle reply, "Always here for you, Justine. Always here, Mary."

As she stood up, Olivia Melrose came across the lawn and stood silently beside her.

"You have made the right decision to return here, my lady," she said softly.

"As have you, to seek new adventures," answered Mary. "I hear Walsingham has already briefed you on your first mission?"

"Yes."

"Then I wish you every success." Mary turned to study the girl's face. "Are you taking the gun?"

Olivia nodded. "I am up to fourteen loads in thirty seconds."

Mary smiled. "I expect no less." She reached out and touched the girl's arm. "Look after it please. I do not want to have to make another one."

Olivia gave a small laugh. "I shall." Then she became serious. "Will I be able to call on you for advice? I would very much value your wise counsel."

"Of course," Mary replied. "Any time, day or night." She turned to face Olivia and put both hands on the girl's shoulders. "I have no doubt you will face great dangers out there, Olivia Melrose, and I know you have the courage, resourcefulness and determination to get through. But if you ever need my counsel, you only have to ask. Any time you need me. Any time."

"I will." Olivia stepped back. "I must be away now, Lady Mary. The carriage is waiting to take me back to London, and I have much to prepare."

"You will not stay to see William and the children? I know they would be disappointed not to see you."

Olivia shook her head. "No, I will leave you to reunite together as a family."

"But you are as much a part of this family as any of us."

"That is kind of you to say," Olivia replied, "but this is your time to be with them, not mine." She leaned forward and enveloped Mary in a warm hug.

"I will miss you, Olivia Melrose," Mary whispered in the girl's ear. "You come back to me, you hear?"

"I will miss you too," Olivia answered. "I will, I promise."

They hugged a moment longer, then Olivia stood back. "On the boat those many weeks ago, when we thought you were facing execution, you asked me to give each member of your family a personal message." Mary nodded. "So now is your chance to give them those messages yourself. In person. As their wife and mother."

With that, she turned and walked back to the carriage.

Mary watched her go, then went up the steps to the main entrance. She gave three loud knocks, then stood back and waited for the door to open.

THE END

A REQUEST FROM THE AUTHOR

If you have enjoyed this trilogy (or even if you haven't!), I would be very grateful if you could give some feedback. Please can you take a moment to leave a review or even just a rating on Amazon? Many thanks in advance - it is very much appreciated!

Please also visit my website at ***jonathanposnerauthor.com*** for more information on my books, and also to sign up for my newsletter – which gives you advanced information on forthcoming books, as well as offers, events and sneak previews.

Thanks

Jonathan ☺

BY THE SAME AUTHOR

Remember Mary Fox, the heroine of the series of books that so inspired Justine? Well, now you can read them for yourself! The first of the Mary Fox adventures is now available.

The Broken Sword

You only discover what dangers you can overcome when you're tested to the limit...

Tudor England
When Mary Fox is ordered to marry a sadistic older man, she decides instead to strike out on her own. As a woman in a man's world, no-one expects her to survive, but Mary is determined to prove them wrong.

Challenged to return the Broken Sword talisman and so break a centuries-old curse, she soon learns how to scheme, fight and outwit those who would drag her back to a life of servitude.

And in doing so, she becomes more than a match for any man.

"Diabolically good! What makes this novel irresistibly readable is the emotional energy generated by the main character Mary Fox, her ups and downs, drawing parallels to our present times." **Gina Flyvholm**

"I would highly recommend this book for its entertainment, historical authenticity and value." **Philip Appleton**

jonathanposnerauthor.com

About the Author

Jonathan has always been captivated by history, particularly the Tudor period, and has also been a lifelong fan of action-adventure novels. So when he decided to write a novel himself, it had to be the kind of adventure he loves to read; one with plenty of action, danger and suspense! And, of course, it had to be set in Tudor England, with a time-travelling heroine finding herself thrown into the deep-end of this fascinating historical era.

The result was **The Witchfinder's Well**, published in 2015. Jonathan decided to end it on a cliffhanger, just to make sure there would be a sequel. This was published in 2019, as **The Alchemist's Arms**. Never one to let a good idea go, Jonathan gave this second book a cliffhanger ending as well – thus paving the way for the third book in the trilogy, **The Sovereign's Secret** in 2022.

Justine Parker, the heroine of **The Witchfinder's Well**, is also an avid reader of Tudor action-adventure; particularly a fictional series of books featuring a Tudor adventuress called Mary Fox. So it seemed a good idea for Jonathan to write these books in reality! The result is **The Broken Sword** – the first Mary Fox adventure. And this one ends on – you've guessed it – a cliffhanger, with more books about Mary's adventures also planned.

Jonathan's other works include a book of short stories called **Once Upon an Ending**, a one-act play called **Private Eyes** as well book and lyrics for three Musicals – **Spirit of History** which premiered in Windsor, **Hot, Mean & Green**, which premiered at the Rhoda McGaw Theatre in Woking, and **A Fine Time for Wine**, which also premiered in Windsor.

Jonathan is father to two adult sons and lives in Exeter. When not writing he is a regular presenter on Phonic FM radio, having previously hosted a weekly show on Marlow FM for over 13 years.

For more information, see Jonathan's website at:
jonathanposnerauthor.com

Printed in Great Britain
by Amazon